Anita Shreve is the author of the acclaimed novels *Eden Close*, *Strange Fits of Passion*, *Where or When*, *Resistance*, *The Weight of Water* and the international number one bestsellers *The Pilot's Wife*, *Fortune's Rocks*, *The Last Time They Met*, *Sea Glass* and *All He Ever Wanted*. She divides her time between Massachusetts and New Hampshire.

Also by Anita Shreve:

ANITA SHREVE OMNIBUS

Eden Close
Strange Fits of Passion
Where or When

An *Abacus* Book

This omnibus edition first published in Great Britain in 2000
by Little, Brown and Company
Reprinted 2001
This edition published in 2003 by Abacus

Eden Close first published in Great Britain in 1990 by Macdonald & Co
Published in 1991 by Futura Publications
Published in 1994 by Abacus
Copyright © Anita Shreve 1989

Strange Fits of Passion first published in Great Britain in 1992
by Macdonald & Co
Published in 1992 by Warner Books
Published in 1994 by Abacus
Copyright © Anita Shreve 1991

Where or When first published in Great Britain in 1993
by Little, Brown and Company
Published in 1994 by Abacus
Copyright ©Anita Shreve 1993

A CIP catalogue record for this book is available
from the British Library

ISBN 0 349 11713 6

Printed and bound in Great Britain by Clays Ltd, St Ives plc

Abacus
An imprint of
Time Warner Books UK
Brettenham House
Lancaster Place
London WC2E 7EN

www.TimeWarnerBooks.co.uk

Eden Close

For John

ONE

THE AIR LAY AS HEAVY AS WATER IN THE SQUARE DARK ROOMS of the farmhouse. The house was still, sounds indistinct and muffled, as if heard through cloth. Upstairs, in the boy's room, the clock over the desk ticked away the minutes just past midnight. In the next room, where the boy's parents slept, there was the soft rattle of an old fan, moving the thick air from outside the house to inside and over his parents' bodies. As they had done nearly every hot night that summer, they had offered the fan to the boy, but the boy, aware that summer for the first time of his parents' age, had refused to take it from them.

In the house, far from town, Andy slept on his back in his bed. He slept badly, his lips lightly parted, his body smothered by the August night. A damp sheet, loose from its moorings, covered his chest. The boy's chest was bony then, without the muscles that would come later, and he had an older boy's summer growth, as if he'd sprouted too fast and had lost the grace of childhood. He was tall now, so tall that he towered over his parents, and his unfamiliar limbs, splayed under and out from the sheet, gave his body a lanky awkwardness, even in his sleep. His skin had an August tan

3

and had all but lost the marks of adolescence. His hair, dark brown and thick and slightly too long, against his father's wishes, was wet at the sides and the back with the heat. He turned, pulling the sheet with him, as if to say, despite his dreams, *OK, now, enough of this.*

The boy's father, in the next room, sleeping on his stomach in a sleeveless undershirt and boxer shorts, moved a hand near his ear to make a mosquito go away. His mother lay beside his father, on her back, like the boy. She had thrown off the sheet entirely, but her body was clothed in her pink summer pajamas. She had curlers at the sides and top of her head. The mosquito, discouraged by the father, alighted on her thigh, and too late, in her sleep, she moved her leg against the air.

Beyond the screen in the boy's room, there was only darkness. The darkness lay over the town and along the road that led from town, and it lay over the two farmhouses that were set two miles along that road like an afterthought, with only each other for company. The two houses were only seventy feet apart, the one facing the road, the other, his own, down a short dirt drive, pointing north, overlooking an abandoned cornfield. Indeed, the darkness had come that day from the north, blanketing that part of the state where the town was and where the boy had been born. In the afternoon, clouds the color of dust had moved along the sky like thick batting, diffusing the sun until it was only heat and blotting out the moon and the shooting stars of August in the evening. The blackness folded the heat back down upon itself and pushed it through the screens and into the rooms where the boy and his parents slept.

Later they would all know and be able to say that it was ten minutes past twelve when the sounds started. It was the boy who woke first, seconds before his parents. He heard a woman cry out, and he thought, as he swam up through his sodden sleep, that it might be his mother. But when he was awake, he knew that the sound was outside, in the darkness past the screen. The boy pushed the sheet from his chest as if the sheet kept him from understanding the sound outside his window. Perhaps, too, he heard then, through the wall, his father or his mother, sitting up. Like him, suddenly alert.

The second sound was a hoarse cry, nearly a shout, from a man, and with that there was immediately the frightened squeal of another female voice, that of a child still, like himself. He heard his father's feet on the floor, the rustle of trousers, a zipper—then his mother's muffled voice, anxious, questioning. The boy moved down to the foot of the bed, where the window was. On his hands and knees, he looked out at the night, waiting for the voices to explain themselves.

There were two shots, the boy and his parents would say later. Two shots fast upon each other, so that they sounded, in the silent night of midsummer, like one explosion shattering the air. The boy knelt frozen, his hands on the sill. He knelt that way for the seconds of silence that followed the explosion, until he heard the loud voice of his father telling his mother not to move. And then calling his son's name through the wall. *Andy.* He could hear his father open the door of the closet where he kept the rifle on a shelf. Then his own door opened. His father, in his sleeveless undershirt, rifle in hand, said, *Get away from the window.* The boy heard his father's footsteps running on the stairs and the soft whir as his father dialed the phone in the hallway downstairs.

Unable to move as his father had commanded, the boy stared at the darkness outside the screen. The last sound began then. It was reedy, a high-pitched wail, rising at first like a tendril of smoke into the sky—a female voice, though nearly inhuman, gathering momentum as it rose. He imagined a woman opening her mouth, her voice rising from her

5

in a thin, quivering stream. The boy heard his father stop dialing, listen and replace the receiver. The keening rose, sliced through the night. The boy shivered with the sound and backed away from the window. The cat downstairs jumped onto the kitchen table and started to hiss. Crows and summer birds, awakened by the unearthly cries, or perhaps by the gunshots, began to chatter and caw. And through the wall, the boy heard his mother say, as if in comprehension, *Oh God, oh Jesus.*

ANDREW WAKES from the dream in the same bed in which he was a boy and is disoriented. The dream lingers, vivid and heavy, pulling him down, causing him to swim in confusion between the night of the gunshots, when he was seventeen, and this night, the night of his mother's funeral, when he is thirty-six and sleeping alone in his parents' house for the first time in his life. He makes the dream linger longer than it might, enjoying the sensation of diving deeply into the boy's body and thoughts, hearing with the boy's ears as he has not been able to do in nineteen years, enjoying even the fear— the ability to feel that kind of fear chasing along the spine.

Andy. He hears again the exact timbre of his father's voice, and of his mother's—muffled, murmuring, anxious. There are details in the dream he hasn't remembered in nineteen years, and he thinks (briefly, because he does not want thoughts to interrupt or block his way back down into the dream) that the dream has worked like hypnosis, giving back sight and hearing that have been lost to him. In his waking thoughts he hasn't been able to see, as he can now, his father as a younger man, the shoulders still muscled under the sleeveless vest, the thin open weave of the undershirt, nearly like gauze, so unlike the thick cotton T-shirts he himself wears now. The midnight stubble on his father's face, the hard stomach lying flat beneath the undershirt. In his waking thoughts he can make his father appear only as he was shortly before he died—clean shaven, the thickened waist straining at the belt, the chest sunken, as though the center, the power, of the body had slipped. Most of the images he now has of his father's youth come from photographs, so that his father is frozen in this pose or that, that expression or this, but has no life, no voice—just as his own son's early years seem locked forever in the photographs and movies Martha, his ex-wife, has taken. His son is seven now, but Andrew cannot reliably remember how he sounded or what he said at two or at four.

He rolls over in the bed, hoping to sink deeper into sleep, to keep the dream alive. He can feel a door closing slowly. The dream is slipping away, and he is losing the feeling of being a boy, but the door hasn't entirely shut: he can still make out some of the details. He had forgotten, but can see now, the way the clouds came on that afternoon, a sour color filling the sky, turning trees and skin in the early evening light a pale, sickish yellow. And he can hear again the excited sounds of the birds just after midnight, when there should have been silence. He had forgotten the way his father held a gun, pointed straight down along the side of his leg, like a brace. And that his mother wore curlers to bed. And he had forgotten (indeed, how could anyone have retained the precise sound?) the terrible pitch of the woman's cries. At any point in the intervening years, he could have said that, yes, there was the sound of a woman crying in grief or in horror, but he couldn't have described it. Occasionally he would, when he was younger and more eager to impress, tell the story to a new acquaintance or to a woman, giving his childhood its only bit of glamour: *The man next door was murdered when I was seventeen. His daughter was raped.* But he hasn't, until the dream, been able to hear the sound.

But is the dream accurate? he wonders. Have bits been added for dramatic effect or for some psychological payoff?

No, he thinks (his thoughts intruding, coming faster, taking precedence over his sleep), the dream is true in the details that are there—nothing that is there is altered (except, perhaps, the part about the mosquito, which must have bitten *him* just now and worked its way into the dream)—but like edited copy, the dream has left out certain messy or seemingly irrelevant complications.

He had forgotten, but remembers now—and this was not part of the dream—the way the heat and the dirty air raised tempers that day, like an irritant chafing the skin, causing his parents, earlier in the evening, to speak in uncharacteristically querulous tones. He remembers that night at dinner—a cold, disappointing meal of ham slices and potato salad (it was too hot to cook, or even to eat)—that when his mother once again offered him the fan, there was an edge to her voice as if she knew in advance that he would decline it and was tired of the minor triumph of her son's refusal and of the larger implication of her son's generosity. And he remembers that after the meal, she rose in silence to get the ice cream from the freezer and put the half-empty carton on the table. The dessert looked to Andy as if it would taste like the cardboard it came in, and he didn't want it despite the heat, despite his usual thirst for sweets. He got up from the table and went out the screen door, letting it bang a little harder than usual, hunching his shoulders slightly against the possibility that his father would swing open the door in anger at his son's sudden sullenness.

But his father didn't come to the door, and Andy walked on down the dirt and gravel drive to the road, his hands in his pockets, thinking that soon he would go away, to Massachusetts, to school. He reached the road and the Closes' house. It, like his own, was a simple, nearly too spare farmhouse of white clapboards. Decades ago, the two houses had been set in a farmer's family compound at right angles to each other, with the back stoops the nearest point of contact, for two brothers to call to each other, or for a mother to watch over her new daughter-in-law. Now, though they shared a common drive, the families were not related, except in that way that two families, living far from town, might come to weave their lives together. Indeed, a passerby, cruising along the straight road from town, would know, at a glance, that the two families were not related: The first house, close to the road, though swathed in lush overgrown vegetation, particularly a profusion of blue hydrangeas in August, was the more derelict of the two. There was always peeling paint, a roof that needed mending, a shutter fallen in a storm. The house behind, facing north, Andy's own house, as if to disassociate itself from the careless house out front, was expertly if humbly manicured, its own hydrangea bushes trimmed neatly to size, its surrounding lawns cut and fertilized with discipline.

Mrs. Close worked nights then, as a nurse at the county hospital, and their car, a black Buick, was not in the driveway. Andy thought, if indeed he thought of it at all, that she'd taken the car and not the bus to work. (Later—hours, days later?—Andy would know that this impression was mistaken. He would be told, or would overhear, that Mr. Close, thinking to escape the heat, had driven his wife to work and then taken the car to the movies. And when his wife's shift was over, he brought her home just minutes after midnight.)

Andy might have wondered then if Eden was at home with her father or was out. He was not able to say later if he saw lights on in the house or not, or if he did, in what rooms the lights were. He tried to explain to the police that he passed that house, looked at that house, a dozen, twenty times a day, every day of his life, so that he could not say for sure if the lights he saw in the living room or the upstairs bathroom were on precisely at that moment, or earlier in the evening, when he was taking out the garbage, or on another night entirely when he had passed by his own screen window and had looked out.

He walked to the road and stood there, looking up and down. He had no plans for the night. He wore a white T-shirt and dungaree shorts and was letting his hair grow, despite his father's sharp comments, long enough for college. The road was flat as far as he could see in either direction. That time of night, after dinner, there were few cars on the road: a family in a station wagon going out for ice cream; an older boy, like himself, about to pick up a girl; a grown man escaping the dishes, heading for the package store. Strangers used the road too, passing through from towns and cities he did not know to other towns and cities. And occasionally there might be a trucker who had a night delivery off the highway.

Across the road, in the fading ocher light, were the cornfields of a working farm; the farmhouse lay on another road, parallel to his own. Sometimes Andy saw MacKenzie and his son, Sam, on tractors, working the fields. Sam didn't play sports at school because his father needed him in the afternoons. The drying and brittle cornfields rose like briers for several acres in both directions, lending the two farmhouses on Andy's side of the road even more of a sense of isolation in August than in December. The corn was feed corn for dairy cattle. Andy was glad his own father was not a farmer.

That evening Andy stood there, alone on the road, hearing only a distant barking of a dog, the faint whine far off of a car along a highway, the clatter of dishes in a dishpan, a faucet running in his mother's kitchen. He looked east and south, across the cornfields, as he had been doing for weeks since his acceptance at college had arrived in the mail, thinking of leaving, of getting out, yet afraid, too, of the leaving and of what might lie ahead. Already he had a sense of leaving for good, though when he spoke to his mother, he talked often of his vacations, of Thanksgiving, of returning to teach at the junior college in the county. But he knew, even then, that this wasn't true, that he would return for Thanksgiving and for Christmas and probably for the first summer vacation, but that he would really never come back. That what he was to be lay not behind him in the small rooms of the farmhouse but across the cornfields he could not, this month, see over.

His mother called to him. He turned. He saw her framed in the screen door, the yellow light of the kitchen behind her. He saw the red smock she wore to cover her heavy breasts and abdomen, the bottom of her shorts cutting into her thighs. And, standing in the road, he saw, too—the vision surprising him—the younger woman she had once been, as though he knew for certain he was leaving all of them. He saw the young woman of the photograph albums she kept on the coffee table—her long thick hair and the white collar of her high school picture; the ivory satin of her wedding dress seen through a blizzard at the church door (his father holding a fur jacket over her shoulders); the dazed expression of sensual pleasure in her eyes as she cradled her infant, himself, in her arms. He always thought of her, in the photographs, as beautiful, and he was startled for a moment to realize— to realize he was *capable* of realizing—that she had no beauty left at all. The subtle color of the once auburn hair was already gone, replaced by short, too bright, reddish curls.

And then, because he was seventeen, he had another realization—one that had possibly been lurking below the surface all along but now became, like many of the insights he was having that summer, a conscious thought: Even though you could love someone as much as he had loved his mother and she him, her only child, you could leave her if you had to. You could even look forward to leaving her.

"Your show is on," his mother said behind the screen.

He went in then and upstairs to shower, to wash away the smell of gasoline that lingered from his summer job at the Texaco station. After the shower, he sat downstairs in the living room watching the rest of the TV show with his parents, not because he wanted to (he would have preferred to be alone in his room), but because it had been the family ritual for years to watch one TV show together before bed. He was very conscious that summer of rituals, and he didn't want to break any of them. He knew his parents would soon be lonely without him, and though he sometimes felt himself wanting to begin the separation, he didn't like to think about his mother's face or his father's tight smile after he had gone. There'd been a time, not so long ago, when the family rituals—the elaborate pancake breakfasts on Sunday morning, the deliberate choreography of the holidays, the small triangle of the supper table—had been the highlights of his days and weeks and years.

Yes, he now sees, his father had already taken off his shirt and was wearing only the sleeveless undervest and trousers. His mother fanned herself with a magazine and got up during a commercial to make them all lemonade. (Oddly, near dawn, they all sat around the kitchen table and drank the remaining lemonade together after the police and the ambulances had gone. How like his parents not to think of whiskey or brandy first in a crisis, as he would now—*does* now.) They all went up to bed after the show, shortly past ten o'clock (he remembers having said so to the police), his father winding his watch as he walked up the stairs, as he had nearly every night Andrew could remember; his mother hoisting her weight up the stairs by her grip on the banister, her tread heavy on each riser, short of breath at the top; and himself, as light as air, flying, bounding, sprinting up the stairs, not an obstacle for him as they were for his parents.

Later, after he left home, he liked to imagine that he had looked out of his screen window, while he was waiting for his mother or his father to vacate the single bathroom at the top of the stairs, and had had a thought of Eden that night—had posed a query or had seen a silhouette of her moving across the window. But it was, in retrospect, impossible to know if he'd thought of her that night or that morning, or when he'd gotten off the bus from the Texaco station. Eden had been too much a part of his life—as much a piece of his geography as the hydrangea tree outside his window, whose white puffy blossoms are turning now to salmon as they do at the end of every summer; or as the way his mother looked each morning at breakfast in her bathrobe, nursing her coffee as she stared out the kitchen window, making, he always thought, some kind of peace with the weather and with how the day seemed about to unfold. He had known Eden all her life and most of his, and though he was too young then to be able to say with any confidence precisely how it was he was connected to Eden, he knew that he was troubled, as the days of August moved toward September, about having to leave her behind.

HE SEES that he has pulled the sheet from the foot of the bed during his dream—during the boyhood fear in the dream?—and it now lies in a damp rough swath across his chest. He brings it to his face and inhales a musty scent; it must be years since anyone has slept in this narrow single bed, he thinks. When he used to visit with his wife and his son, the three of them always slept together in the double bed in the guest room at the opposite end of the hallway—and it was, for him, one of the highlights of those visits, their holding each other in that soft, lumpy bed. As a general rule, Martha didn't believe in letting Billy sleep with them (the child-care books, she said, insisted it would make the boy too dependent), and so they hadn't, except on these rare and wonderful occasions.

Since he left home—and went to college, got married, fathered a child and separated from that wife and child—his room has evolved in the way the rooms of children do when the children aren't ever coming back. At first his mother kept it unviolated, the pennants and the posters on the walls, his desk neat, with his boyhood books and blotter, the few clothes he didn't take with him to school hanging in the closet. They were still there, he saw last night, as he hung up the charcoal gray suit he'd worn to the funeral; but she had used the closet herself, beginning when he didn't know, for her off-season clothes, if such a formal term could be applied to the oversized gaudy synthetics with orange diamonds, green stripes and pink flowers on the sleeves. She never lost the weight she vowed to lose and favored, right up until her death, large loose blouses that camouflaged her ever-swelling hips and thighs.

On the desk now is her sewing machine, and instead of the old pens and half-used notebooks he used to keep in the right-hand drawer, he found there last night an array of bobbins, fabric scraps and needles. There were other rooms she could have chosen to sew in—the sun room downstairs, where the light was good, or the guest bedroom. Perhaps, though, she wanted an excuse to be in this room, to savor some vestige of her son's presence. Or possibly she simply liked the east light in the early morning, or wished to see the other farmhouse, to reassure herself that she was not entirely alone. He tries to imagine what it must have been like for her to have a family and have it fall away: his own leaving and never really coming back except as a visitor; his father abandoning her five years ago with a heart attack. It has happened to him too—Martha and Billy have left him—though faster and without the dignity of these natural milestones. And he had not had time to be defined by the family he'd made, as she was, nor to become rooted to a place.

The still, heavy night mocks the dream, teasing it in and out of his consciousness. He wonders if the weather, so similar to that on the night of the shooting, has brought on the dream, or if it is the coincidence of lying alone in this bed. Or is it that he needs to feel his parents young and alive again, and his dream has willingly obliged? It is a mixed blessing, he thinks, to hold your past again for a few moments, as he sometimes feels when he dreams of Martha as she was (as they were together) when they first met. He wakes from these erotic dreams of his wife as if immersed in a warm bath, and then is chilled by those first few hints of reality — a tie flung over a mirror, a briefcase on a bureau, sheets he hasn't washed.

He swings his feet onto the floor and arches his shoulders. His back aches faintly; he isn't used to such a soft bed. And with Billy gone, he seldom exercises now — though his body remains, despite neglect, reasonably lean. He still has his hair too, for which he is grateful. His father, from whom Andrew inherited his thick dark hair — as well as his pale gray eyes — went bald at an early age. Andrew isn't certain, but he thinks his father may have lost his hair by the time he was forty-five.

Beside the bed, on a table, Andrew sees the sleeping pills. Dr. Ryder, his mother's doctor, pressed a vial into Andrew's palm after the funeral. He imagines the doctor with many similar vials, a drawerful perhaps, kept for similar occasions, the gesture like that of a priest with a rosary card, or of a car salesman handing you a calendar as you leave the showroom. But he doesn't want a sleeping pill just now. He feels restless.

FOUR DAYS earlier, he was in the screening room at the other end of the twenty-seventh floor, watching a videotape of an advertisement for a pain reliever his company manufactures, when Jayne, his secretary, got the call. The videotape had been especially poor, and despite the air-conditioning, he was sweating faintly when he returned to his office. As he walked in, Jayne came to his doorway with her hands clasped uncharacteristically in front of her. "There's bad news," she said quietly.

"Billy?" he said immediately, the adrenaline already shooting toward his fingertips.

Jayne shook her head quickly. Andrew slowly let out his breath. He thought he could bear anything except bad news about Billy, who was uncommonly prone to accidents—already a chipped tooth and a broken wrist, a scar over his right eyebrow. And since the child had left his keeping, Andrew's fears for him had increased exponentially. It was like the panic he sometimes had in airplanes.

"I'm so sorry," said Jayne. "It's your mother. She had a stroke just after breakfast and died almost immediately. A woman named Mrs. Close called to tell you, but I didn't want to break the news to you in the screening room. She says to call her. I have the number."

Andrew sat down. He remembers that his fingers could no longer hold a pen and that already a certain kind of numbness had set in, a disbelief in the truth of the event. He wouldn't need the number, he told Jayne. He had known it by heart since he was four, had been taught it in case of an emergency and later had used it to call Eden.

Although that conversation was days ago, Andrew is not sure even now that he has taken it in. The chaos of a funeral creates a blur inside which one can choose to remain. He has felt, alternately, grateful that his mother died so easily and so quickly; saddened that she might, even so, have known of her death, if only for a moment, and may have called out to him, her only son; relieved that he will no longer have to think of his mother as lonely; and horrified that the burden of being utterly alone has finally passed to him. He has no parents now or any family of his own to go home to, to create rituals with.

He walks from room to room upstairs, switching on lights as he walks, naked but for his shorts. The contradictory feelings have come in gulps, unexpectedly assaulting him and then leaving him to move about in the curious kind of peace that tending to business has always offered him. Like a good secretary to himself, he has made lists: lists of people to call and tasks to be completed to get to this day, the day of the funeral, and a long list of chores to accomplish before he can leave the farmhouse and the town. The list contains notes such as *call auctioneer, call real estate agents, do gutters, select mementos*. He imagines the sorting out, the auctioning off of the furniture, the minor repairs to the house and the arrangements to sell it will take him a week, and he called Martha to say that he will be upstate another seven days. When Martha offered to come to the funeral, Andrew said no, Billy was too young. Their presence, he thought, would distract him. Billy's trusting face and sturdy body would enthrall him as they always did; with Martha, there would be a tension that would inhibit every movement, so that thinking about his mother at all would be nearly impossible.

He has imagined that in lists there is control, but as he walks from room to room, the house seems about to slip from his grasp. His mother's room, now too bright under the overhead electric light, the room she left at dawn one morning five years ago to find her husband cold as tiles on the bathroom floor, the room she then slept in alone, is a labyrinth of snares and complications. There are only so many boxes of things Andrew can rescue from his and his parents' past to take back with him to his apartment in the city. And he sees at once that unless he hardens himself or designs a selection system, he might spend an entire day just in here.

Should he, for instance, take the quilt his mother made when he was ten—a year of her labor (he can recall it clearly) each night after supper, the basket of pieces beside her, her plump fingers nimble with a needle? What will he do with it? He has no wife to give it to, no closet big enough to store it, for it is a massive thing: It kept his parents warm even on the bleakest January nights.

And what of the oak chest of keepsakes at the foot of their bed, things his own mother saved from her mother, and doubtless things that his grandmother saved from her own mother's house? Such a process of distillation, like the corridors of endlessly repeated, though smaller, images in two mirrors; and such a burden, he thinks, these cartons filled with the leavings of lives gone before you. Will Billy one day open drawers in his father's apartment (depressing thought! Will Andrew now progress no farther in his domestic life than his expensive, cheerless condo?), taking objects that seem to contain some essence of his father, or of his own past, and bring them back to his own drawers and closets in Greenwich or Santa Fe?

Andrew picks up the watch his father wore and wound every night going up the stairs to bed. He knows he will take this, a watch his father inherited from his own father, but what of the Omega lying beside it on his father's bureau— the surface of the bureau undisturbed but for dusting? The Omega was a gift to his father when he left the dairy at his retirement. Andrew did not come to the retirement dinner— there'd been a critical business trip, a trip Andrew has always regretted making—and he doesn't know if his father ever even wore the Omega or if he would want it saved.

Andrew's father was plant foreman when he retired. But for most of the forty years he spent at the dairy, he drove a truck. (At his mother's insistence, the more accurate title "milkman" was seldom used in the house.) Andy was always asleep when his father left for work (at a punishing three forty-five in the morning), but when he returned from school, the truck would be there, and if he had a friend with him, they would clamber up into it with its bright green and red Miller Dairy sign, competing for the privilege of sitting on the high burnished leather seat and placing their small hands on the oversized steering wheel, the stem of which came all the way from the floor. Andrew remembers his father's gray overalls with the red embroidered script on the pocket, and the way, in winter, his father would wear so many layers underneath for warmth that he looked nearly stuffed. It wasn't until Andrew went to college and the boys around him spoke of their families that he first thought of himself as a WASP. But so humble were his father's circumstances (and, in truth, the circumstances of all his father's ancestors, most poor farmers) that Andrew wondered for a time if there might not be such a category as failed WASP. Andrew remembers vividly the afternoon his father came home with the news that he'd been promoted to foreman at the plant, releasing him from his position as a driver. He is not sure he ever saw his mother quite so jubilant—the way she kept kissing his father and throwing her arms around him and laughing, as if it were another era and she'd won the lottery.

He sits on the edge of the bed. He wonders who made the bed, for it was here that his mother was found. He assumes it must have been Mrs. Close, who came to his mother after the phone call. ("Your mother called Edith Close at about eight this morning and said she had a terrific pain in her head," Dr. Ryder revealed in his hoarse, authoritative voice on the phone the night Andrew arrived. "By the time Edith got dressed and went over, your mother had already passed away. She found her upstairs. It was a massive stroke, mercifully quick. Be glad for that. But you watch yourself, Andy, both your parents dying of cardiovascular diseases in their sixties; you watch your diet.")

As he sits on the bed, he thinks that a marriage seen

when you're a parent too, an adult, is a different thing than the one seen from boyhood. He wonders if his parents were happy together, if they slept touching or apart (he doesn't really know; they were always private and silent in this room, and he has no memory, as other children do, as Eden said she did, of mysterious and unexplained parental sounds) and whether they had ceased to make love. His parents were older than most when he was born; his mother was thirty-one. She had, she said, nearly given up on a baby before he came, and there was a time when this caused him to imagine that he was adopted, like Eden, despite the fact he looks so like his father that he can't, even today, go into town without a man or woman there saying it: *the image of your father*. Still, as children can be, he was obsessed for months (or perhaps it was only weeks) by this notion of adoption; so much so that he conceived the idea that the two families had gravitated to the two farmhouses set apart from the town because there was about them this unnatural link.

He looks at the marriage bed and sees, suddenly and unbidden, the image of a woman rolling over, turning her back on the man. But it is not his mother he is seeing; it is his wife. He doesn't want to think of Martha just now. He gets up and shuts off the light.

The brandy, kept for company, is in the cabinet with the meat grinder over the fridge. He pours himself a generous amount in a jelly glass. The kitchen, he reflects, sitting on a white-painted wooden chair, is nearly unchanged since he was a boy. And as it did then, it gives the appearance of having been scrubbed raw. It is a farmhouse kitchen, "modernized" during the thirties, with a green-speckled linoleum floor, a white porcelain sink and stove and kitchen table, all with rounded edges. There are painted surfaces everywhere—the white tongue-and-groove boards of the walls, the pale green of the old Hoosier cabinet, the four unmatched white chairs at the table. He thinks about the kitchen in the house in Saddle River he bought with Martha, where Martha and Billy now live, and about the shiny, stainless-steel refrigerator in that kitchen and the expensive quarry tile on the floor and how remarkably cold—literally cold—the floor is there.

When he arrived the evening of the day his mother died—by car, having driven the 270 miles north from the city—and walked in the back door (as did everyone who entered the house), the kitchen appeared as it does now; there were no leavings of a half-eaten breakfast, as he had feared to see. Edith Close again, he imagines, silently officious, cleaning up the clutter of death.

Thinking of Edith Close, he remembers again, and abruptly, the terrible sound in his dream of a woman crying. He swirls the golden brandy in the jelly glass and recalls the sequence of events, an exact sequence he has not thought of for years. His father again picked up the phone and dialed the police. Then he went alone through the kitchen, out the door and up the drive, his rifle tense along the side of his leg. Andy heard his father's unhurried footsteps on the gravel and the heavy patter of his mother running down the stairs. Andy pulled on his shorts and went downstairs to be with his mother, partially out of a desire to protect her, primarily out of a need to be in her presence. She was standing at the screen door, peering out at the darkness. Despite the heat, she had put on a robe (pink seersucker with lace at the edges, he sees now), knowing that there would be the police soon. The shrill wail had stopped; they both knew it had been the voice of Edith Close, but neither yet had the courage to imagine precisely what had caused it. Andy moved closer to his mother, and she shifted slightly so that he, too, could see out the screen door into nothing.

"I told him to wait for the police," his mother said, her

voice tight with strain. It was a strain he is now familiar with, the strain of cautious women with good sense, a voice men often choose to ignore.

"He has a gun," Andy said, knowing instantly she would not for one minute think that a help.

"A gun!" his mother cried. Her voice rose like the other, as if it, too, might spiral up into the night. Was this freedom a special province of women? he wondered. "What good is a gun in the pitch dark? You can't see a hand in front of you out there."

"He'll be careful," Andy said. But he didn't know if this was true. Was his father, in a crisis—a life-threatening crisis—a cautious man? He had never witnessed his father in physical danger; he doubted that his father knew himself how he would react until each footstep was taken.

He could feel the tension in his mother's body, a static current running along her arm, causing even his own arm to raise goose bumps. She stood with her hands clutching her robe closed—still, intent, warding off, as if by her will alone, the sound of another gunshot. His father would say later that he felt no danger, but Andy thought his father must already have been forgetting his fear when he said it. Had his father not imagined the consequences of being seen by a gunman, possibly a murderer, on the dirt drive as the man ran wildly into the cornfields?

Andy and his mother saw the flashing lights just a split second before they heard the siren, coming fast along the straight flat road from town. One, two police cars, an ambulance following—the town's entire force. And then another vehicle, half a minute later: the fire chief. The vehicles swung into the drive and over the lawn, spewing themselves every which way like children's toys, leaving the drive free for the ambulance. The police cars and the ambulance lit up the night with eerie flashing beacons, red and blue, out of sync, so that Andy could see through his own screen door the back door of the other farmhouse and the bedroom windows upstairs to the north and west, awash in the unnatural pulsing lights. Two policemen ran from one of the cars to the back stoop and into the Closes' kitchen. From the ambulance, turning around and backing down the drive to the Closes' back stoop, another man alighted, swinging open its wide rear door.

"I'm going out there," Andy said suddenly.

"You stay here," his mother insisted. "Your father said."

But Andy was already through the door and down the steps. He put his hands in the pockets of his shorts and walked toward the edge of the circle created by the ring of official cars. The humid night was thick with mosquitoes; they whined at his ear, and he slapped at one on the back of his neck. He heard, too, the slap of the screen door behind him and turned to see his mother walking carefully down the back steps on the sagging treads, her curiosity stronger than her husband's admonition. The crows and summer birds, aroused at the wrong hour, had lost their fright and were silent now. Andy could hear the low, muffled voices of men at the front and sides of the house, searching already with powerful flashlights for someone or something, though no one outside the house yet knew what it was they might be expected to find. The headlights of a car—a Chevy?—approached the house, the driver slowing to see what the commotion was, perhaps suspecting an accident. Andy watched the car pull over. A man and a woman got out and crossed the road. They stood at the edge of the drive, staring at the scene, puzzled. And then, he knew from the soft furry breath at his arm, his mother was beside him.

Impulsively, he put his arm around her and jerked her toward him. It was the first time he had ever touched her quite this way, from his full height, as if he were now the stronger of the two. It was a scene he thought he had seen somewhere before, on television possibly, in a show. The son, grown, towering over the mother, assuming the role of protector, steadying her while a husband is taken off in handcuffs or on a stretcher. The image, lasting only seconds, was inexplicably delicious. It was not unlike a similar and baffling feeling he sometimes has even now when he hears of someone else's bad news and has an irrepressible and horrifying urge to smile.

The Closes' back door swung open hard. It was De-Salvo, the thick-necked, heavyset police chief. Andy knew him from the hockey games. His face was pocked along his jowls. He had a son who years ago had made All State as a wing, and though his son had left the town, the father still haunted the games, as if to catch some echo—a shout skimming across the ice, a hand on his shoulder with a reminiscence—of his son's triumph. DeSalvo gestured sharply to the man standing at attention by the ambulance. As swift as skaters, the attendants slid up the back stoop with the stretcher and into the house. (Paramedics? Andrew doesn't know if they were called that then. Were they not simply volunteers, roused from their beds, as he was, by calls in the night?) His mother moved her face closer to his bare chest. Unconsciously, he braced himself for what the night might deliver next. But didn't the urgency of the stretcher imply injury and not death?

Andy could see the man and the woman at the end of the drive edging along closer to the house. A policeman was patrolling the front and spotted them too; he barked at them to move back. Andy thought he could imagine the prurient curiosity of the couple, exciting them enough to trespass, and how they would tomorrow assault whoever would listen with the details, their own status momentarily and satisfyingly enhanced. Then the policeman, turning back to his task at the front of the house, saw Andy and his mother and raised his flashlight to them. Andy brought his hand up to shield his eyes.

"You there," the officer called.

Andy, his arm still raised, nodded. It was Reardon. He saw again the diffused beacon of a flashlight against the steamed-up window on the driver's side of his father's Ford, and Reardon's face, peering and smirking in the darkness as he watched Andy's date worry her hair with her fingers. *Move along now*, Reardon had said with something like amusement or satisfaction on his face. *Not safe to park here this time of night*. Andy and his date, a girl he hadn't known well, had driven home in silence.

Reardon lowered the light. "Where's your father?"

Andy pointed to the Closes' house. Instinctively, he pointed upstairs.

"Either of you hear or see anything?"

Andy looked at his mother.

"We heard some things," she said cautiously.

"You stick around, then," said Reardon. It was an unnecessary command. Where did he think they would go?

The screen door opened, and a stretcher bearer backed out quickly. Andy heard, beside him, a gasp, and before he was even certain himself, his mother said her name. *Eden*.

He felt his thighs loosen, along with the bottom of his stomach, not so badly that he feared he might fall, but enough so that his mother felt the weight and stiffened, becoming a crutch. Their roles, so new and pure just a moment before, were again reversed; he was, after all, still her boy.

Taking a quick swallow of the brandy, he remembers now a white bath towel, darkened by a large black stain, hiding Eden's face. She lay motionless, but Andy knew from the urgent syllables of the attendants that she couldn't yet be dead. She was covered by a bed sheet, a long flower-print one, he remembers, a sheet as smooth as glass over her body, and from that he knew she was naked underneath. He remembers clearly the way her toes stuck out from the sheet, and how the nail polish on them, in the dim light, shone as black dots. He sees, too, the long sticky clump of pale blond hair falling away from the bunched towel.

A force as primitive as running into a street to save a child made him start forward, but his mother held his arm. The attendants raised Eden to shoulder height and slid her into the ambulance as if onto a shelf. One of the men climbed in after her and slammed the door. The door wouldn't fasten properly, and as the ambulance sped out the drive (taking Eden to the same hospital her mother had left only forty minutes before), Andy could see the attendant furiously opening and closing the rear door to get it to catch. As it made the turn onto the road, the driver started up the siren, sending an electrifying wail out over the silent cornfields, summoning all who would listen from their sleep, announcing that something of importance had happened at the farmhouses two miles from town.

Andy watched the receding lights of the ambulance. The driveway was suddenly quiet, too quiet. Something about the scene he had just witnessed wasn't right, wasn't the way it would have gone on TV. He looked at the empty drive, and then he knew at least what the question was: Why had a fourteen-year-old girl been sent alone to the hospital?

It was his mother who said it first.

Where's Edith?

ANDREW FINGERS the quilted sides of the jelly tumbler and gets up to open the back door. He stands at the screen, hoping for a wash of cool night air. But as it was on the night of the shooting, the air is dense and smells unclean. When he was a boy, and the air was bad, his mother would always say, sniffing as she said it, *The dairy*. In the summer, if there was a southeast wind, the sickly scent of sour milk, mixed with the smell of cows, would float over the cornfields. But today, who can say? He doesn't know the industry of the area anymore; and if he did, he thinks, he's not sure he would recognize the odor. The smell could be that of toxic waste, from a plant not unlike the one his own company has in New Jersey. He seldom has to visit the plant, and no one ever talks to him about waste and disposal, but he knows it is a touchy subject. Periodically there are quiet suits and directives.

He takes a large swallow of brandy, draining the glass. Though the air is dull and the night black as a cave, the earth around him is noisy and alive with the castanets of cicadas, relentlessly sending out their frenzied scratchings. Or at least it sounds like scratchings. He doesn't know how they make their sounds, and it has always puzzled him how such a relatively small insect can be so noisy; he thinks the riddle is one that if Billy were with him he would bother to solve.

He looks out the screen door, down the dirt drive to the road. He thinks to himself, in the manner of a pronouncement: *This is the day my mother was buried*. He expects to feel a shudder of grief. When that does not come, he forces himself to think about his mother under the ground, as if that might trigger the appropriate sorrow. He waits for the horror of the image to assail him. But, as has been happening of late, his emotions won't cooperate. The images he tries to bring into focus are like sexual fantasies that no longer do the trick. Instead, at this moment, he is inexplicably distracted by thoughts of Edith Close at the burial. And this distraction, which feels like someone lingering overlong in his bedroom or his office, denying him badly needed privacy, teases him away from his mother.

He sees Edith standing alone, off to one side. She was

27

the only woman there who wore a veil—a hat with a black veil from another era, even in the heat. The other women—women from the Ladies Guild, wives of dairymen—wore sleeveless summer dresses and stood in clumps, stooped, their necks bowed by what seemed to be the thickening of old age between their shoulder blades. Yet she stood erect and alone, in black, the only one there to wear that color. Not family, yet nearly that, the geographical accident of being the only neighbor having given her the status, almost, of a sister.

When he had spoken to her on the phone the night of his mother's death, she was, as she had always been, reserved with him—even if, on this occasion, for a sentence or two, a trace of something softer crept into her voice—and he found he could not call her anything but Mrs. Close, as he had since he was a boy. But at the burial, after the funeral, aware of her presence for the first time that day, he looked up and saw that she was watching him. She looked away quickly, and he remembers her standing on the hill, gazing out over the gravestones, beyond the iron fence, listening but not bowing to the prayers. He thought, or felt, how distant she had always been, even before the shooting. She seemed more fragile than he had, as a boy, known her to be—but though he knows she must be in her mid-sixties, she had at the burial the bearing of a younger woman, a bearing some women never achieve.

After the burial, everyone returned to the church. It had been arranged without Andrew's knowledge. There was coffee in a large green metal urn and brownies and cookies someone had baked, *refreshments*, a woman he didn't know whispered softly, touching his arm on the hill. When his father died, his mother had provided food at home, and he had thought then how macabre it was to entertain, to eat, so soon after you had put a man into the earth. He himself had had no appetite for days after his father's burial, as he has none now and didn't at the church today.

There were old worn green velvet drapes up on a stage and a portrait of Jesus on a wall. Metal chairs were unfolded and placed near the table with the food, as if for a children's dance. He stood benumbed, not from grief but from strangeness. People came and said soft things to him and moved away and chatted with more animation, out of his hearing, to each other. It was the strangeness of being in a room that you had known overwell as a child and that hadn't changed in any detail but now seemed as unfamiliar as death.

She came up to him and explained: *The guild thought you wouldn't want the trouble.* He understood that they saw him now as a bachelor again. She was still wearing the veil, and he couldn't clearly see her eyes. He wanted, almost maliciously, to walk out, for he thought, with a slight irritation, that someone could at least have asked him if he wanted this, but the impulse passed. It was right, he remembers thinking, that she should stand with him; she was as strange in that place as he was.

He looks at the clock over the sink. It reads twelve-fifty. He thinks he might have to resort to the sleeping pill after all, but then remembers that he can't; he's had the brandy.

He looks out the door in the direction of the Close farmhouse, but he can't even perceive its outlines. There are no lights on anywhere—not even the faint glow of a night-light. Somewhere upstairs, he knows, Eden is lying on a bed or sitting in a chair, the darkness irrelevant to her.

AFTER HIS mother had asked *Where's Edith?* they stood together, waiting. Andy had his hands in the pockets of his shorts; his mother had her arms wrapped around his elbow. Andy knew it had to be Mr. Close who was hurt; how else could there have been that awful crying? A policeman opened the back door and called to two others. Andy, straining, could hear bits of grunts and breathless sentences. ". . . is talking now . . . medium height, a mask, yellow shirt, she's pretty sure . . . on the stairs . . . pretty hysterical . . . face blown . . . Christ, you should . . ."

Behind the policeman, Andy saw his father at the Closes' screen door, wanting to get out. His father said something, and the policeman stood to one side. In turn, the policeman mumbled something to Andy's father, and his father shook his head slowly several times—not a gesture of refusal, but rather one of disbelief.

Andy watched his father walk toward him. It was a moment Andrew would never forget, though he wouldn't know until years later that the thing his father had seen, the thing that had changed his father's face and the movements of his body, had, in the space of a few short minutes, soaked in so deep that it would never leave him. Even in the dim, pulsing light, Andy could see the rivulets of sweat running down from his father's temples. His father's walk was slow, the rifle no longer a rigid brace—more like a heavy broken tool he was taking to the garage to fix. When his father stood in front of them, he looked first at Andy and then at his wife. He spoke to her.

"Go inside now. Take the boy. They're bringing Jim out."

"Jim?" his mother said quickly.

"It's bad. You go on in. Quick, now."

But his mother would not move. "What happened?" she demanded. "Tell me."

His father raised his arms, as if he meant to shepherd his family back to shelter. But when he saw she would not move, he lowered them. He stabbed the barrel of the rifle into the gravel, like a stick. He looked at the ground. He sighed—a deep, exhausted sound.

"Jim is dead," said his father. "Eden's been shot, but she's still alive."

His mother brought her hands to her mouth. Andrew heard a high, strangled murmur.

"But how?" she asked. "Who?"

"I don't know. It looks like, *looks like*," his father said, faltering, repeating himself, "and I think Edith was trying to say this, a man broke in while she and Jim were out, Jim was out, and Jim found him in Eden's room. He was"—his father hesitated, looked at Andy, searched for the proper wording—"*assaulting* Eden, and the man had a gun—we heard the shots. . . . Eden somehow got in the way . . . a struggle, I think. . . . Edith saw the man on the stairs. . . . He had a mask. . . . She found them both." His father stared. "I saw her in the bedroom . . . covered, covering . . ."

Andy watched his father's mouth tighten. He was seeing something Andy could only imagine, yet could not imagine at all. The image refused to form. Later Andrew realized that his father must, at that moment, have been in deep shock himself. How could his father, a dairyman, ever have been prepared for that scene in Eden's bedroom? Why did they think, did his father think, sheltered as he was by his homely routines, that he was any better equipped to deal with it than Andy or his mother?

His mother put her hands on his father's shoulders and laid her forehead on his chest. Along the road from town, Andy could see, and hear, a parade of ambulances and police cars, moving fast toward the houses. These would be from the county and the state, he was thinking. When the first ambulance pulled in the drive, they brought out Edith Close from the house.

The black stain was on her white uniform, her shoes, the side of her face, her mouth and her hair, but most of all on her hands. She was supported by a policeman at each side of her. Her feet barely moved. At the bottom of the steps, a pair of attendants or paramedics tried to get her to lie down on a stretcher. She protested wildly, pushing against a restraining hand on her chest, as if she feared she might drown. But the men overpowered her. In shock, in her raving, she raised her knees and spread them, kicking, and Andy saw, up her skirt, the white flash of her underwear. He felt a shiver move through his chest. He thought then that of all the things he had witnessed that night this was something he should not have seen.

HE STANDS up to rinse out his glass. He puts it on the sideboard. He is mesmerized by the quiet. He is not sure he has ever before realized how quiet it is here, how unnerving that quiet can be. He thinks of turning on the radio but realizes the loud voice of a late-night disc jockey will be even worse. And anyway, he tells himself practically, he has got to sleep. There's that list of chores.

He turns out the lights as he goes. In his room, he makes a halfhearted attempt to remake the bed. As he bends to tuck in the top sheet at the foot, he suddenly realizes that the dream *did* get it wrong. Or if not wrong, exactly, then out of sequence. He sits on the bed and replays the dream. In his dream, he has imagined that it was the cry of a woman that first woke him—with thoughts that it might be his mother. He remembers that panic, that struggling to the surface, as if for air. And yet it can't have been a woman's voice he heard first, he thinks logically. It has to have been the voice of a man first, the voice of Mr. Close.

Surely, the woman's cry came later.

I watch you with the sight of years ago. I hear your screen door, and I see you on the driveway. When you walked below my window, then, did you have a thought of me? You are a boy with arms as thin as wood. Your hair is growing longer because soon you'll go away. I teased you at the river, but you wouldn't touch me. You wouldn't touch the buttons or my skin, though I dared you to, and others had already. Which you knew. And when I made you look, your face was calm, though your hands trembled. And you said . . .

I see your collarbone beneath a plaid shirt. Your cuffs are rolled. There's a shimmer on the water.

She said your mother died, though I knew before she told me. She is waiting for you to go away.

I hear your car come in the driveway. It purrs before you turn it off, like a cat. I hear your feet on the gravel and I see you with your hair grown longer over your ears, and I know that soon you'll go away. I hear your footsteps to the road and see you looking over the cornfields. I am forgetting colors, but not the shape of your eyes. I remember how you smell.

TWO

IN THE EARLY HOURS, AN ELECTRICAL STORM ROLLS OVER THE cornfields and the pastures where in the daylight there are always cows, waking children with its thunder, illuminating darkened bedrooms with its flashes of lightning and causing even those who do not wake, like Andrew, to stir in their sleep and alter the course of their dreams. The rain drums against the shingles and tin of the farmhouses and along the smooth cedar shakes of the high ranches closer to town, against the long low flat roof of the mall near the highway and against the windows of the few shops still struggling in the village: the white stucco gas station, built in 1930; the luncheonette across the street, now owned by a Vietnamese couple; the old barbershop that once again gives crew cuts to boys; the small shop next to the barber's, where the TV repairman's sign is; and now, new to Andrew, a mini-superette next to the gas station. After the rain, near dawn, the storm moves out, leaving in its wake a chill wash of air, the first in more than a week, and in the palely lit bedrooms, the relief is palpable. Men and women, some with their children still in their beds, sleep their deepest sleep in days.

When Andrew was a boy, the town, no more than a

patchwork of dairy farms with an undistinguished village at its center, was distinctly rural, devoted to the production of milk and butter and cheese and ice cream at Miller's Dairy. The men of the town, descended from Poles, Irish, Italians and migrating Yankees, tended livestock and cornfields, or they worked for the dairy. Their women hovered somewhere between farmers' wives and suburban matrons, and their children, like Andrew, grew up for a time thinking the universe was cornfields and cows and men who woke before dawn, until they were eleven or fourteen or seventeen and began to feel the first stirrings of a desire to get away, or the first flutter of fear that they might not have the courage to.

For Andrew, who knew for a certainty from an early age that he would go away to college (his parents, with no working farm to leave to him, were united in this goal), the town lost its menace before it had had time even to register, and when he was away, at school, or in the city, he felt, if not consciously thought of, his childhood years in the town as unencumbered by the ethics of a more sophisticated urban life. So much so that he often failed to notice on his visits home, these visits growing less frequent with each passing year, how much the town was changing.

But on this visit home he has observed, with more clarity than he has had before, that the town is not as it used to be. There is a highway now and the mall. There are subdivisions where once there were just farms. In the next town, six miles away, beyond the mall and the biggest subdivision, there is a large insurance company that employs more people than the dairy ever did and a factory that makes cassettes and videotapes. The old dairy itself, so shiny and new when Andrew's father was a foreman, seems hobbled now by time.

Sometimes when Andrew dreams, he sees the town as it once was—the street corners and playing fields and cornfields and railroad tracks that made up the landscape of his childhood. But there will be in the dream an anachronistic conversation, or a person not encountered until years after he left the town, or an object not invented yet when he was living there. And though he will wake from these dreams confused or, more likely, bemused, the dreams, more than his memories, resemble the truth.

Andrew wakes and doesn't want his clothes from the city; in fact, he needs work clothes, although he has brought none with him. He finds, though, a pair of faded jeans, ironed and neatly folded over a hanger in his closet. The cloth is as soft as velvet, and he can see the faint line where years ago his mother let the hem out. When he has put them on, the bell-bottom cuffs look silly and hopelessly old-fashioned, but since he has nothing else suitable to wear, he is glad his mother saved them all these years.

In the kitchen he has a cup of instant coffee and a piece of chocolate cake someone from the Ladies Guild has brought to the house. When he finishes this, he walks out into the yard, letting the screen door slap smartly behind him. He puts his hands in his back pockets and inhales; the air tastes of mint and sage from the tangle of herbs by the back stoop. He can see that the lawn, which badly needs cutting, has shrunk, yielding its borders up, year by year, to the thicket of bracken and fern, of blackberries and wild apple and dogwood marching toward the house—as if soon they will swallow the white clapboards. How quickly a house wants to sink back into the land, he is thinking, to give up the struggle against the grasses and the rain and the sun. He feels inappropriately fine. He circles the house, the grass soaking his old canvas sneakers in a matter of seconds. Perhaps his mother had been ill for some time, he speculates, surveying with more clarity than he's had in days the disrepair of the property he must now offer to strangers. A small bed of badly overgrown zinnias, dahlias and flowers with spindly stems and unattractive red blossoms is a mass of weeds and seems to have no distinct outline. The south wall of the house, he observes, is peeling badly. The shrubs and the hedge need a savage pruning, and there's the falling gutter that must be put right. He notices, with an unreasonable cheerfulness, a screen with an ugly gash that will need replacing.

He can offer the house as it is, he knows, and return to the city and his job—it is not as if he needs the few extra thousand that the fixing and mending will bring—but he finds the thought of the physical labor, the mental list of tasks, oddly appealing. It has been years since he has had such a list of chores. Even when he had a home of his own, in Saddle River with his wife and child, someone else did the work, such as there was, in that new, immaculate structure: a cabinetmaker, a plumber, a lawn service to tend to the shrubs and bushes there. He doubts that anyone in his hometown would ever contemplate buying such a service, just as the women here, he knows, clean their own houses. At best, like the Closes, they might hire a boy to mow. There were always plenty of boys who needed the money.

He should return to the office, of course. He looks at his watch. At this hour he would already be at his desk in a summer suit. There would be a pile of pink phone messages, and some would seem urgent. He would have about him an air of earnestness leavened by an unobtrusive wit he has learned to cultivate, fielding the puns that his boss, like a college sophomore, is so fond of. And he would feel a small pressure, around his shoulders and along the back of his neck, because there would be a deadline and surrounding it a manufactured sense of importance. Though he would not be able to escape, as he hasn't for some time now, a growing certainty that all the efforts of all the men, like him, in offices are merely an elaborate bit of theater, in which the principal actors have so long and so thoroughly played their parts (like the actors in a long-running television series) that they are known to each other—and perhaps even to themselves—only as this character or that.

He remembers, with a slight shudder, how narrowly he escaped accepting, from a woman in his office, an offer of a house in the Hamptons. He can think of practically no worse way to spend a vacation than with strangers in a town nearly as crowded as the city—or so it seems to him from here. He had thought of taking Billy camping in Nova Scotia, but Martha was being unaccountably difficult this summer, insisting that Billy not miss any of his expensive day camp and announcing that when camp was over she was taking him to visit her parents on Nantucket. Andrew likes his in-laws and thinks that Billy should visit them, and it was becoming too complicated to sort out when his mother had suddenly died and inadvertently solved the problem.

He looks north over the cornfields and finds he wants to say the word *beautiful*. The word is strange on his tongue. It is a word he has not said in a long time, and it is all the more strange spoken beside this ruined house—this house, once loved, falling into disrepair. Both houses are now shabby in the sunlight, the back steps of the other nearly rotted out, the privet climbing wild over the sills. He sees a large crack in a kitchen window—from a branch or a bird? he wonders; not now, surely, from a child—and that a shutter has been blown from an upstairs window.

Two women, two widows, living far from town, neighbors with a lifetime of history, but not women who liked each other much, he thinks, not women who called upon each other much for warmth or for talk. He sees now what he has been too preoccupied to see before—the obvious disintegration of two houses that have no men in them, houses patched up as best they can be by women of a certain generation who were never taught how to putty a window and who do not know the names of tools. They make their kitchens gleam, he knows, but if a shutter falls from an upstairs window, it is carried to the cellar and left to stand there.

He will begin with the scraping and the sanding, he decides. The grass cannot be cut until it dries out, and that won't be until late afternoon at the earliest—although he should take a look at the lawn mower before then to see what kind of condition it's in. An oriole darts from among the thick foliage of the hydrangea tree. He wonders if the scrapers are still kept in the same black metal drawer in the garage.

HE HAS been scraping for an hour, and his arm is already sore, when she comes out the back door, gingerly making her way down the rotted stoop. Reflexively he looks at his watch. Quarter to. He knows she works four hours a day, from ten to two, seven days a week, at a nursing home nearby. It was a detail among many in a letter or a phone call from his mother that he'd read or heard quickly, but now the detail comes back to him, and his mother's expression of bewilderment at anyone's willingness never to have a day off. "She even worked Christmas," he remembers his mother saying or writing.

He calls to her when she is at the bottom of the stoop. She looks at her car and then turns to look at him. Delicately, she brings a thin hand to the side of her brow to shade her eyes, for the sun is behind him, and he must be to her a black silhouette against a brilliant sky. But he can see her clearly, as he couldn't yesterday: a pinkish-gray dress, an upturned face, her skin as soft as chamois. Perhaps she forgot that he would be there, but she shows no surprise. He towers over her, and she has to squint to see him. Her hair is ashen, where once it was the color of her bracelets, and is still worn long, drawn back in an intricate knot at the nape of her neck. She has on a strand of pearls—incongruous on a summer morning, driving in a Plymouth to a nursing home, but so in keeping with how he has remembered her that even the greater incongruity of her careful grooming against the ugly ruined farmhouse barely registers on his consciousness.

She walks toward him, each foot grating slightly on the gravel.

"Mrs. Close," he says, and instantly regrets the childish greeting, when he knows her name is Edith and he ought to call her that now, at thirty-six; but he feels diminished in her presence, as if he were a boy again and she'd come out to give instructions. He begins to back down the ladder.

He sees that there are folds beside her mouth where her skin has fallen and that her eyelids are hooded now. And below her eyes, there are smudges indicating that she hasn't slept well; the smudges match the color of her dress. He wants to break free of his image of himself as a boy, but when he says, too loudly for just the two of them, "I thought I'd tackle your lawn too, Edith, while I'm at this one later," his voice seems uncharacteristically boorish and rude.

She looks around at the tall grass and the wild privet, a look of weariness passing over her face.

Again he feels the boyish compunction to please, the awkwardness he has always felt with her.

She doesn't answer him directly. "A fine morning," she says.

How strange that they are speaking to each other in just the same tones of voice, using the same polite vocabulary, as they might have twenty-five years ago—as if nothing had intervened or changed in all those years, as if there had not been all that death and the birth of his own son.

She nods, and there is something in the tilt of her head

or the angle of her profile that gives him a sharp memory of the younger woman he remembers her to have been. He sees a woman's hand on a man's wrist, pulling him up the steps and inside, even though the laundry basket under the clothesline is still half full of wet sheets. He remembers knocking on the back door one afternoon when he was eight, carrying a basket of tomatoes from his mother's garden, bountiful that year, and Edith opening the door, flustered, a red blush staining her throat and chest where he could see it, her hair loose and damp at the temples. She was fingering the top of her dress, where the last two buttons were still undone, and he understood, if not entirely comprehended, that Jim was in the house somewhere, home early, and that they had been doing together something secretive and thrilling.

The knowledge had come before he had even known what it was or what it meant—the suggestion that there might be between a man and a woman something that set them apart, something that could not be shared by others and ought not to be seen from the outside.

And after that day, he would watch her carefully, as if important information could be had by examining her. For other boys in the town, boys who liked to climb onto the high leather seat in the dairy truck or boys he knew from the hockey rink or in the cold tiled corridors of the junior high school, the knowledge had come differently, more predictably, from girls seen naked on a dare in woodsheds or from pictures found in magazines. Sean O'Brien, who was the goalie when Andy and he were in ninth grade, and who would be killed only three short years later, had once told of finding lurid and wonderful pictures of men and women together in a drawer marked "Hinges" in his father's cellar; and later Andrew, when he had grown and had his own house, would sometimes have a fleeting and sad image of a middle-aged TV repairman retreating to the bowels of his house for furtive pleasure.

He was aware that she was different from his mother and from the other mothers—an awareness that was inadvertently encouraged by his mother's disapproval of her neighbor, which hovered somewhere between quiet outrage and thinly disguised envy.

"Edith is not discreet," his mother would pronounce, having caught sight of her across the yard, or remembering a gesture or a remark her neighbor had made that day. "Edith is sometimes quite careless," she would say, and his father would wisely just nod, although Andy sometimes thought he smiled. And one evening his father volunteered, "Well, at least they're well matched," and his mother had said, "Shush," indicating that the boy was in the room. Her tone alerted Andy to a sentence that otherwise might have gone unremembered, and caused him to save it, as children do, until he was old enough to understand it.

He understood also, with a child's unerring antennae, that the woman his mother envied loved only the one person and that she was indifferent to the world outside her door, as if she knew she must be careful not to squander her reserves. She had seemed, for example, always to be spectacularly indifferent to Andy, thinking of him only, he felt, as the neighbor's boy and then later as the fellow who helped with odd jobs around the house to earn money for college. He sometimes thought, in fact, that she didn't actually *see* him in the yard as he trimmed a blackberry bush or raked the leaves from the flower bed. He'd say hello and nod; yet she might just pass silently by, lost in her own vision, unaware of his presence.

She waves once just before she gets into the Plymouth, and Andrew climbs back up the ladder.

Jim, though, Andrew thinks to himself, did notice him

as a boy. He never passed Andy without a greeting or a question or even a piece of gum for the boy in his pocket. When the adults were in the yard, absorbed in each other, it would be Jim who would break away and take him by the hand—or even play a game of catch with him.

Scraping and painting the side of the house, as his own father did every five years, Andrew remembers the way Jim would watch his father when he worked—hands in his pockets, restless, but feeling no urgency to tackle his own chores. Jim was a man who started things but never finished them—unlike the steady, slow progress of Andy's father. And Andrew can remember being asked each August to tidy up a vegetable garden Jim had left too long to the weeds. In the spring, Jim would begin with enthusiasm, having bought exotic seeds from the catalogues and coming home each Saturday morning from the nursery with a shiny new tool or a bag of peat moss. But as the spring wove into summer, Andy would see him on the back stoop, smoking, drinking a beer and listening to the radio as if he had forgotten entirely that there was anything in the yard at all.

He was a tall man, a genial alcoholic, a man whose charm and smile made people say he was good-looking—though he was not, with his long face and its flat planes, a truly handsome man. It was understood that he had appetites—most obviously for women and for drink—though he didn't look the part. He was said to be irresistible to women, and as a teenager, Andy sometimes wondered if his mother's envy of her neighbor didn't spring from an unspoken and unacknowledged attraction to her neighbor's husband. He remembers that sometimes Jim would goose his mother in the yard, and she would, as she twisted away from him, giggle and look girlish.

He was attractive to Andy too, though differently, and primarily because he was not a dairyman, like Andy's father and most of the other fathers Andy knew, but a salesman. That he only sold metal parts for farm machinery didn't bother Andy; it was the fact that Jim frequently left home for other places that seemed so grand. He was the first man Andy ever knew who routinely traded in what seemed to be barely used cars for new models every year—always a Buick and usually black, sitting gloriously in the gravel drive, making his own father's old Fords look like dusty country cousins. It was the traveling, he thinks now, that made Edith panicky in the mornings when Jim left her, sliding his hand down the curve of her narrow hip before he swung open the door of the Buick. He would lay his arm along the rim of the leather seat and back the Buick out the drive, waving cheerfully when he hit the road as if he were the only happy man in town.

And instantly she would be preoccupied, standing in the gravel drive long after he'd gone—as though he'd taken her with him. She would appear surprised and distracted if Andy's mother called to her—which Andy sometimes thought his mother did just for spite—and nearly deaf if he himself had to ask her a question about a chore or the whereabouts of a tool.

The worst, though, was her indifference to Eden. Even when Eden was small and her mother held her on her hip, Edith would seem for long seconds or even minutes to be oblivious to the child's entreaties—Eden, who seemed to have dimension and life in Edith's eyes only when Jim returned from wherever he had been.

HE REMEMBERS it as clearly as a just-told story, or he thinks he remembers it; it is hard now to sort out what he actually remembers on his own—this, his first true memory with a story and a plot—and what he might have been told later by his mother or his father or by Eden herself and then sketched into the picture he sees in his mind.

47

It was summer then too, he remembers, though earlier, fresher, June perhaps. A fine day, the morning, because his father was at work. And Jim, too, was traveling, because Andy's mother that night, using the phone, found him in a motel near Buffalo and called him home. Andy was in the garden with his mother. He remembers the scent of the soil, an evocative aroma he has not smelled for years, and a row of radishes, the fat red globes pushing up from the black earth. He was happy and rather proud, because his mother had said he could pick them. He remembers that he was wearing brown leather shoes and white socks and that the gap between the shoes and the socks was filling up with black dirt.

Edith came across the yard and stood by the gate in the wire fence. She was holding a bundle, wrapped in a yellow towel, in her arms. He knew at once, by the way she cradled it, that it was a baby—though possibly (the thought crossed his mind) it was the Closes' cat, sick somehow. The fact that she might just appear on a random morning with a baby didn't strike him as odd at all; friends of his mother's often just appeared at their door with new babies. It was much odder that the cat might be sick; after all, Andy had just seen it that morning, and it had seemed fine. It wasn't until he saw his neighbor's face, and then felt the way his mother got up from her knees to go to her at the gate, that he knew something was terribly wrong. It was a baby, but perhaps a sick baby, he thought.

"Edith," said his mother. He knew in the name there was a large question.

"I was vacuuming in the kitchen. And when I stopped, I heard a sound," said Edith Close. "It was a strange sound. I thought it was the cat, whining. Or a hurt bird. It was out front somewhere, and I wanted it to stop."

She was wearing, he remembers, the kind of dress she

always wore—a dress with a narrow waist and a top like a shirt, with sleeves she rolled to the elbow. Her forearms were narrow, and she had on gold bracelets. Her hair was parted in the middle and hung straight behind her shoulders, as she often combed it, in a style that would become fashionable years later with younger women. He remembers the bright red lipstick on her mouth, and that her face was white.

"And when I went to the door and opened it, there was . . . there was this cardboard box, out near the road but just inside the privet hedge. It said Oxydol on the side, and I thought someone had thrown their garbage onto the lawn like they sometimes do with the beer bottles. And then I heard the sound again, and I was angry because I thought someone had left us a litter of kittens, and I knew how hard it would be to get rid of them. . . . So I went to look, and the box was open and filled with towels, and this was in it, crying. . . ."

Andy's mother leaned across the wire fence and pulled a bit of the material away from her neighbor's arms.

"Jesus God," said his mother, stepping back quickly as if she'd seen something deformed.

The two women stood looking at each other for a moment and didn't speak.

"What is it?" his mother asked finally.

The other woman didn't understand the question. "What is it . . . ?"

"A boy or a girl?"

Edith looked momentarily stunned. Then she tilted her head back and closed her eyes. "Oh God, I wish Jim were here," she suddenly cried. "I don't know. I don't know." She looked as though she were about to fall, with the bundle in her arms.

"We'll go inside," said his mother quickly, clicking into gear in that way she had when there was a crisis or when he had fallen and hurt himself. "We'll look at the baby and make sure it's all right and call the police. Then we'll find Jim."

She turned to look at Andy, crouched in the dirt. Her face was unusually cross. She spoke in the voice she used when she "meant business," and pointed her finger at him.

"You are not to leave this garden under any circumstances. Do you understand me?" It was not a question. "You stay here and you don't move until I come back for you. I have to go next door with Mrs. Close."

Chastened and frightened, for she had never left him alone with no adults around, he watched them walk toward the other house and disappear inside the back door.

THAT WAS the first intruder, he thinks suddenly to himself, not the man who came in the August night, but the person who brought and left a child on a June morning fourteen years earlier. A parent himself, he tries to imagine what he has never thought of before: a woman stopping her car, the swift movement around the hedge. Had she hesitated, wept, bitten her lip for courage? Had a man or a boy brought her and insisted that she do this? Was she a young girl, a child herself, or an older woman with too many children to feed? Why that house and not another? Had she been driving up and down the road, searching for hours for the perfect doorstep? How had she been certain there was someone at the house to care for the baby?

"It might have been us," his father said that night at supper. His voice was unusually quiet. "It could so easily have been us."

And but for the accident of the other house facing the road, and theirs, seventy feet back, facing north, he came to understand, he might have had a sister, and that the fate of the child who would be called Eden had been determined by geography. And as he grew older and heard the story often repeated, it was hard for him not to think of her as a near sibling, someone who might have been called Ruth or Debbie, as his mother planned to call the daughter who never came, and that she might have been his and theirs.

BUT BEFORE the day was out, she was not anyone's but Jim's. Andy's mother heard it in his voice on the telephone from Buffalo.

"How did he take it?" asked Andy's father when his mother put down the phone.

"He's coming right away. He sounded . . . well, he just sounded very excited. And he asked the queerest questions," she said. "For a man."

"What questions?" said his father.

"He wanted to know . . . well, he wanted to know how much it weighed and how old it was, and what it looked like, and what the doctor had said, in all the details," she said, smoothing her hands along the front of her apron. "Like a woman," she added, but, of course, not like the woman who ought to have asked those questions, her voice implied.

And then his mother shook her head and sighed: "Poor man." For they all knew that the baby would be taken away as soon as the police could arrange for a place in an orphanage or a foster home. When the police had come that morning, accompanied by Dr. Ryder, who examined the child, they had asked Mrs. Close if she would keep the baby until the matter was settled, and she had said yes but had not suggested that she herself wanted it. And yet it was common knowledge, as Andy's mother had reminded his father (and had later incorporated into the oft-told tale of Eden's arrival), that Jim especially wanted a child and that they had been trying for years to conceive one, despite Dr. Ryder's pronouncement that the environment of Mrs. Close's womb was "hostile" to Jim's seed. An irony not lost on anyone.

THE MUSCLES in Andrew's right shoulder are screaming when he sees a red Honda Prelude pull smartly into the gravel driveway. It can't, at that speed, he thinks, be another chocolate cake from the Ladies Guild. A man unfolds himself from the driver's seat and snaps the door to as neatly as a soldier. He wears a tan summer suit and a pair of dark aviator sunglasses. His hair, which Andrew last remembers seeing unwashed and wild behind his ears, is short and trim. The man puts his hands in his pants pockets and grins.

"Andy-boy."

"T.J."

Andrew begins to back down the ladder. Tom Jackson lowers the sunglasses along the bridge of his nose and peers at Andrew. "Nifty," he says.

Andrew looks down at the anachronistic bell-bottoms. "They were in the closet," he says, and shrugs.

"Hey, listen," says T.J., losing the smile and advancing toward Andrew with his hand outstretched. "I'm really sorry about your mother. I just heard this morning. A client said . . ."

The two men shake hands. "It was mercifully quick," Andrew says inanely, parroting the words of Dr. Ryder. He realizes suddenly that the job of the bereaved is to allay the embarrassment of those who come to offer solace.

"Yeah, quick, that's the way to go," says T.J. He takes the sunglasses off and hangs them by a stem from his jacket pocket. "You're looking good, Andy-boy," he says, lightly punching Andrew's arm. "You workin' out?"

Andrew has not been working out, but he knows from the way T.J. has said it and the square look of him that *he* has and that he devotes some time to it. When they were boys, it was always T.J. who would arrive early for practice.

"No," says Andrew apologetically. "I was running for a while, but I moved and I lost it."

"You gotta have discipline," says T.J., the fastest skater Andrew has ever seen, a skater who seemed to hover effortlessly over the ice. "You gotta make it a habit. Every day, no matter what. You gotta stay in shape. Hey, man, forty's just around the corner."

Andrew has not thought of forty quite that way before, if, indeed, he has thought of it at all; but the soreness in his shoulders is telling him that he is not as young as he thought he was.

"Want a beer?" he asks. Andrew's memory of the landscape of his refrigerator is vague, but he thinks there may be the remnants of a six-pack he bought the day before at the mini-superette.

"Sure," says T.J. He turns with a flourish to let Andrew know that he is examining the black BMW in the driveway. He whistles appreciatively. "You must be doin' OK," he says. "Hey, I thought *I* was doing good, but a BMW. Whadda they go for now—twenty, thirty?"

Actually Andrew is embarrassed by his car and has been since arriving at the farmhouse. It sits in the drive looking as out of place as a woman in a mink at a garage sale. It also makes him anxious in a way he can't precisely define.

"To tell you the truth, I'd rather have your Prelude," says Andrew, lying graciously, since he would not for one minute own a bright red car. "The BMW's too temperamental," he adds, compounding the lie; the understated black vehicle runs as smoothly as a panther.

He leads the way up the back stoop and into the kitchen. With relief he sees that there are three Heinekens on the top shelf of the fridge. T.J. takes the tan jacket off and drapes it carefully over the back of a white kitchen chair. He rolls his neck, squares his shoulders and leans against the sink. He pops open his beer. Despite his lack of interest in working out, Andrew is impressed by T.J.'s flat stomach.

"So what's it been? Ten years?" asks T.J., taking a long swallow.

Andrew, leaning against the fridge, calculates. "I think it's more like fifteen or sixteen," he says. "I think the last time we got together was seventy-one or seventy-two. We went to see Tom Rush over Christmas break. I think."

"Sixteen years!" says T.J., exclaiming. "Jesus H. Christ. It sounds like something my old man used to say." He shakes his head. "Holy shit."

He runs his fingers up and down the beer can, making patterns in the condensation. "So whadda you do now?" T.J. asks. "You in business or what?"

"I'm with a pharmaceutical firm in the city," Andrew says. "I'm vice-president in charge of marketing and advertising." In this farmhouse kitchen, his job description sounds absurdly pretentious, but T.J. nods his approval.

"You were gonna be a writer," T.J. says.

"And you were going to be a musician. Keyboards."

"Yeah."

"One thing leads to another," says Andrew, for something to add. He doesn't particularly want to go into the specifics, however, of how smoothly he was "led" into moving to New York and taking his first job with the pharmaceutical firm. Nor into the specifics of how quick Martha was to see, in that move, certain financial possibilities.

"Yeah," says T.J. "Right to the bank."

The two men laugh.

"To money," says T.J., raising what's left of his beer in Andrew's direction.

Andrew raises his can in response.

"You married?" asks T.J.

Andrew shakes his head, "I was. We were separated about a year ago. I have a son, Billy. He's seven."

"Hey, man, I'm sorry," says T.J. "About the split, I mean. That's rough. Your idea or hers?"

Andrew reflects that this is the second time in ten minutes T.J. has said he is sorry for Andrew—three if you count the scolding over not working out.

"I guess it was mutual, the way those things are," he answers evasively.

"Yeah, right," says T.J., draining the last of the beer. He puts the can on the counter.

"Have another," offers Andrew.

"No. Can't. Thanks anyway. I got a corporation this afternoon wants to see the Gunther farm. For condos. Could be a fantastic deal."

"You're in real estate," says Andrew.

"For now," says T.J. "But developing is where it's at. The old farts are selling their land—the kids don't want to farm anymore. So what else is new, right? It's condos now—working couples, retirees, they don't want to have to mow the lawn. I had a deal about a month ago—a developer who bought the Gorzynski place and is putting in a country club with condos, a golf course, a pool, the whole nine yards."

T.J. picks up the empty beer can. He puts it back on the counter. "You gonna be around awhile?" he asks. "I'd like to get you out to the house to meet the kids. I married Didi Hanson, by the way."

"My mother wrote me that," says Andrew. He has an image of Didi Hanson's perfect teeth, a blond flip, and matching sweaters and skirts, long after the girls he knew were wearing jeans. He also remembers that Didi was a cheerleader and that she took it seriously, like a course.

"We've got two boys ourselves. Tom junior's fourteen

55

now, a handful. Ellis, the little one, is nine going on two, if you know what I mean."

Andrew isn't sure he does, but he nods. "I'd planned to stay a week," he answers, "fixing up the place before I put it on the market."

As soon as he says the word *market*, an unwelcome suspicion enters his thoughts. Has T.J. sniffed a potential sale and come looking for a client? Do real estate salesmen routinely read death notices in the papers? Or, to give his friend the benefit of the doubt, did T.J. really hear of Andrew's mother's death only this morning from a client? He can imagine the conversation: *I'm sorry to hear that*, T.J. would have said, immediately calculating how to get the edge, the same quality that, in another era, had made him the best hockey player the county had ever seen. *Her son, Andy, and I used to be real close friends.*

"You selling?" asks T.J., too casually, bending down and peering out the kitchen window, as if something out there had caught his attention.

"I guess," says Andrew.

"Really," T.J. says, standing up but not quite meeting Andrew's gaze. "Well, shit, you need a hand, I'd be glad to help out—for old times' sake, like. To be perfectly frank, I don't really handle such small layouts these days, but seeing as how we're old friends . . ." He looks around the kitchen as if eyeing it afresh, but Andrew has the sudden and distinct impression he's been taking inventory since he walked in the door.

"Whadda you want for it?" T.J. asks.

Andrew shrugs. "I've no idea. What do you think?"

"It's in pretty bad shape," says T.J., "and pretty isolated except for the Close house, and that's not an asset, if you follow me. . . . I dunno, maybe a hundred. One twenty-five."

Andrew nods. He is certain that T.J. has made these

calculations earlier in the day. They fall from his tongue too quickly.

But since Andrew hasn't committed himself to any other real estate agent, and because he wants only to make the transaction as painless as possible, he begins to see the arrival of T.J. as remarkably fortuitous, if not entirely coincidental. He wonders if T.J. feels the same awkward distance from their friendship as he himself does—or if he even cares.

"Be my guest," he says.

T.J. shakes his hand. "Excellent," he says, smiling and giving himself away completely. "I'll be speaking to you later about the details, and as soon as I talk to Didi, we'll have you around. I'd pick a date now, but I have to ask Didi— you know how women are."

Andrew winces inwardly. He doesn't know how women are any more than he suspects T.J. does, but there is something in the use of the cliché that tells Andrew that his friend's marriage isn't good. The knowledge surprises him—and then he wonders if perhaps he's mistaken, if the marriage is only not good that day, that week, that morning. If T.J. had come by last week, he wonders, would Andrew have sensed a different marriage? One more intimate, more hopeful? He knows that for most of his own marriage, its character often changed from one day to the next, depending sometimes on circumstances, sometimes on whether or not he and Martha had made love that morning.

"So," says T.J., shifting his weight against the sink.

Now that business, in its own way, has been conducted, Andrew can smell T.J.'s need to be moving on. It's human nature. Andrew has done it countless times himself.

T.J. picks up his jacket and puts it on. Andrew notices that there are beads of perspiration on T.J.'s upper lip. They move toward the door, open it and stand together on the stoop. They are both looking out at the other house.

"You seen Eden yet?" asks T.J.

"No, I haven't."

"I don't think I've seen her six times in ten years," says T.J. "And each time she was in a car with her mother. Pretty isolated out here. Of course, she was away for so long in that place upstate. . . . Everybody kinda goes his own way, you know what I mean. Sometimes I feel bad I never just drove over and knocked on the door after she got back, but I never knew what I'd say really."

"Yes," says Andrew.

"She was one fantastic-looking girl. You remember?"

"I remember."

"A real knockout. She was—what, fourteen?"

"About."

"A mess, if you ask me."

T.J. squares his shoulders and looks down the drive toward the cornfields on the other side of the road. "I always figured he buried the gun in the cornfields somewhere, but I don't know," he says. "You'd think it woulda been plowed up by now."

"You would think so," says Andrew.

The sun glints sharply off a silver Mazda that speeds along the road, intercepting their view of the fields. Above the fields, a flock of crows makes a half-moon arc.

And as they had done for weeks after the shooting, silently, not wanting anyone to know of their preoccupation, Andrew realizes that once again they are drawing diagrams in their heads of how the unthinkable could have taken place: The father walking into the house, hearing the muffled sounds upstairs, opening the door to his daughter's room, the horror of what he sees there, the frenzied shouts. A hand, reaching for a gun. Eden with a sheet clutched to her breast, moving toward her father. . . . The mother's footsteps on the stairs.

He remembers the terrible sound of the crying.

"You ever see Sean's parents?" asks Andrew.

T.J. makes a movement with his shoulders, as if to shake himself loose from his speculation. "His father's still got the TV repair shop in town, but he's usually pretty far gone by afternoon. The mother died a few years back. Cancer. Bad news, that story. About Sean, I mean."

"Yeah," says Andrew.

"So," says T.J. He grabs Andrew's hand. "So listen, take it easy," he says, moving away and sideways along the driveway, toward his car, reaching in his pocket for his keys.

Andrew watches him from the stoop. With the same economy of movement that made him the most fluid skater in the county, T.J. slips his long body into the Prelude. Andrew is about to wave, when T.J. sticks his head out of the window.

"And for Christ's sake, Andy-boy," he says, turning the key in the ignition, "go buy yourself a decent pair of jeans."

Andrew smiles and shrugs. He wonders how certain qualities in a boy can turn out so strangely in a man. And yet who is he to criticize? Has he not himself, in business, made the same dismal moves?

The beer on an empty stomach has left him light-headed. He goes back up the stairs into the kitchen.

As he opens the screen door, he has an image of Eden naked under a flower-print sheet—and the image startles him.

Why think of that now? He wonders if T.J. knows about this fact. Did he, years ago, tell that detail to his friend?

AFTER JIM had held the baby, there was no thought of ever letting her go. She was his before he even arrived at the farmhouse. Andy's mother was in the Closes' kitchen, waiting, with her neighbor, when Jim flung open the door and let his sample case fall from his hands. She watched the way he bent to the child—his eagerness for the child seeming to be a natural extension of his largesse—and how he held her aloft as gracefully as a baby nurse, as if he'd been practicing in his dreams for years.

And she saw, even in the confusion, the face of Edith Close, who put herself forward to be kissed before giving over the child, but who was not kissed or touched until much later in the night and who sat watching numbly at the kitchen table as her husband danced with his warm bundle over the worn linoleum floor. And Andy's mother saw, too, her struggle to compose her face, to realign her features to match her husband's new expression, to feign a joy she knew she must display so as not to fall behind.

She knew at once not to protest, nor to bring up even one objection—though, said Andy's mother later, there were plenty of them for a practical woman to consider: a distraught mother might, with second thoughts, return; the baby might not be right in some as yet undetermined way; she might herself wake up pregnant any day now, creating two babies to care for (this last objection would immediately be seen as transparent, however, as it had all but been ruled out by the all-knowing Dr. Ryder).

"Eden," said Jim, dreamily skating between the sink and the stove. "We shall call her Eden."

Edith looked up at him; she seemed to be about to protest.

"The Garden of Eden come to us in a basket," he rhapsodized, exposing, Andy's mother was to say later, a hitherto unrecognized and not altogether welcome strain of sentiment, seeing as how the child had actually arrived in an Oxydol box; and creating in that instant a lifetime of confusion by giving the infant a name that sounded so like the adoptive mother's. ("Edith's had stitches?" Andy's father would say distractedly from the dinner table, having half heard a story his wife was telling. "No, *Eden*'s had stitches," she would reply, in endless exasperation.)

And Eden she became, as Andy's mother sat watching her neighbor's face—and saw upon it the struggle give way to the swift sharp knowledge that something irrevocable had happened in her life and that the exact shape of what she'd had before was, in an instant, gone. The hand that had been propping up her chin slipped silently into her lap. Her mouth opened slightly, and Andy's mother could hear beside her a long, slow intake of air.

ANDREW RUBS his sore shoulder and bends down to survey the dismaying contents of his mother's refrigerator. He observes that it seems to contain random pieces of a number of different puzzles—nothing adding up to a satisfying whole. He has never been fond of Edith Close (primarily, he supposes, because she so ignored him—but more, he'd prefer to think, because of Eden), but despite this dislike he cannot help but feel for her the fundamental unfairness of it all: the neat and terrible symmetry of the two intruders—the one on a fresh June morning, a foretaste of what could be lost; the other on a humid August night, taking everything.

AND WHEN the police came the next day, with a social worker, there was Jim at the door. He announced they were keeping the child. If they had to be merely foster parents for a while, that was fine, said Jim. But eventually, he was sure, the child would legally be theirs. The police, unprepared for this, had papers stating otherwise, but these were of no consequence to Jim, who calmly went where he was told, signed where he was bidden, showered his irresistible charm on women who knew shortcuts through the bureaucratic maze, and in that way slipped through the miles of red tape that might have daunted another man.

With motherhood rudely thrust upon her, her hormones ill-prepared for the job, Edith Close performed the tasks required of her as if directed by remote control—a poor connection that might short-circuit at any time and often did. With Jim around, the infant had, at least, a playmate—though Edith's nascent jealousy, a subtle mist through which she floated and which had not yet created the sharp tongue that would come later, often demanded that Jim put the baby down "so the poor child can sleep." But with Jim away, Eden ceased to exist in any tangible way at all—the tree falling in the forest with no one to hear.

Andrew, who has settled for a casserole left by the Ladies Guild, which looks more or less like goulash, remembers the afternoon Edith Close left the baby outside in the carriage without the net and went upstairs to lie down. The Closes' honey-colored cat—whose jealousy, unlike his mistress's, was uninhibited—leapt silently into the carriage and was about to do away with the usurper when the baby's screams brought Andy's mother running from the kitchen. She scooped up the child, giving the sullen cat a remarkably deft kick—thinking the row would alert her neighbor. But even when she went to the back door and called for Edith—rather crossly, Andy thought—it was some minutes before the dazed woman arrived at the door. It was Andrew's mother's impression, as she told his father at dinner that night, that Edith had simply *forgotten* the child altogether.

Andrew doubts, as did his mother, that their neighbor willfully meant to harm the baby. It was rather, as he has thought before, a case of faulty connections: a matter of her fear of losing Jim (who for years had gone off in his black Buick to other rooms in other towns, and about whom rumors of other women often circulated). A child who developed, as luck would have it, an astonishing head of blond curls, several shades lighter than the hair of her adoptive mother. Though she was not a fat child, she had plump cheeks, an appealing pink coloring and remarkably dark lashes for so fair a skin type. Her eyes were blue, like Edith's, causing the women of the town to comment how like the mother the child was (a remark that must have filled Edith with ambivalence), but a more vivid blue, a greenish blue, which on an older girl or a young woman today you'd say was enhanced with contact lenses. She was a child whose beauty was indestructible: You could forget to wash her face or comb her hair, as Edith often did; you could put her in a pair of dull hand-me-downs from the rummage sale—and yet, passing by the playground at the school, it would be she whom you noticed first among the other faces and small bodies on the swings or on the jungle gym.

The more Edith ignored the child, the more Jim spoiled her, as if to redress the deficit—or perhaps it was the other way around: Edith meant unconsciously to temper his excess. But his love being the more passionate and less ambivalent of the two emotional forces in the household, Eden grew up more spoiled than ignored—spoiled "rotten," his mother sometimes said, a phrase that has always suggested to Andrew bruised and softened fruit, a picture distinctly at odds with the beguiling, if willful, child who was growing fast into puberty next door.

Eating the congealed goulash, Andrew remembers scenes he has long forgotten. Jim arrives home from a trip and opens the door of the black Buick. He is in his shirtsleeves, with his tie still knotted. There are packages in his hands. He sees Eden on the new swing set he has ordered from Sears, the one Andy's father had to pour the cement for when Jim could not (or would not) figure out the directions. Eden spies Jim, squeals with delight and looks for the present she knows will be there. Then there is Edith at the screen, peering out, patting her hair. She runs down the steps to her husband. She is wearing a new sweater that Andy, who is playing with an old toy car on his own back stoop and who is wishing Jim would look his way with a stick of gum, has never seen before—a soft white furry sweater with a low jeweled neck. Sometimes she says the name *Jim*. Sometimes she puts her arm around his waist. Then, when he has greeted his wife with a kiss, Edith bends to the child, and in an animated voice neither Eden nor Andy has heard in three days, says how pretty the dress is that Jim has brought her and touches the child for the first time since Jim went away. In the beginning, when she is very small, Eden is happy to have her mother hug her at last. Later she will just be confused. Then she will learn to smirk. And finally she will shrug her mother off with a rude word or a gesture that Edith will publicly ascribe to Eden's "difficult phase."

Andrew, giving up on the goulash and scraping his plate, now understands these domestic jealousies in a way that was impossible for him as a child. Jealousy was there, even in his own house, he realizes, on his father's face, when Andy, with a fever or a scraped knee, would choose his mother's embrace instead of his; and he has felt it himself, more recently, watching a flicker of hesitation pass over his son's features when Billy leaves his mother to come away with Andrew for an evening or a weekend.

But, in an instant, as he grasps Billy's hand or ruffles his hair, the hurt is gone, healed, as quickly as it came. While for Edith Close, there seemed to be no healing, no respite from her own imagination.

THEY WERE FRIENDS, good friends, for a year, possibly two. He was fourteen and Eden was eleven. Before that time, she'd been uninteresting as a playmate, though she'd always possessed the inherent fascination of a celebrity by dint of her arrival. And before she was eleven she whined a lot, having learned early that the thin grating sound was the only one that seemed to penetrate the thickening fog of preoccupation that surrounded her mother, and that it worked miraculously with Jim, who couldn't bear to see his daughter unhappy, no matter how absurd the cause. But by the age of eleven, she'd seen, looking across the yard, that Andy and his friends were considerably more interesting as potential companions than her distant mother and her too attentive father or the girls at school, who had never quite been friendly. And being clever, not to say manipulative, she was quick to intuit that acceptance by these older boys required radical surgery. Thus Eden became, for a brief and happy period in her life, a tomboy.

He remembers vividly the day she first came to them. He and Sean and T.J. were fiddling with their fishing rods by Andrew's back stoop, getting ready to head out to the pond to catch some catfish before supper. It was September or October, Andrew thinks, a school night, because he'd had to finish his homework before he could go. But early in the year, before hockey practice had started. It was muggy; they were in T-shirts, enjoying the last taste of summer and summer pleasures before the cold set in in earnest.

T.J., who was always the quickest of the three, had his rig ready to go, leaning against the side of the house, and was executing an idle tap dance in the dirt by the stoop, his sneakers raising puffs of dust around his feet.

"Come on, you guys," he said impatiently. "It'll be dark soon, and anyway I gotta be home by supper or my old man'll cream me."

"Take it easy," said Andy lightly, threading his line through the guides. "We've still got two hours."

But it was Sean who was having trouble that day, his line hopelessly tangled in a knot he'd been working on with no results for twenty minutes. His brow was knit into a furrow, and his face was nearly as red as his hair from his frustration. T.J. and Andy were both waiting for him to blow,

Andy more than a little worried that Sean would suddenly yell *Shit*, with Andy's mother chopping vegetables right beyond the screen. And then that night at the supper table, there would be the lecture about bad language and comments about the company Andy kept. Though his parents liked T.J., who had, even at an early age, the gift of charm and who had developed a talent for salesmanship, mostly of himself, they were nervous about Sean.

Sean's parents were well known in the town. Both were heavy drinkers, but their reputation had been earned because of their fights: legendary sharp-tongued battles heard through the open window of the apartment they lived in with their three children over the TV repair shop; bitter tirades in the shop itself while embarrassed customers pretended to be studying the contours of a picture tube; or silent, ugly tableaux seen through the rolled-up windows of the family Pontiac, Sean's mother's lined and dead-white face turned toward her husband, who would, like his son, grow red from his fury.

As a boy, Sean was visibly chagrined by his parents' displays of temper, even though, as he grew into his teens, his own temper would betray him when he least wanted it to. But T.J. and Andy accepted this embarrassment and his parents' volatility as a given, much in the same way they unconsciously acknowledged that Andy's mother was too fat and T.J.'s mother was a social climber—these facts intruding upon their childhood, sometimes even causing them a moment's pain or awkwardness, but ultimately easily dismissed as not being pivotal to their lives. The weather was pivotal. And the condition of the ice or the fishing. Or a stolen baseball glove or the offer of a driving lesson or a chance at the playoffs. Their parents, however, seemed more like obstacles to be negotiated than central figures in the daily drama.

(Yet Andrew thinks now how wrong they were to be so complacent. For that legacy of volatility, or perhaps it was the alcohol, ultimately would destroy Sean; and is not T.J., Andrew wonders, just as socially ambitious as his mother?)

Andy didn't notice Eden until T.J. said, by way of a greeting, "Hey."

She was wearing a plaid cotton shirt and a pair of white shorts. She was barefoot, he remembers, and her hair, still long then, was pulled off her face in a low ponytail.

Although she'd sometimes come over when Andy was alone, she'd never approached him when he was with other boys, and Andy was waiting for a message or a summons from Edith or Jim about some task that needed attending to. But she stood there, her hands in the pockets of her shorts, and said, redundantly, "What are you doing?"

It all happened, Andrew thinks now, in a matter of seconds—a deft dance of questions and positions, each one finding, in the space of a few sentences and a look here and there, a role to take on. Sean looked up, the anger draining from his face, replaced by confusion. T.J. shoved his hands into his pockets and said, *Fishing*. Andy, not getting it yet, waited for the summons. Eden smiled, a deliberate smile that made them all stare at their feet, but when they looked up, the smile was gone.

"Can I come too?" she asked quite seriously.

T.J. whirled in a circle on his heel. Andy fumbled with an answer. "I don't know," he said unthinkingly. "You haven't got a rod."

T.J. hooted and punched the air. Andy, realizing the pun, rolled his eyes. Eden stood her ground.

"So?" she said, challenging them.

T.J. put an arm around Eden's shoulder, something Andy had never done. He was sure he himself had never touched her, and T.J.'s touch startled him, caught him off guard, so that he felt in succession annoyed with T.J. and then confused, as he sometimes felt when he was in a room with his friends and his parents and had no idea what to say or whom to be.

"You want to watch the big boys fish?" asked T.J., winking at Andy. "It's a thrill."

Eden shrugged—careful not to appear too eager now that she had made her move.

T.J. put his hands back in his pockets. Andy said, unsure just what it was he was committing himself to, *OK by me*.

Sean, looking first at Eden, then at T.J., then back to Eden, screwed his face into a squint. He peered at Eden as if she were a species unwelcome at the best of times.

"Jesus H.," he said aloud.

As a tomboy, Eden was brilliant. She learned to be tough and savvy as if taking on a foreign language, and in doing so discovered an aptitude for it. After an initial period of disbelief, Andy and T.J. and Sean grudgingly found this new character acceptable, and they were more than a little awed by a tenacity in her that none of them could quite match. No matter how hard they tried in the beginning to shake her off, she stuck, like a stray. She made her mother cut her hair, though Jim had forbidden it; she took to wearing dungarees and white Keds. Though she was inches shorter than Andy or T.J. or Sean, she matched them stride for stride as they walked the tracks, her hands stuffed like theirs into the pockets of a maroon and gold junior high school jacket that was several sizes too big for her, a black knit cap, like the ones they wore, all but covering her bright gold fringe.

It was the year T.J.'s father let him have a BB gun to shoot squirrels with, and after she had wheedled a turn, Eden showed an enthusiasm for tracking and shooting small animals that surprised them—especially Andy, who even at fourteen was hard-pressed to understand why killing animals was fun. In winter, when every afternoon was spent with a hockey stick on the pond behind the cornfields, Eden watched the others at first, hunched in her school jacket, stomping her feet on the ground, both to keep them warm and in irritation. "I want to skate, you assholes," she cried, employing the word that was at the farthest edge of their vocabularies that month. And in the end, she bullied Andy into teaching her. Though she was small, she was, like her demeanor, fast and headstrong. And when she was hit with the puck—on the shin through her dungarees, at the side of her cheekbone, drawing blood, causing a scar that might have been permanent had that particular mark not been obliterated three years later—she, like them, did not cry but rather held her breath and stood perfectly still and let her face go white with the pain.

They played at the pond from early December until late in March. He remembers the way the toes went first, and then the ears, because they'd been bitten by the cold years earlier one day when you hadn't noticed. He remembers the way the ice felt when it was refrozen and bumpy and the sinking in the stomach when you'd caught an edge and knew you were going down on your kneecaps. In early December, after a cold snap, the ice was black and gorgeous, but for most of the season, in the late afternoon, it was snowy with streaks and ruts and graceful arcs, with the sun blinking red-gold behind the lacy silhouettes of the bare tree limbs, the sky already turning navy blue.

He remembers they'd been sitting one afternoon in the snowbank at the edge of the pond, unlacing their skates, timing it so they'd emerge from the cornfields just as it turned pitch, calling each other "shithead" and "fink" in a confusion of vocabularies, trying out words they'd heard at school or from their parents. It was just after Christmas, because Andy and Eden had new skates. He remembers that his fingers were stiff with the intense cold and that he couldn't get the wet knots undone. And then suddenly, raising his head in frustration, in the thickening dusk, he saw it.

She drew from her pocket a pack of Old Golds—casually, as if the pack, wrapped in cellophane, were merely sticks of gum. He can see it still: the pleasure and triumph in her eyes at being the first to have them, thus cementing for herself, with this single gesture, a place among the elect.

One by one they stopped what they were doing to watch her as she expertly opened the cellophane and shook one cigarette from the pack. She lit it. She inhaled deeply, as none of them had ever done, and Andy realized she'd been practicing, possibly for days, watching and waiting for the precise moment to make her move. Sean, his nose running from the cold, tried to disparage the gesture, breaking the silence by saying that she had the only parent who smoked, implying she had an access denied the others, but the moment belonged to Eden, and she knew it. She held out the pack, and they each took one, holding it between their fingers the way, years later, they would learn to cradle joints. She tossed the matches to Andy, fixing him with her eyes. And with this look, she dared him to inhale as she had, though he could hardly breathe from the cold and his earlier exertions on the ice.

They had all smoked the one cigarette, and then they'd had another, till they were nothing but four embers glowing in the dark. And at the edge of the cornfield, as they were about to disperse—T.J. and Sean still with the long hike back toward town, their skates knotted and slung over their shoulders, their heads spinning and their stomachs rising— it was Eden who'd produced the roll of peppermint Life Savers, instructing them each on the importance of masking their breath. And if she had not already truly become one of them earlier when she offered them the cigarettes, she would have done so then—for though they all "caught shit," as T.J. put it, when they arrived home later than they ever had for dinner, none of them yet had to face the shouts and heated lectures that would come months later when smoking among them was already commonplace and they'd grown careless.

By MIDWINTER they were no longer a threesome but a foursome, a mismatched quartet (seen from behind as they walked the tracks with hockey sticks parked on their shoulders) of three tall, reedy clarinets and one short piccolo. Indeed, Eden had become so much a part of them that they minded when she wasn't there.

"So where is she?" T.J. said one afternoon when Andy and Sean got to the pond. T.J. already had his skates on, having arrived first, and was carving impatient circles in the bumpy ice near the shoreline.

Andy, aware that his friends looked to him as a source of information about Eden, his status enhanced by this circumstantial intimacy, knew she was at the dentist and said so, registering as he did a flicker of disappointment in the way T.J. stabbed the ice with his stick. At the very least, it was easier to play a game with four.

Sean, yanking at a lace, was still pretending then that Eden wasn't much more than a pain in the neck and clicked his tongue in disgust; but when he said, with almost too much of a complaint in his voice, "This was the day I was supposed to show her how to do an eagle," Andy thought that he, too, had come to expect her presence.

For a brief time, their days together were a satisfying blur spent on the ice, at the baseball diamond or in the cornfields, looking up at a summer sky that floated too quickly past them. It seems that then he and Eden were always together—sometimes in the larger group, often alone. He supposes now that you could say they were best friends, though if you'd said it to him then, he'd have bristled at the thought, however unfeminine she was. Perhaps it was the circumstance of long summer nights spent tossing a ball after dinner, or the quiet of the fields where they hid to smoke, but when they had things to say then, they said them to each other.

"Edith doesn't like me," he remembers her saying one night as they lay on their backs in the path through the cornfields, just out of sight of the houses. They were eating Fudgsicles; he recalls that a bit of chocolate had melted and had dribbled onto her neck. The ice cream man passed the houses every night after dinner that summer and made a point of parking his truck at the end of the drive and ringing his bell on his way to the next town. Andy and Eden would buy something for themselves, and often Andy would get something for his mother as well. (What a wonderful mix, he thinks now—the innocence of the Fudgsicles and the secret acrid thrill of the Old Gold cigarettes they smoked afterward.) She was wearing a T-shirt and a pair of shorts, as he was, and they smelled of 6-12; the mosquitoes in the cornfields were ferocious on humid summer nights.

"Sure she does," said Andy. "You just think she doesn't. Everyone thinks that once in a while."

"I think it all the time."

Andy could not remember a scene he had witnessed lately that would prove Eden wrong, though he found it nearly incomprehensible, in the abstract, to imagine a mother not liking her child.

"What are we doing tomorrow?" she asked.

"I don't know," Andy said. "T.J.'s gotta do the lawn for his father, and I don't know about Sean."

"Why don't just you and me do something?"

"Like what?"

"Like take our bikes and ride to a town we've never been to before and have a picnic."

"We could. . . ."

The idea appealed to Andy. He tried to remember if he, too, was supposed to do something for his father in the morning.

"We could discover a new lake, go fishing," she said.

"Bring the poles on the bikes, you mean?"

"Sure. I bet it could be done."

Andy pondered the logistics.

"I think I'm going to die young," she said, licking the last of the chocolate off the wooden stick.

"Don't be stupid. Why do you say that?" It was one of the things Andy didn't like about girls, this tendency toward melodrama. He tried to quash it in Eden whenever he thought it was surfacing.

"Because I can't picture myself doing anything as an adult."

"Huh?"

"I can't see myself as a housewife, and I can't see myself as a schoolteacher or a secretary or an actress or anything. So I must be going to die young."

Apart from a vague image of himself going off to school somewhere, and a feverish wish to become a major league baseball player, Andy could not picture himself doing anything either.

"Well, neither can I, and I don't think I'm going to die young," he said.

"Sean doesn't like me very much, does he?" she said.

"Sean's a jerk, and besides, I think he likes you as good as he likes any of the rest of us."

"But you like me," she said.

He sat up, swatted at a cloud of no-see-ums that were hovering about his forehead.

"You're all right," he said, unable to commit himself out loud any further, for the truth was he'd come to prefer her

73

company to that of T.J. or Sean. He turned to look at her lying on the grass.

"But don't let it go to your head," he said, shoving her in the shoulder. She sat up quickly, catapulted a Fudgsicle stick with expert skill. It landed on his ear. He tried to zing one at her and missed.

"I think my real father must have been a jock," she said.

Andy knew that Eden had been told at an early age that she was adopted—even the story, which Jim managed to make charming, like that of a princess in a fairy tale, of her arrival in a cardboard box. According to Andy's own father, Jim was smart to have done this, because it would have been impossible to keep the tale from her once she'd entered school. Indeed, when she did encounter the children of the town, whose parents regarded Eden as a curiosity if not something of a living legend (her arrival itself a historical event in the unofficial town record), she was sometimes the butt of childish and cruel teasing: "The girl in the box! The girl in the box!" the boys in her class would call across the playground.

"He might have been," said Andy.

And then the two of them lay back on the dirt and dried grasses and smoked the cigarettes she stole from Jim (how can the man have failed to notice the two or three packs a week they were putting away then? he wonders now) and thought about these questions and other, more pressing matters, such as whether or not Andy's father would carry through with his threat to keep him off the hockey team if he didn't pass French in the fall. Or whether T.J.'s father was going to get the pool built before the summer was over. Or, failing that, the best way to talk yourself through the gate at the town pool, above which Eden swore she could actually see the chlorine shimmer.

THEY WERE together that first year, through the summer and well into the spring of his junior year. By then he had long ceased to think of her as an anomaly among his friends. She was simply Eden, his friend too, though if pressed, he'd have said that he worried more about Eden, looked out for her in a way that was never necessary with T.J. or Sean—or perhaps with Sean when Andy and T.J. would have to cool him off to avoid a penalty on the ice.

But when he thinks of the summer Eden turned thirteen (the summer he was waiting for his senior year in high school to begin, the summer inaugurated, it seems now to him, by that fateful day on the baseball diamond), it is as if a wave were pulling away from him then with the force of a powerful undertow.

They had let her play third base that spring for their unofficial sandlot team. She was a so-so hitter, but fast and accurate in the infield. He remembers their team was losing narrowly that day. She was on the bench beside him, hunched over as he was, her elbows on her knees. It had rained earlier in the day, but the sun had cleared the mist, leaving only puddles in the depressions in the field behind the school. He saw her sit up, put an arm across her abdomen. He thought her face was especially white, whiter than it ought to have been. She was wearing her cap backward, with the brim pointing down her back. She moaned slightly, almost too faintly to be heard, but he had, and he asked her if she was all right. She looked at him but didn't answer. And then T.J. hit a home run, and they were on their feet, for this brought in two runs, and they were tied.

He sat down on the bench. Eden was still standing. And then he saw it, the dark red stain.

At first he was scared. She'd been hit, injured somehow, and hadn't told anyone. That would be like her, he thought. But then, in the second instant, it came to him.

"Eden?" he said quietly.

She turned to look at him, and when she saw his face, she sat down.

"Don't get up," he said.

He looked down the bench and saw a jacket on the other side of Sean. Leaning behind his friend, he jerked the jacket off the bench, casually laid it on his lap, and then he slipped it to Eden.

She tied it around her waist, knotting the arms in front.

"Hey, look," Andy said to Sean, who was absorbed in the game. "Eden's sick to her stomach." He was surprised how easily the lie came to him. "I'm taking her home. Put Warren in for me, OK? He's been dying to play first." Sean nodded absently without looking at Andy.

Andy turned to Eden. He hesitated. Then he said: "You know what's going on?"

She shrugged. "I guess."

They walked home the two miles from the playground diamond, each carrying a glove, Eden with the jacket tied around her waist. He punched his glove repeatedly, sometimes arced his arm in a pantomine of a pitch. Neither spoke of the reason why they were walking home before the game was finished. Neither mentioned that Andy needn't have come with her. Indeed, Eden hardly said a word. He thought she must be embarrassed, so he tried to talk of other things, tried for a tone just this side of flippant, but there were long pauses in his monologue.

When he thinks about that walk now—now, twenty years later—it is not embarrassment he feels (he smiles to think of their awkwardness and of her delicacy); rather it is sadness that overtakes him. For though she was young and tongue-tied, though she was barely able to negotiate this strange and bewildering matter, he has no doubt now that it was, for Eden, her last pure day of childhood.

THAT SUMMER she quit the team, quit playing sports. She gave no explanation save that she found them "boring"—an explanation that puzzled Andy. For though he, too, was reaching puberty—with his broken voice and faint mustache—he felt himself to be essentially unchanged, still passionate about hockey and baseball, still tied to his friends like a brother. He was busy days with his first summer job—at the dairy, unloading the trucks as they came in, setting up the bottles for the washer. In the evenings, after supper, in this second summer they had together, he and Eden sometimes played catch or escaped from doing the dishes into the fields. But they bickered for the first time. He said he thought her newly pierced ears were barbaric; she stubbed out a cigarette and called him "an infant." She teased him when he couldn't name the Top Ten, and he accused her of doing nothing all day but lying in her plastic chaise longue in the backyard, listening to the radio. That was not all she did, she said, and showed him earrings and rings she'd shoplifted from the Woolworth's in the next town. She got on the bus in the mornings, she said, and got off when she felt like it. She said she'd try for a Timex for him next time, and he said, irritably, "Don't bother." In truth, he was horrified. Stealing frightened him. Finding a ten-dollar bill on the floor of a truck he was emptying just the week before, he'd sought out the driver at once; simply holding the ten had made him feel guilty.

She wore shorts and halter tops and was developing a backyard tan. She curled her legs under her when she talked, and when she smoked, she sometimes absentmindedly ran the tips of her fingers along her arm up to her shoulder and back again. The gesture mesmerized him. She was letting her hair grow out, and she had painted her nails.

By September, the transformation was complete. He remembers the first day of school that year, waiting for the bus. She was late. He could see the vehicle, a yellow dot in the distance, making its way along the straight road from town. He turned and cupped his hands around his mouth and shouted toward her house: *Eden*.

She came around the corner from the back stoop; not running as she would have in the spring, but swaying lightly from side to side, adjusting the strap of a pocketbook on her shoulder. Before she met his eyes, he saw a slow smile crawl across her face. She was enjoying his bewilderment. Out of her mother's sight, she opened her pocketbook and took out a tube of lipstick. She parted her lips slightly and removed a speck at the corner of her mouth. He had never seen her wear lipstick before. Her hair was combed to the side and hung in a long curve across one eye. She was wearing a straight tight black skirt, but it was her blouse that plunged him momentarily into the red heat of confusion. It was a white short-sleeved shirt with a collar—a schoolgirl's blouse or a shirt you'd wear to camp—except that the cotton was thin and he could see that beneath the shirt she was wearing a bra. Her breasts had sprouted overnight, it seemed, too fast for her small frame; they pushed against the fabric. The bus came lumbering to a stop. Quickly, he climbed the steps, walked past several boys he knew and sat on an empty seat close to the window. Too late, he realized his mistake.

In the spring, she'd have sat down beside him, with more of a thwack than you'd have thought possible from her tiny body, and would have said, through the clicking of her gum, where the fuck did he get that wimpy shirt, and he'd have shrugged and felt OK, for it *was* wimpy—a thin white shirt with shiny stripes on it—and he was wearing it only this once, to please his mother, who had bought it the week before.

Instead he watched the leer of the driver and the astonishment of the other boys as this creature he felt he no longer knew at all made her way down the aisle, holding her own as the bus lurched forward, grasping with her fingers the metal bars above the leather seats. Then he saw a brief flash of painted nails and heard the swish of her skirt sliding on the leather seat behind him. He stared out the window, furious with her.

He felt in his mouth, for the first time in his life, the metallic taste of betrayal and longing. With it came the knowledge that the shape of things you had known and trusted as certain could be twisted, overnight, out of recognition.

I think you know. I think, of all of them, you're the only one who knows. You talk like you don't know, but I think you do.

I hear you scraping, scraping, and then you move the ladder. My window is always open. My world is what I hear. I can tell you exactly what time of day it is just by the sounds outside the window.

My life is nothing but this.

She washes my hair. She bends my head back in the sink. Her hands are rough. I am like an old person she has to care for.

I listen to your voice and T.J.'s. His is full of lies. You can hear them when he laughs. He once was in a car with me, and I let him touch my breasts. I opened my blouse, and there were other boys with him. I bet he never told you that.

There was a shimmer on the water. You sat on the ground with your knees up. Your arms were on your knees. You were growing your hair long to go away to school, you said. I made you look at me.

I said, Afraid?

You shook your head.

You said I might have been your sister.

THREE

THE WALK IS SHORT, SEVENTY FEET. THE LAWN IS DRYING, and he could even now be mowing it. He thinks: *In an hour, I'll be doing that*.

He has washed, changed into a pair of khaki pants and a dress shirt, rolled to the elbows. He walks with his hands in his pockets, a walk he made unthinkingly a thousand times in his youth. He heard her car in the drive when he was washing up in the bathroom, and the faint clatter of a screen door; like clockwork, she is home at two-fifteen each day. A dozen large rosy-brown hydrangea blossoms are strewn along the top of the long grass by the drive; the small tree, he notes again, took a beating during the electrical storm in the night. He can't imagine it will last much longer now. His mother planted it the year she and his father bought the house, forty years ago at least, and he has always associated it with his mother, its lush growth with her well-being. Now it seems to him its foliage has grown too dense for its spindly trunk and must soon topple over.

His heart is beating too fast when he reaches the back stoop. Annoyed, he takes a deep breath and squares his shoulders. When he puts his foot on the first step, he feels it give—as if it had accustomed itself all these years only to her weight and could not bear a pound more. It has been nineteen years since he entered this house—and he is aware, as he raps quickly on the frame of the screen door, that he is stepping again into a scene from the past, even though he knows, from the encounters of the last several days, that it won't feel at all as he has remembered it.

She comes to the door at once, wary, then alarmed. Their eyes involuntarily flicker away from each other, in the manner of people who do not like each other much but feel compelled to be polite.

"Andy," she says, not opening the door.

"I came to say hello to Eden," he says almost too brightly, and with this greeting, he opens the door and steps up into the kitchen. Edith backs away from him.

"Eden's asleep," she says quickly.

She is still wearing the pinkish-gray silk dress she had on earlier, a color that immediately begins to fade as he follows her away from the bright sunlight of the doorway into the kitchen. The shades are drawn over the sink and over the window facing the drive, a detail he has not noticed before, coming and going in his car. The effect is of a kitchen shut up for a season, waiting for the summer people or the new tenants to enter. He has a powerful urge to raise the shades with a snap, to see her kitchen and her face in the sunlight.

"I keep them closed to shut out the heat," she says, noticing his glance toward the window. "It's cooler that way."

He stands in the center of the linoleum floor, waiting for his eyes to adjust to the interior dusk, waiting for a cue, but she gives none.

"May I sit down?" he asks.

With an odd nervous movement of her hands, she indicates the chair. She offers to make him a glass of iced tea. She is at the sink and then the refrigerator, getting ice, her back to him still.

"Thank you for everything you did for my mother," he says, although he is not entirely sure exactly what was done.

"I feel badly about your mother," she says, turning now with two tall glasses in her hands. "I ought to have seen it coming on. She did say once she had headaches. And in June, I was in the market when Carol—you remember Carol Turner—Carol said your mother had nearly fainted in the store just the day before. But I thought it was the heat, not a spell."

A *spell*. He hasn't heard the word used this way since he lived at home and his mother spoke of his grandmother— to make him understand why she was sick and couldn't see him. *She has these spells, Andy*, his mother said. And so had his own mother, only there'd been no one at the house to know.

"We see them in the patients at the nursing home," she says. "They're small strokes, and there's medication that can be given. And I should have realized . . ."

"It's not your fault," says Andrew. He takes a sip of iced tea. It has been made from a powdered mix. It has sugar in it, which he doesn't like. Now that his eyes are adjusting, the color is coming up on the walls: a pale green he remembers now, a green of hospitals or of government buildings. He recalls that this particular shade of green, reflecting off the walls, changed the color of your skin. Or was it his mother who said that, shaking her head critically, and he noticed it himself later, coming for Eden or to collect his weekly money? A sickly green, he thinks now, though the effect is muted without the light.

The kitchen is like his mother's in its layout, and both

have the same rounded Magic Chef stoves, but there is otherwise little resemblance. There are no signs on the counters or on the table to indicate that anyone ever cooks here, or ever comes here—not a crusted sugar bowl, not a toaster oven with crumbs on the bottom tray, not a misshapen potholder made by a child. On the wall beside the fridge, where in his mother's kitchen there is a framed collage of snapshots—most of them Billy as a baby—there is only a plastic wall clock. And most disconcerting of all, though perhaps troubling only to Andrew, who has missed the intervening nineteen years of the evolution of this house, there is no sign that Jim was ever here—not a trace. Always, he remembers, there were coats and felt hats on the hooks at the back of the door, a row of heavy leather shoes by the stove, a pile of magazines on the table—*Life, Reader's Digest, Popular Mechanics* (this last a family joke in his own house)—and Jim's bowl of fruit, ready to be peeled, never empty. Not only is there now no fruit in the room; there is not a hint of anything edible at all. Perhaps it's different in the bedroom upstairs. He thinks of his father's dresser in his own mother's bedroom, kept intact, as though any minute his father might come back and need the items on the linen runner. The windows, he notices, have no curtains on them—just the shades. He tries to recall if this was always true.

"You'll be selling, then," she says. She takes a sip of iced tea. He remembers this trait of hers: how she is able to conduct entire conversations without ever once looking at you. He forces himself to study her face, and in doing so sees again, in the dim light, as has been happening of late, the woman she used to be, the profile more defined, superimposed over the face across the table.

"Well, I'll have to sell," he says, knowing his steady gaze is making her uncomfortable. "There's no reason now to keep it."

"No," she says, touching her hair at the nape of her neck. "No, I suppose not. Though with new people coming . . ."

She doesn't finish her thought. Andrew repeats what he has said earlier. "I'm doing some things to tidy up the place—not much; just cosmetic, really. It's no trouble to lend a hand here too, while I'm at it. The grass, of course. And your back stoop needs fixing. It's dangerous. You could break your leg on it. And I could put back that shutter that's fallen from the upstairs window."

"Oh," she says, taken aback. "No. Not the shutter. I . . . I haven't got it. And it's not necessary. The steps, if you like, yes. I'll pay you, of course."

"I couldn't—"

"I'll pay you," she says, cutting him off.

Her face, her aged one, comes clearly into focus. Beneath a faint dusting of powder, he sees a delicate calligraphy of lines around her eyes. Her eyes are hard to look at, but he would say, in telling someone about her (which he thinks he may never have done), that she is still quite handsome. It is not simply that she has aged well (she seems not to have the deep scoring that so changed his mother's face these last several years); it is, rather, a particular something she holds in reserve—her shoulders held back—that something patient and waiting. He thinks, too, about all the longing there was inside her, so intriguing for a boy, from a distance, to observe. Where does it all go to, he wonders, when the person you long for dies?

He turns his gaze away from her. Despite the years, despite his discomfort here, he has a strangely familiar sense of this room. Sometimes when he dreams, this kitchen is the setting. The characters are ones who don't belong here: his boss at work; Billy; a woman he has seen that day turning a corner. They gather in this kitchen; or there will be, in the middle of another dream, a shift in place, so that he is here with them, unfolding a plot begun elsewhere.

"How is Eden?" he asks suddenly. His voice is louder than he has intended.

She looks at the sink. "Eden is not well. She tires easily." The sentence sounds rehearsed, or oft repeated.

"I'd like to see her," he says recklessly.

She shakes her head. "It would upset her."

"I wouldn't upset her. I would just . . ." He searches for a word. "Visit."

"Well, not today." She rattles the cubes in her glass, and her mouth tightens. She raises her chin.

"Why not?"

"She's sleeping. And I've found that memories from the past upset her," she says. "I have to contend with that for days." She brushes an imaginary strand of hair from her forehead.

"But does she see anyone?" he asks. (His persistence surprises him. Why is he being so rude? But he is in it now and cannot stop.) "Does she go anywhere? There must be programs, centers for the blind."

She stands up and rinses her glass at the sink. "I'm a *nurse*," she says, with emphasis on the last word, as if that should settle the matter. As if trying to make him again the neighbor's child. "As you must know, Eden *was* away for several years in the beginning, but we've found she does better with me here. We have a quiet life, and it suits her."

He is about to quiz her once more, when above him he hears a sound, like that of a chair leg scraping against the floor. Or he imagines that he hears a sound. Edith Close says nothing; he examines her to see if she, too, has heard anything. Then he hears another sound, the weight on the floorboards of footsteps moving from one side of the room to the other. Eden's room, in the corner, is above the kitchen. Or *does* she have another room now?

Edith Close walks to Andrew and holds her hand out for his glass. "Will five dollars an hour be enough?" she asks.

He looks up at her. He sees no point in protesting. He knows she won't let him do the work without an arrangement of some kind. He says, *Fine.* He gives her the glass, which is still nearly full. "And there will be lumber for the steps," she adds. "Shall I give you some money now?"

He shakes his head. He knows she wants him to go.

He stands up, and as he does so, he hears music from a radio. He freezes and listens. It is definitely a radio. She hears it too; he sees her shoulders hunch almost imperceptibly, as if wishing to ward off the sound. He thinks he hears a phrase of "Glory Days," then silence, then the voice of a disc jockey. He looks at the ceiling.

She touches him, a hand on his elbow, and the touch startles him. Her fingers are cold on his skin.

"I have to see a patient," she says, guiding him toward the door.

And though he knows this can't be true, and though he wants to say that Eden must now be awake, her touch—that cold, unwelcome touch—makes him feel as if he *were* a boy again, eager to get away, to be gone from the dark kitchen.

She walks him to the door. The radio voice follows them, seems distinctly louder, in fact.

"Thanks for the iced tea," he mumbles.

He backs down the steps with something like a wave, and she quickly closes the door. He forgets the rotting stoop, and with his weight, the bottom step cracks. He nearly falls backward onto the gravel, awkwardly catching himself on the railing. When he turns, his hands are shaking. He thrusts his fists into his pockets to collect himself.

He is almost to his own back stoop when he feels a prickling at the back of his neck. He stops and turns quickly.

One, two. He sees first, at the edge of a shade in the kitchen, a swift settling; and then, in the upstairs window, a gentler movement, a slow blur of a turn, a faint afterimage of a blue dress and a thin white arm.

The image is gone in a second. But he stands straining after the open window, willing it to come back, unable to move away.

She can't have come to the window to see me, he is thinking. *She must have come to be seen.*

HE FILLS the mower with gasoline and checks the oil. He has no idea how old the oil is, or when the machine was last used, but he is too impatient to make another trip out to the gas station. Bending to the pull cord for the fifth time, he gives it everything he's got, more in frustration than with any common sense, and against the odds, the machine belches into life. The sound is harsh and satisfying, shattering the silence. He hopes the loud noise is irritating to the woman behind the drawn shades. He takes a deep calming breath. The noise soothes him. It is a sound that feels good, that he can understand—even though, ironically, it's been years since he has mowed a lawn, anyone's lawn.

The work, he thinks, is equally satisfying. You push the mower down a straight and even path, you look behind you and you see a neat swath, though he is only taking off the top two or three inches this pass—the mower set high, so as not to clog the blade with the damp clippings. He is throwing the grass out to the side; but later on, he'll put the bag on and go over the lawn again, trimming it shorter, picking up the clippings.

The sun is hot and dry on his face. He can feel the tension leaving his body, even as his arms vibrate from the machine. The trick, he thinks, is to keep moving, to move inside the noise, to let the noise drown out the thoughts in his head and the images behind his eyes, until they fade into something distant and manageable. He wants to shut his eyes altogether, but, of course, that isn't possible. He wouldn't mind, though, he thinks, standing just for a second inside the roar, his eyes shut, his face tilted toward the sun.

She was one fantastic-looking girl. You remember?

I remember.

Sometimes he felt as if he hardly knew her then, though he saw her every day. But he heard what was said about her. And he knew the stories. He watched her—as you'd watch a house you once lived in become transformed by new owners.

He saw her on the bus on the way to and from school; in the backyard, meeting in the driveway; in a corridor, stopping for a drink of water from the fountain. She liked to tease him, and he let her. He didn't know how to make her stop. Confronting her, as he did at first when her growing reputation alarmed him, made it worse; he lost the verbal battles. His best defense, he decided, was to ignore her— though she persisted, drawling his name in a husky voice that seemed to have blossomed overnight with her anatomy and that, unhappily, carried the length of the school bus or across a room. And he sometimes wondered, when he was being honest with himself, if he didn't enjoy the odd status that her attention conferred upon him.

She's hot for you.

She is not. I've known her since she was practically born.

She's giving it away, man. Perillo felt her up at the drive-in four times in August. He says her boobs are—

She's only thirteen, for Christ's sake.

She's been doin' it since school started. A chick wants it, she wants it.

Why don't you guys leave her alone?
Leave her alone? Hey, you sure you're not getting any?

IT WAS as if she were changing to suit her body, was some-how growing into the body that was developing too fast for her. He had no other explanation. Or rather, he thought, the basic traits were still there—her nerve, her brazenness—but they'd veered off in a new direction so that she used her talents not to *be* one of the boys but to have power over them.

Sometimes, sitting on the back stoop, pretending to study his French, he would see her across the grass and gravel and wonder about what it would be like to be in a car with her at a drive-in. He couldn't keep from thinking about it: the idea was in the air and in his blood. But the thoughts made him uncomfortable, nearly in the same way that thinking about his parents doing it did. And sometimes he felt guilty, as if he were supposed to have taken better care of her some-how—though that, *he knew*, was crazy. She was beyond his care, or anyone's, for that matter.

And sitting on the stoop, he would sometimes hear raised voices in the Close kitchen, a mother and a daughter scratch-ing at each other like cats: words thrown whining and bick-ering through the screens. The fighting had come on gradually during that summer and the school year following that awk-ward day on the baseball diamond, Eden beginning it (seem-ingly demanding it), taunting her mother with her outrageous dress and behavior, until Edith Close, a novice at this combat, began to learn from her daughter, raising her voice to a new shrillness—born, he imagined, out of bewilder-ment. You cannot, he thought, remain indifferent to a stinging bee.

In the beginning, he and his parents had been mildly

alarmed by the raised voices next door. His own parents rarely yelled at each other or at him. But then, as the weeks and months passed and the bickering voices seemed to find no truce, he began to grow accustomed to the nightly battles— like the rattling of a scheduled train—as though these, too, were part of an evolving landscape.

And sometimes the screen door would slam, and Eden, her eyes inflamed, roughly pushing her hair off her face, would spot him on the stoop. She might put a fist on a cocked hip and narrow her eyes at him. Or she might, with dizzying speed, change her stance and her expression entirely, sashaying across the yard to meet him, a smile skimming her lips as she clutched a pack of Old Golds or Winstons. She would smoke after these battles, in full view of her mother, prolonging, by this gesture, their animosity. (He couldn't conceive of smoking in front of his parents; indeed, he was thinking of giving it up altogether.) She would reach the steps where he was sitting, lean against the rail and shake a cigarette from the pack, deliberately offering him one. She kept her matches in the cellophane. Sometimes, maddeningly, she would ruffle his hair, and he would toss his head sharply to shake her off.

"Enjoyin' the entertainment tonight?" she would say.

When Jim was home, there was no fighting. It was not so much that Jim kept order in his household; it was that in his presence, Edith would not criticize their adopted daughter, nor rise to the bait if Eden dangled it, by wearing a too tight sweater, or by missing supper entirely, or by coming home at eleven o'clock, an hour after her nominal curfew.

"Sweetie," Jim would say, coming out onto the steps on these late nights, intercepting Eden before she entered the house.

"Daddy," Eden would say, though out of earshot she referred to her parents as Jim and Edith, and Andrew had never heard Eden address Edith as "Mother" or "Mom" at all.

"Sweetie, your mother is upset. You should have told us where you were going. We waited supper for you."

And Eden, brilliantly contrite, would tilt her head ever so slightly and murmur, "Sorry, Daddy," in a voice Andy seldom heard, the voice, he thought, of a regular fourteen-year-old girl.

Jim, instantly mollified, poised to be charmed by what he imagined to be his daughter's sweetness, would kiss the top of her blond curls.

"Sickening," his own mother would say of Jim's inability to discipline his daughter, as she witnessed the scene from their kitchen window.

ONE AFTERNOON that last spring, he remembers, he was changing the oil in the car for his father when he heard a sudden and particularly loud spate of bickering, followed almost immediately by the sound of splintering glass. It was Sunday, and Jim had been away for days. There'd been no buildup of voices, no warning of a coming storm. Until the fighting, Andy hadn't even known Eden was home.

The caliber of the bickering was different than he'd heard before, and while normally he would simply register the sound and then go back to what he was doing, this time he slid out from underneath the car and sat up. His father, working that afternoon on the plumbing under the sink, came to the back door.

"What the . . . ," said his father.

But the shouting had stopped by then, and his father turned away from the door. Andy was about to go back under the car, when Edith Close came out of the house, her coat on, her purse over her arm, her mouth set in a thin line. Without acknowledging Andy, she turned down the drive,

94

made a right on the road and walked to the tree where the county bus regularly stopped.

Andy sat on the gravel. His hands were smeared with grease. He stood up and walked to the other house, hesitating below the steps, out of sight of Edith at the bus stop. He wiped the palms of his hands on his jeans. He listened, heard nothing and then climbed the steps. It was April, he remembers; he had on two old flannel shirts of his father's. Edith, in her haste, hadn't closed the door. He put his face to the screen, put his hand up to shade his eyes.

Eden was sitting on a chair by the table. She was wearing a long nightgown and a bathrobe. Her hair was disheveled, uncombed, as if she'd just woken up. She was crying. He didn't think he had ever seen her cry before. She brought her hand up and touched the corner of her mouth. He remembers thinking how small she looked in the chair. He remembers wanting to go in and sit beside her. He wanted to knock, but he didn't.

By May of his senior year, the spring before the shooting, Eden seemed to have settled, in a fairly deliberate way, and in a manner that surprised everyone, on Sean. Andy was never to know what it was exactly that drew Eden to his old friend, if, indeed, she could actually be said to have been drawn at all. For he sometimes wondered, then and later, if it wasn't in keeping with the perverse, self-destructive course she'd been on for almost a year to choose a boy known for his volatile temper and, more to the point and perhaps for Andy's benefit, to strike so close to home.

Andy was sitting on a bench in the locker room when T.J. told him. It was after a baseball game, and Andy, with a towel around his waist, was trying to untangle his underpants, when T.J. said, his back to Andy, "You know about Sean."

"Sean?"

T.J. opened his locker and hunted for a sock.

"And Eden," he said.

"Sean and Eden?" Andy didn't get it yet. Had they had a fight? Got caught smoking on school premises?

"They're like a thing," T.J. said. He looked quickly at Andy and then away. He began to whistle between his teeth.

"You mean they're going out?" asked Andy. He said the words *going out* distinctly, as if they could not possibly apply to the present situation.

T.J. scratched his chest. "Yeah. Like that."

Andy shook his head. There had to be some mistake. "That's impossible," he said. "Are you sure? I'd know if it were true."

"Oh yeah?" said T.J. "And how is that?"

"I'd have seen them together at the house or something."

"No you wouldn't. Her father won't let her bring any boy home. So they hang out in Sean's car. . . ." T.J. stopped, not wanting to lay out the graphic details to his friend.

"But Sean never really liked Eden," protested Andy. "Of the three of us—"

T.J. snapped around. "You know, Andy-boy, half the time, I swear to God, you're livin' in a dream world, you know that? You don't see what's goin' on right under your nose."

"I don't know what you're talking about," said Andy, stung by T.J.'s sudden attack.

"I'm talking about Eden," said T.J. with exasperation.

"What about Eden?"

"Anybody with two eyes could see that it's always been you she liked best, and you're either blind or you're more of an asshole than I thought you were."

"You must be crazy," said Andy defensively. "She's only

fourteen. She was one of the guys. She was like a sister. . . ." He stopped, aware that he was contradicting himself.

"Oh really?" said T.J., buttoning his top button and picking up his gym bag. "Well, that's history now, isn't it."

T.J. slung his gym bag over his shoulder and headed for the door. He didn't wait for Andy, and he didn't say goodbye.

Andy sat on the bench, his underpants balled in his fist. He was trying to imagine Sean and Eden in a car together, she laughing, Sean reaching over to finger the collar of her blouse, but something inside him wouldn't let the image coalesce. He threw the underpants into the bottom of the locker. He slammed the door shut with his feet.

"Fuck it," he said, and pulled his pants on.

AFTER THAT DAY, without appearing to do so, he looked for signs of them together. And he concluded that T.J. had been right: he *was* blind, for how could he have failed to miss the way Sean was always dressed first after a game and out to his car, or the way Sean sidled past him with a greeting but had not really had a conversation with him for weeks? Or the way Sean and Eden sat on the steps behind the gym and smoked during third period, their shoulders touching? And as the days passed, there were more overt signs: Eden missing the afternoon school bus day after day, arriving late for dinner, saying she'd walked home from school, though Andy knew Sean was dropping her off a quarter mile short of the house. And once Andy came around a corner into an empty corridor by the music room at school and saw Sean pressing Eden into the brick wall with his body. They were kissing, and Andy was caught. He couldn't turn around, couldn't retreat. He tried to saunter past them, tried to appear intensely absorbed in the cover of his math book. Eden pulled away just as Andy passed.

"Andy-boy," said Sean, breathless.

"Sean," said Andy, moving past them.

"Hi, Andy," drawled Eden.

He heard giggling behind him.

HE NOW AVOIDED Eden as best he could, stopping short at the screen door if he saw her emerge from her house and cajoling T.J. to pick him up and drop him off for the couple of weeks left before school ended. Sean brought Eden to the graduation party, but Andy had his own date and aggressively pretended to be having a better time than he actually was. After he took his date home, he and T.J. drove for hours in T.J.'s car and got so drunk they had to park by the side of a deserted road before they both passed out. When he got home, well after six in the morning, expecting the wrath of his father to greet him at the door, his father took one look at Andy, shook his head sadly and went upstairs to bed.

ONLY ONCE, in the weeks before the shooting, was he alone with Eden for any length of time. It was a Monday afternoon, he remembers, his day off from the Texaco station. That summer he was working long hours, and his parents let him do what he wanted on his day off, an indulgence that pleased him since it seemed to suggest that he was a man now—a workingman with days off and privileges. He had slept late that morning, and when he came down to the kitchen, his mother was already dressed, already halfway into her day. It was the summer he was reading *No Exit* and *The Stranger* to get ready to go to college in Massachusetts, and he had a book with him at the table. Out in the backyard there was an aluminum reclining chair on which his mother sometimes dozed in the afternoons with *Family Circle* on her lap; and so after breakfast he went outside and lay back on it, shielding his eyes from the sun with the paperback held over his face. It was after twelve, and the sun that day, he remembers, was ferocious. Almost immediately, he unbuttoned his shirt, fanning himself with the cloth.

He was asleep when he felt a large insect crawling over his stomach. He sat up with a jolt, flailing at his chest, trying to brush it off. And then he heard her laugh—a laugh that sounded unpleasant and grating through the fog of his sleep and the pounding of his heart. He fell back against the chair. Her face was over his, too close to his own, blocking out the sun as the book had done.

"Lazybones, get out of bed. The sun is up, the witch is dead."

"What?"

"Andy, it's almost one o'clock."

"*You* should talk."

"Want to go for a swim?"

She was wearing a pair of tight white shorts and a blue sleeveless blouse. Her arms were tanned, and when she moved away from his face, he noticed that her chest, where he could see it, was tanned too. His eyes strayed to her breasts and away again. He hoped she hadn't seen. It was a powerful reflex he was trying to cure himself of—the way, when looking at a girl, his eyes went immediately to the breasts rather than to the face. Instinctively, he began buttoning his own shirt.

"No," he said. "I'm reading."

She laughed. "Right," she said. She picked up his book, which had slipped onto the grass, and squinted at the title: *The Myth of Sisyphus*.

"Jesus Christ, Andy. You're turning into such a fink, you know that? Anyway, you haven't been swimming in weeks. I happen to know that for a fact. It's summer, in case you haven't noticed."

99

She sat on the edge of the chair. "I'm not leaving until you say yes. I'm bored sick, and I want company."

"Where's Sean?" he asked, the name catching in his throat. They had never spoken of Sean.

"Oh, him," she said too casually. "How should I know?"

"You should get a job," he said, "if you're so bored."

"I'm only *fourteen*," she whined. "And anyway, what's it to you?"

"*I* worked when I was fourteen," he said, instantly regretting it.

"Well, la-di-da. You sound like an asshole sometimes, Andy, you know that?"

"All right, all right," he said, capitulating. "Where?"

"The pond," she said. "The pool is *totally* revolting. I swear to God there's half an inch of scum on the water."

"All right," he said again, grudgingly. "I'll get my suit. You go get yours."

"I'm wearing mine," she said.

He checked his eyes just in time, but his visual memory was flawless. That couldn't be true, he thought, but he couldn't very well challenge her.

"Listen, I'll tell you what," he said. "Compromise. OK? I'll walk you down to the pond, and you can swim. I'll keep you company, but I don't think I want to swim myself." Actually what he didn't want was to go through the hassle of looking for his suit and the even greater hassle of explaining to his mother where he was going and with whom.

She shrugged and stood up. "Suit yourself," she said.

"That's good," he said, appreciative of the pun.

She looked blankly up at him.

THEY WALKED through the cornfields, the sun baking their heads, their feet following a path so familiar he was sure he could have found his way blindfolded. Almost at once, away from the shade of any trees or houses, he wished he'd bothered to get his suit. He'd be dying for a swim by the time they got there. Well, what the hell, he'd go in with his clothes on. They'd dry in the sun on the way home anyway.

She walked in front of him, and it was impossible not to notice the way she moved—her narrow hips twitching from side to side in her white shorts. Her hair was in a ponytail, and it, too, swayed back and forth. He thought, fleetingly, of what was said about her. Of what was said about her and Sean. Phrases came into his mind, and he worked to push them away.

He *hadn't* been to the pond in weeks, not since before school let out, and he was surprised by the lush growth there: tall scarlet lilies and Queen Anne's lace and old grape vines. There were trees here at least. He sat on the grass under the shade of one, and to his surprise, she sat down beside him.

"I thought you wanted to go swimming," he said, looking at her.

"So?" She stretched her legs out on the grass and crossed them. She kicked off her sneakers. He looked at her legs. They were tanned, golden, all the way to her shorts. She had lost the bruises of the year before. Now all he saw was the long, smooth shape of her legs and the red polish on her toes. He tore his gaze away.

There was a sparkle on the water. He had learned to swim in this pond when he was a boy, no more than five. His father had taught him, patiently, over many days. Though Andy sometimes suspected his father had subtly planted the notion that there were leeches in the pond—thus hastening the process. He'd been so terrified of touching bottom that he'd learned to float the first day. It wasn't true, though, about the leeches. The pond was crystal clear, even if the color of the water was brassy from the minerals in the soil. He was thinking that any minute he'd just make a run and a flying leap, and the cool water would close in over him.

"Oooh," she said. "Ants." She twisted her body to flick

something off her thigh and in doing so brushed his bare arm with her own. The touch was electric, galvanizing, and instinctively he pulled away from her.

"What's this for?" he asked suddenly.

"What's what for?" she said noncommittally.

"This," he said, gesturing to include the space that surrounded them.

"I don't know what you're talking about."

"You don't?"

Maybe he was wrong, he thought. Maybe she did just want a swim. But if so, why was she sitting so close to him? The sun glinted painfully off the water.

"Andy," she said. There was a question in her voice.

"Let's hit the water," he said quickly. He bent forward, as if to get up.

"Andy, do you ever wonder what it would be like?"

There was a ringing in his ears. "What *what* would be like?"

"You know."

"No, I don't," he said irritably. "You *said* you wanted to swim."

He knew that all he had to do was stand up and begin heading for the water, and that would be that, but instead he waited for what she would say next. He wanted to hear what she would say next. Despite himself. Because of himself.

"*I* think about it," she said in an oddly quiet voice.

"Think about *what*?" he said, trying for a tone of exasperation.

"Us."

The word fell like a leaf to the grass and lay there in front of them—him with his body still poised to stand; her with her legs crossed in front of her. There was a sparkle on the water, so bright it hurt his eyes like a headache. Around them insects buzzed and whined in the heat. The pond always seemed smaller in the summer, he thought, hemmed in by the vegetation. Looking at it, he couldn't imagine playing a hockey game on it.

She moved around in front of him, on her knees, blocking his path to the water.

"Eden," he said.

"You can touch me if you want," she said. "You can touch my blouse."

He looked at her blouse. The longing inside him was so deep and so tight it made his throat dry. He could see the pressure of her breasts against the cloth. He could tell that she wasn't wearing a bathing suit or anything else beneath her blouse. He had never touched a girl's breasts, though he wanted to and he dreamed of it—he had sometimes dreamed of touching hers. He dreamed now of touching the buttons, undoing them slowly, one by one. He looked up at her face. Her eyes, blue-green, were locked on his.

He turned his face away from her. He saw nothing— only a shimmering blur. The color was rising to his face, but there wasn't anything he could do to stop it. He hardened his fists against the grass.

"Eden," he said again.

There was a movement of her hands. He knew what she was doing, and he froze, pretending not to know. He wanted her to do it. He knew what she was doing, and he wanted it.

"Look at me," she said after a time.

And slowly he let himself turn and look at her. He made his face stay calm. It was a test of some kind, and he would make his face stay calm no matter what, though he longed to hide his face in her skin. Her breasts were very white, and the whiteness held him. He could see the tan line of her bathing suit. He brought his hand to his forehead to brush the hair from his face. He kept his face calm, but his hand gave him away.

She said, "Afraid?"

He shook his head, but he was lying. He felt dizzy—loose and big and floating. He knew that all he had to do was touch her.

He raised his face and looked up at the sky. There was a corona around the sun. She was kneeling there, in front of him, waiting. A minute longer, he knew, and they'd both be lost.

He stood up, not gracefully. "I'm going for a swim," he said. His voice was deep, unfamiliar to him. He walked to the water's edge. He bent down to untie his sneakers. He stood up and knifed through the surface of the pond and swam as if his life depended on it, though you could reach the other side in fifty strokes. And when he did, he turned and swam back again, repeating the course over and over until he could barely raise his arm above the water. And then he swam some more, treading water, really, until he knew it was safe to get out.

When he climbed onto the grass, shaking the water out of his ear, Eden was sitting with her knees up.

She had buttoned her blouse. Her face was closed, and she wouldn't look at him. He knew then, watching her, that he had not done the right thing. She looked small and lonely, a fourteen-year-old girl with nowhere to go. He wanted now to touch her skin, to tell her that, yes, he had dreamed of her, had wanted her, that he did often think of them together, that he felt for her something he had been afraid to say even to himself—but he didn't know how.

"You could have been my sister," he said instead.

She said nothing.

They walked back in silence. She was in front of him. His shirt was sticking to his chest, drying some. His hair was plastered in rivulets to his forehead.

When they drew closer to the houses, he jerked his arm forward and tried to take her hand. There was something he wanted to tell her—he *would* tell her now—but she chose that moment, unaware that he was reaching for her, to sprint the rest of the way to the houses. He tilted as if to run after her, but then he stopped himself. He wouldn't catch her. He remembered that she could run as fast as he could.

THE FOLLOWING WEEK, T.J. reported to Andy that Eden had suddenly dropped Sean. It was rumored, said T.J., that Jim had found the pair one night in Sean's car about one hundred yards short of the house and had strenuously forbidden Eden ever to see Sean again, but T.J. thought it unlikely, and Andy agreed. Although Jim's drinking had grown worse over the years—and particularly so in the last year—sometimes causing him to accost Andy's father and harangue him for hours on some arcane subject, or to sit mute on his own back stoop, beer in hand, waiting for Eden to come home for supper, Andy thought it virtually impossible that Jim could be capable of so decisive an act of discipline. Rather it seemed more plausible that Sean had concocted the story to salvage his pride. For from all appearances, Eden had simply tired of Sean. He had served an uncertain purpose for a time and was now no longer very interesting to her—a fate that threw Sean into a frenzy. At first he besieged Eden with pleas and questions, but when his entreaties would not move her, his fury ignited and was boundless.

"I'll get that bitch," he said, to anyone who would listen, his anger growing with each passing day. "I'll kill that bitch," he shouted, his temper ricocheting around the interior of his car. T.J. told him to calm down and get a grip on himself. Then later, when T.J. had wearied of Sean's relentless tirades, he told him to "grow up."

But Sean, enraged and bereft, would not let up. At 2 A.M on the last day of July, he totaled his car on the road leading from town to Eden's house and was arrested for speeding and for drunken driving. On a morning in the first week of August, a summer caretaker at the high school found two windows smashed to bits in the east wing, near the music room. By the middle of August, Jim had called the police station twice to lodge a complaint against Sean, who had been standing across the road for days, waiting for Eden to leave the house to walk to the bus stop.

But that was not the worst of it, T.J. said to Andy one August evening after work when the two of them were going to a movie. The worst of it was this: When Sean had first told T.J. that Eden wouldn't see him anymore, Sean had gripped the steering wheel in his car so tightly that his fingers had turned white. And then he'd gulped once as if for air and had cried like a baby.

When he shuts the mower off, he hears the phone ringing. It's his own, inside the kitchen. He begins to run, leaping over the back stoop, letting the screen door slam, reaching it in three rings.

"Hello?" he says, breathless.

"You're outta shape, Andy-boy. Maybe you should take up jogging."

"T.J."

Andrew puts his hand on his chest, as if to slow his looping heart.

"What were you doin' anyway?"

"I was mowing the lawn," says Andrew. "I ran for the phone."

"You should get a cordless. We got a cordless in the backyard."

"Oh," says Andrew. Is it worth the effort to remind T.J. that he has no plans to stay in this house and to tell him of the cordless phone he and Martha had in Saddle River?

"So listen. I spoke to Didi. Can you come over Friday night?"

Andrew calculates. "What day is it?" he asks.

"It's Tuesday." There is a pause. "You all right?" asks T.J.

"I'm fine," says Andrew, thinking how easy it is to lose track of the time when there is no office to go to. "I'll still be around then. I'd planned to be."

"Excellent," says T.J. "Remember the Conroy place?"

Andrew has a memory of an alfafa farm about two miles east of town, a blue crop undulating like a rolling sea, a tall glistening white silo, a ship, rising from the expanse of unbroken color. "The alfafa farm, right?"

"Yeah. It's houses now. Kind of an upscale subdivision. Water's Edge, it's called. We're on Tudor Lane, the second left, number twelve."

"OK."

"We'll talk about selling your house when you come," says T.J.

"OK."

There is another pause. "You sure you're all right?"

"I'm *fine*," says Andrew.

"All right, all right, I believe you. See you about seven, then, OK?"

Andrew puts his hands on his hips, feels his heart jogging back to normal. It irks him, but T.J. is right: He *is* out of shape. He pours himself a glass of water and sits down on a kitchen chair, his legs spread out in front of him. He is trying to imagine how the Conroy place could now be houses—what did they do with that immense white silo?— when the phone rings again. He thinks it must be T.J., that he has told him the wrong time, and so he answers, casually, "Yeah," but it is a female voice on the other end.

"Andrew?"

"Jayne," he says with some surprise.

"How are you?" his secretary asks. "How are you feeling?"

"I'm fine," he says for the third time in five minutes. "And thank you for the flowers," he adds. "Thank everyone for me, though I know it was your doing."

"We've all been thinking of you," she says. "We've all been wondering how you were. We hadn't heard from you, and we . . ." He can see Jayne in her gray suit with the white silk blouse, her salt-and-pepper hair cut short. Her desk will be impeccably neat. She has a gift, he has often thought, for absorbing the chaos of the office and transforming it into neat, simple packets of common sense and order.

"I'm sorry," says Andrew. "I should have called. They couldn't do the funeral Sunday, and so we had it yesterday, and I've been tied up with details here. I have to sell the house, see to my parents' things. There's no one else, really, to do it." He stops. His voice sounds unconvincing, even to him.

"Geoffrey has asked me to tell you to take all the time you need, but he was just wondering . . . if you should happen to know when you might be coming back. Apparently, there's some trouble with the agency . . . but not to hurry, says Geoffrey." Andrew thinks he can hear some slight embarrassment in Jayne's voice. *See if you can find out when he's coming back*, Geoffrey, his boss, will have said, passing on this onerous task. *See if you can't light a fire under him.*

Andrew runs his fingers through his hair and looks out the window. The patch of grass that he can see looks good— short and trim. He could say, definitely, *I'll be in the office Friday morning*, but he doesn't want to. He could make it by Friday easy, he is thinking; there's no pressing need to stay. T.J. would handle everything if Andrew asked him to.

"I'll try for early next week," he says, waffling.

"I'm sure there must be . . . a great deal to do," she says, "and you must be feeling drained. I'll tell Geoffrey that you have . . . things to attend to."

"Yes."

"Shall I say Monday or Tuesday?" she asks after a moment.

"You can say . . . Jayne?"

"Yes?"

"I need some time," he says in an apologetic rush. "It's hard to explain. A few days. Tell Geoffrey Monday. But it might not be Monday. You understand?"

She misses only one beat. "Perfectly," she says.

He rolls his eyes to the ceiling. He loves his secretary. Although she has been stern with him when he has delayed overlong in returning important phone calls, she has run interference for him more times than he can count.

"You're great, Jayne," he says.

"I think you deserve a rest," she says. He knows that she is smiling. "And don't worry; I'll take care of Geoffrey."

WHEN ANDREW hangs up the phone, he is smiling too. He snaps a bongo beat on the Formica countertop and rolls his shoulders, unkinking his muscles. Another week. He feels, unreasonably, as if he'd won a prize.

Just a week ago, he was overseeing a project that was giving him sleepless nights, an unwieldy ad campaign for a pain reliever that had been his bailiwick—worse, his idea. He thinks he should be worried about the faltering project, from habit if from nothing else, but it seems too remote to fully grasp, as if the mileage alone had sufficiently distanced him from his office. He feels as if he is playing hooky—fishing when he should be taking a physics exam.

And yet, realistically, he knows there is practically nothing he can do to damage his reputation, to change his character in the ongoing soap opera at the office. He has been the unassuming protégé for years—a role he has found easy enough to play, requiring only that he do his work and appear to be committed. He is not sure why he has been so successful, because he has always been aware in himself of a certain lack of an edge to his ambition; rather, he thinks, it has been a consequence of a fairly passive journey through open doors. Martha used to say that it was because Andrew did not appear to be overtly hungry that so many had been moved to open the door *for* him—as indeed (she often reminded him) she had done.

He finishes his glass of water, sets it down on the table, and is halfway out the door when the phone rings again.

"Jesus," he says aloud cheerfully.

"I'VE BEEN calling all afternoon," Martha says at once. "Where have you been?"

It is as inevitable as night falling. No matter how often he has promised himself he will remain immune, the sound of Martha's voice over the telephone sets up a chemical reaction in his blood, which goes immediately to his voice box. His voice withers, sounds hollow, dies.

"Martha."

"I called four times at least. I thought you were supposed to be sorting stuff out."

"I was mowing the lawn," he says quietly. He knows, as surely as he knows the effect of her on himself, that she sounds petulant in this way only with him. It is one of the things they have done to each other.

"Oh. Well, we're on Nantucket," she says.

"You said you might be."

"I called to see how it went."

"It went fine," he says.

"That's all? It went fine?"

110

"There's nothing to it," he says. "You say a few words, you put someone in the ground, you have a cup of coffee, and before you know it, it's over."

There is a pause. "It sounds to me like you're not dealing with it."

"I'm dealing with it. Where's Billy?"

"He's right here. Want to talk to him?"

"You know I do."

He leans against the fridge and waits for the sound of his son's voice.

"Daddy?"

It hits his stomach like a strong drink, the warmth spreading.

"Hi, Billy. What are you doing now?"

"I'm talking to you."

Andrew smiles and nods his head. "I know that, Billy. What were you doing before you were talking to me?"

"Me and Mommy and Nana were getting mussels. But . . . um . . . not the kind of muscles you have on your arms. The kind . . . Do you know what mussels are?"

"They have blackish shells, and they're stuck to rocks in the water?" says Andrew.

"Yeah. That's them. And they're hard to get off. You should see my fingers. And Nana is going to show me how to steam them, and we're going to eat them with melted butter."

"That sounds yummy," says Andrew.

"I don't know," says Billy skeptically. "I might not like them. They look yucky."

"I miss you," Andrew says, trying to keep his voice even.

"I miss you too, Daddy. Where are you?"

"I'm at Grandma's."

There is a silence.

"Billy?"

"Mommy said Grandma's in heaven."

Andrew is surprised by this, since Martha despises religion. Or does she now? Or was it simply the easiest explanation of death to give a seven-year-old? "That's right, Billy. She is. But I'm at her house, packing away her things."

"Oh," says Billy. "Daddy?"

"What, Billy?"

"Don't pack away the car."

He knows that Billy means the wooden go-cart that Andrew's father built for Andrew when he was a boy and that Andrew's mother saved for the time when Andrew himself had a child. During a visit to his mother when Billy was five, he took his son to the high school parking lot and taught him to steer.

"No, I won't. It's safe and sound in the garage."

"Mommy wants to talk to you."

"Billy?"

"What, Daddy?"

"I love you."

"I love you too."

Andrew can hear the squelchy sound of Billy kissing the telephone mouthpiece. He bends to do the same, but the small voice is too quickly gone. He hears a shuffling of the phone, Martha asking her mother to take Billy outside. Andrew braces himself.

"So," she says. He hears a faint sigh. Fatigue? Irritation? Then there is a quick drag and exhale of cigarette smoke. He can see her as clearly as if she were standing next to him. Jeans, a white shirt, a sweater tied around her neck, sandals, her feet tanned. There will be a frown of impatience on her brow. Her head will be slightly inclined because she wears her shoulder-length brown hair parted to one side now, and often there is a wave of hair that wants to fall across her face.

"He sounds . . ." Andrew takes a quick breath of air. "He sounds good."

"He's great," Martha says. "Great. He wanted to talk to you. He was upset when I told him about your mother. But he's better now." Drag and exhale.

Holding her cigarette between her fingers, she will push the hair off her face. He has seen her on the phone a thousand times.

"I'm relieved," says Andrew.

"So listen," says Martha. "You sure you're OK?"

"I'm OK."

"How long are you going to stay there?"

"Another week."

"Oh. . . . I guess there isn't anything I can say."

"No. Probably not."

"You'll come get Billy when we get back?"

"You know I will."

"Well, then."

There is a pause.

"Andrew?"

"What?"

"It's strange, isn't it?" she says.

"What is?"

"You doing this alone."

A PERSON walks into a room and says hello, and your life takes a course for which you are not prepared. It's a tiny moment (almost—but not quite—unremarkable), the beginning of a hundred thousand tiny moments and some larger ones. A random sperm meets a random egg and becomes your child, whom you love more than life itself. Yet the meeting, that infinitesimal beginning, is no more astonishing than the division of a cell.

He had met Martha at an antiwar rally their senior year at college. Not a memorable meeting—she had asked him merely to hand out leaflets in front of the ROTC building— but he had found himself attracted to her, despite, or perhaps because of, her total preoccupation. It was her anger that he noticed, a clear blue anger, so purely defined by the effort to stop the war—an anger that gave high color to her cheeks even as it lent her speech, with its broad A's and its other New England idiosyncrasies, an articulate speed. At first he was content merely to observe her—she was ferocious without being strident in the meetings he attended—but as the year progressed he found himself more and more often paired with her on political projects. Years later, when he would be forced to examine the reasons they had come together, as if puzzling over an insolvable calculus problem, he reflected that it wasn't that the pairing had ignited a passion between them but rather that it had allowed them to drift toward a future that was as much determined by circumstance as it was by desire or will. If they, for instance, had met their junior year in school or later, in graduate school, and had not had to face together the milestone of leaving dormitories and finding another place to live, would they have been impelled to take an apartment they could share together?

Not that he didn't love her. He did, or thought he might, though she, with the admirable bristles and spikes of her anger, was not always easy to love. They were married by then, living in a one-bedroom third-floor walk-up on Fayette Street in Cambridge. The tub was in the kitchen. Martha studied on the bed. He took a table by a window in the living room. At night, when he was finished studying, he'd go into the bedroom. She would be asleep, sitting up, with a book on her lap. Gently, so as not to wake her, he would carefully remove all the papers and books to a table beside the bed and would ease her down under the covers.

And sometimes, having done that, he would watch her, beginning to formulate the calculus problem that would be their marriage. For even by then her anger was starting to become unfocused, more diffuse. The war had ended; it was harder now to find a cause. She was often dissatisfied, discontent. He thought then it was courageous of her, her willingness always to live at the edge, but later he came reluctantly to see that she was this way not by choice but because the anger was herself.

He thinks now how slow he was to understand this, and how often he was impatient with this thing in her she had not wished upon herself, could not control. When they were in New York and living on the East Side, he thought her anger the result of having been uprooted from her home territory and of not being able to find a better job than teaching English in a private school. But by the time Billy had arrived and they had moved to Saddle River, the anger had focused on himself, or, more specifically, on the marriage, or, more specifically still, on the state of being married at that particular place and time. And by then the anger had become contagious, so that he had developed in her presence bristles and spikes, though he would never be as concise or as articulate in an argument as she, and so more often than not lost the verbal battles.

He used to think it was the move that had destroyed them. It had happened coincidentally: a door had opened just when he had wished it to, and so he had walked through it. It was on an afternoon in their last year of graduate school—both of them waiting to hear of jobs for the next year—when he had had an epiphany of sorts following a stultifying session of a freshman course he had taught. He had seen, that day, standing in the classroom after the students had left, a future stretch before him of endless similar afternoons, of dusty books and chalk-filled rooms and freshman themes, and he had realized that this was not what he'd had in mind at all. Yet it wasn't until Geoffrey called, some weeks later, asking Andrew to come and work for him at the pharmaceutical firm, that a plan had taken shape. Geoffrey had been his professor in an American Studies seminar; Andrew had been his favorite pupil—indeed, the two had often finished the seminar with beers at a local bar. *It needn't be forever*, Geoffrey had said on the phone, knowing Andrew would be reluctant after so long an investment to turn his back on academia. *Just come down and give it a try*. And so he had, and the company had offered him so much money that even Martha had been, for once, speechless.

When he tries to think of himself and Martha in Saddle River before they separated, he remembers too much and not enough. The memories flood in upon him like rain, but like rain, they fall through his fingers before he can grasp them. He used to think he could not remember because his memory was failing him, but now he thinks the forgetting is a trick of his mind to protect him. His mind protects him from the good memories, which are painful now to contemplate, and from the bad memories, which make him embarrassed for them both.

When their nights were very bad, he was incapable of remembering the good ones. Or if he did, they were like childhood stories that no longer had meaning or resonance. Yet when there were good times, sparse though they were near the end, he could absolutely not remember the silences or the bitterness or the emptiness that had followed their fights just a week earlier. Or the fear—a persistent image—that the tiny family he had made was coming apart at the roots. He would sometimes not even be able to remember any of the words of a fight they had had just the day before.

They were growing out of love, as if the love itself had always had a finite and predictable life, like childhood. And if they'd been told of this in the beginning, they might have chosen not to marry and have a child, though Andrew could not conceive of ever having made a decision that would lead to a world without Billy. And so they stayed together well past the time when the love had ended, pretending and hoping the hiatus was only temporary, fearful of the future. Until one day when the gulf between them had grown so deep that Martha, having more courage than he and fearing less that she would lose Billy, went to stay with her mother until Andrew was able to move out. He found that night, when he returned home from work, a sad note that, though it offered him a certain kind of relief, nearly drove him mad to read.

And yet weren't those the best years of all—with Billy as an infant, a toddler, a little boy standing up in his crib with his arms wide to greet his father who had come home late from work? A tiny boy with a glove two sizes too big for him, cheerfully missing each ball thrown to him, happy simply to be playing with his father, as indeed the father was happy simply to be playing with him.

Andrew marvels at this conundrum, and he wonders often if this happened only to him, or if it happens all the time, to everyone who marries.

AND HOW MUCH, through all this, did he think of Eden? Did she not rise and bubble to the surface in his dreams?

In the beginning, when he was first at school, he felt uneasy when he met a girl. Pursuing pleasure, when Eden was so damaged, felt to him like an act of disloyalty. On visits home the first few years, he'd pester his mother with questions, but she was oddly reticent, changing the subject, as though she wished to protect him from the facts of the sordid and tragic business next door, perhaps believing the facts might distract him from what she thought was a more important matter—his education. When Martha began making the journey north with him, he found it awkward to ask of Eden, except in the most casual way. And by the time they'd moved to New York (and the journeys north had become even more infrequent), he had news of Eden only when he had a letter from home—in that era of ten-hour days at the office and of Billy's birth.

And yet it seems to him now that Eden was always there, a presence hovering at the edge of his dreams, a fragment of a life not entirely left behind. He would think of her at odd moments, at a hockey game with his son, or when he saw a girl with a head of blond curls on a street corner. Sometimes, when he thought of Eden and himself, the image that came to mind was of two trains on parallel tracks hurtling forward with abandon, until one had stopped short, derailed, while the other, his own, had gone on and on.

AND DID HE NOT, through all this, think often of Sean as well?

The afternoon after the shooting, Sean left town—whether from grief or guilt no one ever was able accurately to say. Nor did anyone know where he had gone, for he had left no note. But T.J., realizing by evening that Sean was missing, told Andy in confidence over the phone that he thought Sean had gone south, toward New York City.

As it happened, this was a shrewd guess, confirmed on the second day after the shooting when a state trooper called at the apartment over the TV repair shop a little after supper to inform Sean's parents that their son had been killed in a hit-and-run accident as he was attempting to cross 178th Street in Washington Heights. The boy had had too much to drink in an Irish bar on the corner, said the trooper, and had, according to witnesses, walked across the street as though blind. It was never known what Sean was doing on the periphery of Manhattan—whether he had got off the bus at the George Washington Bridge by mistake (not realizing there was another leg down into the center of the city, with a stop at Forty-second Street), or whether he had met someone on the bus who had enticed him into the neighborhood. But if there was someone, he or she never came forward. Indeed, none of the witnesses had ever seen Sean before.

After that day and later, Andrew was to think often about that ill-fated bus ride, to imagine what Sean had been thinking on the thruway south to the city and to wonder where it was that Sean had slept that night and why. Even today, when driving north on the Henry Hudson, he catches sight of the George Washington Bridge, or when he crosses the bridge from New Jersey, he never fails to think of Sean—blind drunk and lost in Washington Heights.

The town reeled from the news of the two events (there hadn't been a murder in the village in forty-two years; never a report of a hit-and-run) and waited for Eden to wake up, hoping she would put the pieces of the puzzle into place. And so it was that when Eden came out of the coma that had kept her a silent sleeping prisoner in her hospital bed for ten days and said (her mother vigilant beside her) the single name—one time, never again to confirm or deny it—no one was surprised.

IN THE MORNING, he surveys the gutter. It has come away from the house at one end and sags, as if at any minute the entire trough will break loose. It must be put right, though he has no certain idea how to do it. Walking back and forth along the southern face of the house, he tries to think about the problem logically. He will inspect the supports that are still holding, see how they're fastened, then reproduce that system along the length of the gutter. It isn't as though he has never done repair work before. He has, and still retains a vestigial memory of fixing things with his father in his boyhood. It's that he is, for reasons he can't bring into focus, edgy this morning, his nearly bucolic calm of yesterday morning badly ruffled.

He assumes it is because he slept so fitfully during the night. When he awoke at 5 A.M., having nearly asphyxiated himself with the loose top sheet and wanting, inexplicably, to drink a beer, he had been dreaming of a blue dress in a window. He looks over at the other house. The window, with its four vertical rectangular panes, is bare and lifeless, as if what he saw there *had* been only a dream and not a tangible image.

He gets the ladder and lays it against the house, careful not to dislodge the gutter further. When he climbs up, he sees to his dismay that it is nearly impacted with gunk—a mix of caked silt and petrified leaves. Now is when he could use his father to tell him which task to do first: clear the gutter or refasten it? He may not be able to fasten the trough to the house with the added weight and detritus; on the other hand, any pressure in cleaning it could rip away the entire structure.

The work is irritating and annoying, unlike the pleasure of mowing the lawn yesterday. The payoff is not as immediate, not as showy. No one but him will even know the gutter has been fixed. The wood is rotted out where the nails should go; one entire board should be replaced, but he thinks that if he moves the supports, he may just be able to get away with using the wood that's there. It's not the way his father would have done it, he knows; not the way he himself was taught. But his patience is thin today. Especially thin when the only trowel he can find to clean the gutter (after nearly fifteen minutes of searching for any trowel at all) is too wide to fit into the trough.

He is returning from the garage with a chisel when he sees her open the door of the Plymouth and slip in. She pretends not to have seen him, and he doesn't wave. He wonders how she got herself past the now broken step; he must definitely fix that today. He stops to watch her. She puts the Plymouth in reverse, angles out the drive. It will be quarter to ten; he doesn't need to check his watch. He looks again up at the window in the corner. He waits for a blur of blue to come and disappear, but there is no movement at all, no sign of life anywhere inside that house.

By noon, he has got the gutter three quarters clean. His fingers are scraped raw, and the heat, shimmering up from the tar shingles, has given him a ferocious headache. Periodically, he puts his forehead against the lip of the gutter to rest his eyes, but he doesn't leave it there long. He's nearly done now and is impatient to be finished.

He moves the ladder another two feet along the side of the house. He climbs up the rungs, inclining his head in such a way as to stop the throbbing. Perhaps he should eat something, take a couple of aspirin. What does she do all day? he wonders, unable to rid himself of the vision in the window. He examines his memory closely to see if there are details he has missed, details that might tell him something important—though what details he cannot imagine, since he sees nothing beyond an indefinite shape and an afterimage of color. He tastes the beer he had for breakfast, a beer he suspects is the real reason for the headache, exacerbated by the relentlessly bright sun overhead.

He digs the chisel into the gunk, barking his knuckles again. Wincing, he digs it in again and gets an unexpected purchase. Six inches of gunk comes away effortlessly, throwing him off balance. Panicky, he reaches for the roof, but his hand scrapes and slides to the gutter. He grabs for the gutter, which stops his fall but in doing so comes loose from its supports and pulls away from the house, taking the downspout with it. In the mishap, Andrew has slipped two rungs on the ladder.

He curses and throws the chisel to the ground, where it lands straight up as if he had aimed it. Shaking, he descends the ladder and gives the wrenched downspout a kick. He puts his hands on his hips and breathes deeply. He feels an urge to move fast in his car, to get away, for an hour or two, from the houses.

He'll have lunch in town, he decides, at the luncheonette.

ANOTHER SCREEN DOOR, slapping faintly behind him, and he has never left. The same orange Formica counter with the pencil-line pattern of white and blue boomerangs, the same tall metal revolving stools with their red vinyl seats, stools he and Sean and T.J. spun on endlessly, thinking, talking, cooling down after practice—the kind of soda fountain stool Billy would die for now. The same white Buffalo china mugs, the Kellogg's cereal boxes next to the coffee, the bubble gum machine—providing his first tedious lessons in the fickleness of inanimate objects, mysteriously gobbling nickels and refusing to release the five hard round colored gum balls he'd paid for. Remarkable, he thinks, but it *is* the same machine, still five for a nickel, perhaps the last uninflated buy in America. If Billy were with him now, they'd give it a try.

But, of course, it's not the same place at all. The Vietnamese woman behind the counter nods politely but without recognition. When he came here as a boy, the luncheonette was Bud's, they called it that, *See you at Bud's*, and through the years it has evolved from Bud's to Bill's to other names and now, enigmatically, to Al's—though that cannot be a real Vietnamese name, he is thinking. The place is cleaner than he remembers it ever being—a feeling more than a valid comparison, for it wasn't anything he paid attention to as a boy. But even the old ceiling fan, he sees, has been polished shiny.

The specials are on the blackboard: Beefeater Sandwich Served With Fries / Turkey Health Club With Sprouts And

Avocado—this last the only real clue, besides the new own-ers, to the passage of time. He slides onto a stool near one end of the counter. The Vietnamese woman nods, and he nods back. He orders the Turkey Health Club and a Pepsi.

There is a rustle at the other end of the counter. An older man in a gray jogging suit picks up his sandwich and his glass of milk, walks to the stool next to Andrew and lays his lunch on the counter.

"Andy?"

Andrew begins to rise. He shakes the man's out-stretched hand. "Chief DeSalvo."

"Not anymore. Retired six years. Art. Call me Art. Mind if I join you? I'm here every day. Same time, same station. I get bored of my own company."

"Not at all. Please."

The Vietnamese woman brings Andrew a tall glass of Pepsi filled to within a millimeter of the rim. There is no ice in the glass. Andrew and DeSalvo look at the Pepsi.

"Some things just don't translate," says DeSalvo, and Andrew laughs.

"Sorry about your mother," says DeSalvo. "A lot of memories."

"Thank you."

"You in town long?"

"No. A few more days. Just to pack away some things. Fix up the house."

"You sellin'?"

Andrew nods. DeSalvo's hair is steely gray, clipped short, like a Roman's. A fine gray stubble covers his cheeks, hiding some of the pockmarks on his jowls, but his eyebrows are still thick and unruly and black. Beneath the jogging suit, his body is round and shapeless, what they used to call a barrel chest gone to fat. There's a wheeze in DeSalvo's voice, though the eyes are still a surprising blue and hard.

"My boy was ahead of you—what, three, four years?"

Andrew nods. "Nicky. How's he doing?"

"I dunno," DeSalvo says wearily. "Kids. They're a heartache. You got kids?"

"I have a son. Billy. He's seven."

"Great age. Terrific age. It's later they break your balls. Nicky, he's had a bitch of a time with drugs. Lost his job. His wife and kids left him. Hey, I don't blame her one bit. He's clean now, but big fucking deal. The ball game's over, and he didn't even get to suit up."

"People can change their lives," Andrew says cautiously.

"Yeah, tell me about it. My wife, she cries herself to sleep every night: her grandchildren are in California. Your boy skate?"

"Not really," says Andrew. "He lives in New Jersey. The ponds don't freeze for very long in the winter. Hockey's not the passion there it is up here."

The Vietnamese woman brings Andrew his sandwich, which is stuffed with sprouts and looks surprisingly appetizing.

"He lives in New Jersey, and you don't?"

"I live in New York City."

"You divorced or what?"

Andrew nods.

DeSalvo shakes his head. "I always say to my wife, 'You got your health, you got your family, the rest is bullshit.' "

Andrew nods again, feeling vaguely chastised.

"Anyway," says DeSalvo, "you look like you're doin' good. I seen your car. You're lookin' good. You workin' out?"

Andrew smiles. "No," he says.

DeSalvo turns and examines him. "You haven't changed much. Last time I saw you, musta been—what, ten, fifteen years?"

"More like twenty. The last time I saw you probably would have been the night of the, you know, shooting."

"Did you go to the inquest?"

"No," says Andrew. "Since my mother and I had been together the whole time, they used her testimony instead."

"Yeah, I remember now. Long time."

The Vietnamese woman appears with a cup of coffee for DeSalvo.

"Bothers me, that case," says DeSalvo. "Bothers the fuck outta me, if you want to know the truth. I'll tell you straight out, we blew that one. There was procedures we coulda done sooner—we lost ten, fifteen minutes. It makes a hell of a difference. And we shoulda gone straight for the O'Brien kid. Questioned him at the very least, had him in custody so he couldn't leave town. It had the marks of a hot-tempered son of a bitch like O'Brien—you know, some kid she turned down and he'd gotten pissed. Then he panicked and shot the father. So when she said, you know, that one time to the nurse, it was him, we were ready for it. And, of course, by then, he was already dead, so where was the problem?"

He takes a sip of coffee. He puts his cup down.

"You seen the girl?"

"Eden?"

"Yeah."

"I'm not sure. I might have seen her yesterday in a window."

"Hell of a story, that one. Caught the edge of the shower of the buckshot. They say a piece of it damaged something important behind her eyes. I forget exactly. I always felt sorry for her, even before. Well, she was a little bit of a pain in the ass too, if you want to know the truth, and she coulda gone wild, real wild. I had her in for shoplifting a coupla times. But she had spunk, and I liked her. She had a screw loose somewhere was all. What a waste."

DeSalvo bends his head forward and massages the back of his neck. "This is when I could kill for a cigarette," he says. "Had to give 'em up a year ago. I tell you, though, what really bothers me. You want a cup of coffee?"

Andrew nods. DeSalvo signals the Vietnamese woman and mimes a coffee for Andrew.

"What?" asks Andrew.

"You tell me why she was completely naked," says DeSalvo. "A fellow rapes a girl, he don't wait for her to undress. Take it from me, and I seen some rapes."

"But surely, at midnight, she only had on pajamas or a nightgown," says Andrew.

"We found a long summer nightgown, a pair of under-pants and a book in a heap by the side of the bed. She'd been reading."

"Reading?"

"Yeah. A real egghead book. Reardon knew it. She'd stolen it from the library, by the way. Lemme think. . . . *The Myth of Vesuvius*, or something like that. Mean anything to you?"

The Myth of Sisyphus? Andrew looks sharply up at De-Salvo. He doesn't know which detail he finds more unnerv-ing—the book or the modesty of the underpants.

"He could have made her undress at gunpoint," Andrew says, testing this notion, for he, too, has been subliminally thinking of Eden naked under the sheet.

"Yeah. He could have. But she don't remember that. She don't remember anything, in fact. Wouldn't say a word then and won't now, far as I know. But you think about that. I been thinking about it nineteen years."

THE CONVERSATION with DeSalvo is making beads of sweat break out on Andrew's forehead and between his shoulder blades. For a second or two, he feels the same way he some-times does when he knows he's going to be sick. The fan

126

makes slow revolutions above his head, while beside him, beyond DeSalvo, he hears the clinking of spoons and knives on china. Men eating, a midday break from the job or the house, maybe the highlight of the day, looking forward to the slice of blueberry pie, homemade, now in season, like an earned reward. He has on the slacks and the shirt he wore yesterday to visit Edith, and he can feel the shirt growing wet at the back and under his armpits. He looks at the clock next to the blackboard with the specials, a round face set into a fake copper kettle. It reads five to two. But it might be wrong. He checks his watch. The same. Five to two.

Is it possible?

He has to try.

He stands up abruptly and reaches in his pants pocket. He pulls out his checkbook, a wad of cash, some loose change. The smallest bill he has is a ten. He puts it on the counter. "Cancel the coffee," he says to the Vietnamese woman. He has to say it loudly, because she is at the other end of the counter. One or two of the men glance up, and DeSalvo suddenly looks at him.

"What's the . . . ?"

"I just saw the time. Jesus, I'm an idiot. I'm supposed to be at the house for a conference call from my office at two," says Andrew, improvising wildly. "I'll be screwed."

"You'll make it in that car," says DeSalvo. "But just between you and me, Matheson's got a speed trap going by the Gansvoort place. I can take care of the ticket, but getting pinched will slow you down."

"Thanks for the tip."

Andrew gives a kind of wave and walks out the door. He jogs across the street to where his car is parked. His body wants to bolt, but he fights to keep himself moving steadily and easily toward his car, as if it were only a conference call he was trying to make.

When he slips behind the wheel, however, he can barely

restrain himself. He is not thinking *why*; it is only getting there that matters. He has to make it. He puts the car in gear, guns it, makes an illegal U-turn in front of the luncheonette and, like a kid who's just learned to drive, leaves rubber on the quiet road. He checks his watch. One fifty-eight. On this straight and narrow stretch from town, it can be done in two, three minutes. He knows this from one harrowing race with Sean when they were seniors, the two of them abreast at midnight, himself in his father's car praying there wouldn't be a dog or something larger on the road.

He lets his mind become the racing engine, because he knows that if he allows himself to think about what he is doing, if he can see himself doing it in his mind's eye, he will begin to doubt, and once he doubts, he will be lost. He slows to an irritating thirty-five at the Gansvoort farm, peering out the passenger window to see if he can spot a cop car in the forest of old and rusted '55 Chevys that Gansvoort has been collecting for years, but he sees nothing. A quarter mile past the farm, he brings the car up to sixty. To sixty-five. To seventy.

He's doing nearly eighty when he sees the houses in the distance. He checks his watch. Two-oh-two. He skids into the drive, throwing bullets of gravel as he does so. The Plymouth isn't back yet. He has known it wouldn't be.

He hurls himself from the car. He leaps over the broken step and tries the kitchen door. It opens. Only now does it occur to him that it might have been locked.

He is blinded by the gloom in the kitchen, by the abrupt change from bright sunlight to darkness. He moves, more by instinct and childhood memory than by sight, making his way through a shrouded dining room, through the living room, where he barks his shin on a low table, to the front of the house, where he knows there will be a hallway and the stairs to the second floor.

Memory serves him well. Ricocheting through the rooms, he reaches the front hall and turns the corner. He stands at the foot of the stairs. He looks up.

She is there, waiting, on the landing at the top.

"It's Andrew," he says.

"I know," she says.

THERE IS a shaft of light from a raised shade to one side of her. His heart, which has been beating so fast he is sure he will have a heart attack, thumps loudly against his breastbone. Her hair is long, nearly to her waist, falling in tangles from her shoulders. The blond that he has remembered is now darkened to a dull brass—by time, by neglect. She is wearing a white sleeveless jersey and a pair of blue shorts that are too big for her. There seem to be smudges of gray, like paint, or something else, on her hands. The skin of her bare arms and legs is bone white, flawless, the unblemished white of Buffalo china, or so it seems to him, seeing the long white of her legs from the foot of the stairs.

She turns her head, or inclines it, as if to catch a sound. A bit of light from the window falls on her face as she does so. Her eyes, though sightless and seeming to stare at a point somewhere over his right shoulder, are still the same vivid blue-green, an unsettling color. She moves her hand to push a tangle of hair behind her shoulder, and the movement reveals a delicate haze of small white scars near the temple beside one eye. He sees now that this eye has more of an almond shape than the other, the hood of the eyelid slightly elongated into a slant.

"She'll be coming," Eden says.

Her voice is odd, atonal, as if she seldom uses it.

"I know. I'll be back," Andrew says.

He puts his foot on the bottom step, but she shakes her head. She is fourteen and thirty-three and, towering above him, as insubstantial as a dream, more beautiful than any woman he has ever seen.

He wants to climb the stairs, to see her face more clearly. He wants to peer at her scars and her eye. He wants to touch the white skin of her arm.

"There isn't time," she says, and backs away.

The car was swimming fast along the road, and then I heard the gravel.

When I tell you nothing, you will go away from me.

You broke the shimmer on the water, and I thought that you would drown. I prayed that you would drown. Your shirt is wet and sticking to your skin.

Your weight is on the step. Have you finally come for me?

Your voice is through a fog, but I know your voice, and I have heard it all these years. You will be as I have dreamed you.

I heard you take the car slowly to its place. You stood there looking at my window. You are a boy with arms as thin as wood. Then I heard her car along the road. You didn't go inside. You watched her leave her car, but you didn't speak to her.

This room is very long and empty.

Your father was a brave but foolish man.

FOUR

IT IS RAINING, A HOT FAT RAIN THAT WILL END SOON AND BRING the worms to the surface, so that when he emerges from the house later and stands on the grass or the gravel, the earth will smell of them. Last night, he went finally to the A & P near the mall, and this morning he had his first decent breakfast in nearly a week—cereal, toast, juice, coffee—the meal reminding him of his normal routines, his regular life. The rain drums and splashes against the panes in his mother's room, and too late he sees that he has left a window open during the night. He wipes the wet sill dry with a towel from the bathroom. His mother's papers are on the bed, a random, chaotic spill of papers found finally, after supper last night, under the bed, in a box meant usually for storing winter woolens. She had not known or even guessed she might die, he is sure, for there is no order to the papers, no series of little notes explaining about the insurance or the mortgage or where the key to the safety-deposit box is.

He stands in front of her bureau, with his hands on the brass pulls of the top drawer. It is an oak piece, heavy and Victorian. He has never looked in this drawer, and it has about it, for him, a sense of the forbidden, a sense of the child stealing into the secrets of the adult. His father had a similar drawer—has it still, Andrew supposes, having not yet tackled his father's bureau—which Andrew, as a boy, *did* investigate one night when his parents were at the movies. He must have been young, no more than nine or ten, for he remembers the thrill of discovering a package of Trojans and knowing they were, in some way, connected with sex, but not understanding (not allowing his mind to compose the picture) precisely how. And certain—he laughs now to think of it—that his father was merely keeping them for someone else.

The drawer slides noiselessly open as if it had been waxed only yesterday. The contents are precise and neat, rectangles and squares of differing sizes, arranged to fit in an intimate puzzle. Her spirit was not, he knows now, in her papers, which bear the mark of carelessness and neglect, but here in her top drawer—her treasures laid out as if she were saying to herself or to anyone who might open the drawer: *This is me.* There is an aging, ivory-colored satin nightgown, deftly folded in the left-hand corner, and on it a string of pearls with a diamond clasp, a gift from his father to her on their wedding night. There is a small pink quilted jewelry case behind the nightgown, and to its right a thin packet of letters, postmarked 1943 and 1944: letters from his father in France during World War II. In the right-hand corner are his own baby things: an infant's hand-embroidered playsuit, a pair of tiny brown leather shoes, a baby book with notes and photographs sticking out of it. He has seen this before. He remembers the night his mother brought it out to share with Martha when Martha was six months pregnant with Billy, and how complete he had felt then with his mother and his wife huddled together and with his child coming.

In the center of the drawer there is a cream-colored folder. It, too, is overfull and wants someone to open it, and so he does. In it there are newspaper clippings, mostly of himself in his hockey uniform, and certificates and papers marking a boy's progress through childhood: a homemade valentine for his mother, a second-grade spelling paper with "100" on it, a letter announcing he'd made the National Honor Society.

He puts the heels of his palms on his eyes and rubs them. These were her treasures: a wedding night nightgown, mementoes of her only baby, the milestones of her boy's childhood. No secret love letters from another man; no mysterious rings with enigmatic inscriptions; no vials of tranquilizers; no risqué underwear; no diaries giving clues to bouts of rage or bitterness. Though she has to have had an interior monologue he will never hear, she has put away the tangible evidence of the simple pleasures he has imagined for her. He sits on the edge of the bed and stares blankly at the opened drawer. What will he do with these things? he wonders helplessly. Where will he take them?

There is so much now he'd like to ask of and say to his mother, so much left unsaid these last dozen years, when his own life, his own self-centered concerns—his work, his lapsing marriage, his fatherhood—caused him to think of her less and less, as if she were not as substantial as she'd been, a memory already beginning to fade; and this house, paradoxically, receding further and further into the distance, though you could reach it today, on the thruway extension, an hour sooner from the city than a decade ago.

There was a time, when he was a boy, when he used to think that he could absolutely not survive his parents' deaths, that if they were to die together in a car crash, he, too, would spiral into nothingness. Now it is his son's death he cannot bear to think of or imagine, reading as he does with benumbed horror reports of children with leukemia or falling from open windows. When Billy was five, one of his classmates was struck and killed by a school bus while the mother watched from her front door. The boy, who had been taught always to walk in front of the bus, had dashed behind it instead—no one knew why, except that he was only five—and the driver (a youngish woman with a spotless record, a mother herself) had backed up over him. For a week, the school had hired a psychiatrist to ride the bus with Billy and the other children in the event any of them should show disturbing signs that the tragedy had affected them too deeply. But it wasn't the children who needed the shrink, Andrew thought. It was the parents, like himself, who repeated the tale to each other and to their friends and colleagues over the phone, at the office or in their kitchens for days, as if talking about it endlessly would keep it at bay.

He walks to the window, drawn there by a tease of sunlight on the floor. Though it is still raining, the clouds are moving fast overhead, allowing the sun to break through here and there. The rain will pass any minute now, he knows, and he will go outside. He loves the earth after a fresh rain, has always loved it.

She will be waiting for him.

He checks his watch. Nine-oh-five. Less than an hour to go. He could tinker some with the gutter to pass the time.

He leans his shoulder on the window, his hands in his pockets, and looks over at the other house. A wash of sunlight, like the flight of a bird, passes over the roof and is gone.

He wonders where she would be now had the shooting never happened. If the rapist had not stolen into Eden's room, and Jim, in turn, not blundered after him, who might she be? Wild, as DeSalvo suggested? A married woman, with two children, mired in a loveless marriage? A waitress? A whore? Or would she have rescued herself—or someone have rescued her—so that she might be happily married now in

Boston? Or acting in Los Angeles? Or working, perhaps, in New York, like himself. Might they have met by accident on a street corner or in a bar?

As she is, he thinks, she's oddly pure—untouched, unmade.

HE WAITS by his own kitchen door out of sight, shaded by the screen. It is quarter to. Within seconds, Edith Close will open the door he is watching, make her way down the steps and enter the Plymouth. He checks his watch again, the tenth time in fifteen minutes, and as he does so, he feels faintly ridiculous. A grown man, hiding behind a screen door, unwilling to confront an aging, impotent woman.

He sees a sliver of pink cotton, a flash of gold on a wrist. Of course. Sensible woman. Edith Close has come around from the front of the house to avoid the rotted back stoop. With the sun behind her, he cannot see her face, though she seems not to glance in his direction. Eden won't have mentioned him, then. He didn't think she would. He watches Edith Close back her car carefully out the drive, as he has seen her do several times this week, as she does every day of the year, according to his mother's reports. Angled toward town, she puts the old Plymouth into first and heads south along the straight road to the nursing home.

Even though he could go now, he waits a bit behind the door. A thick peaceful hush settles over the two houses—or does he merely imagine that it does? He hears a buzzing; in the summer there is always a buzzing in the cornfields off in the distance and, closer, the continual hum and whine of insects in the weedy perennials, but this is part of the hush, the hush of two lonely houses set apart from town with only the whiz of a car or, seldom now, a human voice to rattle the quiet. He shuts his eyes and inclines his head toward the screen, listening intently, as Eden might do, this her only world, as cacophonous and distracting as the noise of the city if only he could hear as she does, if only he could tease out the differing sounds and their meanings.

Edith Close will not come back for a sweater or a forgotten purse, he decides. She hasn't done so once this week, so why today? He lets the door slam, to announce his intentions, and walks across the spongy wet grass, soaking his old sneakers. Unlike yesterday, his walk is slow and deliberate, and when he reaches the rotting stoop, he picks his way up over it with care.

He raps once lightly on the door and almost simultaneously opens it. He enters the kitchen, unhurried, again nearly blinded by the gloom. Then he sees her, an image in a photographer's tray, emerging into focus.

Later that night, lying in bed, unable to sleep, or bending to the fridge for a beer, Andrew will recall again the swift surprise of her presence, her back resting against the sink, her arms folded across her chest. It wasn't that he hadn't expected her; he had known she would be waiting for him. It was that her proximity, after all these years, was deeply unsettling, as if a fragment of a dream, a dream he'd thought he lost years ago, had indeed turned out to be real.

"Hello," she says.

She is holding herself still, her gaze seemingly directed toward a window beside him.

"I wanted to see you," he says. He shakes his head. "To speak with you, I mean." He stands in the center of the linoleum floor, uncertain as to whether he should sit at the table, make himself at home, or not. She has not invited him to. Perhaps, he thinks, she has no sense now, as he does, of the awkwardness of a conversation conducted standing stiffly face to face. Though she cannot see him, he feels uneasy in front of her. His arms and hands are appendages that seem no longer to belong to him. He folds them across his chest in unconscious parody of her stance.

"I thought. Yes," she says elliptically.

A quick intake of air she cannot fail to hear betrays his nervousness. "So how are you?" he asks. It is an inane question, and instantly he regrets it.

She gives the faintest of shrugs. "I am always all right," she says evenly.

He searches for the next sentence as if hunting for a trail that will lead him out of an unfamiliar wood. All his choices seem lame.

"It's been a long time," he says.

She doesn't answer him. Instead she turns her head so that she is looking at him so acutely he wonders fleetingly if perhaps he has got it wrong—and she *can* see after all. Her stare is uncompromising. He tries to imagine what it is that she "sees": his presence must be to her a voice in a vast inky sea.

"Your mother is dead," she says.

Her words startle him. The sentence is bald, unadorned. Almost unfeeling. But he realizes that he likes the frank statement. Likes not hearing an expression of sympathy, likes not hearing the words *I'm sorry* for the hundredth time. The fact is a simple one: His mother is dead, and she has said only that.

"Yes. We had the funeral. Your mother came. Did she tell you?"

"She tells me . . . some things. But you always did that."

"What?"

"Call her my mother."

"Well, she's . . ."

"Not."

He nods. He realizes she cannot see the nod. "Right," he says.

It will take some time to learn how to speak to her, he thinks. Everything must be in the voice.

"Jim died here," she says.

Another bald sentence, one that takes him by surprise. During his three brief visits to this house, Andrew has not thought of this fact, but, of course, he knows it is true. Jim died in this house, on the floor upstairs, and Andrew's father found him. He has a sudden, too vivid image of Edith Close being pressed to the ground by the ambulance attendants, of Eden with a bloodstained towel at her head, of his father with the rifle limp beside his leg.

"You have a wife and child," she says, her gaze sliding a few degrees off his face.

Perhaps it is having been alone for so long that reduces her sentences to this simplicity, he thinks. She has lost the etiquette of conversation, having had, he supposes, no experience with small talk. If it were T.J., or anyone else, the sentence would have been looser: "So I hear you're married"—something with a tone of familiarity.

"No," he explains, trying to answer her with equally honest sentences. "I have a son but no wife. We're separated. I live alone, and I see Billy, my son, on weekends."

"I won't have a son," she says.

She says it quickly, without emotion, though it brings him up short. He wants to say, too glibly, *Of course you will,* as he might to almost anyone else, but her statement rings so true he cannot form a reply.

He shifts his weight. He glances down at his feet, then looks at her again. He tries to take it in. All the years spent here. All the days inside this house while he was away; all the years, while he was in college, in the city, at his home in Saddle River. He thinks of what he has had—the grown-up toys and trinkets, the days filled with color and people and work, while she has had only this. Who can calculate, he thinks, even the accumulated weight of one single day: a hundred colors seen in a glance out a kitchen window; a dozen lives witnessed in one brisk walk through an office; the complex wealth of a meal with a wife and child. While her days seem to him, appear to him, impoverished by contrast— weightless, undistinguishable one from the other. Or is he wrong? Is there in her slow universe a life as rich as, even richer than, his own?

Yet for all his advantages, he has the distinct feeling of being at a disadvantage. There is a reality here that he is unprepared for—one seeming to have little to do with the minutiae of the life he has left behind. It is in keeping, he thinks, with the way he has been feeling lately, the way he sometimes does on vacation, the workaday world he has left on hold receding hour by hour so that it seems like something from another period of his life, so that he is no longer sure which *is* his real life, that or this. His world now, circumscribed by the two houses, far from the screening room and the noise of telephones, far from the Thai restaurant where he usually lunches and from the banter of men in offices, is this tiny piece of geography and the three women who have inhabited it for all of the nineteen years he has been gone.

He examines her. He is a voyeur, seeing what she cannot see. She is taller, he observes, but not very tall at all— perhaps five feet four or five feet five. Her arms and legs are slender, her abdomen nonexistent, like a girl's. Meeting her on the street, one would find it impossible to guess her age.

With her hair tangled behind her, her arms folded across her chest, she might be a young housewife, he thinks, barefoot, in old clothes, turning from the dishes in the sink to confront a husband across the room, her children playing in the backyard, seen through the window. He notices again the gray substance on her hands. She is, in some ways, astonishingly ordinary. What had he expected? Someone retarded? Deformed? A character in a dream? Rapunzel in a tower?

And yet she is not ordinary at all. It is in her speech, in the way she tilts her head as if to catch a clue in the silence. Her speech is off—too direct and then too enigmatic, as if rehearsed but never spoken. He thinks of the way he sometimes rehearses in his mind whole dialogues he never actually has.

"What do you look like now?" she asks.

He lets out a small laugh, more a release of tension than because the question is amusing. He puts his hands on his hips.

"Well," he says, "pretty much the same, though older and more decrepit." He smiles. Can she remember what he used to look like, after all these years of darkness, of nothingness? Can she remember what any human face looks like?

"Wrinkled here and there," he continues. "A few gray hairs. T.J. says I'm out of shape, and doubtless he's right."

When he says T.J.'s name, she flinches almost imperceptibly, but he is certain he is not mistaken.

"Are you looking at me?" she asks.

"Yes," he says.

"What do I look like now?"

"Oh," he says. Is it possible she does not know? Of course it's possible, he thinks. Unless she can see herself by touch, or unless Edith has patiently described her features. But he cannot imagine Edith doing this. And would Edith tell the truth?

"You've grown some," he begins, "but you look younger than most women your age. You're slender. Your face is much as I remember it, except for the, ah, eye and the color of your face, which is pale. Your skin is very white. Uncommonly white."

It is this whiteness that makes him cautious, he realizes, that reminds him he is an intruder—as if he'd dived too deeply toward the ocean floor and found in a sea cave a creature not meant to see the light or to be seen. He takes a step closer to her—he wants to see her face more clearly—and a floorboard under the linoleum creaks under his weight.

"Tell me about the eye," she says.

"It's . . ." He swallows. "It's somewhat elongated, shaped more like an almond than your other. And beside it there is a bit of skin that is smoother than the rest. And there seems to be a small patch of very slight depressions. It looks . . . OK," he says, stammering. "I mean that. It looks not exactly normal, but it's not . . . unattractive either. I am trying to be accurate."

"Thank you," she says.

"Does that seem like how you see yourself? Think of yourself, I mean?"

"I didn't know my skin was white," she says. "I can't really imagine that."

"No," he says.

She moves her weight against the sink. She crosses her ankles. Her bones are small and delicate. It surprises him to think of her as delicate: in his mind she was always tough and sturdy, though he supposes she created this impression by her demeanor.

"Perhaps I didn't say exactly what I meant," he says. "You're really very beautiful."

He thinks he sees a smile skimming across her lips, and when it is quickly gone, he finds himself disappointed. He wants, he realizes, a real smile.

The possibility, however, seems remote. The visit is proving more difficult than he had imagined. Reunions are always fraught with awkward tensions—the necessity to account for oneself; the attempt to find, through memories, an ember of the old emotions—but this one has no rules. What memory could he dredge up now without fear of hurting her? *Memories from the past upset her*, Edith said. Is this true?

"So what do you do all day?" he blurts out, unable for a moment to endure the silence, her poise.

"What do *you* do all day?" she retorts quickly.

"Right," he says, and nods. He smiles again. This is better.

He brings his hand up, rubs his cheek with his palm. He has an idea. "Do you ever . . . ?" he asks. "I've heard, or read, about it and was wondering . . . Would you like, would it help, to touch my face?"

He is thankful she cannot see him just now. It is one of a thousand deceits the sighted can practice on the blind. Or do they, he wonders, have ways of deceiving the sighted? Hearing things we did not know we said? He wonders if she will be able to feel the heat in his face.

She shrugs.

The silence in the kitchen is so complete he can hear the refrigerator whining.

He walks to the sink, pauses a moment, and then reaches for her hand. Her fingers are cool, and when he touches her, the touch is so private he feels he might lose his balance, and he nearly withdraws his own hand. But instead he pulls her hand from where it is wrapped tightly around her elbow. She doesn't resist. He brings her hand to his face, to his cheek, in an unnatural gesture. He has the weight of her hand in his, but when he lets his own go, she leaves her fingers on his skin.

At first she seems paralyzed, and he is about to reach up, when she moves her fingers slowly across his cheekbone to the bridge of his nose. He closes his eyes. He feels her touch move toward his brow. The touch is very slow, very light, very tentative. She traces his hairline down one side, pauses, moves up again to the brow and down the other side. She seems about to pull away then, but doesn't. She moves her hand up toward the eyebrows, and delicately she brushes her fingers against his eyelids. Her touch is cool air moving across his face. She skims down along the bones of his nose to his mouth. She outlines his lips, smooths her fingers across them, then dips under his chin to his throat, causing in him a deep internal shiver. He knows that she must feel his shiver, but she gives no sign of recognition. She fingers the collar of his shirt, trails her hand along the bridge of his shoulders and lets it drift away.

When he opens his eyes, she has her head turned from him, her arms again crossed in front of her.

He takes a long slow breath.

"Do I look the way you imagined me?" he asks.

"No," she says.

He puts his hand at the side of her head and turns her so that she is facing him.

"What?" she says.

"Don't move," he says.

He shuts his eyes. He begins on the cheek, as she did, and traces the exact journey she has taken. It is a map he will always remember perfectly, one he knows he will be able to recall in all its detail years from now. Her skin is smooth and dry. He feels the tightness of the almond eyelid, the silky skin directly beside it, with its tiny dots. Her mouth is warm and moist, and when he touches it, she bites her lower lip. He tries to "see" her face in this way, to form a picture with clues only from his hands. The image is different, he thinks, than the one his eyes see. Her skin feels fuller, her lips plumper. He lets his hand trail under her chin to her throat, lets his fingers rest in the hollow there. He traces the line of her shoulders.

He turns and walks toward the table. He sits down and runs his hand along the sticky oilcloth surface.

"What can I get for you?" he asks, changing the subject, knowing the question is condescending, even as he asks it. "There must be something that you need."

"Don't," she says.

"Don't what?"

"Don't bring me anything."

"Why?"

"She'll know you've come, then," she says.

"And if she knew?"

She shrugs again, not answering him. "What do *you* want?" she asks.

He looks at her. "I want nothing at all, except to talk to you," he says.

"T.J. and Sean and others, many others, they always want something. But not you?"

"Sean is dead," he says. "And T.J.?" He shakes his head. If she is talking about what he thinks she is talking about, she cannot mean T.J., surely. Andrew is positive of this.

"There are lies in T.J.'s voice," she says. "I can hear them when he laughs."

He is confused. Her leapfrogging from present to past makes him light-headed with the effort of trying to understand her. It is as if, deprived of time, past, present and future intermingle without context, a day twenty years ago as vivid and as all-consuming as the worries of the morning, or of tomorrow morning.

"What do you mean, T.J. lies? Lies about what?" he asks.

"He lies about himself," she says.

He studies her. "When you asked me how you looked now . . . ," he says.

"Yes?"

"There is something else I meant to say and didn't."

She lifts her head slightly but says nothing.

"Your hair is very tangled."

She turns away, resting her hands on the sink.

He walks to where she is standing. He touches the back of her hair. "I could brush it for you. Now, I mean."

She shakes her head.

But that's all right, because he has another idea.

FILLED WITH PURPOSE, he is competent, the kitchen no longer strange to him, merely a mirror image of his own.

She comes into the kitchen with two towels, a comb, a washcloth and the shampoo, as he has told her to. She puts them on the table. When he asked her to fetch them, she protested, and when she left the room, she was gone so long he thought she might not be coming back. She stands at the table, as if she were examining him. His hands are not steady—from false bravado? feigned confidence?—and he is again glad she cannot see him. To still his hands, he lifts the dishes out of the sink and scrubs it with Ajax until it is gleaming. He lays one of the towels over the lip, making a soft cushion, and puts the shampoo and the washcloth on the drainboard. He tests the water. When he has it as he wants it, he walks to where she is.

"I'm good at this," he says. It is, of course, an untested statement. He has never washed anyone's hair but Billy's, a boy's short crop. He leads her to a chair that he has turned sideways against the sink and guides her into a sitting position. Slowly, against her resistance, he pushes her shoulders back, so that her neck is resting on the towel at the lip of the old porcelain sink. He can feel the tension in her shoulders, a tension that invades his fingers, his palms.

"Relax," he says. "Just try to relax."

Her neck is arched, and he follows with his eye the long

white curve of her throat to where her blouse is buttoned. He puts an arm under her shoulders, brushing her forehead with his chin as he does so, and lifts her up for a moment as he brings her hair over the edge. Her hair is a wild mass that fills the sink. He is at first nearly paralyzed by the sight of the tangled weave of brass and gold; it seems to him that it is something he has no right to touch. He turns on the water, lets it run through his fingers and into the hair. He sees that he cannot wet the entire head with the tap, so he hunts in the cupboards for a pitcher. He finds one and fills it with the warm water. When he pours it over her head, she winces, as though she were expecting it to be too hot or too cold. He tests it again. "Is that all right?" he asks.

She murmurs something he takes to be assent.

He pours the water slowly until her head is entirely soaked. He lifts up her hair with both hands, feels its weight. He opens the bottle of shampoo and squeezes it liberally over the crown of her head. Plunging his fingers in her hair—so thick his fingers are lost—he massages the soap into her scalp, gently at first, so as not to frighten or hurt her, and, when she doesn't protest, more firmly. A faint sigh escapes her, and it is, he thinks—he hopes—a sigh of pleasure. Relieved, he sees her face begin to soften, the muscles letting go, so that, with her eyes closed, she looks nearly asleep. He lingers over the massage, not wanting to disturb her look of repose. A curl of soapsuds edges across her cheekbone, and he wipes it away with his finger. He remembers bathing Billy in the sink, cradling the infant's head with one hand while he soaped his skin with a washcloth. He remembers, later, getting into the tub with Billy when he was two and three, his own long, hairy legs stretched the length of the tub, with Billy nestled between them. Billy would squirt him with a water pistol, and the two of them would make up songs while Martha watched them from the doorway. It was always his job, bathing Billy.

It is only when he begins a succession of pours to rinse out the soap after the second wash that the tangles give way, and when he rinses it for the final time, the hair looks as though he might get a comb through it. He squeezes the excess water out gently and wraps a large towel around her head as he lifts her shoulders off the sink. Her blouse is wet all along the collar and her shoulders. Her body is heavy now, like a drowsy child's. He stands in front of her to dry her hair. Her face is inches from his stomach. He can feel her warm breath through his thin summer shirt. He has a fleeting image of pulling her head toward him so that her mouth touches his skin.

He draws up a kitchen chair next to her and begins to comb out her hair. It is a painstaking process, made more difficult because he does not want to hurt her and he is new at this. He learns to hold the hair in a tight fist above where he is combing the knots out; in that way, she won't feel the pull at her scalp. He parts it in the middle, not knowing how else to do it.

"Best to dry it in the sun," he says. His voice is husky. He clears his throat. "We'll sit on the steps. There should be a bit of sun there."

"I never go outside," she says. "And we only have twenty-five minutes."

He checks his watch. She is right. "How do you know that?" he asks.

"It's just something that I know," she says. "I hear it. Things sound different at different times of the day."

He opens the door and leads her to the back stoop. He tells her that the bottom step is broken, and she says she knows that—she heard him cursing yesterday. He laughs. They sit on the top step, side by side. He sits with his elbows on his knees. Their shoulders are almost touching.

"Why did you do this for me?" she asks.

"I don't know," he says.

They sit in silence. He wishes he could ask her what she is thinking about, but he knows he himself would mind the question, so he doesn't. Her hair begins to dry and turn to corn silk, first at the ends and then near the crown, curling around her face. It was, he thinks, an intrusive thing to have done, full of risk—a thing born not entirely of altruistic motives, were he to examine his motives, which he thinks he may not do. At the very least, it wasn't like him, though he is hard-pressed these days to know what is like him and what isn't. In all the years of his marriage, he never once even combed Martha's hair, never mind washed it.

"I'll have to go inside now, and you have to go," she says when there are only five minutes left.

She stands up, and he stands up with her.

"Eden . . ."

"She will know now," she says quickly.

"That will have to be all right, won't it?"

She doesn't answer him, instead moves toward the door.

"I'll be back," he says.

HE PARKS in front of the TV repair shop. An hour has passed since he was with Eden, and he doesn't know what made him head in this direction, but now, as he looks into the glass window of the shop, it seems to him that, yes, he meant to come here, to see O'Brien, to say hello.

The door is unlocked, but when he enters the shop, the room is so quiet, so still, that at first he thinks that Henry O'Brien is not inside. The shop seems not to have changed much in nineteen years, apart from a thickish layer of dust covering all of the TVs and radios and picture tubes and other components. Even the television sets themselves seem old—all secondhand, some portables, some larger models. He does not remember the dust from before, or this sense of deathly quiet in a hot dusty room on a summer day. As a young boy in the shop, he was fascinated by what then appeared to him as shiny, mysterious, nearly unfathomable pieces of that exciting thing called technology; and as a somewhat older boy, waiting for Sean to finish haggling with his father over a curfew or a five-dollar loan, he often felt uncomfortable in the shop, hoping only that Sean could make his escape before his father lost his temper.

"Hello," Andrew calls.

He hears a murmur, a movement in the back room. He makes his way toward the sound.

"Hello," he calls again.

He thinks he hears a greeting, peers into the open doorway. Henry O'Brien is sitting at a large gray metal desk littered with small electrical parts, white receipts, paper coffee cups, an ashtray overfull with cigarette butts and gum wrappers. Andrew can see only the top of the man's head at first—the reddish hair now paler with streaks of gray, a thinning at the crown—until the man looks up and squints his eyes to get a better look at Andrew or to place the face and body. The eyes are reddened and watery, as though with permanent tears.

"I know you," says O'Brien. "Wait a minute."

Andrew can see the progress of the man's thoughts as they pass across his face: A customer? No. A man from the town? No. Then there is the quick flicker of pain in the eyes, the moment of recognition.

"Andy."

"Yes."

"That's right. Your mother died."

"Yes."

"My wife . . ."

"I know. I'm sorry."

"You need some work done?"

There is no air-conditioning, nor even a fan in the shop, and the back room is airless, with a heavy trace of cigarette smoke. O'Brien is wearing a T-shirt with a hole in the shoulder. His skin is pinkish, blotchy, and there is several days' growth of gray stubble on his cheeks. Andrew notes, from his vantage point standing over the desk, that the coffee cup at O'Brien's elbow is filled with a clear amber liquid.

"No," says Andrew. "I just stopped by to say hello."

"That so."

It is an unexpectedly sullen response, and it takes Andrew by surprise. Why has he come? he now wonders.

O'Brien does not invite him to sit down. He takes a long swallow from the coffee cup. He examines Andrew closely. "You done well for yourself, I know," says O'Brien, looking narrowly at Andrew.

"I guess," says Andrew.

"Better than my boy."

"Well . . ."

"They crucified him, you know. Or maybe you don't know; you went off to that fancy school. But they crucified him in this town—never mind that he was already dead. They wanted a scapegoat, they got one. Killed his mother."

"I . . ."

"The kid never got a trial."

O'Brien takes an angry swallow of the liquid in the coffee cup, but it catches him the wrong way, causing him to cough once, then sending him into a spasm of uncontrollable retching. When he regains his voice, there is a tear of spittle at the side of his mouth, and indeed it seems to Andrew that the man means to spit his words.

"In this country," O'Brien says hoarsely, "you're supposed to be innocent until proven guilty, but the way people look at me in this town, you know they made up their minds a long time ago."

"I'm sure . . ."

"It's all her fault anyway," says O'Brien, wiping his mouth with the back of his hand. "I blame her."

"Who?"

"That whore. That bitch."

Andrew says nothing. He feels the heat rising along his neck behind his ears.

"She done it. She led him on, then turned on him. Made him crazy. And then naming him like that . . ."

A silence, like the cigarette smoke, hangs between the two men.

"She was only fourteen," says Andrew quietly.

"Fourteen. A hundred and fourteen. Makes no difference to me. If it weren't for her, my son'd be here now."

"Well, I'm sorry to have . . . ," Andrew begins.

"That your car?"

Andrew turns to see the tail half of the black BMW just outside the open shop door. The light outside, in contrast to the darkness inside, is so bright that it gives the car an almost surreal aura. Seen in this way, across the shabby bits of the front room, the car seems unforgivably pretentious.

"Yes," says Andrew.

O'Brien sucks his teeth.

"Well, I guess I'll be . . . ," Andrew says, turning back to look at O'Brien, who has deliberately resumed a hunched posture over a small piece of metal with many wires coming out of it. Andrew knows now that he was led to the shop by his desire to find out more about Sean, about the morning Sean left town, but he sees that he will not find the answers here.

"Yeah, you do that . . . ," says O'Brien, not looking up.

Andrew turns and walks back out through the shop. Bitterness hovers in the air like dust. Once outside, he stands for a moment on the sidewalk, letting the afternoon heat soak his head, feeling dusty and grayish and faintly guilty in the white sunshine. He looks across at the man who runs the gas station, waves. The man waves back. Even though Andrew doesn't know the man, no longer knows any of the people connected with the old gas station, the friendly wave is so reassuring that Andrew finds himself waving again.

It seems to Andrew that except for the waving, nothing in the street is moving.

THE HOUSE is now a labyrinth of cardboard boxes, some half filled, some sealed with packing tape, some empty, waiting for Andrew to decide on their contents. Tired, more tired than he has been since arriving, nearly numb with exhaustion, he wends his way through the maze of cartons, up the stairs and to his old room. It is after two in the morning. On a roll, he has been working all night, executing a kind of domestic triage, relegating some few precious items to cartons he will take with him back to the city, appointing more to be sold at auction with the larger furniture in the house, and remanding still less fortunate others to the Salvation Army. The Salvation Army and the auctioneer will come in a few days to collect everything, he has been told over the phone. He has only to transport the boxes he will keep for himself and Billy.

He turns on the light in his room and immediately shuts it off. Walking to the bed by the open window, he sits down, leans his head forward toward the screen and looks out. The night is as dark as a cave. No stars. No moon. He hears the crickets in the grass. Do the crickets live in the grass? he wonders. Across the way, there is the other house, and below his window the hydrangea tree. In the impenetrable darkness, he can't see either one.

In the darkness, he is thinking, he's as blind as she is.

THE DJ on the radio, a DJ who is too loud, too raucous, too juiced for seven o'clock in the morning, announces to Andrew as he eats his cereal that the heat is back—a fact that needs no telling. Already the inland humidity has settled on the land and entered the house like an unwelcome visitor preparing for another languid nap. In August, Andrew reflects, the heat is never far away, hovering as it does on the horizon, waiting for the brief teases of cool, clean air to dissipate and vanish.

The promise of a sweltering afternoon rearranges his priorities. Two jobs that he has planned on tackling—tidying the herb and flower gardens and beginning the paint job on the south wall—must be done in the early morning hours. Later, after he has been to visit Eden again (the anticipated visit anchoring his day, lending his day a sense of urgency he cannot yet quite define), he will find a liquor store and buy a bottle of wine to bring to T.J.'s that evening. He wishes he had been able to think of a reasonable excuse not to have to go to the dinner tonight—though he is looking forward to finding out what T.J.'s children are like; and he is, if he thinks about it, intrigued, as he has always been, by the chance to see how someone else's life, a life he once knew nearly as well as his own, has unfolded.

He finishes his cereal and walks to the garage, where he finds a pair of ancient, dirt-encrusted garden gloves and a small hand hoe. Rummaging through the drawers there, he realizes with dismay that he will have to pack up these items as well.

He crouches in front of the herb garden and tries to read it. It is a tangled mass of differing shades of green fading to brown: some herbs, like the sage and the rosemary, are immediately recognizable: others could be oregano or summer savory or winter savory or thyme. He decides that regardless of variety, each needs the same care—a weeding, a pruning and a watering—and so he begins, working fast, hoping to get the job done quickly so that he can move on to the flower bed and the painting.

He is trimming a small plant that could conceivably be

a weed, though he thinks not, when he feels a light tap between his shoulder blades. The touch is so unexpected that he starts, whirling around in a crouch, with the hoe in his hand.

"She pretends she washed it herself, which she is perfectly capable of doing, but I know you did it."

Edith Close towers over him. Ungracefully, his left knee cracking, he stands to confront her. She has on a summer sundress, with a beige cardigan thrown over her shoulders.

He can think of no reply. It *was* a presumptuous act, and he cannot, for the moment, think of how to justify it.

"And sneaking behind my back," she says.

"I didn't sneak behind your back," he protests.

"You went when I wasn't there."

"Well, yes, but . . ."

"Well, then."

"She seemed fine to me," he says, trying to change the subject.

She has a purse on her arm. One hand is folded over the other at her waist. It is a gesture, common in older women, that he has never seen in a younger woman, a woman, say, of Martha's generation. He wonders, irrelevantly, if it is a gesture women grow into as they age.

"I'd have thought your mother would have told you more," she says.

"Told me what?"

"You know that Eden was away?"

"Yes. At a hospital, and then at a home for the blind."

She shakes her head. "Eden was badly hurt by the . . . incident."

She looks down at the strap of her pocketbook, as if contemplating it. "At first we thought it was physical," she says. "She had numerous operations. She wouldn't talk—to me or to anyone. We thought it was related to the injuries. But the injuries were . . . deeper than that."

He watches as she touches her purse—a talisman. "The injury to her head made her very sick," she says. "The place she was in wasn't, strictly speaking, a home for the blind." She looks sharply up at him, wanting to see his reaction. "It was a mental hospital."

He recalls Eden saying yesterday, apropos of nothing, *Jim died here.* He remembers thinking at the time that it was an odd thing to say.

"She did recover," Edith continues. "Not fast, but after a time. She reached a point where I felt she could come home. It was felt, *I* felt, I could care for her just as well here.

"But she needs *quiet*," Edith says forcefully, contracting her brow. "She needs not to be disturbed, not to be reminded of the past. We never speak of it. I would prefer that you not speak of it. I would prefer that you not visit her at all. You remind her of the past. You may even raise her expectations, her hopes," she says, her voice rising, as if to emphasize her point. "And then you will go away. And where will she be then?"

He again feels the heat seeping into his face. He wants to find her ludicrous, preposterous, but he cannot. Indeed, her speech is to him uncomfortably moving and embarrassingly accurate. For he *has* hoped to raise Eden's expectations, even if subconsciously, and he cannot deny that he will go away. And why should he have assumed that Edith cannot have changed in nineteen years? Rendered helpless, perhaps Eden immediately became more appealing to Edith. Or possibly it was the hole that Jim's death left in her life that allowed her finally to focus on her daughter. And yet, despite these sudden epiphanies, he wants to believe that visiting Eden is good for her.

"Don't you think you're overreacting?" he says, surprising himself not only with his rudeness but also with the word itself, for it is a term he associates with psychobabble, one Martha liked to use on him, a word he normally despises.

But he has never been precise in arguments. The words that come to mind in a tense exchange are not accurate enough, and thus he is often rendered inarticulate, like a child cornered by an adult.

"She is *my* daughter," Edith says, the words stapling the air around them.

The sudden flash of anger is surprising in the quiet backyard.

But in a moment it is gone. She gathers herself together in a deft sequence of subtle movements, gaining an inch as she stands more erect, and recomposing her face until it is the one he saw in her kitchen—calm, cooler and, if wary, then more in control. He watches her, fascinated.

"Andy," she says, as if weary of the effort to teach good manners to the neighbor's boy, "you must see it from my point of view. Eden and I are *family*." She exaggerates the last word. It sounds furry, her voice deep with patience. "She's all I've got now, and I'm all she has. There are aspects to this you can't possibly understand. You've been gone for nearly *twenty* years. . . ."

He is deprived (or relieved) of an opportunity to reply. The sound of a car slowing to turn into the driveway makes them both look up. A small white Toyota rolls over the gravel. DeSalvo hoists himself from the low driver's seat. Some cars, Andrew thinks, are just too small for some men.

DeSalvo waves and makes his way toward Andrew.

"You make your conference?" asks DeSalvo, short of breath, advancing slowly in the heat. "You left your checkbook on the counter."

"Jesus," says Andrew. He turns. "You know Mrs. Close."

DeSalvo casts a canny eye on Edith Close, nods. "How are you?" he asks.

"Fine. Thank you," she says.

"So all I can say is it musta been one hell of a conference

call," DeSalvo says, turning to Andrew and handing him the checkbook. "You got a lotta cash in that account."

"Oh," says Andrew, embarrassed. "You looked."

"Yeah, what the hell," says DeSalvo. "I always look. I called you right away, but there was no answer. I woulda brought it by yesterday, but I hadda take my wife to the hospital. Problems with her hip. And I been tied up there with her all night. I told the luncheonette to tell you I had it, if you called."

"I hope your wife is all right," says Andrew.

DeSalvo scratches his chest. "They're gonna put a pin in, but the doctor says she'll be OK in a month or so."

"I must be getting back," says Edith Close, moving past the two men, giving them a wide berth. She walks slowly down the gravel drive toward her front door. She walks as though she knows they are watching her back.

"Piece a work," says DeSalvo.

Andrew looks at the retreating figure and nods.

By TEN FORTY-FIVE, he has been circling his kitchen floor for nearly an hour. The half-empty beer in his hand is warm; an empty is on the table. His T-shirt is damp at the back and under the armpits. Already the humidity has weight to it. His face feels gritty from lack of sleep. A shower would help, he knows, but he is reluctant to leave the kitchen, as though remaining in the kitchen for a long enough time will finally deliver an answer.

The list of chores now feels more burdensome than it did earlier this morning, but he cannot focus on it. The things of the kitchen, except for the framed collage of snapshots, which he'll keep, and the Hoosier cabinet, which will be sold at auction, are all going to the Salvation Army. A family finally dismantled. It must happen all the time, he thinks, every day, in every town and city in America.

And then who will live in this house? he wonders. A couple looking for an affordable starter home, a couple who will imagine this house to have more charm than it does, a couple who will furnish it with inauthentic country antiques? He envisions the new wife, her brown hair streaked with blond highlights, her lithe, athletic form dressed in khaki shorts and an oversized T-shirt, as she repapers the walls—as if this gesture will secure her dreams.

I should get back to work, he says aloud. He plays the phrase like an old tape that doesn't really interest him anymore but he nevertheless wants to hear again, just in case. Each day away from work makes the thought of returning there more and more foreign. He cannot this moment conceive of ever again having the inclination or the stamina to survive a ten-hour day in a thirty-story building, though he knows he must. Must return, and soon.

It's the heat and fatigue, he says to himself, though not entirely convincingly. This will pass.

He leans against the fridge, finishes the beer, moves away again. He needs a shower, needs a shave, needs a hair wash. A hair wash. His fingernails are black with soil. The knees of his jeans are green with grass stains. Grass stains don't come out, Martha said a hundred times, holding up a pair of Billy's overalls.

There's the wine to get, he reminds himself, trying to refocus on his list of chores. The south wall to paint.

I said to Eden I would be back, but what if Edith is right? he asks himself again. And then again.

He opens the back door, with no clear destination.

Then he has it. He will take the car for a spin, head north for an hour or two, return after two o'clock. He will get in the car and move, stay away. Stop by for a quick goodbye tomorrow or the next day. Leave it alone, forget about it.

Relieved to be moving forward, he hustles down the

steps, walks briskly to the BMW. He puts his hand on the door. He stretches as he reaches for his keys in the front pocket of his jeans. The keys aren't there. They're on the counter in the kitchen.

I knew that, he says to himself.

"I THOUGHT you wouldn't come."

"I nearly didn't."

"She's warned you off."

"She's very concerned about you."

"You think so."

"Yes, I do."

"Then why are you here?"

"Well, I think she's concerned, but I'm not convinced she's right."

"I told her I washed it myself, but she didn't believe me. It's the part. I never get it right."

Her hair is freshly brushed, the part he made yesterday still straight.

"I want to ask you something," he says.

"What is it?" she says after a time.

"Was it very bad?" he says. "In the beginning, I mean. I never knew until today what happened, where you were."

She hesitates. "There are things about the beginning I don't remember," she says. "And what is bad? Worse than before? Worse than now?"

"You must have loved Jim very much," he says.

"He was my father."

"I know."

"No you don't."

It seems to him that she has taken some care with her appearance today. She is wearing a blue sundress with white buttons down the front, and a belt. Her feet, he observes, are still bare. When he entered the kitchen, she was sitting at the table, her body facing the door. There is a blush of pink along the bridge of her nose, across her cheekbones and on her forehead. From the sun yesterday. It wasn't the part that gave away his presence. It was the sun.

"You've been drinking," she says.

"A couple of beers."

"I haven't smelled that in a long time."

"I'm afraid I didn't have any time to clean up," he lies. "I was working in the garden."

"I know. I heard her speak to you."

"I apologize if I . . ."

"Smell like you've been working hard? I don't mind. It's interesting."

He wonders if he should offer to make her lunch. He wonders what she eats. Yesterday neither of them mentioned food.

"I think we should take a walk," he says.

"No." She smooths the fabric of her dress along her thighs.

"It'll be good. Through the cornfields. Like old times."

"There are no old times."

"Well, then, just for now."

"I almost never go outside."

"You said that yesterday. Why?"

"What is there to go outside for?"

"You don't have to be afraid. I'll hold on to you, lead you."

"I won't," she says.

"She never takes you out, does she?"

She shrugs. "When it's necessary."

"Listen," he says.

"What?"

"We're going to do this."

ONCE OUTSIDE, it is as though, in the few short minutes he has been in the kitchen, some unseen hand turned up the heat a few notches, leaving it just this side of unbearable. Or perhaps it is that the gloomy kitchen, with its drawn shades and green paint, has had the unexpected benefit of providing a natural air-conditioning. Whatever the cause, Andrew is assaulted by both the glare and the heat as soon as he opens the door, a double assault that makes him wonder seriously if he should take her out.

Almost instantly beads of sweat form along his brow, on his upper lip and under his nipples. It is real heat, the kind that soaks a man only moments after he has put on a clean T-shirt, that drives children to seek relief under lawn sprinklers. In the luncheonette, the men will be sweating under the laboring ceiling fan. The town pool will be a mass of color and bodies, and in the backyards of the houses closer to town, old women will forfeit their dignity, choosing instead to sprawl in green and white plastic lawn chairs, their white legs, nearly entirely bare, white with purple veins, offered up to a stray breeze in the shade.

The heat makes him want to go to the pond—the body needing to slake its thirst—and this desire pushes aside caution. He holds open the screen door and reaches for her elbow, leading her out onto the stoop. Of course, he sees at once, the glare is nothing to her. Indeed, she keeps her eyes open wide, a stare into the white heat that unnerves him, with his own eyes narrowed into tight painful slits against the sun. He wishes he had a pair of sunglasses with which to cover her eyes. It is as if her gaze, so unaffected by this light, had rendered her naked, too exposed, and he is moved to shield her.

"I'm going to pick you up and lift you over the step," he says.

At her side, his left arm around her waist, he hoists her over the rotted stoop. When he puts her down he takes her hand.

"Do you remember the way to the pond?"

She shakes her head.

"Just stay by me. We'll go slowly."

"I don't want this," she says.

With an authority more assumed than convincing, he leads her along the newly mown grass south toward the edge of the cornfields. The grass is already turning brown in patches. He has cut it too short for August, too short for the heat.

She moves reluctantly, a slight resistance in his hand, a shrinking back from each step taken. Her hand in his is like that of a child who cannot keep up with, or who does not want to keep up with, an adult. He tries to convey confidence in his grasp, holding her hand firmly, not giving way to her resistance. He looks at her face. The too bright light makes it sharp in its clarity, the scar finely detailed, the blue-green eyes vivid and unflinching. He has a sense now of how strange this outing is for her, retracing a journey made in childhood, made then with the easy, unselfconscious movements of a girl, and not made in the nineteen years since. Now the journey must be to her the way a blindfolded walk through a foreign city would be to him, hazard awaiting each tentative step, a sense of complete and frightening helplessness but for the guide.

He shuts his eyes and tries to experience the walk as she must. Immediately he is aware of a sensation of tremendous heat at the top of his head and of the sullen quiet of the noon hour. He is uncomfortable, unsure in his footing, this uncertainty betraying itself through his hand, for he feels her resistance grow stronger. And when he opens his eyes—he can, he thinks, have taken only ten or fifteen steps at best—he sees that he has already veered off course.

At the edge of the cornfields, he can just make out the path to the pond. It is overgrown with wild blackberry bushes and bittersweet. Young boys seldom use it now, he imagines:

perhaps the odd boy, exploring a path from the pond, coming suddenly upon the two stark farmhouses and realizing how far he had strayed.

The heat is producing a faint headache at the back of his eyes. "We'll have to go single file," he says, wiping his brow with the end of his T-shirt. "I'll hold my hand behind me, and you take it. I'll go very slowly so you won't trip."

"Where are we?" she asks.

"Put your arms out," he says.

She does so, brushing the drying leaves of corn.

"Do you remember this?" he asks.

She fingers a corn sheaf but doesn't answer him.

When they begin to move, her walk is even more tentative than before. Once she puts her hand on his back as if to steady herself. The journey is awkward, slow going. He wonders if they'd do better if he walked behind her, with his hand on her shoulder, guiding her.

A fly begins to buzz around his head and won't leave him alone no matter how he swats at it with his free hand. The heat in the cornfields, without any shade overhead, is oppressive. He feels the heat drain his confidence. He is afraid, for a moment, to look at her. What if Edith was right, he wonders, and this expedition is too much for her? And might the sun be harming her in some way he has not anticipated?

She answers his unspoken question with a cry. Her hand slips out of his. When he turns around, she is crouched toward the ground. He sees a shiny object near her foot. It is the pop top of a beer can, the sharp edge curved upward.

"Jesus," he says. "We forgot your shoes. I should have thought. Let me look at that."

She is sitting on the ground, massaging the ball of her foot. He takes her foot in his hand and examines the sole. He can see no blood, no puncture.

"I would like to go back now," she says.

He lifts her up. "We have to get you some sneakers," he says. "You have no sneakers?"

"Don't buy me any sneakers," she says.

"It's all right," he says, thinking. "I can keep them at my house. We can use them when I take you out." He says this as if it had already been decided they would be going outside for walks together again in the future. He says this as if sliding in sideways.

But she hears it. "Soon you will go away," she says.

"Well, not . . . not immediately."

"If she knows that you have been again, she will not go to work."

He ponders this.

"I can be careful if you can," he says.

She doesn't answer him.

"I have to go to T.J.'s tonight," he says. "And I don't want to go."

"You don't like T.J.," she says.

The suggestion surprises him. "I don't know. He and I are different now."

"So are we," she says. She turns in the path. She refuses his hand and holds her arms out instead, letting the cornstalks guide her.

ON THE RADIO, in the car, on the way to the mall, Andrew hears that the heat wave, expected to last for most of the coming week, will break records for this part of the state. This evening and through the night, says the announcer, the temperature will remain in the high nineties. The announcer segues into a follow-up on the lead story, which Andrew has missed. The thirteen-year-old girl who was found raped, sodomized and beaten in her father's barn earlier this morning has died of her injuries at the county hospital. Andrew stares at the digital readout on his radio. The police, says the announcer, have made no arrests, but the girl's sixteen-year-old boyfriend, who appears to have been the last person to have seen her alive, has been taken in for questioning.

The announcer, in a more lively voice, an advertising voice Andrew knows well, reads an ad for an end-of-season sale on pool and garden accessories. Andrew puts his foot on the gas, takes the car up to seventy. Before he knows it, Billy will be thirteen. Eden was fourteen. Just. But she didn't die of her injuries. A line swims up to him through the years from a book he liked when he was a junior in high school. He can't remember the line exactly. He has never been very good at precise recall of quotations. But it was something about there not being much difference between the ones at the farm and the ones in the graveyard, and how the ones in the graveyard were the lucky ones. The book was *Ethan Frome*, and he read it by his bedroom window for English homework one Sunday afternoon in January. He remembers vividly the way the world looked outside that window—a snow cover made bleak by the thin winter light of a January day—and how in keeping the earth was with the book he was reading. He imagines with an unwelcome clarity the face of the mother this morning as she was told the fate of her daughter. In New York, in the papers and on the radio, he has become accustomed, if not inured, to reports of the killing of children, the stealing of children and the sexual abuse of children, and these reports have sickened him and made him wary, and have caused him to be more protective of Billy than his own parents had to be of him. But it is this report, heard in his BMW on the way to the mall, heard not ten miles from the barn where the girl was found, heard nineteen years after Eden was raped and shot, that is the most difficult to absorb. Though he has an understanding of differing sexual proclivities, and a tolerance for tastes he does not himself share, he cannot conceive of a desire that would cause a man to sexually batter a child and then kill her. Nor can he entirely fathom, though a similar act might be said to have shaped many of his adult dreams and visions, how such a violence could take place here. It is the locale, he thinks, this deceptively inoffensive locale, that makes such a news report so incomprehensible. He turns up the volume of his radio so that the sound of a rock song—a piece of music he has never heard before, a loud atonal piece of music with lyrics he cannot decipher—fills his ears.

ALL THE WOMEN of the county without access to a pool or to air-conditioning appear to have converged upon the mall. Inside, the temperature is regulated so that within minutes it is possible to forget the weather. Teenage girls in threes and fours, carrying packages, move en masse from one store to the next, lightly fingering merchandise, using it somehow as material for jokes, creating the mall anew as an activity to while away the long afternoon. Babies in strollers keep watch over their mothers, as the mothers sit on concrete benches along the center of the mall, eating ice cream cones and smoking cigarettes, idly giving the stroller a push now and then, thinking of what to bring home for supper so as to avoid cooking in the heat. There are almost no men in the mall, Andrew observes, and those he does see are in short-sleeved dress shirts and ties, managers, he supposes, of the various shops, or else plainclothes security personnel. He himself is still wearing his sweat-stained T-shirt and his grass-stained jeans, and his appearance seems out of place among all the clean women and babies and girls.

The mall is a long rectangle, with trees lining the center strip. On either side are the stores. He walks the length of the mall and back. There are four stores that sell shoes, not including the Sears at one end and the Caldor's at the other. There is also a store that sells greeting cards, a store that sells books, a store that sells video games and a store that sells fake country antiques. Most of the other stores sell women's clothing but not shoes.

He begins with the most promising store, one that sells athletic footgear, and at once realizes he does not know Eden's foot size. He picks up a sneaker that looks as though it had been designed for an astronaut or by an astronaut and reads the size inside: 6½. The size looks right to him. He is drawn to a rack of plain canvas sneakers in white and pink and blue, but a wiry-haired salesgirl, plucked from her afternoon stupor by the sight of a reasonably young male, steers Andrew away from the simple sneakers to an array of high-tech running shoes along the left wall.

"Jogging? No, I don't think so," says Andrew, who cannot picture the subtly toned blue and gray running shoes, with thick soles and puffy sides, on Eden. On Martha, yes, they would be perfect. His eyes stray covetously to the rack of plain canvas sneakers, but the salesgirl, piqued by his momentary inattention, launches into a discussion of the technology behind (or rather inside) a pair of white and silver "walking shoes." Lest he offend the salesgirl, who has actually stepped between him and the rack of canvas sneakers, he mumbles something about just looking and backs out of the store.

Andrew visits all of the shoe stores and the shoe departments of Sears and Caldor's. He visits some of the stores twice. He lingers over the selections, unable to come to a decision, unable to settle upon what he thinks is the perfect shoe. For he wants the shoes to be right, and he examines each display with the kind of scrutiny hitherto reserved for forays into toy stores in order to buy birthday presents for Billy. He fingers canvas shoes that have no ties, deliberates as to whether they might be a more sensible choice. He thinks of boat shoes as perhaps being more practical. He realizes, in Caldor's, throwing his head back in a gesture of disbelief at his own stupidity, that color is irrelevant. He is, for a time, seduced, despite his natural antipathy, by the endless shelves of sixty-dollar running shoes and lets himself be taught the intricacies of arch support. He passes several times by the first shoe store he entered, hoping the salesgirl there will have gone on a break. Finally, after an undetermined amount of time has passed, and after he has eaten a hamburger and a vanilla shake at Burger King, he walks purposefully into the first shoe store and makes for the rack of plain canvas sneakers. He allows the ambitious salesgirl no time to intercept him, picks out a pair of blue sneakers and says, *Size six and a half, please*, in a voice normally reserved for giving taxi drivers directions. He suspects she will outwit him by coming out of the storeroom with a smile to say they are out of stock, but perhaps she is less interested in him than he thought, for she returns in a minute with a box. He checks to see if they are indeed blue and size 6½, which they are. He pays for the sneakers and walks out with the box under his arm.

Then he begins on the sunglasses.

The quest for the sunglasses takes not quite as long, but standing in line at the register, listening to one teenage girl tell another, enigmatically, that she has burned her blue silk blouse, he looks at his watch and sees that it is already quarter to seven. He is due at T.J.'s at seven. He doesn't even have the wine. He will have to bolt, buy the wine, drop by the house, throw on a clean shirt. No time for a shower and a shave. And even so, he will be late.

He pays for the sunglasses and heads for the exit door. As soon as he opens it, the heat hits him like a thick wall. Nearly seven o'clock, and it still feels like a hundred.

He walks unhurriedly to his car. He is humming a song heard overhead in a store. He has the sneakers and the sunglasses, and tomorrow he will give them to her.

HE RINGS the bell beside T.J.'s front door, turns and glances down the street. Each house is, in its construction, identical to the one beside it. Any individuality, to the extent that characteristic exists at all, is created only by the paint or the trim or the false panes in this window or that. The sign at the entrance to the subdivision reads: "Water's Edge—Center-Hall Colonials," but the houses have little in common with the colonials Andrew knew in Massachusetts years ago. Even the driveways and the lawns and the redwood decks at the backs are clones of each other. What is to prevent a man, he wonders idly, from coming home drunk late one night, swerving into the wrong driveway and fumbling at the wrong door with his keys? Or opening an unlocked door and slipping into the wrong bed beside the wrong wife?

"Andy-boy. Pal," says T.J., opening the door and letting out clouds of frigid air. "Come in quick, before the heat gets in."

T.J. has on a white cotton sweater with the sleeves pushed up to the elbows and a pair of khaki pants with a profusion of pockets. The pants look as though they are meant to be worn on safari. Andrew proffers the bottle of wine wrapped in a paper bag. He has thrown on a clean dress shirt over his sweat-stained back. His fingernails are still black, and he has not shaved. T.J. raises an eyebrow but says nothing. The icebox sting of the air-conditioning, an air-conditioning that makes the interior of the house feel like late November, creates along Andrew's spine an instant and deep shiver.

He is too disoriented, however, to focus immediately on the cold. The two side walls of the hallway into which T.J. has ushered him are mirrored. Andrew feels as though he were floating, not anchored to firm ground. Two black stairways (or is it only one reflected in a mirror?) appear to rise without supports to an upper floor. A chandelier, in black and gold, repeats itself dizzyingly hundreds of times in the play of mirrors reflecting mirrors. A highly polished black chair is the sole item of furniture in the hallway, and even though it, too, has many copies, Andrew edges toward it for support.

"Andy-boy," says T.J.

"T.J.," says Andrew.

"So what'll you have to drink?" asks T.J. before they have even moved from the hallway.

"Drink?"

T.J. frowns. "Yeah, you know, a cocktail, a beer. You all right, pal? You look a little scruffy around the edges."

"I'm fine," says Andrew, reaching for the back of the chair. "Fine. I got waylaid, didn't have time for a shower. I didn't want to be any later than I am . . . was." The sentence trails off as he catches sight of himself and T.J. in the opposite wall. He himself looks dazed, like a prisoner brought from a darkened cell to a room where the lights are too bright.

T.J. eyes him warily. "A strawberry daiquiri OK, Andy-boy? Didi's made up a batch."

"Fine," says Andrew. "Fine."

"OK. Well. Lemme show you around, and we'll make our way into the kitchen."

T.J. reaches for a black handle in the glass and passes through a mirrored wall into what appears to be a living room. Andrew follows and is relieved to see that only one wall is mirrored here. His orientation is momentary, however, as he realizes that the floor on which he is standing is black marble, or some material that resembles marble, and that most of the furniture in the room is also black, a black-on-black effect that causes him to miss a small end table, on which he barks his shin.

The unmirrored walls are covered with a gold-flecked wallpaper. On a solid-black coffee table is an outsized gold ashtray and a gold vase. On the wall opposite is a massive console with an enormous TV screen not unlike the one in the screening room at work, and below it, like the darkened cockpit of an L-1011, an array of instruments and digital readouts.

"State of the art," says T.J., following Andrew's glance. "We got two VCRs just in here. The kids have their own, and we got one in the bedroom. Have to, really, to keep up with all the good movies on. Fantastic picture on the tube. Wanna see?"

T.J. picks up one of three remote-control channel switchers on the coffee table and presses a button. Nothing happens.

"Hold on a minute. Must be the other one."

He picks up the second remote control and presses a button on it. Nothing happens.

"Kids musta been screwing around with these," says T.J., looking mildly flustered as he picks up the third. He presses a button. A life-size image of an evening game-show host appears on the screen.

"Great, huh?" says T.J.

"Great," says Andrew. He ponders for a lucid moment the effort, technology and expense it has taken to bring a life-size image of an evening game-show host into T.J.'s living room.

T.J. passes through an open doorway in one of the gold-speckled walls, and when Andrew follows he finds himself inside a dining room, he guesses, touching the long black-lacquered table in the center. He cannot help but see his reflection again in yet another mirrored wall on the other side. A black and gold chandelier, like the one in the hallway, hangs from the ceiling.

"We're into black and gold," says T.J.

The statement seems to call for some reply. "And mirrors," says Andrew.

"Yeah, well, mirrors are great. Make the place look so much bigger."

"Absolutely," says Andrew.

T.J. opens yet another hidden door. "Here he is!" he announces to the other side.

Andrew hears the female voice even before he sees its owner.

"Andy!"

He steps into a room of black and stainless steel, a room he takes, owing to the especially large amount of stainless steel, to be the kitchen. Didi Hanson, now Jackson, embraces him. He is aware of a white cotton sweater identical to T.J.'s and a strong scent of perfume enveloping him. She stands back and holds him at arms' length.

"Look at you!" she says.

Andrew is momentarily at a loss for words. "It's great to see you," he stammers. "Your house is . . . I think your house . . ."

"Isn't it?" she says, and whisks a frothy pink drink off a stainless-steel counter and hands it to him. He looks at the stainless-steel refrigerator in front of which Didi is standing. He, too, he thinks, once owned a refrigerator like that.

Didi's hair is still curled in a blond flip, a hairstyle he hasn't seen on a woman in years. Enormous gold earrings dangle from her earlobes. She, too, is wearing safari pants. A gold bracelet clinks when she puts her hand near the counter. He takes a sip of the strawberry froth. The deep shiver that began in the hallway takes over his body in earnest when the icy cold drink hits his stomach.

Too swiftly, before he can brace himself, Didi again envelops him, her head nuzzling under his chin. The gesture rattles Andrew's arm, and he tries to steady his drink over her back. A drop of pink froth falls on her white sweater.

"I'm so sorry about your mother," she mumbles into his shirt. They stand motionless for what feels like an uncomfortably long time. She gives a little squeeze and then lets him go.

Andrew can think of no reply. Did she even know his mother?

"So, pal," says T.J., slapping Andrew on the shoulder. "Let's go talk about your house while Didi here fixes us up a gourmet dinner."

"Well, we're just barbecuing," says Didi, smiling apologetically in Andrew's direction. The smile is identical to the smile of her youth—a dazzling display that always seemed to him part of a too vigorous performance.

"Come see where I live," says T.J., steering Andrew's shoulder to yet another doorway.

As remarkable as the black and mirrored interiors of the other rooms have been, nothing is as surprising to Andrew as the room into which T.J. leads him. It is as if, passing through the door, they had entered another era, another aesthetic, another house entirely. The room is what Andrew's mother would have called a den, a pine-paneled room with a maple "early American" sofa covered in plaid fabric. Beside the sofa are two matching reclining easy chairs. A rust-colored shaggy carpet is on the floor, and a small TV is in a corner on a wire pedestal. In another corner is a glass cabinet filled with guns.

"This is the family room," says T.J. "We hang out here."

Through a sliding glass door, Andrew can see the red-wood deck on which is a gas grill, not unlike the one he and Martha had in Saddle River. Andrew wonders when, if ever, the other rooms are used.

T.J. sits on a chair, makes it recline. He takes a long sip of his drink.

"We'll go for one thirty. The furniture gone?"

Andrew stares at T.J. After a blank second, he realizes T.J. is talking about Andrew's own house.

"Nearly," he says, sitting in the other chair. "It's all arranged."

"Can you get someone in to do a good cleaning? I can recommend some people if you want."

"Sure. Whatever you say."

"I'll want to move on this by the middle of next week. You'll be gone by then, right?"

"I may," Andrew hedges. "I hope to be."

"I'd like to open it up. Get some people in quick. Think we can do a fast sale. Certainly we should get some action by early September. Come by the office Monday, we'll sort some things out."

"Sounds fine," says Andrew.

"You're fixing it up, right?"

"I'm doing some things. This heat is slowing me down." Andrew has an intense longing for the heat, looks covetously at the redwood deck. "Where are your boys?" he asks.

"They're at a friend's pool. Maybe they'll be back before you go."

"Do your boys hunt?" asks Andrew. Behind T.J.'s head is the glass gun cabinet. "I didn't know you had so many guns."

T.J. cranes his head to look at the cabinet. "Always had 'em," he says. "You remember. We used to hunt when we were kids."

"I recall only the rifle then. I don't ever remember you with shotguns."

"They were my dad's. He kept his gun cabinet in the basement. Locked. I take Tom junior hunting now and then, but he doesn't have a taste for it like I did. You never really did either, come to think of it, did you?"

"No. I guess not. I liked the skill involved, but I never liked finding the animals after we'd hit them."

"Yeah, my kid's like that. Tends toward the wimp once in a while—no offense."

Andrew is not offended. He thinks he would probably like T.J.'s son.

176

"You've done well for yourself," Andrew says in the silence, changing the subject.

"Can't complain. Can't complain. Course I'm mortgaged to the hilt, but aren't we all? Got a good deal on the house. Knew the developer, got in on the ground floor, so to speak. Didi's really the one with the eye, though. Made this a showplace. Fabulous taste, don't you think?"

"Remarkable," says Andrew.

"She coulda been an interior decorator easy, with her eye, but we decided she should stay home with the kids. Your wife work?"

"Martha? No, not really. But she will now. She's got a teaching job at a private school in New Jersey starting in the fall."

"Your son's how old?"

"Seven."

T.J. nods. "Right," he says. "Great age. You must miss him."

"I do."

Andrew and T.J. take simultaneous sips of their drinks. T.J. drains his glass. He leans forward as if to get up.

"Get you another?"

Andrew cradles his glass, looks into its center.

"When we were kids . . . ," he says.

There is something he wants to ask T.J., a question he must ask when Didi is not in the room. It is a question that has been hovering at the back of his mind since yesterday, but now, in T.J.'s den (or family room), the question seems too bold, too intrusive.

"When we were kids what?" says T.J.

"When Eden was . . . was in that phase of hers before Sean . . . Did you and she . . . ? I mean, did you and she ever have anything . . . ?"

T.J. looks at Andrew with a stare as blank as Andrew's was moments ago. Then he shakes his head.

"Hey . . ." T.J. stretches out the word so that it lasts four syllables. "Wasn't everybody?" he says with a grin.

"You never said."

"You never asked me."

"That's no answer."

"Hey, what is this, the inquisition?"

"Sorry," says Andrew. "Really, it's none of my business anyway."

"Oh, that's OK," says T.J., gesturing expansively with his glass. "You probably don't remember this, but you were pretty touchy about Eden in those days. Like an older brother. I mean, you don't go around telling some girl's older brother you're screwing his sister, even if he is your best friend. Not that we ever screwed."

"Then you didn't?"

"Well, not technically," says T.J. "And I'll tell you something else. I don't want to burst your bubble, but I wasn't the only one. Not by a long shot . . ."

T.J. leans back in the chair, brings his glass to his forehead. "The way things turned out for her, I guess it's just as well she had what she had then. Though I'll tell you something. I never really knew it then, because I was too inexperienced to know this and too—how shall I put it?—*busy* to ruminate on her state of mind, but now as I look back on it, she never really liked it. I wouldn't say she was doing it because she was horny, you follow me. It was more a kind of act. Or more like she was driven. That's the feeling I got—like she was driven, trying to burn something out of her. Course, when you're sixteen, seventeen, who cares what the chick is into, as long as she's putting out, right? But like I say, now, when I think back on it . . ."

Andrew looks at T.J. Didi, on the deck, knocks on the glass doors. She is carrying a platter of small steaks to the gas grill. She mouths the words "You watch the steaks" to T.J., puts them on the grill and disappears into the kitchen.

"Well, you remember what she was like then," says T.J., getting up. "You seen her yet?"

"No," says Andrew, lying.

An image of Eden as she is now, in her blue dress with the white buttons, her hair washed and neatly parted, fills the space between himself and T.J. He feels his glass being lifted from his hand.

"I'll freshen these up," says T.J. evenly, looking hard at Andrew.

THEY EAT dinner on trays in the family room. Andrew wonders how important one has to be to rate dinner in the mirrored dining room. He is just as happy, however, to be eating here; at least from here he can see and imagine the warmth outside. Even so, he is so cold the utensils tremble in his fingers.

Didi serves a bottle of sweet pink bubbly wine with the steaks. Andrew wonders what happened to the serviceable red he brought. Didi, he discovers, has a gift for small talk, a gift Andrew begins to cherish as the evening wears on and his own conversational skills falter. She chats amiably, in response to Andrew's polite questions, about her two sons, about the summer camp they have just finished, about the boom in new houses in the town. She volleys some polite questions of her own. What kind of a place does he have now? What's it like living in New York City? What's his job all about? T.J. embarrasses him by repeating to Didi Andrew's title and managing to make it sound more grandiose than it actually is. T.J. also manages to suggest that Andrew makes a lot of money, which appears to titillate Didi. She glances at him with what feels to him like new respect. She asks about the old house, inquires as to what he's doing with it, asks if he's seen Eden. He lies easily.

No, he says again. No, he hasn't.

"We used to call her—God, isn't this awful—we used to call her Goldilicks."

"What?"

"You know. Goldi licks." Didi blushes.

"Oh," says Andrew.

"I hear she's real deformed," says Didi with an expression on her lips that Andrew takes to be disdain.

T.J. shoots a glance at his wife. Andrew starts to speak, closes his mouth. He puts down his plate. He takes a sip of pink wine, puts the glass on the floor.

"I'm just going outside to stand on the deck for a minute," he says. "To tell you the truth, I'm freezing."

T.J. and Didi look at him as though he has just suggested stepping out of an open window with a long drop below. "Sure," says T.J., recovering. "Whatever."

Andrew opens the door a crack and slips through so as not to let in any hot air. He walks to the railing at the edge of the deck. The heat envelops him like a warm bath. He puts his hands in his pockets and looks up and down the row of redwood decks behind the houses. He is struck by the silence. The grass has little of the symphony he hears outdoors at his own house. Nor are there any human voices at all—only the drone of air conditioners. The door behind him slides and clicks. T.J. is beside him, a short-sleeved T-shirt replacing the white cotton sweater.

"Sorry about that crack," says T.J. "She didn't mean anything, just remembering."

"It's nothing," says Andrew.

"She still gets under your skin, doesn't she?"

"Who?"

"You know who."

"Eden? No. That was years ago."

Next door someone lets a dog out. The dog immediately turns and whines to be let back in.

"Hot out here," says T.J.

"Yes. Sorry to have made you come out."

"You'll be going back to the city soon."

"Yes." Andrew turns, sits on the railing. He looks at T.J. "Sometimes I think I'd like to know what really happened that night, though, before I go."

"What night?"

"The night Eden was shot, the night her father was killed."

T.J. crosses his arms against his chest, looks at his feet.

"For instance," says Andrew. "I've always wondered why Sean, if he didn't do it—and let's suppose for a moment he didn't—why he left town so soon."

T.J. peers up at the hot, starless sky. He puts his hands in his pockets. He looks at Andrew. "Because maybe he thought people would pin it on him. He was always pretty impulsive, not too bright sometimes."

"But how did he know about it?"

"Everyone knew about it."

"So fast? Did you talk to Sean that morning?"

"What are you getting at?"

Andrew looks through the glass door, sees the gun cabinet in the corner.

T.J. had access to shotguns, he is thinking.

I'm losing my mind, he is thinking.

He shakes his head. "Forget it. This town is beginning to get to me. I have to go home."

"No harm done," says T.J. "You've been under a strain, your mother dying and all."

Andrew puts a foot up on the railing. "Where's the water?" he asks.

"What water?"

"Water's Edge."

"Oh, that. It's just a name. You know how these subdivisions go. Tudor Hills, Fox Run, Waverly Manor. They're trying to make it sound like we're living on an English estate."

In the silence they both hear a small plane overhead.

"Don't you miss that big white silo?" asks Andrew.

"You've seen her, haven't you?" says T.J.

Andrew hesitates, shrugs, then nods.

"You be careful," T.J. says.

"How did you know?"

"Whenever you lie, you smooth the hair over your ear. It's a dead giveaway. You always did it."

"Thanks for the tip."

"What's she like?"

Andrew glances at his old friend. "It's hard to say. In many ways, perfectly ordinary. But not really."

"What does she look like?"

"Good. She looks good. There's a scar, but she looks . . . OK. She's not deformed."

"I didn't think so. I told you I saw her a few times in a car—just a peek. She seemed OK but like she was asleep or something."

Andrew puts his foot down, stands up straight. "I'm going to go now," he says. "I'm exhausted. Tell Didi . . ."

"So soon? She probably made a dessert or something," T.J. protests, but something in Andrew's face makes him change his mind. "Yeah, OK. I'll tell her."

Andrew shakes T.J.'s hand. The two men, their hands still gripped, look at each other.

"Don't, ah . . ." T.J.'s voice trails off.

"Don't what?" says Andrew.

"You be careful," says T.J. "Go easy. You never know."

"Never know what?"

T.J. lets go of Andrew's hand. "I dunno. It's been a long time. This isn't your scene here. I can see that. You'd be better off getting back to your job, your kid. . . ."

Andrew nods. "I'll see you Monday, then," he says.

He waves as he makes his way down the redwood steps. He walks around the house to his car. Once inside, he snaps in a tape of Miles Davis and turns up the volume. As he backs into the street, another car starts up T.J.'s driveway. Two boys get out. The boys, in spiked hair and T-shirts, each holding a rolled wet towel, make their way toward the back of the house. Neither enters his home through the front door.

When he is in his own house, Andrew walks deliberately through all the rooms, opening each window as he goes, letting the night air—sultry, luxurious—into the house. Within seconds, his skin is damp. He walks to the bathroom, strips off his clothes and turns the water to hot in the shower. He steps into the steaming cubicle. Later, scrubbed clean and naked, he turns on a light in the kitchen. The kitchen has been stripped; it looks too bare in the summer night. Andrew lifts a carton off a chair, sits on the chair. He bends to open the carton. One by one, he takes each of the items out of the carton and puts it on the kitchen table. When the carton is empty, he gets a beer from the fridge. He drinks the beer slowly and with enjoyment, occasionally fingering the objects on the table.

THE STEAMY weather is bearable now, just, at five in the morning. Andrew takes a cup of coffee, goes outside to sit on the back stoop, thinking that a stray early morning breeze might come his way. The sky is pearly, with a pink wash on the horizon. He slept deeply once he went to bed, but woke too early, too alert to go back to sleep. The landscape is still, peaceful, except for the first birds. Yet Andrew knows that within the hour, it will be uncomfortably hot and humid. He thinks briefly of the chores he might do in the morning to while away the hours until the Plymouth backs out of the drive.

In the distance he hears a drone—a small plane on an early morning flight? he wonders—but when the drone draws closer, he realizes it's a machine, a vehicle. He sees it then across the road, a red tractor catching the first rays of the dawning sun, an old red tractor with its driver, MacKenzie, bathed in coral light, coming down a path between the cornfields. Andrew, with his cup of coffee, walks to the end of the drive, reaching it just as the tractor is about to make a turn onto a furrow paralleling the road. MacKenzie, who has farmed the land across from the houses ever since Andrew can remember, puts the tractor in neutral, waves at Andrew, then gestures with his arm to come across the road.

Up close, the roar of the tractor is too loud to permit conversation, so Andrew hops up beside the farmer.

"Didn't wake you, did I?" asks MacKenzie.

"No. Not at all," says Andrew.

"Have to be out early in this heat." MacKenzie half turns in the seat and holds out his hand. Andrew, switching the coffee cup to his left hand, shakes it. He looks at MacKenzie. The farmer, a tall, lean man, even in his mid-sixties, has a long, weathered face. Below his eyes, which are a watery blue, are deep pale crescents composed of tiny fine lines. MacKenzie has on a plaid short-sleeved summer shirt and a cap that says Budweiser across the front.

"Sorry about your mother."

"Thank you," says Andrew.

"I heard it was quick," says the farmer.

"Yes. It was."

"Good. That's the best." MacKenzie takes a pack of Carltons out of his shirt pocket, lights a cigarette, inhales deeply. "Actually, I was thinking about your family just yesterday," he says. "You heard about the girl?"

"The girl?"

"There was a girl they found yesterday. Thirteen . . ."

"Yes, right," says Andrew. "I heard."

"Made me think . . ."

"Yes. So did I. Awful story."

"Yeah. And the way they think it was the boyfriend," says MacKenzie. "Just like then." The farmer takes a quick drag. He holds the cigarette like a dart, between the thumb and first finger. "Course, they sure as hell tore up my fields, even so."

"How do you mean?" asks Andrew, taking a sip of his lukewarm coffee.

"They came here one morning with about six fellas at first, then a coupla tractors, and dug up half my fields before they gave up. No compensation either. You musta been gone by then."

"I must have," says Andrew. "I don't remember that."

"You working in New York City?"

"Yes."

"That all right for you?"

"It has been. How's Sam?" Andrew asks, shifting the focus onto MacKenzie's son.

MacKenzie rests his elbows on his knees, brings his folded hands to his forehead. The smoke from the cigarette in his fingers curls under the brim of the Budweiser cap.

"Gone."

Andrew at first thinks MacKenzie means that his son is dead.

"I'm sorry," he says. "I didn't know. When did it happen?" Andrew tries to remember if his mother ever mentioned the MacKenzie boy. Had he gone to Vietnam? Died there?

"No, not dead," says MacKenzie. "Just gone."

Andrew waits for MacKenzie to explain, or not to explain.

"Me and my wife woke up one morning. It was his twentieth birthday. He'd taken the cash in the desk drawer. Gave hisself a birthday present. Left no note."

Andrew tries to picture the boy he knew, a boy he always felt sorry for because he was never allowed to play sports. Instead his father made him work the farm, needed him at home.

"Do you know where . . . ?"

"Not a word. Never a word in sixteen years." MacKenzie throws the still burning cigarette onto the ground. "I take care of these fields, but I can't tell you why. I got no one now to leave 'em to."

Andrew looks over the fields, feels the heat already rising from them, wonders if a gun still lies buried somewhere out there, just beneath the probing tines of the farm machinery. All these fathers and their sons, he thinks. DeSalvo, his son a drug addict and now divorced; O'Brien, his son dead at seventeen; MacKenzie, his son gone for good. He thinks of Billy with a pang.

"Well," says MacKenzie, "think I'd better get movin' before that sun gets much higher. My age, you can get heat stroke out here."

"I think any age you can get heat stroke in this," says Andrew, hopping off the tractor. "My regards to your wife."

"You stayin' or goin'?" MacKenzie asks.

"I'm going," says Andrew, shouting from the ground. "Soon."

"Best a luck to you, then," says the farmer, who puts the tractor in gear and lumbers slowly along the path.

Andrew waits for a truck to pass, then crosses the road. There is no sound of movement yet in the Closes' house. He looks at his own and thinks of his father. He wonders if his father was pleased with his son's progress through life, or if he considered him lost, like Sam MacKenzie.

But there is no one left now to ask.

SHE IS SITTING in the same chair, wearing again the blue dress with white buttons. He notes the part is askew today, but that her hair is freshly brushed. He is carrying the new pair of sneakers and the sunglasses.

He is relieved to see her sitting in the kitchen. He has imagined her in her room, unwilling to come down, to be with him again.

"Did she say anything?"

Eden shakes her head.

"I've brought you something," he says.

He puts the sunglasses on the table and bends down with the sneakers. He takes one foot in his hand. He has forgotten socks, he realizes, but no matter. "They're sneakers," he says, cradling her foot, sliding it into the unlaced shoe.

The fit, if not perfect, is adequate. He tightens the laces, then puts on the other shoe. He stands up and looks at her feet. The blue sneakers seem disembodied from her long white legs.

"You shouldn't have done this," she says.

But he is proud of his purchase. When they were kids, he is thinking, girls often wore sneakers without socks. It was the style then.

"And I've brought you these," he says. He picks up the sunglasses from the table and slides them onto her face. He moves the hair over her ears to secure the stems.

"What are these for?" she asks.

"They're dark glasses," he says. "To shield your eyes from the sun. I was worried the bright sun would hurt them."

"Nothing can hurt them," she says.

"How do they feel?" he asks.

"How do what feel?"

"The sneakers."

"All right."

"Let's go, then."

She stiffens. "Where?"

"I'm taking you to the pond."

"Why?" she asks.

"It's hot," he says. "And I feel like a swim. And I want to see it. I haven't seen it in years."

"The pond," she says.

"You remember it?"

"I remember it."

She turns her head. A fall of hair hides the side of her face, so that she looks, with her white skin and her dark glasses, with her long pale hair and her simple blue dress, like a film star making her first public appearance after a lengthy confinement in a rehabilitation center.

"It will be too dangerous," she says.

"Dangerous? Don't be silly," he says, knowing even as he says it that the remark is too glib, too easy.

He takes her hand; her fingers are cool. He feels a rough substance on her fingers and looks at them. "What's this?" he asks, massaging a gray patch.

She hesitates. "It's clay," she says. "I . . . I make things with it. They taught me when I was away."

"What things?" he asks.

"Oh," she says. "Just things. Shapes."

He tugs at her gently to make her stand.

"We'll go as we did yesterday," he says. "Side by side until we get to the path, then me in front and you follow."

She pulls her hand away from his but lets him take her elbow. She looks, he thinks, like a film star who may have been let out too soon.

The sun burns overhead through a zinc-white sky. The grass in the sullen light no longer appears green. Near the back stoop, the leaves of an old lilac bush hang mildewed and curled. On the radio this morning he heard that power blackouts, as a result of the heat wave, have already occurred in certain pockets of the county. The town pool reported record numbers yesterday. A tennis tournament at a local boys' camp has been postponed. At least one elderly woman has died of heat prostration.

He looks at Eden beside him, at the tiny seed pearls of sweat along her white brow. He stares at the small blue feet making footprints in the limp grass. Time has contrived to shorten the distance between them. He has grown very little since he was seventeen, whereas she is taller now by several inches. Still, though, the top of her head barely reaches to his shoulder.

With his free hand he pulls his own sunglasses from his shirt pocket and puts them on. He unbuttons the front of his shirt, yanks the tails out. He wishes he had on shorts. He has said, improvising, that he is taking her to the pond because he wants to swim, but in truth, until he said those words the thought had not occurred to him. He doesn't even have a bathing suit here. Yet the thought of plunging into the water, now that it is spoken, is seductive. He wonders if there will be small boys there seeking relief from the heat in the pond—or if boys nowadays prefer to stay inside their air-conditioned houses watching videos. He thinks of T.J.'s mirrored hallway and of his own twenty-seventh-floor office in New York.

When they reach the path, she makes a movement to shake his hand off her elbow. She touches the cornstalks on her left.

"I can go like this," she says. "It's easier for me."

He walks slowly in front of her. Beyond the point they

reached yesterday, the path is sometimes barred by brambles, toppled cornstalks, densely grown underbrush. He uses his feet and hands to clear a way for her. He takes his shirt off and makes a fan of it, then a towel to wipe his brow. When he turns around to watch her, as he does often, he sees that Eden is stepping cautiously but evenly, with no apparent fear or hesitation. He tries to ascertain, from glimpses of her face, what her thoughts might be, but the set of her mouth below the dark glasses gives no clue. Rather she seems only to be concentrating on the map her fingers read and the progress of her feet.

Deep inside the cornfields—halfway, Andrew reckons, to the pond—he pauses for a moment to allow her to catch up, and it is then that he becomes aware of the sound, an intense resonant hymn of insects and small movements, punctuated at moments by the soughing of a dry sheaf or the quick whomp and flutter of a bird's wing, rising.

The path is shorter than he has remembered it and opens up to a grassy bank. Beyond the bank, the water shines like polished brass. Long vines have overtaken the trees, and the shade is denser at the water's edge than he recalls it having been years ago. A thick profusion of wild red lilies along the embankment, with the gold-colored water scintillating among and between the petals, stops him with simultaneous pleasure at their beauty and the guilty realization that she cannot see them. Should he tell her of them, he wonders, or is that worse?

On her own, she can go no farther than the cornfields, so he takes her hand and leads her to a damp grassy patch beneath the tallest tree, the tree most encumbered by vines and hence the one providing the coolest shade. She sits, leaning against the tree for support, her legs stretched out in front of her. She reaches for the hem of her dress and brings it to her face, wiping her forehead, her upper lip, the top of her chest. Her thighs, uncovered, are white, with a fine down of golden hairs. She smooths her dress along her legs, covering herself.

"You can tell me," she says.

"Tell you what?" he asks.

"How it looks. Is it how it was?"

He surveys the landscape nearest them. "It is," he says, "but more so. The trees are covered with vines. The water is much the same. Do you remember the color?"

She shakes her head.

"It's gold," he says, "from the minerals."

"Gold," she repeats.

"And here . . ." He stands up and walks to the mass of lilies. He snaps one off its stem and brings it back. He puts it in her hand.

"Do you remember these?" he asks. "They're lilies. Red. They've grown wilder, thicker along the banks. It's hard to say if anyone's been here recently. There's no obvious debris left behind, no trampling."

The hymn he has heard before is quieter here. She fingers the long crimson petals in her lap.

"You're going swimming," she says.

"Oh, I don't know," he says, picking up a stone in his hand. He looks at the water. He would like a swim. The surface of the pond is glassy, undisturbed but for the arcs of water bugs.

"You could come too," he says. "You could swim in your dress. It would dry in the sun on the walk back, and you could change before she got home."

She shakes her head. "I don't need to swim. I am just all right here."

He tosses the stone from one palm to the other. She leans her head against the bark of the tree, and he can't tell if her eyes are open or closed behind the dark glasses. Her hands are in her lap, with the flower, wilting now in the heat. Even in the shade, the heat is enervating.

He throws the stone into the water. He stands up and unbuckles his belt. The clink of the metal sounds too loud in the silence. He slips off his clothes and his watch, lets them fall in a pile on the bank. He walks to the edge of the water.

The water at his ankles is cool but not cold. He wades out up to his waist, then lets his body drift slowly forward until he is floating. He raises his arm to begin a crawl, a lazy crawl to the other side. The distance seems longer to him than it did when he was a boy, but he attributes this to being out of shape.

He plunges his head under the water, feels the coolness drive the heat from his brain. He tries a breast stroke on the return lap, sees her through the rivulets of water that cascade off his head each time he comes up for air.

He turns and makes his way to the other side again, thinking that the rhythmic strokes feel good. But after four laps, his arms begin to tire. He reaches the shore closest to her, turns and thinks to make another lap, but stops instead to stand when the water is chest high. He looks across to the other bank, paddles idly in the water, feels the pebbles when he puts his feet down, then the claylike soil of the bottom. Lifting his feet off the bottom, he lets his weight take him slowly up and down beneath the water, blowing bubbles as he does so. The water closes over his head and then breaks again when he comes up for air.

He lies flat on his back, the water sloshing over his belly. With the smallest of efforts, he can bring his toes above the surface. He sculls quietly with his wrists. Squinting, he can just make out a corona in the whitest, most painful, part of the sky. It reminds him of something, but he can't quite seize the memory. He shuts his eyes, lets his head float too, his brow and eyes sinking below the surface, keeping just his nose and mouth free to breathe. The sensation is delicious: the hot sun on the exposed parts of his body, the coolness beneath.

Behind his eyes, images scintillate, shine, disappear. A leaf, translucent with the sun behind it, fluttering . . . Eden turning her head and smiling . . . The sun glinting off T.J.'s sunglasses . . . A sunburst sparkling in the fender of his car . . . Billy with pennies in his palm . . . A window somewhere throwing off the shimmer of a rusty sunset . . .

A fish slithers under his left shoulder, startling him. He tries to stand quickly, is thrown off balance, is blinded by the water in his eyes. His toes scrape a rock on the bottom. It's not a fish; it's her hand. She is standing in the water up to her chest in front of him. She is wearing her dress. Her arms are outstretched for balance, but it seems to him she is reaching for him.

He grasps her hand, pulls her off her feet so that she is floating. The skirt of her dress billows up and around her waist like a parachute. He leads her, as if executing a formal dance, until his feet leave the water and he must swim. He swims on his side, holding her elbow, letting her paddle with his support. He doesn't know what has brought her to the water—the heat, a desire not to be left alone—but he is glad to be beside her, to watch the concentration on her face as she makes her way in the unfamiliar water. He wonders if she has even once been swimming in nineteen years.

A third of the way across the pond, she breaks free of his hand, raises her shoulders and slices through the water with a knifelike crawl. She puts her face in the water, turns to the side for air, repeats the movements in perfect synchrony. Left behind, he swims ungracefully to catch up to her. Years ago, she was an excellent and tireless swimmer, making up in speed what she lacked in power.

"Make the turn now," he says, when they are near the other side.

She makes the turn but rolls onto her back, executing a smooth backstroke. He watches as each white arm rises from the brassy water with mathematical precision. Her hair swims around her, and her legs flutter, keeping her easily afloat.

"You can stand now," he says when they are near the shore.

Instead she makes a swimmer's turn and once again heads across the pond. He watches her for a moment, thinking to stay by her side in case she tires, panics; but so easy are her strokes that he is mesmerized, rooted to the spot. He lets her go.

She swims back and forth a dozen times. He is content just to watch her. When she is finished, she stands and pushes the hair away from her face. She is breathing hard. She rubs the water out of her eyes.

"You're still the best," he says.

She smiles, a real smile.

She has stopped twenty feet from him. He tries to make his way to her side, but the water slows him down. She turns and walks unhurriedly toward the shore. He watches as she squeezes the water out of her hair, then moves around the grass near the water's edge until she finds a patch of sun with her feet. She lies down with her dress on.

He pulls himself out of the pond and stands at her feet, looking down at her.

"I don't think you want to do that," he says.

He means get the dress dirty. It is wet, and the dirt will stick to it. But there is something else he means. Her face is smooth, in repose. The little knots of tension he has seen there earlier are gone.

She doesn't answer him. He studies her. He is looking at a painting in a museum, a painting of a woman with alabaster skin in a blue dress on dried grasses—a masterpiece no one but himself will ever see. Her hair, in a twisted rope, lies to one side of her. He sees the softened knobs of her collarbone, the nipples of her breasts under the wet fabric. He sees the hollow space under the dress where the crease of her breast must be.

He crouches down beside her. Does she know he's there? he wonders. Can she "see" his awkward pose, awkward because of his nakedness?

He touches the rope of damp hair, her brow. She doesn't flinch or pull away, and he takes this as a sign that she is waiting. He touches the knob of her collarbone above the top button of her dress. He hears a sound like a small sigh escape her, and she seems to arch her back slightly.

He takes his hand away. A voice cautions him, tells him that if he does this, there is no turning back. It is not a casual act; she is virtually a child. He sees her as a child, feels again the secret dread in himself, about to touch something he should not. Images come to him from his childhood: Eden sashaying to the bus; teasing him at the pond; pressed against a brick wall.

He undoes the first button, kisses the skin underneath. It seems to him her legs slide together under her dress. She raises a hand, then drops it. The wet cloth is tight across her breasts. He undoes the second button, knows he will not stop now, and peels the cloth back. He kneels, bends his head to kiss her, and as he does so, he feels her hand at the small of his back.

She moves away from him and rolls over. She rises to her knees, stands, then slips off her dress and her underwear. She is smooth, carved but not muscled. Her breasts hang heavier than he has remembered from his dreams, and this is somehow reassuring. Her shoulders are thin, and there is a hollow place where her upper arm meets her body. Her pelvic bones are defined. Around him, the sun glints brilliantly off the water and through the foliage, causing in him a momentary dizziness. His mouth is inches from her flat belly, and he lets himself kiss her there. He lets his mouth slide along her as she drops to her knees in front of him.

He encircles her with his arms, pulling her face into his neck. He calls her name, an urgent summons, as if he were calling to her across the pond, or back across the years. Her name, spoken in that way, makes her shiver, and her poise deserts her then. He feels her break. It is a subtle movement in her shoulders, a letting go, so that he must bear her weight. She begins to cry. He presses her more tightly to him. He is glad that she is crying. There is too much that she is crying for, but he is glad, and he cannot stop himself from saying her name. He kisses her. He makes her open her mouth. He puts his knee between her thighs. She pulls her mouth away once, for air. He feels no hesitation now, no sense of caution. This is where his dreams have led him.

She knew it before I did, he thinks. *She knew it years ago, when I was still a boy.*

She seems unafraid now, though she has said the walk to the pond would be dangerous, and he misunderstood her. His balance lost, he takes her with him to the grass. Her thigh slides like silk over his, and her hair hides their faces like a cool tent. There is heat around them and the dampness of the grass, and a crow cawing irritably from the top of a tree. She clings to him, and he feels the sad frenzy of her nineteen lost years, but she is too shy to guide him or doesn't know how, and so he makes his own way, trying to be gentle, trying not to think of her as a child.

Later he will remember how a shiver rose from her belly and rippled out to her fists against his back. But he will remember, too, her unexpected delicacy. She doesn't make a sound, a silence he finds entrancing.

AFTERWARD she lies in the crook of his arm. He strokes the down on her upper arm. They both smell like the pond. She might be asleep; he cannot tell. He doesn't want to speak. In his mind he borrows a phrase from her, one that he has liked. *I am just all right*, he says to himself.

His body is tired, and he thinks it possible he might fall asleep with her—something he must guard against. He doesn't know the time but guesses there can't be more than an hour left, if that. He wonders if she can tell time here, where she hasn't been in years, where the sounds would be different from those at the houses.

He hears a rustling in the bushes. A small animal, he supposes, until he sees the boy. The boy is eleven, twelve. He comes near to the edge of the clearing, stops short when he sees Andrew and Eden. He has brown hair and glasses and freckles beneath a summer tan. He has a towel around his neck. His chest is bare. He stares at Andrew. Andrew returns his gaze but doesn't move. Then the boy turns and darts though the underbrush the way he has come.

Andrew smiles and wishes to himself that the boy will remember this scene all his life.

AFTER A TIME, he puts her head on the grass and unwinds himself from her. His watch is over by his clothes, and when he consults it, he is somewhat alarmed to see that they have only forty minutes left.

"Eden," he says, waking her. "We have to go now. Quickly."

She leans up on one arm. She seems dazed, disoriented. He helps her to her feet and retrieves the still wet dress from the grass. The dress is dirty and wrinkled. She raises the dress over her head and slips her arms through it, and it is then that he has his first doubts. The dress hangs on her, making her look suddenly very vulnerable. She slips on her underpants. Her hair is damp and tangled, with bits of grass and dirt in it. Her face is wrinkled with sleep. For a minute she seems like someone he had no right to touch, to expose.

"I don't know where the tree is, or where my shoes are," she says.

He finds the sneakers and the sunglasses in the place where they first sat down, but he hands them to her rather than putting them on her himself. The easy confidence he had before, or rather the trumped-up confidence—bordering at times, he has feared, on condescension—has left him. She is again a thing apart from him.

"When we get back," he says, trying again for a tone of authority he does not feel, "I'll take the dress and launder it and give it back to you tomorrow. Your hair should dry completely on the walk back. All you need to do is give it a good brushing and put something else on, but we have to be quick about it."

She nods once and lets him take her hand. He squeezes her hand tightly to recapture the intimacy just left. At the cornfields she goes before him, making her way with a more practiced ease and with more speed. He watches her outstretched arms, her fingers flicking gently against the cornstalks. On the other side of the fields, he takes her hand again and nearly runs with her to her back stoop. By his reckoning, they have only five minutes left. She can tell the time, too, here, on familiar ground, for he sees it in her face.

Once inside the kitchen, she begins to unbutton her dress. She slips the bodice to her waist and then steps out of both the dress and her underwear in one movement. She hands the bundle to Andrew like a child giving her clothes to a parent before she enters the bath. He takes them, moved by the ease with which she has done this, by the way she does not shield her nakedness with her arms. He is moved, too, though differently and more deeply, by her beauty, her beauty incongruous in this desolate kitchen, her feet in her blue sneakers so firmly planted on the worn linoleum floor. He aches to linger, to touch her again. He kisses her on the shoulder, slides a hand down her back. He can think of nothing right to say.

"Jim was my father," she says quietly.

He steps back, still touching her shoulder. "I know."

"No. You don't understand," she says. "I'm giving you something."

He is silent. "What are you saying?" he asks after a minute.

"I was his."

"He was your real father?"

"It's why she hates me."

Her meaning is clear, but his mind balks, unable to take it in.

"How is that possible?" he asks. "I remember the day. I was there when she brought you to the garden. . . ."

"The girl who left me was someone . . . he had been with."

"Girl?"

"She was sixteen."

"How do you know this? Did you know all those years?"

She tilts her head to one side, listens. "That's all," she says. She wrests herself from his touch, and he watches her disappear through the doorway to the darkened part of the house. Galvanized, he moves out the back door, down the steps and across the yard to his own back door. He is just inside with his bundle when he sees the Plymouth turn into the gravel drive.

HE DROPS the dress into the washing machine. The cellar is cooler than the rest of the house. He hopes she realizes in time that she still has the sneakers. He looks at the machine, tries to decide on the water temperature and the cycle. He cannot decide. He pushes buttons. The machine bucks once into life, then begins to throb rhythmically under his hand.

Upstairs, in the kitchen, the air is close, too thick to breathe. Two-twenty. The hottest part of the day. He sits at the kitchen table, brings a hand to his forehead, looks across to her house. He sees Jim sitting on the steps, waiting for Eden to come home. Jim's face, with its long flat planes, comes briefly into focus, then fades. Andrew would have said, indeed people did say, Eden resembled Edith, not Jim, but now he'd like to see the face to search for any likeness. All that comes is an image of height, ranginess, a loose charm when he wasn't drunk. All those years and no one knew. Or did they? Did his mother guess? Did Edith tell her? He sees his mother's back at the sink, slightly stooped, her hands in a stream of water from the faucet. An ache for his mother he is not familiar with knots his stomach. He walks to the fridge, thinking he should have some food, selects a beer instead, the closest thing at hand. Still standing by the fridge, he drinks it down like a Coke, immediately gets another.

Already his memories of Jim are shifting, changing shape to accommodate this new piece of information. He thinks of a scene he remembers from his childhood—Jim coming home from a business trip with presents for Eden, who is playing on a swing—but it means something different now. Indeed, everything about Jim is different now, moving slightly, giving way to something else.

The heat and his empty stomach and the beer, drunk too fast, leave him light-headed. He begins to move about the kitchen floor, pacing from the counter to the table, a slow pace in the heat. He takes his shirt off, drops it over a chair. He can still smell the pond on his skin. He imagines that he can still smell Eden on his skin too. He lets her come into his mind, his head dizzy with images of her. He tastes her skin, remembers how her shoulders felt when she broke. Her hair was dense, shading him. And then she was on her back, arching as if they might merge. She was easy, so easy, and so quiet. Nothing to show how she felt but the quivering.

He leans against the sink, puts his head in his hands. His head hurts badly at the back of his neck, up the sides toward the temple.

You remind her of the past, Edith said. You'll raise her hopes, her expectations.

He thinks of Billy, waiting for him, needing him. He thinks of Jayne in his office, of the job he must return to. He sees his mother, turning now to look at him, to ask him what he is still doing here. From the cellar, he can hear the washing machine switching into the rinse cycle.

He thinks, knows, he should not have made love to her. He feels dry and hollow. He has done the thing that Edith feared, was right to fear. He glances up. For the first time, the room looks to him exactly as it is: no longer a repository of memories—only a faded, shabby, lifeless kitchen.

He cannot tolerate the silence. He turns on the radio nearly as loud as it will go and takes the stairs two at a time. In his room, his changes into a dress shirt and khaki slacks. He empties the drawers, stuffs his underwear and socks into his leather satchel. Slipping on a throw rug in the hallway, he grabs a carton of mementoes on his mother's bed. His arms loaded, he makes his way downstairs and out the back door, letting it slam. He puts the suitcase and the carton in the trunk of the BMW. Back inside the kitchen, he allows the door to slam again. There is another carton in his mother's room, one in the living room. He takes them out to the car. Impatiently, he forces the cartons into the trunk. He is sweating heavily. The cloth along his spine is wet. Returning to the kitchen, he opens the fridge, thinking to throw away any food that might spoil. Instead, he takes another beer, quickly shuts the door. He lifts the phone out of its cradle, starts to dial T.J.'s number, replaces the receiver. He will call T.J. from the city tomorrow.

He finds his charcoal gray suit in his bedroom closet, picks up another carton in his mother's room. Pulling the kitchen door to, he lets the screen door bang shut one final time. He throws his suit and the carton, spilling the contents, into the back seat.

He puts the key into the ignition, but it jams. He tugs at it, tries again. There are shooting pains in his right temple. He thrusts the gearshift into reverse. He whirls around in his seat to back out the driveway, lets the clutch out too fast and stalls.

He slams the steering wheel with the heel of his hand.

He sees his mother coming toward him, and there is something important he wants to tell her, but the image fades before he can reach her. He sees Billy standing in the doorway of the house at Saddle River, watching Andrew pack on the day he left for good. He feels Eden break, mourning what he cannot comprehend. His head sinks below the surface, and he knows he is drowning. Billy is calling to him, but he cannot hear the words through the water. He cannot leave her, not now when she is causing him to drown. He lets the water close over his head. He feels the weight of his own body. He allows himself the sensation of sinking, of letting go.

He leans his head back against the headrest and opens his eyes. He realizes he has been crying.

He sees that he has left the lawn mower out beside the garage. A wasp flies through his open window and begins to crawl along the inside of the windshield. He takes a deep breath, shudders with a last spasm. In the near distance there are cornfields, and over them the heat shimmers.

You are thinking that my world is black. But it is not. When my eyes are open, there is thick fog. Dark fog that turns to white fog when I go to the window and the sun is out. I can make it brighten and then turn dark. The fog darkens, like before a rain.

You are something warm hovering over me.

You said my name, and until then, I had forgotten how it could sound. You were hungry too, for more than you could say. You are not like the others, not like my memories, but I have always known that you wouldn't be.

I am afraid now to dream of you.

I heard your door slam. And again. And I thought that you would leave me.

In the water, I was free.

I was his, which I knew and didn't. She burned me with it when she thought the time was right.

There is light coming into my world, but there is darkness too.

FIVE

SHE IS LYING ON HER SIDE, AWAY FROM HIM, WITH ONE KNEE bent, the other leg outstretched beneath her, while he traces small designs on her back with his fingertips. In the six days they have had at the pond, he has learned this about her— and, he supposes, she has learned this about herself: that she likes to have her back lightly stroked after they have been together.

Beneath them is a cotton blanket that he brings with him every day, and they have now found the coolest part of the clearing. Sometimes he marvels that they have not been intruded upon, or discovered, apart from the boy with glasses who saw them that first day and fled. He slides a hand down her side, along the curve of her hip. Her skin is smooth, like glass, despite the heat and the humidity. He would like to lie here all his life, he is thinking, just repeating that gesture.

She lifts a shoulder, then drops it. She means for him to keep touching her back. She tells him what she likes, not in words but in small movements and gestures, so that he has found himself alert to this communication, eager to move where he thinks she is directing him. This language, new to him, is exhilarating, heightening his pleasure. In all his years with Martha, she would never say what it was that pleased her, as if he must blindly guess at her desires, hoping to read her correctly, though he remembers that too often she seemed disappointed that he had not quite found his way.

In the hot days he has been with Eden, they have made no pretense of their desires. Just as she has no gift for small talk, she no longer knows how to be coy. On Sunday, the first day after they had been to the pond, she was waiting for him in the kitchen. He had brought the blanket, which he told her about. They walked in silence to the pond, and once inside the clearing, nearly dizzy with wanting her, he began immediately to help her off with the blouse and shorts and sneakers she had worn. The pitch of his need was keen, knife-edged—he felt only that he had been away from her for too many hours—and was matched by something both undernourished and generous in herself. And though there is within her a core of reserve he cannot yet penetrate—a repository of things she sees that are still unclear to him—their intimacy is intense, unlike anything he has ever known. Only much later that noon hour did he remember the blanket, abandoned at the edge of the clearing. He shook it out and unfolded it for them to rest on, establishing that day a pattern of resting afterward and then swimming.

When she swam that Sunday he made himself keep up with her. He didn't want her leaving him, if only for that. Twice while swimming, she exclaimed something he couldn't quite make out, and when she stopped, breathing so hard he could see her ribs rising and sinking, she was almost laughing. It has been, he thinks, a remarkable stroke of luck, finding the pond again, discovering together something that gives her so much pleasure.

Sometimes they have talked, though it surprises him when he is away from her how long their silences are, as if they had years together stretching into the future in which to unfold to each other all there is to know. Occasionally he feels an urgent need to ask her questions so that he will understand her secrets, so that they might reach another kind of intimacy, but he has learned, even in the brief time they've had together, that questions unsettle her, cause her to withdraw from him. What she gives, she gives in her own time, small parcels of knowledge.

"She told me in the spring, that last spring," she said, as they walked back to the houses on Sunday.

He was already learning to take a few seconds to determine what she was talking about.

"About Jim, you mean?" he asked.

"We were fighting, and she threw it at me. I picked up a glass and threw it at her. I didn't really try to hit her, and it broke in the sink."

He wasn't sure, but he thought he might remember that day, a day he was working under the car and he heard glass shattering.

"Why then?" he asked. "Why did she wait so long and tell you then?"

"They'd decided together never to tell me, because of what he'd done. But she couldn't stand it anymore. She wanted me to know how he was," she said. "To make me see him differently."

HE HAS given her small parcels too, though of a different nature. One day he fashioned a picnic of sorts out of tuna-fish sandwiches and grapes and cold water in a thermos and cookies from a bakery for dessert. On Tuesday, he bought her a gold necklace, which she wore while she swam. On another day, having searched the county until he found it, he brought her a book in braille from a library in a town nearly twenty miles away. It was *My Ántonia*. She had told him, when he asked, that she had been taught braille when she was first in the hospital but hadn't had a book in braille for years, not since Edith stopped bringing them home shortly after Eden came back to the house to live. He watched her finger the raised dots, trying again to recall the letters. Each day he has brought the book and watched her read. He wanted her to take the book home with her, to hide it in a drawer, but she said no, she didn't want to risk Edith's finding out they'd been together.

"She must suspect something," he said.

"She never says. I'm very careful."

"Why don't we just tell her and get it over with?"

"Tell her what?"

"Tell her we're going to be together when we want to."

"She won't leave, then. She won't go to work."

"But why?"

"She's afraid of you."

"Afraid of me? That's ridiculous."

"It isn't that easy," she said.

HIS LIFE now has achieved a simplicity he would have said was impossible. He lives for the hours between ten and two. He wakes early, with the dawn, and labors on the house. In the coolest hours of the day, he has repaired the torn screen, finished the gutter, repainted the back stoop and sanded the woodwork on the mantel in the living room. He is sometimes vaguely aware that he is doing this work so that he can put the house up for sale, but in the six days since he tried to leave and failed, he has resisted thinking of the future. He cannot now imagine getting into the BMW and driving away for good, nor can he quite sort out the consequences if he doesn't. As a result, he has resolutely decided not to think about it, to savor each day as it comes to him, to experience his days as organic, without a master plan. He has noticed, however, that the things inside the cartons have begun to come out, to spread themselves gradually again over the house. And on Monday, as he was meant to do, he went to T.J.'s office, but not, as T.J. had intended, to drop off the key. Instead he told T.J., who swiveled in a gray chair, eyeing Andrew warily, that he wanted another few days to accomplish all the repair work on the house he had set out to do. He felt he owed it to his parents, he explained rather lamely, to leave the house in good condition. T.J. had let his chair snap straight up with a thwack and had stood, adjusting his belt. "OK by me, pal," he had said, not looking at Andrew, "if you're sure you know what you're doing."

His afternoons are as rhythmic as the mornings. After he and Eden have been together each day, he drives to the mall in search of gifts for her she cannot keep. He has become, as a result of this habit, a devotee of the mall. He has bought her a peach-colored cotton sundress and a copy of *Ethan Frome*, which he plans to read to her. He has bought her a box of chocolates, which they devoured one day after swimming. He has bought her sunscreen lotion for her face and a wide-brimmed straw hat. Today he has bought her something special, the most ingenious of his purchases.

"I'm going swimming," she says, stretching and sitting up.

"I'll come with you," he says.

"No. I can do it myself now."

He is about to protest, but stops. There is no reason she can't swim on her own. Her sense of direction is uncanny. He has noticed that she has entered and come out of the water at exactly the same spot each day. He wonders how she does it: does she feel the path with her feet, or does she hear her way?

Propped up on one elbow, he watches her walk to the pond, wade out up to her waist, then dive forward to begin her crawl to the other side. He likes watching her swim. Her strokes are neat, mathematical, and he takes pride in seeing her strength return with each passing day. She can easily finish twenty laps now, and if they had more time, she might do thirty.

He lies back with his hands under his head. He thinks he hears, very faintly, a distant rumble of thunder. The strangling heat wave, now in its eighth day, has broken all records. It is as if the entire town and its environs were waiting breathlessly for the siege to break. He hopes it is thunder that he has heard, and that it will come soon, this afternoon, bringing with it a soaking, rinsing rain. He imagines the rain, bouncing up from the cracked ground, dripping from the wet leaves, falling onto his face and shoulders as he shuts his eyes and turns his face gratefully up to a cloudburst. . . .

He wakes with a start, annoyed to see he has been dozing. He has no idea how long he has been unconscious: seconds? minutes? He stands awkwardly and too fast, feeling hollow as he does so. He scans the pond. There is no sign of Eden. He glances around the clearing, but she is not there either. He calls her name, the first time hesitantly, the second time abruptly, as he runs to the water's edge.

"Eden!" he shouts, as if he were cross with her.

The surface of the pond is eerily smooth.

"Holy Christ!" he yells now, flailing into the pond. His heart is loose inside his chest. His lungs are huge balloons, pushing against his ribs. The water is molasses. It is like the nightmares he used to have as a boy when he couldn't run fast enough in his dreams. "Jesus God," he cries as he pitches forward to swim, not knowing in which direction to head.

To his right, he sees a ripple, than a hand. She rockets straight up in the water not twenty feet to the side of him, panting hard. She smiles. She listens for him. She waves in his general direction.

"What the hell are you doing?" he snaps angrily, trying to catch his breath.

"I'm just swimming," she says, surprised by his tone. "What is it?"

"I thought you'd . . ."

He turns and heads back toward shore. He holds his chest where his heart is palpitating and walks around the perimeter of the clearing, with the other hand on his hip. She does not follow him, remains in the water where he has left her. When he circles close to shore, he sees her making waves with her fingers, idly stroking the surface. He lunges into the pond, pulling his feet high and clear until the water reaches above his knees. He dives forward in her direction. He bobs in front of her, lifts her in his arms, cradling her, then rolls her in the air and lets her belly-flop into the water. She comes up sputtering, gasping. She makes a broad sweep with her forearm, spewing the water in his direction. He dives, catches an ankle, drags her under. He holds her there, kisses her, but she pushes at his shoulders, propelling herself to the surface. When he comes up for air, she is laughing. He grabs her around the waist, pulls her onto her back, slides her over himself. She turns abruptly, plunges his head under water, and leapfrogs over his body. When he stumbles to his feet, he sees that she is already halfway to shore. She runs dripping up onto the grass, quickly feels with her feet where the blanket is and sits down, hugging herself. Home free.

"You're an asshole sometimes, you know that, Andy?"

The word is a song note he thought he might never hear again. It lifts him up, makes him as buoyant as a child's inflatable toy in a pool. He bobs happily, watching her, then slithers out of the water to the blanket. He sits beside her.

"I fell asleep," he says, "and when I woke up I was disoriented. I thought you'd . . ."

"Drowned?"

"Yes."

She touches his shoulder, runs her hand down his arm. "I'm sorry," she says.

"I just feel . . . ," he says.

"I'm responsible for myself."

"It's more than that."

"It's hard to believe now," she says, "but I once wished that *you* would drown."

He looks at the surface of the pond, returned to its glassy, golden state. "I love you," he says.

She squeezes his forearm. "You think you know me, but you don't."

"I know enough."

"I could say I love you too, but I don't know what it is."

"I do," he says.

"I wish I could see your face when you make love to me," she says after a long silence.

He turns to look at her. He hoots. He drapes his arm around her shoulder.

"I'm glad you can't," he says. "I probably look ridiculous."

After a time, he consults his watch. "I've brought something for you," he says. "I'd better give it to you now."

She no longer protests when he gives her presents, and he likes that. He reaches for the plastic bag he brought with him to the pond.

"It's a battery-operated cassette tape recorder," he explains, taking her hand and letting her touch the small rectangular object. "It's easy to operate, and I've brought you some books on tape to listen to." He fetches the boxed cassettes from the plastic bag. "Short stories by Chekhov," he reads, "and *Smiley's People* by John le Carré."

She fingers the buttons on the tape recorder.

"And here's the best feature." He pulls from the bag a set of headphones. Smoothing her hair behind her ears, he adjusts the headphones and plugs in the jack. "Listen to this," he says.

He snaps the cassette of Chekhov into the tape recorder. "Nod when the sound is the right level," he says. He turns the volume up slowly, and she nods. He watches her listening. He pushes the stop button and moves the headphones off her ears.

"When you have these on, no one can hear the tape. You can play it in your room, and she won't hear you. It's small, so it can easily be hidden."

"I don't know," she says cautiously.

"Trust me. Here, give me your hand, and I'll teach you how to use this." He takes her fingers and shows her how to read the buttons. Play. Stop. Eject. Record. Play. She holds the black box, listens to the words on the cassette. If he can find the right cassettes, he can give her an entire world that has been lost to her all these years.

She pushes the stop button, takes off the headphones.

"When are you leaving?" she asks.

Leaving. It is a question he has scrupulously avoided asking himself for six days. "I don't know about that," he says.

"You'll have to go. You have a life you have to go back to. You have a job and a son."

He flops back onto the blanket and rubs his eyes with the heels of his hands. "I don't want to talk about that now," he says.

"Now *you* have things you don't want to talk about."

"It's different."

She puts the tape recorder aside and crosses her legs, supporting her weight on one hand.

"In the beginning," she says, "I was asleep. Then I cried for a very long time. And then I felt guilty and knew I was being punished."

"Punished for what?"

"For how I'd been."

He is silent.

"You remember," she says.

He ponders this confession. It is another parcel, a small piece of the puzzle. She has given it, he thinks, because she wants him to tell her something, to give her in return a clue about the shape of her future. It has, however, the opposite effect. It irritates him, makes him suddenly want to know more, as if she had merely teased him.

"It's not enough," he says rashly, not looking at her. "Tell me more."

"There isn't . . ."

"Tell me all of it."

"There isn't any more."

"I don't believe you. Was it Sean?"

"I don't remember."

"You know you said it, though. Someone has told you you said it."

"I know I said it one time, but I don't remember it. I have no memory of that time. Please don't do this." Her voice rises at the last sentence.

Even with his eyes shut, the sun is so bright behind his lids he has to squint. He wishes he had his sunglasses on. He sits up quickly, knowing he has gone too far. He touches her thigh with the backs of his fingers. He notices that her hand is shaking.

"I'm sorry," he says.

She sits perfectly still—though inside, he knows, there must be a turbulence he can only guess at. It is, he thinks, a finely honed skill, her poise, a means of coping with too much darkness, too much silence, too many bad memories.

"Is that thunder?" she asks.

He listens and hears nothing. "I don't know. I heard something like thunder earlier. I hope it is, though. Then maybe this awful heat will break."

"I don't want it to break," she says.

"Why?"

"Because then it will be something else, and we'll be different."

He slides his arm along her back and draws her down so that she is lying now on top of him.

"There isn't time," she says. "I can feel it."

He stretches an arm and looks at his watch behind her head. "It's exactly one-oh-seven," he says. He kisses her, pressing her head down toward his face with his forearms. She moves slightly, making small adjustments to accommodate her breasts, her hipbones.

"I think the place likes us," she says. "I think it wants us to stay here."

And as he looks past her head at the trees above them, he believes that what she has said is true—that there is about the pond and its clearing an unmistakable benevolence. Once it offered them its seasons of childhood games. Now, years later, overgrown and neglected, it shelters them as lovers.

WHEN HE enters his kitchen, arms full of grocery bags from the A & P, and a plastic bag from the mall dangling from his fingers, the phone is ringing. He lets his bundles fall to the kitchen table, lifts the receiver.

"Andrew?"

"Jayne."

"You sound short of breath."

"Oh, a bit. How are you?"

"I'm fine, Andrew. I think the real question is: How are you?"

"Better. Better," he says vaguely.

"I've been asked to call. . . ."

"I know. I should have called in."

"You *are* coming back?" she says.

"Yes. Soon. Is it very bad there?"

"Everything that can go wrong . . ."

"And Geoffrey?"

"The usual. Well past hysteria."

Through the kitchen window, Andrew can see a long blanket of tarnished silver clouds advancing on the western horizon.

"Jayne, before you say any more, I've decided to take some vacation time. There's a lot owed me, but I'm thinking in terms of another week, ten days."

There is a pause.

"Jayne?"

He thinks that perhaps they've been disconnected, but just before he is about to hang up, he hears a male voice on the line.

"Andrew."

The one spoken word brings Geoffrey, all six feet four inches of him, clearly into focus. He will be standing at Jayne's desk, his free hand fussing with the knot of his tie. Andrew can see the black aviator frames with the smoky tint, the neatly trimmed black mustache with flecks of gray, the black wing tips, glossily polished.

"Geoffrey."

"Sorry about your mother."

"Thank you."

"But that's not why I called."

"No."

"It isn't a convenient time right now for a vacation. The agency is collapsing under the weight of this project even as we speak. We may have to scuttle them altogether and start anew with someone else. We need you, Andrew, to tighten the reins, to get this thing under control. The product's been ready for six weeks."

"I know."

"So you'll come in, then. Tomorrow?"

"No."

"Then when?"

"I'm not."

"Come again?"

"I can't. Not right now. I'm sorry, Geoffrey."

There is a long silence.

"I think you should give this some more thought, Andrew. Consider what I've said."

"I'll do that."

"I want you to call in tomorrow. Talk to me after you've thought about it. You can take a month's vacation when this is over."

"It's not the vacation per se, Geoffrey. It's that I can't leave here right now."

"I don't want to have to say your job is on the line."

"No."

"We don't want that to be a consideration."

"No."

"So don't back me into a corner on this one, OK, buddy?"

"No."

"Is that all you have to say?"

"I think so. This isn't personal, Geoffrey. I'm not trying to cause a problem."

"Then don't."

"I'll call you."

"Do that."

Andrew holds the phone to his ear long after he has heard the click on the other end. He replaces the receiver and walks to the left side of the window so that he may have a better view of the blanket of clouds on the horizon. He hears, distinctly now, a long roll of thunder in the distance. It is as though a town were waiting for an advancing army to liberate it.

The office must be in worse shape than he thought, for Geoffrey to have threatened him—though Andrew knows the threat is almost certainly an empty one. He would have to be AWOL a lot longer than this for Geoffrey to let him go. This knowledge, however, is oddly disappointing. Getting fired now would come as a relief, absolve him of responsibility for the future.

The phone rings again.

"Andrew?"

The chemical reaction in his larynx deflates his voice by half an octave.

"Martha."

"Where are you?"

"I'm here, obviously."

"I mean, why aren't you in the city? You were only going to take a week."

"I've decided to stay on a bit, take some vacation time."

"Vacation time? But what about Billy? He's been expecting you."

Andrew winces. This fact, which has lain at the back of his thoughts for six days, kept in check by Andrew's attention to the details of his house and of providing for Eden, spirals out of its niche and floods the whole of Andrew's consciousness.

"It's only another week," he says, in a voice that has risen a notch. He clears his throat. "I need to sort some things out."

"Andrew."

"What?"

"You sound odd. Is everything all right?"

"No. Not really."

"What is it?"

"I can't talk about it now. I'm sorry. Tell me how Billy is."

"He's great. All tanned and healthy. But I think you're going to have to talk to him."

"I know. Put him on."

He waits, his chest tight, for his son's voice.

"Daddy?"

"Hi, Billy. What are you doing?"

"Me and Mommy are making a battleship with my Legos. I can't go outside 'cause it's raining. Are you coming to get me now?"

"No, Billy. Not today. I'm still at Grandma's house."

Andrew hears a long sigh, like that from an old man. The sigh enters his own body, goes right to his bones with a shudder.

"Billy?"

"Tomorrow can you come?"

"I can't tomorrow. But soon. I'll come as soon as I can. I love you and miss you."

"I love you too, Daddy."

"I went swimming today in a pond. And guess what color the water is."

"Green?"

"It's golden."

"Are there fish in it?"

"Lots of fish."

"Can we go there sometime?"

"Sure. We'll see."

"Grandpop took me fishing in the ocean."

"Did you catch anything?"

"Nope. Well, kind of. I caught a lot of seaweed."

"You be good, OK, Billy?"

"OK."

"And I'll come soon."

"OK."

"Can I talk to Mommy now?"

"OK. Bye, Daddy."

"Bye, Billy. I love you."

Andrew falls into the chair by the phone, rests his head on his hand.

"So you don't know when you'll be here," Martha says. Drag and exhale. Away from him, she has lit a cigarette.

"I'll let you know."

"You know, Jayne called here this morning. She wanted to know if I knew what was going on."

"There's nothing going on. I'm just exhausted, that's all. I need some time."

"So you say. I'll try to handle Billy. But don't wait too long. You've never not come when you've said you would. I'm not sure he understands this."

"Give me another week. That's all. I'm sure I can sort this out by then."

"You don't sound good."

"I'm actually very good. That's the funny part."

"I don't know if I like this," she says. "You're not making a lot of sense."

"Don't worry. Everything will be all right. Give Billy a kiss for me."

"Andrew?"

"Yes?"

"You take care of yourself."

He stands up, heads immediately to the fridge. Taking out a beer and opening it, he holds it in one hand as he removes the groceries from the paper bags and puts them in the fridge and the cupboards. A half gallon of ice cream he has forgotten about has leaked into the paper bag. Halfway through this chore, he opens the screen door, stands on the back stoop. From there he can see nearly the entire horizon line where the army is advancing. It is a slow-moving storm, beginning only now to flutter the leaves in the trees overhead. Soon the leaves will turn their backs and shine silvery as the clouds slide across the sun. He can see a distant flash of lightning, can hear another slow rumble of thunder.

The phone rings again. He doesn't move. It rings seven times, and then it stops. When he's sure the caller has given up, he reenters the kitchen and throws the empty beer can into the wastebasket. He is nearly through the kitchen on the way to his bedroom when the phone begins to ring again.

"Andy-boy."

"T.J."

"Everything OK, pal? I thought you'da blown town by now."

"Not quite."

"Well, anyway, I got some good news for you."

"What's that?"

"I just had a call from your neighbor, Edith Close. She's sellin' too. Moving right away, she says. This is fantastic. With both houses on the market, we can get a much better deal now."

THROUGH THE NIGHT, storms rattle the town, wave upon wave battering the gates, pausing for a time, then beginning again. The skirmishes—lewd light shows beyond his screen, punctuated by splintering cracks of thunder overhead—sever Andrew's dreams, causing him to start and wake a dozen times before dawn. In the morning, nothing has changed but the rising of a gray curtain of light that reveals the trees' wild careening and a lawn strewn with debris—branches, twigs, leaves and dead hydrangea blossoms. He wakes a final time, his mouth dry, his body soaked from a tenacious humidity that will not break. The sheets on his bed are grainy from too many days of dampness. He curls himself off the bed and slips on the jeans and shirt and sneakers that lie in a pile on the floor. Stumbling into the dim bathroom, he flips on the switch there and is puzzled for a moment when the overhead light doesn't go on. To check that it is not simply a blown bulb, he reaches behind him for the light switch in the hallway and finds there, too, only a deadened circuit. He walks heavily down the stairway, through the living room and out to the kitchen, pausing only long enough to drink a glass of water.

Outside the air feels charged: he thinks he can smell a faint trace of ozone. It is not raining, but he knows the calm is deceptive as he surveys the sweep of sky over the town and sees no break in the clouds in any direction. He heads down the gravel drive, past a faded green shutter that has fallen from an upstairs window at the Closes' house during the night. At the road, he stops. He has no destination, merely a desire to leave the two houses for a time so that he can think. To his right is the town, with its pockets of subdivisions encroaching farther and farther along the straight road out toward his house. To the left is a nearly empty expanse of road through farmlands and cornfields, leading to the next town. He turns left.

He walks on the asphalt, his hands in his pockets, stepping into the ditch from time to time when he hears the whining of a truck or a car. He marvels at the amount of debris on the road and wonders where it is that the wires are down, causing the blackout. He wonders, too, if the luncheonette has opened for breakfast, if T.J. and his wife are even aware, in their insulated capsule, that storms have shaken the county. He tries to imagine how they will survive without their air-conditioning if they, too, have lost their power. He wonders if the women and their babies are getting ready to go to the mall now, or if they will stay home today.

He walks perhaps three or four miles before he is aware

of just how far he has traveled. He has managed not to think too strenuously, which, he realizes, is what he wanted all along. He has reached a spot in the road on either side of which are only cornfields. An angry burst of thunder takes him by surprise, for he has not noticed any lightning preceding it, and it seems to him that the thunder is close, just off his left shoulder. The sky, too, is darkening, as if it would return so quickly back to night. He thinks now that he should turn around, that in his drowsy state he has come too far. It is foolish, he knows, to be walking on an open road, so far from shelter, with the promise of another storm.

He starts to make a turn, when he sees, in the middle of the road up ahead, not fifty feet from him, a small shape that seems as though it shouldn't be there, that doesn't look like a tree branch or a blown cornstalk. He squints at the shape, trying to make out what it is, torn between investigating it and retreating toward his house. He moves a few steps forward, in order to see more clearly, thinking he can discern the outline of an animal. It moves slightly, raising its head. A pencil-thin dagger of lightning in the cornfields to his left lights up the scene: the wet road, the waves of undulating fields, the huddled shape. He feels raindrops on his hair and shoulders—an announcement of yet another storm, followed immediately by a drumming shower. He jogs to the shape, crouches down beside it. A beagle's head turns toward him, its eyes calm and sorrowful. The dog looks at Andrew, as if for an explanation of this calamity, and lays its head down, still watching the man. A bolt of lightning appears to strike the road not a hundred feet from Andrew, startling him. The crack of thunder is so sudden and so sharp the dog lifts its head again. Andrew sees that the creature's hind legs have been crushed, and there is a smear of blood, about three feet long, on the asphalt—washing away now in the rain— where the animal has tried to drag itself. Andrew peers up and down the road. In the distance, coming from town, he sees the headlights of a vehicle. Another bolt of lightning and then another, a pair of jagged wires piercing the space around himself and the dog, make him shudder involuntarily. He has always, even as a boy, harbored a fear of lightning. He bends down and tries to slide his arms under the dog. It gives a faint moan. The headlights of the car are more distinct now, moving fast along the road. Andrew lifts the animal into his arms, feeling the dead weight of the hindquarters. The dog raises its head, tries to reach its nose to Andrew's face. He carries it to a grassy patch beside the road and lays it down as gently as he can. The car whizzes past, showering Andrew and the dog with a fine spray. The center of the storm is upon them now, spewing out its stabs of lightning with abandon. Andrew crouches toward the ground, so as not to be a target, then lies on the grass on his stomach beside the dog. The thunder is so loud—or his sudden fear of the accompanying lightning so paralyzing—that he cannot move, save to cover his head with his arms and hands. He chooses not to watch, but he knows, his breath held, then released in spasms, that all around them there is lightning, dancing gaudily in the cornfields. His spine tingles with the image of his exposed back as an electrical field, inviting the ferocious charge. He stretches his arms out in front of him, feeling the earth. The thunder rises like the crescendo of an orchestra gone mad. He presses his brow hard into the grassy soil and waits.

When he hears the thunder subside, he raises himself off the ground to a sitting position. He tries to clear the rain from his face with his sleeve. The dog's eyes are closed. He puts his hand on the animal's head, lets his hand caress the inert body. The dog has stopped panting, is not breathing at all.

"It's all right," he says, stroking the wet fur. The rain

soaks them both, indifferent to the living and the dead. He thinks about the dog's silence on the brink of death. Did its hind legs not hurt? he wonders.

And then, so completely drenched that he has begun to shiver, he thinks about injury and damage done. The thoughts come warmly and familiarly into his brain; it was what he was trying to dream about all night, an exploration rudely thwarted again and again by the nocturnal chaos of the storm.

Can damage be erased, redressed? he asks silently.

"And who of us is not damaged?" he asks aloud.

He thinks of T.J., lost to his belief in the morality of material things.

He thinks of Martha, twisted from an early age by an anger that refused to explain itself or leave her.

He thinks of Geoffrey, with his wing-tip shoes and his expensive dark suits, committed ten hours a day to the drama at the top of a glass and steel building.

And he thinks of himself, engaged so long in the same enterprise, forfeiting the thing he cared most about—the daily fatherhood of his son.

Is Eden any more damaged than himself? he wonders. Than any of them? And was it folly to imagine that he could, by loving her, ease the hurts of her past? Or she his?

A rusty green pickup truck sails past Andrew, stops short, nearly hydroplaning on the wet pavement, and backs up to where Andrew is sitting. A middle-aged man, wearing a once white T-shirt and a brown felt hat with a brim, leans across the front seat and rolls down the window. Andrew can see the gray stubble on his cheeks, an eyetooth missing.

"That yer dog?" he asks.

Andrew shakes his head.

"What you want to do with it?"

"Bury it," says Andrew.

"Well, then, throw it in the back. You live around here?"

Andrew nods, tells him where he lives.

"Better get in," says the man.

HE BURIES the dog under the hydrangea tree. It is a frustrating process in the rain, since the hole he makes with a spade keeps filling up with water and falling in at the sides. It has to be a largish hole and fairly deep to accommodate the dog and to keep stray animals from digging at it. When the lightning comes again, he has to retreat to the kitchen for a cup of coffee. He looks out the window at the dog and the half-dug hole. The lightning stops, and he goes out to resume the digging. At times he wishes he had not decided to do this, because he knows he has to think now, to plan, to make lists about the immediate future. He is afraid to have an idea and then not remember it later. But when the hole is fully dug, the dog placed inside it, the soil raked over, he is glad that he has done this.

SHE ISN'T sitting in the chair when he enters the kitchen. She is at the sink and turns immediately when he opens the door. Her face seems agitated, hard to read. She is wearing a long blue seersucker bathrobe, and she is rubbing her arms with her hands as if she were cold. He has been worried all morning that Edith would not go to work, and when he heard the Plymouth start up, he raised his head toward the ceiling in grateful thanks.

"What's going on?" he asks at once. He does not go to her. He senses she wouldn't want that yet.

"She found the tape recorder."

"How?"

"I thought she was taking a nap. She said she was going to. I put the headphones on and was listening to the stories when she came into the room. I should have heard her long before she ever got to my room, but with the headphones on, I couldn't."

"I'm sorry."

"She took it."

"What did she say?"

"She didn't say anything. She just left."

"Do you know she's selling the house?"

She nods. "I heard her on the phone. But how do *you* know?"

"It was T.J.'s agency that she called."

"Ah."

"Come over to the chair and sit down," he says. "We have to talk."

"What is there to talk about now?"

"Let's go upstairs," he says, "to your room. I want to lie down with you, talk to you that way."

"No," she says quickly. "Not my room. I'll come sit down."

She makes her way to the chair and perches on it reluctantly, as if about to hear a lecture she intends to resist. She folds her hands in her lap. Her face, he now sees, has become, on the surface, impassive, struggling to keep in check a face underneath.

He reaches across for her hand. She gives it unwillingly.

"Tonight," he says, "I'm going to pack up the house for good. When I come tomorrow, I'm going to help you pack. Then we're going to get in my car and drive to my apartment in New York. We'll leave a note for Edith. When we get to the city, I'm going to take a short leave of absence from my job. We'll get you settled in a good program for the blind, but we'll be together, live together."

He is improvising now. Until this minute he has been unable to think beyond the drive south, the exhilaration of that open highway.

She begins to shake her head.

"What?" he says.

She says nothing, but he can feel her retreating even further, inch by inch.

"What is it?" he asks more forcefully.

"I can't do that," she says. "I can't leave."

"But why?"

"I wouldn't know how."

"I'll be with you every step of the way. It doesn't have to be the city; we can go anywhere."

"You have a son," she says. "And I have Edith."

"You have Edith?" he asks incredulously.

"I have to have Edith and she has to have me. There are things about this you don't understand, things about me you wouldn't like if you knew."

"There's nothing about you I couldn't deal with. I love you. I've told you that. It's simple."

"No; that's just it," she says. "It isn't simple at all."

She withdraws her hand, rises and edges toward the sink.

"I won't leave here without you," he says. "There's nothing more important in my life that I have to do."

She hunches her shoulders forward, rests her weight on her hands at the lip of the sink. He can see the shape of her back, her waist beneath the robe. Her hair is tangled, not brushed. There are dishes in the sink she has not washed yet. She runs her palms along the porcelain rim. She takes hold of the faucet, massages it with the heel of her hand.

The silence worries him. He feels that he is losing ground. "I won't leave without you," he says again, "and I won't let—"

She cuts him off. She whirls around quickly from the sink. "I've changed my mind," she says. "I want to go up-stairs now."

He guesses she is doing this to stop him, to divert him

from his campaign. But he imagines that lying next to him, she cannot fail to hear him.

He follows her through the dining room, the living room, up the stairs and, after they have reached the landing, through a darkened doorway.

A flash of lightning through the sole window lights up the room, illuminating hundreds of faded pink roses on the walls. The paper is peeling badly, revealing another, grayer paper beneath it. Someone years ago, perhaps when Eden was a baby, thought to cover the more somber paper with one befitting a little girl, but having no expertise in wallpapering, as was the case with Jim and Edith, merely covered the one paper with the other. Oddly, he or she also papered the slanted ceiling over the bed, but there whole patches have come away, laying bare a crumbling plaster. The bed is tucked under the slanted ceiling, one side against the wall, with only a foot of space above the edge of the bed where the wall and ceiling meet. The bed has no headboard, only an iron footboard, painted white, but chipped in so many places it looks more mottled than painted. A worn pink chenille bedspread is drawn up neatly to the single pillow. The floor, wide plank boards, is painted a chocolate brown. On the other side of the room is a small desk of maple with a stained green blotter on its surface. There is a radio on the blotter and a hairbrush. Beside the hairbrush is a sealed plastic bag with what seems to be a large lump of moist clay inside. On the chair in front of the desk is the blue sundress.

Another flash of lightning, followed almost immediately by a shuddering crack of thunder. He looks out the window at the rain and at the trees whipping back and forth. The shade at the top of the window is torn along the bottom, and he sees that the panes have not been washed in a long time.

Nearly noon, and it is as dark as a heavy dusk.

It is the first time he has been in her room as an adult, though when he was a boy he was sometimes here while Eden collected a baseball glove or her mittens. Then the room was not barren, at least not as he remembers it. The desk was cluttered in those days with a record player and her records and her sports paraphernalia. Sleeves and legs of clothes spilled from the dresser. In the corner, he remembers, she kept her hockey stick and skates. He thinks, too, he must have been here on a stormy day, like this one, but he can't, for a moment, recall what it was they did here. He has a vague memory of endless games of Monopoly, stretching long past the point when he'd have been glad to concede the game to her if he could have brought himself to do it— or did they go to *his* house on rainy days?

He surveys the room again, returning to the moment. The weight of it hits him now. He imagines how she must sit here with the darkness falling. He wonders if he would be able to stand that, or would he have to find a light? There is a light, a wall lamp near the door. It must be for Edith, for when she comes during the evening.

He watches Eden sit on the edge of the bed, as if momentarily preoccupied with choices, then lie back close to the wall. She raises one knee slightly, and the robe falls open when she does so. She stretches out an arm to indicate that he should come.

There is something uncomfortable about her posture. He tries to read her face. Already she is eons away from him.

He sits in the chair by the desk. He would like to know what she has in its drawers, whether the "things" that she makes are there. The radio is an old one, of round brown plastic. He wishes they could go back to the kitchen, start again.

"I'm lonely over here," she says.

The voice is one he hasn't heard in years. He remembers the afternoon as clearly as if he were at the pond this moment. *You can touch my blouse*, she said, and the voice was the same. But then he was a boy, and he resisted her.

He bends down to loosen the laces of his sneakers. They are still soaked from his walk. He thinks of the dog under the tree. He would like to tell her about the dog. He takes off his shirt, unbuckles his belt. He lays his clothes on the chair, over the blue sundress.

He walks to the bed, lies down beside her. He thinks only that he will hold her, bring her back. But under his weight, when he moves toward her, the bed creaks abruptly and loudly in the silence—the old iron springs protesting a man's additional weight. Yesterday, he thinks, they might have laughed together, but now the sound makes her freeze, as if she had badly miscalculated, as if she had not anticipated this echo. Quickly, he presses his hand against the small of her back, drawing her closer, but she is stiff against his embrace.

"Eden," he says, but she doesn't answer him.

He can feel her fear, or something like fear, along the tendons and muscles of her back. The fear is contagious and travels up his arm to his own chest. Alarmed, thinking he can stop the current by a bold gesture, or by seizing her to him more tightly, he roughly shifts her hips under his. The bed creaks again. He kisses her, but her mouth is empty.

"What is it?" he asks, the fear gathering in his chest like a cloud.

He raises her arms and pins her hands up behind the pillow.

"What is it?" he asks, shaking her wrists.

She lifts a knee as if to twist him off her, but he presses her leg with his own and holds her to the bed under him.

He looks at her closed eyes, the almond eye. She turns her face away.

"Who was here before me?" he whispers hard into her ear.

She gives a cry and strains toward the wall. He lets her go but wraps an arm around her abdomen and pulls her buttocks against him. He puts a hand at the back of her neck, bending her forward. He raises the skirt of her robe until it is bunched at her waist. A sensation, as swift as a kick, moves through his chest when he sees her exposed, too white, too vulnerable. But he is lost now to reason, letting his fear guide him. Holding her hipbone with his free hand, he slips inside her from behind. She cries out again as if he had hurt her, but he doesn't believe he has hurt her. It is something else she is resisting. He can see the buttons of her spinal column rising from her buttocks until they disappear beneath her robe. He moves his hand down to the place where her thigh joins her hip and holds her there.

"Tell me who," he insists, his voice no longer a whisper.

She reaches for the edge of the bed nearest the wall to anchor herself against his pounding. He can see her shoulder quiver with the strain. Beyond her shoulder is the faded paper with the roses and its brittle cracks. But he is suddenly confused, not in her bed but in the pond, grabbing for her hand because she has gone under.

"I was his," she cries out to the wall. The voice is taut, stretched, too high-pitched.

"Who?" he says hoarsely to her back. He holds her tightly now, diving beneath the water to reach her, nearly there.

"Jim's."

It is a wail that comes to him from across the pond. He breaks the surface. The cry reaches him, buffets his ears like a high wind. He takes the name, looks at it, remembers it.

He stops, halted in frenzied midsentence. His eyes refocus on the blue and white stripes of the seersucker cloth. His body slips away from her of its own accord.

He makes a sound like a man coming up for air. He rolls onto his back.

Outside, the lightning comes again, but it is nothing and barely registers. The thunder is more muted than it was when they entered the room. The storm, he thinks, must be moving on. The panes rattle in the loose window frame as if from a farewell gust. He glances over at her desk, at the clothes on the chair, at the clay on the blotter. His eyes stray back to the slanted ceiling directly over him. He squints at the paper. There are tiny holes surrounding the crumbling plaster, he now sees. *Of course*, he thinks, *from the shooting*. And there will be other tiny holes in the room too.

He forces himself to a sitting position. He stands and walks across the room to the window. The window sticks, then gives. On the lawn between the two houses, he can see eddies of leaves and twigs, twisted into dust devils by the wind. On the horizon is a seam of bright light beneath the cloud bank.

Her robe is still raised to her waist. He walks back to the bed and bends across it. He lifts her hand free of the edge, where she is clutching it. He smooths the robe over her legs. He walks to the chair and sits down.

He watches as she turns onto her back. She wipes away a patch of sweat near her temple with the palm of her hand. Already, through the open window, there is the faintest suggestion of a chill in the air.

On either side of the well of the desk are the drawers, the bottom drawers the deepest. He opens the one to his right. Inside is a forest of gray clay shapes. He lifts out one of the small sculptured pieces and puts it on the blotter. It is a figure of a nude woman, sitting on a straight-back chair, not unlike the one he is on. Her head is bent forward, and her long back is curved. One leg is stretched out, the other bent. The sculpture is about fifteen inches high, but he can make out the fine depressions to the side of one eye. The hair, thick and tangled, cascades down the back of the chair. It is an extraordinary likeness, but it is not just the likeness. It is the remarkable softness of the body against the square shape of the chair.

He looks over at Eden on the bed. She has to have heard him open the drawer. He draws out another. It is again a self-portrait, a woman in a sundress with buttons down the front, bending to the floor to pick up a shirt. He runs his fingers along the folds of the skirt, admires the way it opens as the woman has bent forward.

"These are wonderful," he says.

She says nothing, turns her face slightly away from him.

"This is what you meant," he says.

He takes another from the drawer. It is a woman in a nightgown, lying on her side.

"She brings me clay," she says. "But they dry up after a while, and they break."

"But they could be kiln-dried, couldn't they? Or reproduced in metal? They're beautiful." He feels a sensation, something like relief, that she has had this—and then another sensation, one of admiration, that she has been able to create such beauty in this barren room.

She hugs her arms as if she were again cold. She rises to a sitting position. Another gust whistles against the window.

"I'm sorry," he says. "I should never have forced you like that."

"It's all right," she says.

He runs his fingertips along the nightgown of clay. "I went for a walk this morning," he says, "and I found a dog lying in the middle of the road. It had been hit by a car and couldn't move. But it was still alive. I carried it to the side of the road. I lay down beside it while a storm passed over, and when I sat up it was dead."

She draws the robe more tightly around her legs.

"A man came by with a pickup truck and let me bring the dog home. I buried it this morning under the hydrangea tree."

She hunches her shoulders forward and rubs her arms.

"But the thing about the dog is it never cried," he says. "Do you remember any of it—the skating, the railroad tracks, the baseball?"

She tilts her chin up, as if thinking.

"I was remembering this morning," he says, "after I found the dog, that day you were hit with the puck on the cheekbone. Do you remember it? Sean had whacked it, and it caught you right under the eye. Your face turned white, but you didn't cry. I'll never forget it. You never made a sound."

She stands up and walks to the window, her back to him. Her arms are tightly wound over her chest.

"He was always in my bed," she says, "from the very beginning. He would lie down with me to tuck me in when I was little, and sometimes we would sleep side by side."

"You don't have to tell me," he says.

She rubs one of the panes with a finger. "She didn't like it, his being with me, but there wasn't anything she could do. She didn't want to touch me herself."

He watches her from the chair. She is making perfect circles on the glass.

"When I was older, she told him I was too old for him to be doing that. She could say it then, so he stopped. But she started working nights, and he came when she was away. It started then, when we both knew we were hiding from her."

As we have, he thinks suddenly but doesn't say.

She turns toward him, leans against the sill. "I never

said no, not the first time, not ever. It was what I had to offer him. To offer anyone."

He massages the sculpture in his hands. There is nothing he can say. He could say, *It wasn't your fault*, but the phrase seems meaningless, the world *fault* without reference. It is an intimacy he doesn't entirely comprehend. He knows there must be consequences, ramifications to this unnatural life she has had, and perhaps he could say it was this that made her the way she was then, but these would be shallow suppositions, made without understanding.

His eye falls to the chocolate floorboards by her feet. Somewhere on these floorboards, Jim died and Edith found him, and then his father found all of them. The ground lurches when he tries to bring Jim into focus. Soon his memories of Jim will have to be recast, redrawn again. And of Edith too, he thinks dizzily.

"Did she know?" he asks.

She doesn't answer him directly. She leans her head back against the window. "I've had all these years to ask *why*, and I still don't know the answer. I knew the answer better then; I could feel it. Now I can't. She wasn't cold to him. It wasn't that. He liked young girls. He needed to drink before he came to me, but he was always gentle, he never hurt me. It wasn't like you think. I don't know the word you would give it. I don't even remember his face now."

He puts the sculpture on the blotter, walks to where she is. He lays his hands on her shoulders, pulls her head to his chest. He is afraid to form the question, knowing that her answer will be permanent, unshakable. But he has to know.

"You'll come with me now," he says. He tries to say it casually, though she must hear his heart racing beneath his voice.

She doesn't make him wait. She nods, a small gesture.

The balloon inside his chest expands, bursts. He lifts

her, taking them both by surprise, and carries her to the bed. She is weightless, no longer resisting him. He drapes her gently on the pink bedspread. He sits on the edge of the bed, looking down at her, holding her by the wrist. Then he is bending over her, kissing her while he unties the sash at her waist. His hand finds her skin, and she moves to make room for him to lie beside her. He tries to free her arms from the robe, and she helps him. His stomach and chest are suffused with warmth—she must feel the heat radiating from his pores. He slides over her, hunkering down. She is feeling his face, reading him. He tastes the salt at the edge of the almond eye. She murmurs something he cannot quite make out. He thinks she is saying his name into his ear. She opens her thighs and guides him, and he feels, as she takes him in, a gathering there of more love than he thought was inside him. She moves against him slowly: there is no time against which to measure this. She has her arms hooked around his shoulders from underneath. He feels her curl a foot around his calf. Soon they will drive south on the thruway, toward the city. He will buy her clothes, and she will wear them, and she will cast her portraits in precious metals. He will make it up to her; he will give her what was taken from her. The bed creaks merrily and loudly under their double weight. He pictures a pair of ribald characters in a play he read somewhere years ago, and he wants to tell her of this lusty image. He bends his head down to kiss her breasts. He wants to tell her of the drive south, of all there is ahead of them. He is full of images, like bright bits in a kaleidoscope. They are with Billy, and Andrew is making pancakes for the three of them. They are under his mother's quilt on his bed in the city, drinking wine. They are in a concert hall, listening to a piano. He slides his mouth along her neck, reaches his hands down underneath her to hold her there.

But she is pushing at his shoulders. He doesn't understand. He is confused, thrust too quickly away from her, away from the images. He feels her fingernails cut into his skin.

He rises up to see her face, and there is terror there. He hears, too late then, what she has heard, on the floorboards. He whirls around to face the doorway.

Edith is standing just inside the door with something large and strange in her arms—a sight as incomprehensible and as meaningless in the universe they have just created as a code he will never decipher. He struggles for sense, for clarity. He hears Eden cry out behind him. Instinctively, he raises an arm, a hand, to separate himself from the apparition in the doorway, even as it brings the large and strange thing closer to its face. He wants to shout *Wait*, and perhaps he does. The adrenaline hits his thighs then, his calves. He leaps up.

It is the leap of an athlete, a left fielder grazing the sky for a fly ball, a goalie catapulted off the ice to make a save. He will catch the ball, the puck. He knows it. He cannot fail.

But it is not Andrew the gun is intended for.

SIX

THE NIP IN THE AIR TASTES OF COLD WATER. EVEN ON THIS second Saturday in September, he can see his breath, the steam rising from the mug of coffee. The maples are already turning, in the sunlight, a translucent pink, and he knows that down by the pond the leaves of the birches will be the color of brass.

He finds T.J. in the dining room of the Closes' house, standing with his hands in his pockets, surveying the stripped walls. The shades and curtains in the room have been removed, so that the sun makes the newly washed windows gleam. A few last remnants of the old paper, a mildewed and darkened pattern of cabbage roses, fill a plastic trash bag by the doorway.

"I brought you these," says Andrew, handing T.J. a pair of stained jeans and an old blue plaid flannel shirt. "And I brought you a cup of coffee."

"Thanks." T.J. cradles the coffee. "I called Didi, told her I'd be hanging out with you for a while. The kitchen looks great, by the way. Like an ad for *Country Living* or something."

Andrew laughs. But he is pleased with the kitchen. He

has sanded away the green paint on the walls and cabinets, replaced it with a semigloss white. He has torn up the cracked linoleum and sanded and refinished the wide old plank flooring underneath. He threw away the shades and gave the table and chairs to the Salvation Army. The kitchen is now pristine and simple, waiting for new owners to walk in and claim it. He likes standing in the center of the kitchen, drinking his morning coffee there. His only regret is that Eden cannot see what he has done. She has rubbed her bare feet along the satin finish of the floorboards, felt the glossy paint on the cupboards, smelled the fresh tang of new paint in the room. But he could tell, by looking at her face, that to her the room was still green and dark, still contained too many memories. After that day he did not ask her again to "see" his work, and she has not returned to her house, not even when he emptied and packed her own room. She stays now with him at the other house, across the yard.

T.J. finishes the cup of coffee and sets the mug on the sill. Andrew watches as T.J. strips off his brown leather jacket, his expensive safari pants and a vivid lime green and blue cotton sweater. He puts on the flannel shirt Andrew has brought, zips up the jeans.

"You look better," says Andrew. T.J. acknowledges the dubious compliment with a wry grimace.

Actually, Andrew is thinking, T.J. doesn't look well at all. His face has lost its color, and new vertical lines have appeared in the center of his forehead. Although his stylish clothes are the same, the panache seems to be gone.

"How is she?" asks T.J.

"Good. She's sleeping."

"I thought she looked very good when I came around . . . you know, right after. I woulda been back sooner, but you both looked like you needed to be left alone for a while."

"Thank you. We did. But it's better now."

T.J. surveys the dining room. "Where do I start?" he asks.

"I've got the walls down to the plaster, sanded the woodwork," says Andrew. "I'm going to paint the walls a linen white, do the trim in the same color, but a semigloss. I've only got one roller, though. Which would you rather tackle—the walls or the woodwork?"

"I can do the walls," says T.J.

"OK. Give me a hand with the dropcloth, then."

The two men unfold the dropcloth and draw it up to the baseboard. T.J. crouches down, opens a can of paint and begins to stir it with a wooden stick. Andrew, with his own can of paint, does the same.

"It was a great save, whatever you did," says T.J. "I've heard the story now twenty times, and each version is a little different. You're a goddamn hero in the town, you know that?" The statement is an invitation. T.J. looks at Andrew.

Andrew shrugs, a gesture that belies the memory of that moment—the many epiphanies in that single frozen leap.

"I hit the barrel with my hand," he says. "The shot deflected to the ceiling. Then I took the gun. In fact, when I did that, she just sat down."

He remembers how she walked to the chair, and how she folded her hands in her lap, resolutely refusing to look at Eden, who had, in the tussle, risen to her feet and was tying the sash of her robe. Andrew, naked, had held the gun, with the barrel pointing toward the floor, and had told Eden, in a voice that wasn't entirely composed, to go to the phone, dial the operator and ask for DeSalvo's number, then to call DeSalvo and ask him to come out at once. If he wasn't at home, to call the luncheonette. Curiously, his nakedness in front of Edith Close had caused him no embarrassment— in retrospect, he imagined it was because they had all passed, in an instant, onto another plane of guilt and shame—but he walked nevertheless to the chair on which Edith was sitting and lifted his clothes from behind her. He sat on the bed, the gun beside him, and dressed, his hands shaking so badly he couldn't tie his sneakers. He had said to Edith—feeling like a poseur with the gun now in his hands, slightly raised in her direction—to go down to the kitchen. Following her, not knowing exactly what would transpire when DeSalvo arrived, he began composing fragments of stories to see if they might hold, might be plausible, until he reached the kitchen and glanced at Eden, in her robe, at the table, and saw in her body and on her face that she knew that she was free now. She would say whatever she would say, whatever she had longed to say.

"You called the police?" asks T.J.

"I called DeSalvo. I thought I needed advice at that point more than I needed anything else. Later he called the police, and they came and got her."

"And she told the whole story?"

"No. It was Eden who did that. After they had taken Edith away, DeSalvo and I sat down with her, and she told us everything. She was very calm, very clear about it. It was a relief to her. . . ."

T.J. scrapes the drips off the paint stirrer, lays it on a piece of newspaper. He pours a measure of thick creamy liquid into the paint tray. "So it was Mrs. Close all along," he says.

Andrew nods, stands and holds his brush as steadily as he can against the strip of molding nearest the wall.

"She found them in bed together?" asks T.J. The question is rhetorical, or a request for confirmation. T.J. has heard this part of the story oft repeated now from people in the town. For the town, the revelations have been titillating and deeply satisfying, closing an unresolved chapter in its history.

"He was leaving Eden to go back to his own room because he knew Edith would be home soon, but she'd come earlier and they hadn't heard her."

"We all thought Mr. Close was at the movies and came home with Mrs. Close that night," says T.J.

"So she said."

"I guess no one was going to question the story of a grieving widow and a badly injured child."

"Well, they didn't."

Like a flashbulb popping in front of his eyes, the image of Edith Close being pushed to the ground by the ambulance attendants comes briefly into focus. He hesitates, then says to T.J., "They didn't think to question the grieving widow, because she really *was* grieving. You understand that it wasn't Jim she meant to shoot?"

Andrew is surprised by his own desire to tell T.J. these facts—after all, he and T.J. have so little in common now—but there is, in the telling, a kind of relief for himself too. Perhaps it is the shared activity of the work that brings on the atmosphere of confidence, or possibly seeing T.J. in old clothes.

T.J. puts the roller down, turns to Andrew. "And he got in the way?"

Andrew nods. "Something like that." Andrew wonders now if Jim, too, had leapt to make a save.

T.J. shakes his head, gives a low whistle. "She tried to kill her own daughter?"

Andrew nods. "His daughter."

T.J. stares at Andrew, trying to take this in. He turns, resoaks the roller in the tray, lifts it to begin another long strip. "You ever guess that about him?" he asks. "About him and Eden?"

It is a question Andrew has thought about in the three weeks since Eden told him about herself and her father. He knows the answer is no, he did not imagine this of Jim. And yet the clues may have been there, he now thinks. He remembers the way his mother would watch Jim caress his daughter on the steps. "Sickening," she would say, and he thought she meant Jim's indulgence. But perhaps she felt something else too, something she couldn't articulate or even bring to clarity in her thoughts.

"Watch for drips," says Andrew. He opens one of the windows to let out the paint fumes. Immediately, clean air fills his lungs. When he has finished the painting, he will rent the sander again and refinish the narrow oak floorboards. The Salvation Army has taken away the rug and the furniture—indeed, they have taken most of the furniture in the house. Almost nothing, apart from a mahogany sideboard in the dining room, was good enough for auction.

"T.J.," says Andrew. "There's something I feel bad about."

"What's that?"

"Well, for a while, maybe a half hour or a day—I can't remember—I thought it might have been you. Those guns . . ."

"Forget about it. You were under a lot of strain. You weren't thinking clearly."

"You didn't tell Sean, then?"

"No, and I don't know who did, though the news spread fast that morning. His father maybe. My guess is that Sean went crazy when he heard it, didn't know what he was doing."

Andrew watches the shiny paint cover the dull sanded surface. Painting, like mowing, he is thinking, is rewarding work. He cannot tell T.J. how obsessed he has become with this house—seized by the notion of transforming it, sanding it clean, airing it out so thoroughly that the past, like the paint fumes, will drift out the windows and be dissipated in the clean September air. The work has been pleasurable, apart from the one day he was forced to enter Edith's room and remove the belongings there. The room, with its drawn

248

shades, its bleak furnishings and its lone picture of Jim on a dresser, depressed him so much that he sat for long minutes on the worn bedspread, unable to proceed further. The worst moment was opening her top dresser drawer, as he had done in his own mother's bedroom. He was tempted merely to lift the entire contents into paper bags to take to her lawyer, to be given to Edith at the hospital with the suitcases of clothes, but a kind of prurient curiosity compelled him to linger over the items, fingering them, imagining them as clues to an enigmatic woman: a postcard from Jim from Buffalo, dated 1959; a pale blue nylon nightgown that appeared not to have been washed in years; a valentine from Jim that referred to an evening of intimacy; a certificate stating that Edith Close was a licensed practical nurse. Astonishingly, or perhaps not surprising at all, there was not a single trace in this dresser drawer, as there was in his own mother's drawer, that the woman had ever raised a child, that a daughter had ever shared her home. Not a single memento, school paper or photograph. He put the contents in a shopping bag and left the drawer open, unable and unwilling to touch it again.

"What'll happen to her, do you think?" asks T.J.

"You mean Edith?"

"Yeah."

"I think they'll put her away."

"The loony bin?"

"Probably. Even if it comes to trial, which I'm not sure it will do. Eden doesn't want that. No one really wants that."

"She's there now?"

"She's under observation. Sixty days."

He tries to picture Edith under observation, remembers her in the kitchen waiting for DeSalvo to come. She stood the entire time, refusing to sit at the table. Andrew still held the gun, though he knew it wasn't necessary. There was no place now that she would go.

He had not been in a room with the two grown women

before, and he thought how palpable the tension was between them, like an electric current running from the table
to the place where Edith stood, a current so alive he himself
did not want to intersect it. And yet the minutes in which
they waited for DeSalvo were silent ones. Neither woman
spoke to the other or turned her head in the other's direction.
Andrew felt his presence to be intrusive, foolish. He sensed
that even without him, the two of them would have waited
passively for whatever was to happen next. Indeed, the
shooting now seemed like a nonevent, something he might
have dreamed—so much so that he was mildly embarrassed
to see DeSalvo, overweight and breathless, sprint from his
tiny car to the back door, a revolver in hand. That gesture,
and his own posture with the gun, seemed hyperbolic—too
much for the small, plain kitchen. DeSalvo felt it too, first
looking wildly from face to face, then slowly lowering his
own gun. He had handcuffs, but Andrew said he was sure
they would not be necessary. He did think, though, that it
would be better if Edith was taken away from the house,
and it was then that DeSalvo called the police station. Again
they waited in the kitchen. DeSalvo had the sense not to ask
yet what had happened. Andrew thought that he should ask
DeSalvo if he wanted a cup of coffee. He longed to show
him the blown ceiling in the bedroom, to lend their vigil in
the kitchen credibility, but he knew that would have to wait
until the uniformed officers had come.

After a time, they heard the sirens. Andrew raised a
shade and saw two cars pull into the driveway. Men leapt
from opened doors as they had been trained to do, and at
once there were too many people in the kitchen. DeSalvo
took charge then, giving orders, and the tone of his voice and
the flashing lights outside reminded Andrew of the other time
when police cars had come to the two houses. A man took
Edith by the elbow, gently, as if she herself were the victim,

as if it were she who was in shock. She never said a word, never looked back, had no gesture of farewell for the woman at the table, the woman who was meant to be her daughter, the woman she had tried twice to rid herself of.

"But she still wants to sell the house?" asks T.J.

The question brings Andrew back to the present. "So she told her lawyer," he says. "Regardless of what happens, I don't think she'd be able to come back here. Not now."

"No."

T.J. lifts the roller, makes another straight sweep the length of the wall. "So where'd she get the gun?" he says.

Andrew catches a drip, stands back to study the color. "It was here," he says. "It was always here."

"Where?"

"You think the linen white is OK?"

T.J. looks over at the woodwork. "It looks fine to me."

Andrew dips the brush again into the paint. "In a trapdoor under the floorboards of Edith's bedroom closet," he says. "Jim had bought the gun years ago, in the same aimless way he bought everything. He had a farmhouse in a remote part of town, so he thought he should have a gun—just like the way he used to buy seeds and then never plant them. He taught Edith how to use it in case a burglar came while he was on the road, and he had my father build a box—a kind of safe—under the floorboards for him. The funny thing is I *remember* when my father did that. I hadn't realized, I don't think, that the box was for a gun, but when Eden told us about it I remembered the weekend my father built it. It was a joke in our house, how Jim had seen the plans in *Popular Mechanics* but, like always, got my father to do all the work."

"So Edith stashed the gun there after she shot Jim?"

Andrew stops painting, glances at T.J. He is aware of a

feeling of vague discomfort. It wasn't part of the story Eden told, or could have told. She'd have been unconscious then. The discomfort rises to a heat at the back of his neck.

"I don't know," he says to T.J. "She must have."

T.J. sets the roller in the trough, stands back to admire his work.

"Whaddya think?" he asks Andrew.

Andrew examines the wall. "Like a pro," he says.

"Feels good," says T.J. "I haven't done this kind of work in years. Tell you what. I'll do another wall for you, then I gotta go. Tom junior's got a soccer game." T.J. picks up the roller, starts on the second wall.

"I envy you, you know that?" he says.

"Envy me? Why?" asks Andrew.

"Starting fresh. Your life is like this room."

Andrew is about to speak, but T.J. cuts him off.

"Tell you the truth, I could use a fresh start right now."

"Why?" asks Andrew. He faces T.J., who is keeping his back to him.

"The till is empty, Andy-boy. Worse than empty, you follow me. I made some bad investments. . . ." There is a pause. "I may lose the house."

Andrew watches the deliberate way T.J. raises the roller, pretends to be smoothing over a rough spot. The flannel shirt is torn along the shoulder seam. He senses that it has cost T.J. to tell him this.

"Me and Didi, we're supported by what we have," says T.J. "That goes, and I don't know. I don't know how we'd be together without all the stuff, but I don't have good feelings about that. Sometimes I think the till is empty there too."

T.J. stands back to survey his work again, still avoiding Andrew's gaze.

"No one starts completely fresh," says Andrew carefully. T.J. says nothing. "I'm on a leave of absence now," Andrew adds, "but soon I'll have to go back to my job. Maybe not full time. In fact, probably not—as a consultant possibly. I have to have an income, and that's the most efficient way I know how to get one right now. I've got a son to provide for—whom I *want* to provide for. . . ." He thinks of Billy with a tightness in the center of his chest. This is now the longest he has ever been away from his son, but Andrew and Eden will drive to New York soon, and he will have Billy there. He knows that it will be hard for Billy to understand Eden's presence, but he cannot spare his son this. There are things now he cannot control, such as Martha's revelation, just a week ago, that she is getting married again— to a psychiatrist. She had planned to wait to tell him, she said, until she saw Andrew in person, but she had grown annoyed with his delays. Andrew found, over the phone, that he could not respond to this piece of news—immediately he was assaulted with visions of another man throwing grounders to Billy, another man tucking his son in at night. Andrew hopes the psychiatrist, whoever he is, will not be one of those shrinks who insist that everyone in the family unburden himself of his feelings. "I've got to see Eden settled," Andrew says, shaking off the insupportable image of another father for Billy, "with tutors or a good program for the blind. I want to get her set up with . . . Hang on a minute."

Andrew sets his brush down, retreats into the living room, reappears with an object in his hand.

"What do you think of this?" Andrew asks.

T.J. moves closer for a better look. He touches the surface, runs his fingers along the curve of the back, the straight chair back.

"That's beautiful. Where did you get it?"

"Eden made it. It's what she does."

"Jesus."

"But this is clay. She says it will break after a time. She's made dozens of them over the years. And they're all gone. When I think . . ."

"Can't you spray it with something to make it last?" asks T.J.

"I don't know much about the process, but I think it either has to be fired in a kiln, which she never had access to, or she could do them in wax, get them cast in a metal like bronze. My idea is to sell my condo, get us set up in a bigger place downtown, give her some room to do these."

"Yeah," says T.J. He raises his eyes from the sculpture to Andrew's face. The glance is brief but naked. Andrew sees, on his old friend's face, a look of envy mixed with regret. T.J. pulls away first, pivots toward the wall.

Andrew wraps the sculpture in newspaper, returns it to the carton in the living room. He and T.J. work in silence. T.J. paints three of the walls, leaving only the wall surrounding the window that opens onto the gravel drive. Then he changes back into his own clothes. He gives Andrew the jeans and shirt, as if handing over another persona, one he is reluctant to part with.

"Listen," he says to Andrew. "Later on, say four o'clock or so, you want to go for a run with me?"

Andrew accepts the clothes. He watches T.J. slip his arms into his leather jacket. T.J. lifts a pair of sunglasses from his pocket, puts them on. He seems to retrieve something with this gesture.

"Sure," says Andrew. "Why not? I'd like that."

T.J. rests a hand on Andrew's shoulder. He opens his mouth as if to speak, then seems to decide against it. Andrew follows him through the kitchen. He holds open the screen door as he watches T.J. saunter toward his Prelude. His walk is sharper now. T.J. leans against the car, twirls his keys.

He looks over at Andrew's house. "You've really done a lot for Eden. I mean, you've really saved her."

"No," Andrew says quickly. "I think it's the other way around."

T.J. looks up at the sky as if searching for a cloud. "Why didn't Eden leave?" he asks. "Why didn't she just get out?"

Andrew hesitates, but only for a second. "Where could she go?" he says. "What could she do?"

T.J. thinks, then slowly nods. "I'll be back around four," he says, folding himself neatly behind the wheel. Andrew watches the red car back out the drive and swing in the direction of town.

He lets the screen door slap behind him, stands on the stoop, his hands in the pockets of his jeans. The stoop is sturdy now; he finally repaired it last week. He leans against the railing and looks north over the cornfields—a crisp ocher against a bright blue sky. The answer is not sufficient, he knows. The true answer is one Andrew feels but cannot say. To know it as he does, T.J. would have to have seen Eden that first day Andrew came upon her in the kitchen. He could say it was guilt, complicity, fear of Edith's harming her again—but Andrew knows it is more than that. It was, he thinks, an absolute forfeit of will—a sacrifice made deliberately to survive her deprivation.

HE WALKS across the grass, deep green now and soon in need of cutting. The BMW in the driveway is growing dusty, as his father's Fords always were. Looking at it, he can't help but think of the first time he took Eden out in it, just two weeks ago. It was a clear day, crisp like this one, with the first real hint of fall. Perhaps it was the cooler temperatures, or a feeling it was time, but he knew when he woke that morning that he would take her out, that she was ready for an excursion. In the week since the aborted shooting, he had been to the mall and had bought her some clothes, so that she was wearing that day a new pair of jeans and a vivid blue-green sweater that he had picked because it matched the color of her eyes.

"We'll just drive," she said, seeking reassurance, when they got into the car.

"We'll see," he said, not committing himself, backing out the drive and turning onto the straight road through the farms and cornfields. He had discovered, in the short time he had been with her, that she responded to new experiences better if he simply announced that they were going to happen. Asking her if she wanted to do something was likely to make her anxious—though there had not been anything yet that he'd suggested that she hadn't, in the end, enjoyed.

There wasn't a lot of traffic on the road. He took the car up to sixty, edged it toward sixty-five. The clean air made the farms and the fields look washed, and he wished, as he knew he would wish a hundred thousand times in the years to come, that she could see what he could see. He was still tentative about verbal descriptions. He wasn't certain that they helped her—nor even if, after nineteen years, she could "see" his portraits. The visual world, he was coming now more fully to understand, would not be what they shared.

He pressed a button to lower the window on his side, so that she could feel the speed, the air, the day. The wind buffeted her hair; she raised a hand to keep it off her brow. Slowly, he lowered the window on her side, telling her that if it was too much for her, she should say so. Her hair, luminous when the sun hit it, swirled up and around her head like wild bits of silk. She tried to shelter her face with her hands, then gave up and sank back into the headrest. He took the car up to seventy. For the first time ever in his adult life, he wished he had a convertible.

He drove for an hour, changing direction, changing the

type of road when he could or when he had an inspiration. He took a small back road he knew was full of twists and turns, took it just a shade too fast so that she would feel it. She laughed when the centrifugal force pressed her up against the door; once she grabbed for something to hang on to, got the gearshift—he took her hand. He felt reckless, faintly like a teenager with his father's car, a thought he enjoyed—the vestigial memory of the boy pretending to be a man, with his girl beside him in the car—until the thought made him sad, and he put it away quickly: She had missed all of that, all that went with those years, and he would never, no matter how many times he took her out, no matter how fast he drove, be able to give it back to her.

After a time he took the straight road back, but when he reached the houses he said nothing and bypassed them. He looked to see if she knew, but she was still lying against the headrest, her eyes closed, and appeared to be lost to the sensation of the moving car. It wasn't until they got closer to town and passed a school playground, where there was a soccer game in progress on the field, that she leaned forward, listening.

"Where are we?" she asked.

"You'll see," he said.

She stayed bent forward, alert, listening now to the once familiar sounds of men with hedge clippers, children squealing to each other from bicycles, the slightly thicker traffic of a small village. He parked in front of the luncheonette.

"Where are we?" she said again.

"I thought we'd get some lunch."

"No," she said unequivocally, shaking her head.

"I don't have anything at the house to eat," he said.

"That's just an excuse."

"Look, it has to happen someday."

"Maybe, but not here, not now."

257

He sat back in the car, looked across to the gas station, thought a minute.

"I'm going in to have lunch," he said. "You can come with me or you can sit in the car."

He ran his finger along the humps in the steering wheel, waiting for an answer.

"All right," she said after a time.

He didn't know if the "All right" meant all right, she'd stay in the car, or all right, she'd go with him, so he decided to interpret the answer to his benefit. He walked around to her side of the car, opened the door. She hesitated, then got out. He took her hand.

"Trust me," he said.

"You've been saying that for days."

"Well?"

The shooting had happened only a week before; she was a celebrity, the source of rich gossip. Few had seen her in nineteen years, but with the exception of the Vietnamese man behind the counter, who would not have known who she was by sight, may not even have understood all of the stories that had passed from stool to stool that week, everyone in the place looked up, stared at Eden.

Without question, Andrew thought, there were times when he was glad she couldn't see.

But she knew. They took a table by the window, slightly away from the counter.

"Are they looking at me?" she asked, her head lowered.

"Lift your head up," he said. "Look at my voice."

She did so.

"DeSalvo's here," he said. The former police chief had waved when they entered. He would give them a minute, Andrew knew, then come over, a gesture of solidarity as much as of friendship.

"And some men I don't know, and . . . ah . . ."

"Who?"

"Henry O'Brien," he said quickly.

"Oh," she said.

O'Brien was glaring at Andrew and Eden, as though frozen, as though stricken by the sight of an unwelcome vision from the past. The other men, politely, had gone back to their sandwiches—though Andrew noticed that they contrived, by reaching for the salt or the napkin dispenser, to look surreptitiously in Eden's direction. Only O'Brien continued to stare openly.

"Will he cause a scene?" asked Eden.

"No," said Andrew. "I don't think so." But the truth was, he didn't know. O'Brien's eyes were rheumy; he'd already been drinking. There was a slow wave of anger moving across his brow.

The Vietnamese man came to the table. Andrew read Eden the menu from the blackboard. "I recommend the Turkey Health Club, but not the Pepsi," Andrew said to her.

"Fine," she said.

Andrew ordered.

"Raise your head. Look at my voice, " Andrew said again to Eden.

She did so, but she kept her face tilted slightly toward the window, away from the men.

"You're beautiful," Andrew said. "You have nothing to be ashamed of."

She shrugged.

"You're the most beautiful woman in here," he said.

She grimaced, then smiled. "It sounds to me like I'm the only woman in here," she said.

"Well, there's that," he said, enjoying her smile.

Out of the corner of his eye, he saw O'Brien put his leg to the floor, about to stand. Andrew stiffened but kept his gaze on Eden. He hadn't known O'Brien would be here; he should have looked before he brought Eden in.

O'Brien swiveled, bent to stand, swayed a bit. Even if

Andrew wanted to get Eden out, there wasn't time. For one incredible moment, he actually thought he might have to fight O'Brien. He tried to envision the scene, could not imagine himself landing a punch on the man's face.

But DeSalvo had seen O'Brien move too, perhaps even before Andrew had. "Henry," DeSalvo said, instantly behind O'Brien, slapping the red-haired man on the back, lowering him onto the stool. "How ya doin'? How ya doin'?"

O'Brien, momentarily restrained by DeSalvo's beefy hand, mumbled something Andrew couldn't hear.

"Al, cup a coffee for my friend Henry here," DeSalvo said in a loud voice, so that all could hear. "Talk to you in a bit, Henry, but I gotta go say hello to my friend Andy before he blows town."

DeSalvo walked to Andrew's table and, in a gesture that took Andrew by surprise, bent to kiss Eden's cheek, the way a man like DeSalvo might casually greet the wife of an old friend.

"Thank you," Andrew said, meaning O'Brien but also the kiss.

"Mean son of a bitch," said DeSalvo under his breath, "but I'll give you some advice." DeSalvo stood to his full height, hitched his navy blue jogging pants. "You enjoy your sandwiches," he said. "Take your time. That's OK. But Henry's a powder keg even under the best of circumstances, you follow me."

Andrew nodded. He watched DeSalvo return to the place where O'Brien was sitting, take the outside stool, so that he was blocking O'Brien's view of Eden. Andrew could just see the back of O'Brien's head, the longish hair curling over the collar of his jacket, the bright pink skin leading to his ear. No one could help O'Brien now. That was damage that could not be erased, undone.

When DeSalvo had gone, Eden took a bite from her sandwich and said, "I told you it was a bad idea."

He looked across at her. Her hair had taken a beating from the wind. Another woman would have combed her hair in the car before going into the luncheonette. Andrew realized that he would have to be alert to these small gestures for her. The blue-green sweater, a loose cotton, hung neatly from her shoulders, exposing a small white crescent of skin at the neckline. She had the sleeves pushed to the elbows. He reached for her wrist, rubbed the back of her hand. His heart lifted at the sight of her across from him, raising the sandwich to her lips, her hair framed by a Coca-Cola poster behind her—lifted at the thought of the two of them doing something as ordinary as eating in a luncheonette.

Andrew took a bite of his own sandwich.

"It wasn't entirely a bad idea," he said.

WHEN HE enters his own house, he listens for sounds of movement, hears none. There are dishes in the sink he must wash later. He walks through the house and up the stairs, making his way quietly along the floorboards of the hallway, thinking he will not wake her yet. But when he enters his mother's room and sees her lying beneath the quilt, her hair in a braid that trails along the pillow, he cannot resist the impulse to sit on the bed beside her. She stirs slightly, and he says, *It's Andrew*. She smiles in her sleep, before she comes fully to consciousness.

He looks at his watch. He *should* wake her now, he thinks. He has discovered, sleeping with her, that she has lost the common distinction between night and day. She sleeps only three or four hours at a stretch, twice a day, often getting up to prepare herself a meal at three in the morning. He would like to retrain her to a rhythm they could share.

"Where have you been?" she asks drowsily, reaching immediately to touch some part of him. It is her way of looking at him, making contact. She rubs a hand along the cloth of his sleeve by her side.

"I've been with T.J. He came by for a visit, stayed to help with the dining room. You should wake up now. It's nearly noon."

She smiles again. He thinks she is sometimes amused by his efforts to guide her into a normal routine. He wonders if this effort on his part isn't his way of reclaiming for himself some sense of order in his small universe. These have been extraordinary days, extraordinary events, beyond his ken—brought now barely under control.

She yawns, bringing a hand to her mouth.

"I'm hungry," she says.

"Good," he says.

He walks to the window, lifts it open. "It's a fantastic day," he says. "Can you feel it?"

He bends, peers down into the yard. Perhaps it is looking through the encrusted screen that does it—that makes the sound come unbidden into his thoughts. The dream *did* get it right, he realizes suddenly. It was through his own sodden sleep that he first heard a woman's voice cry out, and he thought it might have been his mother. Then there was the second cry, a hoarse shout, that of a grown man, and immediately the frightened squeal of another female, a child still, as he himself was then. And finally, after the shots, the reedy, high-pitched wail, the tendril of smoke rising to the sky, gathering momentum—the anguished voice of Edith Close. He hears again the terrible keening.

"Eden," he says too loudly, shaking off the other sound. "There's something I have to ask you."

"What?" She props herself up and raises the quilt to cover her bare arms. The chill from the day outside has reached her. He returns to the bed, sits on the edge beside her.

"After Edith shot Jim, what did she do with the gun? I mean, how did she get rid of it so fast? My father was there within minutes."

She hugs the quilt around her. She says nothing.

"Eden?"

"I wish you wouldn't ask this," she says.

"Why?"

She doesn't answer him. He waits.

"Tell me," he says. "I have to know."

"It was your father," she says quickly. "It was your father."

"My father?" He lifts his head up sharply to look at her. "My father?" he asks again, unconsciously mimicking her.

She bites her lip, then releases it, giving up a last parcel.

"He saw what she had done, thought he knew why she had done it. Maybe he knew or had sensed it, about Jim. He took the gun and put it back in the box he had built. After the police had finished with him the next day, he came and got it and kept it in his garage. I think he thought she shouldn't go to jail for shooting him. It would have repulsed him, about Jim and me. He didn't guess, then or ever, that it wasn't Jim she meant to kill."

"Did Edith tell you this?" he asks.

She turns her face to him. "We'd long passed the point of having secrets," she says.

Andrew tilts his head back to study the ceiling. He sees his father's face, returning across the gravel drive, the barrel of the rifle limp along his leg. Will there be no memories, no portraits, left intact? His imagination skids out from under him, careens around the room.

"And my mother?" he asks finally. "Did she know?"

Eden nods.

Andrew says nothing, waits.

"After your father died, she came to the back door with the gun. She said, 'I don't have to have this anymore,' and she left."

There is a clock on his mother's dresser. He can hear it ticking. He sees his mother bent over the other side of the bed, making the bed, smoothing the quilt, looking up at him. Already there is something in her posture, in her face, that has changed forever. He remembers the way she would turn away from him, deflect him, whenever he asked about Eden. In time Eden will tell him other stories, small stories of this conversation or that, of that event or this, so that away from them, the houses, too, will change, and the landscape of his childhood will grow branches, sprout wings.

"Is there anything else?" he asks.

"No."

"Would you ever have told me if I hadn't asked?"

"I don't know. I was hoping you wouldn't ask, but I don't know about ever."

From where he is sitting he can see most of the room— the room in which his parents slept, made love, created him: the two screen windows, the pale green wallpaper, the light overhead on the ceiling. Did his parents lie here arguing in suppressed whispers, he wonders, trying to comprehend and possess the object his father had taken to the garage? An object that would alter the homely pattern of their days, that would not let itself be forgotten for even one day, no matter how deeply hidden? And would his father have confided his vision of the scene he had witnessed, his understanding of that horror?

Eden's hairbrush is on his mother's dresser now; his own toilet kit and a list he has written are on his father's. Some of his clothes are still in his suitcase on the floor, hers in a carton on the chair. They will leave soon, drive south to the city.

He slips his hand under the quilt, finds the hem of Eden's nightgown and raises it to her waist. He lays his hand on the flat of her belly, feeling the warmth there. He likes to imagine it is already rounded, swollen, but he knows it may be weeks yet before the shape will change. He is impatient for this to happen, impatient for the visible signs.

"This is everything," he says, touching her.

Her face is ripe with sleep or her condition. She lays her own fingers over his where they are resting.

He leans forward to kiss her at the side of her face. As he does so, he moves into a patch of sunlight coming through the window, forming a bright square on the pillow and the headboard. The sun hits the side of his face, warms his face with its heat. He shuts his eyes. He feels her skin with his mouth, under his hand.

If only his luck will hold, he is thinking.

Your hands erase the memory of others.

A part of you is inside me, and I will always have that.

You have made me give up all the secrets, and I am lighter now.

You talk of days stretching after days, and you believe in them. I do not believe in them, but I believe in this day.

Your mother's quilt has a sweet smell. She had secrets too, and she is lighter, glad that I have told them.

Your face shimmers in the water, and I sometimes think that I can see it.

I will feel and smell my baby, but I will never see its face.

We will leave this place and not come back, and in our dreams it will turn to dust.

Strange Fits
of Passion

Once Again, for John

Strange fits of passion have I known:
And I will dare to tell . . .

William Wordsworth

On my book tours, I am often asked a number of questions: Did he really do it? Do I think that she was justified? Did they do it for the money or for love?

Then, inevitably, the questions come around to me. Why do I write the kind of books I do? they want to know. Why did I become a journalist?

My books are about crimes—cold-blooded acts of treachery or messy crimes of passion—and perhaps some think it strange for a woman to be as interested in violence as I am. Or they wonder why I chose a profession in which I have to spend most of my time chasing down unpleasant facts or asking people questions they'd rather not have to answer.

Sometimes I say that my job is like being a private detective, but usually I answer (my standard, pat answer) that I think I became a journalist because my father was a journalist.

My father was the editor of a newspaper in a small town in western Massachusetts. The paper was called the *East Whatley Eagle,* and it wasn't much of a paper, even in its heyday in the early 1960s. But I thought then, as daughters do, that my father knew a lot about his profession, or his trade, as he preferred to call it.

"The story was there before you ever heard about it," he would say before sending me, his only child and a teenager then, out to cover a theft from a local store, or a fire in a farmer's hayloft. "The reporter's job is simply to find its shape."

My father taught me almost everything about the newspaper business: how to edit copy, set type, sell ads, cover a town meeting. And I know he hoped I would stay in East Whatley and one day take over his press. Instead I disappointed him. I left western Massachusetts and moved to New York City. I went to college there and to graduate school in journalism and then to work for a weekly newsmagazine.

But I did not forget my father or what he had said to me. And in the years after I moved to the city—years in which I wrote articles for the newsmagazine, wrote a book based on one of the articles, which brought me a fair amount of both fame and money, and then made a career for myself as a writer of nonfiction books, almost all of which feature a detailed investigation of a complex crime—I have had to ask myself why it really was that I followed in my father's footsteps. Why, for instance, did I not choose architecture or medicine or college teaching instead?

Because I have learned that it isn't simply a matter of the journalist and the facts, as my father believed and would have had me believe and practice, but rather a case of the storyteller and the story—an ancient dilemma.

Precisely, the difficulty is this.

2

Once the storyteller has her facts, whether they be told to her or be a product of her investigations, what then does she do with her material?

I have thought long and hard about this question. Perhaps I have even been, at times, obsessed with the problem. So I suppose it wasn't so surprising that I was thinking about just this very thing as I sat across the room from the young woman who was perched on the edge of her narrow bed.

I hadn't been in a dormitory room for years—not since my own graduation from Barnard, in 1965. But though the posters on the walls were of rock groups I had never heard of, and there was a telephone and a Sony Walkman on a shelf, the essential facts of the room were not all that different from my own surroundings in college: a desk, a single chair, a bookcase, a bed, a quart of orange juice chilling on a windowsill.

It was February, in the first year of the new decade, and it was snowing lightly outside the window, a gray snow shower that wouldn't amount to much, though the people in this college town in central Maine had not, I had learned earlier at the local gas station, seen the grass since early November.

The young woman sat with her sneakers planted evenly on the floor and her arms crossed over her chest. Not defiantly, I thought, but carefully. She was wearing blue jeans (Levi's, not designer jeans) and a gray cotton sweater with a long-sleeved white T-shirt underneath.

I'd met the girl's mother only twice, but one of those times had been an important occasion, and I had needed, for professional reasons, to remember her mother's face. The daughter's hair was the same—a deep red-gold. But

3

the eyes were distinctly her father's eyes—dark and deep-set. They might actually have been black eyes, but the light was bad, and I couldn't tell for sure.

Whatever else the parents had or had not given the daughter—attributes and traits I would never know about—they had given her an extraordinary beauty. It lay, I saw, in the mix of the white skin and the red hair juxtaposed with the dark eyes—a combination, I thought, that must be rare.

She was prettier than I'd ever been, just as her mother had been before her. I have what might be called a handsome face, but it's become plainer in my forties. Years ago, when I was in college, I'd worn my hair long too, but now I keep it short and easy.

Because she was a natural beauty, I was surprised that she wore no makeup and had her hair pulled severely back into a ponytail, as if she meant to minimize whatever attractions she had. She sat warily on the bed. I was pretty sure that she would know who I was even though we had never met.

She'd offered me the only chair in the room. The package I'd brought was uncomfortable in my lap, and I felt its weight. It was a weight I'd been feeling off and on for years and had driven a very long way to rid myself of.

"Thanks for seeing me," I said, acutely aware of the generation between us. She was nineteen, and I was forty-six. I could have been her mother. I was rather sorry I'd worn my gold jewelry and my expensive wool coat, but I knew that it was more than age or money that separated us.

"I read about your mother," I said, trying to begin

again, but she shook her head quickly—a signal, I could see, not to continue.

"I've known who you were for years," she said hesitantly, in a soft voice, "but I didn't think . . ."

I waited for her to finish the sentence, but when she didn't I broke the silence.

"A long time ago," I said, "I wrote an article about your mother. You were just a baby then."

She nodded.

"You know about the article," I said.

"I've known about it," she said noncommittally. "Do you still work for that magazine?"

"No," I said. "It doesn't exist anymore."

Although I didn't, I could have added that the magazine no longer existed because it had been run on a system that had been ridiculously expensive: Writers, based in New York, had traveled widely to report and write their own lengthy features on the most pressing stories of the week. The magazine had not used foreign bureaus, as successful newsweeklies do today, but instead had sent its writers into the field. The expense accounts had been magnificent and legendary and had eventually led to the demise of the magazine, in 1979. But I was gone by then.

Outside her door, in a corridor, I could hear laughter, then a shout. The young woman looked once at the door, then back at me.

"I have a class," she said.

Although her eyes were dark, by then I'd decided that they were not exactly like her father's eyes. His had been impenetrable, and while hers had gravity, more gravity than I'd have thought possible in a girl only nineteen years old, they were clear and yielding.

I wondered if she had a boyfriend, or girlfriends, or if she played sports or was a good student. I wondered if she, too, kept a journal, if she had inherited her mother's talents, or her father's.

"This belongs to you," I said, gesturing to the package.

She looked at the parcel on my lap.

"What is it?" she asked.

"It's the material I used to write the article. Notes, transcripts, that sort of thing."

"Oh," she said, and then, "Why?"

There was a pause.

"Why now? Why me?"

"I know your mother probably told you what happened," I answered quickly, "but in here there is more. . . . In here your mother makes a reference to the story she would one day tell her child, and I thought that if she didn't have a chance to do that, well, here it is."

All week I'd rehearsed those sentences, so often that I'd almost come to believe them myself. But now that the words lay between us, it was all I could do to keep from telling her that this was not the real reason I'd come, not the real reason at all.

"I don't know," she said, looking steadily at the package.

"It belongs to you," I said. "I don't need it anymore."

I stood up and walked across the small space that separated us. My boot heels clicked on the wooden floor. I put the package on her lap. I returned to my chair and sat down.

I was thinking that in a short while I could leave the dorm, walk to my car, and drive back to Manhattan. I had a co-op there on the Upper West Side that was roomy enough and had a good view of the Hudson. I had my work, a new book I was beginning, and my friends. I'd never married, and I didn't have any kids, but I had a lover, an editor with the *Times*, who sometimes stayed with me.

My friends tell me I'm the kind of woman who lives for her work, but I don't think that's entirely true. I'm rather passionate about physical exercise and opera, in equal doses, and I've always liked men for their company. But since I decided early on not to have children, I've found it hard to see the point of marriage.

I'd wrapped the package in brown paper and sealed it with Scotch tape. I watched as she undid the tape and opened the package. I had let it begin with the memo. I'd included everything.

"I don't have your mother's handwritten notes," I said. "These are my typewritten transcriptions. I've always found it easier to work from typescript than from handwriting, even my own. And as for the rest, it's all here, just as I heard it."

But she wasn't listening to me. I watched her read the first page, then the second. She had shifted her weight slightly, so that she rested on a hand at her side. I shook open my coat. I suppose I'd hoped that she'd glance at a sentence or two, or would flip through the pages, and then would look up at me and thank me for coming or say again that she had a class. But as I sat there, she kept reading, turning pages quietly.

I thought about her class and wondered if I should mention it.

I heard another commotion in the corridor, then silence.

I sat there for about ten minutes, until I realized that she meant to read the entire batch of notes, right there and then.

I looked around the room and out the window. It was still snowing.

I stood up.

"I'll just go for a walk," I said to her bent head. "Find myself a cup of coffee."

I paused.

"Should I . . . ?"

I stopped.

There wasn't any point in asking her if I should come back. I knew now that it would be irresponsible not to, not to be there for her reaction and to answer her questions. And then I had a moment's sudden panic.

Maybe I shouldn't have come, I thought wildly. Maybe I shouldn't have brought the package.

But I had long ago trained myself to deal with panic attacks or doubts. It was simple. All I had to do was force myself to think about something else. Which I did. I thought about how I ought to find a motel room now, and after that a place to eat.

She glanced up at me, her eyes momentarily glazed from her reading. I saw that her hand, turning a page, was shaking.

She looked at me as if I were a stranger who had not

yet entered her room. I could only guess at what she was thinking, what she was hearing, and what she feared.

Yet I knew better than anyone else all about this particular story and the storyteller, didn't I?

And all about the storyteller who came after that . . .

The Notes
and
Transcripts

From: Helen Scofield
To: Edward Hargreaves
Re: The Maureen English story
Date: August 2, 1971

I think we can go ahead with the English piece now, and I'd like your OK on this. If you recall, when I last mentioned it a month ago, I thought we were going to have to kill it because I couldn't get to Maureen English, or "Mary Amesbury," as she now calls herself. I had gone up to Maine with the idea of interviewing her for the piece. I visited St. Hilaire and interviewed a number of the townspeople there and got some good background material. Then I drove to South Windham to see Maureen. I'd met her only once before. She had left the magazine just before I had really come on board. I'd seen Harrold around, of course. I knew him to speak to, but not much more than that.

Maureen met with me, but wouldn't agree to talk to me. I tried everything I could think of to persuade her, but I just couldn't get her to open up. I drove home feeling pretty disappointed. I thought I had a great story, but without her there were just too many holes.

I started work on the Juan Corona story and tried to forget about the English piece. Then, last week, I received a package in the mail. It's a series of notes written by "Mary Amesbury." There are shorter ones, and then some longer ones. It is, I suppose you could say, a kind of journal to

13

herself and for herself, except that in her notes she is sometimes writing to me. Apparently the tape recorder or my
presence in the visitors' room had put her off, but back
in the privacy of her cell she was able to write her story
down. I think that I must have reminded her of her former
life, and that had put her off too.

Actually I'm not sure what it is that she's sent me. I do
think, however, that the basic facts are here, and I'm
pretty sure I can do the piece with this and the interviews
from the others I've already got. I know it's unorthodox,
but I'd like to give it a try. I've received just the one package, but she says that she'll be sending others.

I'm quite drawn to this story. I'm not sure why, except
for the obvious. It's got a lot of strong, raw elements, but
I think that if handled discreetly, it could be a fantastic
piece. And I'm not sure that the issues involved in this
story have really been dealt with before by the media. That
alone seems to me a good reason for tackling it. I think
that it's particularly interesting that this could happen to
them. I know we were all stunned when we found out
what had been going on. And then, of course, there's the
inside angle—the fact that they both worked here. I'm
thinking of in the vicinity of 5,000 words if you can give
me the space.

I should tell you right off that I couldn't get to Jack
Strout. He positively refused to talk to me. But I think the
story can be done without my interviewing him.

Let me know what you think. I'd like to get started on this
right away.

December 3 – 4, 1970

———————

Mary Amesbury

I was driving north and east. It was as far east as I could go. I had an image in my mind that sustained me—of driving to the edge and jumping off, though it was just an image, not a plan. Along the road, near the end, there were intermittent houses. They were old and weathered, and on many the paint was peeling. They rose, in a stately way, to peaked roofs and had els at the back that sometimes leaned or sagged. Around these beautiful houses were objects that were useful or might be needed again: a second car, on blocks; a silver roll of insulation; a rusted plow from the front of a pickup truck, set upon a snowy lawn like an inadvertent sculpture. The new houses were not beautiful—pink or aqua gashes on a hillside—but you understood, driving past them, that a younger, more prosperous generation (the snowmobiles and station wagons) lived in them. These houses would have better heat and kitchens.

The town that I had picked lay at the end of the road.

I came upon it like a signpost in a storm. There was an oval common, a harbor, a white wooden church. There was, too, a grocery store, a post office, a stone library. At the eastern edge of the common, with their backs to the harbor, stood four tall white houses in varying stages of disrepair. In the harbor there were lobster boats, and at the end of a wharf I saw a squat cement building that looked commercial. I thought it promising that the essentials of the town could be taken in at a glance.

I parked across the street from the store. The sign said Shedd's, over a Pepsi logo. In the window there was another sign, a list: Waders, Blueberry Rakes, Maple Syrup, Magazines, Marine Hardware. And to its right there was a third sign—a faded relic from a local election: Vote for Rowley. A boy in a blue pickup truck, parked by the Mobil pump out front, brought a paper coffee cup to his lips, blew on it, and looked at me. I turned away and put my hand on the map, folded neatly on the passenger seat. I put my finger on the dot. I thought I was in a town called St. Hilaire.

The village common to my right was shrouded in snow. The light from a four o'clock December sun turned the white surface to a faint salmon. Behind the steeple of the church at the end of the green, a band of red sliced the sky between the horizon and a thinning blanket of clouds. The crimson light hit the panes of glass in the windows on the east side of the common, giving the houses there a sudden brilliance, a winter radiance. Yet I noticed, above the wooden door of the church, the odd graceless note of an electric cross lit with blue bulbs.

The storm was over, I thought, and was moving east, out to sea. The street in front of Shedd's had been plowed, but not to the pavement. I imagined I could actually see the cold.

I shook open the map and laid it over the seat, with Maine crawling up the backrest. With my finger I traced the route I had driven, from my parking place at Eightieth and West End, up the Henry Hudson and out of New York City, onto the parkways that led to the highways, along the highways and across the states and finally north and east to the coast of Maine. In ten hours, I had put nearly five hundred miles between myself and the city. I thought it might be far enough. And then I thought: *It will have to be.*

I turned to see my baby. She was sleeping in the baby basket in the back seat. I looked at her face—the pale eyelashes, the reddish wisps of hair curling around the woolen hat, the plump cheeks that even then I could not resist reaching back to stroke, causing Caroline to stir slightly in her dreams.

The stuffy warmth from the car heater was fading. I felt the cold at my legs and pulled my woolen coat more tightly to my chest. The horizon appeared now to be on fire. Gray swirls of clouds above the sunset mimicked smoke rising from flames. Along the common, the lights in the houses were turned on, one by one, and as if in invitation, someone inside Shedd's snapped on a bulb by the door.

I leaned against the seat back and looked across at the houses. The windows at the fronts were floor-to-ceiling rectangles with wavy panes of glass. The windows that were lit reminded me of windows I used to look into when I was a girl walking home after dark in my town. The windows of the houses there—warm, yellow frames of

19

light—offered glimpses of family rituals hidden in the daytime. People would be eating or preparing supper, and I would see them gathered round a table, or I would watch a woman, in a kitchen, pass through a frame, and I would stand in the dark on the sidewalk, looking in, savoring those scenes. I would imagine myself to be a part of those tableaux—a child at the dining table, a girl with her father by a fireplace. And even though I knew now that families framed by windows are deceptive, like cropped photographs (for I never saw during those childhood walks a husband berating a wife or hitting a child, or a wife crying in the kitchen), I looked across the common and I thought: If I were in one of those houses now, I'd be sitting in a wooden chair in the kitchen. I'd have a glass of wine beside me, and I'd be half-listening to the evening news. Caroline would be in an infant seat on the table. I would hear my husband at the door and watch as he kicked the snow off his boots. He would have walked home from . . . (Where? I looked down the street. The building on the wharf? The library? The general store?) He would crouch down to pet a honey-colored cat, would bend to nuzzle the baby on the table, would pour himself a glass of wine, and would slide his hand across my shoulders as he took his first sip. . . .

I stopped. The image, filled as it was with critical falsehoods, was a balloon losing air. I looked at my face in the rearview mirror, quickly turned away. I put on an oversized pair of dark glasses to hide my eyes. I draped my scarf over my hair and wrapped it around the lower part of my face.

I looked up again at the simple white houses that lined

the common. There was snow on the porches. I was thinking: *I am a settler in reverse.*

I know you are surprised to hear from me. I think that I was rude to you when you came to visit. Perhaps it was the tape recorder—that intrusive black machine on the table between us. I have never liked a tape recorder. It puts a person off, like a lie detector. When I was working, I used a notebook and a pencil, and sometimes even that would make them nervous. They'd look at what you wrote, not at your face or eyes.

Or perhaps it was your presence in that sterile and formal visitors' room. There was something that you did that reminded me of Harrold. Sometimes he would sit, as you did yesterday, your legs crossed, your face expressionless, your fingers tapping the pencil lead on the table, quietly, like a brush on a snare drum.

But you're not like Harrold, are you? You're just a reporter, as I was once—your hair pinned back behind your ears; your summer suit wrinkled across your lap—just trying to do your job.

Or possibly it was simply the process itself. You'd think that I'd be used to that by now, wouldn't you? But the problem is that I know too much about how it works. I'd be talking to you, and you would seem to be looking at me, but I would know that you were searching for your lede, listening for the quotes. I would see it on your face. You wouldn't be able to relax until you'd got your story, had seen its center. You'd be hoping for a cover, would be thinking of the length. And I'd know that the story you would write would be different from the one I'd tell.

Just as the one I am going to tell you no   will be different from the one I told my lawyer or the court. Or the one I will one day tell my child.

My baby, my orphan, my sweet girl . . .

I took the name of Mary, like a nun, though without a nun's grace, but you will know that, just as you will know that I am twenty-six now. You'll have seen the clips; you'll have read the files.

You'll describe me in your piece, and I wish you didn't have to, for I can't help seeing myself as you must have seen me the day you came to visit. You'll say that I look older than my years, that my skin is white, too washed out, like that of someone who hasn't seen the sun in weeks. And then there is my body, shapeless now in this regulation jumpsuit, and only two or three people, reading your article, will ever know how it once was. I don't believe that any man will ever see my body again. But that's hardly important now, is it?

I know that you're probably wondering why it is that I've decided to write to you, why I've agreed to tell my story. I have asked myself the same question. I could say that I am doing this because I don't want a single other woman to endure what I went through. Or I could tell you that having been a reporter, I suffer from a reporter's craving—to tell my own story. But these explanations would be incorrect, or only partially correct. The true answer is simpler than that, but also more complex.

I am writing this for myself. That's all.

When I lived it, I couldn't clearly see my way. I understood it, and yet I didn't. I couldn't tell this story to anyone, just as I couldn't answer your questions when you came to visit. But when you left, I went looking for a piece of paper and a pen. Perhaps you are a good reporter after all.

If you can find the facts in my memories, in these incoherent ramblings, you are welcome to them. And if I tell this story badly, or get the dialogue wrong, or tell things out of sequence, you will hear the one or two things that are essential, won't you?

When I opened the door to Shedd's, a bell tinkled. Everyone in the store—a few men, a woman, the grocer behind the counter—looked up at me. I was holding Caroline, but the glare of the fluorescent lights and the sudden heat of the store were confusing to me. The lights began to shimmer, then to spin. The woman standing by the front counter took a step forward, as if she might be going to speak.

I looked away from her and moved toward the aisles.

They'd been talking when I walked in, and they started up again. I heard men's voices and the woman's. There was something about a sudden gale and a boat lost, a child sick with the flu and not complaining. For the first time, I heard the cadence of the Maine accent, the vowels broadened, the *r*'s dropped, the making of two syllables out of simple words like *there*. The words and sentences had a lilt and a rhythm that was appealing. The accent grows on you like an old tune.

The store was claustrophobic—you must know the kind I mean. Did you see it when you were in St. Hilaire? A rack of potato chips and pretzels had been squeezed next to a cooler of fresh produce. There were two long rows of cereal boxes and canned goods, but at least half the store appeared to be given over to shelves of objects associated with fishing. I moved along to the back wall and picked up a quart of milk. I held the baby and the milk in one arm and slid a packaged coffee cake into my free hand from the bread aisle. Walking to the front of the store, I passed a cooler filled with beer. I quickly snagged a six-pack with my finger.

When I returned to the front of the store, a man was at the counter, a man about my age and about my height. He had a handlebar mustache and was wearing a denim jacket and a Red Sox baseball cap. The jacket was tight in the shoulders, and I doubted it would button across his waist. It seemed like a jacket he had worn for years—it had a frayed and soft look—but now he had gained a bit of weight across his middle, and the jacket was too small. He wore a navy-blue sweater, and he moved his feet while he stood there. He seemed jazzed up, nervy, in perpetual motion. He tapped a beat on the counter, where he had placed a package of fish cakes, a can of baked beans, a six-pack of beer, and a carton of cigarettes. I thought he must be cold in such a thin jacket.

Across the counter was the grocer, an older man—in his late fifties? He had discolored teeth, from cigarettes or coffee, and an ocher chamois shirt that had an ink stain, like a Rorschach, on the pocket. He rang up the purchases on the counter with only one eye on the cash register. The other one was glass and seemed to be staring at me. My scarf was slipping from my hair; I had my arms full and couldn't fix it.

The only woman in the store was standing by the coffeemaker and reading *The Boston Globe.* She was wearing a green hand-knit sweater and a taupe parka. She was an impressive woman, not fat, but tall and big-boned, and I thought it was possible, though she was well-proportioned, that had she stepped on a scale, she'd have outweighed the grocer. Her eyes were watery in color, bluish, and her eyebrows nearly nonexistent in a roughened face of high color. Her teeth were large and very white, and there was a slight gap between the front two—a trait I would see often in the townspeople. Perhaps you saw it too. Her hair was graying, clipped short, in a style I would describe as sensible. I thought she was probably fifty, but I also thought she was a woman who had early on settled into a look that would last her many years. When she turned the pages of her newspaper, she looked up at me.

"That's five hundred and eighty-two dollars," said the grocer.

The man with the handlebar mustache took his wallet out of his back pocket and smiled at the weak joke. He handed the grocer a ten-dollar bill and began to speak to him. I may not have the dialogue quite right, but I remember it like this:

"Everett Shedd, you're goin' to make me a poor man."

"Don't be bellyachin' to me, Willis. You're poor all by yourself."

"That's so. It's a bitch season. Jesus. There in't a man in town makin' a dime this time a year."

"You pull your boat yet?"

"No; I'll do it on the fifteenth, like I do every year. Tryin' to eke out a coupla more miserable weeks, though the pickin's is pitiful."

"Don't get sour on me, Willis. You're too young to get sour."

"I was born sour."

The grocer snorted. "That's the truth."

The man with the handlebar mustache picked his change off the counter and lifted the paper bag of groceries. I moved forward with the milk and coffee cake and beer and set them down. Quickly I tightened the scarf around my head with my free hand. The man with the handlebar mustache hesitated a minute, then said, "How you doin', Red?"

I nodded. I was used to this.

"What can I do you for?" asked the grocer. The glass eye was looking at me. It was blue; the other eye was a grayish green.

"I'll take these," I said, "and I was wondering if you knew of a motel where I could spend the night, with my baby."

This came out fast, as if rehearsed.

"Passin' through?" the grocer asked.

I touched the items on the counter, reached in my purse for my wallet. The strap from my shoulder bag lurched down my arm, causing me to have to shift the baby.

"I don't know. I'm not sure. I might stay," I said. I lowered my eyes to the counter—a scuffed rectangle of gray Formica, bordered on one side by a canister of beef jerky strips, on the other by a display of candy canes. I knew the grocer must be wondering why a woman alone with a baby wanted a motel room on the northern coast of Maine, possibly for more than one night, the first week in December.

"Well, I'm afraid there's nothing in St. Hilaire," he said, as if genuinely reluctant to disappoint me. "You have to go over to Machias for a motel."

"There's the Gateway, halfway to Machias," said the

26

man with the handlebar mustache, who was hovering near the magazine rack. I looked at the magazines—*Yankee, Rod and Gun, Family Circle*, and others. I saw then the familiar title, and my eyes stopped there, as if I'd just caught sight of my own face in a mirror, or the face of someone I didn't want to be reminded of.

"Muriel has about a dozen rooms. She'd be glad of the business."

"That's so," said the grocer. "Save you goin' into Machias proper. Motel's not much to look at, but it's clean."

Caroline began to whimper. I bounced the baby to quiet her.

"That's three thirteen," said the grocer. He said the number like this: "thuh-*teen*," and I always think of that pronunciation when I think of the Maine accent.

I paid the man and opened my coat. I was sweating in the hot store.

"Where you from?" asked the grocer.

I may have hesitated a fraction too long. "New York," I said. The two men exchanged glances.

"How do I get there?" I asked.

The grocer put the food into a paper bag, counted out my change. "You go north on this coast road here till you hit Route One. Take a right and that'll take you toward Machias. The Gateway is about seven miles up, on the left. You can't miss it—big green sign."

I gathered the paper bag into my left arm, held the baby in my right. The man with the handlebar mustache moved toward the door and opened it for me. When he did, the bell tinkled again. The sound startled me.

The horizon had swallowed the sun. The dry, bitter air slapped my face. My boots squeaked in the snow as I

27

hurried to the car. Behind me, from the top of the steps, in the cold silence of the night, I could hear voices, now familiar, casual and well-meaning in their way.

"She's alone with the baby."

"Left the father."

"Maybe."

"Maybe."

Everett Shedd

You could tell she was in trouble the minute she walked in the door there. She had a gray scarf wound all round her face, 'n' those sunglasses, 'n' I know she meant to hide herself, but the fact is, she looked so unusual, don't you know, with those dark glasses when it was already sundown outside, that you had to look at her. You understand what I'm sayin'? It was like she was tryin' to hide but drawin' attention to herself instead, if you follow me. 'Specially when she wouldn't take the glasses off inside; then you knew she had a problem. And the way she held the baby. Real close, like she might lose it, or it might be took away from her. And then later, the scarf fell back down off of her head, 'n' you could see, 'n' I thought right away that she'd been in a car accident. It was slick as spit outside—had been all afternoon. Not all of the roads had been plowed yet, 'specially the coast road, 'n' so I figured she was going to tell us she'd been in an accident, except that the bruises didn't look exactly *fresh*, don't you know, I mean to say *recently* fresh. And then there was the fact that she'd tried to hide them. You don't try to hide bruises from a car accident. At least in my experience you don't. And I've had a little bit of experience. I expect you know that I'm the town's only officer of the law, apart from when I'm authorized to deputize someone else. Me 'n' my wife, we run the store, but when there's trouble, I'm supposed to sort it out. And if I can't sort it out, I call over to Machias, and they send a car. And I'll tell you something: I hardly ever see a face looks that bad. Not to say we don't have our fair share of altercations. We got some fellas here get to drinkin' 'n' go off their heads, 'n' I seen a few black eyes, even a broken arm here and there, but this was different. Her lower lip, on the right side, was swollen 'n' black, 'n' she had a bump, big as a lemon, at the edge of her cheekbone the color of a raspberry, 'n' I suspect if she'd taken off those glasses we'd a seen a coupla humdinger shiners, and Muriel, who saw her in the morning, and Julia, they say it was bad. This was important, don't you know, what we saw that day, we had to say so at the trial. I think Julia might of said, right there when she walked in, was she all right, and she said, fine, but you could see she wasn't. Dizzy, she was. And it seems to me she had a limp. I thought there was something wrong with her right leg. So I was standin' there, puttin' in the groceries, thinkin' to myself. She in't askin' for help. She says she's from New York. We don't get many people from New York 'tall up here.

So me and Willis and Julia are all three of us lookin' at each other on the sly like, 'n' then she's gone. Just like that.

I can tell you I've pondered many times if I did the right thing that night. I could of quizzed her, you know. Got her to tell me what was goin' on. But I doubt she'd a told me. Or anyone. She was on the run, if you want to look at it like that. And we knew she was probably goin' to be safe at the Gateway, though I didn't like to send her and the baby out in such cold. It was goin' to be brutal that night, they were sayin' minus sixty with the wind chill, so I called up to Muriel to tell her someone was on their way. And then Muriel put her onto Julia the next day, and I think we all figured Julia, she was keepin' an eye on things, had the situation under control, as if you could control a situation like this. But we talked about it later, after she left. We were interested; I won't say we weren't.

She was skin and bones, like them New York models is, undernourished, 'n' I'll tell you something else. You're goin' to think this is strange, but I had the feeling she was pretty. You wouldn't think I'd say that, now would you. But she was. You could see, even with the dark glasses 'n' that hurt lip, she was meant to be a little bit of a looker. She had red hair; alive it was, I've said it since: not orange, like you sometimes see, but red-gold, real pretty, the color of polished cherrywood. Yup. Cherrywood. And a lot of it, fallin' all around her face, framin' it. (Course, I'm partial to redheads. My wife used to be a redhead once; she had pretty hair too, all pinned up at the back of her head. But that's gone now.) It was like . . . let me try to explain this to you. You see a beautiful ancient statue in a picture book, and the statue has been ruined. An arm is gone, or the side of the face has been chipped away. But you know, lookin' at the statue, that once it was perfect and special. You know what I'm sayin'? That's how you felt when you looked at her, that something special had been damaged or broken. The baby had that hair too. You could see it in the fringe, outside her cap, 'n' later, of course. Have you seen her yet?

Have you met Mary yet? Well, I've seen her a few times since . . . well, you know. And I can tell you right now, she don't look the same as she did last winter when she came to us. But you take my word for it, 'n' you write this down when you do this article of yours. Mary Amesbury was a looker.

Not that it ever did her any good. 'Cept with Jack. And that's another story, in't it.

You have to talk to Jack. You talk to him right, he'll tell you some things. Maybe. He's close, our Jack.

Willis will talk to you. Willis will talk to anyone. I only mean that Willis likes to talk, and he was there. He lives in a pink trailer you might of seen just south of town, with his kids and his wife, Jeannine. And speakin' of Jeannine, I'll tell you something confidential. You don't repeat this now, or put this in your article there, but you're probably goin' to hear this around, so I'll tell you now, about Willis. It's said of Willis—that is to say *in connection* with Willis, the way whenever anybody ever talks about Julia they always say how Billy went from the cold afore he went from the drownin'—that Willis's wife, Jeannine, has three . . . that is to say . . . well, breasts. They say that the third one, a little bit of a thing, is located on the right side, up in the hollow where the shoulder meets the collarbone. I've never seen it, of course, 'n' I don't actually know anyone who has, but I do believe it's true, although I would never bother Willis about it.

And Jeannine is as good a mother as they come. Everybody says so, 'n' so I wouldn't want nothin' bad said about Jeannine. It's from inbreeding, tell you the truth, but don't you go repeatin' this in your article there. This is private town business, not for the world. Just an aside, don't you know.

Now, you asked me about the town. You come to the right place. I guess you could say I'm a little bit of the town historian, but I 'spect you know that already, which is why you're here.

I was born here, lived here all my life, like Julia and Jack and Willis. Muriel, she come over from Bangor when she got married. Her husband left her—that's another story—'n' she stayed. We're a fishin' town, you've seen that, lobster mostly, clams and mussels and crabs when the season's on. The main business in town is the co-op on the wharf there. We ship down to Boston. There's some blueberry farms too, just inland; they ship all over the country in August. But the lobsterin' is what we're all about. Me, I inherited the store from my father, never any question about what I was goin' to do. But Willis and Jack, now, they're lobstermen. And Julia's Billy was, afore he died. They're a different breed, you know, not your average Joe. Independent is a nice way to put it. They can be a cussed lot. It's in the blood, lobsterin', handed down from father to son, the way minin' is in a town, because that's the only way to make a livin' here. Don't get me wrong. This is a good place to live, in its way. Can't imagine livin' down where you come from. But it makes you hard, stayin' here. You got to be hard, or you won't survive.

Now, the lobstermen, most of 'em, they'll haul their

boats just afore Christmas, 'n' they won't put their pots back in till the end of March or so. Willis, for example, he drives a truck for a haulage company in January and February. Then in March he'll start gettin' his gear in shape. Some of the men, though, they don't pull their boats till January. Jack don't, usually. Well, he's got a difficult home situation, don't he? His wife, Rebecca, had what we call the blues real bad. Some of the women, they get them in the winter. It's a dreary thing—they can't stand the water when it's gray for days on end, and they start to go a bit melancholy on you, cryin' all the time, or they cut off all their hair, till it gets spring, and then they're OK. But Rebecca, she was melancholy summer or winter, a trial to Jack, though if you want to know the truth, maybe he's not the sort of man she ought to have married. Jack keeps to himself, he does, pretty quiet. Maybe a bit disappointed in life too, if you want to know. He had himself two years at the University of Maine, don't you know, more'n twenty years ago that was, on a track scholarship, but his father got both his arms broke on a shrimp boat and the family run out of money, so Jack come home to take care of his father. He took over the lobsterin' and married Rebecca. He did his best with the kids. He's got two, nineteen and fifteen their ages are, I think; decent kids. The boy, he's in Boston at school there now. Northeastern, I think it is. Jack's puttin' him through.

But anyway, Jack, he'll go out in a thaw or when it's not blowin'. Works on his pots the rest of the time at the fish house over to the point. That's where he keeps his boat—the *Rebecca Strout*. They name 'em for their wives. Well, at least on this part of the coast they do. Elsewheres they name 'em for their sons, don't you know. That's where she was, by the way, over to the point. Mary Amesbury, I mean. You've seen the cottage?

You understand that when they do go out, summer or winter, the water's still so cold a man can't last ten minutes in it. That's what happened to Billy Strout—Julia's husband, Jack's cousin, don't you know. Got his foot caught in a tangle of pot warp, and he went over. Not uncommon, sorry to say. It was November, if I remember correctly. They say he went from the cold afore he went from the drownin'. The medical people up to Machias, they can tell when they get the body. Sometimes we don't ever get the body, but Billy, he washed up over to Swale's Island. We knew, of course, the day it happened. It's a disturbin' sight, I'll tell you, someone findin' the boat, unmanned, the motor still goin', movin' in slow circles. That's how you know. Course, Billy was a drinker, part Indian from his mother, don't you know, so that may have been the problem right there.

I can't allow as Julia was all that sorry to lose him, tell you the truth. Don't write that, either.

Anyway, the town.

About four hundred people, give or take a few. The young ones in their early twenties, they go off, some come back, live at home a few months, go off again, hard to keep track, till they lose heart and settle down here for good, or go off for good. We've sent four boys to Vietnam, and we've lost two. Their names is on the town memorial over there. Most of the boys, they're already lobstermen and feedin' families by the time they get the call—and a lot of 'em don't go. We got some patriots in town, but most folks don't think the war has much to do with us up here.

35

The town was first settled in the seventeen hundreds by the French over from Nova Scotia, which is why we have a French name, like Calais or Petit Manan further south. During the War for Independence, the town was mostly British, I'm sorry to say, so that after the war, they tried to get rid of anything foreign and rename the place Hilary, but it never caught on. There are some families can trace their roots back to the war, others that come from Bangor or over from Calais. We had Indians here too, but now they're on the reservations down to Eastport. I say reservations, but we're talkin' about cinderblock housing projects that'd make you sick to look at. Unemployment and alcohol—it's a sin. What we did to 'em, I mean. Anyway, it's not a problem I can solve.

We got a library, open two days a week. Elementary school. For high school, the kids go over to Machias. The church, the post office, my store. Tom Bonney got sick of lobsterin', tried to start up a marine supply store, don't you know, but it didn't take off—most of the men, they make their own pots, and the gear gets handed down father to son. And Elna Coffin tried to get the co-op to go in with her on a clam shack, but like I say, we're out here at the end of the road—not a road *to* anywhere—and they wouldn't back her.

Those houses over there, they're from the shipbuilding days. A hundred and fifty years ago, this town was big in shipbuilding. We had a hotel too, but it burned down; was at the other end of the common. We had twenty-five hundred people in the town at one time, if you can believe it. You'll see some of the houses on the coast road, abandoned a lot of them. Old Capes, some farmhouses. These houses here now, there's two still in the family, but the people in 'em don't have two sticks to rub together, and they're livin' in only one or two rooms in the winter. Shut the rest off. One of the other houses belongs to the schoolteacher, and the fourth is Julia's. Julia does her best to keep the house standin', but it needs work, you can see that. She come from a bit of money years ago, and she went to college too. Up to Bates. Her mother sent her. Nearly killed her mother when Julia up and married Billy Strout. Anyway, Julia had some money afore Billy run through it, but she kept the house, and she's got the three cottages. We get a coupla dozen summer people. Water's too cold 'n' we're too far north for most people. And the black flies are wicked in June. Still, you wouldn't believe the rents people from the city are willin' to pay in the summer, just to get away from it all. Julia makes a bit of money rentin' out June to September. Uses it to live on the rest of the year.

You read the tourist brochures, the shortest paragraphs are about St. Hilaire. And you won't find a single advertisement for anything in town. There's nothin' here.

So that's about it, as far as the history of the town is concerned. I can't think what else to tell you. 'Cept that we never had a murder as long as I can remember. We've had some violence, what you would call aggravated assault, and I've had to bring in a coupla lobstermen took some whacks at poachers. Dennis Kidder got both his hands broke bad. And Phil Gideon got shot in the knee last year. You take your life in your hands you fiddle with someone else's pots.

And another thing. I know I just said the word *murder*, but you won't find many people in town refer to the events of last winter as murder. They'll call it "that awful business up to Julia's cottage," or "that terrible story about the Amesbury woman," or even "the killing over to the point." But there's not too many willing to say the word *murder*. And to tell you the truth, I guess I feel the same way too.

Mary Amesbury

I drove along the coast road leading out of the village. I was driving only twenty-five, but less than a mile from the store, I felt the rear wheels slip out from under me so that for a moment the car skated sideways to the road. My stomach lurched with that feeling you get when the earth seems to have deserted you, and I whipped my hand around to hold the baby basket in place. I straightened out the car, put it into first, and inched even more slowly than before through a nearly silent landscape. Headlights coming toward me seemed like large ships at sea, and when I passed them I gave them such a wide berth I nearly skidded the car into the deep drifts at the side of the road. I hadn't seen that kind of snow since I was a girl. There must already have been several feet, even before the day's storm, and it surprised me that there could be such an accumulation so near the coastline. Pine trees, with their branches overladen, swept gracefully toward the ground.

I watched for the turn onto Route One that I had

been told to look for. Occasionally I could see a pinprick or a glow of light behind or between the pine trees, the only hint at all that the land was inhabited. I almost missed the warmth of the store then, the bright lights overhead, the reassurance of commonplace objects—a newspaper, a cup of coffee, a can of soup—and I understood why it was that the man with the handlebar mustache had lingered by the magazine rack, why the woman in the taupe parka had wanted to read her paper by the counter. I was looking at the pinpoints of light the way a sailor lost in a fog might strain to find the shore.

At a bend in the road there was the stop sign and the slightly wider road to Machias. I took the right as I had been told to do, and drove for what seemed like too long— perhaps twenty minutes. I was certain that I had made a mistake—that I had missed a turn or had failed to see the motel—and so I reversed direction and retraced my journey. I was impatient; Caroline had begun to cry. I pushed the car back up to twenty-five, then thirty, then thirty-five. I was hunched forward over the steering wheel, as if that posture might help keep the car pinned to the road. But when I reached the village again—the lights surprising me too soon, it seemed—I realized I hadn't made a mistake. I sat for a minute, releasing my hands from the wheel as if they had been sprung, trying to make up my mind whether or not I ought to go back into the store for better directions. I imagined the people in the store looking up at me as I entered, and decided to turn the car around and try again. I glided along the coast road, took the right onto Route One, and looked more closely at all of the buildings I passed, just in case the motel sign hadn't been lit yet. As it happened, the motel was there, a mile or so beyond the point where I had stopped before, the script of the word *Gateway* outlined in lime neon. By the time I angled into the parking lot—it wasn't plowed, and the car fishtailed as I made the turn—Caroline was almost hysterical. I pulled to a stop near the only lighted window.

The proprietor of the motel was an obese woman who was reading a women's magazine when I walked in. She stubbed out a cigarette and looked up at me. A drop of catsup or tomato sauce had congealed on her pink sweater. Her hair, a brownish gray, was permed into tight curls, with two circles caught at her temples by X's of bobby pins. On the counter in front of her was what was left of a TV dinner. In the distance, I thought I could hear a television set and the sounds of children.

The woman breathed through her open mouth, as if her nose were stuffed by a cold. She also seemed to be out of breath. "I been waitin' on you," she said. "Everett called, said you were comin'. Nearly an hour ago, it was."

I was surprised by this. I started to explain why I hadn't arrived sooner, but she interrupted me.

"All I got is rooms with two single beds," the obese woman said to me. She turned back to her magazine and studied an article as if trying to concentrate all the more intensely because I had interrupted her.

"Fine," I said. "How much?"

"Twelve. In advance."

A key was slapped onto the counter. A ledger with a pen was turned around. The motel owner said the words *name and address* as if from very far away.

The baby began to squirm, crying fretfully. Bouncing her against my shoulder, I picked up the pen, tried not to hesitate, tried not to give myself away. I knew I must identify myself; I must now choose a name. I put the pen to the paper, beginning a slow script, composing as I wrote: *Mary Amesbury, 425 Willard St., Syracuse, New York.*

I took the name of Mary; it was my aunt's. But in the forming of that *M*, I thought of other names: Didn't I wish for a name more intriguing than my own? An Alexandra or a Noel? But something sensible—a practical need for anonymity—stopped a possible *A* or an *N*.

The Amesbury had come without thought. It was from my drive that day, the name of a town at the side of a highway. I didn't know if there was a 425 Willard Street. I'd never been to Syracuse.

I put the pen down and studied the black script in the ledger. So be it, I was thinking. This is who I am now.

"What's the baby's name?" asked the obese woman, turning the ledger around and examining it.

The question startled me. I opened my mouth. I couldn't lie about my baby's name, couldn't call her something she wasn't. "Caroline," I said, burying the word in my baby's neck.

"Pretty name," said the owner of the motel. "I had a sister named her daughter Caroline. Called her Caro."

I tried to smile. I shifted the baby to the other arm. I put twelve dollars on the counter.

"Number Two," said the motel owner. "I've had the heat up in Two for an hour now. Put in extra blankets. But you come get me if you and the baby get too cold. Supposed to be minus sixty with the wind chill tonight."

———

Once inside the room, I locked the door. I sat on one of the beds, opened my coat and my blouse as quickly as I could, and nursed the baby. She drank thirstily, making greedy sucking sounds. I closed my eyes and tilted my head back. No one could get to me now, I thought. The realization filled my chest, expanded.

I opened my eyes and looked at the baby. Caroline was still in her snowsuit and her woolen hat. It was freezing.

The motel room felt crowded and dark, even with the single light on overhead. The cloth of the bedspreads and the curtains was a venomous plaid of black and green. The walls were finished with a thin paneling meant to look like knotty pine. I thought the grocer may have been exaggerating when he said the room would be clean.

When Caroline had finished nursing, I changed her, washed my hands, ate a piece of coffee cake, and drank the milk almost as greedily as she had. Then, leaning against the headboard, I opened one of the beers, drank it quickly down. I thought fleetingly that I ought not to drink while I was nursing, but I couldn't get much beyond the thought. The baby was on her back, content, her arms and legs tickling the air. I removed her hat, stroked her head, enjoyed the feeling of the warm fuzz at the crown. My own hands, I noticed, were still trembling. I opened another beer, drank it more slowly than the first.

I liked watching Caroline, sometimes was content to do only this. But that night the pleasure had an undertow I could not ignore. This thought, unwanted, caused other images to press against the edge of my consciousness. I shook my head to keep them at bay. I put the beer can down, picked up the baby, wiggled her out of the snowsuit, and laid her next to me, in the crook of my arm. I thought if I could hold the baby like that, the images would go away. The baby would be my talisman, my charm.

And is it possible that sometime during that night I left the baby safely on the bed and went into the bathroom and took off all my clothes and looked at my body and at my face in the mirror behind the door? I will not bore you with what I observed, or with the feelings I had when I made these observations in that bare frigid bathroom with only a cold metal stall for a shower, except to say that on my body there were flowers—bright bursts of flowers in rainbow hues.

I woke to see that the baby and I had fallen asleep on the bed with the light on. I rolled Caroline over onto her stomach and made a secure place for her with pillows and my duffel bag. Even if she woke up, she couldn't go very far—she wasn't six months old yet and had not begun to crawl. Though she could wiggle herself to an edge if she wanted to.

I put on my coat, my scarf, and my gloves, made sure I had my keys, and went out into the night, closing the door behind me. The cold was motionless—it hurt just to breathe. The lurid green neon script that had read *Gateway* earlier in the evening had been turned off. I had no idea what time it was. I didn't have a watch with me. I walked to the edge of the parking lot, crossed the road, and went into the woods. Only by starlight and a stingy sliver of moon could I keep my eye on the door to the motel room.

I touched the prickly needles of a nearly invisible pine

tree. Already the cold had begun to seep into my boots. I thought I could smell, on the thin air, the ocean, or the scent of salt flats at low tide. Far off I could hear the cry of a gull or an animal, something inhuman.

My insides felt hollow. I was still hungry despite the coffee cake. When I looked at the motel, the baby seemed far away. The distance caught me by surprise, as if I had just discovered that the boat I was on was moving away from the dock. I saw an angry, rigid face, a woman hitting the wall with her back, her arms outstretched to protect her head. I heard a baby cry and was momentarily confused: Was the cry coming from the motel room or the waking dream?

I remembered then a woman I had been in labor with when Caroline was coming. She had occupied the cubicle next to mine on the labor-and-delivery floor, and I hadn't seen her face, but I had never forgotten the sound that had come from her room. It was an otherworldly sound, heard through the wall, like that of an animal afraid for its life, and if I hadn't known that this cry, this howling, had to come from a woman, I would not have been able to identify the sound as belonging either to a male or to a female. The cries grew deeper and louder, and seemed to rock the woman from side to side. The nurses on the labor floor were quiet. Even the other women, in their own cubicles, who had been moaning with their own pains, became silent out of fear and respect for the sound. The woman's doctor, who sounded frightened himself, tried to bring his patient back to reason by calling her name in sharp, angry bursts, but you could tell his presence was nothing to her, less than nothing. I heard the howling and began to shiver. I wanted to talk about the woman, but no one would discuss her with me, as if the howling were too personal to be shared with strangers.

Yet it was pain, pure pain, and nothing more. And it was, I thought then, a useful measure against all future pain, a standard against which I would always be able to quantify my own, even though I knew I would not be able to howl with the freedom of the woman I heard that night. I never saw the woman, but I knew I would never forget her face as I had imagined it to be.

I stomped my feet in the snow and pulled my coat tightly around me. It is possible I heard, on the edge of the silence, the ceaseless ebb and flow of the ocean against a rocky shoreline. I looked across at the motel and pictured my baby sleeping behind the pine-paneled wall.

I have been wondering—you won't mind my asking you this?—are you the sort of writer who changes the quotes? In the early days, when we used to talk, Harrold and I would debate this question endlessly. I was, I suppose, more literal-minded than he was. I thought one ought to report what a person had said, exactly as the person had said it, even if the words were awkward, or had no rhythm, or didn't fit, or didn't precisely say what you knew the person actually meant. But Harrold, who was more used to entitlement than myself, believed in license. He would find the nuggets in a transcript or a file, and keep these kernels, but would embroider the rest, so that his quotes, and thus his stories, would have insight, wit, momentum, even brilliance. Yes, especially brilliance, like rough-cut stones made into polished gems. And only he, and possibly I, and certainly the person whom he was writing about, would ever know that what was written had not been said.

I used to marvel that he was never caught. Indeed, the reverse was true: The more license he took, the more successful he became. The license gave him a style, a pungency, that other writers envied. I think that perhaps the people he interviewed were at first stunned to see their words misstated in print but, after the initial shock, came to like the charming, more intriguing voices Harrold had created for them.

Ironically, it was myself, precise notetaker that I was, who had more complaints from the people I wrote about. For their quotes, though accurate, would sound prosaic, seldom witty, and, even if important, rarely intriguing. Such people would want to disown their quotes. I would, of course, have my notes. I could tell them, if they asked: This had been put just this way; that word had, indeed, been used. And yet I knew exactly what it was they objected to. What had been written wasn't what they had meant to say at all.

And this was the question Harrold and I would debate: In his writing, did the truth get lost? Or did he, with his license, preserve it better than I did?

You asked, when you were here, about my background. I'm not sure what to tell you, what will be relevant.

My mother was the first in her family to make it to the suburbs and to the middle class simultaneously — though it seems to me now, looking back, that this had more to do with geography than with economic status. My mother was a single parent, a working mother, when all the other mothers were at home. She had never had a husband; my father, barely out of his teens, had abandoned her on the day she told him she was pregnant, and he had joined the army within the week. I don't think she ever heard from him again, and he died, in France, before I was born. My father's parents owned a bar on the south side of Chicago, not far from the tenement in which my mother had grown up, and they gave her money after my father died, so that she would not have to work to support me. Instead she used the money as a down payment on a small white bungalow in a town twenty miles south of the city. She went back to work then, as secretary to the president of a company that distributed office supplies. Until I went to school, I was cared for during the day by a neighbor, at the neighbor's house. My mother was determined that no matter what the cost, her own child would not be raised amid the perils of the city, as she had been.

At five-ten every evening, I would walk down the narrow street on which we lived to the austere wooden train station at its foot and meet my mother, who would alight, in her hat and her long woolen coat, from the high top step of the second car on the train. She would be carrying her pocketbook and a satchel, in which she took her lunch to work, and would have come from her office building in Chicago, a trip that took her forty-seven minutes. Our suburb, barely a suburb, was a cluster of prewar bungalows, each like the other, so that the streets had about them an ordered and tidy quality noticeably missing in the city from which my mother had so recently escaped. Our walk up the street—the pastel houses lining each side—was my favorite time of the day, a time out of time, when I had my mother to myself, and she had me, and there were no distractions. My mother would be animated, smiling, and might even have a surprise for me—a gum ball wrapped in cellophane, a paper strip of caps—and if she was tired, or her day had gone badly, she did not share this fact with me. She kept to herself whatever hardships she had to endure in the city, or perhaps her train journey home to her child had erased any discomforts of her job.

During this walk up our street—she would walk slowly to prolong our time together; I would walk backward or twirl around her or, when she was speaking to me in a serious way, would put my hands in my pockets and try to match her stride—she would ask about my schoolwork or my friends or tell me stories of her "adventures," as she referred to them, in which I would be expected to find the hidden homilies. She was also given to heartfelt lectures on various essential lessons of life, which I listened to as though receiving the word of God. There was a hierarchy in the universe, she told me, and I would be happy only if I found my place. Things happened to a person; one must learn to accept those things. One must not rebel too much against the natural order; the price one had to pay would be too high—a life of guilt or loneliness.

I would savor the twelve or fourteen minutes we had together each evening from the station to our bungalow, for I knew that when my mother crossed the threshold, she would be burdened by her chores. She did not complain, but she would become quieter as the evening wore on, like an old Victrola winding down, until it was time for me to go to bed. Then she would come into my bedroom—a tiny room connected by the bathroom to her own—and brush my hair. It was a characteristic that we shared, the color and texture of our hair, and this practice, the faithful hundred strokes, sometimes spilling into another hundred when she was lost in a story or an anecdote, was a ritual we never failed to observe, even when I had grown older and could certainly brush my hair myself.

When I had been tucked into bed, she sat in the living room, on the sofa, and sewed or watched TV or listened to the radio. Sometimes she read, but often when I got up to get a glass of water or to tell her that I couldn't sleep, I would find her with her book or her sewing in her lap while she stared at a distant point on the wall. I don't know what she dreamed of.

When my mother had removed her long coat and her hat, and had changed from her suit or her work dress into something looser, I thought that she was beautiful—the sadness of which I will not dwell upon, for I did not think this sad in my childhood, only now. Maybe all daughters think their mothers beautiful; I don't know. There was her hair, and the color of her eyes, a light green that I did not inherit, and a complexion that has not betrayed her, even in her older years. She was most beautiful, I always thought, on a muggy evening, resting in the middle of her chores, on an aluminum-and-plastic chair on the small screened-in porch off the back door. She would have on a sundress, and her skin would be faintly damp from the heat. Her hair, an untidy but voluptuous mass, would be falling loose from the pins, and she might be smiling at a juicy bit of gossip about our neighbor that I was telling her while we sipped a lemonade. I knew my mother liked me to gossip about our neighbor; it eased her jealousy, the fear that someone else had been a mother to her child.

I was a trial to our neighbor, deliberately so, I think now, and the woman, whose name was Hazel and who had three rebellious children of her own, didn't like me much. The dislike was mutual, or perhaps it was that I disliked living out my childhood in someone else's house. As soon as I was old enough, I begged my mother to let me stay alone at our bungalow after school, and she allowed this privilege, trusting me not to drink or to smoke or to do the other things she sometimes heard that girls my age were trying then. Of course, in time, with my friends, in my house and out of it, I did participate in the wildness she feared—I smoked, I drank some beer—but she was wrong to think that these essentially innocent pastimes would be the traps that would ensnare me.

Sometimes my mother invited men to the house. I did not think of them as her boyfriends, do not even now. They were men who had befriended my mother in some way—single or unattached men who plowed a driveway for which we had no car, or mended broken windows; or men whom she had met in the city and who would come out to the house on a Sunday afternoon for a meal. But once there was a man whom I think my mother loved. He worked as a supervisor for the company that employed her, and she got to know him well at work, for she would sometimes talk about him, in passing, in the middle of a story, and I would notice the pleasure that referring to him, even in this small way, gave her. His name was Philip, and he had dark hair and a mustache and drove a shiny black Lincoln. For a time, he came regularly on the weekends for a meal, after which he would take my mother and me for a drive in his car. I would sit in back; my mother would sit beside him. He would reach over and squeeze her hand from time to time, a movement I never failed to notice. We would go for ice cream, even in the dead of winter. When we got back from these drives, I would go to my room to play, or outside to find my friends. I was eight then, or nine. Philip and my mother would be alone in the living room. Once I came around a corner; Philip was kissing my mother on the sofa. I thought his hand was on her breast, but she moved so quickly away from him when she heard me that the motion is blurred, and I am not sure now what I saw. She blushed and he stood up, as if I were the parent. I pretended I had seen nothing, asked the question I had blundered into the room with. But I hated the moment, and I cringe even now when I think about it. I did not hate the fact that Philip had kissed her—I was glad that she had someone to love after all those years. I hated myself instead, my burdensome presence.

As it happened, however, Philip also abandoned my mother, after a time. For months, I thought that Philip had left my mother because of me, because he did not want to love a woman who was "saddled" with a child, as the expression went then. When other men came to the house—and there were not too many after Philip—I went to my room and would not leave it.

My mother was Irish and Catholic and had been raised in a crowded apartment, one of seven children. She was devout and attended Mass every Sunday of her life, and I am certain that she viewed my birth out of wedlock as the most serious moral lapse of her life. I could not be persuaded, from a very young age, to accept the Church as wholeheartedly as she did, and I know that this minor rebellion on my part was a source of aggravation to her. If we had fights—and actually I remember very few—it would be over this, my irregular attendance at church. But in later years, when I was working in New York City, and when I was already in trouble, I passed each morning, on my walk to the office, an age-darkened brick Catholic church called St. Augustine's, and I would sometimes be overwhelmed by a desire to go inside it and kneel down. I never did, however. I was plagued by the notion that I did not deserve comfort from a church I had scorned, and in any event, I was almost always late for work.

We had other visitors to our bungalow. My mother had many relatives, most of whom still lived in the city. Our tiny suburban house was far enough away to seem like an excursion on a Sunday afternoon. My grandparents and aunts and uncles and cousins would arrive by train at the bottom of the street, and the entire entourage would noisily make its way up the hill to our bungalow, where my mother would have prepared a meal. She knew they did not approve of her single-parenthood, approved still less of her determination to live outside the city and support herself and her child by working as a secretary— a *private* secretary, she always said, as a point of pride— but she invited them faithfully to the house every other week, even cajoled them when they balked. I would not have any brothers or sisters, she knew; and she wanted me to feel that I belonged to something larger than just the two of us. The noisier and more crowded our house became, the happier she appeared to be.

She urged me, too, to have my friends to the house, and there would be food that she had made in the refrigerator or on the counter to tempt us, or she would ask my friends to dinner or to spend the night. She was vivacious when my friends came to the house, as if she were trying to make it seem as though more people lived there than actually did, as if we were, in fact, just like all the other families on the street. I had girlfriends, later boyfriends, and I remember a kind of frenzied race forward through my teens, my energies channeled into my schoolwork and into trying to be more popular than I was constitutionally meant to be. But my fantasies, nebulous though they were, were focused on a distant point, after high school, when I would live away from home. I loved my mother, and I did not like to think of her alone after I had left, but I understood that neither she nor I would be happy unless I did what I was supposed to do, unless I seized for myself those things that she had been denied.

In the daytime, when my mother was off to Chicago to her job, if I was not in school I would walk the tracks with my friends or by myself. We would walk to other towns (more easily reached by railbed than by road), hopping off the tracks when we heard an oncoming train. We felt ourselves "adventurous." The tracks were peaceful and gave a sense of the lay of the land, but the true attraction of this pastime was the illusion of freedom. There would be an endless stretch of rails and ties with no visible impediment and a sense that one could walk forward forever. Even now, when I hear the rhythmic clacking of a passing train, I think of my mother and of the promise of a journey and of that distant desirable point where the rails seem to converge.

Muriel Noyes

What's this story all about, anyway?

I won't be part of no article that is critical of Mary Amesbury, so you can put that thing away right now if this is some kind of hatchet job. Mary Amesbury is innocent. Trust me, I know. How do I know? Because I've been there before. And any woman who has been there knows the truth about this kind of thing.

I had a husband who beat me. The goddamn son of a bitch ruined my life. Goddamn ruined my life. Took away the best years of my life. You can't ever get them back. You know what I'm sayin'? I had my babies, I couldn't even love them. I mean, I loved them, but I couldn't ever enjoy anything, because I had to be so afraid all the time, scared to death every time he walked in the door, scared for them, scared for me. He hit my son in the high chair once, the baby was only seven months old. Jesus Christ, I ask you. Seven months old. I hadda take the baby to the doctor. I hadda lie. I hadda lie every goddamn day of my life because I was so ashamed and scared.

I'll tell you something. I'm not afraid of anyone or anything now. Ever.

So I know all about this. There isn't anything about this I don't know.

Though I will say I didn't realize about Mary Amesbury until the next morning. You catch me while I'm readin' my magazines, forget it. Anyway, she came in, and when I looked at her, I was really lookin' at the baby, so I didn't see it.

But next morning she came into the office, and she had the scarf around her and the dark glasses, and I knew, right then, and she saw I knew, and she looked at me, and I swear to God, I thought she was goin' to pass out. Then she says to me, when she recovers, do I know of a place where she can stay awhile, a cottage like. I mulled it over in my mind and said how Julia Strout might have something. Julia rents cottages in the summer.

I guess it was 'cause I had a feeling of what she'd been through, and with the baby and all, that made me call Julia myself. Up here, we usually don't bother much with strangers, but this was different, you understand?

I couldn't take my eyes off of her. She was tryin' to keep it hidden, but you could see it. You wouldn't of believed it if you'd seen it. It's a nightmare, a goddamn nightmare. Havin' to go out into the world with your life story all over your face.

You're a reporter, right? Well, no one's goin' to tell you the truth about this kind of thing, so I'll tell you a story. I lost two of my top front teeth. I been knocked out. I had a broken arm and a shinbone fracture. I've got scars from cigarette burns where they shouldn't be. For five years I never once had what you would call intimate relations and liked it. Even now I can't think about sex without thinking about what he done to me. So that's another thing he took away from me. One time he thought the police were comin', he stole the kids and ran away to Canada. I didn't see my kids for six months. When he came back, I was so scared he'd take them again, I let him do whatever he wanted. Until he started on the kids. I couldn't take that. I called the police in Machias, he ran away. I prayed it would be for good. That was eight years ago. I hope he's dead.

We had a share in a blueberry farm. I sold it and bought the motel. It was abandoned since the early fifties—an unbelievable mess. Some people from the town, they helped me fix it up. I've got three kids. We get by. They're good kids, but raisin' kids on your own, you better believe it's hard.

I love my kids, but when I said he ruined my life, I meant it. I'm still angry. You can tell, right? I'm still angry. I see other families, they come into the motel in the summertime and they look happy, and at first I'm sad for myself, and then I look again—and I don't trust the happiness.

Julia Strout

Yes, I knew Mary Amesbury. She rented a cottage from me at Flat Point Bar from December 4 until January 15.

The rent was minimal. Is that important?

I saw her first on the afternoon of December 3, when she came into Everett Shedd's store.

I would say that, yes, I thought at the time something was wrong. She appeared to me to be in distress. She seemed ill or undernourished. It was extremely cold that day. Extremely cold. It was all anyone talked about that afternoon. On the news, the weatherman had said that the temperature might go as low as minus sixty with the wind chill. In fact, it went to minus twenty, an actual reading. We aren't used to such low temperatures here, even as far north as we are, because we're on the coast.

I may have asked her if she was all right. I can't remember now.

Yes, Everett and I did discuss her after she left the store. We thought perhaps she might be running away from something. I know I thought about that, and possibly Everett and I talked about it. Everett may have suggested to me the idea that she'd been hurt, but I'm not sure about that now.

My husband died in a fishing accident years ago. I'd really rather not talk about myself. I understood your article was about Mary Amesbury, not about the people in the town, isn't that correct?

I don't think I can participate in this article if you're going to write about the town. I'm here only to talk about Mary, to make sure that the truth gets told. That is to say, the truth as I understand it. I can't pretend to know the whole truth. I'm not sure anyone does, apart from Mary herself.

Yes, of course, I am aware that her real name was not Mary Amesbury. But that's how we knew her here, and I suspect that that is how she will be remembered in this town.

Though Mary Amesbury is gone for good now, isn't she.

I saw her again in the morning. Muriel Noyes called me and asked me if any of the cottages were winterized. I have one winterized cottage, over to Flat Point Bar.

———

I wasn't concerned about making money. I don't normally rent cottages in the winter. The cottage had been winterized by a couple who planned to retire to St. Hilaire, but the husband died, and the widow went back to Boston last summer. I had been renting the cottage to an engineer who was working on a dredging project in Machias, but he left just before Thanksgiving. The timing was fortunate, as it happened, because I hadn't had the water or the heat turned off yet.

She came to my house. She came to the door.

She was wearing a gray tweed wool coat and a gray scarf. Later, when we were at the cottage, and she took her coat off, I saw that she was wearing blue jeans and a sweater and black boots, I believe. She was very thin.

You've met her, I assume.

She reminded me of a thoroughbred. She had what my mother would have called a patrician chin.

I never did any more than any decent person would have done. There are people in the town you have to look out for, give a hand to when you can. I would say it was slightly unusual for Everett and myself to be concerned about a stranger, except that when you saw her, of course, there was no question of not helping her. And then there was the baby.

What happened next? We got in her car, and I took her to the cottage.

One thing I would like to say now, however. Something important I think you should know.

This is a terrible story, and there are many tragedies to think about. But I will tell you this: I believe in my heart that the six weeks Mary Amesbury spent in St. Hilaire were the most important six weeks of her life.

And quite possibly the happiest.

Mary Amesbury

In the morning I opened the curtains. The daylight was blinding—a blazing glare of light, the sun shearing off the snow in all directions. Caroline lay on the bed looking up at me, two tiny teeth winking from the bottom of her smile. I picked her up and began to walk with her. She was happiest when I did this—she liked the view from the top of my shoulder, or she liked the motion—and I felt good and whole when I held her, as though a piece of me that had been missing had temporarily been restored.

I tried to sort out the immediate future while I walked. I didn't like the room, but I knew I couldn't relinquish it until I had found something more suitable. I thought I should try Machias; the larger town might have more to offer in the way of long-term housekeeping units, or even an apartment. I needed a newspaper and food, and that meant having to go into a store again—a task I dreaded.

I decided that I would ask the motel owner for the

room for another night. In that way, Caroline would have a place to nap during the day if I didn't find anything right away.

I dressed the baby and myself, put on my scarf and coat and glasses, and went to the office. The motel owner wasn't there, but I rang a bell and she came. She looked at me as though she had never seen me before. I asked her if I could have the room for another night, and I saw then that she knew.

There was a time when I'd wanted people to know, and I'd been unable to tell them. But now that the truth was apparent on my face, I wanted more than anything else to hide.

I raised my face to the motel owner and asked her if she knew of a place, a rental, where I could stay awhile.

Around the woman, and emanating into the room, there was the stale drift of cigarette smoke. The motel owner peered at my face, at the small bit that was visible, as if trying to confirm her suspicions. She took a long pull at the cigarette, gestured with the cigarette between her fingers.

"There's a woman in St. Hilaire rents cottages in the summer," she said. "I think one or two of them are winterized."

"How do I get in touch with her?" I asked.

The motel owner hesitated, then picked up the phone and began to dial. She kept her eyes on me, spoke to me as she was dialing. "Her name is Julia Strout. She don't rent much in the winter; no one ever comes here. But there's one cottage out to the point, another south of town, I'm pretty sure. The one out to the point that's winterized, there was this older couple from Boston, they was goin' to retire there, and so they winterized it, but then the husband died and she went back to Boston, sold it to Julia Strout, she rents . . . Julia? This is Muriel. . . . I'm fine. Don't know if my car's goin' to start this mornin', though. You survive the cold last night? . . . Good. Good. Listen, Julia. I got a woman here with a baby needs a place to stay, and I was tellin' her about that cottage over to Flat Point Bar that's winterized. . . . Is that right? You think you can get the heat up over there? Be cold out to the point with the wind off the water. . . . There's the baby, don't you know. . . ."

There was a bit more conversation, and then the motel owner hung up the phone, looked at me. "She says she saw you yesterday in the store," she said.

I thought about the tall woman in the taupe parka. I wondered if the motel owner would call the tall woman back again as soon as I'd left the motel parking lot and tell her what she had seen, or what she thought she had seen. I thought then of moving on, to the next town, or to the next.

"Here, let me hold the baby for you while you go try to get your car started, warm her up," said the motel owner. "You can't put a baby in a cold car today. Freeze her tootsies off."

I said thank you and walked out to the parking lot to start the car. The engine didn't catch on the first three tries, but at the fourth coughed anemically. I put my weight on the gas pedal, tried to rev the car into life. I looked up through the windshield, could see nothing. Thick frost coated the glass. While the engine was warming up, I got out and scraped the frost away from all the windows. The sun was brilliant but ineffectual in the deep cold.

When the car felt warm enough for the baby, I packed the duffel bag and threw it into the trunk. I went back to the office. The motel owner was playing a game with Caroline, swinging the baby's arms high into the air. When she did this, Caroline laughed—a deep belly laugh. I felt a pang of guilt. It had been days since I had made my baby laugh, since I had played with her.

The motel owner turned around and reluctantly gave Caroline back to me. "I got three of my own, in grade school now. I miss 'em, the babies. How old is she?"

"Six months," I said.

"You know how to get back to town?"

I nodded.

"All right. When you get to town, you'll see four old colonials across from the store. Julia Strout's is the one with the green shutters. Green front door. She's waitin' on you now."

"Thank you for arranging this for me," I said.

The motel owner began to light another cigarette.

"Don't forget the key," she said.

I took the room key from my coat pocket and put it on the counter.

I circled around the oval common and parked in front of the only house of the four with green shutters. The house was the most prosperous-looking of the group, with a generous wraparound porch at the front. I climbed the steps of the porch, having left Caroline in the car, and knocked at the door. The woman who answered it was already dressed for the cold in her parka, her hat and gloves, and a thick pair of blue corduroy pants stuffed into her boots. She shook my hand and said, "Julia Strout. I saw you in the store yesterday."

I nodded and said my new name; it caught in my throat. I had never said the name aloud before.

"Your car started," she said, locking the door behind her. "You're lucky. They had to call school off today because they couldn't get the buses started. We'll go in your car, if that's all right with you. I haven't taken mine out of the garage yet."

I said yes, that would be fine. She sat across from me in the front seat. She was a large woman, larger even than I had suspected the previous day in the store, and she took up all the space around me in the car. I looked quickly at the woman, but she didn't return my glance, as if she had already seen what there was to see and was too discreet to stare.

"The cottage is just off the coast road, a bit north of town," she said. "Sorry to make you have to double back, but there was no way to direct you to the cottage on your own. The landmark is a pair of pine trees, and I doubt I'd have been able to describe them."

Julia Strout, too, had the Maine accent, but her speech was more refined than that of the grocer or of the man with the handlebar mustache or of the motel owner.

The road was nearly uninhabited and ran close to a serrated shoreline. The view of the water was unimpeded now—a vast, frigid gulf of blue, strewn with islands, stretching out to the Atlantic. There was a wind up; there were whitecaps.

She said, "Here we are. This right."

We turned onto a rocky road, covered by layers of

snow and ice and bordered on each side by tall hedges that she said were raspberry bushes in the summer. We slipped and lurched down this narrow lane until we came, unexpectedly, into the open.

A relentless tide licked at a waterline of dark seaweed. We were looking at a spit of land, with a smooth sand beach on one side and a flat mass of pebbles on the other. In between was a rangy swath of dried grasses, thinly covered with snow. A ruined lobster boat, doubtless tossed by a storm onto the grass, lay on its side, its weathered blue-and-white paint almost too picturesque against the desolation of the beach. Farther along the spit was a shingled shack, no bigger than a single room. And beyond the spit itself, four lobster boats—one a forest green and white—were moored in a channel.

"There's three or four men keep their boats here, not in town," she said, "but they won't be bothering you. They'll be hauling their boats in a couple of weeks, except for Jack Strout, my cousin, and he'll haul his mid-January. And when they do go out, they go before daybreak and are out all day." The shack, she explained, calling it a "fish house," was for the lobstermen when they did not go out in their boats; they worked on their gear there during the winter months.

A pine-covered island, barren of dwellings, made a dark backdrop for the boats, and beyond that a broken necklace of similar islands, each receding island a paler green than the one before, stretched out to the horizon.

"The cottage is behind you, to the right," she said.

I made a turn on a patch of wet sand and found better ground on a gravel drive that led to the cottage. It was on a promontory, with views out to sea on three sides, and when I saw it I thought: Yes.

It was a modest house of white clapboards, like a Cape but not as well-defined, with a screened-in porch at the side. It had a second story with a wide dormer, no other ornamentation. The clapboards came all the way to the ground and were not shrouded by bushes or shrubs. Looking at it, one had a sense of neatness. A square lawn, surrounding the house, had been cut from a profligate thicket of wild beach roses, now dormant and broken here and there from the weight of the snow. The house looked naked, sun-soaked, freshly washed.

"The key is in the doorframe," she said, unfolding herself from the seat.

I took the baby from the back of the car and followed Julia Strout up the small hill to the cottage. She struggled with the key in the lock.

There weren't many rooms inside the cottage—a living room, the kitchen, a bedroom downstairs, the larger bedroom upstairs, the porch. It was a simple house, sparsely furnished, and I must have noticed the white gauze curtains at the windows, for that is a detail I would have liked, but my memory of those first few minutes is of a glistening wash of corners, windows, shadows. I followed where Julia Strout led; she spoke plainly, defining objects, spaces.

We returned to the kitchen. The table was made of pine, but it had a worn green-and-white-checked oilcloth cover on it, and around it were four chairs, mismatched, one painted a dark red. Julia was concerned about the heat—the cottage had been frigid when we entered—and was busy for a few minutes turning up the thermostat and descending into the basement to look at the furnace. She showed me where the hot-water heater was and turned it on. We talked about the lane down to the cottage: She said she would have one of the men plow it later in the day.

I wanted to sit down and did. I kept the baby bundled in her snowsuit and her hat. She began to fuss; I opened my coat and nursed her. I sat sideways in a kitchen chair, one arm resting on the table. Through the window in front of me, I could see a gull rise nearly thirty feet straight up in the air with a clam in its mouth, then drop the shell to break it open on the rocks.

Julia tried the plumbing in the bathroom and switched on all the lights to see if they worked. She was examining a light fixture over the stove when I asked if her husband was a fisherman. It was meant to be a pleasantry. I was looking at a gold wedding band on her finger. I looked at the indentation on my finger where my own wedding band should have been.

"He's passed on," she said, turning to me. Unlike most large women, she stood up straight and was graceful.

She explained: "It was a squall, and he caught his foot in a coil of pot warp when he was throwing his pots over, and he went in too. It was Veterans Day. The water was so cold he had a heart attack before he drowned. Usually they go from the cold before they go from drowning," she said plainly.

I said that I was sorry.

"It was years ago," she said with a movement of her hand. She paused.

I thought that she would go on, but she moved toward

the counter and looked for a light bulb in a drawer instead.

I turned back to my view. The gulls, several of them now, swooped high into the air with their booty, like feathers in an updraft. In the silence of the kitchen I could hear what I'd been too distracted to hear earlier—the business of the day outside the cottage: the gulls cawing and calling; the swell of the waves over the pebbles, the settling of these stones in the ebb; the drone of a motor on the water; the rattling of a windowpane from a gust. The cadence in those natural sounds brought on a sudden sleepiness.

Julia Strout finished her inspection of the cottage and came over to the table where I was sitting. She had her hands in the pockets of her parka.

I was still wearing my scarf and sunglasses. By tacit agreement, I had not removed them, nor had she referred to them. But the scarf and glasses were cumbersome, unnecessary now. With my free hand, I unwound the scarf, removed the glasses.

"I was in a car accident," I said.

"I can see that," she said. "It must have been a bad one."

"It was."

"Shouldn't that lip be bandaged? Or have stitches?"

"No," I said. "The doctor says it will be fine." The lie came easily, but I found I could not look at her when I said it.

She sat in the chair opposite. She seemed to be studying me, making, I thought, a judgment of some kind.

"Where are you from?" she asked.

"Syracuse," I said.

"I used to be at school with a girl from Syracuse," she said slowly. "I don't suppose you would know the family."

"Probably not," I said, avoiding her glance.

"You've come a long distance."

"Yes. It feels like it."

"There's a clinic in Machias—" she said.

I looked up sharply at her.

"For the baby," she added quickly. "And of course yourself, if you should need it. It's a good idea to know where to go in case of emergency."

"Thank you," I said. I reached for my pocketbook on the table. "I'd like to pay you now. What is the rent?"

She hesitated, as if thinking to herself, then said, "Seventy-five dollars a month."

I thought: Even in St. Hilaire in the winter, she could get twice that. I had three hundred dollars in cash in my wallet. I calculated that if I was very careful I might be able to last at least two months before I had to find a job or figure out how to get into my bank account without anyone discovering where I was.

Julia accepted the money, folded it into the pocket of her parka. "You don't have a phone here," she said. "I don't like to think of you here alone with the baby without a telephone. You have a problem, you'd better go up to the LeBlanc place—that's the blue Cape just before we turned in. I'm pretty sure they're on the phone. For other calls, you can come use my phone, but I'm afraid we don't have a public phone in St. Hilaire. You have to go to the A&P in Machias. There's one inside the door."

She shifted her body in the chair and looked at Caroline. "I think you'll find St. Hilaire a very quiet place," she said.

I nodded.

"You'll need a crib," she said.

"I have the basket."

She studied the baby again. She was thinking. "I'll get you a crib," she said.

I noticed that her glance tended to slide off my face and rest on my baby's instead.

She stood up. "I'll be on my way, then," she said. "That is, if you don't mind running me back to town."

"No, that's fine," I said, gathering up the baby and my keys.

"It feels warmer in here, don't you think?"

I did think it was warmer and said so.

Julia moved toward the door. She looked out at the ocean. I was behind her with the baby.

A sharp gust rapped at the glass. I glanced beyond Julia to the seascape outside. I saw the snow-covered grass, the gray-black rocks, the deep navy of the frigid gulf. The sun glinted painfully off the water now. I thought the view was brilliant in its way, but inhospitable.

I had the impression that she was thinking about the ocean or the view, perhaps thinking of her husband, who had been lost in the gulf, for she stood at the door longer than was natural.

I was about to speak, to ask her if she had forgotten something, when the tall woman turned, looked down at my face, then at the baby.

"This may be none of my business," she said, and I felt my heart begin to lurch. "But whoever did this to you, I hope he's in jail."

I am tired. It is late, but you would never know. The lights are on in the corridors, and it is noisy here, very noisy.

I will write tomorrow and the next day, and then I will send this off to you. You will be surprised.

I have traveled so far—farther than you will ever know. Sometimes I remember my life as it was just a year ago, and I think to myself: That can't have been me.

We drove to town in silence, the droning of the motor or the vibrations of the car causing Caroline to drift off to sleep just seconds after we had emerged from the lane onto the coast road. When we reached the village of St. Hilaire, Julia told me to park in front of the store. She would watch the baby in the car, she said, so that I would not have to wake Caroline in order to buy supplies. It was a sensible solution to a logistical dilemma, and I accepted it as that. I put the car in neutral, left the motor running and the heater on.

I shopped quickly, perfunctorily, trying to think of staples, composing lists in my mind as I wheeled the small shopping cart up and down the aisles. The grocer was there behind the counter, making notations in a ledger. He nodded, squinted at me with his good eye, asked if I had liked the Gateway. I told him it had been fine, that Julia Strout was renting me a cottage.

"The cottage," he said. "The one over to Flat Point Bar?"

"I think so," I said. "It's north of town on a small peninsula."

"Yup," he said, satisfied. "That's the one. Tight little

place. You'll be all right there. Well, well. Good for Julia."

The groceries cost me twenty dollars. I felt my own motor revving with the car and wanted to leave the store. But the grocer seemed reluctant to let me go, as if he had questions he wanted to ask, but had to make small talk before he could reasonably get to them. I didn't want him to get to the questions, and was impatient as he slowly put the groceries into the paper bags. I suspected that he functioned as a central source of information, and that he would be expected to report on the new woman who had come to town, the new woman who wore large dark glasses at night and covered her face with her scarf. Or possibly he already knew some of the answers to the questions. Would Muriel have called Julia, and Julia, in turn, have called Everett Shedd? I thought not. I didn't know why, but I trusted Julia Strout, could not imagine her as a gossip or as a woman who would give away much of anything very easily.

The grocer appeared not to like the arrangement of the groceries in the bags; he began to take some of the items out and then to replace them. I inhaled two long breaths to keep myself from sighing out loud. He counted my change with elaborate care. I thought of Julia with Caroline in the car. I did not want to be indebted to anyone. Before the grocer had finished with his repacking job, I whisked one of the bags off the counter and said quickly, "I'll start taking these out to the car."

I put the groceries into the trunk, drove around to the other side of the common, and let Julia off in front of her house. There were people about now—a group of school-age children throwing snowballs near a war memorial, us-

75

ing the large stone monument as a fort; an elderly woman shoveling snow in the driveway of the house next to Julia's. The old woman, lost amid the woolen layers of her clothing, was bent nearly double over the shovel, her progress snail-like across her driveway. Down by the co-op on the wharf, there were capped pickup trucks in soiled rusty colors.

Julia stepped out of the car without ceremony and repeated that someone would be by to plow the lane. I didn't like to think about how Julia had seen my face and had not believed my lie, and so spun off from the curb perhaps a little faster than was necessary. It was only near the end of the drive back to the cottage, alone in the car with Caroline, still sleeping in the back seat, that I could begin to release the crabbed muscles in my back.

At the cottage, I lifted Caroline, basket and all, into my arms and walked with this bundle into the house. Gently, so as not to wake her, I placed the basket on the rug in the living room. As long as the baby stayed asleep, I would have time to bring in the groceries and put them away.

This task pleased me, made sense to me in the same way that caring for Caroline often did. I placed the perishables in the refrigerator, the packages and cans in the cupboards. I looked at the dishes and the silverware. The dishes were white plastic with blue cornflowers, the kind supermarkets offer as promotions. In a cupboard under the counter, I found a cache of pots and pans and serving bowls.

When I had finished with the groceries, I turned to examine the interior of the cottage, as if for the first time. I was thinking that it was mine now, mine and Caroline's, and that no one could tell me how to live here, could tell me what to do. I walked around the corner into the living room. The furniture was spare, even homely: a lumpy sofa covered in a frayed and faded chintz; a wooden rocker with its caned seat coming loose; a maple end table I associated with my mother's house; a braided rug, worn smooth over the years. The walls were plain, painted several times, the last coat a pale blue, but the windows were appealing—large multipaned windows with white gauze curtains at the sides. There were pictures on the walls, trivial paintings of mountain scenes, painted by amateurs for tourists, I suspected. I began to take them down, to stack them behind the sofa. I found a hammer in a kitchen drawer to remove the nails. The walls should be bare, I thought; nothing could compete with that view.

I opened a door and walked into the downstairs bedroom. There was a single bed with a cream chenille coverlet, a tall maple dresser in the corner. The crib might fit in there, I thought, but I wondered if I shouldn't have the baby with me, in the upstairs bedroom.

I climbed the stairs to see if there was space for the crib there. In the center of the room was a large double bed with a carved mahogany headboard. The bed was exceptionally high—I could almost sit on it from a standing position without bending my knees—and on it was a heavy white quilt, intricately pieced together with hundreds of patches in rose and green. I ran my hand over the cloth, admiring the stitches with my fingers. I tried to imagine who it was who had made this quilt and when: Julia as a younger woman, Julia's mother? The widow who had gone back to Boston? To the right of the headboard was a bedside table with a lamp. And to the left was the view—a view farther out to sea than could be seen from the lawn. I sat on the bed and gazed at the seascape through the bank of multipaned windows. In summer the gauze curtains would billow out over the bed.

I could see the boats moored in the channel from a different perspective here—the painted floorboards, the traps stowed in the stern, the yellow slickers hanging just inside the wheelhouses. I could also see the tip of the point, with the gravel beach and the sand beach meeting at a place where the slope cut sharply into the water. To my right, south along the coast, I could make out the map of the shoreline, with a large rock jutting up through the surface of the ocean. Far out to sea, there seemed to be a momentary pinprick of light, a lighthouse, though I thought it might have been a hallucination.

I relaxed my gaze on the horizon and let my eyes drift from the area where I had seen the light, to allow the signal, if it was really there, to come into my vision. It was then that I heard it: it was a small sound, an intrusion. I clutched the fabric of the bedspread, stopped breathing altogether so that I might hear more keenly. It was the click of a key in the lock, the sharp tread of footsteps in the hallway. He was home sooner than I had thought he would be, I was thinking. I must pretend to be asleep. I must turn out the light.

But it was not the sound of a man in a hallway. It was merely a car, an engine straining, in the lane. I released the fabric and looked at my hands.

I listened to the car in the lane, heard it backing up, then the sound of something hard scraping gravel or ice. It must be the man with the plow, I realized. I stood up to peer out the window, but I could not see him from there.

In the living room, Caroline was stirring. I was distracted and busy then—changing the baby, feeding her, putting clothes in drawers. In the background was the whomp and scraping of the plow.

I heard the truck pull into the gravel driveway. I walked with the baby to the living room window, glanced down. The truck was a rusty red pickup with a cap, much like the ones I had seen that morning at the co-op. Below the driver's-side window there was a pattern of scrollwork in flaked gold. The driver alighted from the cab. He was wearing a Red Sox baseball cap and a denim jacket that was too tight across the waist.

He rapped at the glass. I walked with the baby to the door and opened it. He stood on the steps with a crib, staring at me, seemingly unable to move.

Then I remembered.

"I had a car accident," I said.

"Wow. You all right? Where did it happen?"

"New York," I said. "Come in. I don't want the baby to catch cold."

He maneuvered the crib through the door. He asked me where I wanted it. I said I'd like it upstairs, in the bedroom, if he could manage it.

"No problem," he said.

I laid the baby in the basket and meant to help him with the crib, but he was halfway up the stairs by the time I turned the corner. I could hear the crib being opened, the sound of the casters as he shifted it into position. Then he was back on the stairs, pulling a pack of Marlboros from his jacket pocket. He was short and stocky, but he seemed strong. He made his way down the steps as though moving to an inner jittery beat.

"Mind?" he asked as he reached the bottom step.

I shook my head. I walked into the living room. He followed me.

"My name is Willis, by the way," he said. "Willis Beale. I saw you in the store yesterday."

I nodded, but we did not shake hands. "I'm Mary," I said. "Mary Amesbury."

"When did it happen?"

I looked at him. Instinctively, my hand rose to my face, but I lowered it.

"A couple of days ago," I said, picking up the baby.

"Oh," he said. "I thought it mighta been on account of the storm."

His hands were rough, the fingernails cracked and broken. I could see, too, that his jeans were worn, frayed, with grease marks, like finger paint, along his right thigh. He walked to the large window overlooking the point and studied the view. He had a day's growth of beard and used his cupped hand for an ashtray. Despite the sense that he was in constant motion, he seemed in no hurry to leave.

"That's my boat out there," he said. "The red one."

I looked at the boat he was pointing to. I could see the name *Jeannine* on the stern.

"Me and a couple of other guys, we use the point. The channel's deep, and that island there gives good shelter. It's faster out to the grounds from here. You can get yourself a good head start. My father, he used to keep his boat here too. So when it came my turn, I started comin' here."

"Thank you for plowing the lane," I said, "and for bringing the crib."

"No problem," he said, turning, looking almost startled as he again saw my face. He shivered slightly. "Cold out there," he said.

"You should have a warmer jacket."

"I got one; I should wear it. But I dunno, I always wear this jacket. It's a habit. My wife, Jeannine, she's always naggin' at me, 'Put on your parka.' I know, I should. She says I'll get pneumonia."

"You might."

"How old is the baby?" he asked.

"Six months."

"Cute."

"Thank you."

"I got two kids, four and two. Boys. My wife, Jeannine, she'd die for a girl. But we're on hold now. For a while, anyway. They dropped the price of lobster on us last summer; times is tight. You alone here or what? Your old man comin'?"

"No," I said. "I'm on my own now."

The *now* had slipped out without my wanting it to. He heard it, caught it.

"So you left him or what?"

"Something like that."

"Jesus. Winter, too. You goin' to be alone through the winter?"

"Oh, I don't know," I said vaguely.

He reached over and tickled Caroline under her chin.

He looked for a place to stub out his cigarette, could find nothing, walked over to the sink, turned on the water. He opened the cupboard under the sink and threw the butt into the trash basket. He leaned against the counter, his arms crossed over his chest. I thought he must be expecting a cup of coffee, as payment for plowing the lane. Perhaps it was the custom here.

"Can I get you a cup of coffee?" I asked.

"Oh, no, thanks, but I'll take something stronger you got it."

I remembered that he had seen me buy the six-pack at the store.

"I do," I said. "I've got some beer. In the fridge there. Help yourself."

He opened the fridge, took out a can of beer, and looked at the label. He popped open the top, swallowed long and hard. Then he leaned against the counter again, holding the can with one hand, the other in the pocket of his jeans. He seemed somewhat more relaxed, physically calmer.

"So are you from New York City or what?"

"No," I said. "I'm from Syracuse."

"Syracuse," he said, pondering the city name. "That's north?"

"Yes."

He looked down at his feet, at the heavy work boots soiled with dirt and grease.

"So what brought you to St. Hilaire?" he asked.

"I don't know," I said. "I just kept driving, and it was getting dark, and so I stopped."

That wasn't true. I had picked St. Hilaire deliberately,

picked the town because its dot on the map had been small and far away.

He opened his mouth, as if about to ask another question, but I said, quickly, "What is pot warp?" to deflect him.

He laughed. "Yeah, you really aren't from around here. It's rope. Warp is rope, the pot is . . . well, you know, the lobster pot."

"Oh," I said.

"Give you a ride out on my boat if the weather warms up some," he said.

"Oh, well, thanks, maybe," I said.

"Course, I'll be pullin' it the fifteenth, so you want to go, it'll have to be afore then."

There was silence in the kitchen.

"Well, I guess I better be goin'," he said after a time.

He walked to the door. He paused a minute, his hand on the knob. "So, OK, Red, I'll be goin'. You need anything, just give old Willis a call. Watch out for the honeypots, now."

"Honeypots?"

He laughed. "Come here; I'll show you." He gestured for me to come to the door. I walked over to where he was standing. He put his hand on my shoulder, pointed with his other hand.

"You see out there—that salt muck? Low tide in a couple of hours. We get extreme tides here; the bay will be almost drained by suppertime—apart from the channel, that is. Anyway, you look carefully you can see gray patches in the brown, right?"

I looked closely, thought I could see small circles of

gray, about three or four feet in diameter, in the wide expanse of brown.

I nodded.

"Those gray patches," he said, "are called honeypots. They're like quicksand. You walk into one of those, you'll be up to your waist in muck in a matter of minutes. Not too easy to get you out, either. And if you're still stuck when the tide comes in, well . . ."

He released his hand from my shoulder. He opened the door wide, turned on the top step, faced me, his shoulder holding the door open.

He braced against the stiff wind at his back. He nodded, as if to himself.

"You'll be all right," he said.

Willis Beale

That's W-i-l-l-i-s B-e-a-l-e. I'm twenty-seven. I been a lobsterman since I was seventeen. Ten years. Phew. Jesus.

My boat, she's a winner. I don't want to brag or nothin', but she's pretty fast. Every year they have the lobster boat races over to Jonesport on the Fourth of July; I always place in the top three. I come in second this year. She was my dad's afore he retired, but I trimmed her down some. I fish the grounds nor'east of Swale's. My dad fished there, and his father afore him. It's my grounds now, you understand that. No one in town, they'd dare go near 'em. That's the way it goes—handed down father to son, it's your territory. I catch a poacher out there, I put a half hitch on his buoy spindle. I don't give no second chance. The next time I catch the son of a bitch, I cut his pots. My grounds is my livin'. You put your pots out to my grounds, it's just like walkin' into my house and stealin' the food off of my table. You follow me?

When is your article comin' out, anyway? You goin' to put my name in it?

Oh yeah, I knew her. I was around here and there. I keep my boat over to the point, and I had to help her out some. Plowed the lane. Like that.

I thought she was real pretty. Real nice. She was always nice to me. I coulda gone for her, you know what I mean, if the circumstances was right. But of course, I'm married and I love my wife, so anythin' like that was out of the question.

But you see, this whole mess, I have my own ideas about it. It's a complicated problem.

Well, we only ever had her say-so, didn't we? I'm not sayin' she was lyin' or anythin' like that, but you take Jeannine and me. I love my wife, but I won't say that we haven't had our moments. And maybe once or twice we kinda got into a little pushin' and shovin', you follow me. Nothin' heavy. Just a little somethin'. It takes two to tango, right? I'm just sayin' how are we ever goin' to know? And she took the kid, right? Well, I'll tell you the truth: If my wife ever did a thing like that, I'd knock her block off. What guy wouldn't, if you're goin' to get truthful. You steal a guy's kid and run off where he can't find you, that's goin' to make a fellow pretty wild, I don't care whose fault it was. I mean, there's ways to deal with problems in a marriage. You don't have to run away. You got to talk it out or get divorced or whatever, right?

And then there's other things to think about.

Well, I been thinkin' about it. Afore Mary Amesbury come here, this was a peaceful little town, right? Not much to write home about, but the people here is decent, law-abidin', and so forth, you know what I mean. Then she comes, and it's like some hurricane blew through town. Don't get me wrong. I liked her and all. And I'm not sayin' she was tryin' to cause trouble. It's just that she did, didn't she?

I mean, look at it this way. By the time she left us, we got one murder, we got one alleged rape and assault, we got one suicide, and three kids don't have mothers anymore.

I mean, she's got somethin' to answer for, don't she?

Mary Amesbury

I watched Willis Beale make his way down the hill to his truck. He stepped up into the cab and started the motor. I saw him turn the corner, and then he was gone. I moved back from the window, still holding the baby. The tide was going out now. Fast. Already I could see almost fifty feet of salt flats below the waterline. Just a couple of hours earlier, the tide had been high, licking the seaweed.

I didn't know what time it was, but thought it must be the middle of the afternoon. I made a mental note to buy a clock, perhaps a radio. The sun was weaker than it had been; on the horizon there was a darkening, like a gathering of dust. It would be night by four-thirty, I thought. The sun would set behind me.

I stood by the kitchen table, watching the waning sun turn the navy of the water to a teal, the boats in the channel catching the light at anchor. I saw the afternoon and evening stretching ahead of me. Empty time, empty spaces.

I was glad the day would end soon, that darkness would come early. The night had a rhythm of its own, with a meal, with putting Caroline to bed. I could cope with that. Then I remembered that I had no book with me, I had nothing to read.

I heard a car engine in the lane and thought briefly that Willis had come back, that he had forgotten something. But it was a different color truck, a black pickup with a cap. I watched the truck drive along the hard wet sand almost to the end of the point. A man got out, and the wind blew his hair and filled his short yellow slicker like a sail. He wore long black boots, and his hair was the color of the sand. Turning his back to me, he withdrew one oar and several coils of rope from the back of the truck. He walked to one of the rowboats, beached by the low tide, and untied a rope, pulling the boat down to the water. He pushed the boat out, hopped into the stern, and began to scull with the oar, standing up in the boat as if it were a punt. When he was far enough away from shore, he sat down, sculled expertly with the oar in the direction of the green-and-white lobster boat. I watched him tie the rowboat to the mooring and leap onto the bow of the larger boat with his coils of rope. He walked along the narrow deck to the cockpit, jumped down inside. I saw him disappear into the little cabin at the front and then reappear without the rope. He reversed his journey then, from the larger boat to the dinghy to the shore, pulling the rowboat high up onto the beach to the iron ring at the waterline. The small boat tilted onto its side. He carried the oar to his truck. He looked up, saw my car in the driveway, swept the cottage with his glance, but

I didn't think that he could see me. Then he got into the cab of his truck, turned it around, and drove back up the spit, into the lane.

The landscape was suddenly quiet, seemingly motionless. The water lay flat, like a pond. The wind had stopped; there were no gulls. Inside, it was as still as death, except for dust motes that were slowly moving in a beam of sunlight. The baby had fallen asleep in my arms. A wave of something like fear started then, even as I held the baby.

I decided I would clean the cottage. It would keep me busy for hours, keep the fear at bay.

I found the tools that I would need—a broom, a dust mop, rags for dusting—in a broom closet next to the hotwater heater. I had bought a can of Ajax and a plastic bottle of dishwashing liquid. These would have to do, I thought.

I worked on the house. I swept all the floors, wiped down the walls with the dust mop. I ran the rags over all the furniture, scrubbed the tub and toilet in the bathroom. In the kitchen, I cleaned the sink and cupboards and washed the linoleum floor with hot water. I sponged down the refrigerator, scrubbed the shelves.

When I could, I left the baby in the basket to sleep or, when she woke, on the rug to play. Sometimes I stopped to nurse her. Once, when I was mopping the kitchen floor, I looked up to see that she was on all fours, trying to propel herself forward. I watched her make a tentative move. My heart swelled. I looked around as if there might be someone in the cottage I could tell about this feat, this milestone. But I was alone. There was no one there to see my daughter. I went to her and picked her up and kissed her. I held her then a long time.

After the sun had gone down, and I thought it must be close to seven o'clock, I dressed Caroline in her pajamas and put her to bed upstairs in the crib.

Hungry now, I made my first real meal in the cottage—a bowl of canned soup and a salad. I drank a beer while I was cooking, another while I ate at the table with the green-and-white-checked tablecloth that I had scrubbed nearly raw with a sponge and the dishwashing liquid. The soup tasted good to me. I liked looking at the cottage from the table, felt a sense of accomplishment in the cleaning.

When I had finished my dinner and washed the dishes, I decided to reward myself with a bath. I walked into the bathroom. The tub looked inviting, sparkling. I filled it with water as hot as I thought I could bear. I took off my clothes and lowered myself into the tub. The steaming water stung at first, then was soothing. I lay back against the rounded lip of the tub, let the water close over me. I picked up a washcloth and a cake of soap and gently massaged my skin, wanting to make myself as clean as I had made the cottage.

My skin was pink when I emerged from the tub. I dried myself gingerly with an orange towel hanging from the rack. I slipped on my nightgown and put over that a large white cardigan sweater that I had decided would do for a bathrobe. When I sat at the table, to dry my hair with a towel, I could hear that the wind had started up again outside. I heard the press of waves against the rocks, a loose rattling of the windowpanes. I thought that I would indeed like a radio, just to have a bit of music in the background. I had never experienced quite so much silence and wondered if it was good for the baby.

The chores or the beer or, more likely, the long soak in the tub had made me finally drowsy. I did not know whether it was nine o'clock or ten o'clock or even later, but I thought that time didn't matter much, anyway.

When my hair was almost dry, I hung the towels on the rack in the bathroom, turned off the lights there and in the kitchen. I felt my way around to the stairs, climbed them to the landing. Inside the bedroom at the top of the stairs, I could hear the soft rhythm of Caroline's breathing. I waited for my eyes to adjust to the small bit of moonlight coming through the bank of windows, then peered over the crib. I could just make out the dark shape of Caroline's head on the sheet, the bundled body under the blankets.

I drew back the covers of my own bed, took off my socks and the cardigan. The sheets were cool cotton, and I shivered slightly as I slipped between them. I thought I would just drift off to sleep: I was tired now, very tired. The baby would wake early, I knew, and would need to be nursed.

But I didn't drift off to sleep. I didn't sleep at all. Lying on my back in the bed, I had instead a clear and distinct vision of exactly where I was—a luminous vision of myself perched on a high bed at the top of a cottage on a hill overlooking the Atlantic. I had driven to the edge of the continent; there was nowhere else now to go. The slight shiver I'd felt earlier deepened along my spine.

I had been foolish to imagine I was safe. It had been silly to mop floors, wash tables, as if I could scrub away the past. He would not let me get away with this. He would not let me take his child. He would not let me outwit him. He would find me; I was sure of this. Even now, he might be in his car, driving toward me.

In the darkness I covered my face with my pillow— for there was something else that I knew.

This time, when he found me, he would kill me.

June 8, 1967 – December 3, 1970

———————

Mary Amesbury

We met my first day of work. I came around a corner—he was in an office. I saw him only, though it was another man, my editor, I had come to speak to. Harrold had been standing, hovering over a desk, looking at a layout. He straightened up, watched me walk toward the desk. I had on a blouse. It was new, ivory-colored, and I had worn a necklace—a string of beads? I brought my hand up, touched the beads. I had forgotten already why I had come, and I cast about for a question I could ask: It was, after all, my first day on the job, and I had an array of questions to pick from. My editor said our names. We didn't speak, and he felt compelled, I think, to fill in the gaps: She is from Chicago, just out of college; he is off to Israel in the morning. Maybe I asked a question then: What would he do in Israel in the morning? and perhaps he answered, Find a decent cup of coffee.

He was large, I think massive; I have always said massive in my mind, though you could see he'd never had an extra ounce of fat. His hair was large too—that's how I think of it: large and loose and dark, and it curled slightly below his collar. But it was his eyes I remember most clearly. They were black and deep-set, almost lost beneath a wide expanse of brow. They were dark eyes and impenetrable, and when he looked at me I felt lost. I believe he saw this immediately, and it pleased him, possibly even thrilled him. He put his hands on his hips, brushing back his sport coat. His tie was red, loosened at his collar. His shirt was light blue. The sport coat was a navy blazer, and he wore khaki pants. It was a uniform of sorts. He smiled at me. It was a smile that started at one corner and stayed there. You would say, if you saw it, it was a crooked smile, and that would suggest he had charm, and he did. But that day I understood the smile differently. He had plans, and time was short, and he was off to Israel in the morning.

I left the editor's room, and I am absolutely sure I knew it even then. I knew it the way when you're told you have a certain illness you understand you will not get better; or the way when you see a particular house on a particular landscape you think: Yes, that is for me, I am going to live there.

I was given a cubicle in a maze of cubicles. I had a telephone, a typewriter, a small rectangle of desk space, a few drawers, a bookshelf. I remember most of all the noise, a cacophonous crush of telephones and typewriters, punctuated by staccato bursts from the wire services. Even so, everything I said in the cubicle could be heard by those adjacent to me, just as I could hear what they were saying. There was an intimacy in that large room, even as you were insulated by the noise.

I was assigned that day to a section called Farewell and told to write a one-paragraph obituary of Dorothy Parker, who'd died the day before. I had only six sentences to write, and though I put more thought into it than I would ever have time for again, I finished it before lunch. I had the rest of the day to kill. I read past issues of the magazine. I observed the faces in the office—the camaraderie, the hostility, the jealousy. You could see it all, in one afternoon: those who had power, those who didn't, those who thought a lot of themselves, those who had longings elsewhere. I wondered where it was that I would fit. People spoke to me, made jokes, asked questions. They smiled with their mouths but not with their eyes. Even the friendliest were cautious. There were pressures there, and for some the stakes were high. Or seemed so then. It was remarkable, the air of importance created in that office—extraordinary to remember now how much it all seemed to matter.

I saw him too, moving through the office—to his own office, adjacent to the editor's; to a coffee machine across the maze of cubicles; out to lunch; back from lunch; to another writer's desk. In each of these journeys, there was the fleeting look, the sidelong glance, the eyes locking quickly in a turn, and I felt—actually I knew—that I was sealing a bargain with those brief glances. So that when he came to my desk at five o'clock and said some words about a drink at six, I was not surprised, merely nodded.

We went to a bar around a corner. It was filled with men in sport coats and loosened ties. He knew the place well,

moved through it like a regular, took a table in a corner—
I had the feeling the table had been left for him. He ordered a gin martini and I said I'd have a beer. He laughed
at that; he said I didn't look the type to drink a beer. I
asked, recklessly, what type was I? and then he had his
opening: an easy shot straight to the center.

He said that I made lists and that I never would be
late. He said I would be steady, though I'd rather drift.
He said I'd do the job, though my heart would not be in
it—that routine was more important to me than the work.
He said I would be fast and dexterous but that I would
not enjoy reporting: I was the type to listen but not to
pry. He said it was his guess I'd rather edit: It was quiet
work, and I'd be left alone.

A waitress came and brought me a frosted glass. I put
my hand around it—my hand was burning. Was I so
transparent after all? He loved this game; he would always win. It was a dance, and he was leading. I wonder
now, was he not high, too, with the knowledge that
we had found each other, the perfect team, the perfect
symbiosis?

I changed the subject and asked a question about the
Middle East. I knew that there was heavy fighting in the
Sinai. He leaned back, let his jacket fall open across his
belt. His answers were full of understatement, but in the
understatement you could hear his skill, his own dexter-
ity. He had a byline I had seen before: Harrold English.
Already when you saw the name you had images of the
man. I was looking at his wrist, at his wristbone exposed
beyond the cuff of his jacket. It was tanned, and I was
thinking while he talked—fatal, lethal, self-destructive
thought—if only I could touch him there.

You understand that it was physical. Before the night was over, I was in a room alone with him. We hadn't even had a meal. There were silk ropes, or possibly that came later. This was a movie I had never seen before, might never have seen if I had not said yes to his questions. I was frightened, but I was ravenous, complicitous. I thought, believed, that this was love, and before the night was out, I had said the word, or he had. We said the word together, and christened what we did.

He went to Israel in the morning, and I went back to work. I think the others must have seen it: I was like a toy top someone had spun and walked away from. I did not know for how long he would be away. He hadn't told me, and I couldn't ask the editor—it was too obvious. I did my work, took on more and more, stayed late into the night at the office, as the others did. The longer I stayed in that building, the more chance I had of catching some brief word of Harrold, overhearing his name in a bit of gossip from the field. There was nothing else I wanted to do. At night I did not go out. It was enough just to sit in my room and think of him, replaying the same images over and over again in my mind.

I was moved from Farewell to Trends. This was thought to be a step up.

I think it was then that the pattern began—his leaving and his coming back, my never knowing when he would come back, so that always I seemed to be living life on the edge, keen and waiting. I was sitting in my cubicle, on the phone doing an interview, when he walked into the room and looked at me. He'd been gone for seven weeks; I had not had a word from him. He'd been to Israel and Nigeria, Paris and Saigon. I didn't even know for certain if he had another woman; I had imagined, from time to time, that it was someone else he wrote to. I didn't know then that he wouldn't ever write or call when he was away; it was part of his plan, to keep me always waiting.

He came to my desk. I put my hand over the mouthpiece of the phone. He said that he had work to do—two, three days at the most. He asked me how I'd been. I had the sense that we were being looked at, watched by others. I said that I'd been fine. He said that on the third night we would go to dinner. It wasn't a question.

So that's how it began. Do you need other details? He had a large apartment on the Upper West Side, large and mostly empty. I had a tiny room in the Village, and so we lived at his place. He had been to Yale, and his father was a wealthy man. They were from Rhode Island, on the water. Harrold was twenty-eight when I met him, established at the magazine. It was understood that he was meant to be a star. His mother had died when he was a boy, and there was me without a father, and somehow that seemed fitting: Our backgrounds were symmetrical.

What else can I tell you about him?

He had a habit of running his fingers through his hair, and he would seldom comb it. He didn't eat breakfast, he was hard to rouse when asleep, and he almost always ordered eggs for lunch. He typed with two fingers, very fast—a dazzling display, I always thought, of compensation.

He was addicted to the news. He read four papers a day and never missed a TV news program if he was at home. When he read, he always had the radio on, to music or to the news. He said it was a consequence of having lived alone so long. He couldn't bear the silence.

His taste in music was contemporary. He liked Dylan and the Stones and a guitarist named John Fahey. He played them loud and often. But though he liked the music of the moment, he didn't take to drugs: They made him lose control, he said, and made him queasy. Instead he liked to drink in bars—as if he were a character from another era. He liked bars in foreign cities best, he said. The women there intrigued him.

He was often out of town, and later sometimes I was too. When he was home, we'd go to a bar, then to bed, then I'd cook a meal. We'd be up until two or three in the morning. We never had people to the apartment, and we never went to parties. This was essential, that we be alone: My dependence on him must be absolute.

I think now about that isolation, how complete it was. The world around us, as you know, was jagged and screaming. There were the riots, and there was the war. We knew about these things, often wrote about them for the magazine. Harrold was a witness, and sometimes so was I. But strangely the reporting and the writing isolated us even more. What we wrote were words, like the ones we read in newspapers. There would be an event, and we would be above it or beside it. If you were there to tell the facts, you didn't have to feel. Indeed, we thought detachment from the world essential. And if, in the office, we could talk about a protest or a killing because we had the facts, these were not the stories that mattered in the empty rooms at night.

———

We weren't like other couples. How can I make you understand? In the office there would be the heat between us, and possibly others felt it, but in public he went his way and I went mine. I was seen to be friendlier with other people than I was with him. We did not have lunch together or touch in the office or display the kind of public possessiveness that new couples sometimes revel in. What we were and did was secret, and even when we married, the sense of secrets kept us separate from the world, like women veiled in harems.

Later, as a consequence, I would think: There is no one, no one in the world, that I can tell this to.

Sometimes—often, in fact—I would wonder: Why had Harrold chosen me? For I had sometimes found among his things pale-blue air letters from women in Madrid or Berlin.

It was my hair, he'd say, teasing me; it was a flame that had drawn him to me like a moth. But no, really, he'd add later, coming toward me, backing me up against a wall, it was my feet. He liked small feet, and mine were white and neat, and had I ever noticed that before? Or later still, and in a more serious mood, he'd say it was the way we worked together: We had minds that thought alike when it came to putting words on paper.

But once, when we were in a taxi late at night, speeding uptown from the office on a rain-soaked street, the lights swimming on the wet pavement, I asked him why, and he said lightly—his hand was resting on my thigh, his smile had started at the corner of his mouth—*You let me have you.*

———

I wrote my mother. I wrote that I had met a man and that I loved him. I said that he was smart and well respected at the magazine. I said that he loved me too. I told her that he was tall and dark and handsome, and that when she met him she would find him charming.

I knew that she would like this letter.

The things I wrote were all the truth, but they didn't tell her anything like the truth, did they?

The truth was that we drank. There would be the drinking in the bars, with all the world around us. And then there'd be the wine, the open bottle and the glasses beside the bed. Or champagne in a bucket; we often had champagne. The drinking then was festive: Every night was a celebration. The empty rooms in his apartment would be lit with candles, and I would find, in the morning, clothes in a hallway, delicate glasses beside the tub. I cooked in a robe he gave me. It was navy cotton terry cloth, too big for me, and I felt small and lost inside it. There was a round table in the kitchen—a wrought-iron table with a smooth glass top. Around it there were dark-green metal chairs such as you'd see in France. And there would be the red wine on the table for the meal, and it seemed to me that we would drink until the fevers, both erotic and mundane, had burned their way out of us, and we could go to sleep then.

I had had a lover in college, but he was just a child by comparison. He had no dark secrets that he let me see. Of course, I was a child then too, and though we drank sweetened drinks on weekends, it was an innocent pastime, meaningless.

With Harrold, the drinking was different: We were drowning.

I have memories. I remember this: We were in the bedroom after work. It was late, a hot night, and I was in my slip. He lit a cigarette and leaned across the darkness to give it to me. I did not smoke often, but I sometimes smoked with him. His cigarettes were foreign, and I liked them. He bought them on his trips, and they had a dark and fruity scent, like flowers in a damp woods.

He was still dressed in his clothes from work. I remember particularly the cloth of his shirt, a stiff blue oxford weave. He had his tie on, but he had loosened it. We smoked together and we didn't speak, but I had the sense that soon something would happen.

I was sitting on the edge of the bed, my legs crossed, my feet bare. He was sitting not far from me, slouched a bit in his chair, his legs crossed too, one ankle resting on a knee. He was watching me, studying my face, examining my gestures as I smoked, and I felt self-conscious under his scrutiny and wanted to laugh to deflect him.

But then he stood and took my cigarette from me and put it out. He lifted me under the arms and laid me down on the bed. I remember that he was hovering over me, hovering in that way he had, and that he hadn't taken his clothes off. He raised my wrists to the brass bars of the headboard. He undid the knot of his tie. I felt the small stab of his belt buckle against my rib cage, the cloth of his shirt against my face, the silk of his tie against my wrist. I inhaled the cloth of his shirt—I loved the smell of him through the weave. And later, when he was saying that he loved me and was calling out my name, I thought: When he had been watching me, had he read this scene on my face?

It was morning. I was standing by a closet and a mirror, getting dressed for work. I had on a dress I liked—it was cotton, muslin, a long smock from India, and had intricate hand embroidery on the bodice. He was in front of his bureau, lifting socks from a drawer. He had on his pants but not his shirt. He turned to me and examined me—a long, cold stare of examination. He said, You should wear your skirts shorter; you have nice legs. And then: Don't put your hair up. It looks better long.

I took the pins out of my mouth, put them on a table. I unwound my hair, let it fall.

He said, You could look sexy if you wanted to. You've got the raw material.

I had known him three months then, or maybe four.

That day, on my lunch hour, I walked to a department store and bought two skirts that were shorter than those I normally wore. But even as I handed the money to the woman behind the counter, I was thinking: He is changing me. Or rather: He wants me to be different than I am.

The presents started then. Harrold had money and would bring me things from Europe or from California. Or from Thailand or Saigon. At first the gifts were jewelry and sometimes clothes. Then mostly clothes—beautiful, expensive fabrics I could not afford and would not have bought for myself. The clothes were unlike those I'd ever worn before—sensuous and exotic. I put them on to please him and seemed to change as I wore them, to become the person he'd imagined.

And then there was the lingerie. He bought me risqué bits from Paris or the East. He said I had to wear them to the office, and only he would know, and I thought, talking to myself, trying to still just the smallest voice of worry: This is harmless and fun, isn't it?

He said I should stand up straighter; I should unclasp my hands; I should stop a nervous gesture I had of fingering my hair.

He said to me, I tell you these things for your own benefit. Because I love you. Because I care about you.

He was my mentor at the office. I had a modest talent only, but he took me in hand. This was exciting, you understand, being tutored by him. He had power, and I sometimes found that irresistible. In the bar, after work, he would look at a story I had done, suggest improvements. I'd be stumped in my reporting, and he'd have a name to call, a golden source. He told me, too, how to talk to the people above me—what to show them, what to withhold. When I was sick once, he did my story for me; he even wrote it in my style.

He told me I should refuse to write only about trends, and I said no, I'd lose my job. But he goaded me and pushed me, and one day I did as he had said to do, and I didn't lose my job: I was moved to the national desk; I was given a bigger cubicle.

I took everything he offered me, acquiesced to his design. This was the bargain we had made, wasn't it?

We had been together a year, maybe longer. I had gotten home before him. I was in the kitchen, at the table, reading a newspaper. I didn't want a drink. I hadn't gone to the bar to meet him. I had a headache. Actually I had the flu but didn't know it yet. I heard him in the hallway, and I stopped reading. There was his key in the lock, his footsteps in the hallway. I realized with some surprise that I didn't want to see him, I wanted to be alone. Do I need a reason? I was tired. I didn't want to have to give anything—or to have to take from him, either. It was the first time since we'd met I'd felt this way.

He came into the kitchen, and he must have seen it. Perhaps it was in the way I wouldn't look at him and kept my eyes on the newspaper: Something in me resisted this intrusion.

He took his jacket off, hung it on a chair. He pulled his tie loose, unbuttoned his collar. He put his hands on his hips, looked at me. He said, Don't you want a drink? and I said, No, I have a headache. He said, Have a drink; it'll help the headache, and I said, No, but thanks.

He came up behind me, put his hands on my shoulders. He began to massage the muscles at the base of my neck. I should have relaxed for him, but I couldn't. I understood this gesture. He would touch me even when I didn't want it, especially when I didn't want it.

I tried to sit there, pliant, thinking: This will be over soon. But his fingers kneaded the knots in my shoulders too vigorously. I wrenched away suddenly, stood up. I was going to say, I'm not feeling well, I'm better off alone tonight, but he grabbed my wrist, held it.

I don't remember everything that happened—the room

seemed to spin around me very fast. He had me up against the refrigerator; the handle was in my back. His strength was absolute: I'd had only hints of this before. He raised my skirt to my waist. I tried to push him away from me, but he slammed my wrist up against the metal. I felt a sharp stab of pain; I thought that he had broken it. I was frightened then. I knew that he could hurt me, was hurting me. He was a large man—have I said that before?—and though I fought, my fighting him was useless.

And then I stopped resisting and became a part of it, a passive player. And it seemed, when it was over, and he was holding me, and I didn't want to think about the implications of those few moments, that possibly love or sex or violence was simply a matter of degree. Seen in a certain light, was what had happened against the refrigerator so very different from all that had gone before?

He carried me to the bed and wrapped me in a blanket. He put ice cubes on my wrist—it was bruised but not broken. He put his mouth on my wrist and said that he was sorry, but curiously, I understood that he meant he was sorry the wrist was hurt, not that he was sorry for the act.

He made a meal for us, and we ate it on the bed. He seemed grateful to me, and I was aware of a strange sense of our having grown closer to each other, more intimate, as though the more risks we took, the more secrets we shared, the further we pushed the boundaries of what was done, the more entwined we would become.

In the night I got the fever, and it is possible I am confusing the sequence of what was said or felt, but that was when he wrote my story for me. And that was when he asked me to marry him.

In the months and years that followed, it was often like that: He'd take something from me, or hurt me, and then offer me something larger in return. And if I took the something larger—a promise or a commitment or a dream—it was understood that I forgave him.

He never said, then or ever, the word *rape*, and I could not say the word aloud myself.

I said that I would marry him. He went off to Prague to do a story. I had his apartment to myself. I was sick with the flu. I was sometimes feverish. I didn't go to work.

Already I felt addicted, or obsessed. I would drink alone, just as we had done together, because it was a thread, it connected us. I would walk to windows, bare windows looking out at traffic and at buildings, and sit for hours, thinking just of him and of us. I would wander rooms and touch his things, go through pockets to find bits of paper that would tell me more about him. I read his notebooks on his desk, tried to think the way he thought.

Yet even as I did, I knew that we were not like other people. Or if we were like other people, this was a side of love I had not heard anything about. Harrold had had a vision of who I might be, had seen this vision even on the first day we met, was relentless in his pursuit of it. Who I actually was or might have been was merely clay to play with. He saw me as a star, like himself, his protégé, his possession. Perhaps I am oversimplifying this, but I don't think so. I was in trouble only if I resisted the vision he had—only if I spoke or acted or felt in a manner that was incompatible with his design.

Was this my failing, then? My failure to embrace wholeheartedly this new self that was being offered to me, even as I wore the expensive lingerie to the office, short-ened my skirts, listened avidly to his advice?

For always there was something in me, as yet uniden-tified, unrecognizable, that resisted the shaping and the molding. In the beginning it seemed that this resistance was maverick, merely confusing to me, there almost de-spite my best interests or my wishes.

And later, when I did resist at last, his repertoire was extensive, magisterial: subtle scorn, veiled ridicule, icy si-lence, absence, presence, absence. He was skilled, a vir-tuoso, a concert pianist.

But I am getting ahead of myself.

There were good times, have I told you that? At the table in the kitchen, he would tell me stories of his travels, wonderful stories of misadventures and comedies, peo-pled with characters I could clearly see as he described them. He was a gifted raconteur, and he saved for me all the bits he could not put into his articles, so that when he came home from a long trip, I'd be entertained for days.

Or maybe we would lie side by side on the living room floor, with only our arms touching, our heads propped up on sofa pillows, and listen together to music he had chosen. We might smoke together or drink the wine we had brought from the bedroom, and between us for those moments there would seem to be a deceptive feeling of perfect ease.

And sometimes, before the others knew about us, we would be at a large oval conference table in a meeting room at the office, and everyone would be arguing about a cover, or story ideas, and someone would say some-thing that wasn't meant to be amusing but was, and I would seem to turn my head to look at the clock or out the window, and I would catch his glance in that moment and see just the most imperceptibly raised eyebrow or up-turned corner of his mouth, and in that split second between us there would be an invisible smile big enough to last a morning.

When he returned from Prague, he said that we would go to Rhode Island, tell his father that we were getting married. He had not said much about his father, although I knew his name was Harrold, with the same double *r*. It was, too, the father's father's name and so on. Perhaps once, years and years ago, it had been an affectation or possibly a mistake, but now it was so deeply a part of the passing down of the name that Harrold, my Harrold, could not bring himself to drop the extra *r*—even though he himself did not know its origins.

The house was on the water, cavernous, filled with empty rooms, the prototype of the apartment with the empty rooms in Manhattan. It was Victorian, or turn-of-the-century; I never knew for sure. It had gray shingles and a porch and many windows of different sizes. The furniture inside was heavy, dark, and masculine. We drove up the driveway, and already I could feel a sea change in the man beside me. He grew quiet, taciturn. He turned off the radio. There were lines on his forehead, a tight-ening around his mouth. He said before we had even parked the car that this was a bad idea, but I said non-sense, I was dying to meet his father.

There had been, in the city, a sense of manic joy as we'd set out, like opening the shutters and letting daylight flood into darkened rooms. Perhaps we would join the world, after all, we thought but didn't say, by getting married. There had been, after that night in the kitchen, a sense of striving for something like normalcy: We had, just the day before, on his first day back from Prague, told the people in the office that we were getting married. And we had both enjoyed, even more than the announcement, the surprise on the faces there.

His father was a wizened man, a man who had once been large, like Harrold, but now was shrunken, caved in. His face was gray, like his hair. His hair was combed back straight from the brow in a style that seemed to be a holdover from an earlier era. You could see at once that he wasn't well, hadn't been for some time. He had Harrold's eyes, black and impenetrable, catching you suddenly in what might have passed for an indifferent glance. He held a cigarette, and there was a tremor in his hand. There were nicotine stains on his fingers. He was sitting in an oversized captain's chair of darkened wood that seemed to mold itself around him. He was wearing a suit, a formal gray suit that doubtless once had fit him well but now hung poorly over the wasted body.

I remember a housekeeper standing by a window. Harrold walked to the center of the room but didn't go to his father. I had the feeling they hadn't touched in years, so couldn't now. Harrold turned around to look at me— I was behind him—as if he would have me leave the room, as if his father were something I shouldn't see, or the other way around. Harrold seemed lost. I had never seen him like this—smaller, diminished. His father, in the polished chair, was now the larger man. I walked to where Harrold was standing. Harrold said my name, said his father's name. I walked to the father, shook his hand. His hand was dry, like yellow dust in my own.

Get us a drink, Harry, will you, his father said. It was not a question. I heard the diminutive. Harrold was never Harry, though sometimes he was known as English. Once in a while a colleague or the editor would call him that: Hey, English, they would say. I watched Harrold's hand reach for a glass on a sideboard. He made a large Scotch for his father, one for me. I had not been invited to sit down, but I did so, on a leather sofa. The room was not a living room, not a room that people lived in, though his father lived in here. It was a study, leather and wood and masculine, but there was a chaise by a window, with a throw. Beyond the window, you could see the water. The house was quiet, still, with dust motes drifting in the air.

You make your living scribbling for that rag too, his father said to me. There was a scratch of metal in his voice; it turned questions into pronouncements.

By the sideboard, Harrold had downed his drink already, had quickly poured himself another. I was sure his father had seen him do this. You had the sense the eyes saw everything, even though the body was immobile. I said yes, I worked with Harrold, and then because I was nervous and Harrold had not yet spoken, I said inanely, to fill the silence, that I had heard a lot about him, which was not true, and that I'd heard about the textile mills and how he'd made them out of nothing, which was true and which Harrold had mentioned to me, in passing.

The business was his if he'd wanted it, but now it's gone to strangers, said the father, as if the son were not in the room. The bitterness in his voice was unmistakable.

We're getting married, Harrold said in a rush, like a schoolboy in his father's presence who wanted only to change the subject, and I winced that what we had come to tell had been used by him like that.

There was a silence in the room. I thought that possibly Harrold had shocked his father too much, had not prepared him for this eventuality, and that his father, understandably, was at a loss for words.

But then his father spoke.

You can stay to supper if you want, he said, but I won't be joining you. I take my meals alone now.

I glanced at Harrold, but he turned away from me, looked out at the water instead. Perhaps his father was deaf, I thought. The deafness would explain his rudeness. If he had not heard what his son had said, I would repeat it for him, I would tell him that I hoped he would come to the wedding. I would say this loudly, and he would understand then. I opened my mouth to speak, but his father cut me off.

What's your family do? his father said. His voiced rasped, and he coughed.

I knew then that he had heard but had chosen not to give his son anything like his blessing or even an acknowledgment.

Harrold left the room, walked out of the room onto a porch. I heard his footsteps on the stairs, saw him, through the window, walk toward the beach.

I answered his father's question about my family, about my mother. I could see that he was disappointed. He had hoped, despite his air of indifference, that his son would marry well, do that right at least. He gestured to the housekeeper to fill up his glass. I wondered if he sat like this all day, drinking Scotch, not moving much in this tomblike house.

I excused myself. I said I would be back. I went out to find Harrold on the beach, saw him walking in the sand with his shoes on, his good shoes filling up with sand. He had his hands in his pants pockets, with his suit coat and his tie blowing in the wind behind him. We had dressed to meet his father. I took off my shoes and ran down to the beach to talk to him, but he didn't want me there, said he'd rather be alone. I chose not to believe this, ran in the sand to keep up with him. His hair was buffeted by the wind; his eyes squinted against the sun.

We shouldn't have come, he said. It was always like this. His father was an alcoholic.

As if that excused everything—the ice, the scorn, the ridicule. But it didn't, not entirely.

What happened to your mother? I asked.

He didn't answer me at first. He turned and walked toward a dune and sat down. He looked almost comical in his good suit sitting in the sand, and I felt sorry for him. His father was an ugly man, but I couldn't say that.

I sat down beside Harrold.

He was ten, he said suddenly, after a time. His mother was dying of cancer. Breast cancer. He didn't know that she was dying. He'd known about the operations and the hospital stays, but his mother had said to him that she was getting better, and he'd believed her. Had to believe her. He was only ten.

And on this one particular day he was remembering, he had walked into the kitchen for a glass of water. It was a hot afternoon, and there was a swinging door into the kitchen. He'd swung the door open thoughtlessly, as boys do, he said, and he'd hit his father in the back. His father and then his mother's sister, who'd come to help with the care. They'd been embracing—not an embrace of consolation, either, Harrold said. He thought now that probably it was just a grope, a pass on his father's part, meaningless in the long run, but the boy did not see it that way. He was at an awkward age, old enough to understand yet not understand fully. He'd run out of the kitchen and gone outside, had gone into the dunes where we were then. He'd cried, he said. He'd cried for his mother and his father and for the shame of it—the hot earnest tears of a ten-year-old boy.

And then, he said, he'd done the one truly terrible thing of his childhood.

Later that night, thinking somehow that his mother would make it right, he'd half told her, or had begun to tell her, and then had realized he couldn't, ought not to, but she had seen it on his face, had heard too much before he could recover and take it back.

And after that day, his mother had not spoken to his father again. She'd died weeks later, not speaking to her husband, and the father had never forgiven the son.

Mine was the worse offense, Harrold said, looking at me. Telling her like that, hurting her.

He'd understood that almost immediately and had tried to tell this to his father. But his father was a hard man. He'd always been hard, Harrold said—it was how he'd made his family, made his business.

I hate the bastard, let's get out of here, he said.

We drove back to the city in silence. The three quick drinks in the middle of the day had not made Harrold drunk, merely made him silent, almost sullen. I was disappointed for myself too, you must understand. It wasn't how I had imagined it might be; I had hoped we would be happy, like other people seemed to be. I didn't see how we could have a wedding in a church: That wouldn't suit us now, though we would be married. That felt inevitable.

I said that I would go to Chicago to tell my mother. I didn't ask him to come. I knew he wouldn't now.

Was this the reason, then? The reason why the man I loved was so twisted, angry, brutal? And if so, do we forgive him his brutality?

Or if so, what then was the reason for his father's brutality and ice? A father's father's sin? A legacy that I have now dismantled?

I am trying to tell you the truth. I am doing this so that you will understand how it was—how it was that I stayed, wanted Harrold, believed in us. Later, yes, I was afraid to leave, that was simple; but in the beginning, when I could have left, could have stopped it from happening, I didn't want to.

You see, I loved Harrold. I loved him. Even on the day I left, even when I was most afraid of him.

And I wonder now, was this a sickness on my part? Or was it my best self?

I got your letter this morning. I knew that you would be surprised to hear from me, to receive the notes and writings I had sent you. I see you getting the package at your desk, your puzzlement as you look at the first page, wondering what this is, then your face as the wheels begin to turn, realizing you have your story after all, will not have to abandon all the work you've done in Maine, have a story that is viable.

I see you in your white blouse and skirt, your shoes kicked off in the heat. Your suit jacket is behind you, over your chair. You are bent over your desk, reading what I have written. Your hand is at your forehead; you are concentrating deeply. I see your blond hair pinned back with tortoiseshell barrettes, falling behind your ears. Maybe you unsnap a barrette and run your hand through your hair, thinking; it's an excited gesture.

And then you'll have a drink at lunch, maybe a glass of wine. You'll be humming with ideas, your own ideas of how to write the story. You'll think you've got the cover now; it cannot fail to make the cover. You'll have to time it right. The peg will be the verdict. It must come out before the verdict, or the story quickly will grow old. You are thinking—possibly, just possibly—that this story will be the one that will truly make your career. That will let you rise above the others, that will allow the world to see just how good you really are. It's got juice and meat, and you are thinking you can do it justice.

Yet even so, I don't believe it is possible for you ever to know the truth or to write it. For at the end you will have an article, your own ideas, which you will have edited, by necessity, in the process of writing it, and that story will, in turn, be edited by those above you, and *that* final printed story will be read and perceived differently by every reader, man or woman, depending on the circumstances of his or her life, so that by the time all of the magazines are put out with the rubbish, and you are off interviewing someone else, no one will have any idea of my story as it really was at all, will they?

We were married in the winter. My mother came and was radiant, even though we did not get married in the Church. I filled the apartment with flowers, made it seem like a happy place. We were married there and had a party: We invited people from the office.

It was a curious match at the magazine—the subject of much gossip and of speculation: Why had Harrold chosen Maureen? I wore an ivory-colored dress and a wreath of flowers in my hair. I let my mother brush my hair in the morning, and she put it up with combs. I was buoyant with belief in the ritual, drifting lightly with the illusion. If we seemed happy, and had my mother with us, and there was sunlight in the rooms, and there were people there who wished us well, wasn't that enough?

Not long after the wedding, I had to go to Los Angeles to do a story. There was an oil spill off the coast of California, and I was part of a team—two reporters and a photographer.

My colleagues both were men. They had a motel room together; I had the adjacent room to myself. But the three of us moved easily from room to room, sharing takeout, talking of our story, watching television, until it was time to go to bed.

One night Harrold called me on the telephone. Robert, the photographer, was in the room, writing down what I wanted from the Chinese restaurant around the corner. He called out to me as he was leaving, said not to bother with the money, it was his turn to pay. Harrold heard his voice, said, Is that Robert? I said, Yes. He said, What's he doing in your room? I laughed. Possibly that was my mistake. I shouldn't have laughed. I heard the ice in his voice. I said, What's the matter, Harrold? He said, Nothing. I knew that *nothing*. It's what he always said when he was angry and wouldn't talk. I made it worse then; I tried to explain. I said, Robert and Mike are always here. We eat our supper here. It's nothing. Don't be silly.

Don't be silly.

He said, Fine.

I got in late at La Guardia, took a taxi to the apartment. He was waiting up for me, sitting in a chair in the bedroom. There was a bottle on the table. He'd been drinking, quite a lot by the look of him. He got up, hesitated, started walking toward me. I said, Harrold.

Which one did you sleep with? he asked me, moving closer.

I put my hands up. I remember that, I put my hands up. I said, Don't be ridiculous. A tremor in my voice suggested I was trying to wriggle out of it. He made me feel guilty, even though I was not. Harrold, I said, backing up to the wall. For heaven's sake.

He put his hands on my shoulders, shook me once. He said, I know what these trips are like, what goes on.

What does that mean? I asked.

It means I know what goes on, he said.

I brought my arms up, pushed his hands away. I said, You're crazy; you've been drinking. I turned around, as if I would walk away. I wanted to get out of the room, shut a door.

I don't know if it was my saying he was crazy, or my

accusing him of drinking, but I'd said the magic word, ignited him. He grabbed my hair from behind, jerked my head back. I could somehow not believe that this was happening. Revolving as if in slow motion, I saw his hand, his free hand; it made an arc, hit the side of my head. I spun back into the wall, covered my face with my arm. I slid down onto the floor.

I was motionless. I didn't move a muscle. I was afraid even to breathe.

I heard a voice above me. *God*, he said. He hit the wall, put his fist through the plasterboard.

I heard him grab his coat, his keys. I heard the door shutting.

He didn't come back to the apartment or to the office for three days. I covered for him, said that he was sick. I said that a taxi driver at the airport had opened the door when I was bending down and that the door had hit me on the side of the face.

Once you tell your first lie, the first time you lie for him, you are in it with him, and then you are lost.

I want to tell you about something I witnessed when I was in St. Hilaire. Actually it was in Machias, when I was shopping at the A&P. I had Caroline in the baby basket in the front of the cart and was in the fruit-and-vegetable aisle, counting out oranges, when I heard a small commotion behind me. I turned to look and saw a woman walking fast, and with her there was a boy, about six years old or seven. He was crying, trying to catch up to her, trying to hold her hand. She was short and somewhat overweight. She had on a car coat, plaid, and a flower-printed kerchief. She snapped as she was walking, You're the one that lost the money; don't come cryin' to me. There won't be no treats this week. I give you a dollar bill to hold on to, and you lose it.

She was furious, wouldn't look at him.

He ran a little faster then and caught her hand. She whirled around and shook his hand out of hers as if it were a viper, a snake that she had found there. Don't touch my hand! she screamed, and walked away from him.

He followed her; he had nowhere else to go. I knew what he was thinking. He had to get her back. He had to make her like him again, or his entire world would fall apart.

He had on an old woolen winter jacket, a faded navy: a hand-me-down from an older brother? His hair was cut severely short, and his nose was running. He turned the corner after her, and I lost sight of him.

I bought my groceries and paid for them, and went out to the parking lot to put them in the car. Beside my car there was a dented station wagon, rusted here and there from the salt. The man inside was chewing on a cigarette. He had thinning hair that was greasy and dark sideburns that came almost to his jawline. He'd waited in the car while the woman and the boy I'd noticed were shopping. He was sitting in the driver's seat, listening to a story that his wife was telling him in fits and starts, with many hand gestures, some directed angrily to the boy in back. The boy sat sideways in the cargo area, his hood pulled up over his head. He was crying, sniveling, his face bent toward his knees.

The father screamed, Jesus fuckin' Christ! What's the

matter with you, givin' the money to the boy. What are you, some kind of moron? Serves you right he lost it.

And then he gave a kind of hiss of disgust and put the key in the ignition.

The wife turned her head away, inadvertently in my direction. She didn't look at me; she was looking at the brick wall. But I saw it all on her face: that mix of anger and of resignation; a desire there to lash out and a desire to be left alone. She was exhausted, drained. She hated the man beside her, but she would never be able to tell him that. Instead she'd shower anger on the boy in back.

I used to think that, like that woman, I never would be free—that freedom was like that distant point on the tracks. You could never get there.

Harrold went to work on the fourth day, came home that night. I did not know where he had stayed, and he didn't tell me. Already I was learning to be careful, not to ask certain questions, not to use a particular vocabulary. He said that it would never happen again, and I believed him. He was contrite, and he explained it—to me or to himself. He said that just the idea of my being with another man drove him crazy. And he'd been drinking. He would cut down on his drinking, but he denied he was an alcoholic: *not like his father*, he said. He wasn't like his father.

And I must not tell anyone. I must promise not to tell a soul.

I did not go out on stories again. I made excuses at the office. I said that I got motion sick, could not travel well in automobiles or airplanes. I could do a job of sorts if I did not go out, but it would hold me back: I'd have to rewrite files, not report them. I wouldn't get the by-lines.

He did not hit me again for several months, but there are levels of abuse, and some of it is not physical. The other violence was sometimes worse than being hit. It was more insidious, and he was very clever. I didn't understand it quite, and I don't think he did, either. It was something he could not stop himself from doing.

When you have been hit, it is almost a release. You have power then, because he cannot deny what he has done. He can only threaten you more, and he will, but he has lost a little bit of power. Because even though you never do, it is understood that you could now go to the police, or tell someone and say, Look at what he has done to me. But when the violence is invisible, no one knows. It is the violence that is more intimate than sex, that no one ever talks about. It is the darkest secret, the thing that binds you together.

There was a pattern to our married life. We would be close for a day or two or even a week, and I would have hope, and I would think the worst was over now and that we would be happy and have a family. And then, one day, because he had a story that was difficult, or because I had bristled or raised my voice, or because the ions in the air were crazed—I don't know—we would grow distant, and in the distance I would become afraid and tentative, and he would see that and would find that unattractive. Everything about me would suddenly be cause for criticism. I was growing shrill, he'd say. Or others thought me strident. Or I should learn to laugh a little more, loosen up. It didn't matter what it was—there were a thousand faults I had. My faults were legion, dizzying. It was because he loved me, he would again say when I asked him why. Because he cared so much.

And in the distances my anger would develop, so that what he said about me became a self-fulfilling prophecy. I *was* strident; I seldom laughed. The anger eroded joy, dissipated a life. It is a fallacy that anger makes you stronger. It is like a tide running out, leaving you depleted.

And that would be the ebb and flow of our days: the bait, the anger, his saying with derision, *Look at you*. The tears, my silence.

I told myself then that I would leave him. I tried to think of where to go and how to do it.

I tell myself now that I would have left him if I had not become pregnant.

I had the test in the morning but saved the news for the night. I had hope that the pregnancy would end the distances forever.

I had bought a bottle of champagne; we hadn't had champagne in ages. I made a dinner that I knew he'd like, put candles on the table. He knew at once, when he saw the table, that this was special, and he asked. He said, What's the story? And I said, We're going to have a baby.

He kissed me then and put his hand on my stomach. It seemed that he was happy. I felt a rush of giddiness myself: It would go well; I would call my mother after dinner. He opened the champagne, and we toasted babies.

I didn't want to drink much, so he had the bottle to

himself. He said once, during the dinner, What about your job? and I said that I would quit when the time was right. He said, What about us? and I said, We'll be better now—babies bring you closer. I saw a darkening on his brow, but I thought that this was normal: It was only natural for a man to worry some when he had a family coming.

I was drying dishes in the kitchen, thinking of how I would tell my mother, when I saw him standing in the doorway. He had changed into a T-shirt. He was drinking something else now; he had finished the champagne at supper. He said, Come to bed.

I didn't want to go to bed; I had other things to do. I was full of news and plans and wanted to tell more people. But I thought: He needs attention now; I can call my mother later.

I sat on the edge of the bed and began to unbutton my blouse. I felt tender toward myself. You will laugh at this, but I was thinking of myself as a fragile vessel, thinking I should take care now. It was a delicious feeling, that I was something special, and I was savoring it, unbuttoning my blouse slowly, in a dreamy way, thinking then not of Harrold but of babies, of having them inside you.

And then I looked up, and he was standing over me. He had his clothes on still, but he was furious. His eyes were black and glassy. I put my hands behind me on the bed, moved away from him, but he grabbed my blouse, stopped me.

I won't tell you what he did to me; you don't need all the details. Except to say that he pushed my face to the side with his hand, as if he would erase my face, and that what he did he did ferociously, as if he would shake the baby out of me. When he was finished, I curled up on my side of the bed and waited all night to lose the baby. But (strong girl) she didn't leave me.

In the morning, he wrapped me up with blankets and his arms, and brought me tea and toast and said we'd call my mother now, and what grand way could we break the news at the office?

There were other times, four or five, when I was pregnant. I didn't know then, and I don't know now, why it was that the pregnancy angered him so—angered him even as he was denying it, saying that he had never been happier. Perhaps it was that he felt replaced or that he was losing control over me for good; I don't know.

He would come after me only if he'd been drinking. He'd come home late from the bar, and I would be afraid of him. I'd be careful to stay away, but sometimes that would backfire. Somehow, sometime during the evening, I would say a word or a sentence that angered him, and he would hurt me when he took me to the bedroom. Later he would always be contrite, solicitous for my well-being. He would bring me things, make me promises.

I believe he couldn't stop himself. I had opened a door for him that he was unable to close. I think that sometimes he wanted desperately to close it, but he couldn't. In wanting control over me, he lost control over himself. He denied it, or he tried to. He was like an alcoholic hiding bottles in a closet; he suppressed the evidence. If you couldn't see the bruises on my face or arms or legs, he hadn't done it. It was how we lived. Once, when he saw me stepping from the shower in the morning, he asked me if I'd fallen.

I started taking sick days when I couldn't go into the office. Then I used my pregnancy as an excuse and did not go back at all.

In February I was five months pregnant. When I went to the doctor, he said, What is this? It was black, a swath of blue-black paint, on my thigh. There was another on my buttocks, under me, but he couldn't see that one. I said I'd fallen on the ice, on the steps of my building, and he looked at me. He said that if I fell, I should call him straightaway. To check the baby. After that visit, I did not go back for a while. I didn't see how I could tell him that I had slipped again.

Toward the end, Harrold didn't touch me. I grew big, I put on lots of weight, and I think he found me frightening. It was the only time I was ever safe from him, for those two months. I wasn't working then; I stayed inside. Or I walked in the park and talked to the baby. Mostly what I said was that I didn't want the pregnancy to end. Stay inside me, I would whisper. Stay inside me.

Harrold was distant, busy. He was gone for days, and then for weeks. He would say he shouldn't go, that he should be around for when the baby came. I knew I was safer without him, and so I said, I'll be OK, I have friends to help me.

I went to a psychiatrist. I told her what was happening. But I was veiled, cautious. She said, You have longings.

I looked at her.

That was it?

She didn't speak. She waited for me to say something.

I asked a question: Are longings wrong?

I started labor in the night, in June. It was a sultry night, soft and sweet-smelling, and I had all the windows open to the air. Harrold was far away, in London for a story. I got my watch and counted pains, and waited until morning so that I could call the neighbor who lived in the apartment next to ours. She came at once and summoned a taxi for me and went with me to the hospital. I knew her only slightly, just in passing, but I'd been saving her for just this day. In the taxi, she held my hand, this woman I hardly knew, and shouted at the driver to take it easy. She said to me, Are you all right? I thought she meant the baby, so I nodded.

And then she said, I have sometimes thought—

I looked at her.

She stopped and shook her head.

At the hospital, my neighbor said goodbye. I told her I would call her. She said, What about your husband? I said, He's on his way.

There was a woman in the next cubicle, but I have told you that already.

My labor was not too long. Twelve hours or thirteen. They say that that is average. When my baby came, they laid her on my chest, and she looked up at me.

When I came back from the hospital, Harrold seemed at first a changed man, and I had hope. He was calmer; he didn't drink. He came home early from the office. He held the baby and fed her from a bottle, and sometimes sat just watching her. When she woke up in the night, he would walk the floors with her until she'd fallen back asleep. I think he felt that she was his—another possession? He would sometimes say that—*my daughter*—but I understood it differently then, that he was filled with love and pride.

My mother came to visit and said how lucky I was to have both Caroline and Harrold, and I thought when she said it: Yes, that is how I feel, I have my family now, and we will be all right. The past is over, and I don't have to think about that now.

Caroline was six weeks old or seven. It was August, very hot and humid. Harrold had been home for three days. It was his vacation, but we hadn't gone away; we'd said it would be too soon to travel with the baby. There was a fan in the window, revolving slowly, I remember, and he'd had a drink, a tall sparkling one with lots of ice, and then another, in the middle of the afternoon. I thought: It's his vacation after all; if we had a cottage, we might be having summer cocktails.

But the drinking put him in a mood. We hadn't been together for several months. He said, It's all right now? and I nodded. I thought that I was ready and that I needed him. He inclined his head in the direction of the bedroom, and I went in there. We had the baby in a bassinet in the hallway, and she was sleeping.

We began slowly, and he was careful not to hurt me, and I was dreamy, languid, thinking: Babies let you start again; this will be a new beginning.

And then she cried.

I sighed and said that I would have to go to her. I started to sit up, but he held my arm and told me no.

Let her cry, he said, ignore her.

I can't, I told him. It isn't right. He held my arm tightly and wouldn't let me go.

She was wailing now, and I said, Harrold.

He was suddenly angry, furious with me. The baby, baby, baby, he said. It's all you ever think about.

He wouldn't let me go.

It was worse than all the other times, worse by far. Because all the other times, there was only me, and I could stand it if I had to. But this time there was the baby, crying in the hallway, crying, crying, crying, and I couldn't go to her. There is no way, ever in my life, that I can explain to you what that felt like.

We disintegrated after that. My voice grew shrill, everything I said was shrill. I remember standing in a doorway, shouting out, *I hate you*, not caring about the consequences. I had the baby in my arms, and I was thinking: She is hearing this.

He became immensely jealous; he thought that I was seeing men while he went to work. He drank heavily every day; the drinks would start at lunch with martinis, and he would go to bars after work. He couldn't bear to be wakened in the night, and if the baby cried, I had to silence her at once—I was afraid that he might hit her too. I began to hope that he would travel more, that he would go away for weeks, so that I could think, could clear my head, but he traveled less than ever. He was convinced that if he left, I would run away with another man. I began to hope that he'd die in an air crash. Are you shocked? Yes, it's true; I prayed for a crash. It was the only way I knew of to get free of him then.

Perhaps because of the drinking, or because he was in more trouble than even I knew about, his work began to suffer. A story he was working on was killed, and then he lost a cover. There was a new fellow in the office, who seemed to be the favorite now. His name was Mark; perhaps you know him. Sometimes Harrold would talk about him with derision, and I knew that Harrold was threatened by this man.

All his life, writing had been effortless for Harrold, but now it seemed that he had lost his way. He blamed me for this; he said that my constant nagging was destroying his concentration. He said that the broken nights were exhausting him, ruining his career.

Oddly, despite myself, I felt sorry for my husband then. It was coming apart too quickly, and he was powerless to stop it.

In October, there was unrest in Quebec, and Harrold had to go to Montreal. He had whittled the necessary traveling down to two nights, but he had to go. I saw this as my chance. I was nice to him all the week before. I had to make him go, I had to make him believe that I'd be faithful, that I wouldn't run away. I was girlish that week, girlish and sweet and pliant, and as sexy as I could muster. You'd think that might have roused suspicions on his part, but he believed that one day I would come around, turn the corner, and he was always watching for that moment. Perhaps he thought I'd given in after all, that I'd seen the error of my ways. I kissed him when he left, and said to him, Hurry back.

When he had gone, and I felt certain he was on a plane to Montreal, I packed a suitcase and got a taxi for myself. I bought a ticket at the airport, and I held the baby on the plane all the way to Chicago. There I boarded the train for the journey to the town where I'd grown up. I carried Caroline and my suitcase up the narrow street to my mother's bungalow.

When my mother came home from work, I said to her, Surprise! I said I'd had a whim, had come home for the fun of it. I said that Harrold was on a story and I was tired of staying alone. She believed me; she had no reason to doubt me. I couldn't bear to have my mother think that all her dreams had turned to dust.

What was I thinking then?

Perhaps I believed that in a day or two a plan would come to me. Or that in a day or two I would be able to tell my mother that my husband and I were having difficulties and that I needed time to think. I don't remember now. In retrospect, it seems naive to have chosen my mother's house to run to. Where else would I logically go? And he knew that. Knew it at once, knew it when he opened the door to the empty rooms.

He called. My mother answered the telephone. I could not tell my mother not to answer her own phone. Her voice was full of happiness and light, and she said to me, It's Harrold!

I took the phone from her.

I think I had hoped that he would go to the apartment and see me gone, and take some time himself to think.

That he might somehow welcome this reprieve. I had acted, extricated myself, released him from our terrible bond. Perhaps he would be grateful.

His voice was ice, full of clarity and intent. He said, If you don't return at once, I will come and get you. If you run away, I will find you. If you ever take my child away from me again, I will not only find you, but I will kill you.

He said these words, and I was looking at my mother, and she was smiling at me, holding Caroline's arm, teaching her to wave to me. My mother was saying to my daughter: Dada! Dada! It's Dada on the phone!

I can see you shaking your head. You're bewildered; you're confused. You think me unwell, as crazy as he was. Why did I go back? Why didn't I call the police?

Why indeed.

I believed that he would kill me if I did not go back. Or I couldn't tell my mother the truth. Or I thought that I had no right to take his child away from him. Or in my own dark way, I loved him still.

These reasons are all true.

When I returned to the apartment, I was seen to have capitulated utterly. I was punished for having run away, punished for having deceived him with charm the week before, punished for having stolen his child. He would hurt me physically, or he would be cold to me, or he would be derisive.

Look at you, he would say to me.

I went outside infrequently. I talked on the phone only to my mother, and everything I said to her was false.

I haven't told you anything about where I am. I think I should, although there isn't that much to tell.

When I came here, they searched my body. They took my fingerprints and my picture.

I have a cellmate, but she is quiet. She has been convicted of having stabbed her uncle, who functioned as her pimp. She exchanges sexual favors with women now for large quantities of tranquilizers and is sleeping out the rest of her sentence. The guards know this but don't mind. A sleeping prisoner is an easy prisoner to take care of.

Although I have a kind of solitude in my cell, the noise level in this block is deafening. I think I mind that the most, the noise. Even at night, there is talking, calling, laughing, screaming. They make you sleep with the lights on. I haven't yet discovered how to ward off all the noise or the light, but I am learning that the writing helps. I am creating a wall with the writing that is a kind of buffer.

I am in here with women who are thieves and drug addicts, but I'm not afraid of the women. I'm afraid of the staff. The staff have power over me; they determine everything I do.

The women who are awaiting trial or sentencing live in a suspended state, like purgatory or limbo. We say at meals or in the yard, Do you have any news? Or, Do you have a date yet?

In June, on her birthday, they brought me Caroline. She was walking. I hadn't been there to see her take her first steps, and though I was proud that she was walking, watched her walk to the table and fall into my arms, I was heartsick too. I could see that she didn't really know me.

They brought a cake, and I had a present for her I had

made, a doll of yarn and bits of cloth. We sang to her, and I fed her broken pieces of the cake. All around her, they were saying, Give a kiss to your Mummy. This is your Mummy, Caroline. I wanted everyone to leave us, but I knew they wouldn't, couldn't.

You will ask me, Was it worth it? And I will answer, How can it be worth it to be in hell and set yourself free, and then lose your daughter into the bargain?

And then I will answer, I didn't have a choice.

It was the first week of December, and the magazine was having a party for the editor, who was leaving. It had been almost a year since I'd visited the office. I said to Harrold, Do you think I should go?

He thought awhile and said, Why not? Let's show off the baby.

I bought a dress for the party, a black dress with a high neck and a long skirt, and I put Caroline into a red velvet dress my mother had sent her for the holidays. I wore my hair up, pinned it up with rhinestone combs, and when I held Caroline, and we looked at ourselves in the mirror, I thought: You would never know.

Harrold had said that I should bring Caroline to the office at five, when the party would begin. At a quarter to, I put her in the baby basket and drove to midtown where the office was. When I got to the nineteenth floor, Harrold was finishing up some business, but he came out of his office and smiled at me. Smiled at me. He put a proprietary arm around my shoulder, then took the baby from my arms. People came out of cubicles and offices to greet me. Harrold and Caroline and I walked around the office in a kind of luminous cocoon, and I knew how we must have appeared—a proud husband with his radiant wife and daughter. We were smiling, laughing, making easy jokes about my having traded deadlines for diapers, and Caroline was smiling with us. I thought—I remember thinking—Well, this is partially true. We *might* have been this couple.

It seemed there were a lot of people in the office, mostly familiar faces, some I didn't know. Then we all meandered into the dining room or near it, where there was a bar, and you came up to us. Harrold introduced you, and you shook my hand. I was struck first by your height— you must be five ten or eleven?—and then by your dress. It was khaki, I remember, a shirtwaist, belted, and I recall thinking that it was the sort of dress a woman ought to wear on a safari, in a Land-Rover, in the bush of Africa. It suited you. You held the baby, and Harrold went off to get us drinks.

I wonder now: Did you see anything? Did you know?

Did we chat? Briefly, possibly, about the baby, but then you moved away, and a man I'd never seen before came over to me to say hello. He said his name was Mark. He was tall and thin, with light-blue eyes and blond hair. He wore gold-rimmed glasses. I thought he was attractive. We began to talk. He said he knew Harrold, admired my husband's work, and knew that I had once worked for the magazine as well. I was still high from the illusion Harrold and I had created, and perhaps I was laughing—I think I might have touched Mark on the sleeve in the middle of a joke or a story—when Harrold came around the corner with the drinks. He'd been moving through the crowd, smiling easily, accepting compliments on his daughter, but when he saw me standing there with

Mark, he stopped. I wasn't looking at him, but I could feel him staring at me. I turned, against my better judgment, to see him, to call him over.

He was standing motionless, with a drink in each hand. He had on a blue blazer that day; his tie was dark stripes, I remember, loosened at the collar. His eyes were deep circles, fixed on me. He came forward, ignored Mark. He handed me my drink. He said, Get the baby. I want you to hold the baby.

Mark seemed to take the hint and drifted off, or perhaps he saw someone else to talk to, and when he was gone, Harrold said to me, I leave you for a minute, and already you're after some guy.

I didn't say anything. I knew better than to speak. I knew exactly what to do: to hold the baby and to talk only to women until Harrold took me home, and perhaps, if I was lucky, he might forget about what he'd seen or thought he had seen.

I was not lucky. Men came up to me and talked to me and sometimes kissed me; it was only natural. I hadn't seen them in almost a year. They were friends—not even friends, just acquaintances—but Harrold chose not to see that. Each man who came to me, I wanted to say to him, You are sealing my fate, but of course, I couldn't. I waited for half an hour, then I said to Harrold, I'd better go. He said, Do that.

I excused myself, said to anyone who asked that the baby had to go to bed. I drove home, took the baby up to the apartment, changed my clothes. I nursed Caroline, put her to bed for the night in her crib in her room. I made myself a drink; I was frightened. I knew that Harrold was angry, would drink too much, and would come home in a mood as black as his eyes had been. I had another drink, and I thought: Where the hell can I go now?

It was after midnight when he came. He was drunk, stumbling. His features were blurry, and I thought he might have been sick. His tie was missing, and his shirt was rumpled. I knew then that he'd been with another woman. I turned away. I was frightened, but I was filled with rage. I walked down the hallway to the bedroom and shut the door.

I waited.

He burst through the door like a large figure in a childhood nightmare. He said, Don't you ever shut a door in my face again!

It was the only thing I remember him saying.

He threw me against the wall. I put my hands out to protect my face. Perhaps I screamed; I heard Caroline begin to cry in her crib. I prayed that she would be silent, because I was afraid that he might harm her. I didn't cry out again. I put my hands out to protect my face, but he swatted them away like mosquitoes.

He was a machine, a machine of rage and fury. He had never been so frenzied. He didn't seem to care anymore where he hit me, that the bruises would be visible. Instinctively, I let my body go limp. I could not fight him, but I knew it was important to stay conscious if I could. His hands came down upon me, then he stumbled, missed, jammed his hand into the wall. He cursed, held his fingers, and I scooted out from under him. I ran to Caroline's room, swiftly scooped her from her crib, then locked us both in the bathroom.

He came to the bathroom door, shook the knob once as if he would tear it from the door. I didn't move. I waited. I sat on the tile floor and tried to get my blouse open so that I could nurse Caroline. I wanted to keep her quiet. She fell back asleep while I held her there.

I don't know how long I was in the bathroom, but I didn't hear him again. I didn't know if he had gone away or had fallen asleep or had passed out in the hallway. Or if he was sitting in a chair, waiting for me to open the door.

I sat cross-legged for what seemed like hours. When I moved finally, I felt a bolt of pain in my knee, but I knew I had to stand up. I opened the door, could not see him. Tentatively, I limped out into the hallway. He wasn't there. I walked into Caroline's room and put her in her crib. I inched down to my own bedroom, looked in on the bed. He was lying there, half undressed, his shirt still on, his pants and blazer on the floor. He had passed out, was lying on his stomach; he was snoring.

I have never been so quiet or so cautious or so quick. I picked up my duffel bag from the bottom of the closet, put a few things in it, went to the baby's room, packed the bag with her clothes. I walked back into the bedroom, removed Harrold's wallet from his pants pocket, took the cash there. I didn't even count it. I put on my coat and scarf and gloves, slung the duffel bag and my purse over my shoulder, wrapped Caroline in a blanket, and was out the door like a fox with her prey. I couldn't chance waking Caroline to put her in her snowsuit. I would do that in the car.

I took the elevator to the street, ran with my bundles to the car. The baby basket was in the back seat. I'd forgotten to bring it in. I put Caroline in her snowsuit. She woke up and began to cry, but when I started the engine, she was soothed.

The car was nearly out of gas, so I drove uptown to a gas station. I said to the attendant there, Do you have a map?

He said, A map of what?

I said, Anywhere.

He said, Let me look.

I sat in the car and waited. The city was still, unmoving. He came back and said to me, All I got is New England.

I said, Fine; I'll take it.

I turned on the overhead light, shook open the map, and spread it over the dashboard. I let my eye drift until I found a dot that I thought would be safe. I folded the map, switched off the light. I turned the key in the ignition.

I rolled down the window. I took my wedding band from my finger and threw it into the night. I didn't hear it land.

It was four o'clock in the morning, and I was headed north and east.

Jeffrey Kaplan

So how's old Ed Hargreaves? Keeping the magazine together, is he?

Exactly. Exactly.

And Mark Stein. What's he up to now? Taken over Harrold's territory, no doubt.

God, this is an awful business, isn't it? Terrible story, terrible. I was flabbergasted when I heard. I had no idea, none. Absolutely nothing.

I was at the magazine until the first of December, as you know. Maureen English had left the previous year. I knew them pretty well. Well, I *thought* I knew them well. Just goes to show, doesn't it?

She was quiet. But awfully good, awfully good. I thought she would really go places, make a name for herself, until she got that motion sickness. Shame, really. She said the doctors had tried everything with her, she couldn't shake it, something to do with the structure of her inner ear. So I put her on rewrites. God, she was fast. Give Maureen English a file, she'd have the story back to you before the day was out.

She was very attractive. You've met her. You could see right away someone was going to snap her up. I don't think I realized for quite a while that it was Harrold, though. They were cool in the office, very cool. I thought she had a bit of class, actually. You could see that. I don't mean from her background. I didn't really know much about her background, although she was obviously Irish. She was Maureen Cowan, by the way, when she first came. No, I mean the way she carried herself, kept to herself, wouldn't toot her own horn kind of thing. They met in my office, by the way.

Yes, they did. Let me think now. I was in the office. He'd come in. He had a beef with me about a headline, I think. I can't remember now. Something. And it was her first day of work. That's right. And she came in to ask a question. She was very nervous that day, very nervous. I remember she kept fingering these beads she was wearing. Looking down at her feet. I could see Harrold looking at her, smiling, but I didn't think much about it at the time. She'd have caught anyone's eye; it didn't strike me at the time as particularly meaningful. Though as I understand it now, they started seeing each other pretty soon after that.

Now Harrold. He did some great pieces for us then. Those were great days at the magazine. We had Joe Ward, and Alex Weisinger, and Barbara Spindell. Great days. I miss them sometimes. Publishing is a different business. I got out of magazines because the late nights were driving my wife crazy, but the pace is different here. You don't get that adrenaline high; you know what I mean. Books have a different evolution: You see the writers a lot less, hardly at all sometimes. And you've got to love a story. You're working on it for months, for years in some cases. Anyway, enough of this; you want to know about Harrold.

Let's see. He came to the magazine in '64, I think. He'd been working for *The Boston Globe* out of school, then wanted to get into magazines, into New York. He came at a good time. There was a bit of a vacuum—a lot of old blood leaving, retiring. I'd been there a year or two myself; I'd come over from the *Times*. So when he signed on, he was able to move up rather quickly. I had him out reporting almost at once. He was a great reporter. Very aggressive in the field. Wouldn't quit till he got the story. He'd hound them to death, or charm them. I think his size helped, actually. He was very impressive physically. You must have met him. About six four, I think; two hundred pounds, anyway, but not fat, just well-muscled. Played for Yale, I'm pretty sure. But he wasn't a blow-hard like some guys from the Ivy League you meet. Kept to himself most of the time. And those eyes. Black as coal. They could pin you to the wall, make you squirm. I saw him do it a couple of times. Pretty impressive.

Harrold English was a real pro. We weren't what you would call friends, but we had some lunches. You know the kind of thing; you get to really talking after the second martini. He said once that he'd had a bit of an unhappy childhood, despite the money. His mother died when he was a kid, and he never got along with his father.

Bit of a son of a bitch, from what I gather. They weren't close. I never heard about any other family.

I liked his writing style. It was clean, straightforward, not too much of the "I," and I liked that. You could feel his intelligence in the piece, but he didn't let it get in the way. He wasn't one of those let-me-show-you-my-dazzling-virtuosity kind of writers. Just straight. Always got his facts right. The fact checkers loved his pieces.

Maureen, she had a different style. I'd say more feminine, except that would probably get me in trouble. Her rhythms were different, more fluid. I liked her writing, but you had to push her a bit to dig a little deeper for the story. She had a hard time asking the really tough questions. One time she came in to see me and said she didn't want to write only about trends anymore; I'd had her on Trends. I was a little bit taken aback, but I could see her point, so I moved her over to National. She was very good there, detached in a way, but good. Until she couldn't travel anymore.

I think it was a good six months before I knew they were seeing each other. When I heard about it, I have to tell you, I wasn't too happy about it. I've seen these office romances, and they always lead to trouble. You have a fight at home, what are you supposed to do at the office? But Maureen and Harrold, like I said, they were cool. If you didn't know, you'd never have known, if you know what I mean.

That's why it's so—Jesus—unbelievable. I have trouble believing it even now. I just can't see it. I mean, you hear about these kinds of stories once in a while, but it's always some poor woman with six kids in Arkansas or

147

Harlem, and her husband is an alcoholic kind of thing. Rarely do you hear about this kind of thing with people like Harrold and Maureen.

You would think there'd be a hint of something somewhere. And Harrold was no alcoholic. I mean, he drank like the rest of us drank. A martini at lunch maybe, maybe two if the occasion called for it. Cocktails at dinner, that kind of thing.

Although I will say, the last couple of months I was at the magazine, he did seem to be in a bit of a slump. We all get them; I really didn't think too much about it. Was he drinking more then? I really can't remember. I do remember thinking that maybe he was bent out of joint a bit by Stein. Stein was straight out of Columbia, a whiz kid. Very sharp. Very. He was at the magazine a couple of months, and already he was stepping on Harrold's toes. Flavor of the month, that kind of thing. It coincided with Harrold's slump, put the edge on the slump, but I knew Harrold would pull out of it. He'd just had a baby. I could remember what that was like—up all night, out of it all day. I figured he was cutting some slack for a few months, then would pick up speed. And then I left, and really never gave it another thought.

Until I heard. Absolutely stunning. Really.

But it's a hell of a story. In fact, I don't know if you've given this much thought, but you might have a book there. You know, maybe an *In Cold Blood* kind of thing. It depends on what you get, how it shapes up. There are some interesting themes here: the secretiveness of it all, the fact that it was them. Like Scott and Zelda run amok kind of thing.

Yeah, it's a possibility. Tell you what. You put the

piece together, send it over to me when you've finished it, before it comes out. I'll take a look, let you know.

She had a lover up in Maine, didn't she?

For the book, we'd want to know about that. These complexities. Makes a better story. It might have some bearing on her motives, don't you think?

December 5, 1970 – January 15, 1971

———————

Mary Amesbury

I heard a sound. A muffled sound of tires crunching over gravel. A car or a truck was moving slowly down the lane, as quietly as it could, a sleepy vehicle at daybreak. I tossed back the covers and went to the window. I found my cardigan on a chair and put it on. The floorboards were cold underneath my feet. Outside, there was a field of gray, that half hour of lightening before the sun would rise. I watched the black truck roll along the sand to the dinghy. A man got out. It was the same man as yesterday, although I could see only the yellow slicker clearly through the field of gray; his features were indistinct. The water was still and flat, and when he sculled out to his boat, there was a perfect rippled wake behind his oar.

The rumble of the motor was a complaint, a boat disturbed too early and grumbling under her skipper. I saw flashes of the yellow slicker on the bow, in the wheelhouse, then moving in the boat in its graceful arc out to where the sun would rise.

I sat on the edge of the bed and watched the boat disappear. I wondered where he was headed, how he knew where to go, what it would be like when he got there— another expanse of gray, with colored buoys bobbing in the water? I didn't know what time it was for certain, but I knew that it had to be early: no later than six-thirty, I imagined. To be on the water by six-thirty, I thought, required rising at five-thirty. In the dark with his wife at his side, his children sleeping in another room. And this was in December, with the longest nights of the year. What must a lobsterman's life be like in June, when daybreak came at four or earlier? Do lobstermen eat their supper in the late afternoon, I wondered, go to bed before their children?

I touched a finger to my lip; it was swollen still, and tender. I was aware, too, of other places that I didn't want to touch. There was something wrong with my knee. I wasn't sure what, exactly, but it burned under the knee-cap, as if I'd wrenched it in a fall. I thought that perhaps the cleaning yesterday hadn't helped it much, the crouching and the bending.

I heard the baby stir and went to her and lifted her out of the crib. I carried her to bed and pulled the covers up high over us so that we were a warm package together underneath. I nursed her this way and she drifted back to sleep, and perhaps I did too, but I remember listening to the sounds of my new surroundings, trying to orient myself to where I lived. There were the gulls, roused now and cawing over the point, and there was a breeze that was coming with the sunrise.

I slipped out of bed, humped up a secure niche for Caroline, and went downstairs to make myself a cup of coffee and a bowl of cereal. The sun had risen; the day would be clear. The water went from gray to pink to violet even as I watched from the table. I heard another vehicle in the lane, saw a blue-and-white pickup truck emerge from the brush and stop in front of the gray fish house. A man in a pea jacket and watch cap got out, carrying a cardboard box of rope and bits of hardware. He went inside the shack, and in a few minutes I saw smoke rising from a chimney. When he opened the door again, I heard the jarring patter of a disc jockey from a radio inside. The man walked to the back of his truck and removed several lobster traps and carried them into the shack. He didn't come out again.

After a time Caroline began to cry. I brought her down, bathed her in the sink, dressed her, and set her on the braided rug. She seemed intent on mastering the art of crawling, or at least the art of balancing on all fours, despite a few comical false starts and a tendency to propel herself backward. But I was tickled by the look of concentration on her face, the tongue tucked into the corner of her mouth, the goofy expression of surprise when her coordination betrayed her and she collapsed on her tummy.

I had another cup of coffee and made a list. I needed a clock and a radio and a laundromat. The soiled diapers were piling up, and Caroline was running out of clothes. I wanted to see if I could find a baby sling too. I thought if I had one I could walk on the beach with her if it warmed up some. Carrying her in my arms wasn't practical. Even though she wasn't all that heavy—only seventeen pounds— it was an awkward position for long distances, and my arms would grow tired.

In lists there was a kind of order: creating purpose out

of aimlessness; rescuing a day from a vast expanse of time. It didn't matter so much that I didn't actually have the clock; it was enough just to have written it on the list. That was progress. I thought that I would dress myself, find my pocketbook, put Caroline into her snowsuit, and make my way into Machias, but for the moment I was content just to sit and look out the window, drink a cup of coffee and watch my baby daughter on a rug, or the water change its color out the window. I had forgotten the fear of the night before, or I had put the taste of it aside. This was a new sensation, drifting with the moment, *enjoying* the moment, with no urgency for the next, and I savored it, or rather, I simply let it happen.

Machias is, I think, considered a small city by the people who live around it, but I was reminded of a suburb. It had more shops and buildings than St. Hilaire, but it, too, was quiet, an only somewhat larger fishing town, on the banks of the Machias River. I saw a lumber mill, a furniture factory, a restaurant, a fish store, a five-and-ten, a gift shop, a church, a hardware store, an A&P, and one historical house that was open for tours in the summer. There *was* a laundromat. There were strollers for sale in the five-and-ten, and I would have liked one, but I was concerned about the money I had left, how long I could make it last. I bought a clock radio, however, thus crossing off two items on my list with one purchase. Along one wall, there was a small shelf of books—a paperback shelf of doomed love. I selected three: *Anna Karenina, Ethan Frome, The French Lieutenant's Woman.* In another aisle, I bought a sling and two presents for my daughter: a string of toys to hang across a crib that she could bat at, and a fuzzy yellow duck I could not resist. As I put the duck on the checkout counter, I was suddenly struck by the idea that just as Harrold had had his legacies, so also did I have mine: I was alone now with a daughter. I was alone now with a daughter for good, just as my mother had been. The woman behind the counter, a woman who looked as if she might be related to the woman who owned the Gateway Motel, had to ask me twice for my money.

I wondered then, as I was walking to my car with the baby and my purchases, what Harrold was doing. He would not, at first, go to the police; he'd be afraid that I might tell them what had happened. He'd try other ways of obtaining information: He would call women I'd known at the office; he would quiz my neighbor; he would keep a careful watch on our bank account. I didn't think he would call my mother. He would know I hadn't gone there again. And then, when I did not return, he might call a private detective whom he had gone to school with and whom he had sometimes used on a story. Harrold would have to be careful; he'd have thought the dialogue through in advance. He would say, in a voice rich with male camaraderie, that he had a ticklish situation, could the fellow help him out? He would explain that I had gone away on a trip and hadn't returned, and he was worried that something had happened to me. He'd tell the man he didn't want a fuss, we'd had a little row, and that all he needed to know was where I was. He'd ask his friend not to tip me off, and he'd say that he himself would drive to where I was, sweet-talk me into coming back—

you know how women can be, he'd say—and then they'd laugh together, and one of them would say, Let's have a drink when you're in the neighborhood.

He wouldn't say I'd kidnapped his child. Not yet. That would be his trump card, his ace in the hole. He'd save that for later, in case I did speak up, went to the police before he got to me. What was hitting a wife, he would reasonably argue, compared to stealing a baby?

There were three trucks in front of the fish house when I returned from Machias; one of them I recognized, a red pickup with gold-leaf scrollwork under the driver's-side window. Indeed, no sooner had I entered the cottage and put the baby down than I heard a knock on the door. Willis had a package in his hands, and he spoke to me. This is how I remember it:

"Brought you some fish," he said, walking into the kitchen. "Haddock. Caught this morning. Not me. André LeBlanc brought it in."

I took the package from him. He put his hands into the pockets of his jeans and hunched his shoulders up underneath his denim jacket. He looked as if he were freezing. I said that I had to get some packages from the car.

"Don't you move," he said. "I'll get them for you." And before I could respond, he was out the door.

He brought in all the packages from the five-and-ten and the bundle of laundry from the laundromat. I saw that he was wearing the same pair of jeans as yesterday, the same navy sweater.

"I have to put the baby in for a nap," I said.

I thought that he would leave then, but he said instead, "No problem," and walked over to the window, looking out at the point.

I took off my coat and scarf and carried the baby upstairs. I sat on the bed and nursed her, and when she was finished, I laid her down in the crib and pulled her blanket over her. Below me, I could hear footsteps on the floorboards, the refrigerator opening, a chair scraping the linoleum.

When I came downstairs he was sitting at the kitchen table. He had an open can of beer in front of him.

"You don't mind," he said, lifting the can in my direction.

I shook my head, stood uncertainly in the middle of the kitchen floor.

"Get one yourself," he said genially, as if it were his kitchen, as if we were old friends.

I quickly shook my head again. I turned the heat on under the coffeepot, stood by the stove while I waited for the coffee to warm up.

"Let me pay you for the fish," I said.

He waved his hand. "Wouldn't hear of it. Think of it as a housewarming present." He laughed. "No, seriously," he said. "I didn't even pay for it. LeBlanc gave me a coupla pounds of fish; I just skimmed off a pound for you. I been waitin' for you over at the fish house. I got pots do to myself, but it's too fuckin' cold out there. Anyway, I feel like takin' a coupla days off."

He looked around the cottage. He snapped a beat with his splayed fingers on the table. He bobbed up and down in his chair for a measure or two. I wondered what music he was listening to. "You like the Dead?" he asked.

I nodded noncommittally.

"I gotta get a tree," he said. "Jeannine likes it early. Says it gives her somethin' to look forward to. She puts it in a corner of the trailer. I worry about fire, that's the only thing."

"Fire?"

"You have a fire in a trailer and you're dead. Just like that." He snapped his fingers. "It's like fryin' in an aluminum box. It's the biggest problem with a trailer, fire. So I only allow the kids to have the lights on when I'm in the trailer with them—the lights on the tree, I mean. And I'm a son of a bitch about keepin' it watered. The minute the needles start fallin' off, I get rid of it. But any tree I get won't shed until Valentine's Day." He laughed again. "I'll cut it myself, in the woods across from the Coffin place. Sit down, take a load off your feet."

I poured the heated coffee into a mug, took the mug to the table. He kicked out a chair with his boot, an invitation. I sat down, took a sip of coffee. I'd let it boil, and it burned my tongue. Willis looked at me, seemed to be studying my face. He looked away toward the living room.

"Baby asleep?" he asked. He looked back at me.

I nodded.

He stood up, walked to the refrigerator, took out another can of beer. He opened the can and drank it almost entirely down. He returned to the table, stood just to the side of me. He was looking out at the point, with the can in his hand.

"So what's the story?" he said. "You and your old man are definitely split, right?"

"Something like that," I said carefully.

"You're on your own now," he said, more to himself than to me.

"For now," I said vaguely.

There was an awkward silence. I felt his presence beside me. He was standing close to me, calmer, not moving now.

The back of his finger brushed the bruise at the side of my cheekbone. I flinched, more because of the shock of his touching me than from any pain.

"Oh, did that hurt?" he asked, as if surprised. "Sorry. Didn't mean to hurt you. It must still be pretty raw."

I stood up. The chair was between us. I put my hand on the chairback. "I'm tired," I said. "I didn't sleep well. I think you'd better go now. I'd like to take a nap."

He put his hand on my hand. His fingers were dry and cold. He looked at the place where our hands were touching.

He said, "You wouldn't like to—you know—like fool around, or anything, while the baby is asleep?"

I slowly pulled my hand from his, crossed my arms over my chest. My chest was tight, and for a moment it was hard to breathe.

"No," I said. And then again: "No." I shook my head.

He quickly withdrew his hand, put it into his pocket. "Yeah, well, I didn't think so."

He nodded, as if to himself. He took a last swallow from the can. He sighed.

"Sometimes," he said, "a women gets left by a guy, she needs a little lovin', you know what I'm talkin' about. Nothin' heavy, just a little comfort. I thought maybe . . ." He shrugged.

I didn't say anything.

"So no hard feelings, right?"

I looked down at my feet.

"Come on, Red, let me off the hook."

I looked up at him. On his face was an expression of genuine, if mild, anxiety. Perhaps he had been opportunistic, but there had been no malice behind his request, I thought. He had tried and failed, and that was all right with him; he would think that it had been worth trying.

"No hard feelings," I said.

He made a show of relief, letting his breath out, wiping imaginary sweat off his brow. "Well, good," he said. "That's settled." He began again to move his shoulders from side to side.

I was thinking how long it had been since I had been able to say no to a man and not be fearful of the consequences, since I had been able to say no to a man at all. I was almost glad that Willis had asked, despite the minute of awkwardness between us.

"There's Jack," Willis said, turning away and walking to the window.

I followed him and looked out at the water with him. The green-and-white lobster boat had entered the channel and was closing in on the mooring. We stood together and watched as the man in the yellow slicker snagged the mooring, hitched the boat to the buoy, and jumped back into the cockpit to turn off the motor—a fluid motion, a graceful maneuver.

"He's crazy," said Willis. "You wouldn't catch me out there on a day this cold, but Jack, he don't give a shit, excuse me, about the weather."

We watched as the tall man with the sand-colored hair unloaded buckets of lobster into the dinghy that he had pulled alongside the larger boat. He returned to the cabin then, appeared to be fastening a door.

"Course if I had his home life, I might be out on the water year round too. His wife has got the blues real bad. She don't clean the house or nothin'. Jack does it all. Him and his daughter. I used to feel sorry for his kids. They're good kids, but it's a sad house. My wife, Jeannine, she tried to go over there once, sort some things out; Rebecca was in her room, wouldn't come out. Jeannine swore she heard her cryin' through the door. They got a Cape down the road here. Cries herself to sleep most nights, so I'm told. Jack, he don't say much about it, but you can see it on his face. I'll hand it to him, though, he's stuck by her all these years. She waited for him when he went away, and he came back and married her."

He peered closer out the window, as if something interested him there.

We watched the man in the slicker scull toward shore. The water was a deep, crisp winter blue.

"Rebecca didn't start gettin' sad till after she got married and her babies come. They say that happens to women sometimes. But it's the sea and the weather what does it. The gray and the long winters—that really does 'em in."

The man in the slicker beached his boat, made it fast on the iron ring.

"He's stuck with her for the kids, of course. Although sometimes I think he mighta done better by the kids if he'd got out of there, married someone else. Well, you can't ever know why a person does what they do, can you. Maybe he still loves her; you never know."

Willis turned away from the window.

"I gotta go," he said. "The guys at the fish house,

they're goin' to want to know what happened to me. They'll start makin' jokes. And if I drink any more of these, I'll fall asleep; then they'll really be ribbin' me."

He put the two cans in the trash, walked to the door.

"So," he said, "you're all set, right?"

I nodded. I thanked him again for the fish.

He waved his hand as if to toss my gratitude away. He looked at me.

"I gotta go fix some pots," he said.

As it grew toward evening, Caroline began to fret, then to cry. Nursing didn't help; she refused me, twisting angrily away and scrunching up her features in a grimace of discomfort. I thought: If she won't feed, how can I help her? She wasn't content to lie or rock in my arms, and seemed to be trying to jam her fist into her mouth. This convinced me again that she must be hungry, but each attempt to feed her ended in tears and frustration. I put her then up against my shoulder and began to walk with her. She was quiet as long as I was actually walking. If I sat and tried to duplicate the sensation of bouncing up and down from the walking, she quickly saw the ruse and cried almost at once. What was it about the walking? I wondered. It was mysterious and exhausting. I walked in a circle through the kitchen, the living room, the downstairs bedroom, around and around until I thought I would drop, or go mad from the tedium. I was sure she would fall asleep against my shoulder, but as long as I walked, she remained contented and alert. If I stopped, even for a minute, she would begin to cry again. I thought: If whatever hurts her doesn't hurt when I am walking, how can it hurt when I sit down?

I walked for at least an hour, maybe two. Toward evening I remembered the baby sling, endured her wrath as I dressed her and myself for the cold, and struggled to get her into the new contraption. A change of scene might save my sanity, I thought, and the fresh air might let her drift off to sleep.

The air stung: I shielded her face in my coat. The sling allowed her weight to rest on my hip rather than in my arms, and it was such a relief to be out of the cottage, I didn't mind the cold. The sharp air was bracing, but not as bitter as it had been the day before—or perhaps the damp by the sea had taken the edge off; I don't know. I walked down the slope to the pebbled side of the spit, made my way along its expanse. My boots, even with their modest leather heel, were inappropriate for the rough surface, and the walking was slow going. I thought immediately that I would have to be careful, that I could not afford to stumble or to twist an ankle. Apart from the damage to Caroline from a possible fall, there was the total isolation of the point. Would anyone hear my shouts if I was in trouble? I looked around and thought not. The nearest cottage, a blue Cape up on the main road, was too far away to call to: I would not be heard against the white noise of the surf and wind, particularly if all the windows and doors in that cottage were tightly shut, as they must be on a cold night.

Dusk was gathering quickly, seeming to rise in a mist from the gray gulf itself. Already I could no longer make out the horizon—only the blip of the lighthouse at rhythmic intervals. There was seaweed on the stones, some old weathered boards—driftwood—empty crab shells, bits of blue-violet mussel shells. As I passed the fish house, I could smell the lingering scent of a dampened fire. I was intrigued by the fish house. I walked over to it and peered into the windows, but I could not see much in the gloaming: two or three aluminum-and-plastic lawn chairs; a stack of slatted traps in a corner; a low wooden bench along one wall; a small, untidy fireplace. I thought about the men who gathered there during the day, imagined their voices as they sat in the stuffy warmth, mending their gear. I wondered what they said to each other, what they chatted about.

I crossed the ridge of grasses to the beach side of the spit, enjoying the comfort of the hard sand underfoot in place of the uneven stones. I thought briefly of the honeypots that Willis had warned against, but I wasn't sure I believed in them; anyway, I reasoned, if I kept close to the high-water mark, I wouldn't step in one.

When I reached the point, the green-and-white lobster boat had lost its color. There was a faint outline of its shape, a sense of rocking from side to side. Only a set of yellow foul-weather gear, hanging on a hook by the pilothouse, caught what was left of the light. The gear looked like a man moving with the boat—so much so, in fact, that I felt as if someone were watching me.

I was thinking about the man Willis had referred to as Jack, and about his wife, Rebecca, who had become melancholy, when I idly stuck my little finger into Caroline's mouth for her to suck on. I sometimes did this if I thought of it, because it seemed to soothe her, but when I put my finger in this time, she immediately bit down on it, and I felt the tiny sharp surprise. That was it, then, the source of her discomfort and irritation: My daughter had another tooth, one on top this time. I could feel only a sliver of a rippled ridge in her gum; I couldn't see the tooth in the darkness. She looked up at me and smiled. She seemed almost as relieved as I was that I had solved her mystery. I remembered then that I didn't have any baby aspirin with me. I wondered what the women of St. Hilaire used when their babies teethed—a sluice of brandy along the gums, a frozen crust of bread to gnaw on, or the prosaic baby aspirin I'd have used if only I had thought to buy it at the store?

I heard a motor on the lane. I turned to look back in the direction from which I'd come, but darkness had fallen so swiftly I could no longer see the cottage, only a flicker of headlights as a vehicle bounced along the dirt road toward the beach. I thought it might be Willis, wanting company—perhaps thinking to try his luck again now that it was evening and I'd been softened by an entire day alone with the baby. But when I saw the headlights make their way steadily along the beach, I was inexplicably frightened, as though I were trespassing and would be caught or scolded. I was standing just south of the point; the truck was moving along the northern edge of the spit. I was sure the headlights would soon pick me out, but the truck stopped just short of where it would have found me. The driver left the headlights on and got out of the cab. He still had on his yellow slicker; you could see that right away. I stood motionless behind a small hillock of sand. I put my finger in Caroline's mouth to keep her from crying, but it wasn't necessary; she had finally fallen asleep.

I watched as the man called Jack walked along the sand to his dinghy. He bent into the boat to retrieve a metal box, like a toolbox, but as he straightened up, he seemed to hesitate. He laid the box on the edge of the dinghy and bowed his head, as if thinking for a moment. He replaced the box in the boat, walked back to the truck, and turned off the headlights. I was puzzled. I could barely see him now—just a hint of a yellow slicker moving across the sand to the dinghy again. He got inside and sat down. He didn't move.

I could have turned and walked back to the cottage along the gravel beach. He'd have heard me, but I'd have been walking away from him by then, and there'd have been no need to call out to me or to speak. I could have done that. But I didn't.

I stood at the edge of the point, cradling the baby, my finger in her mouth. I was watching the man in the dinghy—only a suggestion of yellow against the black of the sand and the water. The natural light, what little remained, was playing tricks with my eyes. Already it was impossible to tell where the water met the shore, and I was no longer sure I knew where the truck was parked. The man lit a cigarette. I could see the sudden flare of the match, the red ember.

I stood and he sat for perhaps five minutes. I don't know what I was thinking then; I was just watching, trying not to think. I did not consciously decide, yes, I will speak to him; I did not have a reason to speak to him beyond a vague curiosity or wonder about what his life was like, with his wife and his children and his boat. Possibly I felt that I wanted to dispel the image of trespassing, that I didn't like the image of myself sneaking away. I crossed over the hillock to the northern side of the point, walking toward him, saying as casually as I could—as if it were noontime, summer, and I were having a stroll on the beach with my daughter—*hello*, as I walked.

I startled him, I could see that. He'd been far away, or he was surprised to see another human being. Probably, I thought, he was used to having the point to himself, had forgotten there was a car at the cottage.

He stood up, stepped out of the dinghy, faced me. I said hello again, and I think he must have answered me or nodded.

I walked close to him. Now that I had intruded upon him, I had to let him see me—though I must have appeared to him as only a gray shape in my coat and scarf.

My first impression of him is distinct and clear. I am not overlaying this with later images, seen in the sunlight, or by firelight or at daybreak. His face was angular, and I was aware that he was taller than I'd thought. There were deep lines running from his nose to the bottom of his chin at either side of his mouth, but I didn't think these were from age, even though he looked as if he was in his forties. They were from weathering; his face was weathered. You could see this even in the darkness: the roughened skin, the wrinkling at the eyes. His hair was average length and curly. You could not see the true color in the darkness, but I knew already it was the shade of dry sand. He wore an off-white Irish knit sweater underneath his slicker; there was a hole unknitting itself where his collarbone would be. He threw his cigarette onto the sand.

"You've got a baby there," he said. His voice was deep and slow, hesitant, but he didn't sound surprised. He had a bit of the Maine accent; it was in the lilt of the words and in his vowels. But he spoke more like Julia Strout, his cousin, than Willis Beale.

I looked down at Caroline.

"She was teething—I just discovered that—and I was trying to get her to stop crying, so I brought her out for a walk in the sling."

"Looks like it worked," he said.

"Yes," I said. I smiled. "I've taken the cottage there."

That seemed to register. He looked in the direction of the cottage.

"I heard someone was there, and I've seen your car."

We didn't tell each other our names, and we didn't shake hands. Why? I thought at the time it was merely economical, as if we imagined we would not know each other long, or at all.

"I've seen you," I said. "And your boat."

"I bring it into town if we get some weather. Otherwise, I leave it till mid-January. We sometimes get a thaw in early January."

"Oh."

"Cold tonight, though."

"But you went out today."

"I did. Didn't get much for my trouble."

"Willis Beale was delivering some fish when we saw you come in. He said he thought you were crazy to go out today."

He made a sound, a sort of laugh. "Willis," he said, as if I shouldn't pay much attention to Willis. But I already knew that.

He was glancing out to where he'd have seen his boat if there were any light left, and I was looking at the side of his face. Ravaged, I remember saying to myself, by the elements or by something else. What was it about the face? The eyes—they were old eyes, or were merely tired. Yet I was drawn to his face, its shape, the sense of calm around the mouth, or what I took to be calm in the dim light. His body was lean, but you felt its weight, as if it were anchored to the sand. Or its stillness. I had a feeling of stillness when I watched him, when he moved.

A breeze came up, blew a strand of hair across his brow.

"I have to put her to bed," I said, shielding Caroline's head with my arms.

"Getting late," he said.

He bent down to retrieve the toolbox from the dinghy. I walked away.

We didn't say, "So long now," or, "Nice meeting you."

I was halfway down the beach when I heard the motor of the truck start up. For a minute I was walking in its headlights, conscious of my back in the headlights, and then they were gone, veering up the lane. I stopped to watch the progress of the truck, the jostling of the light on the rough dirt, the left turn onto the coast road, the swath of light moving south toward town.

There was a rhythm to my days. It established itself before I had even become aware of it, an insistent pattern pushing at the edge of my consciousness.

Each day I woke with the low rumbling of a motor on the lane. There would be just a hint of gray beyond the window, the first sign of daybreak. I would listen as one or several trucks made their way down the sand, and after a time I began to be able to recognize the sounds of routine: a truck door shutting, the dragging of an object along a truck's metal bed, the small splash as a dinghy was put into the water, the creak of wood under a man's weight, the slap of a wake against a larger boat. And then the other motor would start up, grumble a bit as if it wanted to quit, and there would be the quiet whine out to silence as a boat moved away from the mooring.

Each day I made the high double bed. I smoothed the sheet, drew up the quilt. There was about these gestures a monastic purity, a return to the single self. If the baby was not awake yet, I would go down to the kitchen and make myself a cup of coffee and sit in my nightgown and sweater at the table and watch the water change its colors as the day began.

At first I was unable even to read. I had the books, but for days they lay unopened on the table. I wanted just to look.

It was winter, the dead of winter, when everything was dormant, and yet I was continually surprised by the constant mutability of the landscape. Sometimes the tide would go out so far that what sea was left was only puddles. At other times, when the tide was high, the spit in front of me would seem to have shrunk to a spindle.

I knew so little. For the first few days, I couldn't predict the tides at all; they were a constant surprise. I somehow always had it wrong. I could spot the gulls, but there were other birds I had never seen before. Sometimes I thought I saw seals, I was sure of this, and yet when I'd look again, the dark hump I'd thought was a seal was only a rock with the water lapping against it.

I had my chores, of course. I took to washing the clothes by hand, boiling the diapers and putting the wash out on a line behind the house. I liked the way our wash looked—the tiny undershirts and my jeans whipping in the breeze.

There was industry all around me, and perhaps I took my cue from that. How could I be idle when every morning men came to the point to mend their broken pots and traps or go out onto the water? First there would be the trucks, then the sound of a boat's engine or a curl of smoke from the fish house. There might be three trucks on the point, or four. From time to time, I'd hear a voice or a bit of music, sometimes a shout and then a laugh. And in the early afternoon, I'd see the green-and-white lobster boat come from behind a pine-darkened island. This would be a milestone in my day, a mark of punctuation, and I never failed to watch the man in the yellow slicker perform his returning ritual.

But when the black truck had gone back up the lane, the day would seem to lose its momentum. The rhythms I had heard and understood and counted on disappeared, and those hours until darkness were somewhat harder for me to negotiate. I tried to fill them with a drive or a walk or a nap. But I understood that these were gestures of defiance, skirmishes against empty time.

Eventually, in the second week, I established a routine that suited me, that didn't feel at odds with the world around me. I bought a few skeins of yarn and began to knit, a sweater for myself and one for Caroline. In the mornings, when the baby napped, I would knit. My mother had taught me how when I was a child, but I hadn't taken it up again since I had moved to New York. I felt it as a link to her, to something she had given me, translated now into something I could give my daughter.

I liked also the sense of working with my hands—a kind of counterpoint to the men working around me.

I called my mother once a week on Saturdays, from the A&P in Machias. It was a habit we'd established, and I knew she'd be alarmed if she didn't hear from me. I didn't tell her where I was or what had happened. I pretended everything was fine.

Willis came by almost every day, on one pretext or another. He might have fish for me or want to warm up in the kitchen. Once he had whittled a small wooden figure for Caroline. Each day he took a seat at the kitchen table. He would look at my face. The bruises were healing, I knew, and didn't appear as raw as they had when I had first come to the cottage. But when he examined me, I would look away.

I almost always let him in, from politeness if nothing else, and he seldom stayed long. I think he felt proprietary toward me. He never asked again if we could "fool around," as he had put it that day, but the question always seemed to be in the air: If he was persistent enough, would I not change my mind?

You will perhaps wonder why I permitted these visits and I sometimes ask myself that too. I believe I didn' want to alienate Willis—or anyone else from the town, for that matter. Nor did I want to draw attention to myself any more than I had to. I think I hoped that Willis would grow tired of my lack of response and stop coming.

After Willis had left, I would feed the baby and then make a lunch for myself. Usually I'd done my chores by noontime. Then I'd go out with the baby. If the day was reasonable, I'd put Caroline into the sling, and we would walk to the end of the point and back, or south along the rocks. I had bought for myself, on one of my forays into Machias, a pair of sneakers so that I could make my way better along the stones. Sometimes I'd look for things: smooth mauve pebbles one day, pure white shells the next. There were jars and cups of stones and shells collecting on the sills in the cottage.

After a walk, I'd put Caroline into the car, and we would drive into St. Hilaire. I shopped every day at the store there, selecting in the early afternoon what I would have for supper. I learned to weather the baleful glass eye, the small talk, and the questions—even, after a time, to look forward to them, a tenuous thread of connection to the town.

Two days a week, when it was open, I'd go to the library. I'd begun finally to read, and once I'd begun, I became hungry for more books. I read in the evenings and long into the nights, sometimes devouring a book a day. I hadn't ever had this kind of time, it seemed to me, and the books were a luxury I'd rediscovered.

The library was a poor one, I suppose, as libraries go—there wasn't much new in it—but it had the classics, plenty to keep me occupied. I read Hardy, I remember, and Jack London, and Dickens and Virginia Woolf and Willa Cather.

I looked forward to walking into that small stone building. There was a woman there, a Mrs. Jewett, who balked at first when I requested a library card, since I was only renting, but finally, after much wheedling from me, she gave in. An extraordinary reticence on her part, now that I think of it, since I was almost always the only visitor she had, and I know that she looked forward to these visits.

Eventually I took to going around to Julia Strout's for a cup of tea. Yes, I was sometimes lonely—even if I savored my solitude: an odd paradox—and it was this loneliness, after a long spell of gray days in the second week, that prompted my first visit to the tall woman with the gapped teeth. I'd come out of Everett's store and seen Julia Strout's house across the common. I thought: I could just stop by on a pretext—the kitchen faucet leaked? I needed extra blankets?—but when I climbed her porch steps with the baby in my arms and knocked on her door, pretext left me, and I said, when she answered, her eyes momentarily startled but her face not giving away much of her surprise, that I'd just come by to say hello.

I had not been inside her house before and had the idea that it would look fussy, if homely, with knick-knacks and knitted tea cozies. Did I think this only because she was of a different generation than myself? But her rooms were not fussy, were rather surprisingly spare and inviting. I remember most of all her floors, burnished dark hardwood floors that she later confessed to me she polished on her hands and knees. She had a ritual, she said, of rising at six every morning and spending her first two hours cleaning and polishing, so that she did not have to think about chores the rest of the day. Her kitchen was quite large, with white vertical boards on its walls and a gray-green slate floor. She invited me into her kitchen and said she'd make us a cup of tea. There was a fireplace and a large round oak table. She was wearing that afternoon, as she always wore, a pair of thick corduroy pants and a sweater. I don't think I ever saw her in a skirt the entire time I knew her. She had strong, muscular hands and forearms, which I noticed particularly when she brought the kettle to the stove. I remember, too, that there were a great many books in her kitchen—not cookbooks but novels, biographies, and histories—and I had the sense that she lived in this room, at least in wintertime.

I put Caroline on the floor and let her creep around, always keeping my eye on her and the fireplace. Julia put the screen across, and she, too, kept watch, once getting up and bringing Caroline, who had wandered too close to the hearth, back to the other side of the room.

"You settling in?" Julia Strout asked as she fetched two mugs from her cupboard.

"Yes," I said. "The cottage is wonderful. Very peaceful."

"You have any idea how long you're going to stay?"

It was an idle question—I'm not sure she really cared—but it took me by surprise, and I must have hesitated, or she must have seen the alarm on my face, for she quickly added, "It's yours for as long as you need it or want it. There's no one else signed up for it."

"Oh," I said.

"Milk or brandy?" she asked.

"What?"

"I prefer brandy on a cold afternoon," she said, "but suit yourself."

"Brandy," I said.

I watched her pour large dollops of the amber liquid into the mugs. Perhaps she wasn't as sensible as I'd imagined.

She brought the steaming mugs to the table. I took a

sip from my own. The liquor was strong, and I could feel it hit my stomach, the warmth spreading.

She sat across from me, took a swallow of her tea.

"Are you going to be looking for work?" she asked.

I wasn't sure of the answer to this question. I looked at Caroline.

"I don't know," I said. "I suppose I'll have to eventually. But there doesn't seem to be much work available. I'm not sure what I'd do."

"You have a certain amount of money," she said carefully.

"Yes."

"And when that's gone . . .?"

"Yes."

"I see." She turned in her chair.

"I like living alone myself," she said, "though this house is ridiculously big for just one person. The cottage is nice, though."

"Very nice," I said.

"I've shut off most of the rooms here. Can't imagine living with anyone else now. Comes from too many years on my own."

I heard the hidden message—that I did not have to be afraid of living alone. I took another swallow of tea. Caroline was making cooing sounds in a corner, entranced by the carved and spindly legs of a tall wooden chair she'd found there.

"You're on the run, aren't you?" Julia Strout said suddenly and plainly. "You've run away."

At first I didn't speak.

"You don't have to tell me," she said. "It's none of my business."

"I had to," I said finally.

She stared for a time at her knee, which was crossed over her other leg. She wore work boots, laced up over the ankle.

"Not a good idea to be alone with a baby all the time," she said. "I can always take her for a couple of hours if you want a break."

"Thank you," I said, "but I couldn't . . ."

"Well, you think about it."

"I will."

A silence descended upon the kitchen. In the corner, up on all fours, Caroline lost her balance and bumped her head on the chair leg. I went to her and picked her up. I had nearly finished my tea, anyway, and said I ought to be going. Julia seemed at first reluctant to let me go, and I thought that possibly she was sometimes lonely too.

She walked me to the door.

"You come again for tea," she said to me.

I thanked her and said that I would. She watched as I put Caroline into her snowsuit, wound the scarf around my head.

"He won't find you in this town," she said.

That day I did not go back to the cottage but instead drove into Machias. There was something at the five-and-ten that I wanted to get. I went into the store and bought a night-gown for myself—a long flannel nightgown in a pattern of small blue cornflowers, a long prosaic nightgown to keep me warm in my solitary bed, the sort of nightgown that might grow soft and threadbare from use.

A nightgown that Harrold would not have approved of.

———

In the middle of December, about ten days before Christmas, there was a flurry of activity on the point, as three of the four boats in the channel were hauled onto cradles for the winter. There were boat trailers and winches and heavy pulleys and more men on the point than I had ever seen before. One of the boats that was being pulled that day was *Jeannine*, Willis's boat, and he made a show of coming to my cottage twice, once for coffee, and once for a drink when the boat was safely hauled, as if to suggest to the men on the point that we were old friends and the cottage nearly a second home to him. I wondered if the other men ever asked Willis about me, and if they did, what he told them. Would he confine himself to the little that he knew, or would he feel compelled to embellish these few facts so that I might appear more mysterious or intriguing in his stories? The green-and-white lobster boat did not get hauled that day, was not even in the channel. It had gone out at daybreak, as was its custom, and did not return until nearly dusk, when all the other boats had been hauled and the men had gone home to their suppers.

On the day after the boats had been hauled, I dressed Caroline and myself for an excursion. I was short of coffee and dishwashing liquid and a baby cereal I had begun to give Caroline, and thought I would just run into town and pick up a few things at Everett Shedd's. It was a gray day, cold and overcast, with a hint of snow in the air, and I was thinking that I had better do the errand before dusk and possible bad weather. I put Caroline into the basket in the back seat and started the car. I was halfway down the gravel drive, however, when I realized something was wrong. The steering wheel kept pulling to the right. I stopped the car and got out. I had a flat, the right front.

You will probably be amused by this—I see you as someone who prides herself on being competent—but I had not actually ever changed a tire before. I had been shown how to do it by a male friend of my mother's, who had taught me how to drive, but I had never done the deed myself. Out of habit, I looked around me, as if someone might materialize—where was Willis when I really needed him?—but the landscape was particularly cheerless that day and empty. Now that the boats had been hauled, the men seemed to have taken a day off. And the green-and-white lobster boat had not returned yet. I thought to myself that I could wait until the next day, when someone might appear, but I did not like to think of myself and the baby stranded without a car, in case of an emergency. I carried Caroline back into the house, so that she would not freeze in the back seat, and laid her in the baby basket on the braided rug. All the coming and going had thoroughly woken her up, and she was crying.

I mumbled something to her about being right back, which was, in the circumstances, wildly optimistic, and went out to forage through the trunk of the car. I found the jack and the spare and a lug wrench. I understood the theory of changing a tire. I got the jack to work, but I could not get the nuts off. I stood on the wrench, but even my weight wouldn't budge them. Inside the cottage, I could hear Caroline wailing.

I was thinking that I might have to wait until she was asleep, but by then it would be dark outside and the task even more difficult. I thought that if I jumped up and down on the wrench, that would loosen the nuts, and so it was that I was standing on the wrench, jumping up and down for all I was worth, holding on to my car so that I would not lose my balance, perhaps even cursing my bad luck into the bargain, when I heard a voice behind me.

I hadn't seen the boat come in. From the gravel drive, the channel was not as visible as it was from the cottage. And I hadn't heard the familiar sound because I'd been too distracted by Caroline's cries.

"The way they put them on, it's a wonder anyone can get them off," he said. "Here, let me give it a try."

He bent down and gave the wrench a hard push. I could only see the back of his head. His ears were red from the cold. I had never seen him wear a hat. He loosened the nuts and tossed them into the hubcap. Caroline sounded hysterical in the cottage.

"I have to see to the baby," I said.

He nodded once, took the flat off the axle. I went in to Caroline, lifted her into my arms, and returned to watch the man in the yellow slicker fix my tire. He worked with dispatch, methodically changing the tire as if he'd done it a hundred times before. He turned the damaged tire carefully in his hands, examining it. Then he put it into my trunk.

"Can't see offhand what the trouble is. You take it into Everett's, he'll fix it for you if he can." He was wiping his fingers on a rag in my trunk.

"I'm glad you came by," I said. "I don't know what I'd have done on my own."

"Someone would have come along," he said. "Is she still cutting teeth?"

I looked at Caroline. "Not any more since that night," I said. "She's been pretty good, actually."

I glanced up. He was staring at me, at my face. I hadn't given a thought to the scarf while I'd been trying to change the tire. He looked hard at me for four or five seconds, not speaking, and I didn't look away. I was thinking how unusual his eyes were, how they didn't seem to belong to the rest of his face. He seemed about to speak, then stopped.

He threw the rag into the trunk, shut it.

"Thank you," I said.

"It's nothing," he answered, and turned.

Just then a red pickup truck came around the corner of the lane at a fairly fast clip, pulling to a stop beside my car, spewing gravel so that it hit my car like bullets. The man in the yellow slicker, on his way back to his own truck, gave a wave to Willis but kept walking.

Willis jumped down from the cab, looked toward Jack Strout, then at me.

"What's the story?" he said, sounding out of breath.

"What story?" I said.

"With Jack. What's he doing here?"

I thought, all in all, it was an odd question.

"I had a flat," I said. "He saw me trying to fix it and came by to help."

"That so."

He shook a cigarette from a pack in his jacket pocket, put the cigarette to his lips. He seemed particularly jumpy.

"I've got to go," I said. "I have to get the tire fixed at Everett's."

"Let me take it for you," he said quickly. "I'll bring it right back, put it on for you."

"No," I said, "but thanks, anyway. I have to get some things." I moved toward my car.

"I come by to tell you about the bonfire," he said.

"The bonfire?"

"Yeah; it's a town tradition. Every Christmas Eve, we get together on the common, the whole town, and we have a bonfire and sing Christmas carols. Everybody goes. The women from the church, they make hot cider and sweets for the kids. You should come; wrap the baby up. You'd be amazed, the heat from the bonfire, it keeps you warm, even on the coldest nights." He looked up at the threatening sky. "Think we're going to have another storm tonight," he said.

I thought he must be running out of excuses to come to the cottage. Christmas Eve was more than a week away.

"Well, I'll see," I said.

He took a long drag on his cigarette.

"Want me to follow you into town? Make sure you're all right, with no spare now and all?"

"No," I said. "I'll be fine."

"You're sure about that now, Red."

"Yes," I said, moving toward my car. "I'm sure."

"OK, then," he said, looking down at the figure in the yellow slicker moving toward the end of the point.

"Think I'll go see how old Jack is doin'," he said. "Too bad I didn't get here sooner. I could of changed the tire for you; you wouldn't have had to bother old Jack."

"I didn't bother old Jack," I said. "He just—"

"Yeah, whatever," Willis said, cutting me off. "Watch yourself now, in the storm, if it starts snowin'."

"I'll be fine," I said, with more firmness than was perhaps necessary. I got into the car, put Caroline in the back, shut the door. Willis was walking down the point, his shoulders hunched up inside his jacket. I put the key in the ignition, took a long, deep breath. I had a sudden image of Harrold coming fast around the corner, spewing bullets of gravel up onto my car. I had a sudden image of myself and Caroline in the car, with Harrold hovering over us, trying to get in.

I wondered where he was now, what he was thinking, what he had done to find me.

There are stretches of my stay in St. Hilaire that are hazy to me now. The several days before Christmas, for instance. I remember clearly only Christmas Eve, the bonfire, but the days preceding it are now a blur.

On Christmas Eve day, Caroline cried a great deal; she was cutting two more teeth simultaneously and resisted my efforts to console her. Even the baby aspirin I had finally bought seemed ineffectual. As a last resort, I put her into the car and drove aimlessly up and down the coast road for at least an hour, so that she might sleep. The day was clear, transparent. To my left, as I drove south toward town, the gulf was strewn with jewels— glinting, restless, sparkling—in the high sunshine. I wore my dark glasses from necessity as much as for camouflage. The green-and-white lobster boat had been gone when I bundled Caroline into the car, and as I drove— first south, then north, peering across the passenger seat out to sea—I suppose I looked for a speck that might have been a boat, emerging from the lee of an island or idling amid a scatter of buoys.

During the day, men came and went on the point. I would be aware of a motor, then perhaps a voice calling to another. Short words, bursts of words on the wind, with a hint of gruffness in them, the greetings of men who do not stop working when they talk to each other.

I think I imagined I would just have a look at the

bonfire, stay a minute or two, and then take the baby home. I was curious about this event, and I would have liked the sense of having somewhere to go, something to cap my day, but I was worried about having Caroline out on such a cold night.

I had not been on the coast road after dark, except for that first confused drive to the motel, but now that I knew the road better and had landmarks to refer to, I could more easily pick out houses that had grown familiar to me. The sky that night seemed immense with stars, and there was a moon, cream and low on the horizon, sending a rippled shaft of light across the sea and illuminating, from the east, the simple outlines of the Capes and cottages and farmhouses.

Many of the houses had Christmas lights strung up along the gutters, or electric candles in the windows. Here and there, I could see a tree in a living room, and detached as I was that night, I was thinking about what an odd custom it was—to take a tree into your house and dress it with gaudy bits of glass and paper and put colored electric lights all over it. I was trying to imagine what I'd think of this custom if I had happened to visit Karachi or Cairo in the summer, and the people there, for a Muslim holiday, had brought a flowering tree into their house and decorated it in the same fashion. But I was not so detached that I did not sometimes have sharp memories when I looked into the windows on the coast road, memories of holidays with my own mother, memories of holidays she had made for me—stockings hanging from a bookcase; the fragile glass ornaments on the higher branches of our Christmas tree; our own electric candles in the windows; the pile of presents (handmade sweaters and gloves and hats; an array of toys).

You could see the glow of the bonfire from the edge of town. I parked in a small clearing behind the church, put Caroline into the sling, and wrapped my coat around her, so that only her head, in her woolen cap, peeked above the buttons of my coat. She had settled down some since late afternoon, and I thought she would probably sleep as I walked around.

I made my way toward the light of the fire, hanging back at an outer ring of celebrants. Already there were what looked to be a couple of hundred people in the common, most surrounding the fire. Closest to the fire were the young boys, their faces lit orange, darting recklessly toward the fire and back to the circle, throwing bits of twigs and debris onto the pyre, their faces upturned as a plume of sparks arced over the crowd. The fire was noisy, crackling, popping, and around it there was an equally loud commotion: boys squealing, adults admonishing, buzzing, greeting each other, slapping their hands together in the cold—although even in the outer ring, I could feel the fire's heat. Once or twice I saw an older teenager moving through the crowd, flashing a peace sign; another boy had a cardboard poster: "Stop the War." Where there were gaps in the ring, the light flickered outward, against the stone war memorial, against a green Volkswagen parked by the common's edge, against a tall straight tree I could not see the upper branches of.

To me the bonfire seemed dangerous, as if the sparks could easily ignite the old boards of the store or of Julia's house, or the trees overhead—but the townspeople seemed unconcerned about the danger. Perhaps they had had so many years without incident that they were complacent about hazard, or perhaps they had taken precautions I was unaware of. Possibly icy-cold branches do not easily ignite; I don't know.

There was comfort in the darkness of the outer ring, in being a voyeur, muffled in my coat and scarf, although I did occasionally get a knowing look. Probably most had heard already of a new woman in town with a baby; perhaps some thought me a relative who had come to spend Christmas with a family in St. Hilaire. Most of the men and women were wearing bulky car coats, scarves wound around their necks, and knitted caps. The night was frosty with puffs of condensation, warm breath on cold air. Some of the men took occasional nips from bottles concealed in paper bags, and once or twice I passed through the sweet drift of marijuana, but I did not actually see anyone with a joint.

"It's made from wormy wood from the pots."

Startled, I turned to the voice at my shoulder. Willis had a beer can down by his side, the other hand in the pocket of his denim jacket. There was frost on his mustache, and when the fire lit his face, I could see that his eyes were badly bloodshot.

"The fire," he said. "We make a pile of our rotted pots and so on. Makes a blaze, don't it."

He was looking at me, appraising me, while he said this. His leg was jiggling.

"Where's your family?" I asked quickly.

"Jeannine's taken the boys into the church for cider and whatnot. I saw you from across."

He took a last swig of beer, dropped the can onto the ground, and crushed it with his foot.

"So what do you think of our fire here? Wild, huh?"

"It's really something," I said.

"We been doin' this fifty years, anyway. My old man used to talk about it. You want me to get you a beer?"

"No," I said. "I'm fine."

"You want a toke, then? I could get us some joints."

I heard the *us*, didn't like it. I also did not like the picture that came to mind: Willis and myself smoking grass in the shadow of the church.

"I'd like to meet your boys," I said.

He swayed. He seemed confused.

"Yeah, sure. They'll be out soon," he said vaguely.

The singing began from nowhere, at no visible signal. There was a single man's voice for a bar or two, then half a dozen voices joining him, then a crowd, as people heard the carol, stopped chatting with their neighbors. By the end of "Silent Night," the town was in unison, the deep bass of the men offset here and there by the high trilling vibrato of the older women.

They began a heartier tune next—"Hark the Herald" or "God Rest Ye, Merry Gentlemen"—and I was watching the men and women singing. I had begun to sing myself; it forestalled conversation with Willis. He was moving beside me—swaying or jiggling, I couldn't tell. It was in the middle of that carol, or another, that I saw Jack, two or three people in front of me. He had his back to me but was slightly turned and bent toward a teenage girl beside him, so that I saw his face as he spoke to her. She had spilled her cider onto her gloves—that seemed to be the

189

problem. I saw Jack take her gloves off and put them in his pockets, then remove his own gloves and give them to her. He held her cardboard cup of hot cider while she put his gloves on. I couldn't see her face—her back was to me—but I was struck by her hair spilling out from her hat: It was the color of her father's and was long and curly.

Possibly there was a subtle shift in the crowd, or a man in front of me moved and blocked my view, but I must have strained or craned my neck to watch the scene with Jack and his daughter, for I became aware suddenly that Willis was staring at me. He examined my face and then looked at the thing that had caught my attention. Then he turned back toward me. I met his glance; I looked away. I think I was embarrassed. I hadn't been able to read his expression—he'd been thinking—but his eyes had seemed clearer, sharper, than they had before.

"I'm getting some cider," I said quickly, and moved away from him.

The church was warm, brightly lit. People began shedding scarves and hats and gloves as soon as they entered, and those who wore glasses had to take them off and wipe the steam away. The cider was in the parish hall, I was told, a room adjacent to the sanctuary. I followed the others to a long table covered by a red tablecloth. On it were black ironware pots of hot cider, plates of cookies and cakes, and candles wreathed with holly. The tangy scent of the cider was delicious and filled the room. Garlands of silver tinsel had been strung from a green velvet curtain up on a stage, and there was a tall Christmas tree in a corner.

Caroline woke up and looked at me and rubbed her

eyes. I thought fleetingly that I might have to nurse her soon and wondered if I should just drive straight home. I was hot in my scarf in the church. The cider smelled good, yet I was too uncomfortable to stay there any longer. I thought, also, that Caroline might begin to sweat, and I didn't relish having to unfasten her from the sling and undress her, just for a cup of cider.

Outside, the cold was almost a relief. I stood on the steps and watched the scene before me. A stiff wind had come up off the ocean, fanning the bonfire, causing it to intensify in brightness and sending even larger plumes of sparks out into the sky. A woman came out of the church, stood beside me on the steps as she put on her gloves, adjusted her hat. They were singing "Joy to the World" now, and I thought both the singing and the fire seemed to have reached a feverish pitch.

The woman beside me appeared to be thinking the same thing.

"I know we do this every year," she said, shaking her head, "but I said to Everett only this morning, one of these years he's goin' to have a fiasco on his hands."

She nodded briskly at me, tugged at her gloves, and marched down the steps and into the crowd.

I may have wanted to stay longer, but I didn't mind the prospect of returning to the cottage, nursing Caroline, and climbing into my high white bed. Caroline's teething was exhausting me, and I knew she would wake early. I made my way down the steps, feeling vaguely pregnant and ungainly again, with Caroline strapped to my belly, and was about to turn the corner to the clearing where I'd parked my car when I heard a shout, then a kind of gruff rumbling. The singing stopped, but the circle remained intact, still facing the bonfire. I edged toward the circle, wondering what the source of the sudden silence was. The wind blew hard across the common and stung my cheeks. I raised my scarf over my face, kept Caroline hunkered down inside my coat.

I reached the crowd, stood on my toes to see. There was fighting near the fire. A group of older boys were pitching back and forth, rolling toward and away from the flames. The "Stop the War" poster was on the ground. Men from the crowd moved forward to contain the fight or to stop it, and those who watched but were not involved had made a space, backing up into the crowd, compressing it. Those in the outer ring had moved forward, and it seemed that everyone was straining toward the center.

There were grunts and shouts, arms flailing, heads thrown back. I saw Everett in the fray. He held a boy by the zippered edge of his leather jacket, and then he was hit or slammed from behind, and the grocer's hat fell off. Willis was in the midst, wild and inarticulate with fury. I couldn't tell which side he was on, but I saw him kick a boy in the groin. Women closest to the scuffle were screaming and shouting, calling out names: *Billy! Brewer! John! John! Stop it! Stop it now!*

I backed away from the crowd, wound my arms around the baby. A jostle in the center might ripple outward, and I was afraid that Caroline might get hurt. The fire roared beside the fight, but no one was paying it much attention now.

The crowd parted, and Everett emerged. His face was flushed, his coat torn, and he had not retrieved his hat.

He had a boy by the collar, and despite his age, Everett was racing the boy faster than the boy could walk. Other older men, in their forties, had boys in tow too, and the crowd turned to watch the procession. Everett took his charge into the church, and the others followed. Where else would they go? There was no police station.

The crowd then turned inward on itself. There was excited murmuring, the confusion of many witnesses. Someone said a group of kids had wanted to turn the bonfire into an antiwar demonstration. I heard a man near me tell his wife that the boys had been drunk, as if that were all the explanation anyone needed.

The fire burned unheeded; it couldn't compete now with the stories that were being passed from one puzzled or knowing face to the other. I looked over at the white houses lining the common, saw Julia standing on her porch. I thought that I would walk over to her, speak to her, wish her a happy Christmas. But I was reluctant to leave the crowd just at that minute, or to leave the fire. I was concerned about the fire, perhaps more so than I ought to have been. I had the idea that if I left, I would hear in the morning that a building or a tree had ignited, that something had burned down. Then I thought that I should mention my fear, but I didn't want to call attention to myself. I thought that I could say something to Julia Strout; she would know what to do.

I remember standing there, feeling somehow paralyzed with indecision, looking at the fire and the people. Images from the fight began to blur with images of the faces around me. I was sure I saw Willis again, striking a boy on the side of his head, his hand making an arc in the

cold air. But the air was thin, leaving us. The fire was
sucking the air from around us, and I was having trouble
breathing. I looked around me to see if other people were
having trouble breathing too. My heartbeat felt shallow,
insubstantial. Then I looked up, and the trees began to
spin.

Everett Shedd

After Christmas Eve, of course, everyone in the town got
to know who she was, even if they hadn't heard any of
the stories earlier. I don't know what caused it, exactly;
the fight, I think it was. Maybe she saw things that brought
back bad memories to her, don't you know. Or maybe
she was just in a lot worse shape than any of us thought.
I know Julia Strout blames herself, but she shouldn't. You
can't be responsible for a person just because she rents a
cottage from you.

Every year at Christmastime, we have a bonfire on the
common there. It's a ritual; we been doin' it now, let me
see, since probably 1910 or thereabouts. It started one year,
the men made a fire outta their rotted gear on the green
there, 'n' some folks got to singin' 'n' that, and each year
it got a little more elaborate, until now we have a right
fire from the traps that are useless—wormy, they are—
and the townspeople, they gather 'round the fire and sing
carols every Christmas Eve, 'n' the kids run around 'n'

drink cider 'n' eat goodies, 'n' some of the older boys, they get a little wild and drunk, 'n' it's a way for folks to get together to celebrate 'n', to tell you the truth, to let off a little steam. My wife, she's a doomsayer; she's always tellin' me every year the bonfire is goin' to be a fiasco, but usually I think the bonfire is a good idea—keeps the boys pretty quiet for most of the rest of the winter, till they can go out on the water again—but this year things got a bit out of hand, 'n' we had ourselves a pretty good scuffle.

What happened is that a coupla the kids—Sean Kelly's boy and Hiram Tibbett's son—they had an idea to have a protest, don't you know, and there was this other group of kids—town boys—they got ahold of a couple of fifths of bourbon, 'n' I didn't realize it, they were drinkin' behind the church, 'n' then they come over to the fire, and the two groups, they got to exchanging words and then they got to fightin'—you know how boys are when they been drinkin'—'n' then somehow all hell let loose, 'n' the men were in it too, 'n' I had to go in and lay down the law. So all this is by way of explainin' to you that I was in the church when it happened, 'n' to tell you the truth, I'd been hit pretty bad, 'n' though I pride myself that I didn't let it show, I was feelin' a bit woozy, don't you know, so I didn't react as fast as I ought to have done.

The first I heard is Malcolm Jewett comes tearin' into the church where I got these boys under control 'n' we're sortin' out the damage to each other, 'n' he shouts that it's the woman with the baby, she's on the ground. Right away, I know who he's talkin' about, because I saw Mary earlier in the evenin'. Wanderin' around with the baby.

He says she just fell, 'n' one of the women has got the baby off some contraption on the woman, 'n' the baby is OK but cryin'. So I leave the boys with Dick Gibb and hotfoot it out to the common, but already I can see Jack Strout has got her on her feet and is fixin' her scarf. Julia is there too; I think she seen Mary from her porch, where she always stays to watch the bonfire. She worries every year that sparks from the fire is goin' to blow over to her porch, so she stands there with a coupla buckets. I park the fire truck behind the store just in case we ever do lose control of the bonfire, but it never happened yet. We had years where we couldn't get much of a fire goin' because of a snow, but knock on wood, we never had an accident yet. Then Julia, she takes Mary 'n' the baby into her place. Jack, he didn't go inside, I'm pretty sure. But like I say, that's when anyone who didn't know who she was, they all knew by the time the night was done.

She just passed out, apparently. Fainted.

She was damn lucky, you want to know the truth. If she'd a fallen the wrong way, she could have really hurt the baby, don't you know. According to Elna Coffin, who was standin' beside her, she just went. Just like that. One minute she was standin' there, the next minute she was on the ground. At first Elna thought she'd been hit or bumped by the crowd, 'n' then the baby started cryin' 'n' then Jack was there, 'n' she came to. And that's about it, far as I can remember.

The next day people were askin' Julia 'n' me, whenever we saw anybody, and maybe they asked Jack too, I don't know, but he wouldn't have known anything anyway, how she was 'n' all, but Julia, she don't say much, 'n' she never had much to say about Mary Amesbury to people who was just curious or lookin' for a bit of gossip. And I think people, they kind of got the idea that Mary was in trouble.

So when that man come, you know, that fella from New York City—oh, let's see now, it was a coupla weeks later, don't you know, after New Year's—askin' questions about a woman with a baby, nobody would say much of anything. They took their cue from Julia; she carries a lot of weight in this town. If Julia had her reasons, people figured, those reasons would be good enough for them.

Though of course, I'm sorry to say, not everybody felt that way, did they? I mean to say, in the end, someone told that fella somethin'.

I have my ideas, 'n' I know Julia, she has her ideas, but I think that's about as far as I'm prepared to go right now.

Julia Strout

Mary Amesbury sometimes came to my house with the baby for a cup of tea. And then I had her in the house on Christmas Eve. She fainted on the common on Christmas Eve.

I was on my porch, and I saw it happen. I had been thinking of walking over to Mary. I specifically wanted to make sure that Mary had somewhere to go on Christmas Day. I didn't like to think of her alone in the cottage, with nowhere to go on Christmas. I didn't want to leave my porch just then, however, as it seemed to me the bonfire was burning too intensely.

Everett has explained to you about the bonfire? I know we've never had an accident, but still I like to be prepared. I stay on my porch with a few buckets of water just in case of stray sparks. I do this, too, on the Fourth of July, when we have fireworks on the common for the children. Everett is in charge of the fireworks too. I know he says he's got his fire truck behind the store, but all it takes is one stray spark. These houses are very old and entirely built of wood, and if one were to go, there'd be no stopping it.

As I say, I saw her fall. I thought at first that she had been pushed, but when I got there, her face was white. I do mean white; you could see this even in the dark. This does happen to a person. I've seen it before. They say that my face turned white when they told me about my husband's drowning, but that's neither here nor there.

Jack Strout, my husband's cousin, was bent over her when I got there, shouting for people to give her air. Elna Coffin already had the baby out of the sling. The baby had been scared. That was all. You could see she was all right. And when I got the baby inside the house, I undressed her and checked her all over. Jack helped me get Mary to her feet. You couldn't leave a body on that cold ground. She would get pneumonia or worse. And as we got her up, she came to. I have salts in my house, and I think I might have told someone to go for them, but they weren't necessary. She came to right away. She was terribly embarrassed and kept asking me about the baby. She was badly shaken. There might have been an injury to the baby if she'd fallen the wrong way.

I took her into the house and tried to get some brandy into her and some hot tea, and I didn't want to let her leave until she'd had a meal, but she was in shock then and couldn't eat much. I thought she might have fainted because of malnutrition, that she wasn't taking care of herself, but she said no. She'd just gotten dizzy, she said, and I had an idea that the fighting had upset her.

Yes, if you want a reason, that's it. The fighting had upset her. Possibly it had triggered some unpleasant memories for her. That would be my guess. She didn't say much, and I didn't like to pry.

She'd taken it to heart, if you understand my meaning.

I offered to drive her home, but she said no, that she would be all right. She was quite insistent. She thanked me for the invitation to come to dinner the next day, but she said she didn't feel comfortable yet in front of other people, and she thought she would probably not come. But she did say that she had to make a phone call, and she asked if it would be all right if she came by the next day to use the phone, since the A&P would be closed on Christmas. I got the idea that she wouldn't want to be there when Jack and Rebecca and the children were there, so I told her to come by about noon. The others weren't due until three or so.

Yes, she did come to make the call.

She made the phone call in private, so I don't know who she called or what she said, and I'm not sure it's any of our business, anyway. But she did give me four dollars for the call. I wouldn't take the four dollars, so we settled on two.

———

I didn't see Mary for some time after that. I was very busy with whatnot, and after Christmas I always like to rest a bit, so it was nearly two weeks before I was able to get over to the cottage.

I mention this only because it took me somewhat longer than it might have to realize what was going on.

Mary Amesbury

I fainted on the common. I had never fainted before. It happened. It just happened.

I recognized a man's face over mine. His eyes were old, and his face was weathered. He was telling me that the baby was OK, and asking if I could stand. Then I saw Julia and remembered Caroline. Where was Caroline? I asked, looking frantically around. A woman next to me showed me Caroline but wouldn't give her to me. Caroline was fine, they kept saying.

I went inside with Julia and the baby. I felt the man's hands at my side, and then he was gone. I drank the brandy Julia gave me, but I had trouble eating the food. I couldn't tell her of what I had seen, of the images that had confused me. I was aware only that I had caused a scene and that people had been buzzing around me. I was aware, too, of how lucky I had been. When I thought of what might have happened to Caroline . . .

I don't remember Christmas Day at all. There is nothing about the day I remember. My mother says that I called her at midday and told her that Harrold and Caroline and I were just sitting down to Christmas dinner, but I don't remember any of it.

I did not sleep that night or the next.

I got your letter this morning. Yes, I understand about September and the timing of the article, and I will hurry with the next batch of notes.

I write all night now. I seldom sleep. My cellmate and I are a perfect pair. The more I am awake, the more she sleeps, as if to redress the deficit.

I sometimes wonder about your life. I have written you so much about myself, and yet I know almost nothing about you. I think about that imbalance, wonder what you will do with all these pages that I have sent you.

Several days after Christmas, a thaw, as predicted, warmed the coast. And with the thaw came the fog. One morning I awoke knowing something was amiss. I hadn't heard the motor on the lane. I went to the window but could not see out. I went downstairs and opened the bathroom window and watched the fog spill in over the windowsill.

I stood in the kitchen. I heard the foghorns then, one to the north, one to the south, slightly out of sync, one a low mournful note, the other slightly higher, speaking to each other across a vast expanse of wet gray air and water. In between the foghorns you could hear a gentle lapping of the water.

We had six days of fog, off and on. On two or three mornings during the thaw, I woke and there wasn't any fog. And then, in the late morning, while I was feeding the baby or washing the dishes, the fog drifted in with stealth, blotting out the colors, then the shapes, then the sun. First there would be puffs of fog blowing across the bar, and soon the island would be gone. That was it—gone just like that. It didn't exist.

The green-and-white lobster boat did not go out on the first day of the thaw, or the second, but I heard the truck on the third morning. It was a day on which the fog had not come in yet, and I, not understanding the pattern of the fog, felt buoyant at the sight of the islands becoming visible in the distance at daybreak. When I saw how my own spirits had lifted with the return of the sun—and we had only had two days of continuous fog—I began to understand better the depression Willis had described, the depression that sometimes settled upon the women of the town. I wondered why it was that Willis had mentioned only the women becoming depressed in the winter. Did the men not mind the days of grayness too? Or was it easier for them because they were able to meet the grayness as a challenge when they went out on the water?

Caroline seemed to catch my mood and was unusually contented and cheerful that morning. She had been practicing balancing on all fours for a couple of weeks now and had learned how to pitch herself forward. Crawling, I could see, as I watched her from the kitchen table, was imminent. But I had no impatience for anything. With Christmas behind me and no need to go anywhere or to do anything, I was becoming more and more content to allow the days to dictate themselves to me.

I was reading, and Caroline was napping upstairs, when

the fog came back. First there were wisps, ethereal and transitory, and then the fog became a shroud, blanketing everything. The light dimmed so that it seemed like dusk when it was only midday. I had to turn on a light to read. With the fog, the room turned chill as well, or perhaps it only seemed that way, with the sun gone. I went to the window. I could not even see the fish house now, although I could make out the barest hint of the back of a red pickup truck. The end of the point had disappeared entirely.

There was a knock on the door.

Willis came in like a figure emerging from the sea. The fog seemed to cling to him in the form of billions of droplets of moisture—on his denim jacket, on his mustache, on his hair. He carried a mug of coffee.

"Brought my own this time," he said, shutting the door behind him.

I was glad I had gotten dressed early.

"Socked in," he said.

"I thought the fog was over," I said.

There was a recording of a string quartet playing on the radio. The elegiac music seemed to underscore the view outside my window.

He made a disparaging sound, the sort of sound you make when the other person has just said something incredibly naive.

"No way. We'll have fog for days yet. Hey, Red, better get used to it. Bother you?"

"No," I said, lying. "Not at all."

"Well, that's good." He took a seat at the kitchen table. He looked at my face.

"Jack's out," he said.

"Oh," I said.

"Probably thought he could beat the fog back."

"Oh."

"Wouldn't catch me out on a day like this."

"No."

"So what you goin' to do all day?"

"Same thing I do every day," I said. "Take care of the baby."

"You don't miss it?"

"Miss what?"

"Your old life. Where you come from."

"No," I said.

"Musta been pretty bad," he said. "Your old man."

I said nothing.

"Syracuse, huh?"

I nodded.

"Nice place, Syracuse?"

I shrugged. "I like it better here," I said.

"You're lookin' better," he said.

"Thank you."

He sighed.

"So OK, Red, I'll be off now. Goin' home for lunch. I'm supposed to start drivin' for a haulage company next week. I hate doin' it, but we got to have the money. You need anything?"

He asked me this every day.

"No," I said.

Caroline began to cry. I was glad.

"Hope I didn't wake her," he said.

I shook my head. He got up to leave. He walked to

the door, opened it, and hesitated. The fog blew in around him.

"Keep your eyes peeled for Jack," he said, and smiled.

The green-and-white lobster boat did not come back at two o'clock, as was its custom. I thought that probably the fog would delay it some, so I wasn't exactly worried. It was merely that I was alert to the fact that it had not returned. As I have said, it was a kind of punctuation to my day to see the boat emerging from behind the island, and without it the day felt incomplete, like a sentence with no ending.

I was knitting a second sweater for Caroline, and I was halfway through the back piece. Caroline was in bed for her afternoon nap. I picked up the knitting, with the radio on in the background.

It's odd, now that I think of it, that I didn't write. Or perhaps not odd at all. To write would have required remembering.

The boat did not come back by three o'clock or by four. I had become attuned to all sounds emanating from the water or the point, and I went to the window frequently to peer out into the grayness. By four, it had grown dark, and all of the trucks but one were gone. Indeed, when it was foggy, night fell early on the point. I carried Caroline, or I nursed her. I made myself a cup of tea. I listened to the news on the radio. Eventually I made myself some supper. At six, the darkness outside was impenetrable. I began to wonder if I oughtn't to walk up to the blue Cape and alert someone that the green-and-white lobster boat wasn't back yet. Was this my responsibility?

I wondered. Who else would know that he hadn't returned? His wife and his daughter? Would they resent my alarm, my interference? Was this natural, not to come back from time to time? And what if he had decided to moor his boat at the town wharf? He had mentioned that when the weather was bad, he took his boat into town. Perhaps he had done that earlier, knowing of the fog to come, and I had waited all day for the boat's return for nothing. If I raised an alarm then, I would simply look foolish, as naive as Willis had indicated, and I would only draw even more attention to myself.

At six-thirty, I bundled Caroline into her snowsuit and into the sling and took us both for a walk. I could no longer bear it in the cottage. I didn't care that I wouldn't be able to see much of anything. I had to have some fresh air.

I made my way gingerly along the spit. I felt I knew the way well enough to walk without any danger to myself or the baby. I would feel the gravel underfoot, or the grasses, or the sand, and would be able to navigate with my feet.

The air was drenching. You felt it soak you through almost at once. I kept Caroline close to me. I could feel the pebbled beach under my sneakers. I hadn't walked fifty feet when I turned to look back at where I had come from. Already the cottage was gone. The lights burning in the living room were extinguished. I could see only about two or three feet ahead of my feet along the ground. That was it. The sensation was eerie and otherworldly. I don't think I was frightened, exactly, but it was a feeling I shall never forget. The world had disappeared entirely. There was only my baby and myself. I could hear, from time to time, sounds from the world I had come from—the foghorns, an occasional car along the road at the end of the lane, and a strange squealing overhead, like that of bats—but in that darkness you could not really believe in the world. Perhaps I *was* frightened, but I was also exhilarated. The anonymity, the privacy, the safety—it was perfect. No one, no one, could ever get to us now: not Harrold, not Willis, not even Julia or my mother, well-meaning though they might be. It was as I had imagined it in my dreams: my baby and myself, protected and enshrouded.

I heard the motor then. I knew its idiosyncrasies by heart. It grew louder; louder still; then it stopped. I wondered how he had found the mooring. I heard the slap of the dinghy, the sounds of the return ritual. Perhaps I walked in the direction of those sounds. Perhaps my feet knew the way better than I had imagined.

I wonder now, and I have often wondered this: whether things would have developed as they did if we had not come upon each other in the fog, if we had not had that perfect sense of isolation, of the world around us vanished.

He appeared out of the dark mist, as if emerging in a dream, and I must have too. It occurred to me that he'd be more startled to come upon me than I him, and so I spoke at once.

"You're back," I said.

I thought my voice sounded casual, cheerful.

He *was* startled. He'd been walking from the dinghy to the truck, but he stopped. He had two buckets, one in each hand. I could hear the lobsters inside those buckets more than I could see them.

He put the buckets down.

"Are you all right?" he asked.

"Yes," I said. "I'm fine."

"What are you doing out here?"

"I was just taking a walk. I'd been feeling cooped up."

He looked at my face, then at the baby in the sling.

"You shouldn't be out here," he said. "This fog is nasty today. You could lose your way."

"I don't see how," I said, but my voice lacked conviction.

"I've lived here all my life. I know the coastline and the water as well as I know my own kids. But in the fog, I'm a stranger. You don't trust anything in the fog. Nothing."

"Why did you go out, then?" I asked.

He looked out toward the water. "I don't know. I thought I'd beat it back. But I got caught the other side of Swale's. Took me all day to creep back in. Foolish. It was a foolish thing to do."

His voice was low, and he spoke matter-of-factly, without much emotion, but I understood that he sometimes took risks too. That he had been foolish was merely a statement of fact, not cause for much remorse. Beyond his voice, you could hear the foghorns.

"Your wife will be worried," I said.

"I've been on to her on the CB. She knows I'm in."

He looked at me as if he was thinking.

"You come with me to the truck, let me put these in, and then I'll walk you to the cottage."

"I'll be—" I started to say.

"I couldn't leave you out here without seeing you were safely back," he said, and picked up the two buckets as if there were nothing more to discuss.

I walked a little ways behind him. He had long sloping shoulders beneath the yellow slicker. His hair was covered with mist, and his slicker was wet. He wore tall waders that came up high over his knees, over his jeans. He had large hands with long fingers. I was looking at his hands gripping the handles of the buckets.

At the truck, he slid the buckets onto the bed.

"Well, then," he said.

He turned, and we walked in the direction of the house. He seemed to know better where to walk than I, and so I followed his lead, again a few steps behind him. He'd been right; I realized it at once. The fog was disorienting. I'd have gone in a different direction, south along the coast. I'd have missed the house at first, but I did think I would probably have found it after a few tries.

The cottage loomed out of the mist. First there was the glow of light from the living room, then the outline of the house itself. The light inside the rooms looked warm, inviting.

He walked me up the slope to the door. I had my hand on the latch. I felt like a schoolgirl who'd been seen home by a teacher who was too shy for conversation.

"Thank you," I said.

He looked at me. "I wouldn't say no to a cup of tea," he said.

His voice was so low I wasn't sure I had heard him right. "Would you like a cup of tea?" I asked.

"Thank you," he said. "I've got a chill on from the damp."

"Will your family . . . ?"

"They know I'm in. They won't be worried now."

I opened the door, and we both walked into the cottage. I went directly to the stove and got the kettle, filled it, and lit the burner.

"Keep your eye on the kettle," I said. "I have to go upstairs and put Caroline to bed."

In the living room, I wriggled out of my coat and removed Caroline from the sling. I carried her upstairs, put her into her pajamas, and nursed her on the bed. After a time, I could hear the kettle whistling, then the sounds of cups and saucers being fetched from the cupboard. I heard him at the sink, washing his hands. The refrigerator was opened and closed. I heard him rummaging through the silverware drawer.

When I came downstairs, he was sitting at the table. The slicker was on a hook on the back of the door and was dripping water onto the linoleum. He had removed his waders and was in his stocking feet. I could smell the sea in the room, from the slicker or the waders. I watched him for a minute from behind, and if he knew I was standing there, he gave no indication. His back was very long, so long that his sweater rode up over the waist of his jeans. But his back was broad, and he was not as slope-shouldered as he'd appeared in the slicker. He sipped his tea and did not turn around. At the place at right angles to his own there was a cup of tea for me. He'd let it steep, taken out the tea bag. He'd put milk and sugar on the table.

I sat down. I looked up at him. I had never seen his face in bright light. He was still, and his eyes moved slowly. I was again struck by the deep grooves at the sides of his mouth. His face had color, was permanently weathered. He looked at me, but we didn't speak.

"It's some warmth," he said finally.

"Did you get many lobsters today?" I asked.

"I was having some luck before the fog," he said. "But all told, it wasn't much. Doesn't matter, though."

"Why?"

"Whatever you get this time of year you're grateful for."

"Why do you do it? Go out when no one else does?"

He made a self-deprecating sound. "Because no one else does, I suppose. No, I like it out there. I get restless. . . ."

"It seems dangerous to me," I said. "It seems I'm always hearing about men drowning."

"Well, you could. . . ."

"If you're not careful?"

"Well, even if you're careful. There's things you can't control. Not like today. I should have been smarter today. But you can't always control a sudden blow, or engine failure. . . ."

"What do you do then?"

"You try to get back the best way you can. You try not to make any mistakes." He leaned his weight on one elbow, turned slightly toward me.

"You've been all right, then," he said. "Since Christmas Eve, I mean."

"Oh. Yes. Thank you. It was awful, fainting like that. I've never fainted. I don't know what came over me."

"Just a bunch of kids protesting the war," he said. "My son probably would have been in it too, except he was home with . . . my wife. You looked shocky. Like you were in shock."

"Oh," I said, looking down. "Did I?"

"What happened to you?" he asked quietly. "Why are you here?"

The question was so sudden, I felt I had been stung. Perhaps it was the quiet of his voice, or the way I had come upon him in the fog, or the way the simplicity of his question required a truthful answer. I put a hand up to my mouth. My lips were pressed together. To my horror, my eyes filled, as if I had indeed been stung. I couldn't speak. I was afraid to blink. I was afraid to move. In all of the days since I had left the apartment in New York City, I had not cried. Not once. I had been too numb to cry, or too careful.

He reached up and took the hand away from my mouth and put it on the table. He held my hand on the oilcloth. He didn't say a word. His eyes were gray. He didn't look away from me.

"I was married to a man who beat me," I said after a time. I let out a long breath of air after I had said it.

It sounded appalling, unreal, in the cottage.

"You left him," he said.

I nodded.

"Recently. You've run away."

"Yes."

"Does he know where you are?"

I shook my head. "I don't think so," I said. "If he did, he'd come and get me; I'm sure of that."

"You're afraid of him."

"Yes."

"He did that to you?"

He made a movement with his head to indicate my face. I knew the bruises were healing, were yellowish or light brown rather than purple or blue, but they were still visible.

I nodded.

"What do you think the chances are that he'll find you?" he asked.

I thought for a minute.

"Fairly good," I said. "It's what he does, in a way. Investigates things. He knows how to find out things."

"And what do you think will happen to you when he finds you?"

I looked at the place where he was holding my hand. His hand hadn't moved; it was firm on mine.

"I think he'll kill me," I said simply. "I think he'll kill me because he won't be able to control himself."

"Have you gone to the police?" he asked.

"I don't think I can go to the police," I said.

"Why not?"

"Because I've stolen his child."

"But you had to do that, to save yourself."

"That's not how it will appear. He's very clever."

He, too, looked down at where he was holding my hand. He began then to stroke my arm from the wrist to the elbow. I had a sweater on, and the sleeves were pushed up over my elbows, so he was stroking my skin, slowly and softly.

"You have a wife," I said.

He nodded. "My wife isn't—" He stopped.

I waited.

"She's sick," he said finally. "She has a chronic illness. We're together, but we don't have what you would call . . ."

"A marriage."

"No."

He was stroking my arm. I might have pulled it away, but I couldn't. I couldn't move. It had been so long since anyone had touched me this gently, this kindly, that I was nearly paralyzed with gratitude.

"We haven't . . . been together," he said, "for years."

"You haven't even told me your name," I said, "although I know it."

"It's Jack," he said.

"My real name is Maureen," I said. "Maureen English. But I've become Mary. I've taken it on. I'll stay Mary."

"Your daughter's name is Caroline," he said.

"Yes."

"That's her real name?"

"Yes," I said. "I couldn't call her something she wasn't."

He smiled. He nodded.

"I can't do this," I said. "I'm no good at this anymore."

But even though I said this, I did not pull my arm away. The stroking of his fingers was soothing and rhythmical, like a warm wave washing over me, and all I knew was that I didn't want it to stop.

"I'm afraid," I said.

"I know."

"You're old enough to be my father," I said. It was

something I'd been thinking—just that minute or for days?—and I thought it ought to be said, soon, to get it over with.

"Not really," he said. "Well, technically maybe. I'm forty-three."

"I'm twenty-six."

He nodded, as if he'd already guessed my age, give or take a year or two.

Outside, the foghorns were relentless—insistent and scolding.

He took his hand away and stood up with his teacup. He took his teacup to the sink.

"I'm going to go now," he said. He walked to the door, where his slicker was hanging. "I've been gone long enough. I can't leave my wife alone too long."

I stood up. I didn't say anything.

"But I'll be back," he said. "I can't say when. . . ."

I nodded.

"You shouldn't be afraid of this," he said.

I woke when I heard the motor on the lane. There was just a smear of gray outside the windows, but I could see the tops of the trees. The fog had not come yet. I heard the motor stop, but it was not at the end of the point; it was below my cottage.

I threw back the covers and ran down the stairs to the kitchen. Harrold *can't* have found me yet, I was praying. My heart was drumming in my chest.

Then, through the window on the door, I could see just a glimmer of a yellow slicker.

I unlocked the door.

Jack came in and put his arms around me.

"Willis said you went to college and had to come back."

He snorted. "Willis," he said.

I watched him as he ate his cereal.

"I did," he said finally. "I was in my junior year; my father broke his arms on his boat. I had to come back to take it over."

He didn't elaborate further.

"Were you disappointed?" I asked. "Disappointed you couldn't finish school?"

At first he didn't answer.

"I might have been, for a time," he said slowly, not looking at me. "But then you settle in, have your house, your work, your kids. It's hard to regret the things you've done that have led to having your kids."

I looked at him. I knew what he meant. Even though my own marriage had become unspeakable, I could not now imagine a life without Caroline.

Just then the sun broke over the horizon line, flooding the room with a bright salmon light. Jack's face, in the sudden fire, was aglow. I thought his face was beautiful then, the most beautiful face I had ever seen, even though I hated the sun, for I knew it meant he would have to leave. I could see it in his gestures, in the sudden tensing of his muscles, in the way he pulled back from the table.

He stood up, walked to the back door to get his slicker. He put the oilskin under one arm, came to stand behind my chair. With his free hand, he lifted the hair from the back of my neck and kissed me there.

"I can't give you much," he said.

I could feel his breath on my skin.

For a minute, I couldn't speak.

Then I said: "You smell like the sea."

"I think it's permanent," he said.

Later, before the sun had fully risen, we left my bed and returned to the kitchen. He had carried his clothes with him, and dressed standing on the linoleum floor. He showed no self-consciousness when he dressed, even though he knew I was watching him.

I had put on my nightgown and my sweater in the bedroom. I made us a breakfast of coffee and cold cereal. We did not speak while he dressed, and he lit a cigarette and smoked at the table while I made the coffee. I brought the bowls of cereal to the table.

"I usually make a breakfast before I leave the house, but I couldn't eat this morning," he said, putting out his cigarette on an ashtray I'd given him.

I smiled.

"Couldn't sleep, either," he said, and smiled back at me.

I wanted to climb upstairs to the bed and curl up against his chest and go to sleep with him, the blankets pulled up high over our heads.

"When did you decide to come?" I asked.

"Sometime in the middle of the night. As soon as I decided it, I wanted to get up right then and there and come, but I couldn't. . . ."

I nodded. I knew he meant his wife.

"Do you mind having to get up so early for your work?" I asked.

"It's all right," he said. "You get used to it. It suits me."

He left before the other trucks had come to the point. He drove his own truck down to his dinghy. He went out that day in the green-and-white lobster boat but came back before the fog had settled in. As it happened, when he returned, I was walking on the point with Caroline, and though he waved to us from the truck—a wave that would be construed by the men who were in the fish house as merely a friendly gesture—we did not speak. Later he took to parking his truck at his dinghy and walking back to the cottage, staying until the sun had risen. There was an understanding between us, though unspoken, that no one should know about his visits. There were his wife and children to think of.

He came every morning at daybreak. There would be the motor on the lane and then his footsteps on the stairs. I kept the kitchen door unlocked. I'd be sleeping when he came, and it sometimes seemed to me that he would enter into my dreams. It would be dark in the room, with just a tease of light, and I would see the shape of him standing at the foot of the bed, or sitting on its edge as he bent to remove his shoes. And when I rolled toward him, in the bed that I had warmed all night, it was as if our coming together were already one of the rhythms of the point, as natural and as necessary as the gulls who woke and called and foraged for food, or as the light that would be lavender or pink on the water when he left me.

After the first morning, I had moved Caroline to the downstairs bedroom. It was hard for me to separate us in that way, but I knew that the time had come for me to do this. The walls were thin in the cottage, and I could hear her easily from my bed when she cried.

Do you want the details? There are moments I will

never give away for any purpose—memories, words, and visions that I hoard and savor. But I can tell you this much. He never asked from me more than I could give, and he was careful, as though I hurt all over. Sometimes he would hold me; that would be enough. At other times, I offered what I had.

On the third day, or the fourth, I waited until the sun had almost risen, so that there was light in the room. I got out of the bed and stood in front of him. I let him look at me. I made him look at me. I knew that I was damaged in some places, ugly in others, but I didn't mind his eyes. I felt no shame in myself, nor any sense of judgment from him. I didn't want him to say that I was beautiful; that wasn't what I hoped for. I think I wanted only to have it behind me, to have it done. But then he did a funny thing. He got out of his side of the bed. There was a line across his abdomen from a ruptured appendix, which he pointed out. He stood on one foot and showed me a dent from a rope burn on his shin. His hands had many nicks, he said, displaying them, and I saw a mark, like something made with jagged scissors, on his upper arm. He'd been a boy, he said, pegging lobsters for his father, and he'd gotten stung by a bee, lost control of the lobster, and it had clawed him. I began to laugh.

"All right," I said, and crawled back into bed.

"They're battle scars, that's all," he said, touching this one and then that one and then that one on my body.

We were intimate but not possessive. Oddly, we never said we loved each other, although I was certain that this was a form of love, one I had never thought to have. I think it was simply that although we trusted each other, we no longer trusted the word. I imagined that he, like myself, had once told his wife that he loved her—and had been perplexed and dismayed when certainty had become uncertain, then had turned to disappointment.

There was so much about each other that we didn't know, could never know. His life on the water had shaped him, formed him, as had my life in the city and with my mother. He would never know about deadlines and the pressure of putting words and sentences together in offices, just as I would never know what it was to be lost on the water in the fog and to have to rely on wits and instinct to make it back to shore alive. I did not know much about his marriage, either. By tacit agreement, he did not talk about his wife, and I asked few, if any, questions. It was an area of old sadness for him, around which I trod carefully, just as he was reticent to probe too deeply into the madness that had been my marriage. Although once he did speak up. I had said to him that I thought I had brought the abuse upon myself because I had been a catalyst for my husband's anger. Jack held me by the wrist and made me look at him. I was not responsible for the beatings, he said clearly. Only the man who hit me was responsible. Did I understand that?

One morning when we were in the bed together, I thought I heard a cry. I stiffened, to listen, and I felt Jack pull away from me, listening too.

It was Caroline, who seemed to be crying in pain. I thought to myself: I must go to her—but I was strangely paralyzed, thrust backward in time to another bed, another set of cries. For a minute, I almost couldn't breathe, and there must have been on my face an expression of alarm, for Jack said, pulling even farther back and looking quickly at my face, "What's wrong? Are you OK?"

"It's Caroline," I whispered.

"I know," he said. "Go to her. Or do you want me to?"

The question snapped me back to the present moment. I flung back the covers and threw on my nightgown. I ran down the stairs to her bedroom. She was on her back, in her crib, her knees raised. She was indeed crying in pain. I picked her up and began to walk with her around the well-worn path through the kitchen, the living room, and her bedroom, but even the walking this time could not quiet her. Jack came down the stairs in his shorts. His hair was mussed, and he was barefoot—the floorboards were freezing.

"Give her to me a minute," he said on my second pass.

I handed her to him, and she looked at him curiously before she started again to cry. He walked with her to the sofa under the window and placed her, stomach down, on his knees, which were slightly apart. Then he began to make an up-and-down motion with his knees—in effect massaging her under her stomach. Almost immediately, she stopped crying.

"I don't know why it works," he said, looking pleased with himself, "but it does. I had to do this with my daughter all the time when she was a baby. It moves the gas bubbles up, I guess, or down. I can't remember now who taught it to me."

I stood across the room watching him with Caroline. They were a funny sight—Jack in his shorts, his eyes puffy, his hair flattened, Caroline stretched out on the tops of his long legs, looking up at me as if to say, *Now what*. It was so cold in the room, I'd begun to shiver. I went to him and picked up Caroline. She burrowed into my shoulder as if she wanted to go back to sleep.

"You're good with children," I said. "I saw you with your daughter at the bonfire."

"Good with children, lousy with wives," he said, getting up from the couch.

"You've had more than one?"

"One's enough." He crossed his arms over his chest and rubbed them to warm them.

"Is your marriage really so bad?" I asked, swaying lightly from side to side with Caroline.

He shrugged. "You make a mistake, you lie with it," he said.

It was an interesting choice of words.

"Why don't you leave?" I asked.

"I can't leave," he said. "It's not a possibility."

There was an air of finality to this pronouncement, and as if to underscore that finality he turned to look out the window, out to the horizon, where he saw the same thing I did—a crimson sliver of sun breaking over the water.

I was afraid that he had misunderstood me, and so I said, "I don't want you to leave; that's not what I meant."

He turned back to me.

"I know," he said.

We stood there looking at each other, and it seems to me now, remembering that moment, we spoke volumes to each other.

"I'd better go now," he said finally.

I went over to him and touched him lightly on the

side of his arm, stroking his arm, as he had once stroked mine. It was all I could think of to do.

I did not know much about his life on the water, although one day near the end, on a Sunday, when the men did not come to the point, he took me out on his boat. When he first suggested the trip, I immediately thought of Caroline, but he said we would take her with us, in the sling if I liked. He used to take his own babies out onto the water, he said. Babies almost always fell asleep at once, from the rocking of the boat or from the vibrations of the motor. Indeed, when the men's wives had babies that were colicky, he said, the women would often beg to come aboard the boats with their babies for a day's fishing, just to get some rest.

I woke Caroline early, and we were ready for him when he came. The air was cold but still, and I could see all the way out to the lighthouse. The water's surface was unruffled, but I knew that by midmorning, the breezes would make it rougher. He untied the dinghy from the ring, slid it down to the water's edge.

"Get in the punt," he said, "at the bow."

The dinghy was pretty beat; even I could see that. He said that he'd been meaning to replace it all year, but somehow he hadn't gotten to it yet.

"We'll go slowly," he said.

I sat in the bow with the baby, as he had told me to do. He knelt in the stern rather than stand, so that he would not inadvertently tip us. When he got in, our combined weight seemed almost too much for the dinghy, and when I looked over the side, I could see we were riding pretty low to the water. I didn't move as he sculled us out to the channel and the boat, a distance of perhaps a hundred and fifty feet. Despite the short distance, the journey made me anxious. I wished I had a life vest, although I was remembering how Julia had said her husband went from the cold before he went from the drowning. I was, in fact, so frightened at one point that I surreptitiously dipped my hand into the icy water and made the sign of the cross on Caroline's forehead—a gesture that astonishes me now, when I think of it. I had not had Caroline baptized, and I could not bear the thought of being separated from her for all eternity—even though, if you were to ask me now, in this room, I would have to tell you that I don't believe in eternity.

As Jack sculled, I had a clear view of the point, seen from the eastern end, and of my cottage. From the water, the cottage had even more of a sense of isolation than it did when you were on land. Surrounding it, in both directions for as far as the eye could see, there was only low-lying brush and coastline.

Jack managed somehow to get us all into the larger boat, though I was ungainly with the baby strapped to my middle and in the end had to be hoisted over. He told me to sit on a box in the cockpit while he got us under way. I watched him open the pilothouse, lift the lid off an engine box, and start the engine. He foraged forward and handed a life vest back to me. It was a regulation Coast Guard type, but I could see that it hadn't been used much. I put it on, over my coat, and when he looked back at me, he shook his head, raised his eyebrows, and smiled. Then we were off.

The port side of the boat was enclosed, with the foul-weather gear hanging from a hook. The starboard side was open. The wheel was there and a kind of hydraulic setup for pulling the pots. Above the wheel was a CB radio, but he didn't use it that day. There were other bits of equipment near and around the wheel—a depth sounder, he explained, and fuel gauges. In the cockpit beside me there was a bait barrel. He stood at the wheel and saw us around the island. Then he gestured for me to come up beside him.

I hung on to a center pole and watched the land recede behind the boat. It was hard to hear each other over the engine, so we didn't talk much. He shouted that he would take her straight out to the grounds, pick up twenty traps he'd set a few days before. At the end of the week, he said, he'd have the boat hauled. After he'd picked up his pots, he added, he'd take us over to Swale's Island. It was beautiful, he said. It had the prettiest beach in eastern Maine.

As soon as the engine started, Caroline fell asleep, and she did not wake up until we stopped the boat in the natural harbor of Swale's. The air was frigid, but if I stood close to Jack, inside the well of the pilothouse, I did not feel the wind. I thought that Caroline was probably warm enough, though I did not like to think of all the possible things that could go wrong and how quickly a person could die out there.

Jack was relaxed and loose and amused, smiling at me in a way he seldom did at the cottage. Perhaps he was enjoying the incongruity of myself and the baby on his boat, or perhaps he was just continually tickled by the way I looked with the baby at my front and the life vest tied around me. There were few boats on the water. Indeed, once we had put the coastline behind us, and there were only islands, I had a sense of being very far away. At first, I had been able to see the village of St. Hilaire from the water, but now that was gone, even the white steeple of the church. The sun was up, but the shore was just a hazy blue.

After about forty-five minutes, we reached a point where he cut the engine, idled the boat. He took the foul-weather gear from its hook, put on only the pants. He already had on his yellow slicker over his sweater. He wore the bib of the pants over the jacket, like an apron. I asked him how he knew where he was. He pointed to a small cove in a nearby island, then to a rocky ledge. They seemed identical to all the small coves I'd seen, all the rocky ledges. He laughed. He said he had the depth sounder too. And then, of course, all around us were his buoys—red on the top and bottom, with a yellow band in between.

I watched as he hauled his pots. As each came up, he would remove the lobsters, band the claws with elastic, put the lobsters into one of the buckets that he had filled with water, throw back into the sea any detritus that had been in the lobster pot, and stack the pot on those he had already retrieved.

"Normally I'd rebait them, throw them back, but I'm hauling them for the winter," he said.

It was hard work, and it had a certain kind of ugliness to it too. I did not think it was romantic, the actual hauling of the pots, only cold and difficult. He wore long cotton gloves, but I thought his hands must be freezing. The water splashed up on his bib and around our feet.

When he was finished, the small cockpit was jammed with buckets and pots and buoys, and I had lost my seat on the box.

He turned the boat south then, toward Swale's Island, which he pointed out to me when it became visible. On the north side of the island, as we approached, I could see several large wooden houses and what looked like fields.

"It's privately owned," he said, "though we all use the beach on the other side in summer. It's where we take our families for a picnic or whatever."

At the mention of families, he looked away from me and busied himself at the wheel. He checked the depth sounder, looked westward toward shore. I knew that it had cost him to give me this time on a Sunday, and that there might not be any more Sundays. The boat we were on had his wife's name on it, and I was sometimes reminded of this, as when he would say—a common enough expression—"I'll just take her out to the grounds."

He took the boat in close to the western shore of the island, so that I could see the rocky ledges there or catch a glimpse of a seal. Then he negotiated the cut, and we were in the harbor—a crescent bordered by a nearly pure-white beach. It was a wild beach, undomesticated. The only way to get there was by boat. He cut the engine and threw an anchor overboard. The baby woke up.

"I've brought us a picnic," he said.

"I have to nurse the baby," I said. I had never nursed her in front of him. He cleared two seats facing each other in the cockpit. He helped me off with the life vest and extricated Caroline from the sling. As he held Caroline, he said to me to go forward and see if I could find an old beach towel he thought was there. It would make a kind of tent, he said, to shield Caroline from the breezes while she nursed.

I went forward into the small cabin. I supposed there was an order to it that Jack understood, but to me it looked chaotic. There was hardware and ropes, a canvas tarp and rags. I opened a door to a cabinet. It was the books that first caught my eye. There were half a dozen paperbacks. I remember a book of poetry by Yeats, Malamud's *The Fixer*. The books were worn, dog-eared, and some had water stains. Also inside were old charts, folded and refolded a hundred times. A flashlight, some flares, a flare gun. A bottle, a third full, of whiskey. I saw the towel, picked it up. Under it was another gun, a pistol. I picked the pistol up, held it in my hand, put it back. I returned to the cockpit with the towel.

"I found the towel," I called to him, emerging, stopping a second to watch him holding Caroline, "but I also found a gun."

"Oh," he said. He seemed unconcerned, as if I'd found a watch he'd misplaced and not a gun. "We all have them," he added. "We all keep a gun for poachers, to warn them off. I'll fire it from time to time to keep it from getting rusty, but that's all."

"It's loaded?" I asked.

"Wouldn't be much point in having it if I didn't keep it loaded. Anyway, no one's ever on board except me."

"I also found some books," I said. "Paperbacks. Do you read when you're out here?"

He looked startled for a moment, embarrassed.

"If I get the chance," he said. He laughed. "Well, sometimes I make the chance. It's peaceful out here."

I took the baby from him and sat down. I opened my

coat and raised my sweater. I immediately felt the cold air on my bare skin. He shook out the towel and placed it over my shoulder to shield Caroline's face from the cold. He went forward into the cabin and returned with the bottle of whiskey. Then he sat down and began to unpack the picnic. Occasionally, such as at that moment, I would shut my eyes, for just a second, and let the smallest picture come into my mind of what my life might have been like if I had met Jack years ago and not Harrold, but I immediately shook these pictures away. It was treacherous ground—shifting shoals.

He had made bacon sandwiches and a thermos of coffee. It was all he had made, but he'd made lots, and I was ravenous. My God, you cannot imagine how good bacon sandwiches are when you are hungry. He had toasted the bread, and even though the sandwiches were cold, they were indescribably delicious. He poured a generous amount of whiskey into the coffee. It seemed to be the custom here—to lace your coffee or tea with spirits. He gave me my coffee in the cap of the thermos; he himself drank from the canister. Around us the sun was brilliant and doing its best to try to warm us. It reflected off the white beach and the water. He sat across from me; our knees were touching. I ate with one hand, held the baby with the other. The boat was rocking gently. I looked at his weathered face, the wrinkles, his gray eyes. He had the collar of a flannel shirt up high under the sweater. It was just the two of us and all that water and all that sand and all that sky.

"This is . . .," I started to say, but I couldn't finish.

He looked at me.

He adjusted the towel on my shoulder.

He nodded and looked away.

Perhaps we talked while we sat there eating the sandwiches. We must have, because I have bits of information I might not otherwise have now. We tended not to talk much in the mornings, and he was reticent by nature, not used to sharing thoughts and feelings—or possibly he was just long out of practice. I thought that in this way we were alike, for I had learned to be guarded, too, in conversation. If you cannot talk about the thing that is at the center of your life—cannot let bits slip out for fear of revealing the entire story—you develop what might pass for a natural reticence, a habit of listening rather than of telling stories yourself. But that day, I think he did speak of his family: not of his wife and children, but of his father and his grandfather. They'd been lobstermen too, or at least his father had, he said. His grandfather had fished for cod, then had switched to lobster when the demand for it had begun to increase after World War II. His grandfather was dead now, and although his father was still alive, living just south of town with his wife, he could no longer fish. I don't remember exactly what words Jack used to describe his father's accident, but I understood it and the early retirement it necessitated to be a calamity of serious proportions.

Though I never met Jack's father, I did sometimes have an image of an older, smaller version of Jack, a man with withered arms, sitting in an armchair in the living room of a Maine Cape, looking out across the gulf.

When we had eaten all the sandwiches, Jack said that

we ought to be heading in. He would drop me off at the point, then take the boat over to the wharf to wash her down and set his pots on the dock. Easier to pick them up there, he explained, than to ferry them in the dinghy.

We didn't speak on the voyage home—again the engine was too loud—but the ride was comfortable and strangely warm. We were going with the wind.

We rounded a pine-thick island, and I could just make out the point and my cottage.

"Damn!" he said.

I tried to see what had caught his attention, but his eyes on the water were sharper than my own. I squinted in the direction of the cottage. And then when we had drawn a little closer, I saw it. A red pickup truck at the shack.

"There's a truck at the fish house," I said.

"You know whose it is?"

"Yes."

"We can't turn around. . . ."

"No, we can't," I agreed.

"All right, then," he said. "Jesus Christ, what's he doing here on a Sunday?"

I knew, but I didn't say.

He brought the boat to the mooring, lowered me into the dinghy, and sculled us to the shore. By the time he had pulled the dinghy far enough up onto the sand so that I could step out, Willis had traversed the length of the beach.

"Jack."

"Willis."

The two men greeted each other, but Jack did not look up in Willis's direction. Willis was smoking a cigarette.

"Red."

I nodded, bent my head to the baby.

"You out for a spin or what?" he said to Jack.

"Hauling some pots."

"On a Sunday. Good for you. I always said you were a hard worker, Jack."

Jack pushed the dinghy back into the water, prepared to get in.

"And you took Red here along for the ride."

Jack looked up from the dinghy at me. "Yes," he said. No excuses. No explanations.

"So what'd you think, Red? You like it or what?"

Willis had sunglasses on, as I did. I couldn't see his eyes, but I looked straight at the sunglasses.

"It was instructive," I said. "Very instructive."

Jack pushed himself away from the shore with the oar. I thought he was smiling.

"So long, then," he said.

"Thanks for the trip," I answered as casually as I could.

I was thinking: In a few hours, I will see him again.

Perhaps he was thinking that too.

Willis walked me back toward the cottage. He said, "I saw your car was here. I tried the door a coupla times, no answer. I got worried, thought maybe you'd had an accident or something, or fallen into a honeypot. Another half hour and I'd a gone for Everett."

"That would have been silly," I said.

"It's dangerous you goin' out on a boat in the winter with a baby. You got to think of the baby, you know."

"I think of the baby all the time," I said. "And don't worry about me. I can take care of myself."

We were at his truck by then. I was not going to invite him in, even if he asked, and I suppose he sensed that, because he did not ask.

"Is that a fact," he said, touching the baby on the cheek.

Willis Beale

Well, I suppose someone's goin' to have to tell you the whole story about Jack and Mary. I don't mean to say that this has any bearin' on the crime itself, I wouldn't want you to think that. I'm not sayin' she did it because of this, that's not what I'm sayin' 'tall, although maybe you got to think of that a little bit, but the truth is she didn't waste much time before she hooked up with Jack Strout.

Has anybody told you the whole story yet?

Not too much of this came out at the trial, because nobody who testified would give too many details. That is to say, it was mentioned, and Mary, she had to say, didn't she, but the prosecutor, he didn't really get into the details. But I think if you're goin' to do this article of yours, you ought to have all the facts, even though I don't want you sayin' it was me or anything that told you. This is—what do you call it—undercover information.

Well, OK, background information.

So long as you don't put my name with this. But the truth is, it didn't take her too long, if you understand my meaning. I can't tell you for sure when it began, but I can tell you this. By Christmas Eve, I had kind of an idea about the two of them. Just call it an instinct. I got a nose for people, you know what I mean? I didn't actually see them together until, oh, at least a week or more later, but I just began to get this idea from watchin' 'em. Now you think about that. She got here on December 3. Christmas Eve was only three weeks later. Is that a fast worker or what?

So you think about that for a while, and you start to get a little bit of a different picture of Mary Amesbury. You know, maybe she wasn't quite the injured party she made herself out to be. Maybe she went after the fellas in New York City a little too often, and her husband had what you would call a real case against her, you follow me. I don't know, I'm thinkin' if I had a wife played around a lot—hey, you know, what if the baby wasn't even his?—well, that could turn a fella's head around, and he might get a bit hot under the collar.

All I'm sayin' is, it bears some thinkin' about, that's all.

Now, Jack, he was your basic family man. Never a hint of any funny business from either him or Rebecca. And to tell you the truth, this whole thing is a really sad story. When I think about what happened . . .

So what I'm tryin' to tell you is, I don't think Jack made the first move, you understand me? I know Jack. He's as straight as a die. Loyal to his wife, even with all his troubles. Never even looked at another woman, far as I know, and I'd probably know. So you tell me what happened. I mean, Mary Amesbury, she was a pretty good-lookin' woman, even with all what happened to her, and I suppose even Jack, I mean if a woman really goes after you, sometimes, well, we're all human, right, and maybe she was just too much for him. What I mean to say is, I just can't see Jack makin' the first move. He's not the type.

Yeah, I saw 'em together. Caught 'em red-handed, so to speak, although they weren't actually . . . you know. It was a Sunday afternoon, and I was over to the point to get some gear from the fish house, and I thought I'd just stop by, see if she was OK. You know I felt responsible for her a little bit, seein' as how I was practically the first person she met in town, and I noticed that her car was there, but she was nowhere to be seen. I started to get worried after a while, that she'd had an accident or something, and then I saw 'em comin' in. He took her out on the boat. On a Sunday, no less. So right then you knew it wasn't on the up and up. 'Cause how come he takes her out when he knows no one will be on the point? Right? So I go down to say hello, be friendly, and they're both lookin' guiltier than shit. All over their faces. And there she is with the baby, no less. I'd like to know what they did with the baby when they . . . you know. Anyway, that's none of my business, is it?

Fact is, he used to go there in the mornings, afore he went out on his boat. It got to be kind of general knowledge around town, though whether it got to be general knowledge afore or after is hard to say now. I can't really remember. I knew, but of course I wouldn't a told anyone. Except possibly Jeannine. I might of told Jeannine.

239

I was pretty disappointed in Mary Amesbury after that. I thought she was what she was, but she wasn't, if you follow me.

So, like I said, probably this is neither here nor there. I just thought you ought to have all the facts, that's all.

Mary Amesbury

That night I woke up to the sound of Caroline crying. The cries were high-pitched and insistent, and when I reached her room, she was on all fours in the crib, trying to pull herself up the bars. Her face was scrunched and reddened with pain. I reached for her, and I could feel at once that she was feverish. I put my hand on her forehead. She twisted away from me. I'd never felt such hot skin before.

Immediately, I went into the kitchen and crushed a tablet of baby aspirin. It dissolved imperfectly in the apple juice, and when I tried to give the juice to Caroline, she flung her head back and screamed, refusing the bottle. Not knowing what else to do, I walked with her around the familiar path, but the walking was useless. I tried to hold her close to my chest to comfort her. When I did so, however, she kept twisting her head away and then flopping her face from side to side against me. I wanted to stay calm, to think clearly, but this flopping alarmed me.

Jack came just before daybreak, as was his custom. I had Caroline on the orange mat in the bathroom. I had stripped her of her pajamas and diaper and was trying to give her a sponge bath with cool washcloths to bring the fever down. The touch of the washcloths must have been searing on her skin, however, for she shrieked even louder when I did this.

Jack stood at the door. He had his slicker on and his high boots.

"What's wrong?" he asked.

"She's hot, feverish. I can't make out what's wrong."

He crouched down to touch her face.

"Jesus," he said. "She's burning up."

I had been trying to convince myself that her fever wasn't all that serious, but when he said *Jesus*, I knew it was. "I was going to wait for the clinic in Machias to open," I said in a rush. "But I don't know. What do you think?"

He looked at his watch. "It's five-thirty now," he said. "There won't be anyone there till nine."

He stood up, unfolding his long body. His boots and slicker crinkled.

"I'll go up to LeBlanc's," he said. "Call the doctor on duty."

"You can't do that," I said, looking up at him. I was thinking that his going up to the blue Cape on my behalf would give him away, be too risky for him.

"I'll say I was on my way out to the boat when you came to the door and called to me and asked for help."

"They won't believe you," I said.

"I don't know," he said, "but I don't think you can afford to worry about that right now."

When he returned I was in the bathtub with Caroline. The water was dreary and cold and felt miserable even to me, but I couldn't think of anything else to do. Bringing the fever down was all that seemed to matter.

"Let's go," he said from the doorway. "The doctor's going to meet us there."

I looked at him questioningly. His eyes, his gray eyes, were focused and alert.

"Should you . . .?" I started to ask.

He shook his head, as if to toss away my question. "I'm taking you. Get dressed."

I stood up and handed Caroline to him. He wrapped her in an orange towel. He held her while I went upstairs and dressed myself. Then I came downstairs and dressed the baby. Through all of this, she continued to scream, twisting her head from side to side, alarming even Jack, who I had thought was unflappable. Once, when I had her on her back and was trying to get her foot into the leg of her sleeping suit, she began to bat at the side of her face. I looked at him, but he wouldn't return my gaze. I abandoned the thought of dressing her then, simply wrapped her in a woolen blanket.

Jack held her as I climbed up into the cab of his truck. The sky was violet, and on the western horizon I could still see stars. There was no traffic on the road to speak of, but in the houses there were lights on in the bedrooms. The town of Machias was still and silent when we drove though it, as if it had been abandoned.

The doctor was at the clinic. He had turned on the light by the door. He came around a corner as we entered the waiting room, and I was surprised to see how young he was. He couldn't have been more than thirty, and he didn't look like a doctor. He wore blue jeans and a wrinkled blue work shirt, as if he had stepped into the clothes that had been lying on the floor by his bed. He ushered us into an examining room and asked me to unwrap the baby. As I did so, I told him of how she'd been shrieking and twisting her head, of how she'd batted at the side of her face.

He didn't take her temperature. He seemed not to need to do that. He examined her throat, then looked into each of her ears.

He stood up. He felt her forehead then. "Ear infections," he pronounced matter-of-factly. "Thought it might be that. She's got a couple of lulus."

He reached into a cabinet for a small bottle and put a drop of liquid into each ear. "This'll stop the pain for a bit," he said. "But we'll have to put her on antibiotic straightaway. Actually I'd like to give her an injection right now, if that's all right with you, and then you can get a prescription when the pharmacy opens up. Quite frankly, I don't really like this fever, and I think we probably want to get that down as soon as possible." He felt her forehead. "I'll take her temp, but my guess is the fever's close to a hundred and five." His voice was calm, but I understood that the fever worried him.

The room went hollow then, airless, like the inside of a bell jar. The floor sank perceptibly. I put my hand out for the edge of the leather gurney. I tried to think, to remember. But what I needed to remember was just beyond my grasp, like a mystifying calculus problem that will not yield up its secrets.

"Oh, no," I said quietly, almost inaudibly.

The doctor heard me, but he misunderstood me. Jack

looked puzzled too. Ear infections were good news, weren't they? Compared to what it might have been?

"She'll be all right," the doctor said quickly to reassure me. And perhaps there was a note of false heartiness in his voice. He removed a rectal thermometer from a glass jar filled with liquid and held Caroline's legs while he inserted it. She twisted and wriggled in protest, but his grasp was firm. "I wish I had a nickel for all the ear infections I see in a season, believe me," he said. "If I give her an injection now, the fever will probably break before the day is out. By tomorrow, she'll be her old self, though you'll have to continue the antibiotic for ten days."

I shook my head.

"What's wrong?" It was Jack. He was looking at me oddly. In the harsh light of the examining room, his roughened skin and the two deep grooves at the sides of his mouth were pronounced. I thought that my bruises, though nearly healed, must be prominent too. I wondered if Jack had been here before, if he had stood as he was standing now, with his wife where I was, with his own child on the gurney.

"She's allergic to one of the antibiotics," I said as calmly as I could, "and I don't know which one."

"Well, there's no difficulty there," the doctor said, extricating the thermometer. "Yup," he said. "One-oh-five on the nose. Don't want to fool around with this. I'll give her something for the fever too. Who treated her? I'll make a call. It must be on her chart."

Jack understood then. He shifted his weight, looked at me again.

"She was three months old," I said, more to myself than to the doctor or to Jack. "She had a fever, but her pediatrician couldn't figure out what was causing it. He gave her something, and I don't know what it was, but it made her break out in hives and swell up. So they gave her something else, but I don't know what that was, either. I'd say it was penicillin, but I'm not positive. They also gave her a sulfa drug, I think, and I just can't remember which was which."

There was a silence in the room.

"I'm sorry I can't remember," I said. "I wasn't very—"

"Well," the doctor said, interrupting me. He sounded impatient with my inability to grasp the ease of the solution. "It *is* important. An allergic reaction like that can be fatal the second time around. But it's not a problem we can't solve. As I said, if you can give me the name of where she was treated, I can call up her chart."

Jack's face was impassive. "Is there any drug you can give the baby that wouldn't be either of the ones Mary mentioned and that might be safe?" he asked.

The doctor looked at Jack, then at me. You could see on his face that he was beginning to understand.

"I'll make the call," I said quickly.

The doctor shook his head. "No," he said. "I think I have to. They probably wouldn't give you the information, and you might not understand it, anyway. And I don't think we want to lose any time."

I started to speak, then hesitated.

"There's a problem here, isn't there?" the doctor asked.

Caroline, whose pain was temporarily gone but who was wrung out from her fever, looked up at me from the gurney.

"No," I said quickly, and perhaps too loudly for such a small examining room. "No, there's no problem here."

I gave the name and address of Caroline's pediatrician in New York City. I even knew the phone number.

We left the clinic and walked to the black pickup truck parked out front. Jack carried Caroline. He said to me that it was a long shot, that my husband wouldn't have thought of the pediatrician, that the odds were a million to one against it. I, in turn, to reassure him, said that I agreed with him, the odds were a million to one.

But I didn't agree with him. I didn't at all.

Jack drove me back to the cottage with the baby. Dawn was breaking as we bumped and jostled down the lane, and already the ocean was turning a bluish mauve. The air was clean and crisp, as though washed through, and cold. It had been clear and frigid for three days, and I sensed that the thaw was over, that we would not have any more fog or moderate temperatures for some time now. Jack had said the day before that he would soon be hauling his boat.

He left me off at the cottage and drove back into Machias to wait for the drugstore to open so that he could fill the prescription for me. This would mean that he would be delayed going out onto the water and that he might be seen by the men in the fish house coming to my cottage with the medicine. I had said to him that I would go into town to get the prescription, but he wouldn't hear of it. I should be inside with Caroline, he said. He would go.

As it happened, the red pickup truck was at the fish

house when Jack returned. He came to the door and gave me the package. He asked me how Caroline was. I told him that she seemed better, was sleeping now. I willed him to come in, and I sensed that he, too, wanted to step over the threshold, to close the door to the point behind him, for he held the door open with his shoulder and hunched forward as though poised on the brink of a decision.

"Come in," I said, knowing even as I said it that he would have to refuse. It was full daylight now, and I sensed that Willis was peering at us from the salted windows of the fish house. I expected him to emerge at any minute from the door.

"I can't," Jack said.

I reached my hand forward and tucked it inside the collar of his flannel shirt and his sweater. It was a gesture that could not be seen from the fish house. His skin was warm there. I was trembling from the cold and from pure longing. I saw on his face the same need I had. Beyond us the gulls twirled and looped in an early-morning feeding frenzy.

Time had become compressed—perhaps even more so since the events of the morning. I knew that Jack felt now as I did, that minutes together could not be wasted. When he hauled his boat in a few days, he would not be able to come to me any longer in the early mornings—not until the season began again in the spring. He couldn't come to me while he was working on his gear at the fish house; the others would see. And he couldn't leave his bed at four in the morning. He would have no boat to go to, which his wife would know. Did we have three mornings left or four?

"I have to go now," he said.

I withdrew my hand.

"You'll come tomorrow?" I asked.

"Yes," he said, and turned abruptly to jog down the small hill to the end of the point.

I nursed Caroline through the day and the night, dozing when she slept, just holding her when she was awake. The antibiotic had knocked her out, but she didn't seem to be in much pain, for which I was grateful, and her fever was abating as well. Toward evening, she recovered a bit more of her spirits, and we played together on the braided rug. I lay down on it and she crawled over me, then I'd capture her and whisk her through the air or lay her down beside me and tickle her. She giggled and laughed—deep belly laughs that made me want to squeeze her all the more.

Jack came just before daybreak. I was awake and waiting for him. His footsteps seemed urgent on the stairs. He was already shedding his yellow slicker as he opened the door to my bedroom. I rose in the bed to meet him, and he embraced me before he even had all his clothes off. His need was high-pitched and keen that morning, and we roiled in the bed like a churned-up sea. I felt in him something new—a frustration, the wanting of more than we could reasonably have. Afterwards, he rolled onto his back.

"I want to leave her," he said. "I want to come here and be with you."

I started to speak, but he stopped me.

"I can't leave her," he said. "Yesterday morning, when you gave the doctor the name and the number in that way you did, I thought for a just a minute that if you could risk so much, so could I. And all day I was trying to work it out, trying to figure a way I could leave her without harming her and come to you, but I couldn't. There just isn't any way to do it. Because it isn't a question of my risking anything for myself. I'd be risking her things—her family, her home, what little stability she has. And I can't do that to her. I don't have that right. She's too fragile, and this would just—"

I rolled over onto him and pulled the covers up to our shoulders. I put my hand over his mouth, laid my head on his chest. "Don't think about any of that," I said. "Let's just have this."

He wrapped his arms around me, held me close to his body.

"I'm sorry," he said.

There was a silence in the room.

"You know," he said after a time, "I don't want you to go, but maybe you should think about that, just to be on the safe side." His arms had stiffened against me. "Just to another town or something, somewhere a little further north maybe."

I had had this thought too, almost immediately, at the clinic in Machias, but I had rejected it even before it was fully formed. I couldn't leave the cottage now. I couldn't leave Jack. I didn't have the strength. I knew that.

"When does the season start up again?" I asked.

"April," he said. "But I could push it a little. Get her in mid-March."

"Do that," I said.

———

Later, when he was sitting at the kitchen table and I was making tea, I asked him what it was that he had studied in college, what he had thought he might do with himself after he graduated. It was still dark outside, and I could see our reflection in the windows: myself in my flannel nightgown and my cardigan sweater, my hair too long and loose over my shoulders; Jack in his flannel shirt and sweater, his body half turned toward me so that he could watch me at the stove. We looked, in the windows, like a fisherman and his wife, who had risen early to prepare her husband's breakfast. I thought that we did not look anything like a love affair—rather something homelier, more familiar. This vision in the windows held me for a moment; we appeared to be something we were not, could not ever be.

"What's wrong?" he asked.

I shook my head. I brought the tea and some toast to the table.

"You'll laugh," he said, "but I suppose I thought I'd be a college teacher one day. I went to school on a track scholarship, and I thought I'd be a track coach myself. I loved running—there's nothing like it, not even lobstering—and then I had a great professor for English lit, and somehow I sort of thought I'd do both: teach and coach."

"Do you ever think of going back to it—school, teaching?" I asked. I was thinking of the books I had found on his boat.

"No," he said quickly and dismissively. "Not since I left."

"Do you mind?"

"No." He said it with finality, as if it were something he had put behind him years ago.

We ate the small breakfast. He said that he would haul his boat on Friday if the weather was decent, and that he would then begin to mend his gear. He always took his wife and daughter on a small trip in February, he added, a kind of vacation. He wasn't sure where exactly they would go this year; he himself wanted to go down to Boston to see his son, who was at school there, but his daughter was vigorously lobbying for somewhere warmer. There was an edge to his voice; he talked more rapidly than he usually did, and I responded the same way, as if we sensed that whatever it was that we had wanted to tell each other, or might want to tell each other during the winter months, we had better say it now. I was wondering if I would continue to wake early, before daybreak, after he was gone.

The sun broke the horizon line. I could see there a sliver of molten red. I thought how odd it was to hate the coming of the day, as if we were night creatures who disintegrated with the light. I stood up and went to the door, waiting for him. I always hated the moment when he left the cottage. I watched him rise from the table, put on his waders and his yellow slicker.

"Maybe I won't let you through the door," I said playfully, snaking my arms around him between the slicker and his sweater. "Maybe I'll just keep you here all day."

He buried his face in my hair. He put his arms around my nightgown, lifted the nightgown so he could feel my skin.

"I wish you would," he said.

The next morning—it was the Wednesday—Jack didn't come. I woke, as usual, just before daybreak and waited, but I didn't hear his footsteps on the stairs. I lay in bed, straining for the sound of his motor on the lane, but I heard nothing except the first cries of the gulls, the lapping of the waves against the shingle. I watched as daybreak came, then the dawn itself. When the sun broke above the horizon line, I knew that he would not come at all. It was the first time since the fog that he had failed to visit me, and I felt empty, as though the day itself had lost its color.

Caroline woke shortly after sunrise. She seemed, as the doctor had predicted, perfectly fine, but I continued the antibiotic as I had been told to do. I put her on the braided rug after I had fed her, and looked out my windows to the end of the point. The green-and-white lobster boat bobbed in the water as though mocking me. Eventually trucks came and parked by the fish house, and men got out, but Jack was not among them. I tried to think of all the reasons why he had not come. There had been a crisis at home. Perhaps Rebecca had caused a scene of some kind. Possibly Jack had told her after all. Or Jack had decided to make a clean break with me—that would be like him. Yes, that was it. When he'd said goodbye yesterday, he'd known it was for good, and that's why he'd held me in that way. He'd said goodbye, only I hadn't known it.

I tried to come to terms with this possibility, tried to believe it and accept it. But I couldn't. I walked around the rooms, empty-handed, while Caroline played on the floor. I couldn't sit still. Was he telling me I should go now? Leave this town and find another?

But I couldn't leave. I had no will to leave. And I couldn't go without first speaking to Jack. I had to know if he meant never to come again.

I dressed myself and then the baby. I wanted to drive into town and find his house and ask him why he hadn't come, but I knew I couldn't do that. Down by the fish house, I could hear men talking. I wanted to go down there, ask of Jack—the hell with Willis—but I knew that was an absurd idea too. Instead I bundled Caroline into the sling and took her out for a walk. I didn't think a walk would harm her, not if she was dressed warmly enough.

The air was dry and light and stinging, like chilled champagne. It hadn't been the weather that had prevented Jack from going out on his boat, I knew that. I walked fast down to the edge of the point and back again. If someone had seen me walking, he would have said that I looked angry. I glanced up at the cottage, but I didn't want to go inside it yet. I veered south, walked along the shore toward town. Because I was walking fast, I went farther than I ever had been before. The tide was peeling back, leaving a firm patch of sand. The low-tide smell drifted in on a breeze from time to time and then wafted away on the fine, dry air. I walked until my legs ached and my back was sore from the weight of Caroline in the sling. But it was what I had wanted, I realized—to tire myself out.

I walked back more slowly than I'd set out. I'd been gone almost two hours when Caroline began to cry. It was past the time when I should have fed her again, and I knew I had to get back to the cottage soon to do that. I picked up my pace.

I rounded a bend and saw the cottage on its promontory. Outside the cottage, on the gravel drive, there was a car I hadn't seen before, an old black Buick sedan. Julia Strout was standing on the steps to the cottage, looking out over the point.

She saw me then and waved. I waved back. I made my way up the slope.

"Thought you might have gone for a walk," she said. "The baby's OK?"

"She's hungry," I said. "I've got to nurse her. How are you?"

Julia said, Fine, thank you, and held the door for me; we both entered the cottage. I took Caroline out of the sling and shook off my coat. I sat on the couch in the living room and gestured for Julia to sit down too. She did so but did not take off her coat.

"I got a call from Jack Strout this morning," she said, looking at me carefully as she said this. I tried to keep my face composed, but almost immediately I could feel a sharp squeeze inside my chest. I took a deep breath of air. I wanted to open a window.

"He said that the baby had been quite sick," she said. "And that you'd asked him for help morning before last and he'd taken you into Machias, to the clinic."

I nodded.

"Baby's all right now?" she asked.

"Better," I said. "A lot better." I realized that I was sitting stiffly in my chair, that I was breathing shallowly. I also became aware of the fact that the milk was no longer flowing. Caroline had stopped nursing and was looking up at me. I tried to breathe evenly and deeply to relax, to let the milk flow again. Take it easy, I said to myself.

"Anyway," she said, "he wanted me to tell you that he had meant to come by today to see if the baby was OK and if you needed anything, but his wife, Rebecca, got sick in the night herself—a bad stomach virus, he said—and he couldn't leave her. And he thought, if I was coming out this way, I could look in on you myself."

"That was . . . that was nice of him," I said feebly. "And of you," I added quickly. "You can tell him that Caroline is fine now. I'm fine. We're all fine."

Julia looked at me oddly. My voice sounded high and tight in the small room. I was trying to figure out how to get a message back to Jack through Julia, but I couldn't think clearly.

"Actually," she said, sitting back in her chair and unbuttoning her coat—it was warm in the cottage—"I was on my way out here, anyway. This may be nothing, and I don't want to alarm you, but I thought you ought to know. I saw Everett at the store early this morning—I go over every morning to get the milk and the paper—and he said there was a fellow from New York into the store last evening asking questions about a woman named Maureen English."

I may have blanched then, or perhaps the shock registered some other way on my face, for Julia said quickly, "Are you all right?"

"I'm having some trouble," I said, making a gesture that indicated the nursing.

"You're sure?"

"Yes," I said. "This man. . .?"

"Everett thought the fellow was some kind of private detective, although the man didn't say exactly," she continued. "Everett said he knew of no one named Maureen

English, and then the fellow described the woman he was looking for and said she was traveling with a baby, and Everett said he didn't know of anyone like that, either."

I shut my eyes.

"The man left and hasn't come back," Julia said. "Everett thinks he's gone on to another town. He told him to try Machias, but the man said he'd already been there that afternoon. He said he was trying all the towns along this part of the coast. He'd had a tip the woman he was looking for was in the area."

I opened my eyes. I tried to breathe normally. There was no hope of any more milk now, and Caroline had begun to fuss.

"I have to make her a bottle," I said, and got up.

Julia followed me into the kitchen.

"I think you'll be OK," she said. "Everett thinks the man believed him. He thinks he's moved on."

I nodded. I wanted to believe her.

"Does Everett know if this man spoke to anyone else in town?" I asked.

Julia shook her head. "He doesn't know, but he doesn't think so. It's only logical that someone would try the store first. It's the only place that looks half alive in town."

Normally, I'd have smiled at that.

"Let me hold her while you fix the bottle," she said.

I gave Caroline to Julia. I warmed some milk on the stove. My shirt was sticking to my back, and I realized I'd been sweating.

"You should go to the police," Julia said. "I don't mean Everett. I mean the real police, in Machias. If you're that afraid."

I shook my head. "I can't do that," I said. "I'm better off if he doesn't know where I am at all. If I went to the police, they might have to notify my husband and tell him where I am. I don't know how this sort of thing works, but I can't take any chances."

I took the bottle from the stove and retrieved Caroline. We went back into the living room. Caroline resisted the bottle at first, but then settled down to it. Julia sat across from me, as before. She still had her coat on.

"Would you like a cup of tea?" I asked.

"No," she said. "I can't stay."

She said that, but she did not get up to leave. She watched me giving the bottle to Caroline. I thought that she might be lingering to make sure that I was all right before she left.

"Jack's been around?" she asked.

I kept my face focused on Caroline. The meaning in Julia's question was unmistakable. She hadn't said, "So my cousin was helpful, was he?" or, "So you've met Jack, then." She'd said, *Jack's been around?*

I didn't know how to answer. Perhaps she was only fishing.

"Well, he helped me that one time."

She nodded slowly.

There was a long silence in the room.

"I'd be glad if Jack had some happiness," she said finally after a time.

It was, if she really didn't know anything, an extraordinary thing to say. But even as she said it, I could feel the ground begin to shift. I sensed that somehow we had entered new territory now. Where it was better not to lie.

It was tempting territory. Or perhaps I only interpreted it as such, because *I* wanted not to lie, to tell someone the truth.

"I think he's had some happiness," I said cautiously, looking away from her and out the window.

She changed the subject then. "Your face looks better," she said. "A lot better."

I nodded and tried to smile. "Well, that's good at least," I said.

She stood up then.

"Now I've *got* to go," she said, all business. "I'm on my way into Machias. Can I get you anything in town? Anything for the baby?"

I shook my head. "No," I said. "We're fine." I stood up too. "Thanks for coming by. I mean it."

She put on her hat and gloves and walked toward the door, and I thought she would leave then, as briskly as she'd come in. Instead she paused, looked out at the cars parked by the fish house. I sensed that she was on the verge of saying one thing more, of saying the one thing she'd really come to say, but that her reserve, her code, inhibited her.

"I'll be by to check on you again in a day or two," she said. "Or Jack will."

"I love him," I said recklessly.

She turned. She looked stunned at first, but I knew that this was because I'd spoken, not because she didn't suspect the truth. Then she nodded slowly, as if confirming her own imaginings.

"I thought that might be it," she said.

She studied me then as if I were a daughter who had

grown too fast for safekeeping, who was now beyond a mother's reach.

"You be careful," she said.

Jack did not come the next morning, either. It was the Thursday, and I thought that he would be hauling his boat on Friday. At best we had only one more morning left. I waited in the bed until the sun rose. Then I got out of bed and walked downstairs to the windows in the living room. I looked out at his boat. The white paint had taken on a salmon hue.

In the afternoon, I went into town, to the store. I did this almost every day, from habit even more than from necessity.

That afternoon, when I parked my car across the street, I saw, in front of the Mobil pump, a black pickup truck with a cap. I knew this truck well, knew its dents and rust marks even better than those of my own car. In the front seat, on the passenger side, there was a woman. I turned off the ignition and looked at her. Her hair was gray, pulled back severely off her face. She wore a silk-like kerchief in a navy-blue print. She had high cheekbones in a face you sensed had once been beautiful but now was painfully thin and white. Her lips were narrow, pressed together tightly. She had on a navy-blue wool coat, and it seemed that her hands were folded in her lap, although I couldn't see them. She must have sensed that someone was looking at her, in that way that one does, for she turned slowly to look in my direction.

I saw then her eyes, and looking at them I felt what it was that Jack had had to live with. Her eyes were pale, a milky blue, or perhaps I have that impression of their color because they seemed cloudy, clouded over. And yet they had a hunted look, a haunted look. They were pinched at the sides. Looking at them, you could not describe what it was these eyes were seeing, but you sensed that it was something terrible. I had the immediate impression that this was a woman who had lost her children to illness or to an accident, but I knew that wasn't true.

I looked away—as much because I didn't want to see those eyes as because I didn't want her to know I'd been examining her. When I glanced up again, she was facing straight ahead, waiting.

I thought then that I ought to start the car up, go home. But I knew he was inside the store. I couldn't pass up this chance to see him, even if I couldn't talk to him.

I got out of the car and removed Caroline from the baby basket. I walked with her around the back of the black pickup and up the steps into the store. The bell tinkled overhead, announcing me.

He was standing with his daughter at the counter. She wasn't wearing a hat, and her hair fell in curls down her back. She had on a red woolen jacket and a white scarf. She turned to see who had entered the store, and when she did this, he turned too. Everett nodded, said hello. I was looking at Jack. I didn't know if he would speak, if he would dare to acknowledge me. He looked at his daughter and then said, in as casual a voice as he could, "How's the baby?"

"She's better," I said.

Everett was looking at both of us.

Jack said to his daughter, "I don't think you've met Mary Amesbury, have you? She's living in Julia's cottage over to the point."

And to me, "This is my daughter, Emily."

I said hello to Emily, and she said hi in a shy way, as fifteen-year-olds do.

I saw Jack glance briefly through the window at the truck. I knew he was wondering if I'd seen Rebecca.

"Mary's baby had a fever the other day," he said to his daughter. He turned to me. "But she's better now?" he asked.

I nodded.

Around me, the canned goods and the fluorescent lights began to spin. It was a reprise of that first evening in the store, only now there was Jack. In the spinning, I had locked onto his face, and I became aware that I was standing there longer than would have been natural. With an effort of will that seemed monumental, I made myself walk forward, made myself say lightly, "I need some milk and things. . . ."

I waited at the rear of the store until I heard the bell over the door. When I walked back to the counter, Everett said, "Julia told me the baby was sick. Looks OK now, though."

He rang up my purchases. I had no idea what I had bought. Outside, I heard the truck start up, the familiar motor.

"Rebecca's poorly," Everett said, nodding to the sound. "Jack's had to do for her."

That night I was lying in the bed. I heard a motor on the lane. The room seemed darker than it ought to be, and I was thinking that he'd come earlier than usual. This would be our last morning together, and like myself he'd been impatient. Perhaps he'd told his wife that he'd be leaving early, that he had a lot to do before he could haul the boat.

I heard his footsteps on the linoleum floor in the kitchen. He didn't come straight up the stairs as I had thought he would, but instead seemed to be getting a glass of water from the sink. Then I heard him open the door into Caroline's room. Yes, I thought, he's checking on the baby. He's been worried about her.

Finally, I heard his footsteps on the stairs. I rose in the bed to greet him. He opened the door.

"Jack," I said with relief in the darkness.

A figure loomed into the room, hovered over the bed. It wasn't Jack.

January 15, 1971

———————

Everett Shedd

You're askin' me now did I know about Mary 'n' Jack afore that terrible business over to the point. Well, that's a hard one to answer. I know Julia 'n' me, we talked about it at length, but whether it was afore the killing or after it, I'm not sure I can say now. Memory is a funny thing. 'Specially so in this case, because I do know this, that when Julia did say somethin' to me about Mary 'n' Jack, I remember thinkin' to myself that I already had an idea about that.

She came into the store just afore the end. And Jack was here with Emily, 'n' the two of 'em, Mary 'n' Jack, they had a little bit of conversation between 'em, and I think even at that point I might of been sayin' to myself, Those two know each other. Course I did know that he'd helped her with the baby the morning the baby got the fever. Do you know about the fever? It's important, because that's how she got found.

As I understand it, the baby got the fever on the

Monday morning, 'n' Jack come by—well, who's to say; maybe he was there already—'n' he drove her into Machias to the clinic there, 'n' Dr. Posner, he's this young fella from Massachusetts come to take over the clinic when Doc Chavenage retired, he saw the baby, 'n' somehow because of the baby bein' allergic to some kind of medication, he had to call down to New York for the baby's records, 'n' I guess he had to give his name 'n' all, 'n' the husband, he'd already alerted a nurse in the office there to Mary's disappearance, 'n' so forth. So it wasn't too long after that morning that the private detective come by askin' questions.

He didn't waste much time, I'll tell you that, 'cause it was Tuesday evenin', 'n' I was gettin' ready to close down the store for my supper, when this fellow walked in. Actually he kinda caught my attention afore he walked in, due to the fact that he was wearin' these shiny black shoes 'n' he slipped on the steps 'n' caught himself, 'n' I heard him cuss on the steps. So he came in, 'n' he was blowin' on his hands; he didn't have any gloves—I tell you, some people don't have the sense God gave 'em—'n' he asked me if I'd seen a woman named Maureen English around. I didn't know the name, of course, but I had an idea, right off the bat, what was up, so I asked this fella to show me some identification, 'n' he did, 'n' then I told him I was the town's only officer of the law, 'n' this seemed to please him. I suppose he thought he'd come to the right place for help. And then I asked him what the woman was wanted for, and he said it was a private matter, she'd run away from home, 'n' so forth. And then he showed me a picture, 'n' if I'd a had any doubt, I wouldn't have then, but of course, I didn't have any doubt in the first place, so I told the fella I'd never seen anyone like this, 'n' if anyone in town would know, I would know. Then I wished him well and told him he ought to try Machias.

That's when he told me he'd already tried Machias. He'd got a tip that she'd been to the clinic there, as I told you. Dr. Posner, I got to hand it to him, he didn't let on much more'n he had to. I don't know whether she didn't give the doctor her address, or she gave it 'n' he wouldn't give it to this fella, but the fella told me the doctor told him he'd treated the baby but had no idea where she was; in fact, he'd had the idea she was just passin' through, on her way north.

Course, none of this matters much now, does it? I mean to say, someone got on to this fella, didn't he? My guess is the fella was on his way out to his car 'n' saw some trucks down by the co-op, and thought, just for the hell of it, don't you know, he'd go down there, snoop around, ask a few questions. And someone down there must of said they'd seen her and where they'd seen her, and that was that.

I got the call 'round five-fifteen in the mornin'. I picked up the phone, 'n' this voice said, *Everett.* I said, *What?* And the voice said, *It's Jack.* And I said, *Jack.* And he said, *You better get out here.* And I said, *Rebecca?*

And then there was a long silence, 'n' I thought he'd gone off the phone.

And then he said, *No, Everett. It's not Rebecca.*

Mary Amesbury

I think you aren't like me. I think you wouldn't have let this happen to you. I see you in your khaki dress, your summer suit, your eyes clear and unwavering, like your sentences, and I think you couldn't have loved Harrold. You'd have left him after the first night.

Do you have a lover? Do you go to bars after work at night? Do you stay at your lover's place, or does he come to you—when *you* want, when *you* say?

I imagine you reading this. I imagine you thinking to yourself: Why did she let this go so far?

I write all night and all day too. I have learned to write through the light and the noise and the numbing routine. I sleep badly and infrequently, napping under the lights, amid the din.

When I dream, I dream of Harrold.

Harrold stood at the foot of the bed. I was kneeling on the mattress with the covers pulled up to my neck. He reached for the switch and flipped it on, lighting the lamp on the table.

The bright glare momentarily blinded us both, and when I looked at him, he was squinting. He had on a heavy crimson sweater and a pair of jeans, with his navy cashmere topcoat over them. The skin of his face was mottled and drawn, and I could see that he hadn't had a haircut since I'd left. He rubbed his eyes. There were dark circles under them, and the whites were bloodshot.

"Why are you naked?" he asked.

I said nothing, didn't move.

"Put something on," he said. "And come downstairs. I need some coffee." His voice was flat, as if drained.

He turned and left the room. I heard his footsteps on the stairs. I was nearly as stunned by his sudden departure as I'd been by his entrance.

My blocking the light behind me cast a long shadow on the opposite wall. I was still frozen on my knees, with the bedcovers drawn up to my chin. Below me I could hear a chair scrape on the linoleum floor. He was sitting at the table. I had a vision of myself slipping out the dormer window, shimmying down a drainpipe, crawling in the window of Caroline's bedroom, snatching her, getting into the car, driving off. But I didn't even know if there was a drainpipe; I had locked Caroline's window to keep out drafts; my coat was on the hook at the back of the kitchen door; my keys were on the kitchen table.

I looked down at my own nakedness. What time was it? Two-thirty? Three?

I dressed as quickly as I could. I put on layers: A long-sleeved T-shirt, a shirt, a sweater, my cardigan over that. The layers felt protective. I put jeans on, and my boots.

When I came down the stairs, he was slouched in a chair by the table, his head thrown back, resting on the top rung. He had his eyes closed, and I thought for a moment that he was dozing. When he heard my footsteps, he sat up and looked at me.

"I drove straight through," he said. His voice was low, husky with lack of sleep. But it was also without inflection, as if he were on automatic pilot, or as if he were trying hard to modulate his emotions. "I haven't slept in a couple of days," he added. "I need some coffee."

I walked to the stove.

I took the percolator from the burner, filled it with water and with coffee from a canister. I knew that he was watching me as I performed this task, but I didn't return his gaze. He'd been drinking—I'd guessed that when I'd seen his eyes, and I'd smelled it when I passed him—and I was afraid to look at him, to say or do anything that might be a trigger.

"I'm not going to hurt you," he said, as if reading my thoughts. "I've just come to talk."

"To talk?"

I put the percolator on the stove, turned on the gas underneath the pot. I stood in front of the stove with my arms crossed, staring at the flame. Just beyond me, to the left, was the door to Caroline's bedroom. I imagined I could hear her turning in her sleep, crinkling the plastic that covered her mattress under the crib sheet.

"How's she been?" he asked. "How's the fever and the ear infections?"

How had it worked? I wondered. The pediatrician had

called Harrold? Harrold had called the private detective he'd used on his stories, and the man had driven north, talked to the doctor in Machias? The doctor had known Jack, given the detective Jack's address?

No, Jack wouldn't have said anything, I knew. And Everett wouldn't, either. Someone else had. But who?

"How did you know?" I asked.

"Your mother called, did you know that?" he said, slightly off the subject. "When you talked to her on Christmas Day, apparently you sounded so out of it that she called back to talk to you again, and I had to tell her, of course, that you weren't there, you'd left."

I shut my eyes. I thought of my mother, of how she must have worried. I realized, too, with some surprise, that I hadn't spoken to her since Christmas.

"But it was Caroline's doctor's office put me onto you. I'd told a nurse in the office to give me a call if she heard from you, and she did. She called Monday morning. So I got in touch with Colin—you remember Colin—and he drove up here that night, and found you the next day, apparently. Didn't take him more than a day. I knew it wouldn't. Some guy in town—Williams, Willard: something like that—told him there was someone new in town staying at this house, so Colin put two and two together." He leaned forward in his chair. "Listen, I don't want a scene here. I didn't come for that. I just came to get you, and take you and Caroline home where you belong."

I watched the coffee begin to perk.

"Your mother was relieved when I called her," he said. "I told her yesterday I was bringing you home, and she was relieved."

I watched the bursts of coffee in the glass bubble at the top of the pot.

"Caroline's fine," I said. "The fever's gone now."

He shook his head.

"She wouldn't have had any fever if you hadn't had the *idiocy* to come up here," he said suddenly. I froze. "The nurse told me it was high, *life-threatening*, for God's sake."

I didn't move.

He must have seen that he'd frightened me. He opened his hands. "But we won't talk about that now," he said in a more conciliatory tone. "That's behind us. All that nonsense is behind us."

I wondered if by nonsense he meant my coming up here or the way that he had been just before I'd left.

"Look, I'll go into therapy if you want," he said, answering my question. "It won't ever happen again. OK, I was in the wrong. You had to leave. But now all that's behind us. We can be a family again. Caroline needs a father."

I turned off the gas under the pot. I brought the pot to the counter and poured coffee into a mug. I took the mug to the table. I put the mug in front of Harrold. When I did, he looked up at my face, took my hand in his.

I may have flinched. I wanted to withdraw my hand, but he held it tight. He began to knead my hand with his fingers.

"You look good," he said softly.

There were faint traces of the bruises still on my face, but I knew that he would not allow himself to see those.

"Sit down," he said.

I sat in the chair at right angles to his own. He let go of my hand.

"How long will it take you to pack?" he asked. I could see that he hadn't shaved in a couple of days. "I think it's best if we get out of this place as soon as possible. We can drive for an hour or so, stay at a motel. I don't think I can make it all the way home unless I get some sleep."

"How's the magazine?" I asked carefully.

He rubbed his eyes. He looked away from me. "Oh, you know. The same," he said. "I'm taking a few days off now."

He moved his hand in front of his face. I could smell stale liquor on his breath. He took a sip of coffee, winced as he burned his tongue. He blew over the rim of the coffee cup, met my eyes.

"So let's go," he said. "You want me to help you pack?"

I put my hands in the pockets of the cardigan, drew the pockets around to my lap. I crossed my legs, looked down at my knee. Around us there was silence, though not silence at all. There was the wind against the window-panes, in the dormant beach roses; a drip in the sink. The refrigerator hummed behind me.

"I'm not going," I said quietly.

He put the cup down slowly.

"You're not going?"

I shook my head. "I'm not going," I repeated. I sat very still. I was waiting for the reaction. Instinctively, I had tensed. To ward off his raised voice, perhaps even a blow.

"Is there anything to eat?" he asked.

275

"What?" I thought I couldn't have heard him right.

"Eat," he repeated. "I'm hungry. Have you got anything to eat?"

I felt dazed, thrown off guard. "Eat," I said slowly. I thought. "Yes," I answered finally. "There's food in the refrigerator."

He got up from the table and went to the refrigerator. He stood there with the door open for a moment, looking at the contents, the light spilling out around him, and then he withdrew a bowl. He still had on his navy overcoat. Was this a tactical maneuver, or was he simply hungry? Was it possible that Harrold had changed while I'd been away?

"What's this?" he asked.

I tried to remember. "It's sort of a macaroni and cheese," I said.

"All right; I'll eat this, then."

He took the plastic wrap off the bowl and set it on the counter. He moved slowly, deliberately, as if he had to think about his movements in advance. He seemed whipped. He opened a cupboard over the sink and removed a small plate. He pulled out a drawer, looking for silverware, but the drawer contained pot holders.

"Where's the silverware?" he asked.

I gestured toward a drawer at the end of the counter, near where I sat at the table. He walked toward the drawer, bent down over it, one hand on the counter, one hand on the drawer. He was bent like that, rummaging through the drawer, when I stood up.

"So that's all right with you," I said.

"What's all right?"

"That I'm not going with you. That I'm not leaving here."

He stayed bent over the drawer. I could hear the rattle of cheap metal as he searched for a fork. I was thinking—what was I thinking?—that now was the time to say what had to be said, to say it all.

I was, in that moment, not afraid of him. Perhaps it was the curve of his back, or the domesticity of looking for a fork. I took a step forward. He looked tired, punished. I was thinking: I used to love him. We made a child together. We made Caroline, and she is as much his as she is mine.

I had a sudden brief vision of the bed in the apartment in New York City, the kitchen table there.

I put my hand out toward his back, withdrew it. I was thinking that we would simply get a divorce like other people, and he'd have visitation rights, and that would be all right, he would see that.

"I think you and I can work this out," I said, tilting my head a bit to speak to him.

The movement was swift and stunning. I did not actually see the arc of his hand, merely felt the rush of air, like an electric charge, then the shock of something sharp on my face. He'd straightened up in a flash, swung his arm around. There was a silver object in his hand. It was a fork. I put my hand up, looked at my hand. There was blood on my fingers. The tines had scraped my cheek just below my eye. He could have blinded me.

I whirled around to get away from him. He grabbed my hair. He snapped my head back, so that I lost my balance, staggered, but he was holding me up by my hair. He pulled me to my feet. He wrenched my hair tightly with his fist; his forehead was against the side of my head. He pressed the tines of the fork into the hollow below my neck. I thought: It's only a fork. What can he do with a fork?

But I knew that he could kill me with the fork. He could kill me without the fork.

"Did you really think you'd get away with this?" It seemed he hissed the last word. "Did you think you could humiliate me, take Caroline, get away with this?"

"Harrold, listen . . .," I said.

From the back of my head, he shoved me into the living room. I fell against the couch, regained my balance, sat down. I pulled the cardigan tightly across my chest. He held the fork in his fist, as a child would. He took his coat off, slipped the fork through the sleeve.

"Take your clothes off," he said.

"Harrold . . .,"

"Take your clothes off," he repeated. His voice had risen a notch.

"Harrold, don't do this," I said. "Think of Caroline."

"Fuck Caroline," he said.

The air around me billowed out, then in, like a sail that had filled suddenly with wind and then emptied. Nothing—nothing—Harrold had ever done or said up to that point was as palpable as those two words. They were words I'd have said a human being couldn't pronounce together, as if, in combination, they were unintelligible. But Harrold had said them.

I knew then that he was beyond reaching, that in the days I'd been away from him he'd crossed a line.

"Take off your clothes," he yelled.

I began to undress slowly, stalling for time so that I

could think. There was a knife in the same drawer in which he'd found the fork. Could I get to it? And if I did, would that help me? What in God's name could I accomplish with a knife?

I pulled the sleeves of the cardigan from my arms. He stood across from me, watching. He looked impatient, annoyed with my slowness. I laid the cardigan on the couch, actually thought of folding it, crossed my arms to slip my other sweater over my head. I had the sweater up over my face when he grabbed my arm, pulled me toward him and onto the floor.

"You fucking bitch," he said.

He unsnapped my jeans, yanked the zipper down in thrusts with his free hand. I did not resist. This was not important to me, being raped by him; I had survived this before, though it hurt: His body was abrasive against mine, he tore at me, and he kept the fork pressed hard against my neck. It was only near the end, when in his frenzy he had the fork pressed too tightly against my skin and I thought that he would puncture me, that I tried to lift my shoulders, shake him off. He rose up over me then and slammed his free hand into the side of my head.

I was unconscious only seconds, I think, though when I came to, I lay still, did not open my eyes. I let him think that I was out cold. I did not have a plan then, but I sensed that if he thought I was out, he might loosen his grip.

How long did I lie there? A minute, five minutes, ten? At first I felt the full weight of him, and then he seemed to slip to the side, to roll over onto his back.

I didn't move; I was completely limp. This, at least, I did well.

I listened for sounds of Caroline awakening, but I heard nothing. In the distance a dog barked.

After a time, I felt Harrold get up from the floor, heard him pull up his jeans. He walked away from me, but I didn't open my eyes. There was the clink of something metallic on the table. Then it seemed that he had opened the door, and he was gone.

I lay still and listened. I thought. He hadn't taken his coat. That meant he would return. There was no point in leaping up, grabbing Caroline, and making a run for it. I wouldn't get past the door.

I was careful not to alter my position on the floor, though I was exposed—my jeans were down below my knees—and that exposure was painful, as though a spotlight were aimed at me.

The door opened, and he came in again. I felt his eyes on me. I heard him walk to the couch, sit down. I heard the slosh of liquid in a bottle, heard him take a swallow.

Was he concerned that I hadn't come to yet? If he was, he didn't show it. He didn't bend down over my body, or pull my jeans up, or speak to me, or slap my face. He just drank, almost rhythmically, with a minute or two between the swallows. I knew it was whiskey. I could smell it, and I knew he'd never drink gin straight as he might whiskey.

How long did I lie there then? Twenty minutes, forty-five? Sometimes I imagined that he was waiting for me to twitch, to make the slightest move, so that he could pounce. But that was just my imagination, wasn't it? What he was doing was drinking himself into a stupor.

Eventually I heard the sound that I'd been waiting for. It was faint at first, then heavier, deeper. He was snoring.

I moved just a foot, then a hand. Then I pressed my teeth together for courage and rolled over, away from him. The snoring didn't stop.

I sat up, turned my head, dared to look at him. His mouth was open, his head was leaning at an angle against the back of the couch, the bottle was in his lap. A bit of the whiskey had spilled out onto his thigh.

I pulled my jeans on and zipped them up. I stood up. How much time did I have? A minute? An hour?

I thought: If I get Caroline and run to the car with her and drive away, he will find us again.

I thought: If I run up to the blue Cape and call the police, they will arrive and see that a husband has come to reclaim his wife and his child.

I thought: If I tell them that he has raped me, they will look away. A husband cannot rape a wife, they'll be thinking.

I walked to the silverware drawer, opened it as quietly as I could. I removed a long kitchen knife with a black wooden handle. I held the knife in my hand, tested its weight. I put the knife behind my back and walked toward Harrold. He was lying on the couch, still snoring. I brought the knife from behind my back, held it in front of me, not two feet from his chest. I said to myself, *Do it, just do it*, but my hand didn't move. Instead I found myself wondering if the knife would go through the sweater and the shirt. And if, when I got to the skin, I'd have the strength to push it through.

I looked down at the knife. It seemed preposterous in my hand.

In the end, it wasn't so much a question of strength as it was of physical courage. I didn't have the courage to thrust the knife forward. Perhaps if he'd awakened and lunged toward me, and I'd held my ground, I might have gotten the knife into him, but short of that, I knew, I couldn't do it. I lowered the knife. I eased back into the kitchen, put the knife silently back in the drawer.

I put my head into my hands. *What*, then?

I lifted my head up.

I had it.

Because I had my boots on, my progress was slow and clumsy on the smooth round stones of the pebbled beach, and several times I had to catch my balance to prevent a fall. I had put my coat on, but I felt the cold air, like the sting of dry ice, on my hands and face and through the cotton of my jeans. I was not cold inside, beneath the coat, however; I was trying to run, and that kept me warm.

I abandoned the south side of the point for the sand beach. Because I was running, the heels of my boots sank and caught occasionally in the sand. It was low tide, I could smell it, though it was so dark I couldn't see the tideline. A layer of cloud had pasted itself over the moon. I moved more by instinct than by sight. I was bent over a bit, my knees in a slight crouch, my arms extended in front of me, in case I should suddenly hit a dinghy or a rock or a large piece of driftwood.

The sand grew softer, muckier, wetter, sucking in my boots, making a squelching sound when I pulled them free. I guessed that I had veered too close to the low-tide mark, that the harder sand was to my right. My progress seemed absurdly slow; I felt that I was trying to run through molasses, the sticky medium of childhood nightmares. I thought of Caroline and pulled a boot free with a smack from the muck. What if she woke up and began to cry? Wouldn't that wake Harrold? And if she woke Harrold, mightn't he just take her with him, leave with her in his car? I plunged on more frantically.

I turned to my right, in the direction of the harder ground of the spit, expecting the ground to begin sloping upward to the dunes. But the ground seemed flat all around me. I stood still, disoriented. I took a deep breath, tried to think clearly. I could see nothing, not even a shape I thought might be the fish house. Above me, the paste was moving slowly over the moon. If there were a break in the clouds, I thought, the moon might provide enough light for me to see my way.

I took a step forward, then another. It seemed to me that I had badly miscalculated somehow; the ground was growing soupier, not firmer. I backtracked, tried another direction. This was slightly better, but my inner compass was spinning in confusion: This certainly was the wrong direction. I retraced my steps, went back to what I thought was the position I'd been at before I began to maneuver. The moon broke free just at that moment for only a second or two, but I could clearly see the end of the point, the dinghy, the boat. Confidently, I took a step forward.

The ground gave way like a trapdoor in a stage. My leg vanished up to my knee. I fell to the sand, as if someone had yanked my foot from under me. When I put out my hands to stop my fall, my arms plunged into a vat of glue.

It felt like that in the darkness—a vat of gritty glue; it had that consistency. I couldn't pull my arms out. I couldn't pull because I didn't have any leverage. The vat of glue seemed to have no bottom. My foot was sinking, and my arms could not find firm ground.

I thought, in rapid succession: *Honeypot. Willis. Caroline. This can't be happening to me. Caroline. Jesus God, Caroline.*

Lie flat, I told myself. Had I read this in a childhood story about someone caught in quicksand? I tried to spread myself out and lie as still as I could. Nothing happened. I didn't sink. If I didn't pull and twist, I realized, I'd be better off. I felt hard spots under my shoulder and the knee that was free. I used these for leverage, and as slowly as I could, I began to roll over, away from the muck. I could feel the muck in my hair, in my ear, inside my collar. Close to me, I could hear the crawling of a wave up the sand. A crab or something small scurried over my face. I made a sound and tried to blow it off me. Gently I rolled and began to pull. One arm slipped free, then another.

Inch by inch, I slithered back onto the harder ground. Pulling my leg out was more difficult than freeing my arms had been: My knee was bent, and heavy with the muck. If I called out for help, the only person who could conceivably hear me would be Harrold.

I began to shiver then. The soupy ground was cold and wet with icy salt water. The water had already seeped through my woolen coat, my sweater. I was thinking: If I lie here any longer, I will die from exposure, and dying is not a possibility, because I can't leave Caroline.

I gritted my teeth and groaned audibly with the effort. Then I said out loud, *Goddamn fuck*, and I didn't care if Harrold heard me.

I pulled my leg free.

I rolled over and over, away from the honeypot. I was crying, mixing tears with the muck that covered my face.

The paste slipped past the moon. I could see my way. I rose to my feet, stumbled forward. I began to run then to the dinghy.

The rest was nothing by comparison. I pushed the dinghy into the water, got inside. I lay forward in the bow, paddled with my cupped palms over the edge. The water stung, felt colder than ice.

I tied the dinghy to the mooring, slipped along the bow of the lobster boat, and fell into the cockpit. I opened the door to the cabin. Only then did it occur to me that it might have been locked. This thought took my breath away. I so easily might have gone through all of that horror with the honeypot only to find the bulkhead door locked tight. But it wasn't.

I found this fact momentarily encouraging, as if the ease of opening the cabin door were a sign that I was doing the right thing.

I felt for the cabinet with my hands, fished around in the darkness for the small object I had come for.

When I got back to the cottage, Harrold was in the same position as when I'd left. What I should have done, what I ought to have done, is to have walked straight up to him and fired.

Instead I sat at the kitchen table with the gun in my hand. My hands were shaking so badly that I was afraid I might shoot myself. I put the gun on the table. I could not stop the shaking. I felt a sudden wave of nausea, got up quickly, and vomited into the sink, trying to stifle the sound of my retching. I wiped my mouth, saw my reflection in the window over the sink. My face and coat and hair were black with muck. It was as if I had on a mask, were not really myself at all. I smelled like low tide.

I went back to the table, sat down. I thought it astonishing that Harrold had not come to when I had vomited.

I tried to breathe deeply so that I could stop the shaking. I felt another wave of nausea, fought it back. I was waiting for the shaking to stop. I was thinking: I have no life as long as he exists.

I put the gun in my hand, felt its weight. This weight, or the cold metal of the object, calmed my hand. I stood up, walked to where Harrold was sprawled against the couch. I heard only a high ringing in my ears. I raised my arm and aimed. I was thinking: Is it better to aim at the heart or at the head?

Behind me, I heard a hoarse, whispered shout and a gasp, or perhaps it was the other way around. I turned to see. It was Jack, in his yellow slicker and his boots. He had come at the accustomed time. Our last morning together. I stood with the gun in my hand. He looked at me, then at Harrold, then at me again. I must have seemed to him a sea monster, a mucky creature from the deep with an incomprehensible object in her hand.

But he comprehended soon enough. He started to cross the room.

"What the . . . ?" he said.

On the couch, Harrold stirred.

I thought: If he exists, I have no life.

I was aiming at Harrold's heart. Jack's hand was only inches from my arm. I fired. Harrold bounced forward from the couch, clutching his shoulder.

Jack shouted and turned toward Harrold. Harrold opened his eyes, looked, understood, didn't understand.

"Maureen . . . !" he said.

I shook my head.

"My name isn't Maureen," I said.

I fired again.

Or perhaps I fired first, then said my name wasn't Maureen.

I lowered my hand.

I stood as if paralyzed, rooted to the floor.

Above me and around me then I could hear a strange sound. It was a sound that began slowly at first, then gathered pitch. I looked at Caroline's door, but the sound wasn't coming from there.

I looked at the couch, but the sound wasn't coming from there, either. Harrold had fallen forward onto his knees, and I was certain that he was dead.

I looked at Jack, as if he might tell me about the sound, but he didn't seem to be able to. I could see that he was not its source. He was looking at me, saying my name. He was wearing his yellow slicker. His face was weathered, he had deep grooves at the sides of his mouth, and he was saying my name. I remember that he had his hands out, palms upward, as if he had an object in them he wanted me to see.

The sound became a keening.

I looked out the window to the end of the point. I could see the green-and-white lobster boat bobbing in the water. There was a mist of daybreak just above the horizon.

I thought then of the woman in the hospital, of the woman behind the wall in the labor-and-delivery room.

The sound became a howling.

I think it was then that Caroline began to cry.

January 15 – Summer 1971

———————

Everett Shedd

When I got there, good Lord, there was a sorry sight. I hope I don't ever see anything that sad again, 'n' that's the truth.

Mary was on the floor, holdin' this man in her arms. Jack was cradlin' the baby, walkin' with her in the living room. There was blood everywhere—on the couch, the floor, on the wall behind the couch. All over Mary Amesbury.

Well, Mary, you wouldn't of believed Mary. She had her coat 'n' her boots on, 'n' she was covered with mud— from the low tide, don't you know. On her face 'n' hair 'n' everything. And that mixed with the blood . . . well.

Mary, she just kept her eyes shut. She was holdin' this man—course I know now it was her husband, Harrold English, but I didn't then, not right away—'n' makin' this sound 'n' rockin' back 'n' forth, 'n' it was the sorrow you felt in that room, not the horror of it all at first, but more like somethin' very deep 'n' sad had kind of settled itself in there.

I went out to the car 'n' called over to Machias to ask for a car 'n' an ambulance, even though I knew that was a dead body in that cottage. And then I went back inside.

Jack, he was as white as a milk sky, he was. But he hung on to the baby 'n' tried to get her to stop cryin', 'n' he kept lookin' at Mary, 'n' then I said to him, *Jack, what happened here?*

Jack, I think he'd been waitin' for me to ask this. He cleared his throat and stood over by the sink. He's got a deep voice, don't you know, husky, and he spoke slow that mornin', like he was thinkin' as he spoke. He said he'd come around four forty-five. He didn't say *why* he had come, 'n' I pretended to make out as how he was just goin' down to his boat, but I think he knew I knew that wasn't strictly the case. Anyway, he said he saw the car, 'n' then the lights on in the cottage, when normally there wouldn't be any, 'n' then he thought he saw this man get up from the couch 'n' hit Mary at the side of her face. So Jack, he started up the slope to see what was goin' on, 'n' by the time he made it to the back stoop this man had Mary up against the table 'n' was beatin' her. He said the man looked as if he would kill Mary, 'n' Jack opened the door, 'n' then there was the shot.

A shot? I said.

Just the one, Jack said, 'n' I think he regretted that straight off, because even I could see there'd been two shots.

Whose gun was it? I said.

Jack was holdin' the baby, mind you, 'n' I think this question might of stopped him a second, but then he said, straight up, it was his, he'd given it to Mary Amesbury a week or so earlier, for protection, one night when she was scared 'n' thought she'd heard a prowler.

Then Mary said, from the floor where she was holdin' the man—her husband, that is—*Jack, don't.*

Jack, he looked at her 'n' then at me, 'n' then he just turned away from me.

And then Mary got up 'n' came over 'n' sat down at the table. And as I say, she looked pretty dreadful, 'n' I was wonderin' what had happened to her she got all that muck all over her, 'n' she began to talk.

This is what she said that mornin', 'n' she never wavered from it, neither.

She said her husband had come around two-thirty or three in the mornin', 'n' he'd been drinkin'. He raped her, she said, 'n' hit her once while he was rapin' her, 'n' knocked her out. And he'd attacked her with a fork once afore that.

A fork? I said.

And she said, *A fork.*

After he'd raped her, he'd fallen asleep or passed out, 'n' she had gone out to Jack's boat, 'n' got the gun in the cabin there, 'n' come back 'n' shot her husband while he was asleep. Once in the shoulder 'n' once in the chest. And then she said that Jack had come in the door after he heard the shots, but that Harrold was already dead by then.

And then Jack started to say, *That's not—*

And then Mary interrupted him and said to me, *That's what happened*, 'n' she got up 'n' went to Jack. They stood there for a minute just lookin' at each other, 'n' I'll tell you, I was embarrassed to be in the same room with 'em, to have to look at 'em, at somethin' that *raw* between 'em, 'n' then she kissed Jack on the mouth, with the baby between 'em, 'n' then she took the baby from him 'n' sat back down again at the table.

And I thought to myself: If she tells this story to the police from Machias when they get here, they aren't ever goin' to see each other again.

The trouble was, Mary was her own worst enemy. It wasn't that she was proud of what she'd done, or that she was glad of it in any way. That wasn't it 'tall. It was more that this was the most *important* thing she'd ever done, 'n' she wasn't goin' to lie about it.

So there we were, the three of us—well, the five of us, if you want to get technical—'n' the sun come up, 'n' I said to Mary, *Why?*

And she thought a bit, 'n' then she said, *Because I had to.*

And that was it.

They were goin' to put her in the county lockup, don't you know, but they couldn't really keep her there, 'cause it wasn't a fit place for a woman prisoner of any duration, so they made arrangements with the state, 'n' Mary, she's at the Maine Correctional Center now in South Windham, which is where the women go.

Now, since that mornin' I've had lots of time to think about all this 'n' mull it all over, 'n' this is what I think now. I think Jack was in the house with her when she shot Harrold English, but he couldn't say that, could he? Not because he wouldn't want to implicate himself. Oh, no—that's not our Jack. But because he saw right away her only hope was in self-defense, 'n' she's got no self-defense case if he's standin' right there beside her. I don't know exactly how it went—maybe he tried to get the gun away from her. And Mary, she wouldn't say he was there because she didn't want to get him involved. Sort of like that great old story "Gift of the Magi." You ever read that one? By O. Henry, it was. My kind of story, don't you know. Well, it weren't exactly like that, but the feelin's were the same, you follow me?

Anyway, at the trial, all this was confusin' to the jury, weren't it? The defense lawyer, Sam Cotton, local boy from Beals Island, his argument was this: Mary shot her husband while he was asleep—they allowed as that's what happened, even though actually, Mary said, he'd woken up when she pointed the gun—but she did it in self-defense because she believed that *eventually*, that day or that night, he would kill her.

Tricky.

It was the "eventually" that was the problem, wasn't it?

The prosecutin' attorney—Pickering—he argued that Mary had had time to call the police—me, if it came to that—'n' have Harrold English arrested for assault. But the problem was that Mary didn't go *up* the hill to the LeBlanc place, where there was a phone; she went *down* the point to Jack's boat, where she got the gun 'n' come back 'n' shot her husband in cold blood.

Now, Mary, she kept talkin' about the rape 'n' the blow that had knocked her out, but the problem is, in Maine, a husband can't legally rape his wife, and maybe everywhere else as far as I know, so the prosecutin' attorney, he made short shrift of that one—settin' aside the blow almost as easy as he set aside the rape.

And then there was the fork.

Unfortunate, that, the fork. Well, I mean to say, a

fork. How much damage can you do with a fork? Pickering, he made mincemeat out of the fork. Even got a laugh out of the jury, if I remember correctly.

So you see, Mary Amesbury, she just didn't help her case 'tall, did she? And even with me 'n' Julia 'n' Muriel testifyin' as to how beat-up she looked the first day she come to us, it wasn't enough, was it? Particularly so when you had Willis Beale testifyin' that Mary herself had told him the bruises were from a car accident, 'n' Julia, she got recalled 'n' had to say Mary had told her the same thing too—very damagin', that was—and in light of the fact that Sam Cotton couldn't produce a single witness from New York City to say they'd ever suspected anythin' amiss between Harrold English and his wife, or who had ever seen any bruises on Mary.

Well, that was it, wasn't it? And I guess it was too much for the jury—got ourselves a hung jury, didn't we? Pretty much split down the middle, far as I can make out.

After the trial, don't you know, the judge thanked the jury for their services and dismissed them, and straight off, Sam Cotton, he asked for a dismissal, but Pickering stood right up and said there was goin' to be another trial, and he asked for a date.

And then about ten days ago, Sam, he must have heard who the judge assigned was, 'n' it was Joe Geary, who everybody in Machias knows has a soft spot for women. He gives 'em light sentences, don't you know. So Sam, he decided to waive Mary's right to a jury trial—I think he figured she'd make out better with Geary—'n' so the whole thing gets thrown to Joe Geary in September, when they have the next trial. It was in the papers.

So there you are.

It's in his hands now, in't it?

The muck? That was from a honeypot. Those are nasty patches in the flats. Can suck you in, give you a fright, I'll tell you. Like quicksand. Mary Amesbury had a run-in with one, tryin' to get to Jack's boat.

The baby? Julia Strout asked to take her. Has her still.

Willis Beale

Well, I'll tell you right off the bat what I think happened that night. This guy, this Harrold English, he done what any guy woulda done; he drove up to get his wife and kid and bring 'em back home, and he surprised Mary and Jack in bed, in flagro delecti, if you catch my meaning, didn't he? And there was some kind of a scene between the three of them, and there was Jack with his gun, and one or the other of them shot the poor son of a bitch, and that's what I think.

There's your motive, if you're lookin' for one.

Mary's coverin' up somethin' for Jack. Even Everett, he thinks so. He didn't say so to me, but I heard this around.

I think, near the end, they didn't care who knew what was goin' on. You ask LeBlanc. He'll tell you Jack was there five-thirty in the morning the day the baby got sick. It was Jack went up LeBlanc's place for the phone. And I myself saw Jack comin' and goin' all that day to Mary's cottage, like they was real old friends. I saw him from the fish house. He didn't kiss her in public, but they weren't foolin' anybody.

Maybe they had a plan. Who's to say? I mean, what were they goin' to do when Jack hauled his boat? How was he goin' to see her every day? You ever think of that?

At the trial I had to say, didn't I, that she said the bruises were from a car accident. I was under oath. I know some people from town, they don't understand that, but bein' under oath is serious business to me.

I don't know how she got found. I do recall this fella up from New York City, he come down the co-op askin' questions. I mighta said, if he asked was there someone new in town, that there was this girl with a baby, but I wouldn'ta let on where she lived or anythin' like that. If Mary didn't want to get found, that was her business, wasn't it?

I'm real curious now about Judge Geary's verdict in September. She'll probably get off, 'cause he's partial to women.

Julia Strout

Yes, I had to testify at the trial. I testified as to the condition Mary Amesbury was in when she first arrived in St. Hilaire. Then I had to say that she'd told me that the bruises were from a car accident. But I was quick to say, before the lawyer interrupted me, that I hadn't believed her.

I could not have done what Mary Amesbury did. I don't believe so. I don't think I could have shot a man, but who is to say what a person might be driven to? I know that they say she killed this man, her husband, in cold blood. She could have asked Jack or Everett for help. She could have done any number of things, I suppose. But then who is to say that an act of passion, of hot blood if you will, has a finite limit of only a minute or two? Who's to say an act of passion couldn't last all the way through going out to the boat to get the gun and returning with it and shooting the man who was hurting you? Who you were sure would hurt you again. Who might eventually kill you. Who's to say an act of passion couldn't last for weeks or months if it came to that?

So I can't tell you what will happen to Mary in September. They say she might get off, and I hope that's true.

But when I think about this terrible business over to the point, what I feel most is . . . distressed. I feel distressed for Mary and for Jack, and distressed about Rebecca, and most of all now, worried for Emily and this little baby I'm taking care of now. It's Emily and the baby I feel for.

Listen. Do you hear that? That's the baby now. It always takes me by surprise. It's a strange sound in this house after all these years. But a welcome one. My husband and I, we didn't have any children ourselves, and I was always sorry about that.

I just have the baby until Mary gets out.

Would you like to see her? I saw his picture. . . . She looks like her father.

The Article

The Killing Over to the Point

by Helen Scofield

Sam Cotton seemed preoccupied. He looked uncomfortably hot in his best blue suit and in his shiny black wing tips, which were getting ruined in the sand. It was unseasonably warm on Flat Point Bar this September afternoon, and the talk in this small coastal town of St. Hilaire, Maine, 65 miles north of Bar Harbor, was that the temperature would hit 85 before the day was out.

Cotton put a finger between his collar and his neck, then wiped his bald pate with a handkerchief. He was headed for the end of the bar, also known as "the point," so that he could get a better look at a green-and-white lobster boat that was bobbing in the channel. When he finished examining the boat, he made his way back to the other end of this small peninsula that juts into the Atlantic. There he stood next to his car below a modest white cottage that overlooks the point and the water. Apart from the odd wave to a fisherman heading for shore in his dinghy, Cotton said nothing and spoke to no one. The entire round trip, including the time he spent gazing at and thinking about the boat and the cottage, took about twenty minutes. He does this every day.

Defense attorney Sam Cotton, 57, has been practicing criminal law in eastern Maine for almost 30 years. But his current case, at the Superior Court in Machias, may be the most complicated defense he's undertaken. It is certainly the most celebrated. The case is known around here as "that awful business up to Julia's cottage," or "that terrible story about the Amesbury woman," or "the killing over to the point." Sam Cotton must prove his client, a 26-year-old woman, innocent of murdering her husband last January in the small white cottage Cotton has spent so much time studying. And

305

there isn't much time. Next week, at the conclusion of the second trial of a woman known both as Maureen English and as Mary Amesbury, Judge Joseph Geary is expected to deliver his verdict.

As Cotton has told it, the bare facts of the case are these:

Following two years of domestic violence at the hands of her troubled and alcoholic husband—including repeated rapes and physical assault, even while she was pregnant—Maureen English left her home in New York City last December 3 with her infant daughter, Caroline, and drove 500 miles to the small fishing village of St. Hilaire to seek refuge. There, under the alias Mary Amesbury, she rented the white cottage on Flat Point Bar and settled in to a life of quiet tasks, centered around caring for her six-month-old daughter and nursing herself back to both physical and emotional health.

In the early morning of January 15, after six weeks in hiding, Mary Amesbury was surprised and frightened by her husband's sudden appearance in her bedroom. Harrold English, 31, a successful journalist with this magazine, had driven to Maine to confront his wife. He'd been tipped off to her whereabouts by a physician at a local health clinic Mary Amesbury had visited.

Sometime during these early-morning hours, English assaulted his wife with a sharp instrument, raped her, and hit her so violently in the head she was knocked unconscious.

Believing her life was in danger, Mary Amesbury waited until her husband had passed out from excessive drinking and then made her way to the end of the point. There she crossed a short expanse of water and located a gun she knew was kept on a green-and-white lobster boat moored in the channel. She returned to the cottage, and fearful that her husband would kill her when he came to, shot him twice—once in the shoulder and once in the chest.

Cotton claims she acted in self-defense. So does Mary Amesbury. "I had to do it," she says. "I had no choice."

Last June, a jury was unable to reach a verdict in Mary Amesbury's case, and the trial ended in a hung jury. There were seven votes for acquittal; five for a guilty verdict. Cotton immediately moved for dismissal, but D. W. Pickering, the prosecuting attorney, asked for a new trial date in September. In a surprise move in early July, Cotton announced that his client would waive her right to a trial by jury. Cotton has not commented on his strategy, but sources close to the defense attorney suggest that Judge Geary's reputation for leniency toward women may be the explanation.

At both trials, Cotton likened his client to a modern-day Hester Prynne, the heroine of Nathaniel Hawthorne's classic *The Scarlet Letter*. Both, said Cotton, were wronged women, romantic figures, living out quiet exiles in cottages by the sea and both fiercely protective of young daughters. Both women were outcast and doomed by love to carry the scarlet "A" on their breasts. In the case of Mary Amesbury, the "A" stood not for adultery, but for abuse.

When Mary Amesbury tells her own story, however, she comes across as somewhat more complex than just a "wronged woman." And her story sometimes raises more questions than it satisfactorily answers.

To prevent her husband from finding her, Maureen English assumed the name Mary Amesbury when she arrived in St. Hilaire on December 3. She refused at both trials to answer questions when addressed as Maureen English. The prosecuting attorney solved the problem, addressing her as "Mrs. English/Mary Amesbury." Cotton deftly avoided using either name when he addressed his client on the stand.

For seven weeks this summer, I conducted a series of exclusive interviews with Mrs. English while she was awaiting her second trial. Despite the tension and fear she was obviously feeling, Mrs. English was often eloquent. She was also sometimes sad and occasionally angry, but she was always forthcoming, even at times appearing to contradict testimony she had given in court. One of these interviews was conducted in person. The rest were carried on through the mail.

Because there were no adequate facilities in Machias for long-term female prisoners, Mrs. English has been remanded to the custody of the Maine Correctional Center at South Windham. As she sat in the visitors' room, she looked older than her 26 years. Her skin was pale and lined about the eyes and on her forehead. Her red hair, one of her most striking features, had been cut short, and there was a thin streak of gray over her left eye. Her posture was tense and angular beneath the gray sweatshirt and pants of her prison garb. When she spoke, she had a nervous habit of twirling a strand of hair between her fingers. Those who knew Maureen English less than a year ago find the changes in her appearance startling.

I had met Mrs. English only once prior to our prison interview—at a party at this magazine's office in Manhattan. Although she had once worked there, she had left before I joined the staff. At the party she wore a black velvet dress and looked radiant as she showed off her infant daughter, Caroline, to her former colleagues. She struck me that evening as a happy woman, well-off and well-married, and content to take a few years off to start a family. Harrold, her husband, was almost constantly at his wife's side and kept what appeared to be a loving and protective arm around her shoulder. The idea that he might be beating his wife in the privacy of their home was inconceivable.

During the course of telling her story, Mrs. English spoke at length about her childhood and her upbringing. The illegitimate daughter of a soldier and a secretary whose immigrant Irish family hailed from Chicago's south side, she spent most of her youth in child care, while her mother worked to support them. Mother and daughter lived in a small white cottage in the suburban town of New Athens, 20 miles south of Chicago. Mrs. English appeared to have been close to her hardworking mother and to have respected her values: "My mother would often tell me that things happened to a person and that you should learn to accept those things," Mrs. English said, "but I also understood from an early age that neither my mother nor I would be happy unless I did what I was supposed to do. Unless I seized for myself a life she had been denied—a life with a husband and a stable family."

A talented student, Mrs. English was accepted at the University of Chicago in 1962. She studied literature and eventually became an editor on the university paper. A svelte, redheaded beauty with pale skin and large hazel eyes, Mrs. English eventually made her way to New York City. In June 1967, she was hired as a reporter with this magazine. She met Harrold English on her first day of work.

Colleagues recall Maureen English as a diligent worker who learned her trade quickly. Although she was well-liked, she was something of a loner. With the exception of Harrold English, she made no serious lasting friendships at the magazine. Still, she was promoted in near record time to the National desk.

"She was fast," says a former editor who worked closely with her. "Give Maureen English an assignment, and she'd have a solid story back to you before the day was out."

Despite the disparity in their backgrounds, Maureen and Harrold appear to have been attracted to each other at once. Harrold came from a wealthy Rhode Island textile family and was educated at Yale. A tall, well-built, dark-eyed young man whose good looks and journalistic successes made him attractive to his female colleagues, he had been a reporter for the *The Boston Globe* before moving to New York City. He distinguished himself as both a national and foreign reporter and was a 1966 Page One Award winner for his series on the race riots in Watts. "He did some great pieces for us," says Jeffrey Kaplan, editor in chief during most of English's tenure.

"He was an excellent reporter and was very aggressive in the field. His writing style was clean and straightforward. He was an extremely intelligent man."

The pair began dating almost at once, and were seen as a "perfect" couple, both up-and-coming journalists, both very much in love. According to Maureen, Harrold gave her presents, tutored her in her reporting, and significantly aided her career.

"I loved him," she said. "Even on the day I left him, I loved him."

Co-workers maintain that there was never the slightest hint of friction between the couple, who almost immediately began living together in Harrold's Upper West Side apartment. "These reports of friction between Maureen and Harrold are unbelievable," says Kaplan. "I have trouble believing it even now. You hear about stories like this once in a while, but it's always some poor woman with six kids, married to an alcoholic. Never, I mean never, do you hear about this kind of thing with people like Maureen and Harrold."

Yet alcohol and abuse are exactly what Mrs. English asserts formed the fabric of her marriage. The violence began even before the couple were married, she said. It started one night when she refused to have sexual relations with Harrold and he became angry. He'd been drinking a lot, she said. Eventually that became a pattern: Excessive drinking would often trigger violent mood swings in her husband. He assaulted her in their kitchen that night, she said, and "raped" her.

Later, Mrs. English said, Harrold repeatedly had sex with her against her will and then physically assaulted her—striking her in places where the bruises wouldn't show.

"I think he believed if you couldn't see the bruises, it hadn't ever happened," said Mrs. English.

She also said that her husband raped her and hit her even when she was pregnant. "I don't know what it was about the pregnancy that angered him so," she said. "Perhaps it was the fact that I was doing something that

310

was beyond his control. He seemed to be happiest only when he was controlling me."

Curiously, however, Mrs. English described herself as sometimes "complicitous," and hinted at S&M sex games between herself and her husband that may have turned rougher than she anticipated. "I was part of it," she said, referring to "silk handcuffs" tied to a bed on their very first date. Sometime after a particularly brutal evening of sex that she subsequently began to think of as "rape," Mrs. English found herself wondering, "Was what had happened that night so very different from all that had gone before?"

At other points in her account, she suggested that she was "a passive player" in the ongoing, furtively violent drama that was her marriage.

In her interviews, Mrs. English came across as a passionate woman. Beneath the cool, contented, and hardworking exterior she presented to colleagues at work is a woman who uses words such as "ravenous," "lost," and "burning" to describe herself in relationship to her husband. "I was a toy top someone had spun and walked away from," she said, of their first date. She also described herself as being under the influence of "erotic fevers," as being "ensnared," and as having struck a "secret bargain" with her husband. For example, she described in detail a night of unconventional lovemaking but gave no hint that she thought the episode distasteful. To the contrary, she suggested she found it pleasurable. The implication in these revelations is that something in her own passionate nature may have contributed to the couple's unusual relationship.

This ambiguity about the nature of the violence in the English household is crucial to any moral or legal judgment about the murder.

One witness at the trial, Willis Beale, a lobster fisherman and something of an old salt, even at the tender age of 27, addresses this issue of the relativity of domestic violence from another angle. "I'm not saying she was lying, or anything like that, but we only ever had her say-so, didn't we?'' says Beale, who seems to have made a point of befriending Mrs. English while she was in St. Hilaire—walking daily over to her cottage from the fish house where he mended his lobster pots on Flat Point Bar, to see if she was all right. "Most couples get into a little pushing and shoving at some point in their marriages. Nothing heavy. Just a little something. It takes two to tango, right? I'm just saying, how are we ever going to know?''

The relative severity of the domestic feud between Harrold and Maureen English raises troubling ethical questions—particularly insofar as it casts a shadow of a doubt on her self-professed motive for the shooting—but there is an even more serious legal difficulty with Mrs. English's assertions of abuse and alcoholism in her marriage: No one has been able to produce a single shred of evidence to support them.

Despite Mrs. English's testimony at her two trials, and her interviews with me, there has been no corroboration of scenes of violence between husband and wife. Although Mrs. English now says that her husband beat her up on at least three occasions and hit her repeatedly throughout their marriage, there is no evidence that she told anyone about this violence while it was happening.

At the office party they attended together, none of those present had any hint of discord. While it is certainly possible that the scars of domestic violence might have been hidden, there were no visible marks on Mrs. English. She left the party early, telling former colleagues that she had to put her baby to bed. Now she asserts that her husband made her leave because he had seen her talking to another man and that when he arrived home from the party, he beat her severely. It was this beating, she said, that prompted her flight. "I prayed for my husband's death," she said.

But if her situation was as bad as Mrs. English now asserts, why didn't she go to the police? Prosecuting attorney Pickering raised a similar issue at both trials: "If these allegations of violence are true, why didn't Maureen English leave her husband sooner, when the abuse began?''

Upon arriving in St. Hilaire, Mrs. English told townspeople that her bruises were caused by a car accident. She also falsely claimed to be from Syracuse, facts that several St. Hilaire residents had to testify to at both trials. She declined to go to the police even after she ultimately told about the beatings.

Mrs. English's charges that her husband was drinking heavily during their marriage have also been called into question. Editor Kaplan dismisses the claim: "Harrold was no alcoholic," says Kaplan. "He drank like the rest of us drank. A martini at lunch, maybe two if the occasion called for it. But that was it.''

Whatever actually happened between Harrold English and his wife, there *is* evidence that friction began to develop not long after the wedding. According to Mrs. English, the traveling demanded by her job incited Harrold's jealousy. Like most national reporters, Mrs. English often had to travel around the country with male reporters and photographers. While she always had her own room, she acknowledged that there was usually an easy camaraderie among the crew and that her colleagues would often visit her in her hotel room. Her husband, she said, found this familiarity intolerable and once beat her badly upon her return from a business trip. She was then forced to lie to her editors, telling them that she suffered from motion sickness and could no longer travel in airplanes or automobiles. Her editors released her from reporting duties and relegated her instead to rewriting other people's stories, a move that effectively derailed a promising career.

Mrs. English said that she was driven to seek the help of a psychiatrist, and that at one point she considered suicide. It's also possible that her pregnancy aggravated her despair. She quit her job at the magazine unusually early in the pregnancy and seldom left her apartment after that. On one occasion, she ran away to her mother's.

Alcohol, too, may have exacerbated her downward spiral. Both she and her husband, she said, were drinking excessively during this period. "We drank like we were drowning," Mrs. English explained. They drank in bars and then drank at home. Curiously, Mrs. English continued to drink in Maine. By her own admission, there was always beer in her refrigerator at the cottage on Flat Point Bar, and she often offered Willis Beale a drink when he came to visit.

Even after she reached St. Hilaire, Mrs. English's emotional health appears to have been unstable. At one point, she said, she began to have hallucinations, to hear her husband in the cottage long before he actually found her. She also apparently passed out from fright at a community event—a festive holiday bonfire on the town common on Christmas Eve.

Undoubtedly Mrs. English was under great stress during her stay in St. Hilaire. She had taken her baby from the apartment in New York City and driven 500 miles to a strange town. When she arrived, the temperature was 20 degrees below zero. Both her own and her baby's health were fragile. She was living on funds she'd taken from Harrold's wallet on the night she left him. She'd been unemployed for nearly a year and had no clear prospects for employment in Maine. She was lying about her name, lying about her background, and telling varying stories to those she met. She was trying to begin a new life—that of "Mary Amesbury."

Everett Shedd's general store has always been the hub of the small fishing village of St. Hilaire, but these days it is bustling. Each day, after "the doin's over to Machias," residents of the town gather in the small store filled with groceries, sundries, fishing gear, and cold beer to talk over the case. They speculate as to who came out on top that day in court, and comment about how "Mary Amesbury" looked on the stand.

On the surface, St. Hilaire is a classic New England coastal village—charming, picturesque, and sleepy. There's the typical white steeple, the common, the old colonial houses, the tidal rhythms of the harbor. But underneath, life in St. Hilaire is not always as simple as it seems. According to Shedd, who has one glass eye, a thick Down East accent and doubles as the town's only officer of the law, St. Hilaire has seen better days.

"The town was big in shipbuilding 150 years ago, but now it's economically depressed," he says. "Most of the houses are abandoned. The kids, when they get out of high school, they lose heart and leave town."

The fishing for lobster, clams, and mussels makes up the heart of the economy of this and other towns like it along the coast. Further inland, a few residents have been able to eke out meager livelihoods on scrubby blueberry farms, but an aura of hard times permeates the area. The houses, while charming, do not look prosperous; small pink and aqua mobile homes, many of them rusty with age, mar the landscape. It is a town, says Shedd, where women frequently become depressed during the winter months, where insularity has led, on occasion, to inbreeding (according to Shedd, one local woman has three breasts; others have what appears to be a ubiquitous familial trait—gapped front teeth), where men sometimes drown off their lobster boats, where unemployment and alcoholism are pervasive. It is a town of lapsed ventures and failed hopes.

"You read the tourist brochures," says Shedd. "The shortest paragraphs are about St. Hilaire. There's nothing here."

Into this bleak and frigid coastal town came Mrs. English on the night of December 3. She spent one night at the Gateway Motel just to the north of town and then rented a cottage on Flat Point Bar from Julia Strout, a prominent local widow. Mrs. English then, according to her own testimony, settled down to a tranquil, Hester Prynne–like existence. Like Hawthorne's heroine, she even took up needlework. "I loved the cottage and my life there," she said. "I read, I knit, I took care of the baby, I took walks. It was a simple life, a good life."

Indeed, this tranquil domesticity might have helped her more at her trials were it not for one critical detail that some observers have found at odds with her assertions of a simple life.

Barely a month after she arrived at St. Hilaire, Mrs. English took a lover—a local fisherman with a wife and two children of his own. He was Jack Strout, 43 (a cousin of Julia Strout's husband), and he was there on the morning Mrs. English shot Harrold English.

"By Christmas Eve, I could see there was already something between Jack Strout and Mary," says Beale. "And I can tell you this: It wasn't Jack who started it. He was always, before he met Mary, very loyal to his wife. I always liked Mary, but I have to say, in retrospect, she was a pretty fast worker."

Strout is a tall, lanky lobsterman with light-brown, curly hair. His daughter, Emily, 15, is still at home, and his son, John, 19, is a sophomore at Northeastern University. Strout attended the University of Maine and hoped to become a college professor. But after his sophomore year, his father broke both of his arms in a fishing accident, and young Jack returned home to take over his father's lobster boat. Strout refused to be interviewed for this article, but he appears to have been well-respected in St. Hilaire. For years he has kept his green-and-white lobster boat moored off Flat Point Bar.

According to Mrs. English, she met Strout on the point one night while taking a walk. The two became lovers shortly afterward. She has described the affair in some detail in her interviews. Strout came to her bed at daybreak and made love to her each morning before he went out on his boat. She said that their relationship was very "natural"—that they needed each other.

The two appear to have been discreet at first, but Beale, who was often on the point, mending his pots, recalls seeing them together.

"I saw them come back on Jack's boat on a Sunday," he says, "and I would see them at her door, acting in a very 'friendly' way."

The need for discretion was important because Strout's wife, Rebecca, was almost incapacitated by depression, which appears to have begun shortly after the birth of her first child. Strout was afraid of what his wife might do if the affair became public.

Even so, on the Monday before the shooting, Strout accompanied Mrs. English to a clinic in Machias when her infant daughter developed a 105-degree fever. After this visit the local doctor called the child's pediatrician, who subsequently alerted Harrold English to the whereabouts of his wife. It was on that Monday, too, that Beale saw Strout in broad daylight at Mrs. English's door, acting in a "friendly" way.

According to Mrs. English, she and Strout were anticipating an end to their daily predawn trysts because he would soon have to haul his boat, and then he would no longer have a reason for leaving his home before daybreak. The prospect was causing them both anxiety about the future. In her interviews, Mrs. English stated that she knew the last time Strout would be able to come to her cottage would be on Friday morning, January 15— the morning she shot her husband.

More than just calling Mrs. English's character into question, the love affair has crucial significance because prosecuting attorney Pickering contends that it was this, and not self-defense, that was the true motive for the murder of Harrold English.

In court, D. W. Pickering, a 32-year-old graduate of Columbia Law School who moved north from Portland to practice law in Washington County two years ago, has presented a formidable contrast to his older opponent, Sam Cotton. Pickering, whose height (6'5"), booming voice, and penchant for theatrics have given him at least a performer's edge in court, has seemed at home and unruffled, first before the jury and now before Judge Geary. Unlike Cotton, who sometimes sweats in the courtroom and who has a slight but noticeable stutter, Pickering seems positively to be enjoying himself. And perhaps never more so than with the business of the fork.

According to Mrs. English, her husband attacked her in the cottage in the early hours of Friday morning, January 15, with a sharp instrument. Upon cross-examination during the first trial, it was revealed that this object was a fork with which Harrold was about to eat a casserole he had found in the fridge.

"You mean to say you were worried that your husband would kill you with a fork?" Pickering asked her under oath. There was, in his tone, an unmistakable note of disbelief.

"Yes," Mrs. English replied, in her quiet, straightforward manner.

"The same fork he'd just eaten the macaroni and cheese with?" the prosecutor asked. The disbelief in his voice had risen a notch.

"He hadn't started it yet," she replied.

A wave of laughter washed over the courtroom.

Each side then called "expert" witnesses to the stand to attest to the fact that a fork could or could not kill a woman, but Pickering's amused incredulity tainted the testimony, giving it a frivolous backbeat and mitigating Harrold English's intent.

Pickering was no less incredulous when it came to the shooting itself. As he pointed out at both trials, if Mrs. English was truly concerned for her life, she certainly had time, after her husband fell asleep, to go up to a neighbor's house at the top of the lane, barely 200 yards away, and telephone either Everett Shedd or the police in Machias.

Instead she made an extremely difficult journey in the dark out to the end of the point, where she got into a dinghy and rowed out to Strout's lobster boat, on which she had once seen a gun. She had some difficulty en route with the wet sand of low tide, once falling into a treacherous quicksand-like pocket the locals refer to as a "honeypot."

When she returned to the cottage, she says her husband was still asleep. He woke up just before the bullet hit his shoulder. Then she fired again. Strout, she has said in court, entered the cottage after the two shots were fired.

According to Pickering, at his summation at the first trial: "Maureen English had obviously hurt Harrold English, if not disabled him entirely, with the first bullet. If all she were concerned about had been self-defense, she'd have achieved that then. But she fired again. She meant to kill her husband."

Instead of self-defense, Pickering maintains, the murder was premeditated. Because Mrs. English was now in love with Strout—and her husband, who had driven 500 miles to reclaim her, was unlikely to agree readily to a separation or divorce—she believed she had no alternative but to rid herself of her husband altogether. Hence the difficult trek to the lobster boat instead of to the neighbor's house. Hence the shooting in what Pickering has called "cold blood."

Both Mrs. English and Strout have testified under oath in court that they were "friends," and Strout admitted that he went to the cottage on the morning of January 15 with the intention of "visiting" Mrs. English. When Pickering asked the defendant if the "friendship" included a sexual relationship, she would say only that she and Strout had "a relationship."

Both have testified that Strout entered the cottage seconds after she shot her husband.

In her written interviews, Mrs. English has been somewhat more revealing. She states that Strout entered the cottage just seconds *before* she fired two bullets at her husband. Even allowing for the confusion of the moment, it seems apparent, if we are to believe Mrs. English's statements in her interviews, that Strout was physically present in the cottage when she shot her husband. "I raised my arm and aimed," she said. "I heard a noise. It was Jack. He started to cross the room. I aimed the gun at Harrold's heart. I fired."

Shedd, who arrived moments later, believes that the two have publicly denied Strout's being in the cottage at the moment of the shooting to protect each other: "If Jack were to say he was in the cottage when Mary shot her husband, there would be no case whatsoever for self-defense. And Mary has changed the moment of Jack's appearance because she doesn't want to involve him."

However, if Strout entered the cottage before Mrs. English fired, *why did she shoot her husband?* Wasn't Strout's presence in the room security enough? Or did she, as Pickering has argued, have an additional motive, above and beyond that of self-defense, for wanting her husband dead?

Mrs. English insists her motive was self-defense, and she will say only this: "If Harrold lived, I had no life of my own."

Although Pickering claimed in his opening remarks that the love affair was the motive for the shooting, he was noticeably gentler with Strout on the stand than observers had anticipated. At neither trial, for example, did he ask Strout if he had had a sexual relationship with Mrs. English. At Shedd's store, Pickering's treatment of Strout has been the subject of much speculation. Some have suggested that the prosecutor has been unwilling to harass Strout about the affair because Mrs. English's statement about "a relationship" said enough. Others have maintained that there may have been some local reluctance to trouble a man already racked by guilt and grief—and that badgering Strout might have sat poorly with both a jury and a judge.

For perhaps the saddest aspect of the story is the death of Strout's wife, Rebecca, less than twelve hours after the shooting.

Upon returning home on the morning of January 15, Strout appears to have told his wife of the shooting at Flat Point Bar. Whether he also told her of his affair with Mrs. English, he has never said. But later that day, while Everett Shedd was taking him to the police station in Machias to give a statement, Rebecca drove her husband's black Chevy pickup truck over to the point.

Mrs. Strout was a tall, thin woman of 43 who had once been a beauty queen in high school. In recent years, however, as a result of her chronic depression, she was seldom seen in public.

On the day she drove to Flat Point Bar, she wore a long navy-blue coat, a blue kerchief, and a pair of black rubber boots. She appears to have taken her husband's rowboat out to his lobster boat—a boat named after Rebecca herself—and climbed aboard. Then she stepped off the boat into the Atlantic Ocean.

Her pockets and boots were filled with stones from the beach. The autopsy indicates that she drowned at once.

Townspeople searched for her all night long and found her body the next morning. Mrs. Strout had washed up on the low-tide flats of Flat Point Bar—ironically, just below the little white cottage where her husband's lover had committed murder the day before.

"When I think about Rebecca, I just get so upset," says Julia Strout. Mrs. Strout has asked for and received temporary custody of the Englishes' baby daughter, Caroline.

"It's the children I feel for now," she adds. "Rebecca's children, John and Emily, and now this baby. . . . It's such a tragedy."

Throughout both trials, Cotton has retained his mild demeanor. Cotton's father was a fisherman off Beals Island—an island connected by a causeway to Jonesport, just south of St. Hilaire—where the lawyer still lives, with his wife and three children. A familiar presence in these parts, he has defended local fishermen who have taken well-aimed potshots at poachers. Rumor has it that he might be tapped for a seat on the bench this year—making this case particularly important for him.

Cotton has two advantages. The first is that while Mrs. English's initial trial ended in a hung jury, the final split was tipped in her favor. One juror, a Native American woman from Petit Manan, seemed to speak for those who had voted for acquittal when she said on June 23, "You couldn't *not* believe that woman." Although Mrs. English's presence on the stand has occasionally been a problem for her, she has, at times, struck a distinctly sympathetic chord.

Cotton's second advantage is the previously mentioned tendency of Judge Joseph Geary to be particularly lenient toward women. Although Geary has not shown Mrs. English any favoritism in court so far, the word over at Shedd's general store is that with Geary on the bench, "Mary Amesbury is in good hands."

Still, Cotton has been dogged by several key aspects of the case. The most serious is the core of the defense itself. Because Harrold English was asleep when Mrs. English shot him, she cannot claim that her life was immediately in danger. Instead she has stated that she believed that her husband would *eventually*, that day or that night, kill her. Trickier still is the fact that Mrs. English herself says that while her husband was physically abusive toward her, he did not actually verbally threaten to kill her that morning. She simply *believed* that he would seriously harm her, if not kill her outright, sometime that day.

The allegations of abuse themselves have also been a problem for Cotton. As previously mentioned, he has not been able to provide a single witness to testify that Harrold English beat his wife. He did, however, put several residents of St. Hilaire on the stand—Shedd, Julia Strout, and Muriel Noyes, the owner of the motel where the defendant spent her first night in Maine—to testify that when Mrs. English arrived in St. Hilaire on December 3, her face was covered with bruises and her lip was cut and swollen. This testimony was later somewhat weakened when both Beale and Mrs. Strout testified that Mrs. English herself had told them that the bruises were the result of a car accident.

Lastly, Cotton himself seems to be baffled by the love affair between his client and Strout. In court, he tried feebly to skirt the issue, but to no avail. Cotton will not comment on his strategy during the trials, but sources close to the defense attorney have suggested that he was loath to put Mrs. English on the stand because of the damage the revelation of the affair might do to her case. It was only when he was unable to locate any witnesses to the domestic violence that he was forced to let her tell her own story—thus leaving her prey to Pickering's skillful cross-examination. The tragedy of

Rebecca Strout further complicated the case. It suggested that the affair not only provided a motive for Harrold English's murder, but also led directly to the death of Strout's wife.

Cotton knows, perhaps better than anyone, that the case is a complex one. During a brief telephone interview, he said only that "this is an extremely serious case" and that his client serves as an important test case for all women.

The defense attorney must wonder if he has taken too great a risk in advising Mrs. English to waive her right to a trial by jury, and if her presence on the stand has done her more harm than good. Whether or not Cotton's gambles succeed, in many's people's minds there are larger issues at stake; and even after Judge Geary reaches his verdict next week, many of them will linger:

· What really constitutes domestic abuse between husband and wife? In the privacy of the bedroom, where "normalcy" is an elusive concept, where is the line drawn between sex play and abusive behavior?

· What role did Mrs. English actually play in fostering the dark undercurrent of sado-masochism that she admits to condoning, however passively? Was she an innocent victim or an unwitting accomplice?

· If Mrs. English's motive was self-defense, as she has said, why did she fire *after* Strout entered the room?

· And finally, did she have a motive above and beyond that of self-defense? Was the shooting truly prompted by a will to survive? Was it the result of an unstable frame of mind? Or was it a love affair with another man?

Cotton reached his blue Pontiac. He put his hand on the door of his car, but before he got in, he raised his eyes to the cottage. It has been uninhabited since Mrs. English was taken from it on the morning of January 15. Surrounded now by wild beach roses, it sits spare and lonely on its small promontory. To one side is a weathered lobster boat on the sand, abandoned years ago. The water was unusually still, but gulls swirled about the roof and the dormer windows. Cotton took one last long look at the cottage, as if it would yield up its answers.

But the answers he was looking for are ones only Mrs. English, or "Mary Amesbury," can reveal now.

Perhaps Willis Beale put it best: "Before Mary Amesbury came here, this was a peaceful little town. Then she came, and it was like a hurricane had blown through. I'm not saying she tried to cause trouble. It's just that she did, didn't she?

"By the time she left us, we had one murder, one suicide, and three kids had lost their mothers.

"She's got something to answer for, doesn't she?" ■

*N*ight had fallen by the time I returned to the dormitory. I had guessed at how long it would take Caroline to read the notes and transcripts. Now I would have to let her confront me.

The corridors were quieter than they'd been earlier. I didn't announce myself by calling up to her room. Instead I simply knocked on the door.

She said at once, "Come in."

She was standing by the only window, holding a small doll made of yarn and bits of cloth. She looked straight at me when I entered. Although I could see at once that she was shaken, she didn't avert her eyes from mine. The notes and transcripts were in a neat pile on her desk.

"You've finished it," I said.

She nodded her head.

"Are you all right?" I asked.

She nodded again.

"It wasn't so much the article that upset me," she said, setting the doll on the windowsill. "I had guessed about that. It was the pattern of my mother's words. That was how she spoke, did you know that?"

I hadn't known the mother well enough to be able to answer that question.

"Have you had dinner?" I asked, gesturing toward the door. "We could go to a café or something, have a late supper."

She shook her head quickly. "No," she said. "I'm not hungry."

I edged closer to the center of the room. I felt uncomfortable in my coat and scarf. Although I didn't want to stay long—indeed, I wanted this interview to be over as soon as possible—I thought it would be better to sit. So I did, again on the only chair in the room.

She herself did not move to sit down, but instead rested her weight on the sill.

"I'm not sure I understand why she wrote all of that to you," she said. "Why did she tell you all that? Why did she contradict what she'd said in court?"

I shifted in my chair, unwound my scarf from my neck. It was hot in the room—a fact I hadn't noticed earlier in the day.

"I've often asked myself that question," I said to her. "I'm not sure what your mother's motivation was in sending the material to me. I think that at first she was trying to comply with the interview process, but on terms she could manage. Later the process itself became a kind of catharsis for her and may have brought her some relief. So she wrote in great detail, almost as if she were writing a memoir. I think she wanted to tell her story once and for all, and it was for herself that she did this. And because it was for herself, she had to tell the truth."

"The truth? But you didn't accept it as the truth! It's outrageous what you did!" she screamed. She sat up quickly and wrenched her hair out of her ponytail. "Outrageous! How could you have done this to her?"

I turned my head away and looked at the wall. Oh, yes, I wanted to tell the daughter, I had known her mother's story was the truth. In spite of what I'd done.

"I'm sorry," I said. "I know that's not much, but I *am* sorry."

She shook her head violently, as if to toss away my apology. Her hair fell all around her face.

"Why?" she asked, gesturing with her hands. "Why did you do it?"

I took a deep breath. The answer was complicated.

"That's a complicated question," I said.

I paused, searching for the answer.

"The truest reason, I suppose, is ambition," I said. "I know that's inexcusable, but that's the truth. I was looking for a cover and a book contract. I knew that to get a book contract, I had to leave the reader with unanswered questions—make it seem like a real puzzle. I knew I also had to suggest that I had more material from your mother's notes—material I could reveal at a later date."

She looked down at her feet. Her lips were pressed tightly together.

"But there are other reasons you should know too. Not to excuse myself. You should just know them."

She didn't speak, so I went on.

"It's true that my article was different from the story your mother told in her notes. But I don't think that when I wrote the article I deliberately set out to hurt her. It seemed to me, at the time, that the truth of the story lay in its complexities—in its different voices, different angles."

It was now extremely hot in the room, so I took my coat off.

"And there's something else," I said. "There's the process itself. It's hard to explain, but in the process of writing an article, a writer has to pick and choose. He has to edit a person's words, select some quotes and discard others, perhaps even change what a person said to make the meaning clearer. When you do this, it's almost impossible not to change the story in one way or another. . . ."

Outside, in the corridor, I could hear students talking.

"And another thing," I continued. "The article was a product of its times. It couldn't be written today. We didn't know a lot then about domestic violence. I mean, we didn't know *anything* about domestic violence. Wife-beating wasn't part of our thinking in 1971. To a lot of people it wasn't even considered all that terrible. . . ."

Truth was sometimes relative to the era in which it was spoken, I was tempted to add, but I didn't think the girl in front of me would find that much consolation.

"She was in there twelve years!" Caroline shouted from across the room. "That was my childhood!"

I leaned my head back, looked at the ceiling.

"I know," I said.

My article had gotten more play than anyone had anticipated. It had been picked up by the wire services, had been quoted on TV. Judge Geary, in rendering his verdict, had said he had not been swayed by recent reports in the media. But I had wondered. Judges are not required to sequester themselves during trial, because it is thought they have the professionalism to remain immune to publicity. But I didn't think he had remained immune when he had found Maureen English guilty of first-degree murder and was then required to sentence her to life in prison, with a possibility of parole in twenty years. Basically, he'd thrown the book at her.

Today, I thought, she'd have gotten five years for manslaughter, if that.

I'd been afraid when the article had come out that Pickering would subpoena my notes. But he hadn't. After Geary had found Maureen English guilty of first-degree murder, what was the point?

Maureen English's sentence had been commuted by the governor of Maine after she'd served twelve years. I knew that Julia Strout, along with various feminist groups, had lobbied for the commutation. I had even thought of joining their efforts, but I didn't.

When I looked down at the girl across from me, I saw she'd been crying. She took a tissue from her pocket and blew her nose. She'd been crying earlier, too, I suddenly realized.

"She wasn't complicitous, was she?" Caroline asked in a small voice after a time.

"No," I answered as truthfully as I could. "But I didn't know that then. Your mother often describes herself in the notes as complicitous, but I didn't know in 1971, as I do now, that most victims of marital abuse feel as your mother did. I didn't know then, as I do now, that this sense of guilt and complicity is part of the destructive process that the victim suffers."

I paused.

"What did your mother die of?" I asked, changing the subject. "The obituary didn't say."

Caroline didn't answer me at first. Then she moved to the bed and sat on it.

"Pneumonia," she said finally. "She'd had it on and off when she was in prison, and was prone to it. Jack and I were always careful. . . ." She trailed off.

Her face seized, as if she might be going to cry again, but she gained control of her features.

"I'm sorry," I said.

There was a long silence in the room.

I cleared my throat. "I was glad to see from the obituary that she'd been survived by Jack and yourself," I said. "I mean I was glad to see that she had married Jack in the end, and that she had been able to eke out some happiness for herself."

Caroline nodded dully. "They were happy," she said.

"If you don't mind my asking, I'm just curious, but I was wondering what happened to some of the people."

She looked up at me, her eyes vaguely unfocused. "Who?" she asked.

"Well," I fumbled, "Julia, for one."

She answered me, but she seemed preoccupied.

"I lived with Julia until I was twelve," she said. "My grandmother asked for custody, but my mother wanted me near her in Maine. And then, when my mother got out, she and Jack and I moved into his house. This was . . . this was hard for me at first. I loved Julia. I thought of her as my mother for a long time. . . . Emily had left by then. She's an engineer in Portland."

330

"And you," I said. "Will you be a writer, like your parents?"

She shook her head slowly.

"No," she said. "No, I don't think so. I'm thinking about a program in architecture right now."

"Jack stayed a lobsterman?" I asked.

"Oh yes," she said, as if it were a silly question.

"Oh. And Willis?"

"I was taught to hate you," she said. There was a sudden anger in her dark eyes, almost threatening; but more than anger, there was confusion.

I'd been prepared for this, but the heat came up into my face even so. I made a small gesture with my hand. I couldn't remember how I had planned to respond.

"Well, not taught to hate you," she said, "but it was understood."

I nodded. It was all I could do.

"I've felt bad," I said. "I feel bad. It's why I'm here."

She looked away from me.

"Why do you do it?" she asked.

I thought a minute. Hadn't I already answered this? She saw the incomprehension on my face.

"No, I mean," she said, "why do you write about violence, about crimes?"

I looked down at my hands. I twirled a gold bracelet on my wrist. It was a question I had, over the years, often asked myself—sometimes with alarm, sometimes with complacency. Why was I so drawn to other people's stories of murder, rape, and suicide? It seemed to me a question that went to the very heart of my existence, my life's work.

Could I possibly explain to this young girl the draw of the unnatural act unfolding naturally? Or tell her of my fascination with the violence and passion just beneath the veneer of order and restraint? Could I admit to this girl that it was precisely that excess, that willingness to permit—to commit—excess, that had so drawn me to her mother's story? Could I reveal to this child the trembling of my hands when the packages from her mother had arrived at my desk?

"I'm interested in the extremes to which people will go," I said.

It seemed to suffice.

"When I read of your mother's death in the *Times* last week," I said, "I spent an entire afternoon walking the streets. The memory of your mother triggered many powerful associations for me, many questions that I'd tried for years to brush aside. And when I got home, I went into my files and dug out this material and reread all of it. It's a very different thing reading something in the heat of ambition and then twenty years later. . . . When I had finished it, I felt you should have it."

She shook her head slowly back and forth.

"There was a book," I said.

She nodded. "I know. I've never read it."

"I have a copy here for you, if you want it," I said, bending and reaching into my briefcase. "Though it's just a longer version of the article, the same themes and so on."

But I saw when I looked up that she was shaking her head again.

"No," she said. "I don't want it."

I put the book back into the briefcase.

"The truth is," I said, "your mother's story made me rich."

I stopped. I looked down at my boots.

"She trusted you," she said. "Despite her reservations, despite what she knew of the process."

It was an indictment I could not protest. I gathered my coat into a heap on my lap.

"The title of your book . . .," she said.

"*Strange Fits of Passion.*"

"It's from Wordsworth," she said. "We read the poem last year. I'd heard the title years ago, from Jack or Julia, and was surprised when I came across it in class."

"He meant the phrase differently than in the modern sense. He meant it to describe grief," I began. But the mixture of gravity and grief in her own eyes stopped me.

"Look, this is difficult," I said, bending forward and reaching into my pocketbook. "But the truth is, I made a lot of money from your mother's story. My success with the book enabled me to write other books—have other successes. Over the years I've tried to share some of the income with her, but every time I sent her a check, the envelope came back unopened. I have a check here that will help you with your education. I hope you won't refuse it merely on principle. I believe that your mother should have shared in the money from the book."

I had no hope that she would take the check. I felt foolish as I held out my hand to her. I saw myself as she must have seen me—a middle-aged woman with a bribe. She stood at the desk a long time, longer than was necessary to humiliate me. So I was stunned when she took the check and put it into her pocket.

Stunned and then immensely relieved.

"I need the money," she said simply. "My father's legacy has run out. Jack hasn't much, and I don't like to ask."

She didn't thank me. I thought she understood and believed the money to be her mother's, and therefore hers.

"Well, I'll go now," I said, standing up and putting my arms into my coat.

Her taking the check, that was an unexpected bonus. There was absolution in that.

"There's just one more thing I have to ask you," she said.

"Sure," I said, perhaps a bit too flippantly.

I was thinking already of finding a place for a late supper and then returning to the motel room I had taken earlier in the day while she'd been reading. And then tomorrow I could return to my apartment and to my work.

"Do you think my mother told the truth?" she asked.

I stopped in mid-gesture, my coat half on and half off. Caroline had turned her back to me and was looking out the window. But there was dense blackness outside the window, and the only thing to be seen was the wavy reflection of both the young woman and myself.

"What do you mean?" I asked. I was confused. "Do you mean, did your mother tell the truth in her notes?"

"Yes," she said, turning to face me. "Mightn't she have edited her own story a bit, changed a quote here and there, exaggerated or altered something in order to help herself?"

The question lay between us like an abyss. An abyss in which the story and the storyteller were endlessly repeated and diminished like images in two reflecting mirrors.

Who could ever know where a story had begun? I wanted to say. Where the truth was in a story like Mary Amesbury's?

And then I wondered if she was thinking of her father. If she wanted to see him in a better light.

"I don't know," I said to the daughter.

Outside, a bell rang. From a campus church tower, I imagined. I counted eleven tolls.

She seemed to shrug, unsatisfied with my answer. I continued getting into my coat.

"I'll be at the Holiday Inn if you have any more questions," I said. "I won't be leaving until around nine tomorrow morning. And you can always reach me at home. My address and phone number are on the check."

"I won't have any more questions," she said.

"Well, take care, then," I said.

I turned to leave.

I had my hand on the door.

"Don't forget this," she said behind me.

When I pivoted, I saw that she was holding the stack of pages.

"No," I said, shaking my head. "It's for you. I brought it for you."

I was aware that I had backed away from her. To my embarrassment, I had actually put my hands out in front of me, as if warding her off.

She took a step forward. "It doesn't belong to me," she said. "It belongs to you."

I shook my head again, but she put the neat stack of typewritten pages into my hands, a final gesture.

"Julia died," she said, "a year ago. And Everett still has the store."

I walked down the long corridor to the stairs. Behind some of the doors I heard voices and music. Outside, on the stone steps in front of the dormitory, I saw that it had begun to snow again, and so I tried, with my free hand, to pull my scarf over my head. In doing so, I dislodged the stack of papers in my arm. They cascaded in a fan down the wet steps.

Perhaps I thought then about how my father had once told me that the story was there before you ever heard about it and that the reporter's job was simply to find its shape, but when I put down my briefcase and began to gather up the already soggy pages, I saw that they had spilled in total confusion.

There was no hope, in the darkness, of remaking a neat bundle.

Where or When

For Ozzie

Acknowledgments

To Claire and Ginger – who stood by me.

Existence permeates sexuality and vice versa, so that it is impossible to determine, in a given decision or action, the proportion of sexual to other motivations, impossible to label a decision or act 'sexual' or 'non-sexual.' There is no outstripping of sexuality any more than there is sexuality enclosed within itself. No one is saved and no one is totally lost.

MAURICE MERLEAU-PONTY

ONE

I remember everything.

A kiss at the nape of the neck.

You said you used to have a dream. When we were children, you dreamed that the nipples of my breasts burst through the fabric of my blouse. And when we were grown, you said the dream came back to you, and you had not had it in all the years in between.

When we were children, we whispered words like novices at vespers. We were children and afraid to say the words aloud. I believe this gave us longings that would last a lifetime.

But that afternoon, what did I know of indelible connections?

It was a September afternoon, a Sunday afternoon, and I remember that it was raining. There were a hundred people in the wood-paneled library at the college, and a stack of books on a table by the door. Some friends were there, and my husband, Stephen. My daughter was not. I watched my husband gesture with his glass, embrace with a sweep of his hand (the wine spilling a bit over the rim) the entire room of people, as if he might still his own anxieties by becoming my most exuberant supporter. It was Stephen in a gray sweater and a blazer, who was standing by the table with the books – the books and that day's newspaper, with my own picture in an advertisement.

Earlier that day, when we had driven to the college, Stephen had been quiet in the car. The onion sets that spring had been washed away by heavy and unexpected rains. Stephen had missed one payment at the bank, might miss another soon.

It wasn't anything that Stephen had done or had not done. All the onion farms were going.

The farm that Stephen might lose was set upon the dirt. They called it 'black dirt,' a soil as black as soot. Each year, in the spring, when the water had receded, if the sets had not been washed away, the tender shoots sprouted up from the soil in perfect rows and turned the black dirt to a shimmery onion green.

But the farm was not mine. Never mine.

It was the first time there had been a party, though there had been other books, other collections. The book, as you saw, was a slim volume with a paper cover in a matte finish, a slim volume of some thirty poems. This book would gain little more attention than the others had, though there was the party this time and money for an advertisement, just the one.

For the picture for the advertisement, I had been asked to wear a black jersey, and at the studio the photographer had removed my glasses, had taken the clips from my hair and mussed it with his fingers. The result was a likeness, recognizable as me, though essentially dishonest.

At the party, I stood at the edge of a small room while people moved around and past me and sometimes stopped with a sentence or a word. I remember that my editor came up to me and said, in a moment of unwarranted optimism, a friendly unwarranted optimism meant to deflect attention from the fact of the disappointingly small printing, that this slim volume would change the direction of my life. And I had smiled at him as if I, too, might share this optimism, though I had thought then that my life would not change, not beyond the small, seismic vibrations of a child growing, of a house slowly settling into the soil, or of a marriage – in unmeasurable, infinitesimal increments – disappearing.

I am in disgrace now. Removed from a state of grace.

When you and I were children, we learned of death. It was in the inevitability of a final separation, a death against which we were helpless. And even as adults, leaving you was always brutal.

I always wanted to ask: Did your wife give you the leather jacket? Did you wear other clothes, a tie perhaps, a shirt, that she had given you and that I touched?

Toward the end of the party, my editor made a toast. When it was over, I looked up. Within the crowd, I searched for Stephen. He was by the door, his back against the wall, draining his glass.

I watched my husband set the glass upon the stack of books, leaving a wet circle on the matte finish of the top cover. I watched Stephen leave the party without a backward glance.

EVEN ON THE BAY SIDE, the waves are spiking, spitting their caps off the crests. He likes it this way – hard and bright; these are the best mornings. The gulls, the rats of the sea, push against the wind, then swoop and dive for their catch. The old men are on the bridge, as they are every Sunday, braced against a railing that cannot last another year, even though he has been thinking this for years and the railing never gives. The bridge is wooden, nearly a mile long, the ride rattling in good weather, slick and treacherous when the spray freezes over the thick wooden slats. The bridge connects the mainland to a slender sliver of beach, and in the summer the bridge shakes under the weight of the Dodge Caravans and the Jeep Cherokees with their women and children, their beach umbrellas and blankets, their coolers of sodas and sunblock. But by now, the second week in September, the summer people have cleared out, and Charles and the old-timers finally have the place to themselves.

Charles sails the aging charcoal Cadillac gracefully along the rough planking. He nods and waves at the men in their stained parkas, plaid jackets, and baseball caps, their shoulders hunched against the wind, watching their lines for a tug that looks slightly different than the pull of the current. He drives this bridge two, three times a day, takes the car each time to the end. Sometimes he gets out to cross the dunes to the ocean side, to look out toward Lisbon or Rabat, or to watch the fishing boats come in around the bar to the harbor, south of the bridge. At other times he simply sits in his car, listening to Roy Orbison, nursing a beer, maybe two, until it's time for his next appointment or to drive back to the house, where Harriet and his children seem always to be waiting for him.

Today they need milk for breakfast, and he knows he shouldn't have taken this detour. But the morning is too fine, he rationalizes, to have missed. Beside him there is the half gallon of two percent, a heavy Sunday paper this week, and a greasy bag of jelly doughnuts he has bought for the kids, although he knows that by the time he arrives home, his children already will have eaten a breakfast that did not require milk. Harriet will disdain the doughnuts, will not even open the package, will set them aside on the counter until, inside the spotted bag, they will grow hard around the edges and finally be inedible. Thinking this, Charles is determined to eat at least one, even though, as a rule, he doesn't like sweets. He parks the Cadillac in the small circle of blacktop that grows more circumscribed each year by the encroaching sand, takes a doughnut from the bag, gets out of the car, and walks toward the dunes, which prevent him from seeing the ocean side. He has on his jeans, a white dress shirt he's been wearing since Friday, and a black hooded sweatshirt over that. Unthinkingly, he has worn his leather shoes with the tassels, his dress shoes, and as he walks they quickly fill up with sand along the edges. He bites into the doughnut; the jelly squirts over his fingers. With his free hand he tries to remove his shoes and his socks. He licks his fingers; the sand is cold on the soles of his feet. How quickly the warmth leaves the sand in September, he is thinking.

The view from the top of the dunes is always worth the small climb. The sea is charged, yet still a vivid navy. Whitecaps appear and vanish like blips on a radar screen. He descends the dune and walks toward the water. The gulls hang motionless in midair, unable to make headway against the wind. Even the sand, a thin sugar above the crust left by high tide, echoes the spray off the whitecaps, stinging as it does against his bare feet. But it is the blue, a deep inexhaustible blue, which speaks to him of clear uncomplicated days, that stops him. He wants, as he always wants, to have it, to possess it, to take it with him, to take it out when he needs it. For he knows that by this afternoon, this particular blue will be gone – replaced by muted colors, grays or greens.

'Hey, Charlie Callahan. You takin' in the rays, or what?'

Charles turns to see the speaker, but he already knows by the gravelly voice that it is Joe Medeiros, a presence in town, a client. Joe made his money as a draggerman and looks the part: two-day growth of beard, a plaid quilted jacket worn so badly in the elbows you can see the polyester, stained chinos. One of Joe's front teeth is badly discolored. Medeiros is a man embarrassed by his teeth and consequently never smiles. Charles can smell the stale breath even in the salt air. He knows it's Bourbon.

'Fishing?' Charles asks.

'Had my line in. Saw your car. Can't pull anything but pogies.'

Charles waits, shoes in one hand, the other in the pocket of his jeans. He knows this won't be a casual visit. Joe is wheezing from the awkward climb up the dunes. Joe won't be interested in the view either.

'How's business?' Joe pulls a pack of Carltons from his jacket pocket, lights one away from the wind.

Charles shrugs, a practiced and familiar shrug. 'Hanging in there. Same as everybody.'

'You got that right.' Joe exhales. The wind sends the smoke under his chin, into his collar. 'Hadda sell two boats last week. Hadda give 'em away, I should say.'

Charles looks down at the sand. Jesus Christ, he thinks, here it comes.

'So here's the deal.' Joe studies the harbor as if searching for one of the boats he had to give away. 'The fuckin' bank slashed my credit line. You know me, Charlie: I been doing business with Eddie Whalen with a handshake for years, and I've paid the bastard faithfully every month. And this is the reward I get.'

Joe Medeiros coughs on the smoke or on his anger, hawks up a glob of phlegm to make his point, spits it onto the sand. 'So I go down to find out what's the story with the credit line, and I find Eddie sweatin' bullets. Thinks *he's* going to get the boot now. The FDIC's been goin' over his stuff, and they're tellin' him now that he might of made some loans shouldn't of been made, you follow me. Fact is' – and here Joe Medeiros looks away, unable to meet Charles's eye – 'the cash I was gonna use for the premium? I gotta have it for the mortgage payment. It's that simple.'

Charles looks out toward Morocco. He has never been to Africa, nor even to Europe. He wishes he had the ability to banish Joe Medeiros from the dunes, make him disappear. He minds his Sunday morning invaded, the scene soured by the talk of business, the panic he doesn't usually feel until Monday's dawn beginning the slow crawl up his spine.

'Same old story, isn't it?' Charles says casually, as he has had to say too often in the past ten months. He is not surprised that the feds have been looking at Eddie Whalen's books. Eighteen months ago, Whalen was giving money away. Sign on the dotted line. As Charles and half the men in town had done.

'Stop by the office tomorrow or the next day,' Charles says. 'We'll talk. We'll figure something.'

With his toe, Charles scratches idle markings in the sand. He knows he ought to have gotten Medeiros's premium up front. The $15,000 commission check would have paid Costa. Tomorrow he will have to call Costa, cancel the construction on the addition. And Costa is a client – Charles will lose his business.

Christ, it never ends, it seems.

'So when are the fuckin' banks going to have a dime to put out on the street? That's what I want to know,' Joe says, looking at Charles now. The fisherman takes another drag, throws the cigarette onto the sand, business concluded. Small sparks from the lit end blow toward Charles's bare feet.

'The wife?'

Charles nods.

'The kids doin' OK? I gotta hand it to you, Charlie. You got the whole scene. Am I right?'

Charles hates this part, the denouement, the ingratiating banter after bad news.

'The kids are fine,' he says carefully.

Another case shot. Charles fights the panic by looking out to the ocean, imagining the Azores. He focuses on a fishing boat trying to negotiate the gut in the chop.

'So I'm goin' back to my line. Probably snagged a shitload of seaweed.' Joe turns as if to leave, then stops. 'Listen, Charlie, I'm sorry as shit about this. You know what I'm talkin' about. I know you do. I don't ever forget how you drove out to Jeannette's. After Billy . . .'

Charles looks up at Joe. The fisherman's nose and eyes are running in the wind. Medeiros's son, dead before he was twenty-five, drowned off his father's fishing boat. Charles had sold Medeiros insurance on both his sons, and he remembers the drive out to Billy Medeiros's wife with the check. After he'd heard of Billy's accident (seven years ago at four-thirty on a summer afternoon, and Charles was in The Blue Schooner; the news had rippled down the barstools like a loose and slippery eel), Charles had done the paperwork at once, gone that night to the funeral home for the death certificate, cut out the obituary from the local paper, and sent the required documents in to the home office. In ten days he had a check, which he carried in the breast pocket of his suit coat up the steps of Billy Medeiros's small bungalow on the coast road. Charles had seen grief before – it sometimes went with the job – but never anything as bald as on that day. Jeannette, a small woman with thin dark hair, met him at the door, and at first he didn't recognize her. Her face was fish white, years older, and swollen with her pregnancy. Beside her was a daughter, not four years old, who sucked her thumb.

Charles remembers how he took the check from his pocket and handed it to the woman and how her face changed as she comprehended the meaning of the check, how she once again experienced the irrevocability of her husband's accident. And Charles remembers how Billy Medeiros's wife seemed to fold in upon herself, fold in upon the high soft moans that sounded to him almost sexual in nature and struck him as too intimate for witnesses. He recalls wondering what his own grief would sound like if Harriet died, recalls thinking guiltily that it probably wouldn't sound like Jeannette Medeiros's. He had stood helplessly, not knowing if he should touch Billy Medeiros's wife to comfort her, his hands seeming to float huge and useless in his pockets. Finally he had picked up the silent and frightened daughter and taken her out of the house. They'd gone for a Dairy Queen and a round of miniature golf.

Remembering that day and watching Joe Medeiros recross the dunes, Charles thinks again that his job is an odd one to have fallen into – and that is how it seems to him, something he has fallen into, wandered into, not chosen – a far cry from the seminary, though sometimes not. He has few illusions about how his job is perceived by others: an unwelcome (if often necessary) chink in the machinery, a job falling somewhere between that of a CPA and a tax lawyer, the occasional butt of jokes on late-night TV. Usually he thinks of himself as simply a businessman, a salesman with a product, a man who is better with people than he is with the paperwork. Though once in a while, on days when he is filled with hope, he likes to think of himself as a Life Agent, with all that the title, as metaphor, might imply – an agent for Life, an insurer of life, even a kind of secular priest – and he imagines his clients, an entire town of clients (his flock?), as motivated by love, buying insurance from him because they love a woman or a man or a child.

But inevitably there are the bad days, the ones when he wonders if he isn't after all only a paradoxical and unwitting harbinger of mortality.

Last Tuesday was the worst. Just the visual memory of Tom Carney sitting behind his desk makes him shiver involuntarily beneath his hooded sweatshirt. He looks out to sea, as if to shake off the memory, but it is in place now, and though he is watching Cole Hacker tack his Morgan through the gut, it is Carney that he sees.

Charles had pulled into Tom Carney's gas station at twelve-thirty, left the Cadillac by the pumps. A teenage boy with spiky black hair came out of the office.

'Fill her with special,' Charles said. 'Tom in?'

'He's in the office,' the boy told Charles.

Charles walked to the office, opened the door. Tom Carney, an inch taller than Charles's six feet three, sat sideways to his desk, a desk littered with receipts, one greasy rag. Carney was bald already, had lost his hair early. The two men had joked about middle age: hair where you didn't want it, none where it was supposed to be. Carney's face, in adolescence, had been badly scarred by acne, and sometimes he still got pimples. Charles had told Carney that this was a hopeful sign – the man's hormones were still working.

Carney was smoking when Charles walked in, and his face was a grayish color that looked like fabric. On the desk was a Styrofoam cup of milky coffee, also grayish-looking, not touched. When he visited this office, Charles often had an impression of metal, as if the room and its entire contents were constructed of metal – metal walls, a metal desk, a metal chair – and this somehow was in keeping with the ever-present stink of gasoline in the air.

'It's right there,' Carney said to Charles. Carney indicated an open letter with his hand. Charles remembered then that Carney didn't smoke; he'd given it up years earlier. Charles took the letter from the desk. Clipped to its top was a check. Charles read the relevant sentence.

He remembers a sensation of being buffeted – as if the air had been blown out of the room.

'Jesus Christ,' Charles said softly.

Charles had gone to school with Carney, had played basketball with him, and the two boys had made it as far as the regional championships together. Then Charles had gone off to college and into the seminary, and Carney had stayed to work at his father's Mobil station. Carney owned it now; the father had retired. That was how Charles's business worked; he insured his friends, their referrals. Carney had held off for years, though, had had his children late. Usually it was the fact of the children that brought the new clients in.

Three weeks earlier, Charles had sent in Carney's application on a $300,000 policy, and he'd thought little of it until he'd opened his mail Tuesday. Carney's case was what the home office referred to as 'a flat declination.'

'Your client is unacceptable for medical underwriting reasons,' the letter had read. 'No further details are available. The initial deposit is being returned to the client with a letter of explanation.'

13

Charles had been mildly worried for himself financially (another case shot); more seriously for Carney. Such a flat refusal didn't simply mean your client had high blood pressure.

Charles looked at Carney in his metal office. Through the window, Charles could see the boy replacing the cap on the gas tank, moving the Cadillac away from the pumps. The boy's gestures seemed choreographed, dreamlike.

'I've got two kids,' Carney said.

Charles held the piece of paper, read the sentence again. He wanted to say to Carney that there must be some mistake, but he knew it wasn't a mistake. The blood tests never lied.

'And my wife . . . I've got to tell my wife.'

Charles put the letter back where it had been. He wanted to know how, but would not ask. He wanted to say he was sorry, but that seemed an insult.

'You want a drink?' he asked Carney.

Carney was quiet, wouldn't answer him. Carney's hands were large, had always been large. He'd been brilliant, fast with the ball.

'Let's get out of here, Tom, go get drunk at least,' Charles said.

Carney was staring at a spot on the opposite wall. He shook his head slowly. 'About five years ago, I had some encounters . . .,' he said.

Encounters. The word hung in the air. It was an oddly restrained and formal word for Carney to have used, and it didn't necessarily mean one specific thing or another, but Charles didn't have to know more.

After a silence, Charles had left Carney in his office, left the gas station. He'd gone to the Qwik Stop, bought a six-pack, and driven over the bridge to the beach. He'd drunk the six beers as fast as he could, on no lunch. It had seemed to him then that if he hadn't tried to make the sale, Tom Carney would never have known. It was illogical thinking, Charles knew, but he couldn't stop himself from making the loop. He'd thought of Portugal that afternoon, of emigrating to Portugal. He had wanted to be sitting at a café in the hot sun, eating braised octopus with Portuguese sausage and – for a change – looking out the other way across the Atlantic. He'd missed two set appointments.

Charles watches Medeiros disappear behind the dunes, relieved to be alone again on the beach. Charles likes the bridge and the beach, and he thinks of the drive here as the 'drive to nowhere.' He imagines the drive itself, the drive alone even without its eventual destination, as a balm, a respite from the business in town. And sometimes, when he comes here and when he is absolutely certain he is all alone, he sings: show tunes, oldies from his youth, once in a while a current hit that has captured his imagination on the radio and that he has bothered to learn the lyrics to. He likes his voice – a good Irish tenor – and occasionally he wishes he could join a church, any church, just for the pleasure of singing in a choir, though immediately, when he has this wish, he thinks of having to endure the rest of the service or the mass, and his fantasy deflates. So he sings alone. Often, if he can, he brings Winston with him, his dog, his black lab, and if he can get him going, he will sing too – a high, lonesome, off-key wail that drives the gulls crazy and almost always concludes with Winston bounding out of the car along the dark muck of the bayside, chasing the gulls and plunging into the frigid waters if need be.

It was why he'd bought the oversize Cadillac, a car big enough, he thought at the time, for himself and his dog. (Charles thinks of himself as getting bigger too, with each passing year, as if life itself were causing him to inflate, though except for the occasional pound or two, he knows this can't be true.) There were other reasons as well for the purchase, all of them nebulous but of equal weight, the sum total of which urged him to make this uncharacteristically showy gesture. He'd driven a Cadillac in Milwaukee on a business trip, and the car had reminded him of the big cars of his boyhood, the mythic Bonnevilles and Chevrolets of his early teens. And when he'd come home from the business trip and passed the Cadillac dealership and seen the sign announcing the sale, he'd pulled in, knowing as he did so that he'd be seriously chastised if he bought such an ostentatious American car, by Harriet and by his friends and even by many of his clients, and somehow this had perversely pleased him, though not as much as turning in the Saab – that everpresent symbol of New England yuppiedom – had done.

Charles crosses the dunes twenty minutes behind Medeiros. He takes the bridge fast; by now, he knows, Harriet will have passed from merely impatient to tight-lipped. He reaches down in front of the passenger seat, snaps the cooler lid, brings a bottle of beer between his legs. With a practiced gesture, he twists the cap, inhales a long swallow. It's ten o'clock in the morning. But it's a Sunday; it's OK. His soul is not in jeopardy. Yet.

At the end of the bridge, the road forks. To the north is a tight string of low-rent beachfront houses, a wall of thin shacks that stretches along the coast to a power plant at the end of a rocky beach. To the left is High Street, residential until the harbor and the village itself. Here the houses are more substantial – two-story, wooden-frame homes with peaked roofs, most of them year-round. The yards are small, postage-stamp, some bounded in the chain-link favored by the first-generation Portuguese and Irish, others bordered by the hedges and white picket fences preferred by their children and the newcomers.

16

Sometimes now, driving this road, Charles imagines that there has been a war or at least a skirmish – something to explain the bombed-out landscape, the physical and psychic eyesore of stalled construction, additions that will never be completed and that now lie covered with torn blue tarps, condo complexes aborted even before the windows got their glass. Where once there were weathered saltboxes surrounded by sea grass, now there are abandoned foundations, signs that say No Trespassing – ugly, half-built concrete objects that mar the blue of the ocean. He passes such a sculpture, with its rusted girders pointed toward the heavens, and thinks of Dick Lidell. Two years ago, Charles sold Lidell a policy for three million, and when the home office wanted to look at Lidell's tax return, Lidell had shown four million five in cash. The man could have retired. Instead the four million five went into the Tinkertoy with its orange girders up on the hill, and Lidell, Charles knows, is now renting someone else's two-bedroom condo.

The stories are legion. Charles passes his office, a modest white Cape with dark green shutters. In the front, hanging from a wrought-iron post, is his sign: Charles A. Callahan/Real Estate and Insurance. Each year Harriet tends the garden around the front porch of the office and hangs a basket of geraniums on the post with the sign. It was Harriet who found the old wicker rockers at a garage sale, rewove them, and painted them green to match the shutters. The rockers have been on the porch for three years now, though no one ever sits in them. He hates passing his office, hates thinking of having to go to it in the morning. The building will be the bank's within a matter of weeks. He will have to move his business into his home then, a move that doesn't bear thinking about.

He knows, of course, that it was greed: an unfamiliar sin

17

of boyhood, a ubiquitous sin of middle age, or so it seems to him now. But nearly as bad, he believes – almost as damning, almost as venal – was his carelessness, his recklessness.

At the time, the idea seemed to Charles like a certainty: All he had to do, Turiello explained, was take the equity out of the office, then leverage that cash into a one-third share of a three-million-dollar loan on the proposed office-condo complex the other side of town. Turiello had been a good client; the idea had been too seductive to walk away from. The location was ideal – a commanding precipice on the coast road, visible for miles. If the plan had worked, if the real estate market hadn't crashed, Charles, like Lidell, could have retired, and Harriet and his children would have been set. But timing (and he now knows the precise truth of this bromide) is everything. Almost immediately the market had begun to collapse, and neither he nor Turiello nor the third partner, Turiello's brother Emil, could lease or sell any of the space. At last calculation, Charles was into the bank for a million, his commission flow had trickled to almost nothing, and he now has on his desk a stack of policy lapse notices nearly half a foot high. If the bank can't sell the office soon for a decent price, Charles knows he will almost certainly lose his house as well. Already the newly compounded mortgage is crushing; his savings are nearly depleted. When he wakes in the middle of the night, the sheet below him soaked with sweat, the question he ponders is this: Will he have to put his next mortgage payment on his MasterCard?

Sometimes in the middle of the night he allows himself to think he is particularly plagued by bad luck or timing – but he has only to make this drive, as he does each day, to know he is but one of many. He can catalog the names: John Blay, Emil Turiello, Dick Lidell, Pete French ... the list is long. Each with bombed-out fantasies, chill sweats in the night. Each scrambling now just to keep his home.

Charles rounds the last bend just before the village. Here there are Federal houses, white or pale yellow with black shutters, fading square mansions with widow's walks and larger lawns. Ship captains once built these, Charles knows, and then later sold them to the owners of the mills. Now there is only one mill owner in residence; the rest are professional offices. Two stand empty. Out in front of several there are For Sale signs. Charles's name is on some of the signs.

As a summer place, the town has always been marginal, not a town that attracts the Volvos and the Range Rovers. It is and always has been a Rhode Island fishing town, mostly Portuguese and Irish, too working-class to have supported the massive summer places farther south and west or along the coast of Connecticut. For the most part, the town has remained undiscovered, not yuppified, and Charles is glad of this, though he thinks he shouldn't be.

He passes the bank at the end of the village – The Bank – the largest building in town, an imposing stone edifice with beautifully proportioned windows and two monstrous white columns that make it look deceptively solid. It is a singular institution, a family bank, not part of a chain, the only game in town. If Charles hates passing his office, he hates having to pass this building even more, loathes particularly the fact that lately the bank is almost always on his mind. From habit, he averts his eyes, studies a knitting shop across the street.

He takes the first right at the end of the village, brings the car to rest in the driveway of his house. A hundred and forty thousand on the clock. Christ, he wonders, can the old Cadillac make it another sixty?

Charles steps out of the car, looks at the incomplete addition at the side of his house, the foundation with no building, the addition that was to have been a new kitchen for Harriet, then later an office for himself, and will now stand empty, filling up with water in a rain, and he knows it is folly to imagine oneself as the repository for all the economic troubles, that somehow it all ends with oneself. For beyond him is Antone Costa, then Costa's three sons, one of them married already, two grand-children in eventual need of college educations. And beyond them, who? Carol Kopka, a single mother with two kids, at the checkout counter down at the A & P, the last to have been hired before the troubles? Bill Samson at the Dodge dealership, who's running thirty percent behind this year in sales? Christ, even Tom Carney at his gas station? He wonders if there is anyone in town who has escaped unscathed.

Harriet, he sees at once, has already been on the mower. The front lawn has shot up in the cooler weather, but the back lawn is trim. He could put the office in the front, he knows, where they have now a living room they hardly ever use, favoring, as they do, the family room, off the kitchen. He has been thinking about this for weeks, has reached no conclusions. He likes his house, though it is too grandiose and impractical. The house is frigid in winter, and the plumbing is mystifying – yet it's an elegant building, even if its nineteenth-century lines have begun to sag. Harriet mows the lawn, keeps the exterior tidy and painted, and minds that Charles has not solved the riddle of the plumbing – his part in this particular unspoken marital bargain.

Harriet is in the kitchen, wrestling with a large white softball of dough in a mustard-colored bowl. She has on her Sunday clothes – a pink sweatsuit and sneakers – and Charles can see that she hasn't had her shower yet: Her short, nearly black hair is still matted at one side from sleep, and there are smudges of teal blue below her lower lids. She doesn't speak as he walks in. He could tell her that he ran into Joe Medeiros, that Medeiros is pulling out of a deal, and that this will mean another stall on the addition, thus eliciting, possibly, a glance of sympathy or, at the very least, a change of subject, but as he watches her kneading the dough angrily, he decides to forgo the solicitation. More than likely, the news will simply frighten her. He puts the doughnuts on the counter, the milk in the fridge. He asks, 'Where are the kids?' and she answers, not looking at him, 'Outside.'

He takes the newspaper into a small room off the porch that is a kind of sanctuary, a library if one were to be so formal, which he is not inclined to be. This, too, is a room that could be turned into an office, though it is a bit cramped, and he does not like having to think of giving up his retreat.

There are books in uneven stacks on the floor of the room, nearly covering the small Oriental Harriet gave him last year for Christmas. Across one of the books is a tie he wore a few days ago. A second pair of dress shoes is in a corner, and for some reason he cannot quite fathom, a pair of jeans is flung over a chair. It is another unspoken marital bargain that Harriet never enters this room, and as a consequence it is seldom cleaned, seldom tidied.

He drops the heavy Sunday paper on top of his desk, itself awash in inches of unopened mail, half-read magazines, and more books. Slipping the sweatshirt over his head, he tosses it in the direction of the chair with the jeans. On a bookshelf he has his turntable, and he puts on the Brahms Second Piano Concerto, a piece he plays often, never tires of. It seems to him a hopeful concerto, nearly a symphony, appropriate somehow for a Sunday morning, even though the news this particular Sunday morning has not been especially hopeful. Outside, Hadley, his eldest daughter, is squealing as she takes the long, looping ride on the rope he hung for her from the tall walnut, a sail through the air that ends with a whomp in a large, forgiving pile of leaf mulch. Jack, his son, two years younger than Hadley's fourteen, is with her and is loudly demanding a turn for himself. Charles can see him through the small window of his study, squirming with impatience. He wonders briefly then where Anna, his five-year-old, is – not with them, for he would see or hear her. But he quickly dismisses the query; Harriet will know, will be watching her. For the moment he can relax.

He picks up his reading glasses from the desk, puts them on. Usually he begins with the magazine: a quick perusal of the cover story, a glance at the recipes, a longer look at the crossword to see if it's one he might tackle. This week the recipes are about blueberries – not interesting. He would study them if the dishes were Italian or Spanish or Indian. He is the cook in the family, though Harriet likes to bake, and his children often complain that what he concocts is inedible. The cover story is about the savings-and-loan scandal. He will look at that later. He picks up another thin magazine inside the paper, the weekly literary supplement.

He is thinking, as he turns the pages, of a book he has ordered at the bookstore and forgotten about; he must call to see if it is in yet. It's a volume by the French philosopher Paul Ricoeur; it must definitely be in now: he ordered it – what? – in July, he is sure. Perhaps, he is thinking as he idly peruses the table of contents, the bookstore did call, and Harriet answered and has simply forgotten to mention it to him. And it is then, in the middle of this thought, that he turns the page and sees the photograph.

His hand stops. He looks at the photograph. He lays the paper flat.

He lets his breath out slowly. He looks at the picture, reads the print around it.

It is Siân Richards. Of course he knows by the name.

Another woman might conceivably have this name as well, though he thinks that unlikely. More than the name, it is her photograph that makes him certain. It is, without question, the same face, the same expression in the eyes. He brings his hand up to his face, smooths his jawline with the back of his fingers. He puts his hand down on the desk, on the newspaper, and notices that it is trembling.

He studies the photograph. The woman in the picture is now forty-five, he knows, the same age as he is. Would he know this from the photograph? He cannot say for sure. Her hair is loose, wavy; he remembers it as a kind of pale bronze, particularly in the sunlight, with glints of fresh copper wire, though it seems from the black-and-white photograph that the highlights may have become muted over time. Her face is somewhat tilted, slightly turned, so that though she looks directly at the viewer, the sense is that her face is in profile. She is not smiling, but the gaze is steady – serious yet not sad. The suggestion from the eyes is that she is poised or waiting somehow, though he cannot imagine what precisely it is that she seems to be waiting for. She is wearing large gold earrings, simple circles, and what appears to be a black sweater or soft shirt with an open neckline, like that of a ballet dancer. The photograph stops just below her breasts. He remembers her mouth.

The mouth is generous; he has not forgotten that.

He reads the print again. She is a poet. She has a book.

He holds the newspaper up – looks across the desk at the picture. He remembers the high white forehead. He cannot escape the feeling that she is looking at him.

How many years has it been? The number staggers him. He remembers with absolute clarity the first time he ever saw her. He puts the paper down again flat on the desk. He reads the smaller print about the book of poems. He notes the publisher's name. He hears then a sound, the soft brush of fabric on wood, and he looks up to see that Harriet is in the doorway. She stands, arms crossed over her chest, resting against the jamb, observing him. Her face is not angry, but it is closed. She seems about to speak, to ask a question.

He might lift up the literary supplement and show Harriet the picture. He might say to his wife, You'll never guess who this is. Instead he does something that surprises him, that makes a faint blush of heat rise from his neck to his face and lodge behind his ears. He leans forward over the desk, arms spread, elbows cocked. With his left forearm, he shields the picture of the woman in the newspaper.

That night, when I had already entered your thoughts, I drove my husband home from the college. I had found him in a bar around the corner from the party. He'd been drinking Guinness and Bass, a string of half-and-halfs. He was sitting alone, and he tried a smile when I approached.

I said, Stephen.

He collected his change from the counter and slid off the stool. He was a gentle, brooding man, though large and muscular. He had pale blond hair, nearly white, and the high, pink color of a man who spends his days in the sun. On the right side of his face near his jaw, was the shiny seam of a scar.

He let me lead him to the car and let me drive him home. He did not speak on the way, and I did not know if his silence was composed of embarrassment or bitterness or worry.

A fine dust of black dirt almost always covered the house despite the washings by the rain, and though the house had been painted white, it looked, from a distance, gray. The black dirt got in over the thresholds and through the cracks in the caulkings of the windows. I would find it in my drawers on sheets that I had hung out to dry. The black dirt was nourishing and fertile, the richest soil in the state, but it seeped in everywhere, blew across the floor, coated sills and mantels. I sometimes scrubbed the woodwork until the paint wore through.

I went upstairs to see my daughter. I opened the door to Lily's room, peeked in to see the tiny body in its bed.

Then there was my study, Stephen's office, the bedroom that we shared. Stephen went into his office and shut the door.

When I had paid the baby-sitter and taken her home, I went back into the house and sat at the kitchen table. I had made an effort to give the room warmth, and there was a vase of mauve and brown hydrangeas on the pine table. I took off the jacket I had worn over my dress and laid it along the back of a chair. I took off my shoes, undid the pins from my hair. I sat down.

It was raining, a light drizzle that had come with the afternoon clouds, and on the windows the droplets lit up in the headlights of a car. Beyond the front yard, I could hear that particular sound of tires on a gravel road. I thought then that I should go to Stephen. There are always, in any partnership, balances and debts and payments. But I know I hoped instead that he had fallen asleep on the couch in his office. He often slept there.

Perhaps, as I sat at the kitchen table, I replayed certain phrases from the party. Perhaps I thought about the morning, about a class I had to prepare for. Possibly I did actually wonder if anyone from my past would see the advertisement in the Sunday paper. Or did I merely peer into the vase, a polished ceramic surface that gave off a rose sheen like a mirror, and study the distorted image of my face?

When visitors came over the mountain and first saw the valley, the dirt was so astonishingly black and the landscape so unrelievedly flat that the visitors thought what they saw was tar. And sometimes they said that: A parking lot? A landing field?

I often wonder now: What would have happened if that first letter had not been sent on to me, if it had lain unattended in a folder or on a desk? Or if it had been lost?

I have your shirt still, but the scent is fading.

HE HAS BEEN back in his study now for twenty minutes, and he cannot find anything suitable. Outside, a cloud bank from the west has begun to cover the sun, letting through only a thin wash of light. His children are in the house somewhere: Hadley, he thinks, is upstairs, finishing her homework; he is not sure where Jack and Anna are. He can still taste the roast from Harriet's mother's, a leg of lamb that was, inevitably, too well done. No one in Harriet's family can cook, he has long decided, and the table invariably looks stingy – even on Thanksgiving. He had forgotten that they were expected at his in-laws' until Harriet had come to the door of his study to remind him. He was distracted at dinner, focused on a face.

He has the paper folded to the ad and has arranged it so that it looks casually tossed upon his desk. He has found a box of Audubon bird cards, is not sure that they will do. Harriet, he knows, may have stationery, but he certainly cannot ask her. In any event, it's unlikely to be appropriate for the occasion; he has an idea that her writing paper will be the color of cotton candy and will have scrollwork down the sides. He sifts through the papers in his top left-hand drawer. There's a Hopper print, but it's of a middle-aged couple in front of a house, and they don't look particularly happy. Does he have nothing plain and simple? He pulls out a thin sheet of blue airmail stationery, looks at his watch. Five past four. What's open?

He puts on the hooded sweatshirt, checks his back pocket to make sure he has his wallet. He slides his keys from the kitchen counter, snaps the screen door shut. Harriet is raking along the ell, already removing the first leaves of the season.

She has her back to him. He watches as she bends and pulls. She has on jeans, an aqua sweater. The tines of the rake scrape along the dirt, obscure the sound of his leaving. She doesn't turn around. He hesitates, observing her.

He loves her more than he used to, he does know that. He does not like to think about the early years of their marriage, when he would sometimes wake in the night, his heart racing, stricken with the knowledge that he and she had both made a terrible mistake. That fear, foundering and bobbing in the early mornings like a stick tossed upon a chop, would make him irritable, and they often fought. He remembers the fights – shrill words he thought could never be taken back. But then Harriet had become pregnant with Hadley, and their life together – the pregnancies, the babies, the house, the building of his business – had become a project that made them quieter, easier together, and he no longer allowed himself to ponder the question of whether or not he had made a mistake. How could he regret the decisions he had made that led to Hadley and to Jack and to Anna? It was to him almost a physical impossibility, like juggling, which he has attempted several times to impress his children but has never mastered.

He watches her stoop to remove a rock. Her jeans are tight along the backs of her thighs. Since Anna she has not lost the extra ten pounds she has wanted to lose, despite her vigorous and sometimes comical early morning walks with the hand weights. He has tried to tell her that she looks fine as she is, which is true but does not explain why they seldom make love anymore. He does not understand it himself exactly, except that it is harder now to get through the day without the small irritations that lead to resignation.

He knows, too, that it is not Harriet who often demurs in the bedroom at night, but rather himself. Always, his wife asked for and accepted their sexual life as a given – even in those early years, when there was little love between them. For that he might be grateful, though he often feels that while she is essentially present in the bed, perhaps even in the entire marriage itself, he somehow is not.

The fan rake catches on a rock, bends the tine. He thinks of calling to her, taking the rake, straightening the tine for her, but he stops himself, watches instead as she ignores the rake's bent finger and drags the tool even more aggressively across the ground.

They are not alike, he and Harriet, a fact that he knows was a source of his tension in the early years of their marriage. A tension that has become a mild discomfort whenever he has to be alone with her. They do not talk much together, and he knows that despite the children and the house, they have little in common. It is not just the obvious dissimilarities – that he is an Irish Catholic and she a Yankee Congregationalist, despite the fact they virtually never attend church (nor do the children); or that he grew up in working-class Providence while she spent her childhood in the suburbs; or even that he cannot quite escape the old thought patterns of sin and redemption, while she seems never to have imagined a life in terms of transgressions and payments. No, it is instead, he thinks, the smaller truths, the almost inconsequential ones, that carry with them the greater weight: That she has plans for any given day and seldom deviates from them, is almost never late, and at the end of the day can add up the experiences, the completed tasks, and find among them some satisfaction, while he squanders time, resists the effort necessary to complete a task, thinks of his drives to the beach as the highlights of his day. Or the small truth that she has never once, in their entire marriage, played a piece of music for herself, never put a cassette into the tape recorder, never put a record on the turntable, and that when she drives she prefers silence to the radio. Or the small fact (although perhaps, he thinks, this ought to be a larger fact) that she believes wholeheartedly in the ritual of the family dinner at six, even though his stomach almost always seizes up at that hour and doesn't begin to relax until later in the evening. Many nights he stands at the kitchen counter at nine o'clock and eats alone a dish that he has made, and if she walks through the kitchen then, she almost always asks him what he's doing there.

Sometimes this information – the small truths and the larger ones – puzzles him: how one can be with a woman for so many years, ostensibly have shared so many intimacies (how many times have they made love, he wonders – two thousand? three thousand?), and yet still feel fundamentally unknown in her presence.

She did not hear him leave the house, but she will hear the car starting, so he calls to her.

'Harriet.'

She turns to face him. Her hair is fixed in place, and she has on her makeup.

'Where are you going?' she asks.

'Out,' he says. 'An errand.'

'What errand?' She frowns slightly, a reflexive gesture more than a comment. Her hand is poised on the top of the rake.

His mind flails and leaps. What errand on a Sunday afternoon?

'Tires,' he says.

'Tires?'

'I'm worried about the tread. Thought I'd get them checked out. Before the weather turns.'

'Oh.' She looks puzzled.

Charles flings open the door of the car, puts the key in the ignition. Although he does not look at her again, he

31

knows his wife is studying him as he backs the Cadillac out of the drive.

Costa's Card & Gift is just past the pharmacy. He flips his blinker on to pull into a space in front of the store, then abruptly turns it off. Jesus Christ, he can't go in there. Janet Costa, Antone's wife, is a class mother with Harriet, and Janet owns and manages the store. He can hear the dialogue: Saw Charles on Sunday in the store. Charles? He was buying stationery.

Stationery? What kind of stationery?

He will have to drive to the mall. The bookstore there sells note cards and writing paper. He checks his watch again. It's a twenty-minute ride. The mall should still be open.

The route to the mall takes him along 59, a county highway so densely packed with fast-food restaurants and discount stores that it looks more like Florida than the coast of New England. Yet even here the recession has claimed its victims: an appliance center is boarded up; the windows of a ski shop are empty, the fake snow still cascading across the glass. He thinks briefly of Joe Medeiros, pushes the thought from his mind.

The bookstore is small and appealing – surprisingly so for a shop located in a mall. There is, when he enters, an abundance of wood and Essex green, a wicker rocking chair by a pot of coffee, books with glossy jackets arranged on tables and shelves. Along one wall, he sees several stands of note cards. He heads in that direction.

He turns the wire stands slowly, looks at the rows of cards. A young woman in a black sweater asks him if he needs help.

'I need paper,' he says, looking at the woman. 'Writing paper. Simple. Heavy.'

The woman bends to retrieve a box in a cabinet beneath a counter.

'I don't have paper,' she says, 'but I have these.'

He takes the box from her and opens it. Inside are stiff heavy cards, about the size of wedding invitations. Below them are envelopes that match. The color is ivory.

'They're our best,' she says.

'This will do,' he says, 'and I need a good pen, if you sell them. A fountain pen.'

This last request has occurred to Charles only as he has uttered it. He will have to write the note in the car. He cannot write it at home.

They walk together to the register. Charles hands the woman a credit card, wonders fleetingly if he's already over the limit – a staggering amount of money in itself. 'Wait a minute,' he says. 'I have a book on order here. And I need another book too, although I don't know if you have it.'

He tells the saleswoman the names of the books. He adds that the second is a book of poetry. She checks in the computer, says that his order came in and that they have five of the volumes of poetry – the shipment arrived last week.

'I'll get it for you,' she says.

When she hands the small book to him, Charles studies the jacket, turns the book over. The photograph he saw in the advertisement is on the back. He reads the short biography that accompanies the picture: 'This is Siân Richards' third collection of poetry. She lives in eastern Pennsylvania with her husband and daughter.'

This last sentence seems impossible to him – as if he had been told that the earth had four moons. Or that the tides had stopped.

The bridge is desolate, empty at five-twenty on a Sunday. He parks on the blacktop at its end. The cloud cover is thick now, a grayish-brown batting, darker behind him in the west. Soon there will be splashes on the windshield. The temperature has changed too; it's dropped ten, fifteen degrees since noon, he thinks. Beside him is the book of poems, the box of stationery, the pen. He picks up the book, rests it against the steering wheel, turns each page slowly. He reaches down in front of the passenger seat, fumbles for a beer in the cooler. Still cold; the label is wet.

He reads each of the poems, then closes the book. He makes a desk with it on his lap, resting one edge on the steering wheel. He unscrews the pen, slips in a cartridge, makes a few practice scrawls on the paper bag from the bookstore. The rain begins, tentatively at first. a slow, uneven rain of fat drops. He likes the sound of the rain on the roof of his car, the isolation of the beach. He takes a card from the box, lays it on the book. He puts the pen to the card.

He cannot think how to begin. He takes a long swallow of beer, then hears a phrase, a single phrase of a song. Jesus Christ. He turns the book over to look again at the picture. The phrase comes to him again, blown off across the sand. He plays it in his mind, and then again, even as he played the 45 over and over as a boy.

Fragments rush in upon him now. A young girl's face. A high white forehead. A blue dress just below the knees. A stone courtyard.

Images and ideas scud along the crust of sand in front of him, pockmarked now with the beginning of the rain.

The song may be on a jukebox somewhere, he thinks. He cannot remember all the words, just the tune, bits of phrases. He looks down at the thick white card on the book.

He thinks: I cannot do this. I have a wife and three children, and I may lose the house soon.

Then he thinks: How can I not do this?

'Dear Siân,' he writes.

TWO

Dear Siân,

When I saw your picture in this morning's newspaper I had the same feeling as I had the first time I saw you, in the courtyard of The Ridge thirty-one years ago. I bought your new book of poetry today. I have read all the poems once, and will need to spend more time with them, but I was struck initially by the way the bleak emotional and physical landscape you describe takes on a unique beauty. Beauty out of deprivation. And how this theme holds true as well in the several poems about the migrant workers. I hope you have not had to experience what you write about.

Congratulations.

Charles Callahan

September 23

Dear Charles,

I was delighted to get your note. Can it really have been thirty-one years ago? I have an image of the boy you were then – and somewhere I have photographs of you, even one, I think, of the two of us. Weren't you called Cal, or did I dream that?

*I live on a farm with my husband and my daughter, Lily,
who is three. Two days a week, I teach poetry at Stryker
University, not far from my home. Thank you for your
comments about the poems. The landscape I write about is
familiar to me. As are the migrant workers.*

*You know what I do and what I look like. I am more
than a little curious about what you do and what you
look like.*

Siân

September 26

Dear Siân,

Somewhere my children still have a gold identity card
hanging from a chain, with 'Cal' written on the front and
'Siân' written by you on the back.

I am married, with three beautiful children – fourteen,
twelve, and five.

I am surprised your daughter is so young. I suppose I
just assumed you had married earlier and that your child
would be nearly grown.

I plotted the bike ride between my house and yours
several times, but a 200-mile bike ride across three states is
pretty difficult for a fourteen-year-old boy. Did your father
ever tell you that I called about a year after we had each
graduated from college?

Concerning what I do, I sell both insurance and real
estate. I'm doing brilliantly at neither at the moment.

To know what I look like, you'll have to meet me for
a drink.

Thank you for not making me write to you through your
publisher. That would be tiresome.

Charles Callahan

October 15

Dear Siân,

I am just a little concerned that you have not responded to my last letter. I hope this correspondence has not put you off in some way.

I remember I saw you as soon as I arrived at The Ridge. I can picture this vividly. You were standing in the courtyard, in a cotton dress with short sleeves, and it came down below your knees. It must have been just after we had arrived. I remember, too, the first time we spoke to each other.

We were painfully shy with one another. I do remember that. I remember walking down to the lake in an agony as to whether or not I would have the courage to hold your hand. I believe I also gave you a gold bracelet that said 'The Ridge' on it. I remember the badminton game. And, of course, I have never forgotten the bonfire. Do you remember that?

I find it extraordinary that I should have the same feeling looking at your picture in the advertisement that I had thirty-one years ago looking at a beautiful young girl in a courtyard.

Charles

October 20

Dear Charles,

No, I have not been put off by this correspondence, though I am unclear as to just where it is going. But perhaps I am being too linear. It doesn't have to go anywhere,

I suppose; it might just circle and loop around in our memories.

I am fascinated by your memories. I would love sometime to compare them – yours and mine. Did you perceive that week as I did, I wonder? I do see myself with you. I am wearing a white sleeveless blouse and plaid pedal pushers, and my hair is pulled back in a ponytail. You are beside me, quite a bit taller, and you have a crew cut. I must have this image from a photograph. I will go through my trunk and find all of the photographs one day soon.

I do remember the bracelet and the badminton game and the night of the bonfire. I also remember having an epiphany of sorts, down by the outdoor chapel at the water's edge, that the essence of religion was love, pure and simple. I am not religious now, by the way. I haven't been inside a church, except for a wedding or a funeral, in twenty years.

I would, of course, meet you for a drink, but I think you will be disappointed. I am not quite as interesting or as mysterious as my photograph makes me out to be.

> *Siân*

October 23

Dear Siân,

I received your letter yesterday. I saw the review of your new book in last Sunday's literary supplement. I was thrilled when I saw it, and I thought it was quite good, all in all. I know it must be hard to have your work hanging out there for anyone to take aim at. I confess I seldom read poetry – at least contemporary poetry: I am more likely to read philosophy or history – so I was a little lost and befuddled in the paragraph of comparisons to other poets, but I felt the reviewer was absolutely right when he referred to you as a transcendentalist.

I can remember being with you at the outdoor chapel by the water. If the essence of religion is love, and you love someone as I'm sure you do, then I guess you're religious. Those are words from a former seminarian. After college I entered the seminary and was there for two years. Mostly I wanted to avoid the draft, but I probably received my best education there. I haven't been to church in twenty years either.

There is a line in a book I read recently about the curiosity of lives unfolding. I guess that is what we are doing. I know you are interesting. The part of you that I believe is mysterious we could hold on to by not meeting, but I wouldn't be satisfied with just holding on to a mystery.

Just tell me where and when. Whatever is easiest for you. I'm looking forward to meeting you. Again.

Charles

October 28

Dear Charles,

I would like to meet with you sometime, although I confess I am a bit uneasy. My larger difficulty, however, is that I feel uncomfortable in the position of having to arrange a meeting. I don't know quite what else to say at this point, except that I will think about it. I don't mean to put you off, but I am a little daunted by the hows and wheres.

I'm sorry you had to see the review in the literary supplement. It is probably a classic example of a 'mixed' review, but it stung nevertheless.

I smiled at the image of you plotting the bike ride from your house to mine. My father still lives in the same house in which I grew up in Springfield, but I really left western Massachusetts when I went to college. I attended a Catholic college for women in New Hampshire and barely escaped entering religious orders myself by joining the Peace Corps. My mother died while I was in college. In the Peace Corps, I taught elementary school in Senegal. When I returned to this country, I went to graduate school for a time, and I met my husband there. Then we settled on his farm.

What is it like where you live, and what are the names of your children?

I am sorry my handwriting is so poor. I could type these letters if you'd rather – your handwriting is remarkably beautiful.

I am intrigued by how you happen to have a postbox.

Siân

November 1

Dear Siân,

I had already ordered from my local bookstore your two previous books, and several days ago your first book of poetry, about Africa, arrived. I think the poems are beautiful – that goes without saying. There are threads and currents that run through your poetry, but each poem is somehow a surprise. I'd also like to say, and I hope this is not disturbing to you, that I think there is a kind of sadness associated with your poetry. This is easier to see in the later poems – a kind of awful loneliness, I think. Or do I only imagine that?

I'd like to see you smile. You seem fairly serious, and I'm sorry about the 'sting' of the review.

I knew that your mother had died. Your father told me when I spoke to him on the telephone.

Our lives seem to have been running on parallel tracks. I mean by that only the coincidences of having small children, of both having entered or nearly entered religious orders, and of both having lapsed. Perhaps when we meet, we will discover other similarities.

I live in a middle-to-working-class coastal fishing village, in a large white house badly in need of repair. Unfortunately I'm fairly lazy, so it will probably stay in need of repair.

I went to Holy Cross, then to seminary in Chicago. After that I drove a city bus. I was driving the city bus when my sister's husband was killed in a car accident, and I had to come home to help her take over her husband's business. Then she remarried and went off to Los Angeles, and I got stuck with the business. The rest, as they say, is history.

The town I live in is about a half-hour from Providence, where I was living when we met as children.

My children are Hadley, fourteen; Jack, twelve; and Anna, five. I think each is beautiful and unique.

When I first wrote you, I thought we could have a casual meeting. Now every letter I write you, I feel I risk scaring you away. Putting the burden of the 'where and when' of our meeting on you was really just the concern of someone who knows what it's like to have a three-year-old child. I can set up the time and place and arrange for a chaperone.

I'd rather write you in longhand, and thanks for the

compliment about my handwriting, but I had to get this out in a hurry. The only reason I have a P.O. box is that I run my business out of it, and I can get the mail earlier.

It takes time to read between the lines.

I notice that you don't say much about your husband.

Charles

November 5

Dear Charles,

I am leaving for Cambridge, England, on Thursday and will be away teaching a poetry seminar for two weeks. I wanted to say, before I left, that I like the letters you write to me, that I like the things you choose to say.

Yes, I am often too serious, and no, you are not wrong if you sometimes see sadness in my work. These are characteristics I don't seem to be able to do much about.

Thank you, but I won't need a chaperone.

I notice that you say little about your wife.

Siân

November 7

Dear Siân,

Touché.

Going to England is one hell of a good excuse for not being able to meet with me. For whom are you teaching? Do you do this sort of thing often?

I am disappointed. If I knew what flight you were taking, I'd drive to the airport and see you off, though that would be incredibly frustrating.

Please send me a postcard from England. I probably won't get it before you're home, but do it anyway.

I miss you already.

Charles

November 10

Dear Charles,

My plane is leaving in a few hours, but I had to send these pictures off to you before I left. For some reason I cannot explain, I was seized this afternoon with a desire to go through my trunks and find the photographs I thought were there. I am sending you these two – the one of us together in the courtyard and the shot of the lake taken from the outdoor chapel. I'm sure that the one of us was taken on the last day, just before we had to leave. How extraordinary what the memory got right and what it didn't. You look much as I had remembered you (do you still have somewhere that wonderful old Brownie that is in your hand?). But I look very different. I didn't remember the Bermuda shorts or that my hair was quite that light ever. Nor that you and I were the same height. Your arm is around me, but just barely, and I'm unable at all to meet the gaze of the camera. I seem to be studying my feet.

Aren't the photographs concrete proof that somewhere in time we did actually meet and know each other? What did we know? I wonder. And what did our voices sound like?

This archaeological dig has consumed nearly all my afternoon, and I'm not even packed yet. I must run, but I

*wanted you to have this. One day I will find the bracelet.
I'm sure I must have it. I never throw anything away.*

I promise a postcard.

Siân

November 15

Dear Siân,

I drove to the beach today to look out toward Portugal,
but there was a haze on the water, and the view was
obscured.

Actually, I often go to the beach and look out toward
Portugal. This activity consumes more of my time than it
ought to.

This letter is hard to write, knowing you are far away
and won't even read it for at least a week. I wonder what
it is like for you in England, what you are doing. I imagine
you with a long scarf wrapped around your neck, walking
along a path toward a beautiful stone building where your
students are waiting for you.

I was moved by your archaeological dig and by the two
photographs. It was the last day of camp, and we had asked
someone to take the picture of us together. I remember
that my parents had arrived already, before yours, and that
they were standing off at some distance, watching us, barely
masking their impatience. I also remember that I cried all
the way home in the car and that when I told my mother
I had given you a gold bracelet with the words 'The Ridge'
on it, she said to me: 'So where's my bracelet?'

What happened to me thirty-one years ago was love at
first sight. I don't understand the phenomenon entirely,
and I'm more than a little embarrassed at having to resort

to the clichés of old 45s, but I can remember vividly that gut-wrenching feeling. I am less clear about what happened to me when I saw your picture in the newspaper two months ago. Last night I was reading Paul Ricoeur, and a line of his stopped me: 'the fulfillment of an antecedent meaning which remained in suspense.' He meant the irrational irruption of Jesus Christ in the context of the New Testament, but I tend to take bits where I find them and apply them to my own life. The difficulty for me is that I can't completely absorb what happened thirty-one years ago or on September 15, because I don't have enough access to the antecedent.

All this means is that I want to meet the woman who has grown from the girl I remember.

Time has taken on a new dimension. I feel the chaos of time, but I'm trying to comprehend it in relationship to loss. I spent all of August with Stephen Hawking, thinking about 'quarks' and black holes, but he didn't mention how waiting for a letter or recrossing a warp of thirty-one years to a young girl's face can make time fold in upon itself. My daughter is now the same age as we were then, a 'fact' of physics or of nature that baffles me.

Perhaps I am looking only for an open connection.

Today has more warmth than you would imagine for the fifteenth of November. The ocean was a dusty blue when I drove to the beach earlier, with the haze on the horizon. There was a stillness this afternoon, both visual and sensual, that was soporific – or at least that's the excuse I am using to explain why I dozed for twenty minutes in my car with the sun warming the front seat through the windshield. At the beach, across a long wooden bridge from the mainland, you can hear the bells from the church tower in the center of town, and I like listening to them, interspersed with the calling of the gulls. Even the gulls were half asleep

49

today, though – enjoying this short Indian-summer respite from a string of cold gray days. I nearly missed my lunch appointment.

You mention my wife, and I mention your husband, and we receive in reply only further questions or silences. I might one day be able to speak to you or write you about my marriage, but I am more engaged now (and have been for some time) with the sound of bells from a church tower or the mysterious physics of time. What to reveal and what to conceal is perplexing to me.

For the same reason that I cannot focus on my marriage, my business is shot to hell. I used to be better at compartmentalizing. I'm supposed to sell insurance and real estate, but the entire town is under siege, and every dime is frozen. I could write you more about this, but I'd like to keep the shit out of this correspondence. I'd like to transcend the shit, is what I'd like to do. Actually, I do not always hate my job. I used to like to talk to people about what was important to them.

Where does the pain in your poetry come from?

I imagine going to a market in Cambridge and buying ingredients for a meal that I would make for you. I love to cook. Am I going too far?

Yesterday I called The Ridge to see if it was still there. You will probably not be surprised to learn that it has been turned into an inn. I asked the woman who answered the phone if she had a brochure with a photograph so that I could see what it looked like now. She said the only exterior shot was the building itself with the fountain. Did I remember the fountain? I said yes, but that my most vivid memory was of the girl I met there thirty-one years ago. She said: 'Did you marry her?' I said: 'No, but I should have.'

Now I know I am going too far.

Sometimes I think we are both too serious. If you want me to stop, just tell me. I know this can end in an instant.

I know we have to meet. I think you know that as well.

I could tell you so much more, but I really just want to hold your hand.

As I sit here trying to compose a letter that will mean something to you, I can't take my eyes off your picture. You said in a letter that you are not interesting and not mysterious, but you didn't say that you are not beautiful.

Charles

November 16, London

Dear Charles,

Today I took a walk in Regent's Park. I'd love to see it in the summer when the roses are in bloom. I'm in London for talks with my British publisher. They've put me up at a wonderful hotel on the Strand. Downstairs in the pub, they serve forty different kinds of malt whiskey. Last night I tried three and was nearly paralyzed. Today is my birthday.

Cheers,

Siân

November 28

Dear Charles,

I want this to stop. I'm sorry.

It has been a very long time since anyone wanted to, or wanted only to, hold my hand.

51

I do not know you, but I sometimes think I have felt who you are in your letters.

   Siân

November 30

Dear Siân,

   Regarding your last letter, there is a wonderful story about Jack and Bobby Kennedy during the Cuban missile crisis. You probably already know it, but I'm going to tell it to you anyway. Reducing it to its essentials, the story goes like this. At a crucial moment in the negotiations, Jack Kennedy gets a telegram from Khrushchev that's fairly conciliatory and suggests that Khrushchev is going to back off. Just as Jack and Bobby are about to celebrate, however, Khrushchev fires off another telegram. This one is hostile and essentially tells Kennedy that he's changed his mind about backing off. What to do? Bobby has a brilliant idea. Ignore the second telegram, pretend they never got it, and immediately go on national TV, thanking Khrushchev for his humane gesture – thus ending the crisis.

   Your comment about holding your hand will haunt me forever.

   The enclosed device has many possibilities, but I hope you'll use it to listen to the tape I am sending with it. Sorry for the sound quality, but some of these songs are as old as I am. A number of them had to come off a jukebox.

   I know you could order a similar tape with an 800 number and your credit card, but it wouldn't be the same. I tried for the time that might bring us back together, if only for a moment. My favorite song is 'Where or When.' The B side of that record, 'That's My Desire,' is a close second.

This may mean nothing to you. There is a gap on one side where I screwed up. Just be patient. If you can't be that, just put it in the trash compactor.

We have a reservation for lunch at The Ridge for next Thursday at twelve noon. I'm including with this letter directions from your house.

I thought it unfair to meet for lunch and not allow you to know what I look like when I know what you look like, so I am sending along this picture. It isn't very good, but I don't have many. My daughter took it last summer when she and I were fishing. The fish is a striped bass. On Thursday at noon I won't be holding the fish and I hope I won't be left holding the bag.

Charles

THREE

I was working in my office when I heard the familiar sound of the engine of the mailman's jeep, the squeak of the mailbox being opened, the firm slap of metal upon metal. It was a signal, as it almost always was, to leave my desk, as if I had been summoned by the outside world. Lily was at the house where she was watched during the mornings by a neighbor. Stephen was in the barn, working on the cultivator.

It was chilly as I walked out front to get the mail, and I was thinking that when I went back inside, I would make myself another cup of coffee. Inside the mailbox, there was a large envelope from my publisher, and inside that a smaller envelope, with my name on it. I took all the mail inside.

The envelope with my name on it was the color of thick cream; the ink was a dark navy. My name had been written in a beautiful hand, strong and large and steady. Simple, not pretentious. I thought: This must be an invitation. I remember I ran my finger across the ink of my name, as though it might have texture.

And when I read the letter, I thought: *Cal.*

I saw a boy, a tall boy with soft brown eyes and a crew cut – and for weeks, even after we had met, when I thought of you I would see this boy.

I could see the lake with the wooden benches, a wooden

cross, not ornate. I could see the length of you, the span of you from your waist to your shoulders, in your arms and in your legs. In those days, boys wore white shirts and black pants, even in the summer.

I could see the woods, a patch of woods, in the moonlight.

I went upstairs and put the letter in a drawer, under other papers, where it would not be seen.

I made my husband's lunch and called to him. I put on my jacket and walked to my neighbor's house, where I picked up my daughter. My life went on as usual. I put dishes in the dishwasher, held my small girl, ran my fingers through her fine blond hair. Stephen came and went, and there were long silences between us. There was a kind of tightness around his eyes, which was new to me. He had migraines – two, I think – from the time your letter came until I answered it.

Some nights, after dinner, Stephen and I would talk about the farm, replaying worn scenarios. There was my father, but we had borrowed from him already, and he had almost nothing left. There were more acres we might sell if we could find a buyer. It was the second year of a failed crop, an insupportable burden. Stephen had taken on another job, as a part-time instructor at the agricultural school.

After we had talked, however briefly, Stephen would go up to his office and shut the door. Often I would find him there in the mornings, asleep in his jeans and a sweater.

I didn't mind sleeping alone; in fact, I believe I welcomed it. But sometimes, waking in the middle of the night and walking down the darkened hallway to look in on Lily, I would have a hollow sensation within me, a certainty that I had failed with

Stephen, a fear that my life would be defined by this missed connection. Stephen had needed me to fill his emptiness, to assuage the intensity of the black dirt and of his ties to the farm, but I hadn't been able to do that for him.

Stephen had always been secretive – a gentle man, but a hard man to know. Once when I'd asked him about the scar, that shiny seam on his jaw, he said he'd had an accident with a gun some years before I met him and that a bullet had grazed his chin. But when he told this fact to me, he averted his eyes, and I saw something in his face more revealing than the telltale scar. And always, after that, I was watchful.

Had I really ever loved my husband? I think I must have in the beginning, drawn as I had been to his reserve, his anomalous grace, and what I thought, mistaking silence for self-containment, was an appealing dignity. But love, I now know, is an imprecise word, a relative term. I believe you loved your wife, in your way. I believe Stephen thought he loved me.

I waited for the second letter and the third, I learned to listen more keenly for the sound of the mailman's jeep, and I began to anticipate the cream envelopes with the navy-blue ink. I tried to imagine who you were and what you looked like as a grown man, but I could not think beyond the tall, thin boy with the crew cut. I would take the letters you had sent and reread them in my office, trying to extrapolate from the boy, trying to feel who you might be. I wondered what you could remember and how it was you had developed such a clear hand. And in the mornings, before waking, I began to dream of you.

On the day I left for England, I was thinking about meeting you again after all those years. It was late, and I had not finished packing, and I knew that I should concentrate on that activity. Stephen was at the college. I had clothes out on the bed – sweaters and skirts, stockings and a robe. I looked at them and thought: I have to find the picture.

The attic was a cramped crawl space, an alcove into which I tossed things from time to time – the Christmas box, winter quilts, summer quilts – and tidied once a year. I could not stand up in the attic and so made my way, bent over from the waist, to the place where I had stored my trunk. It was a large, heavy wooden trunk that had traveled from Springfield to Dakar and back to this country and to the attic of this farm. In it were letters from my grandmother, scented letters on lavender stationery written in a small hand with purple ink. I had saved the corsages from high school dances, flat brown mementos in waxed paper, with the names of boys attached. There were diaries, ribboned piles of more letters, African sculptures in black wood, a grade school picture in a gold frame, a piece of cloth from Senegal I'd forgotten about, an oval photograph of my mother as a young girl that I took out and dusted off and thought resembled Lily and how I would put it on the piano in the living room for her to see.

Then, at the bottom of the trunk, there was the album of photographs, an album I had put together when I was fourteen. In it were three photographs from the week we had together, and I kept one. You and I are standing in front of the fountain, and again you have your arm around me. But the photographer (who was it, I wonder now – a girlfriend of mine? my mother? a counselor?) has caught us in the act of laughing or of moving apart, and our bodies and our faces are turned away from each other. Your arm is still on my back, and in the picture my eyes are closed, and I am smiling.

When I returned from England and saw the letter waiting for me, I became afraid. Stephen had put it on my desk, unopened. I did not think he would ever open a letter addressed to me, but I could not be certain. Already the correspondence would have been impossible to explain: Why was I writing to you at all?

I wrote you that I wanted it to stop, but I know I hoped you wouldn't hear me.

The package with the tape recorder and the headphones was sitting atop the mailbox, and I thought when I saw it that it must be visible for a hundred miles, even through the thick planking of the barn. I held it cradled in my arm as I walked into the house, thinking: I don't want this, I don't want him to send me gifts.

The photograph alarmed me. You didn't look at all like the boy I had been imagining. Your face was turned to the side. I couldn't see your eyes. You were wearing a windbreaker, and your hair was blowing from what seemed to be a stiff breeze. I could see that you were tall, or possibly, I thought, that was only the angle of the camera. Behind you there was a lighthouse and a cliff.

I hid the tape recorder and the headphones in the drawer with the letters. I went downstairs to make Lily's lunch. I put on my jacket to walk to my neighbor's house to get my daughter.

All the farms backed onto the dirt as onto water – a vast, inky sea. Some houses were not five feet from the black dirt; it seemed to run straight to the foundations, a dark flood. I was still often surprised by the colors of the houses – pink and aqua and mint green – and I thought they must have been painted that way to dispel the monochrome of the landscape. Behind most of the farmhouses there were metal barns in brittle pastels, and in the yards there was often wash on the line. It was a fine day, sharp and clear and cold.

Almost all of the farmers now were Polish. The Rutkowski

farm; the Bogdanski farm; the Sieczek farm; the Krysch farm. St. Stanislaus was the center of the town. When I met Stephen, I had thought the life of farming romantic. I did not know how hard it was – how lonely.

The walk to my neighbor's house took only minutes. By many of the farms there were onion crates stacked like lobster pots. I liked the piles of onions at the edge of the black fields behind the houses; the piles were red and rust and a shiny, tawny yellow in the sunlight. At harvest, the eyes stung for days.

The farms had little privacy. They were exposed to the black plains, a geological accident. I passed an old graveyard with Dutch names, and beyond that a wooden barn in disrepair. Out of sight over the hill was migrant-worker housing – long, low, flat buildings, two windows and a door to each unit, gray cement blocks. Out in front of this housing was a rusted swing set the children never used.

I could not leave the town or Stephen. We had had a boy early, and after he was gone, I didn't think of leaving. Our son was buried in the Polish cemetery behind St. Stanislaus, where we had been married.

Lily was waiting for me with her jacket on, her nose pressed against the glass of the front door. We made the journey back to the house slowly. Lily played as we walked, picked up stones and bottle caps, treasures to save in the pockets of her jacket. She had soft, pale hair from her father, which I liked to feel with my fingers.

I put Lily to bed for a nap and went downstairs to begin the laundry. Stephen was sitting at the kitchen table, in early from the work in the barn. He wore his jacket still, was rubbing his forehead as if there might be another headache coming. I asked him if he wanted lunch. He shook his head no. I sat down, waited.

I saw a package, he said, on the mailbox. I meant to bring it in to you. Did you get it?

I said yes.

What was it? he asked.

Extra books, I said. I looked away.

He said, Oh.

I decided then that I would reseal the package and send it back to you. I thought that I would tell you again that this would have to stop. I tried to tell myself that the consequences might be severe, that already I had committed a kind of betrayal that would not be understood. But I did not reseal the package, and it remained hidden in my desk for days, untouched and unreturned.

On the night before you had asked me to meet you, Stephen was called away to a meeting at the college. I had put Lily to bed. I took the tape recorder and the headphones from the desk drawer and walked with them into the bedroom. It was a small room, in which a double bed was dominant. I had made a quilt, a white quilt with patches of rose and green, to give the room color and light, but it was always dark even so. There was just the one window, which looked out over the black dirt, and on the glass there were rivulets of a fine dust that had been disturbed by the rain.

I can tell you about the bedroom. It doesn't matter now.

I had a glass of wine with me that I had poured after supper. I lay down on the bed, did not turn on the lights. I fumbled with the machine in the dark, plugged the headphones in, put them on. I had never listened to music with headphones before, had never experienced the way the music seems to be inside the brain.

I played the first song, and I smiled. It reminded me of CYO dances as a girl; of dark gymnasiums with loud, slow, dreamy music; of awkward embraces with boys who were often shorter than myself then. Of my face sometimes muffled into a taller boy's shoulder.

I played the second song and sat up in bed. I laughed. I thought: This is a kind of excavation.

I played the third song, and the memories flooded in upon me. A kiss at the nape of the neck. A butterfly.

I played the fourth song, and I began to cry.

HE WAKES for the fifth time and can see, to his relief, by
the faint suggestion of light at the edges of the shade at the
window, that it is finally early morning. He stirs slightly, not
wanting to disturb Harriet, but something in his movements,
the slight tug of the sheet perhaps, makes her turn toward
him, murmuring in her half sleep. He feels then her fingers,
her hand reaching for him, the practiced, sleepy gesture meant
to massage, to bring him along. He sucks his stomach in, shifts
slightly so that he is just beyond her reach, hoping that she is
not yet quite conscious enough to notice this gentle rebuff.
Not this morning.

He studies his wife in the gray light of predawn. She seems
to be burrowing, lying on her stomach with the pink strap of
her nightgown meandering down her shoulder. Her mouth is
pressed open against the sheet; her eyes are still closed. Her
hair is matted against her ear, half hidden by a pillow that
has fallen partly over her head. He watches his wife sleep,
this woman he has lived with for fifteen years, watches her
breathe, and as he does so, he feels again, as he has felt at odd
moments over the past several weeks, the tremulous drag of
guilt, a line snagged with seaweed. In a file cabinet in the room
below the bedroom, there are in a manila folder six letters and
a postcard that could not be easily explained, that are, in their
seeming innocence, as treacherous as motel receipts. Yet he
resists this drag of guilt, knows he cannot afford to let it take
hold of him. Not today, not this morning.

He rolls over, squints at the clock. Nearly six forty-five.
Christ, it has to have been the longest night of his life, and
there are still five hours and fifteen minutes to go. He knows

65

already that the morning is lost to him, held suspended in anticipation: Will she be there? Will she come at all? He has no reason to expect her. She has written that she wants it – the nebulous 'it' they have created only with words – to stop, and he has ignored her. He's done worse than ignore her: He's sent her the goddamn tape!

He slips out from between the sheets, walks naked into the bathroom. The tile floor is ice against the soles of his feet, the air so frigid he begins almost immediately to shiver. He minds that he pays six hundred dollars a month for heat and can still see his breath in the morning. He turns on the shower, watches as clouds of steam boil over and around the plastic curtain. His face in the mirror disappears; the bathroom fills with mist. He steps into the shower, adjusts the water temperature so that it is just below scalding. He turns, bends his head, lets the water pummel the back of his neck.

It has not, he knows, been an innocent correspondence. In the beginning he tried to tell himself that it was harmless, simply intriguing, but he knew, even then, that from the very first sentence of the very first note, there was nothing innocent about it. If he wrote her, as he had, that he had the same feeling looking at her picture as he had when he first saw her in the courtyard of The Ridge thirty-one years ago, what did that imply? And although he has not permitted himself to think of Siân Richards sexually – he cannot, despite his childhood memories, despite the temptation, for to do so might allow the 'it' to spiral out of control – he knows that however chaste his thinking is, it is not innocent. Not to have told his wife, to have shielded Siân's picture with his elbow, was to have given the 'it' a life. He remembers sitting in the car at the beach that rainy Sunday afternoon, drafting and redrafting that first letter, trying to strike just the right chord, find the right tone – a tone somewhere between revelatory and careful

– and how he waited for days after that, convinced that the letter had been lost in the mailroom of her publisher, that it had not been forwarded after all.

But then she had replied. He remembers still the delicate blue surprise of that letter, how his hand trembled as he withdrew the envelope with the unfamiliar hand from the postbox, how he sat outside in his car and opened it and read the letter, not once but many times, before he was calm enough to start the Cadillac and move away from the post office. Her handwriting was tiny, cramped, with the capitals strangely pointed, and he had to look at several words twice or three times before he could decipher them. But she had used the word 'delighted,' had remembered him as Cal. And at the end of the letter she had all but invited him to write to her again: If he knew what she looked like and what she did for a living, she said, oughtn't he then to tell her what he looked like and what he did for a living?

He got her letter on the twenty-fifth of September, had responded the next day. And then there was what seemed like an interminable wait for a subsequent letter. Each day he went to the post office, looked for the small, cramped penmanship. He thought of what he had written her, became convinced that something he said had put her off. Perhaps he'd been too forward, too bold. Too suggestive. Once, telling Harriet he had business in Boston, he got into the Cadillac and drove across Connecticut and New York and into Pennsylvania, to the town on the return address of Siân's envelope. He had no intention of making an unannounced visit; he simply wanted to see where she lived, as though from that he might derive more clues as to whom she had become. He knew, even as he was making the drive, that he was behaving like a teenager, not a grown man with a wife and three children, but he was unable convincingly to talk himself out of making the journey. (He thinks now, standing in the shower, perhaps that was the point of the trip after all: He was reliving something he hadn't been able to do as a teenager – the bike ride across three states.)

The trip through Connecticut and New York was exhilarating. He had Roy on the tape player and another tape he'd bought in September, in search of the song he remembered at the beach, a tape of golden oldies from what he had already come to think of as 'their' era, and the day was fine. Crisp and golden, pure fall.

But he wasn't at all prepared for the sight of her town, stranded, it seemed from his vantage point as he followed the map across the border and over the mountain, amidst a vast black desert. He knew only from the poems that what he saw had to be the 'black dirt' she wrote of; if it wasn't for the poetry, he'd have thought he'd spun off into the surreal, that the land west of the small mountain was sealed with tar, that he'd somehow stumbled upon a foreign landing strip. He descended the winding road cautiously and drove straight into the town, and as he did so he felt the exhilaration of the journey dissipating. The light over the black dirt was unearthly and pale, and even though the sun still shone, the houses looked washed out or smudged. He decided then that the effect was created by the blackness of the soil; the light was sucked up, he thought, swallowed by the dirt itself.

In the center of the small village was a dark Catholic church with a parking lot to one side and a cemetery in the back. Opposite the church was a row of storefronts – a video store, an uninviting bar with faded blue curtains covering the windows, a real estate agency, and a restaurant, The Onion Inn. He had a sandwich there, asked the waitress if she could direct him to the street he was looking for. He wondered, while he ate his sandwich at the bar of the inn, if he would know Siân Richards if she walked in now, if when their eyes met she would know him. He'd been replaying various scenarios for days, imagining their first encounter after thirty-one years. Sometimes he imagined kissing her before he even spoke to her. He examined every woman in the restaurant – those at the tables, those who entered while he sat there – but none of them remotely resembled Siân. He didn't know what he'd do if he did encounter her that afternoon. She'd have thought him deranged if she knew he'd driven more than four hours just to see the town in which she lived. And almost certainly that information would have frightened her off. Yet it was all he could do to refrain from asking the waitress if she was familiar with the name.

He followed the waitress's directions to the address he had asked about. The road wasn't hard to find; there were only three leading from the village – one to the north of the onion fields, one to the south, and one that seemed to bisect the dark desert like a canal. Hers was to the north, the farms arranged along it as along a shoreline. He drove by the house twice before he realized it was the address he wanted: The number was hidden from view behind a post on the front porch. It was a gray house with black shutters, a farmhouse with an ell. Out on the front lawn was an ancient elm, its leaves this time of year just beginning to catch fire. He saw, in the three or four times he passed the house after he realized which was hers, that there were white curtains at each of the windows, that the red barn in the back belonged to the farmhouse, and that there was a flower garden at the side. To the other side was a massive yellow tractor in the driveway. Each time he passed the house he slowed the car down and held his breath, wanting to see a woman and yet not wanting at all to see a woman, but there was no activity as he came and went – not a movement behind a window, not a child playing in the yard, not a man walking toward the barn. He'd wondered where she was, what precisely she was doing then.

Later, after he'd driven the other roads leading from the village and had seen all there was to see of the town – primarily other farmhouses, most of which had been painted in odd, pastel colors that seemed to obliterate whatever charm the buildings might intrinsically have had in some previous era – he crossed another small mountain in order to reach the university, and he had thought that the bleakness of the valley, however dispiriting (but was it bleakness, he wondered, or was it simply the fear of being swallowed up by the black dirt oneself?), was somehow encouraging: If he had discovered Siân Richards living in a pretty village, on a sunlit street, with a Volvo station wagon in the driveway and a ten-speed Motobecane on a front porch (or, worse, in an imposing fortress on Manhattan's East Side, with a doorman out front and a Porsche in a garage somewhere down below), might he not have felt more inhibited in his pursuit of their much-imagined reunion? And yet he had to concede as well that possibly Siân Richards was perfectly happy at her farm and in her marriage, that the despair suggested in her poetry – the suggestion of pinched lives – did not come from her own circumstances but was a metaphor for something larger, which he might better grasp if he knew more about poetry.

The university was a small one in population, though it did have a large agricultural school, and it was through fallow fields that Charles drove to reach the main campus. Classes were in session that day, and he wondered if Siân was there, teaching. He hadn't seen a car of any kind in the driveway of her house. He walked a series of footpaths under bare trees and between red-brick buildings until he had crisscrossed most of the central campus. Girls in thick sweaters and boys in neon parkas looked at him as they passed by. He studied each older woman he encountered – hopeful and panicky at once that he might stumble upon her. Occasionally his own years at Holy Cross came back to him. He was certain, when he left finally (too late to make it home in time for dinner, and he had to compose yet another lie in the car), that he had not come face-to-face with Siân Richards, though it was easier to imagine her there, on that campus, than it was to envision her in the gray house by the onion fields.

After that day, he developed a habit of going to the post office three, four times a day in search of a blue envelope in his box. For weeks, it seemed, there was nothing, and then finally she wrote him. Hers, he thought, was an odd correspondence, one that was, at its heart, not always easy to decipher. Sometimes she seemed encouraging; at other times, occasionally even in the same letter, she appeared to withdraw. It was a kind of feinting: a touch here, then a retreat. His own correspondence to her, he was certain, was not difficult to read. He was pushing her, he knew, even at the risk that she might close up altogether. He thought that he had taken a terrible leap by describing the 'awful loneliness' of her poetry, but she hadn't seemed to mind that. And sometimes he thought he detected humor in her letters, as when she echoed his comment about her husband in her comment about his wife, or when she said thanks, but she wouldn't need a chaperone. (He imagined – hoped for? – a dry wit.) Yet she could unnerve him as well. She said that he would be disappointed when he met her. What did 'disappointed' mean? he wondered for days.

And just at the point when he was poised to suggest the where and when of a meeting, she wrote that she was leaving for England. He was thrown into the unreasonable confusion of a teenage boy. It occurred to him when he got that letter that something was seriously wrong with him; it (again, the nebulous 'it' they'd created – *he'd* created – only with words) was merely a fantasy, a figment of his imagination. How could he miss a woman he'd never even met? He'd met the child, the girl, but he couldn't say, in any lucid moment, that he knew the woman. And yet he remembers vividly the night he got her letter, how he walked outside into the backyard and looked up at the night sky with all its stars and imagined a jet taking her to England. And he wrote the next day that he missed her already. Surely that was madness.

But then there was the letter with the photograph, the one she found and sent to him before her plane was leaving. He'd been moved by the picture – it was one thing to remember himself as a child with her as a child; it was quite another actually to see the two of them together, with his arm around her, her eyes cast down, the two children clearly in the throes of some charged emotion – yet even more moved by the way in which she'd written about the photograph, by the very fact that she'd had to find the picture at all. Yes, it did mean that once they had been together, that she was, after all, just as he had imagined her. But didn't it also mean that she had needed to see some tangible proof as well?

From that he took encouragement and wrote her the longest letter, the one in which he told her he'd once fallen in love at first sight and that something similar may have happened when he saw her photograph three decades later; that he was looking for an 'open connection'; that he wanted to hold her hand. And she wrote that she wanted him to stop. He had no choice then but to push blindly ahead, to ignore her request. He was, after all, a salesman. He had to be able to see her again.

Yet even so, he doesn't know if she will come today. It was risky to have arbitrarily set a day and time: What if she has a class? What if she's already arranged to be in the city with her publisher? He knows, however, that he has at least to try to meet her, to try to bring the 'it' to fruition. He can no longer focus on his work; he hasn't been able to concentrate on his business for weeks now. He cannot somehow put aside the notion that meeting this woman is the single most important task he must accomplish, and he hopes (or is it that he fears?) that seeing her will somehow take the edge off – that Siân Richards in the flesh will dispel the fantasies he has created.

He emerges from the shower, and the tune and the words are still with him. He hums a bit, takes it to the end. The song is with him all the time now, sometimes as a repeated melody, sometimes as a code he cannot entirely crack. He knows he has sung it silently hundreds of times since September. After that afternoon at the beach, the afternoon when he first heard its echoes floating across thirty-one years, he sought it out, found it finally, as more phrases came back to him, on an old album in a secondhand-record store. The familiar rendition, he discovered, was by Dion & The Belmonts (he ought to have known that), but he is aware now that there have been many other versions, and he has unearthed some of them. The song is old, 1937, Rodgers and Hart. He remembers playing the 45 endlessly as a boy (that and its flip side, 'That's My Desire') during the era he met Siân Richards – the song hit the charts in the summer of 1960, the summer they met at camp. He is puzzled now, however, by how the boy he was can have interpreted the lyrics, can have understood them at all, apart from the sense of pure longing. They seem almost to require the mystery of loss and rediscovery – states of being he can't possibly have been familiar with at fourteen.

Beyond his humming he can hear activity in the house. Harriet will be up now, will be negotiating the children through their breakfast. He wonders, not for the first time in the past several weeks, how his wife can have failed to notice his distraction. He hasn't slept or eaten well in days. He wipes the mirror of condensation, peers at his reflection. He looks like shit. His eyes are bloodshot from lack of sleep, the skin below them is wrinkled; he has bags under his eyes for the first time in his life. His hair is thinning, considerably more gray than brown now. He thinks of the tall boy with the crew cut in the photograph, the promise of that boy. Christ, couldn't this have happened to him when he was thirty-five, when he had all his hair and a flatter stomach? He looks more closely into the mirror, sees the beginning of a pimple under his cheekbone. That's all he needs. He shaves carefully, puts a Stridex tab on the incipient pimple. He brushes his teeth twice. He has planned to wear his gray suit, wonders now if that mightn't be too conservative. No, he'll stick with the gray suit, a white shirt, a dark tie. Keep it simple.

When he enters the kitchen, Harriet is at the counter, making school lunches; Hadley is thoughtfully working her way through an English muffin. She has a textbook open beside her. She is the only one of the three children who resembles him — wide brown eyes, prominent ears, straight teeth, slightly off center, light brown hair as his once was. He feels the guilt again, the seaweed. He pours himself a cup of coffee, sits across from Hadley. He asks her what she's reading; she looks up at him and answers, Geography, a test. Like him, Hadley has always been an early riser and even as a small child dressed herself and was down for breakfast before any of the others. He thinks of her, too, as the most responsible of the three, though that might simply be her age. He cannot say, however, that he loves her more than he loves the other two; he has never been able to compartmentalize his love like that, to feel more for one than for the others. His love for them is of a piece, and that is how he thinks of it — a vast, diffuse, protective warmth that surrounds and envelops all of them.

Harriet asks him from the counter what his day will be like, a question she asks him nearly every morning so as to determine better the shape of her own day, and he tells her, as he has rehearsed, that he will be away in Boston, two clients and a late lunch, and as he does so it seems to him that his voice thins out, that the sentences sound not only rehearsed but also blatantly untruthful. He watches for a sign that she has perceived the falsehood – a shift of her head, a tensing of her shoulders – but instead she deftly slices three sandwiches, packs them into plastic bags. He is aware of the heat in his face, and when he turns to Hadley he sees that she is staring at him. He smiles at her, takes a sip of coffee.

'I'm off, then,' he says. 'Just get some papers.'

He pushes his chair into the table, bends over and kisses his daughter. Harriet does not turn around. Some years ago he gave up the custom of kissing his wife when he left the house. He cannot now remember what year it was, though he remembers well the morning he decided to forgo the ritual. He had passed through the kitchen and was standing at the door when he realized he could not possibly walk the seven or eight steps to his wife at the sink, could not experience again the reflexive and pursed pecking at the mouth, their bodies not touching, as if they were birds, or distant, strained siblings. And oddly, though he watched for some sign of unease on her part and was prepared to resume the custom if she pressed him, she seemed not to mind the lapse at all, nor even to notice that they no longer touched outside of the bedroom. He sometimes wonders guiltily what messages they are giving their children by never being demonstrative, but it seems to him a small, forgivable parental transgression that he lacks the will to do much about now.

He leaves the kitchen and walks into the office, the old front room, a room now swimming in papers, unopened boxes, and electronic equipment, a room too small to absorb the contents of the building he once called his office and has now irretrievably lost. He puts a sheaf of random papers into a briefcase, tucks his briefcase under his arm, walks again through the kitchen. He takes his topcoat from a clothes tree in the corner and watches as Harriet turns, gives a small wave with her hand. Have a good day, she says, and smiles, and he says back to her, You too. He does not look again at his daughter.

Outside, the day is gray and raw, not unusual for the first week of December, but disappointing to Charles, who has wanted sunshine, some bright omen. He has planned his route – west on 95, north on 7 – and it should take him just under three hours. He'll be there before ten, but that's all right. He needs to see the place, walk around, gather his wits before she comes.

He puts a tape, *the* tape, into the tape deck. He's made a duplicate of the one he sent Siân. He has in his office dozens of rejects – tapes on which the sequence wasn't perfect, on which there were gaps that weren't acceptable, on which he'd put songs he decided wouldn't do after all. At first he was tickled by the project, then he became obsessed. He sequestered himself each evening in his study with his turntable and his tape player, listening to albums and 45s he'd found in old-record stores, sifting through his own albums. He spent hours with his Sony in quiet bars, hunting down old tunes on jukeboxes. Astonishingly Harriet did not ask him once what he was doing in his study in the evenings (what can she possibly have thought of the music emanating from the room night after night?), though she has mentioned once or twice that she is concerned about his 'stress level.'

Then he actually sent the tape, the small player, and the headphones. It was the most reckless gesture of all, one he regretted the minute he watched Harry Noonan behind the counter at the post office toss it into the Priority Mail bucket. He expected the box back unopened almost immediately, dreaded going to the post office each day and finding the little pink slip announcing that there was a package waiting for him. He was positive, too, that the picture he sent along with the package, the picture of him holding the fish, was going to backfire. It was a terrible picture, but it was the only one he could find that showed him alone – without one of his children or Harriet.

He listens to the first song on the tape, Dion's 'A Teenager in Love.' He has tried, in the correspondence, for a tone of lightheartedness, and he sent the tape in the same vein, though he is certain – and he suspects this has been all too obvious to her as well – that his entire life hangs in the balance of her response. He *has* felt like a schoolboy, a teenager, with a teenager's innocence and longing.

He is confident, too, though he understands this less well, that she has been there all along, all through the years, a kind of subterranean rhythm or current. He knows this because he has always favored women who looked like Siân – tall, small-breasted, blondish (and it has often puzzled him that he married a woman so unlike this image) – and he knows Siân was the first, the antecedent. And her name, her strange Welsh name, has bubbled up into his consciousness over the years, often when he has least expected it. In college, he roomed for a year with a boy named Shane, and he frequently slipped and called him Sean, the spelling different but the pronunciation the same as hers. He remembers, also, a client he had seven or eight years ago, a Susan Wain, and how he twice addressed correspondence to her, Dear Sian, without the accent, somehow transposing letters subconsciously from the last name to the first, but again echoing the antecedent. He hadn't realized his mistake until the client pointed it out to him.

He knows as well that through the years he has been drawn to things Welsh, a subconscious draw, as if one were trying to find something lost in childhood – a piece of music, the shape of a room, the way the light once filtered through a certain window. He remembers reading Dylan Thomas and Chatwin's *On the Black Hill* not too long ago, and another book, Jan Morris's *The Matter of Wales*, and deciding that if he ever got to Europe he might begin with Wales and then make his way south to Portugal. (Though when he drives to the beach and looks out, he never imagines looking at Wales – it's too far *north*, he thinks.) He will have to ask her, but he thinks he has remembered this correctly, that she has a Welsh father and had an Irish mother, both first-generation immigrants after World War II, and though there was no lilt in her own voice, as there was in her father's (he remembers the father's accent vividly from that phone call he made when he had returned home from college: the strange vowels, the crescendo and sudden swift fall in the rhythm of the sentences), it was evident, looking at her (particularly on that first day at camp and, more recently, even in the photograph in the newspaper), that she had Celtic origins. It is in the shape of the mouth possibly, or in the high forehead, or perhaps it is the eyes with their pale eyebrows.

The second song is on now: 'Angel Baby,' Rosie & The Originals. He loves Rosie's nasal twang, is not sure they ever had another hit. Great slow beat on this one, though. For months after they left each other at camp, he and Siân corresponded. He wonders if she might still have those old letters – hers to him, he knows, were lost when his parents' basement was flooded and everything that had been stored there for him was destroyed. He doesn't now know why the correspondence ended; he suspects it began to seem more and more hopeless as the months wore on. He had thought and planned endlessly, he remembers, to find a way to see her again, and these adolescent schemes now seem comical and sad to him. However was a fourteen-year-old boy to make his way across three states to see his girlfriend? At that age, one was a prisoner of one's parents. He certainly had no car, did not even know anyone with a car except for people his parents' age, none of whom was likely to drive him to Springfield, Massachusetts, from Bristol, Rhode Island. If only he and Siân had met at sixteen, when seeing her again, seeing her continuously over the years, might have been possible.

He turns up the volume. He loves this one: 'That's My Desire.' He waits each time for the falsetto at the end, sometimes tries to imitate it himself. He remembers as vividly as if it were yesterday the agony of that final and irrevocable separation, the anticipation of that separation all that last morning of camp and, indeed, even the entire day before. If one week at camp were the experiential equivalent of a lifetime together, then the last day and a half has to have taken on, in the savoring of each minute, the totality of years.

He woke that last morning with a strange feeling in his stomach, a mixture of dread and guilt and deep sexual excitement. (Odd how clearly he can remember this – more clearly, it seems to him, than more recent events, from college or from seminary, or even from the early years of his marriage.) He'd had a counselor (what was his name?) who played 45s on a turntable in the boys' dorm. Johnny Mathis at night to soothe the overheated psyches of adolescent boys; The Silhouettes and The Shirelles in the morning to wake them up. 'Get a Job' was on that morning. He'd woken after a restless night, a night full of wild dreams and schemes, as if he were a prisoner of war planning their escape – his and Siân's. He imagined hiding in the woods until all the parents had left, and then he and Siân would get on a bus. He had no idea where the bus might take them – he hadn't been able quite to make that work, and that was the point at which he'd begun to panic: Where could they go? What would they do for money? How long could they hide out from their parents or from the police? He smiles now to think of that boy, of his frantic and desperate imaginings.

He met her that morning in the dining hall. They'd sat at the same table all week. She was next to him, the bracelet on her wrist. She didn't speak. He remembers that she was wearing Bermuda shorts and a white blouse, a sleeveless blouse. Neither of them could eat. She'd pushed her eggs around; he hadn't even been able to do that. He'd sat with his fork in his hand, unable to speak to her in front of the others, unable to move. He wanted to touch the bracelet on her wrist, touch the hairs on her arm. To his right, on the other side of him, was his counselor (what *was* his name?), a big guy with a crew cut and a short-sleeved dress shirt that showed his muscles. They'd had to wear white shirts, he remembers that. He also remembers that his counselor had seemed unreasonably happy that morning, and Charles (Cal then) had formed an instant and lasting hatred for the man.

(It strikes him suddenly, as he engages the cruise control in his car, that the counselor was probably only a kid, a college kid then, someone he'd now think of as a child, and that at this point in time the man has to be in his early fifties at least.)

There was a blue plaid tablecloth on the table, heavy white crockery at each place. Prayers were said before the meal, and then again at the end. Siân had pushed her chair back; Charles was paralyzed with confusion. All he could think was that he and she would never share a meal together again. Very shortly they would never do anything together again at all. He had to be with her, had to be alone with her again, before they said goodbye.

He stood and asked her if she had packed. She said yes, looked down at her feet. She was wearing sneakers, he remembers, and no socks. Though she was tall, she had small feet. White sneakers. White Keds.

All week he had been with this girl as he had never been with anyone before – not his mother, not his father, not his best friend, Billy Cowan. How could he allow this person to be taken away from him? And why could he find no words at that moment to tell her what he felt, what he wanted?

And then she'd spoken, a miracle, a deft slip through the knot of his inexperience: Would he like to play badminton? she had asked. They could skip chapel just the once on this last day and play badminton before the parents came, before they had to leave. Just the two of them . . .

There it is now. 'Where or When.' *The* song. (Their song?) He'd planned it fourth, like a clean-up batter. The song is sung almost entirely a cappella. He listens to the whole of it, rewinds the tape, plays it again, as he almost always does. He plays the entire tape (fifteen songs) twice through, then turns the tape deck off. He chooses silence over the radio. He cannot focus on the news and doesn't want to hear any other music just now. He hasn't been able to read a newspaper in days, hasn't watched a television program with any kind of concentration since he saw her picture. He has to get this meeting over with, he knows, if only to return to some kind of normalcy.

He follows the map, the directions that were sent to him from The Ridge. The town in which the inn is located is in northwestern Connecticut, close to the New York border. He finds the town, drives with the directions between his thumb and the steering wheel. The town itself is a New England classic, recently refurbished, he suspects, during the boom of the eighties, the broad High Street lined with eighteenth-century three-story houses, all white, all with black shutters, all set back from the street, with well-manicured lawns leading to the front porches. (From force of habit, he counts the number of For Sale signs – seven in five blocks.) The inn, however, is at the outskirts of town, on the edge of a private lake. He discovers the road just south of the town park. A discreet sign indicating The Ridge with an arrow – carved gold letters on dark green – tells him that he's made the correct turn. He hopes that Siân, too, will see the small sign.

The houses dwindle in number as he drives; the inn appears to be at least five miles from the village center. The day is still damp and overcast, though not as chilly as it was earlier in the morning. Driving through town, he noticed a liquor store and a deli. After he locates The Ridge, he wants to pick up a bottle of champagne, a six-pack, and some ice. He has the cooler in the trunk, put it there last night after Harriet went to bed. He is not quite sure exactly how this will work, but he somehow envisions himself and Siân sharing a glass of champagne together on the grounds of The Ridge, or possibly in his car, before they go in to lunch. He would rather meet her that way, would rather have a drink alone with her, than greet her for the first time in a formal dining room, with waiters hovering.

He reaches the end of the road, comes to a stone wall with an open wrought-iron gate. Another sign in green and gold announces that he has arrived. He turns into a twisting drive of brick herringbone. Bare plane trees line the drive at precisely spaced intervals.

He has always known that the mansion and the grounds, before they were an inn or a camp, were privately held. He remembers now that the money came from shoes in the 1920s and that the last owner, sometime in the early 1950s, died and willed it to the Catholic Church. He wonders if the church owns the inn.

The long drive takes him through a thicket of birches, then opens to a panorama of the main house itself, behind a maze of formal gardens. He slows the car to a stop.

It's exactly the same. Nothing ever stays the same, he is thinking, but somehow this has done so. Amazingly, astonishingly, the estate is as he has remembered it.

He puts the car in gear, slips it into a parking space at the side of the inn. With some difficulty, as if he had suddenly aged, he steps from the car.

The house is a well-proportioned three-story building in gray stone, with wings to either side. The roof is slate, a greenish-gray, and the shutters at the windows are a faded pale blue, so faded and so pale they seem almost colorless, and he remembers with a clarity that startles him that they were nearly colorless even then, when the estate was a camp. They remind him now, as they cannot have reminded him then, of the shutters on French country houses in paintings and in photographs. The wings of the house are set at an angle so that they embrace a center courtyard of square, hand-cut stones. Frost and time have heaved some of the stones, and wisely no one has tampered with the uneven surface. In the center of the courtyard is the fountain – a patinaed bronze well with a graceful arc of water into which he tossed pennies and wishes as a child.

There are no signs in the courtyard or at the front door, nothing to indicate that the camp of his memories has been transformed into an inn.

He looks out to the west wing, where the boys slept. He can see his room, the fourth window to the left on the top floor. He shared it with three other boys. A waiter in a black tuxedo emerges from the front door, nods at Charles, and makes his way across the courtyard to a door at the end of the east wing. A gust of wind comes from behind Charles, makes a swirl of dry leaves eddy in a corner. At a window on the second floor of the east wing, a curtain is drawn.

Charles hikes the collar of his navy wool coat, puts his hands into his pockets. A wash of light, the sun through a break in the clouds, moves swiftly across the facade of the house, then disappears.

The girl arrived first. She had her parents with her and one hard blue suitcase. She held the suitcase in front of her with two hands and walked from the car to the courtyard, where she had been told to go. She put the suitcase down beside her and stood near the front door, on the uneven stones. Her parents, curious, wanted to explore and left her alone. She herself was not anxious to explore; she knew that by evening the place would be known to her. She held her hands loosely clasped and stood quietly, watching the others arrive with their parents. She was wearing a blue dress, a thin cotton dress that fell just below her knees. She had worn the dress because her mother had insisted, but as she watched the others enter the courtyard, she saw that the girls were dressed in shorts and sleeveless blouses. Her hair, which was long that summer, was pulled back into a ponytail, yet even so, she was uncomfortably warm. It was the beginning of summer, midday, and the sun beat down upon the courtyard. Overhead, the sky was a deep blue and cloudless. She was wishing that all the parents would leave so that she could change her clothes. She was thinking about a swim. There was a lake, she had been told, and a pool, and even if the lake was not for swimming, she knew it would be cooler down by the water's edge.

When the boy arrived, he, too, was carrying his own suitcase, though he was tall enough and strong enough to hold it in one hand. He walked to the center of the courtyard, his parents behind him. His mother wore red lipstick and sunglasses with white frames. Her dress had a wide white collar, and she was having trouble on the stones with her high heels. His father was a tall man, with broad shoulders beneath his suit coat and a summer tan on his face and neck and wrists. His mother lit a cigarette, and even from across the courtyard, she could see the red lipstick mark on the mother's cigarette. The mother examined the families in the courtyard and turned to her husband with commentary behind her white-gloved hand. The boy stood still, in the center of the courtyard. He had on a white shirt, the sleeves rolled to the elbows, and a pair of black chinos. He wore black shoes, dress shoes, the sort a boy then would wear to mass. He had his hands in the pockets of his pants, and on his wrist she saw the silver glint of a watchband. There were perhaps twenty or thirty other people in the courtyard.

When he turned his head in her direction and looked at her for the first time, she did not glance away. He had soft brown eyes and a crew cut, and like his father, he had a summer tan. Her own face, she knew, was white; her skin would not brown no matter how much oil she used. The boy looked at the girl for a long time, and she thought that possibly he smiled – a shy, nervous, unpracticed smile. He looked at the girl for so long that his mother noticed and turned to see who or what had caught her son's attention. And when the mother examined the girl – a frank stare of examination – the girl blushed finally and turned her head away.

Years later, I looked in the mirror and I thought: I cannot let him see this aging body.

In Africa, the sun had scalded my skin and left a residue of spots and wrinkles. I had a belly with a scar from a caesarean.

My breasts were small, they had always been small, but there was no girl left; I had nursed two babies. My hair was graying at the sides.

Sometimes, when I was with you, I felt betrayed by my body.

When I drove to The Ridge, I played the tape loudly to drown out my imaginings. When I came into the parking lot, 'Crying' was on, announcing me.

I saw the building with the blue shutters, and I thought: We were only children.

I emerged from my car, and I noticed, across the parking lot, a large American car, the sort of car I would not know, might not ever look at. The door opened, and a man got out. He had on a navy coat, a dark suit. His hair was graying, thinning at the top. His face had an elegant line. His body seemed elongated, and his gestures, as he shut the door, were poised. I was thinking of photographs of T. S. Eliot and of Scott Fitzgerald. I was thinking: Someone from another era, another decade.

The man looked at me, and I turned away.

Down at the lake, the wind rippled the water so that it appeared to be moving, one large body of water, like a river, moving. The lake was gray, and the sky; the trees had lost their leaves.

We sat on the wooden bench in our coats, side by side, and watched the water moving. And it seemed to us that what we saw that day was time.

I T I S O N E M I N U T E P A S T N O O N when the small black car –
a Volkswagen Rabbit? – makes its way along the drive. The
car executes what seems to be a practiced turn into the parking
lot, comes to an abrupt stop. It *is* a VW, perhaps five years old.
A woman is behind the wheel – a woman his age, and he has
just the briefest sense of prettiness, in her profile, in her chin
– and his heart leaps. But from her short, quick gestures as
she emerges from the car, snaps the door to, and locks it, he
thinks: Someone who works here, the hostess perhaps. He
opens his own door, turns toward the VW, and stands, but
the woman's face and body are a blur as she spins away from
him. She wears a long black coat over what appears to be a suit,
and she has on dark glasses despite the overcast day. He can see
black high heels, a pocketbook slung over her shoulder. The
hair may be the right color, though – a kind of dark blond
with just a hint of red – and the woman wears it up, pinned
back at the nape of her neck. It could conceivably be she, he
thinks. He watches as she walks without much hesitation to
the entrance of the inn. She disappears inside the building.

The heavy door opens to a long foyer tiled in black and
white squares, in the center of which is a highly polished
wooden staircase. He remembers the staircase now; it was on
its wide steps each night that the entire camp, the children and
the counselors, assembled for an event called 'Stairway Sing'
just before bedtime.

He opens large glass French doors to the left and to the
right of the foyer and finds unoccupied sitting rooms. He then
remembers that the dining room is at the top of the stairs; his
memory is jogged when he hears sounds tinkling down the

stairway. He climbs the stairs, his hand on the banister, a serious knot beginning in his stomach.

On the landing, he is aware of an abundance of brass and wood, thick white paint, massive bouquets of freesias and lilies, a rose Oriental at his feet. A small, thin man in a tuxedo offers to take his coat. As Charles turns obligingly, pulling his arm from the sleeve, he sees her standing by the maître d's desk. She is watching him speculatively, making no sign or gesture to commit herself. She has on a black suit with a white blouse, a silk blouse with soft folds along its deep neckline. He can see the bones of her clavicle, and a thin gold chain around her neck. She has on her sunglasses still, but he recognizes the gold earrings, simple circles, heavy gold circles at her earlobes.

'Siân?'

His voice cracks slightly on the name, as if he has not spoken in some time. He clears his throat.

She tilts her head.

'Charles?'

She takes the dark glasses off, allowing his scrutiny. Her eyes are nearly navy, with flecks of gold, and he remembers that now, the contrast, almost startling, of the dark eyes with the pale skin. There are wrinkles at the corners of her eyes and below them, but her forehead is unlined – high and white and unlined. He pauses at her mouth.

'I'd have worn the bracelet,' she says, 'as a sign. But I ran out of time and couldn't find it.'

She smiles, her lips together, and tilts her head again, as if questioning him, or waiting. She is tall in her heels, nearly as tall as he is. He supposes she is five nine, five ten in stocking feet, the length of her, he can see at once, in her legs. The skirt she is wearing is simple and straight, falling slightly above the knee.

But her voice is new to him. As he knows his must be to her. In their voices they must be strangers. He wonders if his voice had already changed when he met her, or was changing that summer. Her voice is deeper than he expected. She speaks slowly.

'I didn't need the bracelet,' he says.

It seems she smiles again, glances in the direction of the maître d', who has been waiting behind Charles. Charles, feeling that he must gather himself together and take charge somehow, gives the man his name, says nonsmoking when he is asked, then wonders. He turns to her, but she shakes her head. He thinks of his mother, smoking in automobiles with the windows shut tight. He waits while she puts the dark glasses into her pocketbook, takes out another pair of glasses, clear glasses with thin wire frames. She removes them from their case and puts them on. He did not know she wore glasses, and he tries to remember if she had them when they were children. Thinks now that she may have, though she almost never wore them.

He follows her through the dining room, his breathing tight, his heart missing beats. Other diners look up at her when she passes, in the way that people notice a tall woman walking through a room. The maître d' leads them to a banquette against one wall. He pulls the table out, gestures for her to sit. Charles sits beside her, turning his body slightly in her direction. He lays his arm along the back cushion of the banquette. She seems uneasy with the side-by-side arrangement, crosses her legs. Her skirt rides up slightly on her thigh. He allows his eyes momentarily to fall on the span between her knee and the hemline of her skirt. Her stockings are sheer, with a dark tint. He orders a Stoli martini, bone dry, with a twist, and wishes he could inject it. She orders a glass of wine.

'The tape,' she says. 'At first I didn't want it. I didn't want you to be sending me things. But last night I listened to it finally. It was . . .'

She stops, unable to find the word.

He waits, and when she doesn't finish the sentence, he says, 'It was meant to be lighthearted. A joke. Kind of.'

He thinks it may have been partially intended as light-hearted, but he knows, and he knows she knows, its true intent was something larger and deeper.

'I hadn't heard any of those songs in years,' she says.

'They . . .' She puts her fingers to the gold chain at her neck. 'It was a kind of excavation. I felt it as that.' She looks down, as if she may already have said too much.

'This is very strange,' she says.

'It certainly is.'

'Can you remember it? What do you remember?'

'I remember some things,' he says. 'Some things very vividly. Other parts are a blur now.'

A waiter arrives with the drinks. Charles picks up his glass, swirls the ice, takes a swallow. He watches as she brings her glass to her lips, pauses, then looks at him. She moves her glass in his direction.

'To . . . ?'

He does not hesitate. 'Reunions,' he says.

'And time passing,' she adds, nearly as quickly.

He nods. He catches her eyes as they both simultaneously take sips of their drinks. When they are finished, he says, recklessly: 'To the next thirty-one years.'

She seems startled. As if there were no reply to this.

She surveys the room. 'I was surprised,' she says, 'that the place is so unchanged. I thought somehow it would be different.'

He studies her profile, the same profile he saw briefly in the car. It has always intrigued him how much one can tell about a person with one quick glance at a profile – age mostly, also weight, sometimes ethnic background. Her profile is classic, but she is not a classic beauty, he thinks, and he suspects she probably never was, the forehead too high, the eyebrows too pale. Yet he is certain he has never seen a more arresting mouth. And he doesn't know if this is because it is a feature he has remembered all these years, the prototype by which he subconsciously judged others; would he find it so if he met her today for the first time? Her neck is long and white. Closer to her now, he can see that there are small discolorations, like freckles but not, on the backs of her hands and inside the neckline of her blouse. Her nails are cut short, unpainted. Like him, she wears a wedding ring.

He examines the dining room with her. To one side are floor-to-ceiling windows that, he knows from memory, give onto a sloping lawn leading down to the lake. The windows are arched at the top and let in a diffuse light that spreads across the room. The ceiling is high, vaulted, with fading cherubs depicted in blue-and-peach mosaics. He remembers now that there were jokes at dinner about the naked cherubs. When they were children, they ate at refectory tables – eight, ten, twelve to a table. The chairs scraped the floor. Now there are banquettes against the south wall, small dining tables covered with heavy damask linen, upholstered chairs in red-and-white-striped silk. There are white flowers in delicate vases on each of the tables.

'Do you suppose the food is any good?' she asks.

'It can't help but be an improvement over what we ate when we were here last.'

She smiles.

'It was actually kind of a classy camp, I think now,' he says. 'As camps go.'

'Yes, it was,' she answers. 'Though I don't suppose we knew enough then to appreciate the fact.'

'I don't think I noticed much of anything then,' he says, 'apart from you.'

He lets his hand slip off the banquette cushion and rest on her shoulder, the shoulder closest to him, and as he does so he can feel her stiffen. The touch to him is momentous, charged, the first touch since he last saw her. Of course, she is a stranger to him, a woman he has known only minutes; and yet he is certain he has known the girl forever.

He removes his hand.

He wonders, briefly, if she might be reticent about physical love, and then he has, almost simultaneously, another thought, an unwelcome one, a way to measure out the time lost, the thirty-one years, the measurement being the sum total of all the sexual experiences she has had, all the boyfriends, all the nights with her husband. The realization buffets him, makes him slightly ill, so that when she speaks, he has to ask her to repeat the sentence.

'Tell me about your wife,' she says again. She reaches forward to the table, picks up her glass as if to take a sip.

He stalls, still awash in the confusion of his previous thought. He thinks about her question and then understands that it is for the hand on her shoulder. He drains the vodka, bites into the lemon peel. 'She has short, dark hair,' he says. He hesitates; he feels lost. 'She's a good person,' he says lamely.

'Do you love her?'

He pauses. He must get this right. He must not lie. He senses she will know a lie. He swirls the ice cubes and the lemon peel in his glass. 'I love her more than I used to,' he says slowly and deliberately.

She brings the glass to her lips, as if pondering his reply. As he looks at her, the space between them becomes flooded with images: the two of them as children; the picture she sent him; the girl she might have been at seventeen; the woman she might have been at twenty-eight or thirty-five; herself in the embrace of another man – her husband? Her husband, about whom he knows almost nothing but who almost certainly has more hair than Charles does and probably (Charles winces inwardly) a flatter stomach. He imagines her lying on a bed with her hair undone. He sees her nursing an infant. The images elide and collide. He feels light-headed, signals the waiter for another vodka.

'Do you want another glass of wine?' he asks her, and she surprises him by finishing her drink and nodding.

'It's hard to take it all in, isn't it?' she says. She shakes her head slightly, as if she truly cannot digest the fact, as if, like him, she can barely believe she's been alive thirty-one years, let alone known someone that long. Though of course they haven't known each other, he thinks.

He looks out at the other diners in the restaurant: a table of businessmen, several tables of couples, mostly older couples. The waiter brings them menus, recites the specials of the day. Charles dutifully listens to the man, as does she, but for his part he cannot absorb a word. He won't be able to read the menu either – he's left his reading glasses in the car.

'Are you hungry?' he asks her when the waiter has left.

She shakes her head.

'You're right,' he says. 'You don't look like your picture.'

She seems embarrassed. 'I think they were trying to make me out to be more interesting and glamorous than I really am,' she says with a wave of her hand.

'That's not what I meant,' he says. 'I meant you look more familiar to me now than you did in the picture. You look very familiar to me.'

She turns away from him toward the waiter across the room.

'Oh?, I almost forgot,' she says. 'I've brought something. I found it in the trunk with the pictures.'

She bends down to retrieve her purse, a black leather pocketbook with a long strap, opens it, and removes a mimeographed newsletter, several pages stapled at one corner. She hands it to Charles.

'It was a kind of newspaper they gave us on the day we left. It has a brief history of what happened that week, and at the end there are all the addresses of the campers and the counselors.'

Charles riffles through the newsletter, looks again at its cover, at the hand-drawn cross with the words 'The Ridge' above it, and the dates of their attendance below. He puts the newsletter on the banquette between them.

'I've left my reading glasses in the car,' he says.

'It's odd,' she says, 'but I didn't recognize a single name there, except yours.'

Her eyelids are slightly hooded; a soft tint in her glasses takes the edge off the navy of her eyes, makes them appear almost charcoal. She wears little makeup, at least as far as he can tell, and there is just the faintest suggestion of a dark rose color on her lips. He knows he should ask about her husband, as she has asked about his wife. And there are facts he would like to know about her marriage, though not necessarily from her. He does not want to hear her speak of her husband – not today, not right now.

'You certainly don't look like the wife of a farmer,' he says lightly.

She laughs for the first time. 'Well, you don't look like a salesman,' she says.

'What's a salesman look like?' he asks. He would like to ask her what she thinks of him – has he aged hopelessly? is she disappointed? – but, of course, he cannot.

She glances again at the newsletter with the cross. 'I don't remember much religion from that week,' she says. 'It's strange when you think about it. Except for the epiphany I wrote you about, and the services down by the water. Though they seem, at least in my memory, not very Catholic. Not very ornate. Having more to do with nature than with God.'

He thinks this is true. There was a priest, he recalls, a tall, athletic fellow with thick black hair – Father Something; Father What? – who doubled as a swimming teacher. A number of lay counselors. Not a single nun.

'What was the priest's name?' he asks.

She thinks a minute. 'Father Dunn?' she asks tentatively.

He smiles. 'Thank you. You're right. They soft-pedaled the religion. Mercifully. And wisely too.'

'I remember the pool, but I didn't see it on my way in.'

'We can take a walk,' he says.

She shifts slightly, moving her shoulder away. As if she might not acquiesce to a walk.

'You don't look like a poet either,' he says, 'Though I don't really know what a poet is supposed to look like.'

Her hand is on the banquette, resting there between them. He covers her hand with his own.

The room spins for a second, as if he were already drunk.

'Does this upset you?' he asks her quietly. She shakes her head but doesn't look at him.

They sit there for minutes. She seems unwilling to withdraw her hand; he is unable to remove his. He feels the warmth of her hand beneath his, though he is barely touching her. He sees the waiter across the room. He will kill the man if he comes to their table now.

When she speaks, her voice is so low he is not sure he has heard her correctly.

'When you wrote about holding my hand . . .'

He waits, poised for the conclusion of the sentence. He rubs the top of her hand lightly.

She leans slightly toward him, an infinitesimal, yet highly significant, millimeter closer. She looks down at his hand over hers. She slips her hand from his, but gives her face to him. Her eyes are clear, unclouded.

'I had a son,' she says quickly. 'He was killed in a car accident when he was nine.'

'I'm sorry,' Charles says.

'His name was Brian. It was six years ago.'

She tells him these facts in a steady voice, as if she had planned to tell him, as if she could not proceed without his knowing. He feels then the full weight of all that each of them has lived through, all of the separate minutes she has had to experience, to endure. The time they have been away from each other has been a lifetime – a lifetime of other people, other loves, sexual love, children, work. She has had to bury a child. He can barely imagine that pain. They once knew each other for one week; they have not seen each other in three decades. The imbalance staggers him.

'I'm not hungry either,' he says quietly. 'Why don't we get our coats and walk down to the lake. We can always eat later if we want to.'

She opens her mouth as if to speak, closes it. She seems to be trying to tell him something, but cannot. She touches the back of his hand on the banquette lightly, briefly, with her fingertips.

He places the coat over her shoulders. She wraps herself in it as if it were a cape. In the foyer, he finds the door to the back, the one leading down to the lake. When she steps outside, she pulls the coat around her more tightly. The breeze is stiffer here, the day still overcast and cold. They hear a windowpane rattling. The wind loosens her hair a bit, makes stray wisps at the sides.

He has his arm at her back, guiding her across a wide stone porch.

'Wait here a minute,' he says. 'You'd probably rather have a thermos of hot coffee right now, but I brought something to celebrate our reunion.'

When he walks to the car, his legs feel loose, boneless. He's aware he's moving too quickly, but he does not want to leave her alone, even for a minute, as if, after so brief a reunion, she might disappear again. He has few conscious thoughts, no plans. In his ears there is a pounding, a kind of desperate beat. His fingers tremble as he unlocks the trunk. The glasses are plastic, bought in the deli. He minds now that he didn't think to bring champagne glasses.

When he returns, she is standing at the edge of the porch, leaning against a stone railing, looking down toward the lake. She has the collar of her coat up, her arms wrapped around her. Before her, there is a sloping lawn, then a thicket of trees. Beyond the trees, they can see the far edge of the lake, a thin silver oval.

'The path is here somewhere,' he says.

'Yes, I remember it.'

'Can you manage in those shoes?'

'I think so. I can give it a try anyway.'

She puts her hand on the railing, balances herself as she descends the stairs. She has a slight limp, and she explains: 'My knee. From a skiing accident.'

(He adds then another image to his mental collage – she's in a ski outfit, her poles dug into the snow. But whom is she with? Her husband? A friend?)

He walks slightly behind her and to her right, the bottle in one hand, the glasses in the other.

'Do you think they mind us drinking our own champagne,' she asks over her shoulder, 'walking all over their property?'

'This is America. We can do anything we want.'

She looks at him and smiles. They are on the lawn, and he is at her side. She seems brighter now, more relaxed, the sadness in the restaurant momentarily dissipated.

'Well, we know that's not true,' she says quickly. 'I hope you're not going to tell me you're a Republican.'

'I knew you were going to ask me that. Is it important?'

'Yes, of course it's important.'

'Well, I've never voted, so I guess that lets me off the hook.'

'You've never voted?'

'And another thing you're going to hate.'

'What's that?'

'I drive a Cadillac.'

The backs of her heels are sinking into the lawn. When they reach the lake he will offer to clean them for her.

'So it was you in the parking lot,' she says.

He laughs. 'You looked right at me. I couldn't believe you looked at me and walked so quickly away. I thought I'd scared you off.'

'Well, I didn't really look at you, and even if I'd known it was you, I can promise you there wasn't a chance on God's earth I was going to walk across that parking lot and introduce myself.'

'I thought you were the hostess.'

She seems taken aback. 'The hostess?'

'You drove in so quickly, as if you were late for work. As if you knew the place.'

'I was just nervous.'

'Why?'

They reach the pathway in the woods, the one that will

lead them down to what was the outdoor chapel by the lake.

'I was just about to call you *Cal*,' she says. 'It's hard to think of you as Charles now. I had the tape on. Roy Orbison. "Crying." A wonderful song.'

'He not only sang all those songs, but he also wrote most of them.'

'I don't know much about that music then. But I do remember it.'

'I went to a concert of his once. In Providence. An incredible concert. Now, there was a man with a lot of pain in his life. He was riding motorcycles with his wife, and his wife was hit and killed instantly. And I think he lost at least one and possibly two sons in a fire.'

As soon as he has spoken, he realizes what he has said. She is in front of him, walking single file along the path, watching her feet so that she will not stumble.

'Jesus Christ,' he says. 'I'm sorry.'

She shrugs slightly as if to say it doesn't matter. They walked along the path in silence for perhaps a hundred yards. Overhead are tall pines, their tops swaying in the wind. Down below, on the path, it is quiet, with few sounds – the rustle of an animal in the bushes, a flock of geese he can hear flying and calling somewhere out of sight.

They emerge to a clearing of simple rough-hewn wooden benches on a carpet of pine needles. The clearing opens to the lake, an expansive view across gray rippling water. In the center of the clearing, at the edge of the lake, is the place where the cross – a wooden cross vaguely a man's height – used to be.

'I remember this,' she says beside him.

He steps ahead of her and walks to the bench closest to the lake. He sits down and looks out. He puts the two plastic glasses on the bench, works the top of the champagne bottle. She sits, her hands in the pockets of her coat, on the other side of the glasses. The cork pops, flies toward the lake. He catches the spill of champagne in a glass, hands it to her. He fills the other glass, takes a sip. He wants to make another toast, looks out at the water instead. The water seems to be moving, an optical illusion. He wants to say the word 'destiny' but does not. He remembers their sitting there as children, can remember holding her hand as if it were yesterday – the deep, sexual thrill of that gesture.

'What I tried to tell you in the restaurant and couldn't,' she says, breaking the silence, 'is that somehow a death keeps you together, even if you shouldn't be. . . .'

He waits.

She waves a hand outward. 'To help remember, is what I think I'm trying to say.'

'That's the pain in your poetry?'

'Oh, I don't know,' she says. 'That's a hard question to answer. And I'm not sure it's pain exactly.' She takes a long swallow of champagne. He raises the bottle to fill her glass again, and she lets him.

'What did you mean by "the shit"?' she asks. 'You said in your letter you were trying to "transcend the shit."'

'It's not important,' he says. 'It's just financial stuff. I'm not in particularly good shape at the moment.'

'No one is these days.'

'I suppose that's true. I didn't like it when you went to England.'

'You're funny. You don't even know me.'

'I'm not so sure about that. I loved the postcard you sent.'

'You'd have loved the pub.'

'The forty kinds of malt whiskey. It was your birthday.'

'Yes.'

'So how old are you now? Forty-six?'

'Yes. When's yours?'

'New Year's Day.'

'So you're . . .?'

'Forty-five now.'

'Then I'm older than you.'

'By two months. An older woman.'

'Did we know that then? I wonder. My sister named a goldfish after you. Cal.'

'And you think *I'm* funny.'

'I guess I talked about you incessantly when I got home from camp. When did you give up the name?'

'Sometime in high school, I think.'

She looks out at the water, as if at an apparition there. He looks to see what she is seeing.

'Charles, what happened to us that week?'

'I think it's simple,' he says. 'We fell in love.'

'Is that possible, for two fourteen-year-olds to fall in love?'

'What do you think?'

She looks off to the side, into the woods beyond the clearing. 'Where is it? Do you know?'

'I think it must be in there, where you're looking.'

'It's strange. For months afterward, possibly even longer, I thought that I would marry you.'

'I cried all the way home in the car,' he says. 'My mother never let me forget it. It was a three-hour car ride. I told you what she said when I told her I'd given you the bracelet.'

'I wish I could have found it.'

'It probably disintegrated or turned green. I think I paid a dollar and a half for it at the camp store.'

'That was a lot then.'

He laughs. 'I remember that summer I saved up twenty-four dollars from my paper route and bought a turntable and a bunch of forty-fives.'

'The songs you sent. They were from then?'

'Most of them. "Where or When" was from the summer we met. I played it endlessly.'

'The lyrics . . .,' she says. She takes a sip of champagne, swallows thoughtfully, as if pondering the words of the song.

'They're extraordinary,' he says. 'Though what's more extraordinary is how I can possibly have understood them then. I suppose . . .' He looks out over the lake – a flat surface of sterling. 'If I played it so often after I met you that summer, which is what I did, I had to have been envisioning a future reunion. In other words, I wasn't experiencing the song as it's meant to be experienced – a man remembering a former love – but rather I was the boy already imagining meeting you again after some time had elapsed. For instance, the line "The clothes you're wearing are the clothes you wore . . ." I'd have been thinking of finding you one day, and you'd be wearing the thin cotton dress that came just below your knees.'

'Or Bermuda shorts.'

'Or Bermuda shorts.'

'"It seems we stood and talked like this before . . ."'

He looks at her, adds another line: '"We looked at each other in the same way then . . ."'

'"But I can't . . ."' She seems unable to finish.

'". . . remember where or when," ' he says quietly.

He sits, one leg crossed at the knee, a glass in his hand. He wonders if these are the exact same benches they sat on when they were kids. He shakes his head. He knows he will never understand this. They are, simultaneously, the children they were then and the man and woman they are now. As the water itself, this ancient lake, is the same and yet not. As the trees overhead are the same and yet not. He has never been able fully to comprehend time, now knows it is infinitely more mysterious than he ever imagined.

'There's another line I like,' he says after a time. 'It's in the original version, but not sung by Dion & The Belmonts. "Things you do come back to you, As though they knew the way."'

A flock of geese flap noisily overhead. She bends forward suddenly, her face in her hands.

He puts his hand on her shoulder, tries to pull her up toward him, but she resists.

'What is it?' he asks.

His heart is tight, his chest in a vise.

He is going to lose her, he is thinking. After all these years of not even having her.

'Oh, God,' she cries.

'Charles will do.'

She sits up quickly, her mouth in a sudden, wide smile. Her eyes are wet.

She looks at him. Her eyes dart from his eyes to his mouth to the top of his hair, as if examining him for the first time. Back to his eyes. She seems to be trying to find him. To read him.

He knows he will not be hard to read, that it must all be there on his face.

He puts his hand at the side of her chin, holds her face steady and kisses her.

Her mouth is soft and large. He can feel her give. A loosening along her spine. He puts his arms around her, pulls her toward him, and she comes, so that her face is against his shoulder, inside his coat.

She inhales deeply into his shirt. 'I can smell you,' she says with evident surprise. 'I remember how you smell.'

He kisses the top of her hair. She puts her mouth against the weave of his shirt. She slides her fingers through a gap between the buttons of his shirt, touches the skin there. He wishes she would unbutton his shirt, thinks if she doesn't, he might do it for her. Instead she takes hold of his tie and loops it twice so that it is wound around her hand.

'You're fond of my tie?' he asks.

She laughs lightly.

He puts his hands inside her coat, inside her suit jacket, holding her rib cage, the warmth of her through the silk of her blouse. He kisses her again, finds the inside of her mouth, and feels lost and light-headed, as if he were spinning.

She makes a small sound.

He puts a hand on her chin, tilts her face more sharply toward his. He kisses her again. She slips her face slightly to the side, finds his fingers. She kisses one finger, then another. He slides a finger inside her mouth. She closes her lips around it, holds it, then lets him withdraw it. He does it again, explores her tongue. Then again, and again.

He withdraws his finger. He slides his hand to her breast, feels the breast through the cloth. He unfastens the top button of her blouse, pushes the fabric of her bra aside. He kisses her nipple, licks it with his tongue, astonishing himself with the boldness of this gesture.

She breaks away, as if they had been tussling like schoolboys.

It has not been a minute since he first kissed her. How did they get to this point so quickly?

Her face is flushed, her mouth reddened. Her hair, at one side, has begun to come loose. There is a faint mottling at her throat and on her forehead. Her blouse is open, exposing the top of her left breast.

'Is this a sacrilege?' she asks.

He takes a breath. The question is light, from someone who no longer believes in sacrilege.

'Absolutely not,' he says, matching her apostatic tone. 'In fact,' he adds, going her one better, although he really believes this now, 'I think God is going to be pretty annoyed if after bringing us together again – finally, after all these years – we don't do something about it.'

She smiles, but she withdraws. He watches as she fastens the top button of her blouse, tucks her hair up under an invisible pin.

'It's so odd that I remembered how you smell,' she says. She leans toward him, breathes his chest through his shirt, but before he can seize her, she has moved away. 'I love your shirt,' she says, laughing. She sits up straight.

He cannot move.

She looks at him, but in her eyes she seems to withdraw even further. She frowns slightly.

'I think I've been frozen,' she says, looking away.

She stands up, gathers her coat around her.

He stands up with her, flustered, wanting to keep her there, to tell her that surely now she is becoming unfrozen, but he cannot find the right words, does not want to have misunderstood her. He remembers the empty bottle, the glasses.

He follows her along the path, up across the lawn, and toward the parking lot. He tosses the bottle and the glasses into a bin.

'We haven't eaten,' he says, catching up to her.

'I couldn't. Not now.'

'No.'

'In any event, I have to get home.'

He nods.

'You picked a lunch and not a dinner because you had to go home to your wife?'

He doesn't lie. 'Yes,' he says. 'And also I thought it would be easier for you.'

They reach her car. She stands at the door, looking in her pocketbook for the keys, a casual gesture, as if she were a client, and he, out of politeness, were walking her to her car. When what he feels is a longing and a regret so achingly deep, he wants to bend over.

When she finds her keys, she turns so that she is facing him. She opens her mouth as if to say goodbye, as if she had so quickly forgotten what they have just done down by the lake.

'I might not be able to do this,' she says.

Thursday night, 9:40 P.M.

Dear Siân,

I want to pick up the phone. I want my hand held. I want to call you and lie all night with the phone receiver next to me and know that we have an open connection.

I won't call.

I watched you drive out of the parking lot this afternoon, and I felt desolate.

These letters are so volatile now, I do worry about sending them to you. What happened today was not innocent. I would like to say to you that it felt innocent, but I know that's not true.

I want to make love to you and have it stop time.

If I call the literary supplement and tell them you kissed a man who drives a Cadillac, your reputation will be ruined.

Charles

Friday, 2 A.M.

Siân,

I have picked up the phone and put it down fifteen times. I want to call you to tell you to meet me later today back at The Ridge. I want to hand deliver this letter.

You said you might not be able to do this. I want to persuade you that there is nothing more important in life that we have to do now.

I can't sleep. I've been up reading. I dug out one of my old philosophy books and came upon a passage. It's by

the French phenomenologist Merleau-Ponty, and it's about
sexuality. 'Existence permeates sexuality and vice versa,'
he writes, 'so that it is impossible to label a decision or
act "sexual" or "non-sexual." There is no outstripping of
sexuality any more than there is sexuality enclosed within
itself.' He also says that no one is saved and no one is
totally lost.

I found that last bit reassuring.

I think that I have been somewhat frozen too, but I don't
fully understand why.

Your face is as familiar to me as my own.

Just think – it could have been worse: We might have
met each other again at sixty-five, not forty-five.

　　Charles

　　　　　　　　　　　　　　　　　　　　　　Friday, 5 A.M.

Dear Siân,

I am still in my suit. I may never take this shirt off. I am
going to frame my tie. I look like hell. I've been listening
to 'Where or When' all night. About half an hour ago, my
wife came down to my study and asked me if I was sick.

You and I have lost thirty-one years. I cannot bear to
lose another day.

My study is in ruins. I haven't been able to find your
last book of poetry, and I've turned the place upside down
looking for it. Now that I've met you – again – I want to
read each of the poems – again. I want to know everything
there is to know about you.

This house is fucking freezing. I pay $600 a month for
heat, and I have to sit here in my overcoat.

I want to kiss your other breast.

Anita Shreve

I want to believe that this thing that we are doing would
have happened – it was just a question of time. My timing
in this could not have been worse, and it could not have
been better. To meet the woman you were meant to be with
is timing that cannot be argued with.

Charles

Friday, 11 A.M.

Dear Siân,

I still cannot sleep. I haven't eaten since Wednesday
night. I've been drinking Coors Light since I got home
from The Ridge, but it hasn't made a dent. I know I should
try to lie down, but I have to tell you one more story
before I mail these letters off.

I went to the bookstore to buy another copy of your
book of poems. The first copy, I discovered earlier this
morning, is on my wife's dresser. I went in to change my
shirt, and it was sitting there like a radioactive isotope. Why
she should have chosen that book out of all the books in
my study to read, I have no idea, but I certainly can't touch
it or ask her for it back.

I went to the front desk at the bookstore, and a man
and a woman were behind it. I asked the man to find the
book for me. The man started to enter the name into
the computer, and I said, 'I know you have it, or had it,
because I bought a copy here several months ago.' Then the
woman said, 'Yeah, it's got a picture of some blond all over
the back cover.' I said, 'Yes, I guess that's the way they
market books these days.' Then she said back to me, 'Yeah,
even the academic stuff, they make the women take their
blouses off.'

110

I said to her, 'She's pretty embarrassed about it herself.'
'You know her?' the woman asked.
'She was my girlfriend when I was fourteen,' I said.

Charles

HE HAS ALWAYS LIKED watching volleyball: the movements of the players, the high leaps to block shots, a dozen arms in the air at once, the smash at the net. They are late, Hadley is already on the court, and the gym is half filled with parents and siblings who have rushed an early dinner. He spots Hadley at once in her blue T-shirt and white shorts, her ponytail whipping behind her as she rises straight off the ground. Charles follows his wife and two other children to the side of the gym where there are bleachers. He has not wanted, for Hadley's sake, to miss this game, but as he quickly scans the crowd he wishes he could disappear. Whalen is there, and Costa. Charles has twenty-seven messages on his machine just from this day alone that he hasn't returned – though he knows already whom they are from. Whalen from the bank, who will probably nab him tonight. GMAC pressing him for a payment on the Cadillac. The telephone company. Optima. His Citibank Visa. Master-Card. He is fairly certain that Harriet doesn't know yet just how bad their (*his*) financial situation is, an intuition that is borne out when his wife waves at Eddie and Barbara Whalen, sitting downcourt. Charles lifts Anna onto his lap and in doing so catches Muriel Carney's eye. Tom is in the hospital. Has been there since Thanksgiving.

The gym is large, part of a building that was once the town's high school and has now passed on to the middle school. The girls at the center of the blond wooden floor look small and innocent, children still, though they mimic, as Jack does when he plays baseball, the movements of the older athletes they have seen on television or at high school games. Odd, Charles thinks, how many of his peers have girls Hadley's age. Whalen, Costa, Carney. Lidell's Sarah is there too. He cannot make out who is winning, asks the woman beside him for the score. Hadley's team is down two. He can see that his daughter, at the net, is sweating slightly. She is among the tallest of the players on her team, though he knows, she doesn't have all her growth yet; he guesses she will be close to five ten before she is seventeen.

Hadley leaps, blocks a shot, spikes it straight to the floorboards. The crowd cheers. Charles calls her name. He looks at Harriet, who is smiling broadly, and in doing so he can see that Whalen is making his way along the bleachers, decorously holding his topcoat closed with his hand in the vicinity of his crotch, sliding with apologies past the other parents. Asshole. Whalen will nail him, with Harriet sitting beside him. There is no escaping this. He feels a twinge of the panic, can feel his blood pressure rising. He stares straight ahead, knowing his face is suffused with color.

'Callahan.'

Whalen has perched himself behind Charles, up over his left shoulder. Whalen has soft white skin, thin wisps of hair combed across a bald pate. Charles, glancing quickly at Whalen, makes a silent promise to himself to go bald without attempts at camouflage.

'Eddie.'

'Called you all last week. Today.'

'I know.'

Charles looks over at Harriet, who returns his glance and frowns slightly. She seems surprised to see Whalen sitting behind Charles.

'I don't have the money,' Charles says, turning away from Harriet toward Whalen.

'You've missed three months.'

'I know that.'

'We can't carry this mortgage forever, Charles. If you could just give us some indication of when . . .'

Charles is silent. He hates Whalen's whine. It comes through even on the telephone. Charles knows he cannot pull out of this but doesn't want to have to admit it to Whalen, not right now, not in front of Harriet.

'I'd like to cut you some slack, Callahan,' Whalen says, the whine rising a notch. 'You know that. But times are tight right now. We're down to the bone ourselves.'

Charles removes Anna from his lap. He shifts slightly on the bench so that only Whalen can hear what he is saying.

'Listen, asshole,' he says slowly and deliberately, punctuating *asshole*, knowing as he does so that he is sealing his fate. 'I'm watching a fucking volleyball game in which my daughter and your daughter are playing, and I'm sitting here with my wife and two other kids, and I'm not going to fucking discuss my fucking mortgage right now. Is that clear?'

He looks at Whalen long enough to see the man's face turn the color of his shirt, a grayish white. He watches Whalen open his mouth and close it. Charles swivels back to the game, a din ringing in his ears. It's his blood pressure, and his right hand is balled into a fist. Behind him he can hear Whalen stand abruptly. On the court, Hadley is serving. She faults twice, forfeits the serve. Charles winces inwardly for his daughter.

There was no letter today. He went to the post office two, three times. He has calculated that the earliest a letter could have arrived from her would have been today, though she'd have to have written it and mailed it almost immediately upon returning home from The Ridge on Thursday, which seems highly unlikely. He's not sure she could have made it home before five o'clock, the hour the post office closes. He doesn't even know if she will write him now, if he will ever see her

114

again. He sent his own packet of letters to her on Saturday morning, calculating that they would arrive tomorrow. It's entirely possible that she will not respond, will refuse to meet with him. She said at the car that she might not be able to do this . . .

He lets his eyes wander to the court. He has no idea who is winning. Did Hadley's lost serve cancel out the gain of the blocked shot? He could ask Harriet but does not want to speak to her just now. She might ask him about Whalen. There are several good players on the other team, he can see, focusing on them for the first time. The visitors are wearing black shirts, red shorts. There's a small girl from the other side with a surprisingly powerful serve; no one from Hadley's team can return it. Costa's daughter makes a valiant try, misses. He sees then another girl, a girl from the visiting side who is at least Hadley's height, a girl with dark blond hair pulled into a knot at the back of her head. She's standing in the back row, waiting for the serve. She glances down at her feet, puts her hands together briefly, poised for the shot. A coach calls for a time-out; the girl relaxes her posture. She brings her hand up to the back of her neck, idly touches her hair. She does not have the obvious stance of an athlete, but her pose is graceful, self-contained. The players wait while Costa's daughter reties a shoelace. The tall girl from the visiting side is sweating slightly, on her upper lip, at her temples. She glances up at Charles, across the court, as if she knew that he was watching her.

He might be hallucinating. He *is* hallucinating, he decides. The girls move, the game resumes, but he sees only Siân, a central presence in a swirling collage of outstretched arms and small thin bodies leaping from the shiny wooden floor. He feels light-headed, dizzy, but he is certain he is watching Siân. He knows the hallucination is a product of his unraveling. He hasn't eaten or slept in days. And yet the vision seems also to be a gift, a peering into a past that has been denied to him. He watches the girl arc her body off the ground and knows that it is Siân he sees. He aches sharply for the loss of her, feels his eyes fill suddenly, as if he'd been stung. He glances quickly at his wife, realizes that Harriet has been staring at him. He looks back at the game. The hallucination fades as quickly as it came to him. He wonders then: Was he seeing Siân as she really was, or as he imagines her to have been?

He feels a hand on his knee, looks down. It is Harriet's, reaching across Jack and Anna, their children.

'Charles,' she says.

In bed that night, when his wife reaches for him, he knows that this time he cannot refuse her. It is not exactly a challenge – he and Harriet do not engage each other in that way – yet he knows that in the gesture there is a question. He lets her touch him, prays that his body will respond, but in the darkness, even with his eyes shut, he sees only other faces, other images, that distract him. Siân as a young girl, Siân's face by the lake, her breast exposed to him. The images are not sexual; they make him want to cry. He is afraid he will cry, thinks instead of Whalen's whine. His body is hopelessly limp, unresponsive. He does not want to hurt his wife.

'I want you to come first,' he whispers, shifting his body quickly, putting his hand to her, hoping she will allow this, will accept this, will let his own failure go.

She puts her hand on his hand, makes him stop.

'I'm just exhausted,' he says feebly.

She takes his hand away from her body, rolls over with her back to him.

He is at the post office before eight, the Cadillac humming, waiting for Harry Noonan to arrive and open the front door to the postboxes. This morning, Charles was out of bed before Harriet, so as to avoid a reprise of the previous night. He showered, shaved, dressed, drank some coffee, and sat in his office, trying ineffectually to clear the debris off his desk while he listened to the early morning sounds of his wife and children in other rooms. He thinks briefly of his outburst with Whalen at the gym last night, nervously taps the steering wheel as a familiar knot forms in his stomach. It was not smart, he knows, to have let his anger boil to the surface. The bank will foreclose, he is certain of this now, but with children in the house, they'll have to give him at least sixty days to find another place to live. Harriet and the kids will have Christmas in the house, and it's conceivable he may not even have to tell Harriet until the new year.

Christmas. New Year's Eve.

She has said she may not be able to see him again. There may, at this very moment, be a letter inside the post office repeating that intention. Or worse (or perhaps not worse), there may be no letter at all.

Four past eight. Harry Noonan finally drives up in his gray Isuzu Trooper. Charles nods through the windshield at Noonan, waits for Harry to unlock the front door before getting out of his car. Charles's early arrival at the post office is not unprecedented – he often begins his day by getting the mail – but he does not want to appear particularly overeager today. After a minute or two, however, he follows Noonan through the lobby with the postboxes – the mail won't be in them yet – and into the main room, where Noonan is already sorting through a large stack of envelopes, his parka still on.

'Callahan.'

'Harry.'

'You heard anything this morning about the storm we're supposed to get?'

'No. It'll probably just be rain. Freezing rain. Screw up the roads.'

'Probably so.'

Noonan sets aside a small pile of familiar-looking envelopes – one from the phone company, others from Citibank, the cable company, the bank (The Bank) – and one large unfamiliar manila envelope. No blue envelopes, but Charles focuses on the manila envelope, reaches for it. The handwriting is hers; there is no return address. His hand begins at once to shake; he feels his chest constrict. He tucks the envelope under his arm, puts his hands, to still them, into the pockets of his overcoat. He wants to get back to the safety of his car, tear open the gummed seal.

'Thanks, Harry,' he says, turning to leave.

'Callahan.'

Charles looks back at Noonan, who is studying Charles over the rims of his half-glasses.

'You forgot your mail.'

Charles holds the envelope in the car, taps it twice against the steering wheel. He feels as he used to as a kid, opening his report card or an admissions letter from college – pausing on the brink of relief or disaster, mumbling incoherent prayers. He takes a deep breath, exhales. He slits open the seal. Inside are three blue envelopes, marked '1,' '2,' and '3.' He opens the first envelope, quickly scans the letter, devours it like a junkie. His eyes fill; he blinks. A strangled, muted sound – something between a sob and a sigh – escapes him. He cannot read the other letters here. He lays the opened letter and the two unopened letters on the passenger seat, puts the key into the ignition, and, nearly blind, backs out of the parking lot.

A sharp, stinging rain begins on the windshield. He drives to the bridge and the beach.

Thursday night, 11:20 P.M.

Dear Charles,

I will write this letter. My hand has been poised over the paper for fifteen minutes – the equivalent of a kind of speechlessness that comes from having too much to say and not being able to find the right words with which to say it.

It is easier to sit on a wooden bench or to listen to imagined music than to explain why I can think of little else and why, walking across the lawn to the parking lot, I felt different to myself. It is possible that today I have begun to become unfrozen. That would seem to be a good in itself, yet I wonder what it will do to myself and to my family.

I found your presence reassuring, your body and your voice familiar to me, as I seem to have been to you. How that can be so, I cannot say. The two of us together, down by the lake – it seemed that we were both reality and metaphor at once for something I barely understand.

My fantasies are simple ones and are products of what I think is a kind of emotional exhaustion – the result of trying to hold myself and my family together all these years. I dream of having my hand held. I don't really dream of sexual passion. That, this afternoon, was unexpected.

You did not ask about my husband, though I asked about your wife. I tried at lunch to convey something of my marriage, but I suspect I did it badly. When I met Stephen in graduate school, I mistook his silence for a kind of appealing reserve. I didn't know then that I had met him during the two happiest years of his life, when he was as far from the farm as he had ever been.

He is wedded to the farm, even more than to me, but he has never really been happy here. It is, for him, his own peculiar kind of destiny.

I feel extremely disloyal writing even this much:

I must go to bed now, but I doubt that I will sleep.

I imagine us meeting intermittently over a period of many years – possibly even into old age – a thread running through our lives.

When I move a certain way, I can smell you on my skin.

Siân

Friday, 9:20 A.M.

Charles,

I'm glad I wrote that letter to you, and I will send it along with this one, but in the early morning light of family and a child and a house and a life, I know this is not going to be possible. I think somehow, somewhere, you know this too. There is, probably, a great affinity between us – perhaps that's what drew us together as children and again yesterday. But I know this is not going to be manageable. There must be, on your part, some relief in reading these words.

It was tantalizing for me, the vision I had of how this might work. But did I really imagine I could see you from time to time and then forget about you and go on with my life in the intervals?

I know that you understand that what happened yesterday was not casual, that it was, potentially, the first step of a thousand steps, and that ending it now is essential.

What happened between us on that bench, for those few brief moments, was dangerous.

Yesterday, driving home from The Ridge, I felt deliciously female and wanted, as though I were carrying around inside me, a wonderful secret.

I did not sleep all night.

I do not want you to do anything to hurt your wife or your family.

Siân

Friday, 6:45 P.M.

Charles,

You will think me deranged, or descending into madness.

I wrote the letter to you this morning, then I took my daughter to the playground. It was very quiet and peaceful there – it's really too late in the season to go to the playground, but Lily was bundled up and warm. She went immediately to a small sandbox, and I was grateful for the opportunity to sit on a bench and think.

All I can think about is you.

You held my shoulder in the restaurant. And then you held my hand, and I turned my head away, and you asked if it upset me, and I said no, when what I really wanted to say was, 'I can't breathe.'

And then I thought, sitting on the bench, with my daughter playing in the sandbox: This is madness. I just wrote this man a letter telling him it couldn't happen, when all I want – all I want – is for him to make love to me.

I am walking around in a feverish state. I am not sleeping, not eating.

I know it would be better for everyone if we didn't see each other ever again.

I want you to know that I take at least equal responsibility for what happens now.

I ask myself all the time, every minute, every hour: What is this?

   Siân

HIS HANDS are so wet and frozen he can barely make the phone work. He's forgotten his glasses and cannot see the digits, taps the numbers in as if working braille. The phone is exposed, an outdoor box at the side of the Qwik Stop. He hopes no one he knows will pass by: What's Callahan doing at a pay phone in this filthy weather, with his own house not two miles away? Needles of frozen rain sting the back of his neck. He turns his collar up, wishes he had an umbrella. The sleet drips off his nose.

'Hello?'

It is a woman's voice; it is Siân's. But her voice sounds tentative, as if she had not wanted to answer the phone.

'Siân?'

There is a silence. A long silence.

'This is – '

'I know who it is,' she says slowly. He hears a small sound, a tiny sound from the back of her throat. 'Oh, God . . .,' she says.

'Charles will – '

'I know. I know.' Her voice is strained. He thinks she may be crying, but he can't tell without seeing her. 'I thought when I said I might not be able to do this I'd never hear from you again,' she says in a rush.

'You had to have known that I would call,' he says. 'Did you get my letters yet?'

'No.'

'You'll get them today. I just got yours.'

There is a silence at her end, though he thinks he can hear her breathing.

'Siân?'

'Yes?'

'We have to meet again. You know that.'

'Yes.'

'I want to meet you today, now.'

'I can't – '

'No, not today. The weather is awful. Is it snowing there?'

'Freezing rain.'

'Same here. Tomorrow?'

'Tomorrow?'

'I don't want to wait. I won't wait. I have to do this.'

'I'll try.'

'Same place?'

'All right.'

'But earlier. Can you get there by ten?'

She seems to be thinking, calculating. 'Yes,' she says hesitantly. 'I think so.'

'Good.' He lets out his breath. 'Siân?'

'Yes?'

'I know you'll think I'm crazy, but I want you to know, in case something happens to me and I don't get there, that I love you.'

The silence at her end is so long, he thinks she may have hung up. He wishes he could see her face.

'And there's something else,' he says.

'What?' Her voice is quiet.

'I don't know how I know this on the basis of only one meeting,' he says, 'but I'm sure of this . . .'

'What?'

'I know I always have.'

He is standing at the side of his car when she drives into the parking lot. Ten past ten. The day is frosty and translucent; the storm from yesterday blew the front through, leaving in its wake a sky so blue it looks almost neon. She emerges from the car, slings her pocketbook over her shoulder, shuts the door. He watches as she crosses the parking lot to the Cadillac. They stand facing each other for an instant, and then he embraces her, folds her into him. She comes willingly, as if she, too, has been anticipating this moment for days. He can feel her trembling, and she says so: 'I'm shaking,' she says, as if embarrassed. 'I'm just shaking.'

He holds her at arms' length, looks at her face, kisses her. Her mouth opens; he feels as if he is pouring himself into her.

He breaks away. 'I've got a room,' he says.

She composes herself then. He thinks for a moment that she may protest, may not be ready for a room yet and what that implies, but she says nothing, seems to be waiting for him to lead the way. He takes her hand, walks with her across the parking lot, up the steps of the inn and into the lobby. Again she is wearing black – a black coat, black high heels – and he senses, rather than sees, the slight limp as she walks. Inside the lobby, he turns to her and says quietly, 'This is the hard part, walking past the front desk. I've already checked us in.'

'I don't feel guilty,' she says. 'It's all right.'

He cannot remember the last time he booked a room in a clandestine manner with a woman. Certainly not since he has been married. He has been faithful to Harriet throughout their marriage, as he imagines she has been to him. Yet it is not guilt he feels so much as awkwardness – as if he were a young man who has had little experience with women. He wonders, too, not for the first time, if it will work – if, in the throes of an emotion he can barely define, he will be able to make love to Siân Richards. He has tried, over the past several days, to envision making love to her, but he has not been able to bring these fantasies into clear focus. He can only remember them as children. He would like to say to her that the room is simply for convenience, for privacy, so that they can talk out of earshot of others, get to know each other again, but he knows that would sound disingenuous. She walks slightly ahead of him, to his right. He gives directions behind her. The room is on the top floor, on the west wing. The wing in which the boys once had their rooms. The view from the room is out to the back, to the lake. He has already been to the room, inspected it.

He puts the key into the lock, opens the door, and lets her pass through. In the center of the room is an austere four-poster, the bed covered with a white duvet. The other furniture in the room – a tall dresser that conceals a television, a washstand on which there is a white porcelain bowl and pitcher, two silk-upholstered chairs – is of matching cherry, either authentically eighteenth century or intended to resemble that era. Entering the room again, he marvels at the transformation. When he was a boy here, the rooms contained two sets of bunk beds, four crates intended as storage cabinets.

Siân stands with her hands in the pockets of her coat, walks to the window to see the view. He joins her at the window, puts a hand at her shoulder, looks out with her. The sun glints harshly off the water. He makes a gesture so as to remove her coat; she lets the coat and her pocketbook slide off. She is wearing a black dress with a gray jacket. Again she has worn her hair up, twisted into a knot held with a clip.

He bends down, puts his lips to the nape of her neck. She seems to shiver. She lets her head fall slightly forward.

'You remembered,' she says, her voice barely a whisper.

'Of course I remembered,' he says.

He turns her to him, walks with her the two or three steps to the bed. She sits at its edge, he beside her.

She opens her palms. 'I'm not . . .'

She looks at him, a question on her face. She opens her mouth as if to finish her sentence, but he kisses her, brings her with him onto the bed. Her mouth is open, welcoming, but he feels, too, as if at any minute she might pull away. He puts his hand under the skirt of her dress, feels the skin of her hip, her belly. Her stockings stop at the top of her thigh. He raises her skirt so that he can see her body.

She has on a short black slip, the lace falling across her abdomen. She lets him remove her underwear. He finds her then, slips one finger inside, then another. He moves his fingers back and forth slowly, savoring her. He bends toward her, his fingers still lost inside her, and lets his mouth hover over hers. She opens her mouth slightly, as if to receive him; he can see her teeth, her tongue. He opens his mouth but does not kiss her yet. Their mouths are not an inch apart. She lifts herself slightly toward him, waiting for him. He can feel her breath on his lips. He removes his fingers from inside her, puts them to her mouth. He traces the outline of her bottom lip. She reaches for his hand, pulls his fingers toward her, into her mouth, lets him move them slowly back and forth there as he did inside her.

Quickly he unfastens his belt buckle, enters her. He raises himself up on his hands; he has to be able to see her face. She watches him, closes her legs around him. He can feel the cool smoothness of her legs on the backs of his. She watches him steadily, closes her eyes briefly, intently, only at the end. He is not far behind her, and he knows, when he comes, knows it for a certainty, that he will never want to make love to any other woman but Siân Richards again.

After a time, under him, she turns her face to the side. He raises himself up so that he can see her. She is smiling.

'What is it?' he asks, beginning to smile himself.

She shakes her head slowly. She turns back to him, gazes at him steadily, seeing him as he knows he has never been seen before – not by Harriet, not by any other woman. Her smile is full of knowledge, beyond the circumstances of just this day, just this bed.

'I've been waiting for you,' she says.

She is sitting on the edge of the bed in her black slip. She has removed her jacket, her dress. Her hair has fallen down to one side, barely held with the clip. He is nearly naked, under the covers, propped up against the pillows. He likes watching her move in her slip.

'Do you always wear black?' he asks her.

She shrugs, crosses her legs. 'I suppose so. It's easier that way. Everything goes with everything.'

'I think I'm going to kill every man who's ever heard you have an orgasm,' he says.

'There haven't been many,' she says. 'And in any event, if we keep this up, we'll soon surpass our marriages.'

They have made love three or four times. He is no longer sure how to define the act of making love, or how to count the experiences, each time somehow merging into another, exciting another. They haven't even had lunch yet.

'Well, it's not going to take *me* long,' he says.

She laughs. 'That's a sweet thing to say.'

'It's true.'

'It's odd,' she says, 'how the fourteen-year-olds really didn't know what was happening to them, and now the forty-six-year-olds don't really know what is happening to them either.'

'One of us is only forty-five.'

She raps him on his arm. He flinches in mock pain.

'*I* can't define this,' he says. 'I can only relate it to how I felt about you at fourteen.'

He sits up, lifts her hair, kisses her again at the nape of the neck. 'When I do this now,' he says, 'I smell a sexual odor. It's something about my breath on your neck.' He pulls back, looks at her neck. 'You have a stork bite,' he says.

'A what?'

'A stork bite. At least that's what it looks like. A birthmark. It's just inside your hairline.'

She touches the back of her neck. She stands up, walks to the window, looks out at the lake. He gets out of bed, stands beside her. He is wearing only his shirt, unbuttoned.

'That was very strange,' he says, 'when we sat down there last week, looking out at the water.'

'What did it mean to you?'

'I don't know,' he says. 'It seemed like John the Baptist himself was going to emerge right then from the lake.'

'That's not a very Catholic image.'

'No.'

'Where's it coming from?'

'I suppose I just wanted to jump in and be cleansed. I didn't want to have to imagine you with anyone else.'

She puts her hand on his shoulder, slides her hand down his back.

'I think this was supposed to happen,' she says.

'Can we trust that?' he asks.

She is silent for a moment. 'I think if you can't trust this, you can't trust the universe.'

The room, his chest, expand. He wants to open the window, call out to the waiters.

'I think we were meant to have mated,' she adds.

He smiles. He loves the word 'mated.' It suggests to him something primitive, simple, animal-like, beyond thought, or before thought, like the way she has recognized his scent.

'Yes,' he says. 'I believe that.'

'And I've never even seen your children.'

'Nor I yours.'

'We won't ever have children together,' she says. 'Well, we probably won't have children together. What I mean is, we ought not to have children together.'

A new thought enters his mind. He is appalled that he has not been concerned about this earlier – more appalled by his next thought: While he is worried that they have made love unprotected, he wishes fervently that he could make her pregnant.

'I ought to have mentioned this sooner,' he says, 'but . . .'

She shakes her head quickly. 'No. I didn't bring anything. But I'm not sure it's an issue for me anymore.'

He is not altogether certain what she means by this, but he lets her statement go. 'We have enough children,' he says.

'We've only known each other six days.'

'Six days and one week.'

'Six days, one week, and thirty-one years,' she says.

He folds her into him, brings her head into his shoulder. She has asked him in a letter, 'What *is* this?' The question of meaning, he knows, might not be able to be answered. Is this relationship, he wonders, regressive or progressive? Are they each merely trying to recapture an immature childhood love? Or is this a chance – the chance of a lifetime – to have a rich, mature, sexual love with the person you were meant to be with? Odd how these very questions are implicit in the song he has found again and now likes so much. *Things do come back to you as though they knew the way.*

She touches the cloth of his shirt, brings it to her face, inhales deeply.

'I love the smell of you,' she says.

She has put herself together as best she can, has redone her hair, though she had no makeup with her to cover the faint mottling at her forehead. Her gray jacket is wrinkled. 'Next time,' she said in the room, his heart lifting at the words, 'I'll have to bring some things with me so that I can shower, fix myself before lunch.'

They are sitting at the same banquette they had before. The room is much as it was last week, except that sheer white curtains have been drawn across the large floor-to-ceiling windows to protect the diners from the trapezoidal blocks of bright sunlight that fall at this hour across the dining room. He has had a vodka, she a glass of wine; he, oysters; she, salmon. Surprisingly – or perhaps not surprisingly – he was hungry for the first time in weeks. He feels exhausted but exhilarated. She sits slightly turned toward him, her knee just touching his thigh. He has his hand on her leg, on the skirt of her dress. Though she is not precisely smiling, her face gives off a glow as if she were.

'*You're* beautiful,' he says. He knows that she does not have an unflawed body, as he does not; and he knows that she is forty-six, not twenty-six. And yet he cannot, at this moment, conceive of another woman being more appealing to him than she.

'*You're* beautiful,' she says.

'I don't think anyone's ever said that to me before.'

She puts her hand on his knee, touches him lightly there. 'I've never done this,' she says. 'I mean I've never been unfaithful.'

'Nor have I.'

'I don't have what you would call a very bad marriage,' she

says slowly, removing her hand. 'But Stephen and I are not close. We don't . . . We hardly ever . . .' She makes a gesture as if to include the experiences they have just had together in the room in the west wing.

He puts a hand up quickly. 'Don't,' he says. 'I can't. Not yet.'

She looks down at the table.

'We have to be careful,' he says.

She agrees quickly. 'I don't want your wife to be hurt.'

'No. I didn't mean that. I mean we have to be careful with each other.'

She studies him. 'I sometimes think about the next thirty-one years,' she says.

'So do I.'

'I wonder, how much time do we have left? The second half? The third third? And it's all so serendipitous. If you hadn't bought the Sunday paper that morning, we wouldn't be here now.'

'Does it matter, the number of years?' he asks. He can hear the sudden heat in his voice. 'Isn't it worth it even to have one year, one month? Isn't that just as valuable – or is it really the accumulation of hours?'

She sits silently. He knows she cannot answer this question. She reaches into her pocketbook. 'I brought some pictures,' she says. 'To give you an idea of the years in between. And I wanted to show you my daughter.'

He takes the small, neat pile of photographs from her hand, puts on his glasses.

'That's me in high school,' she says, pointing to a picture of a girl in a pageboy haircut, a simple sweater and pearls. She is not wearing glasses in this picture, and he is struck by how much older than a girl she looks. She has to have been only sixteen, seventeen at best. Yet her eyes have an ageless quality

— a gravity that belies her youth. 'And that's me in Senegal.' He looks at a photograph of a tall, thin, angular woman in dark glasses with a colored cloth wrapped around her breasts, forming a dress. 'It's all the women wore there,' she explains. There are other people in the photograph as well, but no men. She shows him other pictures — some of a small, pretty child with long blond hair. None of her husband.

He stops suddenly at one photograph, can go no further. It's of Siân and a baby. She looks to be in her late twenties or early thirties, and she's cradling the baby in her arms, as if she were nursing the infant. This has to be the son who died.

He puts the packet of photographs in his lap, looks across at the far wall.

'It hurts that this is you, and I wasn't there,' he says.

He hands the photographs back to her. He can feel the pressure of the minutes left to them. He glances surreptitiously at his watch, but she sees him.

'What time is it?' she asks.

'I don't want to tell you,' he says.

'I'll have to know,' she says.

'I was hoping we could go back to the room, but I know you can't.'

'We'll come back here.'

'When?'

'I'm not sure. It'll be hard to get away.'

'But we have to.'

'Yes.'

'Can I call you?'

She looks down at her hands. She raises her head, sighs. 'He's almost never in the house between four and five,' she says. 'But I have Lily then. It won't be easy.'

As he pays the bill, she gathers her coat around her. They leave the dining room. He puts his hands in the pockets of his pants, hunches his shoulders against the cold. He's left his overcoat back in the room, will have to retrieve it when she has left. They walk together across the parking lot to her car, the small black Volkswagen.

'If we think about what might have been,' she says, taking his arm, 'we'll drive ourselves mad.'

They reach her car. She puts the key in the lock. She looks up at him. He is aware only that within seconds she will leave him.

'Will we be allowed to do this?' she asks.

'I can't conceive of not doing this,' he says, answering her.

He puts his arms around her, brings her head into his shoulder. As he does so, a car pulls into the parking lot. The driver, making the turn, is an older woman with short, graying hair, a waitress perhaps, or a chef in the kitchen. The woman looks at him, smiles broadly, gives him a thumbs-up sign. He smiles back at her.

'This is it,' he says to Siân.

Minutes later, entering the room to retrieve his coat, he sees the bed, still unmade, still rumpled. He sits at the edge of the bed, notices a stain on the bottom sheet. He touches the stain with his fingers, closes his eyes. How can they be apart, he wonders, with this evidence of their union?

The girl knew, on the second day, that the boy would speak to her. All the afternoon before – inside the rooms of the old mansion and out on the lawns, and even by the pool when finally they had been allowed a swim – she knew that he was watching her. He wore red bathing trunks and dove with his body pointed like a knife, and when he came up, his hair, though short, was flattened, and he was looking at her.

On the second day, just before noon, she left the art room, where the others were, and walked along the path to the lake. Such a walk was not on the schedule, but it was not forbidden either. She was not a recluse necessarily, though she did often prefer to be alone.

Walking from the wide lawn into the thicket of trees was, she thought, like entering a cathedral where the walls were made of tall pines rather than the large hand-cut stones of the Catholic church near her home. The breeze from the lake drifted up the path through the trees, and the walk was dark, in shadow, sheltered from the glare of the midday sun. She made her way with her hands in her pockets, and when she heard the footfalls behind her, she kept her pace steady, did not hesitate or turn around. She entered the clearing, walked along the aisle between the wooden benches, sat at the one closest to the water. In front of her was the cross, and beyond that, the surface of the lake stretched to the other shore. Her being at this camp, she knew, was not about the cross. She understood already, even at fourteen, that the cross was historical, that it was but one of several ways the adults around her had seized upon to define hope, though she liked the discipline and the ritual of her church, the cadence of the Latin words.

He sat on a bench not far from hers, facing toward the water as she was. He said Hi in a shy voice, glancing at her sideways, and she said Hi too, looking at him quickly. He told her his name, and she said hers, though each knew the other's already. He asked her where she was from, and she asked him where he was from, and they gave their answers casually, not knowing that these answers sealed their fate. He seemed like her, she thought, not withdrawn, but someone comfortable with his own company. He said he'd left the room where the others were because he already had a wallet and couldn't see the sense of making another, not one held together with gimp anyway. She nodded and smiled. She said she wasn't much for crafts herself. She preferred other activities – the swimming and the archery, badminton. He said, smiling at his own cockiness, tempting fate, that he was pretty good at badminton and that they ought to play sometime. She said then, matching his self-mocking tone, that she was all right herself, and she might, if he was lucky, give him a game. They sat silently then, looking out at the water, both with smiles still left on their faces, until the smiles, after a time, faded.

He stood up, moved over to her bench. He sat beside her. He held a stick, etched figures in the dirt beneath their feet. They talked of their families and their schools, their new counselors, the routine at camp, each knowing that the casual questions and answers masked another dialogue, one spoken with averted eyes, small gestures. She crossed her legs; he scratched his arm.

The lake was not for swimming. At the shoreline, the

bottom turned dark with roots and weeds. There were fish in the lake, and sitting there, even under the hot sun, they could sometimes see the movement of a bass or a perch at the surface. A bell rang a melody, tolled twelve chimes, signaling lunch. They could not be away for this event, would be looked for, spoken to. She thought she might not mind that, except that then the others would know they had been found together and would be watching them.

She stood first and said they would have to go up the path now to the dining room. He flung the stick into the water. She watched it sail and fall. It was understood already, even on this first meeting, that they must return separately, and so he said, chivalrously, that he just wanted to inspect the boathouse before going back – allowing her to walk up the lawn first, accepting for himself the greater risk.

She hesitated, then acquiesced. She knew he saw her hesitation, that he knew she did not want to leave the clearing, this tentative beginning. He put his hands in his pockets, made markings in the soft dry dirt with the toe of his sneaker. Beyond them up the hill, they could hear the slap of a screen door, the muffled clatter of the others.

This afternoon, he said, and she nodded.

When we were children, you held my hand. And later, when we lay together on the damp, rumpled sheet, when I said, This is overtaking us, you said to me, This is only holding your hand.

The summer that I met you I began to bleed. The winter that I met you again, I stopped. I used to think that that was what we had missed together – my womanhood.

At the room at the inn, the room that used to be a dormitory room, you slid your fingers inside me, and I thought to myself: This is as intimate as I have ever been.

At the room at the inn, I lay under you. Your face was over mine. I looked up at you, at your mouth and at your eyes, and I thought: I know this man. It was the shock of recognition.

I brought pictures to the inn, to show you who I'd been, but I saw at once my mistake, the hurt in your eyes, and you said, It hurts that I wasn't with you.

You sat in a chair in the room. I sat astride you and looked at your face. You were wearing a blue-striped shirt, a red tie loosened at the collar. I looked at the outline of your face, the elegant jaw, the brown eyes, the mouth, the straight lower lip, and I saw the boy who had left me, the young man I had never known.

I watched you sit at the edge of the bed and bend to put your shoes on. I was standing behind you, and you didn't know I was watching. I saw the curve of your long back, the vulnerability of that long back, and I thought: I will always love this man.

I wanted to ask you questions, but could not. Did you know when you made your babies? Did you kiss your wife when she was in labor? When did you tell your wife that you loved her? Did you think your wife was beautiful?

And now I wonder this: To what extent does time distort memory?

HE IS AWARE, as he stands in line, that he is an object of scrutiny. He is not certain, however, if the cause is his unshaven appearance or if it stems from something else altogether – a demeanor that is both distracted and focused, is lost and yet edgy. He has been up all night writing letters, four of which he now holds inside a large manila envelope. He slept only two hours, after the kids left the house this morning, on the couch in his clothes. Since returning home from The Ridge, he has been unable to enter his and Harriet's bedroom, to look at the marriage bed, as if to do so were a kind of double betrayal – both to his wife and to the woman he made love to yesterday.

He feels trapped, third in line, at least seven people behind him. Possibly, he thinks, the reason everyone is staring at him is that they know he has lost his office, will almost certainly lose his house soon. Another recession casualty. Even Harriet has lately been attributing his bizarre behavior to his financial difficulties – an attribution that makes him feel both relieved and guilty. She no longer even asks why he doesn't come to bed, why he doesn't eat, as if she had decided to let this minor breakdown take its course.

He has come to the post office at the worst imaginable time, twelve-fifteen, lunch hour, and in the pre-Christmas rush too. He thinks of leaving, returning later, but he knows he must get these letters out of the house, get them off to Siân. Moving up to second in line, he reaches to the counter, snags an Express Mail address label, finds his pen in a jacket pocket. He thinks, as he has done all morning, of what they were doing at precisely this hour yesterday, reliving the day in fifteen-minute intervals. At twelve-fifteen, he recalls, they were still in bed, hadn't gone down to lunch yet. His mind swims with erotic images. Today he will call her at four. He needs to hear her voice.

The elderly woman in front of him puts her purse on the counter, removes her wallet, and painstakingly counts, in coins and bills, the cost of her transactions. Even Noonan, normally stoic, looks impatiently at his watch and then at the long line that has opened the door, letting in the cold, and sighs.

'Callahan,' he says, nodding slowly over the woman's head.

'Harry,' Charles says.

'Cold out there.'

'Bitter.'

'Whatya got there?'

'Express,' Charles says.

The woman in front of Charles moves away. Charles puts his packet on the counter. He wonders what Noonan will think about the address. The second time this week – an address he's been writing to all fall. Noonan looks at the package, weighs it, begins to attach the Express Mail label Charles has filled out.

The idea comes to him then. He looks at the long line of people behind him, glances at Noonan across the counter. Noonan has just indicated an amount of money, is waiting for Charles to pay.

No one will understand this, he knows. But she will. *She* will.

'Hold it a minute there, Harry.'

Charles strips off his topcoat, then his suit jacket underneath, lays these garments on the counter. He loosens his tie, slips it through his collar. He unbuttons the front of his shirt,

141

then the cuffs. He takes the shirt off, folds it into as compact a bundle as he can manage. He reaches across the counter, stuffs the shirt inside the packet with the letters, seals it again, slides the packet back to Noonan. Noonan looks at Charles. Charles puts his jacket and his topcoat back on, slips the tie into a pocket. He buttons the overcoat all the way up to the collar. He takes out his wallet.

'What do I owe you now?' he asks Harry Noonan.

FOUR

The air was soft and moist, the early morning air of a day that later would be hot but now was cool from a breeze off the water. She liked best, she thought, the way the pink light filtered through the leaves and highlighted the foliage along the banks. It was the third day or the fourth, and they had found a way each day to be together. He had said the night before to meet him early, at the boathouse.

He was there already. She could see him through the wide entrance, a white shirt in the shadows, bending to a boat, wrestling with a line. She walked beneath the wooden canopy to the dock. When they arranged to be together, neither ever said, We shouldn't be here, or, We might get caught. She had left her room before the others had awakened.

He rowed from the center of the boat, while she sat in the stern. She liked the smooth rotation of his arms as he pulled the oars, though sometimes, in his haste, the oars slapped the water, spraying them. Once, when he shifted in his seat, their knees touched, his through the cotton of his slacks, hers bare. He looked up at her quickly then, glanced away. He rowed to the middle of the lake, then let them drift out of sight toward the westward shore. He banked the oars in the boat and rested.

A sweat had broken out already around his neck and on his forehead. He took off his shoes and socks. He handed her his watch, and when he dove into the water, she thought later that he had done it as much to break the tension as to cool himself. He came up laughing and told her that if he drowned, she should give the watch to his little brother. She smiled. She wished that she could dive in with him, but she knew that they could not both go back with wet clothes, and besides, she reasoned, they couldn't abandon the boat, not without a line or a mooring.

He swam away, then back again. He swam on his side, then cut the water with a crawl. The water around them was dark in the early morning light, though away from them, the surface had a pink shimmer.

He returned to the boat, circled it on his back. He looked happy; his swimming seemed effortless. He spouted water like a whale, enjoyed showing off. He asked her questions, questions that were easier to ask from the water: Had she ever done anything really bad? Did she have a boyfriend at home? And she answered him. She did not have a boyfriend, she said, and once she had hitched a ride on the highway with a truckdriver.

What happened? he asked her, hanging on to the side of the boat with one hand.

He drove me to the next town.

Then what? he asked.

She was sorry now that she had chosen this story to tell.

He tried to kiss me, she said.

The word hung between them, a charged word at fourteen, a word that lay at the center of their thoughts. He looked stricken, would not ask the next question, though she knew she had to answer it.

I didn't let him, she said. I ran away from the truck, walked all the way home.

How long? he asked.

Five miles.

He flung himself back into the water, sank down as if with relief, bobbed up again.

That's not something bad that *you* did, he said.

Sure it is, she said. I got into the truck, didn't I?

He seemed to think about this. Well, that was stupid, but it wasn't bad, he said.

I thought it was bad, she said.

Did you tell your parents? he asked.

Of course not, she said.

I'll bet you told it at confession, he said. I'll bet you thought it was a sin.

He grabbed hold of the side of the boat, hoisted himself in. His shirt was a translucent peach, stuck to his skin. His pants were molded to the contours of his body. She looked away.

She was slightly irritated: She *had* thought it was a sin. Did still. She had put herself in jeopardy.

He rowed quickly, came in close to the shore. She could see the boathouse and the cross. Soon the others would be down, for morning chapel. She wondered then what Cal would do about his wet clothes.

When he entered the dock underneath the cover of the boathouse, she handed him his watch. She could not see his face in the gloom, not with the sun off the water behind him, but she knew that he could see hers. She felt his fingers briefly in the exchange with the watch.

You're like me, he said to her.

When the others came for chapel, she was sitting on a bench already. A friend asked her why she had missed breakfast, and she answered that she'd gone for a walk. The others were noisy, took seats, changed seats. She leaned slightly sideways on her bench, her arm outstretched to prop her up, as if she were tired, waiting for the priest. In this way, she saved a space, so that when Cal came, she sat up straight and he sat down beside her. His hair was wet, but his shirt and pants were dry. They didn't speak.

The priest entered the clearing, stood beside the cross. The children rose and knelt and sat again. She looked out toward the water, noticed that the pink had turned to blue. Her hands were clasped loosely on her lap. She thought that she could feel the warmth of the boy through the sleeve of her blouse.

With one swift movement then, as if it had been rehearsed, thought about, practiced in the mind, the boy swept her hand off her lap and held it on the bench between them. His hand was cool and dry from the swimming, though she felt it tremble. He held her hand more tightly to stop the trembling. She felt something flutter deep inside her abdomen and knew that her face was hot. She looked at her feet, heard the priest intone his words. The water and the sun spun around her.

THE SKY IS HEAVY and gray, a fine snow beginning, like ashes from a fire. He has been waiting in the parking lot for more than half an hour, is worried that she won't arrive before the storm begins in earnest. He has listened to weather reports at least half a dozen times this morning, has determined that since the storm is moving in from the west, she's probably been in it for some time. The prediction is for heavy accumulation, the first substantial snow this season. His children at breakfast were hoping for a day off from school, though they will begin their Christmas vacation tomorrow. He thinks of Harriet in her pink flannel nightgown this morning, of the way she walked him to the door, wished him a good trip, worried over his driving in the bad weather, and he winces. He has had to tell her he had business in western Connecticut, will have to stay overnight.

He gets out of the car, buttons his overcoat, tucks in his scarf. The parking lot is slippery; his shoes make elongated footprints in the thin wet covering. He walks to the neck of the drive, scans its length. It is the first night he and Siân will have together, the first time they will be able to sleep in the same bed. They've never even been together in the dark. Always before, she has had to leave shortly after lunch to get home to her daughter or to make supper. He feels like a man less than half his age who might never have been with a woman, the promise of an entire night sleeping next to a woman an incomparable gift. Yet even so, he senses as he always does the press of time, of minutes passing already, of a finite number of hours that he will be with Siân before she has to leave him; and that when she does leave him, time will stop, as

149

if he were about to be executed. He remembers, as a boy, lying in his bed, trying to imagine what it would be like to be a condemned prisoner, watching the clock tick away the minutes left of life. It seemed to him the worst imaginable fate – to know precisely when one would die.

They have been together now four times, including their first lunch. Always, since that day, they have met here at the inn, gone straight to the room. He is known now, is greeted warmly on the phone when he calls for a reservation. The last two days they had together, the management put them into a suite that had at its entrance two successive locked doors; Siân joked immediately that they'd been put into a soundproof room. He aches with wanting her, and his body tightens. He looks at his watch for the tenth time in the half-hour. He cannot think of her now without also seeing the erotic images they have created together: Siân with her back to him, pressed against a chaste, blue-flowered wallpaper; Siân in a hot bath, the room filled with steam (her glasses, until she took them off, opaque ovals), while he sat, fully dressed, on the lid of the toilet seat, drinking beer from a water glass, watching her breasts float above the waterline. Siân bending her neck while he unzipped her dress, the long line of her white back open to his hand. The muscle of her inner thigh made wet from both of them.

It is not so much, he knows, that he or she, or they together, are particularly skilled or adventurous; it is rather that their bodies want each other, fit, are trying to say something that cannot be said with words. He understands, too, that somehow, at least for the two of them, eros is linked with time. It is in the very urgency of time, the sense that their minutes together are short and numbered, that he must say what he has come to say before she leaves, that gestures and words cannot be wasted. But it is, paradoxically, also in the vast expanse of the lost years – the keen sense, whenever he is with her, of all the days and hours missed, the youthful bodies not known, the thousands of nights he might have touched her easily, without loss, without guilt and anxiety. They will never know together the sense of time squandered. To the contrary, he thinks of their hours together as time stolen or salvaged – time-outs from their separate realities.

He turns in his pacing, faces into the snow, walks in the direction of the parking lot. The inn, in the gloom of the lowered skies, is inviting, the door laced with holly, the windows lit with small electric candles on the sills. He has brought Siân a present, and he will give it to her this evening before they go down to dinner. This will be, will have to be, their Christmas together; he knows they will not be able to see each other again before Christmas, perhaps not again before the new year. He does not know how they will survive the holidays, and thinking this, he feels again the seaweed on the line, the drag of guilt, the chaos of the facts and his inability to sort them out. He has a wife and three children – each blameless, each believing in the rituals of Christmas Eve and Christmas morning, each ignorant of his infidelity. He has betrayed his family in the absolute and common sense of desiring and sleeping with another woman, *loving* another woman, but he cannot escape the notion that he has betrayed them as well with the debacle of his financial ruin. Within days, unless he can work a deal at the bank, he will have to tell Harriet that they will not only lose the house and all their equity in it, but they will almost certainly have to declare bankruptcy to ward off the creditors who have been hounding him. He hardly knows which is worse – to tell her that he loves another woman or to tell her that he can no longer provide for her as he has promised to.

These large betrayals, he believes, will not be forgiven, but he sometimes wonders if it isn't the smaller betrayals that are worse. He thinks of the dozens of times in the past several weeks that he has lied to his wife: He left a Christmas party in their neighborhood twice last Saturday night, saying that he wanted to check up on the children, when what he actually did was drive to a phone booth to call Siân, who he knew was alone for the evening. ('This is torture,' he remembers telling Siân that night.) He has surreptitiously poured milk down the sink, then told his wife that he would go to the store for her to make sure the kids had milk for breakfast (surely that cannot be forgiven, he thinks – the use of fatherly love in the service of adultery), when what he intended to do and did do was to drive to yet another phone booth and call his lover. He knows the location of every phone booth in his town and in the neighboring communities. He knows precisely at which phone booths he is likely not to be disturbed, which connect him immediately with AT&T, which are better to use during the day, which at night. He can punch in Siân's number and his credit card number in seconds, with or without his glasses, in the dark or in the light. He presses the numbers blind, like someone trying desperately to reach his drug dealer.

He wonders, too, not for the first time, how Siân manages in her own home. He can tell immediately, from the way she says hello on the telephone, whether or not her husband is present in the room when he calls. They have had dialogues that would be comical if they weren't so serious. He talks to her; he asks her questions; she responds obliquely as if answering a phone solicitation from a PBS television station or a political cause. He believes he has communicated more to her, said more to her, in the several weeks they have been together than he has ever shared with anyone. Certainly he has never talked to his wife the way he talks to Siân.

He has never been inside Siân's home, but when he talks to

152

her on the telephone, and when he thinks of her during the day (a continual series of images and thoughts, interrupted only by a momentary and strenuously willful effort to concentrate on a task at hand or a question posed to him), he tries to envision her life with her daughter and her husband. Sometimes he imagines her in a T-shirt and ponytail, leaning against the lip of a counter, holding a phone in one hand and preparing a meal with the other. Often, when he calls, he shares her attention with Lily, her three-year-old, who seems to chatter constantly at her feet. He thinks she is a good mother; he likes the way she speaks to her daughter, speaks of her daughter. He has a less clear sense of what she is like as a wife. He cannot bring to focus the image of Siân sitting at a table with another man, embracing another man, lying in a bed with another man. He senses – she has allowed him to believe – that the marriage is not a good one, perhaps never was. She has alluded to an emptiness in the relationship, which he has seized upon and possibly embroidered; and he knows that he has extrapolated from her poetry a kind of deprivation, an emotional desert. She has said little of, and he has not asked about, her sexual life with her husband (though it is this question that haunts him, that seems always to be at the edge of his tongue when he is with her, that he is sometimes afraid that he will, despite his best intentions, ask), apart from her comment early on that she was 'frozen.' Sometimes he hopes this means that she and her husband no longer make love; at other times he knows this can't possibly be true, and that knowledge sickens him. Is it really conceivable that she and her husband have not been together since he first kissed Siân?

He brushes the snow from the top of his head, stamps his feet to shake out the cold. He says aloud, once, the words 'Screw it,' as if by that he might ward off a sense of hopelessness that he feels coming upon him now, like gathering fog. He feels it particularly when his thoughts have led him to images of Siân with her child, in her home, or when he watches his own children in his own home. He does not want to imagine a life now without Siân, yet he cannot begin to sort out in his mind how a life with her will be accomplished. Even if he were able to walk away from Harriet and his children (which seems to him at times nearly as unimaginable as cutting off a foot), is it at all likely that Siân would do the same? Would she *want* to do the same? Would her husband just meekly leave the marriage and his farm? Impossible. Then what? Would Siân bring her daughter to Rhode Island to live with him? Could they live somewhere in between? And if so, what then of his business? Even as anemic as his business is, it is still grounded in a particular locale. If he's ever to salvage it, if he's ever to wait out the recession, it has to be done within the community. Or *would* it be possible to set up shop somewhere else?

He hears rather than sees the car coming – the slippery hiss of tires on the drive. He turns, she puts on the brakes; the car skids gently a foot or two. She rolls down the window, her face flushed from her impatience with the weather or (he hopes) with her impatience to be with him. He bends down, kisses her on the mouth. She smiles broadly; she seems as exhilarated as he is to have this whole day together.

'I thought you'd never get here,' he says.

'I'd never not get here,' she says.

He unlocks each of the double doors, follows her inside. There are electric candles at the windows, a fire in the fireplace, a large bowl of fruit on a table between the windows. She turns to him, a look of mild surprise on her face.

'Did they . . .?'

He nods.

'They know,' she says.

'Of course they know.' He smiles. The fire and the fruit seem an omen – a sign that others have seen them together and approve. She takes off her coat, lets it slide into a heap on a chair. She has worn her hair pinned at the sides, and it falls loosely along her back. There is more gray at the temples than he has noticed before; she seems self-conscious about her hair, touches it, smooths back a strand. Her face is bright from the cold. She has worn a black dress with long sleeves. She sits on the chair, removes her leather boots. The melted snow from the soles and the heels make small puddles on the highly polished wood floor.

He kneels, buries his face in her lap. She puts her hands to the back of his neck, bends her head to his.

He feels the warmth of her thighs at either side of his face, the soft wool of her dress on his cheeks. She is holding him as she might a child, and he wants to weep. What they want seems so simple – time together, a lifetime together, or what is left of a lifetime together – and yet that small goal, he knows, is fraught with endless complications: a maze of responsibilities and commitments, deceptions and betrayals. Why, why, why, he asks himself silently for the hundredth time, couldn't they have remained somehow connected – in touch, with all that the phrase implies – until they were old enough to find each other again? How maddening that they should have met when they were children and had no control over their lives.

His anger and his grief and his specific lust for this woman fill him with a need so sharp he shudders. He raises her skirt to her hips. He wants to devour her, and he is afraid that he might inadvertently hurt her. He lifts his face to hers so that she can see this. She touches his face with her hands. Perhaps he *is* weeping. He draws her down off the chair, onto the floor. He moves her skirt up toward her waist, slips off her underwear. He finds her with his tongue, kisses her, caresses her with his mouth. He waits for the tiny sound she makes at the back of her throat, a faint cry of helplessness, as from a small animal, and watches now the delicate arch of her white neck, her head thrust back, her mouth slightly open.

And when she comes, he thinks that possibly the most erotic image of all may be the tilt of her nostrils seen across the long expanse of her body.

'It's lovely,' she says, turning once for him. The robe is short and silk, ivory, and barely covers her in the back, a fact that makes her laugh and blush at the same time. She sits on an upholstered chair, crosses her legs, and tries to look demure, a task she seems to know is hopeless. The robe falls open slightly, draped just so along the curve of her breasts, and she makes no move to close it. He likes sitting on the bed, looking at her in the robe. He enjoyed choosing it for her, thinking of her in it, though he knows she will have to conceal it when she goes home. He wishes they had a place of their own, however small, so that she could hang the robe in a closet and it would always be there. He wishes he could cook a wonderful meal for her.

'I love you,' she says.

'I know.'

'But I feel bad.'

'Why?'

'I didn't bring you a present. There was nothing I could find that you could have taken home, that seemed to say what I want to say to you.'

He ponders this. 'What might you have gotten me that would have said what you wanted to say that I couldn't have taken home?'

156

She smiles, thinks. 'A lake, maybe.'

He laughs.

'Or a small country.'

'Possibly this hotel?' he suggests.

'Perfect,' she says. 'Or a plane.'

'A plane?'

'Mmmm. And flying lessons.'

'I'd like a biplane. I've always wanted a biplane.'

'Or years,' she says.

'How many?'

'Thirty or so.'

'Past or future?'

'Both. How many years do you think we have left?'

His heart leaps. She *does* think of them together. 'My grandfather lived to be ninety-six,' he says, 'in full possession of all his faculties. *And* he drank Jack Daniel's and smoked half a pack a day.'

'I've got it,' she says, looking pleased with herself. 'The ideal present. A videotape of us together here when we were kids. Of the whole week. What we sounded like. What we looked like.'

He tries to imagine what she sounded like as a fourteen-year-old, wishes he could, for a moment, hear her voice. 'We know what we looked like. From the picture. Anyway, I don't need a present. I don't want a present. Your being here is enough.'

'It's not enough,' she says.

'No. You're right. It's not.'

She leans forward, folds her hands across her knee. 'I wonder,' she says, 'if we had all the time in the world, if we knew we could be together for the rest of our lives, would we not care anymore, would we grow bored with each other – or fight?' She laughs.

'I doubt it,' he says.

'We'll never know.'

'Don't say that. Please.'

'And I also wonder,' she says, 'if we *had* been together all this time, what would we be feeling now? Would we be as happy as we are now? Would we even know what we had? Without having known the loss of it, I mean.'

'I'd like to think we'd know,' he says, 'that we'd have known all along.'

'You probably wouldn't have liked me when I was younger,' she says. 'You'd have thought me too stiff or too repressed or too serious or whatever. I was a virgin, technically, until I was twenty-two. And even then, I didn't really get it. I think my erotic life got lost or was buried somehow – possibly by the church. It's one of the reasons I won't send Lily, though Stephen's mother thinks I'm damning her.'

'I lost my virginity when I was nineteen,' he says. 'It seemed late at the time.'

He looks away, unwilling to linger on the image of Siân losing her virginity – at any age. 'No,' he says, turning back to her. 'I'll tell you this: No matter when I'd met you in my lifetime, no matter when, I'd have left what I was doing or who I was with to be with you.'

A flicker of alarm passes briefly across her brow.

Though he has thought of little else, and he knows now that she has to have thought of this too, they have never actually mentioned leaving their respective homes to be together.

'You know we have to be together,' he says quietly.

She shakes her head. She says nothing.

'Siân.'

She turns her face away. 'Not now,' she says. 'Please.'

158

He takes a breath, exhales. 'All right,' he says, 'but you know we have to talk about this sometime.'

'I just want this one night to be a happy one,' she says. 'Without complications. Or is that not possible?'

'I'm sorry,' he says, getting off the bed and walking to the chair where she is sitting. 'It will be.'

He slides the robe gently off her shoulders so that it falls open and along her arms. He kneels, looks at her breasts. They are small and round. Below them there is the curve of her abdomen – from her babies. He bends forward, kisses her belly, then her left breast.

'Is this the one?' he asks.

'What one?'

'On the bench, that first day.'

She thinks a minute. 'Yes, I suppose it is.' She gathers the robe across her chest, covering herself.

'They're small,' she says.

He looks at the crumple of fabric where she is holding it with her hand. 'Well, look at it this way,' he says. 'They'll never sag.'

She laughs. 'Yes they will.'

'No they won't.'

He bends to her again.

'They're little,' he says, 'but I know for a fact they like to be kissed.'

'Mr. Callahan.'

The maître'd nods at Charles, indicates that he should follow him to what has become, in the several weeks they have been visiting the inn, their table. The snow outside the windows is thinning out; the storm, it seems, is nearly over. Charles follows Siân across the long dining room, his hand lightly at her waist. She has worn her hair down; it falls in a

159

loose fan along the back of her dress. Pearls circle her neck. Charles orders immediately, as he has planned, a bottle of champagne.

They sit side by side, and he takes her hand. Siân crosses her legs, touches a heavy silver spoon. He surveys the room. Only three other tables are occupied tonight; he suspects that the storm has kept most people away, though he has never eaten here in the evening. Instead of flowers in the center of the room, there is a Christmas tree – a small, simple tree with white lights. Boughs of spruce, interspersed with white candles, decorate the fireplace mantel.

'Pretty,' he says.

She nods. Her mood seems altered, shaded.

'What's wrong?' he asks.

She shakes her head. 'Nothing's wrong.'

'You seem pensive.'

She smiles. 'It *is* pretty. I'm sorry.'

The waiter brings the champagne, pops the cork, fills the glasses. Charles raises his to Siân.

'To presents we can't give each other,' he says.

'Yet,' she says.

She takes a sip, doesn't meet his eyes. She puts her glass down.

'What's it like?' she asks. 'Your Christmas?'

He sighs. So that's why she is pensive. He studies her mouth, the long curve of her lower lip. 'Are you sure you want to hear this?' he asks. 'It might be better if we didn't.'

'No, I'm sure. I'd like to be able to picture what you're doing that evening, that day.'

He hesitates. He has a feeling that he has often: a sense that no matter how he answers this question, the answer will be the wrong one. 'Are you writing?' he asks instead.

She turns her head slightly away. She seems surprised by the question. 'Not much,' she says. 'I write to you. I can't work well now. I'm too . . . preoccupied, I guess you would say.'

'I know the feeling.'

'You're trying to change the subject.'

'OK. OK. Here's what happens. My wife's parents and my parents and my wife's sister and her kids come over on Christmas Eve, and basically I hang out in the kitchen, cooking.'

'You have Christmas on Christmas Eve.'

'The adults do. We open our presents in the evening, after the children are in bed. The kids open theirs in the morning.'

'Oh. And do you go to church?'

'I don't. And Harriet doesn't . . .' A flicker of something crosses Siân's eyes. He wishes he hadn't mentioned his wife by name. '. . . but my parents go to midnight mass, and maybe my daughter Hadley will go with them. I'm usually doing the dishes.'

She is silent next to him. He knows what she is picturing, what she is imagining, what she wants to ask and won't: Do he and his wife exchange presents? When do they do this: when others are present or when they are alone? He watches as she drains her glass, pushes it forward on the table as though to ask for another. Silently he fills her glass again. She raises it, nearly drains it at one go.

'Siân . . .,' he says.

'Do you want to hear about my Christmas rituals? So you can picture what I'm doing?'

'Siân, don't,' he says.

'It's quite interesting. Really, Charles, you should let me tell you.'

There is a slightly manic note to her voice that he has never heard before. She drains her glass, nudges it forward yet again.

'The champagne is delicious,' she says. 'You have excellent taste. I feel like getting drunk tonight. Why not.'

Reluctantly he fills her glass again. 'Why don't we order?' he suggests.

'In a minute,' she says. 'I'm going to tell you about Christmas Eve on a Polish onion farm. You haven't lived until you've had Christmas on a Polish onion farm.'

'Siân, why are you doing this?'

'Actually, I used to like this ritual. I used to like rituals of any kind to break the silences. I used to like as many people in the house as possible . . .'

'Let's talk about something else.'

'It's called Wigilia,' she says, 'the Christmas Eve dinner. We have it at our place, all the relatives – well, all Stephen's side of the family. We visit my father the day after Christmas. I cook for days beforehand with Stephen's mother. I bet you can't picture that, can you, his mother and me in my kitchen, making pirogis. Well, I do. You can't imagine how good they are. You like to cook. You should learn how to make them . . .'

'Siân.'

'I fill them with sauerkraut or potato or farmer's cheese and potato or prunes. The prune ones are especially delicious . . .'

'We can go upstairs, come down later to eat if you want,' he says. Her face is flushed, her eyes too bright.

'And we never have meat. Only fish. We have pickled herring. Do you like pickled herring? And pike and carp. And borscht. And sometimes cabbage soup. And sauerkraut and sardines. And a kind of poppyseed bread. And figs and dates. And everybody eats as much as he can. And oh, I almost forgot: You have to leave a place for the unknown visitor. You know who the unknown visitor is, don't you?'

He looks out across the long dining room. The heavy white

linen seems extraordinarily beautiful to him – comforting, weighed down by anchors of silver. When he turns to glance outside the long windows, he sees that the snow has finally stopped. Within the dining room, and without, there is an unearthly quiet, the quiet of a building surrounded by a new snow. And is it only his imagination, or is everyone in the room actually frozen, listening intently to Siân's voice, at once animated and brittle, as if it were a piece of crystal that might soon shatter?

'Well, it's for Jesus Christ. That's who.'

She puts her glass down on the table. She stands up slowly, with inordinate care, and slips through the small space between the banquette tables, as though each movement had been choreographed. She turns delicately without looking at him. He watches her walk the long distance through the dining room, her pace unhurried, her back straight. Her heels click rhythmically on the wooden floor. He follows her with his eyes until she rounds a corner and he can see her no more.

The champagne was a mistake. They have not eaten all day. He will give her a minute, then follow her back to the room. Perhaps she ought to have a short nap before they eat. He will suggest it, rub her back. The dining room must be open late; he'll speak to the maître d'. He knew it was risky territory; he tried to warn her off. And yet, he thinks, this had to happen. It's his own anger too. At what might have been and wasn't. Will he ever be able to listen to her talk about her life, or she his, without the hurt?

He looks up. A waiter is at his elbow.

'I'm sorry, sir,' the man says, 'but I thought you'd like to know.'

'Know what?'

'Your friend appears to be ill.'

Charles stands up. 'Where is she?'

'She's in the ladies' room, sir.'

He finds her kneeling in a stall, her feet splayed out behind her. A waitress, standing in the center of the room as if not wanting to approach any nearer, is the only other person present. Charles nods to the waitress, dismisses her. 'I'll handle this,' he says.

Siân retches once into the basin, reaches up with her hand to flush the toilet. Charles moves in beside her, squats down with his back against the stall. Siân's face is white, with pearls of sweat on her forehead. He holds her hair back with one hand, puts the other to her forehead to brace her.

'It's all right,' he tells her. 'Let it out. Let it go. Don't fight it.' It is what he tells his children when they are sick in the night.

'I can't do this,' she cries. 'I can't do this.'

'It's OK, Siân. It's OK.'

'No, it's not OK. It's not OK at all. My daughter is at home without me. I have to lie all the time. We didn't have all those years, and now it's too late, we won't be able to have any time at all. We have families, and they need us.'

'We'll work it out,' he says quietly.

She retches again into the bowl, wipes her mouth. He flushes the toilet for her.

She sits back against a corner of the stall, her knees raised. She doesn't seem to care about her ungainly posture, her knees spread as if she had on jeans and were resting against a stone wall. He takes a handkerchief from his suit pocket, hands it to her. Her face is bathed in sweat, her hair curling along its edges in wet tendrils. In the fluorescent light, her face washed of color, she looks every bit of her forty-six years – a middle-aged woman, he would say now – and curiously, studying her, he can see all of her, all the women she has been or will be, from the young girl to the old woman. The clarity of the images frightens him, but he is aware only that he loves her, that he wants nothing more in life than to be allowed to take care of her.

'You don't understand,' she says, her eyes rimmed red, her cheeks wet. She reaches up for toilet paper, blows her nose. 'My husband gets up early and makes doughnuts on Christmas morning. He's giving me a leather-bound edition of my book. On Christmas morning, we drape a blanket across the entrance to the living room, so that Lily can't peek at her presents, and then we ceremoniously drop the blanket, and she squeals with delight. My daughter loves Polish food. Even I like the pirogis. Don't you see? We can't undo that.'

Her voice has reached a pitch he has never heard before. He watches as she leans her head back, sighs deeply.

'I'm finished,' she says. She closes her eyes. She looks worn, exhausted. 'Families once took us away from each other, and now families are taking us away from each other again.'

'I'll help you,' he says.

She shakes her head. 'You can't help me,' she says quietly. 'Neither one of us can help the other, and that's the truth.'

He lifts her to her feet. He watches while she washes her face at the sink, towels it dry. She sloshes mouthfuls of water, spits them out. She runs her fingers through her hair, pulling the wet strands back.

'I need some fresh air,' she says.

'I know,' he says. 'I'll get our coats.'

He returns from the room with their coats and scarves and her boots. She exchanges her shoes for her boots in the hallway.

'Wait here,' he says to her before they go outside. 'I'll be right back.'

When he rejoins her in the hallway, he is carrying a broom.

'I got it from the kitchen,' he says.

'What's it for?'

'You'll see.'

Outside, the snow across the lawn is a vast cascade of white, unmarred by footsteps of any kind. He calculates, as they make their way down to the path, that the accumulation must be somewhere between four and six inches. A moon has risen and shines through the last patches of cloud. It will be a clear night and cold.

He takes her arm, helping her through the snow. Her boots are dress boots with heels, not meant for hiking. When they are halfway down the lawn, he turns to see the inn behind them. The facade is ablaze, the glow from inside making golden pools of light on the snow. In the darkness, it seems as if inside the inn there were a large party, a Christmas party, with many guests dressed in velvet and gold and black, holding champagne glasses, smiling under holly, their faces lit by candlelight. He has a fleeting sense of having left something important and warm behind.

Amidst the pines, the going is rougher, the light from the moon partially obscured. Beside him, Siân has begun to breathe more normally. He carries the broom over his shoulder like a rifle.

When they reach the clearing, they can just make out the shape of the benches in the snow. He walks with Siân to the one closest to the lake, the one they sat on a few weeks ago, brushes it off with the broom.

'That's what the broom was for?' she asks.

'No, not exactly,' he replies.

She sits on the bench, her hands in the pockets of her coat, her body drawn inward against the cold.

'I'm going to test the ice,' he says.

The snow on the lake is faintly blue from the moon. He is

not sure exactly where the shoreline ends and the lake begins, but when he reaches the ice, the soles of his shoes slip against the hard surface. He is destroying his shoes, he knows, and his feet are frozen from the snow. He walks twenty-five feet out onto the surface of the lake, takes a test jump; the ice feels solid. He begins then to sweep. The snow, so new and light, blows effortlessly away like dust. When he has cleared a patch the size of a small bedroom, he slips across his newly created rink and walks to where Siân is sitting.

'We're going to walk on water,' he says, reaching for her hand.

'You're crazy,' she says.

'Well, we knew that.'

He holds her hand, then her whole arm when they reach the ice. She makes one small tentative movement onto the ice, leans into him for support. When he takes her weight, he is afraid for a moment that his footing will give and they might both go down, but his shoes hold and he steadies her. Together they slide forward, first one foot and then the other.

He lets go of her arm, but not her hand. They glide across the ice, she occasionally clutching him when she feels herself about to lose her balance. They are dark shapes on the lake; he can barely see her face.

'I'll always love you,' she says.

'I know,' he says.

A bird – an owl? – hoots at them from across the lake. But the snow, all around them, is a buffer, smothering the sounds of the outside world.

In the center of the small square he has made, he turns to her, then holds her arm out in the classic dance posture. They execute a few slippery steps, draw closer to each other for support.

'What are you listening to?' she asks.

'You won't believe this,' he says.

'I might.'

'The Brahms Second Piano Concerto. Do you know it?'

'I think so. Where are you?'

'I'm in the third movement. The quiet one. The one that begins with the cello.'

'Oh.'

'It's a concerto, but it's like a symphony,' he says. 'I used to think it was the most beautiful piece of music I'd ever heard, and I'm not sure I don't still think that. Sometimes, when everyone is out of the house, I put it on full blast and just luxuriate in it. I believe it's the longest concerto ever written. Brahms himself was the soloist at its premiere. God, how I'd love to have heard that. I have a number of versions, but I'm partial to Cliburn with the Chicago Symphony Orchestra. Although the Rudolf Serkin is absolutely – '

'Charles.'

She puts her gloved hands to his face.

'What?'

'Stop.'

'Stop?'

'You're as bad as I am with the Polish food.'

Her face is white, drained by the moon. She looks, despite her warm coat and scarf and gloves, naked to him, her face unmasked, her eyes, in the cool light, black and open. This is, he knows, one moment that they have, one moment in time, one pearl on a short string.

'If you're skating on thin ice,' he whispers into the frosty night, 'you might as well dance.'

Around the curtains there is light. They are naked in the bed, she folded into him, like spoons. He is hard when he awakens, knows it instantly, knows too that this is not generic lust, that she was there in the dissipating dream: He sees her face in a fragment before it drifts away. He finds her breast, the small nipple, nearly always erect. Her belly, the softness there. She does not exercise, and, somehow, this appeals to him. He makes a light circular motion with his hand, and she awakens, turns onto her back. He knows he must look like a pterodactyl, his thinning hair in a sculpture all its own, but she smiles, embraces him, shifts slightly so that in one movement he is above her. He enters her immediately without needing to be guided in. She is slippery already, as though waiting for him in her dream. *Was* it a dream that produced this, he wonders, or is it left from an earlier time – how many hours ago? – in the night? He straddles her legs; he feels welded to her, and he can see her face. Her excitement is contagious, fuels his own, as his, as his, he knows, triggers hers. He watches now as her mouth opens; he circles her tongue with his own. He smooths her hair from her forehead. He raises himself up, his weight on his hands. Her eyes dart from his face to his shoulder and back again. He watches as a flush of color begins at her throat, suffuses her face. They are locked in a deep, slow rhythm, the ebb and flow of waves. In time, studying her, he sees the slight arch of her neck that tells him she is close. He has wondered if it might be possible, but now it seems almost inevitable. He feels himself there, holds back, examines the tilt of her chin. In a few hours they will leave each other, sucked back into lives of lost meaning. There is only this now; this is everything. The frame of the world around them increases his urgency. He waits for her to close her eyes, as she almost always does but this time, she opens them immediately, astonishing him.

'I want to see you,' she whispers.

And saying that, she comes, and he is with her, and it is only seconds later that he hears again the mingled bewilderment and pleasure of their simultaneous cries.

It was brief, and yet it was a lifetime. I used to think it was something I would never have, that the era in which I was raised and the church I nearly wed had bred it out of me, or had leached it out. But you gave it to me, or I gave it to you, and now I cannot separate your body from your words, nor mine from my thoughts. I cannot separate what we did from who we were. Every image is erotic, or within the fold, etched in stone now, engraved blossoms.

In December, the black dirt held the warmth long after the other soil had frozen, as if, along with the light, the dirt had swallowed up the sun. Consequently, the early snows melted on the onion fields, like snow falling into the sea.

That December, I touched my daughter often. Stephen worked on machinery and taught at the school, and when we chanced upon each other, in the kitchen or in a hallway, he held himself away from me, in self-preservation. I believe now that he knew before I did that I was leaving him, that he felt it in the silences, in the unbreachable distance, even as he denied it to himself, refused to imagine it.

We spoke sometimes and were careful with each other – unwilling yet to disturb the separate peace each of us had made.

The week before Christmas, I went into the attic, where I had found your picture, and brought out garlands and tinsel, colored lights and a star. The ornaments were heavy, the garlands weighted, and it was an effort to raise my arms to the tree. Lily asked me often what it was I was looking at, and I answered her that I wasn't looking, I was thinking.

I was thinking about equations: Is one hour spent doing X equal to thirty-one years of doing Y?

On Christmas morning, my husband left the bed early. I waited until I could smell the fried dough and the coffee, and I went down to join him. He was wearing an ocher flannel shirt, and I was thinking: Are you wearing a similar shirt, one that I have never seen, may never see at all? Are you with your wife, your children? Do you hold your wife in the bed when you sleep? Do your children join you in the bed on Christmas morning, making a sandwich of bodies, as Stephen and I sometimes did with Lily and had done with Brian when Brian was with us?

It wasn't possible, of course, ever to forget Brian, or that he should have been there with us. Christmas was the worst, though I don't know how I can say that. Every day was the worst; the pain was not dulled by time, not filled up, not muted. He had died in a friend's car on the way home from a soccer game at school, died when the car in which he was traveling was hit by a metallic-blue Corvette that had run the light. In the few seconds just before the intersection, the last few seconds of his life, Brian, for reasons that will never be known to us, had unfastened his seat belt. For days, for weeks, for months afterward, I replayed that scene in my head, willing time to stop, so that I could crawl into that car, into the back seat, and refasten the seat belt for my son.

Stephen finished frying the doughnuts. In his flannel shirt, he made an effort to be festive. Lily came, with a bright anticipatory smile. With a flourish, Stephen let down the curtain, and Lily ran to the tree.

We ate the doughnuts as Lily opened up her stocking and

her presents. Stephen and I made a show for each other, each pretending to be happy. I opened the leather book: It was beautiful, and I said so. I had given Stephen an easel and a set of costly oil paints, and I saw at once the confusion behind his smile: How could he take up again this hobby while he was under siege?

We were sitting in the living room, awash with colored paper, toys underfoot. Stephen made a fire, brought us more coffee. I was thinking that in each house on the street, in all the pastel houses, there were children and colored paper, and women and men who might or might not love each other, who might or might not have indelible connections of their own. And it was then that I remembered another present for Lily, one I had hidden away. It was a sweater, a rose-colored sweater that she could wear through the winter.

I laughed. I've forgotten a present, I said.

Stephen said, You do this every year.

I said, I hide them so well I sometimes forget about them. I'll just get it now.

Stephen was standing. No, I'll get it, he said. I'm already up.

I looked at him against the window, the overbright light from the snow outside causing him to be in silhouette.

Yes, OK, I said. It's in the dresser in my closet, the third drawer down.

I sat back, took a sip of coffee. Lily had on her lap a jewelry box with a secret compartment that intrigued her. The hot coals from the fireplace filled the room with warmth.

I sat up quickly then; the coffee spilled onto my robe. I was paralyzed, unable to speak or move. Lily said, Mum, you spilled your coffee.

I waited a minute, possibly an hour. I heard Stephen's

foot-steps through the kitchen, looked over to where he stood in the doorway.

I saw it all on his face – that peculiar mix of confusion and horror that accompanies a fear confirmed.

In his hands he held your shirt.

THE WIND FROM THE NORTHEAST rips along High
Street, stinging the side of his face with a cold rain that
smells of the sea. Charles watches as a string of Christmas
lights loops high over the traffic, dislodging a wreath, which
bounces once onto the street, then scuds along the sidewalk
like prairie sage. Last-minute shoppers, their faces pinched
with cold, bend toward the storm. From his vantage point
on the top step of the bank, Charles looks out over the row
of storefronts toward the harbor. Even sheltered, the water
is rough; a grizzled sky meets a muddy sea not two hundred
feet from shore, obliterating the lighthouse at the end of the
point. He hopes each of the draggermen has made it back in;
there is nothing worse than a boat late or lost over Christmas.
He remembers two or three scares from the past, the news
spreading with Christmas greetings until no one in town could
pass a window without looking out to sea and mumbling a
prayer – as though no celebration could begin until all boats
were in and accounted for.

The storm will hurt the shops, he thinks, the small busi-
nesses struggling through the worst Christmas season in
memory. Already McNamara, with his lumberyard at the
end of High Street, has declared bankruptcy; and Janet Costa,
at the stationery store, has told Harriet she won't make it
through February. The decline is contagious, the failure of
each enterprise a harbinger of other failures to come. Charles
wonders if the street soon will resemble a ghost town, with
rows of empty storefronts.

He takes one step down, hikes his collar to cover his ears.
He should go home, he knows, to help Harriet with the tree,

but if he goes now, he is certain she will see it on his face – their own failure, *his* failure. He feels the anger, but oddly there is now as well a kind of relief. It can't get much worse, and in that there is some comfort. The particular struggle to save his house is over.

He looks across at the coffee shop; he could go in there, get himself a sandwich, wish a few clients a happy Christmas. But it isn't what he wants – it won't take the edge off the anger. He looks down the street in the direction of The Blue Schooner: a pint, a bowl of hot chowder, wish a different set of clients a happy Christmas. The wind howls up the steps, buffets his coat. Nothing keeps out the cold in a storm like this, he knows. He feels the raw air inside his sleeves and close to his chest.

Hunched in his coat, he jogs down the steps of the bank. On the sidewalk, he turns to look up at the imposing edifice. The thick white columns support a wide stone portico. An oversize wreath, decorated with tiny jewels of light and golden bows, hangs over tall wooden doors, as if promising access inside to wealth and taste and power, when what the bank has really done is suck the town dry. Charles wants to give the bank the finger, suppresses this juvenile urge.

He hates the bank, The Bank, the institution itself and not really the people who work inside it. He hates the institution that has siphoned millions of dollars out of the community with its stock offerings that have all gone to shit, the one that has lent out other millions and now lost all of it. He can't even count the number of people in town who've had to forfeit, in the last several months, their retirements, their IRAs, everything they had. Now the bank has no money to lend to keep people like Medeiros afloat – literally.

The meeting was brief, stunningly brief and clearly point-less. Whalen had called the meeting deliberately for the twenty-fourth, and Charles knew this was punishment for his having crossed the banker at the volleyball game. He felt sorry now for that encounter; he knew the financial fiasco wasn't Whalen's fault, and when Charles arrived at the bank – twenty minutes late for his eleven o'clock appointment (twenty deliberate minutes spent sitting in the Cadillac in the bank's parking lot; they could all be children when they wanted to be) – he wanted to say that to the banker. Charles studied the sweating pink face, the remarkable shine on the bald pate, and said simply, 'Whalen.'

Whalen looked down at the papers on his desk, shuffled them. 'You're four months behind on your mortgage payments, Callahan,' he said. 'What are you going to do about it?'

Charles knew immediately he shouldn't have come. What was the point of talking to Whalen anyway? If the bank was going to foreclose, then let it be. The process was inevitable. 'You know I can't bring it up to date,' he said.

Whalen looked at Charles. The man's reading glasses enlarged his pupils. Charles thought idly of hot frogs on a railroad track, felt truly sorry for the man. 'The bank examiners are looking over our shoulders right now,' Whalen said, 'and they're forcing us to act on all our problem loans.'

Charles felt his own face grow warm. He knew he should shrug his shoulders, walk out the door. It was what any sensible man would do. Or perhaps he should beg, plead the Christmas season; or lie, say the money would be there the first of the year. But why lie? There wouldn't be any money in January, or in February, for that matter.

'I know it's not your fault,' Charles said. 'I know you're only doing your job. To tell you the truth, Ed, I feel sorrier for you than I do for myself.'

Whalen looked sick, even in the glow of incandescent light

and warm wood. Charles knew that when the feds got through with Whalen, he, too, would be out on the street, and possibly on his way to jail.

Charles leaves the bank, passes the coffee shop, then makes his way toward The Blue Schooner. A Salvation Army Santa is out in front of Woolworth's. Charles gives the can some change. A pickup truck passes, a wreath on its grille. Charles ponders what degree of holiday spirit would possess a man to put a Christmas wreath on his car, decides it must have something to do with kids. Halfway to The Blue Schooner, he comes upon a pair of phone booths on the sidewalk. He cannot pass a phone booth now without studying it, considering the possibilities. Generally he does not ever call her from a place as public as the center of town, but today everyone is so huddled, warding off the storm, that he is certain no one would notice him. Yet even so, he thinks again, it is too risky. They have agreed, tentatively, not to call each other all day Christmas Eve or on Christmas itself, with the understanding that neither is likely to be alone. He stops at the booth, looks at the black phone. He wants to tell her about Whalen, about losing his house. He wants to tell her that he thinks about her every minute, even when he is dealing with the bank; she is always there, hovering in his thoughts. He tries to imagine her in her kitchen, making pirogis with her mother-in-law. He picks up the receiver, puts it back. He leans on the shelf. How bad could it be? Even if the mother-in-law is there, or Lily is there, she could talk to him for just a minute, just long enough so that he could hear her voice, so that he could tell her that he thinks her feet are beautiful. He wants to hear her laugh. He picks up the phone again, dials the familiar number. The phone rings twice, three times, four times. He wonders idly where she is. At the store? Out in the car with her daughter? Is it raining there too, or snowing?

The phone stops ringing. He hears a man say hello. The man sounds breathless, as if he had run in from outside. The man says hello again, and Charles is paralyzed, unable to speak, unable to put the phone down. Once again the man at the other end says hello, this time with exasperation. The voice is deep; the 'hello' has resonance. And yet the man does not sound cheerful or friendly, or is Charles extrapolating again, reading too much into a simple greeting? Charles hangs up the phone and backs away from the booth as if he had been barked at, nipped at, by a dog. He has imagined her husband, has known on one level that the man must exist, and yet the image has been disembodied, willed away when he wants it to be gone. But this he cannot will away – the resonance of that voice across the wire. The man does exist, is standing in her kitchen. Where *is* she?

Subdued and frustrated, he enters The Blue Schooner. The bar is thick with men, off early from work, in now from the water, or simply escaping the ennui of a day at home with no structure. Charles makes his way through the wet heat of the crush, finds Medeiros on a stool at the end of the bar. Charles hesitates, says hello.

'Callahan.'

'Joe.'

'Buy you a beer?'

'Thanks.'

Medeiros is sweating under his wool cap. His eyes are rheumy in the dim light. Medeiros will be going home to a Portuguese meal with his clan – squid and octopus; each family has its rituals. Charles leans on the bar, unbuttons his coat, shakes it out. He loosens his tie. The beer is sharp and cold, deeply satisfying. He returns the favor, orders Medeiros a bourbon.

'What's the matter, Callahan? You look like shit. You been losin' weight, or what?'

'Something like that.'

'The kids OK?'

'The kids are fine.'

'The wife?'

Charles starts to smile. 'The wife is fine,' he says.

'So what's the story, then? You broke?'

'Yeah, I'm broke.'

Medeiros takes a long swallow of bourbon, looks at Charles. 'Yeah, so what else is new? We're all broke. There's something else. You in trouble?'

Charles looks up at the ceiling, down at the condensation on his glass. He drains his beer, signals the bartender for another.

'You could say that, Joe. You could say I'm in trouble.'

'I knew it. I knew you were in trouble. I told Antone you was in trouble. I could see it on your face. With the government? With the IRS? With that deal that went sour? What?'

Charles leans on his elbow, looks at Medeiros. 'I'm in love.'

Joe Medeiros seems stunned, stupefied by Charles's words – as if he hadn't heard a man say those words in a very long time, cannot quite compute them. The draggerman looks embarrassed, takes a thoughtful sip of bourbon. He shakes his head, out of his depth.

'I didn't figure you for that, Charlie. I never figured you for chasin' skirts.'

'This isn't chasing skirts.'

'Who is she?'

'No one you know.'

'Where is she?'

'With her husband and daughter in Pennsylvania.'

'Wow. Shit.'

'Yeah. Shit.'

'Does the wife know?'

'Harriet? No.'

'You gonna tell her?'

'I don't know, Joe. I'm not sure what I'm going to do.'

Medeiros looks away over the noisy crowd, as if pondering Charles's options. Defeated by the lack of easy solutions, he turns back to Charles.

'Well,' Medeiros says, settling on a bromide, 'you gotta do what your heart tells you.'

Medeiros lets out a long sigh, acknowledging that even that was complicated. What if the heart wanted the lover but wanted the wife and kids not to be hurt?

'I guess,' he adds lamely.

'Yeah, I guess,' says Charles.

Medeiros looks at Charles, slides off his stool, not wanting to be in the proximity of such a thorny problem – not on Christmas anyway. 'I gotta talk to Tony over there, find out his boats made it in,' Medeiros says. He puts a hand on Charles's shoulder. 'Hang in there,' he says.

'Thanks, Joe. Have a happy Christmas.'

Charles takes Joe's stool, orders a bowl of chowder. The chowder tastes good; nothing better than Rhode Island chowder, with its thin broth. He orders another pint of beer, listens to the cacophony in the room. The bar is close, overheated, redolent of damp wool from the fishermen's caps and jackets. A dozen clients are at tables or standing at the bar. Last Christmas – and at Christmases before that – Charles used the occasion to spread goodwill, rekindle contact with lapsing clients. But today he knows he cannot manage that. He feels disoriented, shut off from the men, shut out from a world in which the usual standards and words apply. The voices in the room seem overly loud, out of sync with the mouths forming the words, as if a sound track were a split second off. Charles shakes his head to clear it. He doesn't belong in here. He has to get out, but he can't go home either. Not yet.

Charles crosses the street, walks back toward the car. He is wet inside from sweating in the overheated bar; soaked outside from the nasty weather. He bends into the wind, watches as a car's spray washes along the street. Already the traffic is thinning out, everyone off work early, closing shops, going home. He was supposed to pick up something for Harriet – what? He tries to concentrate. Milk? Eggs? Bacon? Paper towels?

He reaches the bank parking lot, puts his key in the lock. As he does so, he glances over the top of the Cadillac, sees the back of St. Mary's, the town's Catholic church. He removes the key from the lock, crosses the lot, then makes his way through a wet mossy cemetery. He enters the church by a side door.

He hasn't been inside the church in over a year, not since the Fahey funeral. The interior is dimly lit, with electric lanterns high overhead. Votive candles flicker in bubbly red glasses. He walks in twenty feet, looks at the altar, nearly smothered today in poinsettias. He has always hated poinsettias; their color alone seems poisonous to him. He studies the cross suspended above the altar, a particularly grotesque crucifixion, the skin of Christ abnormally white, with magenta blood from the wounds dripping along the feet and hands. Why do this to children? he wonders, not for the first time. He walks to the front pew, sits down, his hands folded limply in his lap. He examines the cross on the altar itself, a simpler gold cross, without a body. He focuses on the cross, tries to formulate a prayer. But the old words still do not work, and he cannot create the necessary sentences. He wants to ask for help and to kneel, as if in those simple acts he might be forgiven – not so much for what he has done as for what he is about to do. His longing for forgiveness feels enormous, a large indefinable longing, but he knows the request is futile. He will never give up Siân; therefore, according to the rules of the game, asking for forgiveness is out of the question. And in any event, it has been too long since he has had any clear idea of what or whom he was asking for forgiveness.

A chill shakes him. He stands up to leave, glances again at the flickering votive candles, remembers now what it was he was supposed to get for Harriet: light bulbs. He hurries to the car. He has been gone too long. He needs to get home, be with his children. And Christ, he forgot: the ducks – he has to marinate the ducks.

Pulling into his driveway, he sees the twinkling Christmas tree behind the window of the family room. At least Harriet has finished the lights, he thinks, emerging guiltily from the car. When he enters the kitchen, his children and his dog run in to greet him. His children's love is physical; they climb up his legs, tug on his arms – even Hadley, who snuggles into his shoulder. They squeal at him that he is wet and that his coat smells from the damp. As he removes his coat and jacket, he gently shakes off his children, one by one. He slips his tie through his collar, rolls his sleeves, and squats to nuzzle Winston's head in affection.

The children lead him into the family room to admire the tree. Harriet is perched on a stool, trying to repair the star atop the tree; it lists to port. She has on jeans, a hunter-green sweater. He studies her broad shoulders, the swell of her hips below her sweater, the way the jeans pinch in at the crotch. But when he looks at her, he feels nothing, not even a certainty of what her body looks like beneath her clothes. Sometimes he cannot even remember what it was like to make love to Harriet, what it was they did together, as if his time with Siân had somehow erased that particular loop. He watches his wife's sweater ride up in back as she reaches again for the top of the tree. He studies the sliver of pink skin above her waistband. The skin seems foreign to him, skin he has never touched.

'Let me get that,' he says behind her.

'Oh,' she says, turning to him, flushed with her effort. 'Thanks.'

'I got the light bulbs,' he says.

She steps off the stool. They exchange places.

'How did your appointment go?' she asks.

'Fine,' he says. 'It went fine.'

He hasn't told her yet about the bank. At breakfast he announced only that he had an appointment. The ubiquitous and genetic 'appointment.'

'You've been gone awhile,' she says, looking at her watch. 'I was worried you wouldn't get home in time to do the ducks.'

'Had to buy a couple of rounds. You know how it is at Christmas.'

Charles secures the star with picture wire. It's still off five degrees, but it will do.

'How have the kids been?' he asks, stepping off the stool, facing her.

She stares at him a moment, puts a finger to his chest, strokes the cloth of his shirt in the vicinity of his left nipple. Idly, as though lost in a memory. Her eyes are uncharacteristically vacant, staring at the skin above the top button of his shirt.

'Harriet.'

She looks up at him, dragged reluctantly from her reverie. Her eyes are a vivid blue-violet and large – her best feature. He has sometimes thought her pretty; she *is* pretty. But not beautiful. He tries to remember if he ever told her she was beautiful. Perhaps at the beginning. He must have then. He hopes he did.

'Jack is in orbit,' she says slowly, removing her finger from his chest. 'Hadley has been helping me with the tree. She wants to make cookies when you've finished with the ducks and the pâté.'

She opens her mouth again, then closes it. She seems to want to say something more, something that is hard for her to say, and he knows that if she does, he will have to tell her. He wants to tell her that he is sorry, that whatever has happened or not happened between them, it was not her fault. That it wasn't because she wasn't beautiful or that he didn't want to love her. Or that he has been recognized, at last, in a way his wife has never known him. He puts his hand on the sleeve of her sweater, rubs her arm between her elbow and her shoulder.

She moves away from him, turns her face to the side. 'Keep your eye on Anna,' she says. 'I have one or two more presents to wrap.'

'Harriet?'

'Yes?'

She looks at him, wary now, the vacant look gone entirely. She narrows her eyes, seems almost irritated, impatient to leave the room.

'My parents will be here at four,' she says.

Handel's *Messiah* blasts from the kitchen speakers. He has played it so often through the years that he knows almost all the words by heart. He likes particularly to belt out the 'Hallelujah' chorus and does so as he puts the ingredients

185

for the marinade – teriyaki sauce, fresh ginger, soy sauce, garlic, shallots, sherry, and a splash of red wine – into the several roasting bags. He has cut the breasts and legs and thighs off six ducks; purple carcasses line the yellow Formica kitchen counter. Winston stands by his feet, nose pointed upward, alert for a tidbit that might deliberately fall his way. Somewhere between the second and third ducks, Charles sliced the tip of a finger; he has stanched the bleeding with a kitchen towel, which is now wrapped untidily around his hand. Hadley, leaning against the counter, studies her father thoughtfully. He glances down at her face, at the steady gaze of her large brown eyes. She looks concerned.

'Dad,' she says.

'What?'

'Are you all right?'

He slides duck pieces into a roasting bag with a flourish, sets it along with the other bags in a large pan on the counter. He is on a roll now, four cookbooks open on the island. His menu did not really come together until somewhere between 'O thou that tellest . . .' and 'All we like sheep . . .,' and he has been into town twice for extra ingredients for his meal – once to the fish market, once to the Italian deli – emptying his checking account in the process. He is aware that his menu is somewhat eclectic and that possibly all of the proper components are not quite there, but he has always preferred to cook because he felt like making the separate dishes, not necessarily because they formed a perfect whole – and he thinks that somehow this spontaneous and haphazard desire might be applicable to his life and his financial ruin as well. In addition to the duck carcasses on the counter, he has now two fillets of salt cod for the baccalá; five pounds of mussels (he hadn't planned on the mussels, but he couldn't pass them up at the fish store – he will serve them in a brine of tomato, basil, capers, and white wine); one fillet of salmon, which he will coat with salt and sugar and dill, and marinate in plastic wrap so that it will cook itself (they'll have the resultant gravlox for an appetizer); and a medley of scallops, shrimp, and smoked salmon, which he will do up in squid ink pasta, along with red pepper slices, as an accompaniment to the duck. Into a massive teak salad bowl he presses out several garlic cloves, then mixes the paste with the anchovies, along with Worcestershire sauce, lemon juice, mustard, capers, and hot sauce. He tastes his efforts with a spoon and makes an extravagant gesture of approval for Hadley, kissing his fingers with a moue of his lips. The Caesar will have a good scald on it, he tells his daughter. The counter is awash in body parts, spilled sugar, chopped dill, empty sauce bottles, bottle caps, wet spoons, and flour from the sourdough bread. He kneads the bread in a baking bowl, trying to camouflage into the dough the inadvertent smears of blood leaking from the wet kitchen towel around his hand. Jack comes into the kitchen, looks at the carnage on the counter.

'Ew, yuck, Dad. What are you making?' he asks.

'Don't ask,' says Hadley.

Charles feels almost happy now – or a state as close to happy as he has been able to achieve in this house, in this town. If he keeps moving, he is certain, his dinner will be a success. He has to choreograph his pots, conduct the play between the stovetop and the oven so that the ducks won't conflict with the sourdough bread, so that his largest pot will be free for the mussels after he has made the pasta. He doesn't worry much about timing, however: Though his timing in love and finance have been appalling, he has been blessed with an uncanny sixth sense when it comes to cooking. Cooking is orchestral, he decides, resembling something of a symphony or at least a concerto, the movements allegro or largo, depending on the tempo of his swoops and turns as he reaches between the island and the fridge, between the stove and the counter, as he plays the butter of a roux, the garlic of a sauce. He has Bing on now. Can't make a Christmas dinner without Bing, he says to his younger daughter, Anna, who has come into the kitchen to observe the performance. He reaches up to pour himself another tumbler of the Kendall-Jackson, a nice dry red, which he opened because he needed it as the finishing touch to the marinade, and as he does so he notices that the bottle is nearly empty. His dress shirt and the pants to his suit are spotted with olive oil and flour and bits of something brown that might be blood. He has an apron somewhere in the kitchen, but he has been unable to find it.

Outside the warm kitchen, a gust of rain sweeps against the windows, rattling the windowpanes. He takes a sip of the dregs of the red, looks through the panes to the sheets of water beyond. He wonders where she is, what she is doing at this precise moment. He glances at the phone, thinks fleetingly of calling her, then shakes off the desire: He cannot risk hearing the resonant voice of her husband, having to hang up on the man once again. He tries to imagine what her husband looks like, tries to envision the body that might go with the voice; Charles has never asked Siân, and she has not volunteered any details, about her husband's appearance. With the heel of his hand, he punches down the rising dough in the bread bowl, pummels it roughly. He wants her now, with an ache that is not physical, or not entirely physical. His body feels taut, stretched with wanting her, wanting simply to be in her presence. He bends suddenly at the waist, touching his forehead to the surface of the island. He wants to lower himself to the floor. His insides feel hollow, empty without her.

'Daddy?'

Charles glances up quickly, remembers his children. Hadley looks quizzical.

He forces himself upright, smiles.

'Dessert,' he says.

'Dessert?'

'I have to think about dessert.'

'I want Christmas cookies,' says Anna.

He opens a cookbook on the island. He contemplates the ceiling. Winston, who has come to him, nuzzles his knees. He has an image of a French tart; no, of a flan. He thinks about custard; does he have the ingredients? He could do a crème brûlée possibly. Yes, that's it, he decides, cracking open another bottle of the Kendall-Jackson. A ginger crème brûlée – the ginger will be a perfect holiday nuance for the end of the meal. What will he need? he wonders. Eggs? Cream? He has fresh ginger from the marinade. Sugar, of course. And a blowtorch. Can't caramelize the top without a blowtorch. He tries to think where it was he learned this: in the kitchen of a restaurant just outside Providence. He'd inquired of the waiter, as he sometimes did in restaurants, how a dish was prepared (in this case, a particularly fragile peach crème brûlée) and had been summoned into the kitchen by the chef himself, who'd demonstrated the blowtorch technique: Sprinkle a thin layer of granulated sugar along the top of the custard; blast it with the torch. The process – definitely overkill and probably not ecologically sound – was repeated until the top of the crème was a paper-thin disk of caramelized sugar, like a perfect circle of delicate brown ice.

He gathers on the island the eggs and cream and sugar and ginger, finds a clean bowl and the eggbeater. He stands on a stool, investigates the top shelf of the cabinet over the fridge. He has an idea that there is behind the champagne glasses a set of custard dishes, ramekins, perfect for the crème brûlée.

He sees them, snakes his hand through the champagne glasses, then hears his name spoken by his wife in a tone that reminds him of a teacher he had in seventh grade.

'Charles.'

He teeters for a moment on the stool, turns around to face his family. They are standing there beneath him, aligned at the end of the counter – Harriet, Hadley, Jack, and Anna. The tableau they make is characterized by composite alarm. He knows how he must look to them – the singular embodiment of the chaos he has created, both within the kitchen and without. He holds a champagne glass in one hand, a ramekin in the other. His shirt is soaked under the armpits, smeared with duck entrails and flour; the kitchen towel is still ineffectually wrapped around a hand. They stare at him as if at any moment he might be able to explain himself. From his considerable height, he surveys the kitchen – a bloody and ungentle mess, a manic attempt to stave off the unbearable sadness of Christmas.

He looks at his children and his wife, at the walls of a house he no longer owns.

'No one is saved, and no one is totally lost,' he tells his assembled family.

The sun had set not a half-hour before, and in the west there was still an orange dust at the horizon. The air was dry, the evening lit up already with the summer constellations. He walked her down with the others to the water's edge, where tonight there would be a bonfire, a small celebration for the Fourth. In his hand he carried sparklers. He gave one to her, lit it for her with the matches he had in his shirt pocket. The golden sprinkles from the sparklers illuminated their faces. In front of them, and behind them, there was laughter and chatter, as the others walked singly or in pairs, some with sparklers of their own. It was exciting, this walk in the darkness down to the lake, the path known but not certain, the event producing in the air a sense of freedom, an element of risk.

The counselors had made the pyre already, were hovering importantly nearby. The children took their places in a semicircle around the wood and the straw, facing the lake. It was the last night of camp, and friendships had formed, delineated in the shapes that drew closer to each other. She sat beside him on the ground, their knees raised, their arms touching from the shoulder to the elbow, and for a time it was all that she could absorb — the length and dizziness of that touch, a thin delicate line along her skin. Until he moved his arm and put it around her, finding with his fingers first the capped sleeve of her blouse, then the skin beneath it. Neither spoke or dared to look at the other.

The straw was lit, bursting noisily into flames, crackling toward the sky, letting loose a shower of sparks that arced upward and died before they could fall on hair and bare skin. Someone, a figure lit by the fire, led the group in songs, summer camp songs and songs for the Fourth. The boy sang beside her, his voice nearly a man's, but she could not sing. She felt the pressure of his arm along her back, the imprint of his fingers on her skin. The fire obscured the cross, obliterated the lake.

When the singing was over, the counselors produced long sticks and marshmallows. The boy hesitated, moved his arm away from her, stood up. She watched him walk toward the counselors, take a stick and a marshmallow, poke it toward the fire, which had settled some. She watched his back, his body just a silhouette. He spoke to another boy.

He returned, sat facing her. He removed the gooey marshmallow, charred on the outside, and held it out to her. She exclaimed, started to speak, so that when he thrust it toward her, it caught on her lips and teeth, smearing her mouth. In the confusion, laughing at the mess, she licked the marshmallow from his fingers as he tried to push it in. She caught one finger between her teeth, released it. Embarrassed, she laughed again and said that he was mean.

He licked the stickiness from his own fingers. When they were clean, he put his hand into his pocket and withdrew an object. She couldn't see in the darkness what the object was. He held it for a moment, then seized her arm at the wrist. He put the object into her palm, closing his hand for a moment over hers. She fingered the object, rolled it in her palm. She felt the links of a chain, the sharp edges of metal charms.

'It's a bracelet,' she said, holding it in a fist. Her breath was tight and shallow.

'I wanted something to give you,' he said beside her.

When she looked at him, she could see only that half of his face that was lit by the orange of the fire, a light that made shadows in his eyes and with his cheekbones.

He took her hand, and she thought that he might remove the bracelet from her fist and put it on her, but instead he made her stand up. He led her up the path, away from the others; the chatter and the laughter around the bonfire faded as they walked. Above them, trees rustled in the night breeze. In the distance, up the hill, she could see the glow of the lights in the main house, the lights from the dining room, some individual lights in bedrooms where they had been left on.

When they were halfway up the path, the boy stepped off the worn track and into the woods. She was not sure exactly what he meant to do, but strangely, she was not afraid. She followed closely behind him, sometimes touching his shirt, as he led the way, held branches for her, pointed out to her where there was a rock or a log. She wondered briefly how they would find the path again, then dismissed her worry. All she could think was that within hours her parents would come to the camp to fetch her and drive her north to Springfield, and that she might never see this boy again.

An owl hooted, startling them both. She laughed nervously, reached out for him. He stopped, turned to face her. She could barely see his eyes in the moonlight, the strong moonlight that had been on the path obscured now by the overhead trees. She sensed rather than saw him, felt his presence near, his own shallow breathing, the heat from his chest and arms. 'The stars are amazing tonight,' he said, looking up at the sky. 'Can you read the constellations?'

'The Big Dipper,' she said. 'And sometimes the Little Dipper. But that's all.'

'Mmmm. Me too.' He took a step closer, so that his face was just over hers.

He tilted his head slightly, bent to kiss her. Instinctively she raised her chin. He caught her at the side of the mouth, held his lips there. The kiss was dry and feathery, so tentative she was not certain they were actually touching, though she could feel his breath on her cheek. He put his hands on her arms; she lifted her hands so they touched his back. She had never kissed a boy before, had never even held hands with a boy until she met him. Each touch was new and exhilarating, but she knew that he would not hurt her.

He found her mouth, the whole of it, and drew her in to him with his hands at the back of her waist, so that she lost her balance, was leaning against him for support. He swayed with her weight, then together they knelt. He lost his own balance then and carried her onto the soft mulch of the forest floor. Lying that way, as if on a bed, they became aware simultaneously of what it was they were doing. He pulled his face away to look at her in the dim light, to see if there was alarm there, if he had transgressed. She returned his gaze, but she could not speak. He kissed her once more, not so tentatively this time, and she felt something of his urgency, her own awkwardness. He kissed her for a long time, and there was again the fluttering in her abdomen. His hand moved along her rib cage. She thought that possibly she should move his hand away; it was what she had been taught. He touched her breast, enclosed it with his palm. The touch caught her breath; the fluttering sensation spread out from her abdomen and along her thighs like the spill of a warm liquid. He looked down at her breast, to where her nipple was hard against the cotton of her blouse. She could hear his breathing, faster now, like her own, a rhythm against her face and in her ear. He kissed the side of her face. She unfastened the top button of her blouse, then the next. He pushed aside the cotton fabric, exposing her breast to the night. He touched the skin with his fingers, delicately and gently, as if caressing something fine and fragile – a spun-glass ornament, or the face of a newborn. He kissed her again on her mouth. She could feel him shift his body, move a leg over hers. He raised his face up, looked again at her eyes. He looked at her breast, lowered his mouth, touched the skin of her breast with his lips. She felt him press against her. Her leg was between his; his between hers. The fluttering deep inside her became a pressure, an exquisite urgency. He put his mouth on her nipple, opened his mouth, and sucked her. She moaned faintly with this pleasure, whispered his name. She felt the urgency burst inside her, spread through her and along her legs. She felt the boy shudder against her, a tight helpless shuddering, her nipple still caught in his mouth. He said her name sharply, pressed his forehead hard against her breastbone.

In her fist, she still held the bracelet.

They lay on the dirt and mulch without moving for a long time, long enough for the moon to shift slightly overhead and shine down upon them through a gap in the leaves. The white fabric of her blouse was blue in the moonlight, and she could see clearly now the length of the boy, from the top of his head, where it rested on her chest, to his feet. As they lay there they could hear the voices of the others, moving up the path to the house, young silvery voices laughing in the darkness not fifty feet from them. She thought then that they ought to try to make their way back, so that they would have the voices to guide them, but she did not want to disturb the boy. When after a time he looked up at her, she saw that his eyes were wet, that he had been crying.

'It's all right, Cal,' she said.

He covered her breast with her blouse, buttoned it for her. He lifted himself up, knelt beside her in the piney mulch. He saw her clenched fist. He opened her fingers, took the bracelet, fastened it on her wrist. She sat up, slid the bracelet along her arm.

'What we did . . .,' he said.

She touched the bracelet. 'I'm all right, Cal,' she said. 'It's all right.'

'I've never . . .'

'I know.'

'Do you understand . . .?'

She looked down at the bracelet, dangling from her thin wrist. 'I'm not sure, but I think so,' she said.

'I'm not sorry,' he said.

'No. I know,' she said. 'How could we be?'

He helped her to her feet. Together they brushed bits of bark and leaves from her back, her shorts. They would be in trouble when they returned, required to say where they had been, but that seemed unimportant, meaningless.

'We'll just say we went for a walk, lost track of the time,' he said. 'They won't like it, but we'd probably both better have the same story.'

She nodded. He walked in front of her, held branches for her till he had found the way back to the path. They held hands as they climbed the hill, their footsteps reluctant and slow. At the main door of the house, the door that would admit them to the bright light of the hall, to the stern queries of their counselors, to their separate wings and separate beds, they paused. He kissed her quickly on the cheek, lest anyone was watching them.

'I won't be able to say goodbye to you,' she said.

THE RAIN has stopped. The night is still. A hush envelops
the house, both inside and out, and except for the occasional
whine of the refrigerator or the rumble and whomp of the
furnace, all is quiet. He holds in his hand a glass of warm
champagne, which he poured from the dregs of a bottle on
the kitchen counter. Harriet and his children are in bed. He
has no clear idea what time it is; he took his watch off
to scour the pots, cannot remember where he put it. He
thinks it must be after two o'clock. His parents returned
from midnight mass nearly an hour ago with Hadley, asleep
on her feet as she stumbled to her room. Harriet has already
filled the stockings, cleaned up the bits of crumpled wrapping
from the adults' presents, set out the children's gifts under the
tree. For Christmas Charles gave his wife an astonishingly tiny
video camera that the salesman promised would not only be
easy to use but also take brilliant movies of his children, an
enterprise that now fills Charles with sadness and remorse.
Harriet gave Charles two season tickets to the Red Sox, games
he already knows he will never attend. In another life (*what*
other life? he asks himself – *this* is his life) he'd have loved the
tickets, would have taken Hadley and Jack; the tickets would
have framed his summer, would have given him something to
look forward to, a way to punctuate the long, hot weeks. But
now he feels only a vague sense of loss, as of having misplaced
one's childhood.

(He thinks, oddly, of the O. Henry story about the couple
who buy each other presents they can no longer use, because
of what they've sacrificed to afford the gifts. Might he have
used the camera to take movies of the kids at the Red Sox

games? Without the games, or any similar outings, will Harriet want to take movies at all?)

He finishes the warm champagne, sets the glass on the counter. He has had an extraordinary amount of alcohol to drink today, and yet he has not felt high or drunk or even buzzed. He has been drinking to anesthetize himself, he knows, an exhausting and futile effort. He walks through the living room, observes the classic picture: the stockings at the mantel, the presents arranged artfully under the tree. Only Anna this year believes in the miracle of a white-bearded man who visits every house in the universe with presents on this one particular night. He realizes with a pang that he doesn't even know what is in the brightly wrapped packages. He has not bought a single gift for any of his children, a ritual that in the past used to give him pleasure. In a few hours, his kids will be awake and demanding that he and Harriet join them downstairs to see what Santa has brought. If he doesn't go up to bed now, he'll get no sleep at all.

The room in which he and his wife share a bed is at the front of the house. White gauze curtains cover the windows, letting in only a pale glaze of light from a streetlamp across the road. The dark shape in the bed is unmoving; he is certain she must be asleep. At dinner, Harriet was cordial but not animated. He thought she seemed preoccupied, distracted, possibly annoyed by the dinner, which, in the end, did not really work as a whole. The children barely ate anything apart from the duck. The others seemed confused by the menu, as though presented with a puzzle in which certain key pieces were missing. The crème brûlée was a hit, however, and he felt inordinately pleased with this finale – the delicate sugar crust flambéed to translucent perfection.

He removes his sweater, a clean shirt he changed into before the relatives came, his shoes and socks and slacks. In his underpants, he slips under the heavy quilt, a practiced and delicate movement that disturbs the covers as little as possible, the movements of a thief stealing into a house undetected, the movements of a man who does not want to engage his wife. He knows instantly, however, that he has been heard. When he holds his breath and listens intently, he cannot hear his wife breathing, as he ought to. He turns slowly so that his back is to her, so that he might, with luck, fall asleep at once, but as he does, he feels the covers tug and pull, hears her turn in his direction. A hand is at his back, moving up to his shoulder. He turns his head, but not yet his body.

'Harriet?'

She pulls gently at his shoulder, asking him to face her, a request he cannot deny. He rolls over, his head on the pillow, and looks at her. Her face is grave, as he knows his must be to her. They examine each other in this way for what seems like minutes. She does not speak, but he knows that she will.

'Harriet, what is it?'

She says quietly in the thin artificial light, a light in which he can barely make out the expression in her eyes, 'I want you to make love to me.'

He opens his mouth to protest, to say, reasonably, that it's after two in the morning and they will have to be up at dawn, to say that he's exhausted after all that cooking. To say that he'll make her come, or rub her back. But he knows he cannot say any of those things, that his voice alone will give him away, will announce that he has betrayed her. Instead he draws her to him, embraces her tightly.

'I've been waiting for you,' she says, the words muffled into his chest, and he understands instantly that she means more than just this night.

'Oh, Harriet,' he says.

And there is no help for him now. He begins to cry. He

holds himself still, not breathing, so that she won't detect his tears, holding the ache deep in his chest and in his throat, but she has known him too long, knows the context of every sigh, of this stiffening of his body. She pushes herself away, studies him. She seems alarmed now, even more alarmed than she appeared to be in the kitchen earlier.

'Charles, for God's sake, what is it?'

He rolls onto his back, his arms out, looks up at the ceiling. The tears leak out of the corners of his eyes, trail down his cheeks. He knows by the tone in her voice that she will not let this go. He knows, too, that he cannot lie to her, not now.

'I have something to tell you that's going to make you sick,' he says.

She sits up abruptly, kneels on the bed facing him. Her bare arms are white in the dim light. He winces as he sees for the first time that she has worn her black silk nightgown, a revealing nightgown with lace at the breasts, which she wears when she wants him to make love to her.

He cannot say what he has to say from a supine position. He sits up, puts on his shirt.

'Where are you going?' his wife asks quickly.

'I'm not going anywhere. I'm just putting on my shirt. I'm cold.'

'What is it? What is this thing you have to tell me?'

He buttons his shirt, sits on the edge of the bed, half facing her, half turned away.

'I'm in love with another woman,' he says.

He waits for the ceiling to fall, for a tree to smash against the windowpanes. He has been imagining these words, cannot hear even his voice saying them without also hearing a crash of cymbals, the pounding of timpani. The silence then, the absolute silence of the bedroom, astounds him. He is afraid for a moment that he did not actually say the words, that he will have to repeat them, louder this time.

But he hears a sharp intake of breath, sees Harriet's hand rise to her mouth.

'Oh my God,' she says.

'Harriet, I'm so sorry. I never meant for this to happen.' He shuts his eyes, appalled at the sound of his own voice. The words are offensively trite, each syllable a lie. Of course he meant for this to happen. He *made* it happen.

'I'm going to leave you,' he says, more honestly. 'I'm in love, and I'm going to leave you.'

He dares to look at her now, at the shock on her face. He, too, is stunned by his words, by the baldness of them, by their incontrovertibility. He cannot take them back, should not take them back. He does not want to hurt his wife, but he has to make her understand that this is not casual.

'What are you saying? Who is she?'

'She isn't anyone you know. She lives very far from here.'

'Then how do you know her?'

'I met her thirty-one years ago. We spent a week together at camp when we were fourteen, thirty-one years ago.'

'You spent one week together thirty-one years ago and you love her?' she asks incredulously. 'Or have you known her all along?'

'No. No. No. I just remet her a few weeks ago.'

'A few weeks ago?' He hears the bewilderment in his wife's voice, knows how truly mad this must sound.

'Have you slept with her?'

It is, of course, *the* question, the one he has anticipated, dreaded. He hesitates. He will not lie. 'Yes,' he says.

He hears the moan, the single note of pure pain in his wife's voice.

'How many times?' she asks bravely.

'Not many,' he says. 'Four times.'

'Four times?' she asks incredulously. 'You've been with her four times? When? When were you with her?'

'Harriet, does it matter when?'

'I trusted you,' she says, loudly now. He cannot ask her not to shout, not to wake up the children. It is her right. He realizes with horror that of course he should not have done this now, not on Christmas Eve, not when the children are in the house, not when they will wake up soon, anticipating the stockings and the presents, and will find what instead – a mother devastated? Harriet slips off the bed, stands up. She shivers in her nightgown. He, too, stands up, reaches for her bathrobe on a hook at the back of the door, hands it to her. She bats it away to the floor.

'I love her,' he says, as if to explain. 'I always have loved her. We were lovers, even as children, all those years ago.'

'And what about me? I thought you loved me.'

'I do,' he says, 'but it's different.'

'What's different?'

'It's just different.' He hears the evasiveness in his own voice, but he knows he will never tell his wife that it's different because he never really loved her, because he believes that he and Siân were meant to be mates. This is the worst heresy, not something that Harriet ever needs to know.

'Is she married?'

'Yes.'

'And does she have children?'

'Yes. She has one, a girl. She had a boy, but he died when he was nine.'

'And you're going to be a father to someone else's child?' This last is said in a high-pitched wail, as though this, more than any other betrayal, hurts most. She flails out at him with her fists held together, like a tennis player grasping a racket for a tough backhand shot. She hits him in the rib cage. He holds his arms aloft, does not stop her. She hits him again, and then again. She whacks him a fourth time, then whirls around, sobbing.

'How could you?' she cries.

He cannot tell her why. The why is clear and not clear, as simple as animals mating, or as complicated as a physics problem – a labyrinthine equation of time and distance.

She falls back onto the bed, puts her hands over her face. He cannot tell whether or not she is crying; he thinks she may still be too stunned for tears. He reaches down on the floor for his pants, puts them on, buckles the belt. Hearing the clink of metal on metal, Harriet takes her hands away from her face, watches him dress himself.

'Where are you going?' she asks quietly from the bed.

'I don't know,' he says. 'I can't stay here now. Not tonight.'

'But the children. It's Christmas tomorrow.'

The realization seems to strike her even as she announces the import of the morning to her husband. She twists her head and moans again, a terrible, plaintive sound that he has never heard before from his wife, not even when she was in labor with Hadley, the worst of them. Harriet throws an arm across her face, covering her eyes.

Charles looks at his wife on the bed, at the black silk night-gown on the white sheet, at his wife's breasts, small and flat under the open lace. It is conceivably the last time he will ever see his wife's body. No, he thinks again: It is positively the last time he will ever see her body. A body that he has made love to thousands of times. A body that carried and bore and nursed his three children.

'I'll come back,' he says. 'Before the kids are up. I'll spend the night, or what's left of it, someplace, maybe a motel, and then I'll come back to be with them when they open their presents. We'll tell them together, tomorrow night or the next day.'

She lies still on the bed, her face shielded. He thinks she will not speak, that she acquiesces with her silence, as bewildered on this foreign territory as he is. But then she sits up sharply, facing him. Her mouth is tight, a thin line of anger. There are vertical lines above her upper lip that he has never seen before.

'Don't you dare to come back here,' she says evenly. 'Don't you come back here ever. You want your things, you can send someone else for them. Or I'll put them out on the street. This is my house now, and you are not to come here again.' She turns her head away, puts a hand protectively across her stomach – an unconscious gesture she used to make when she was pregnant.

'But, Harriet, the house . . .'

As soon as he has said the words, he knows he has made an unforgivable mistake. She twists quickly around, poised for more pain. He can see it on her face, in the fear in her eyes. It was her mentioning the house that caused him foolishly to blurt out the one thing he has not intended to tell her yet, certainly not on this night. His mind leaps, somersaults. He tries desperately to think of how to extricate himself.

'What?' she says anxiously. 'What?'

'Harriet . . .'

'What?' she cries. She turns, springs off the bed. She faces him, her arms locked across her chest. 'What?' she cries again, defiantly.

'Harriet, I feel sick about this. You can't know how bad I feel about this . . .'

'For God's sake, spit it out,' she screams. 'We've lost the house, haven't we?'

He walks around to her side of the bed, extends his arms to embrace her. For a moment, she lets him, leans into him.

'How could you . . .?' she asks. 'How long have you known this was coming?'

'I've known for a while,' he says. 'But I just found out for certain this morning. I was at the bank.'

She sits down abruptly upon the bed, as if she has fallen.

'I'll take care of you, Harriet,' he says. 'I'll always take care of you and the children. And they've got to give us at least sixty days before they foreclose. Perhaps . . .'

'I'm going downstairs,' she says, almost in a whisper. 'I'm going to sit down there until you're gone. Don't be long, because I'm very, very tired.'

She stands, walks slowly to the other side of the bed, bends to the floor, and retrieves her robe. She slips her arms through the sleeves, wraps the robe tightly across her chest, securing it with the sash, as though she realized she was exposed, does not want him to see her skin.

Charles watches Harriet leave their bedroom, shutting the door behind her.

He stands for a time in the center of the room, staring at the shut door. Numbly, he turns, puts on his shoes and socks. He takes a jacket from a hanger in the closet. From the drawers of his bureau, he makes a pile of socks and underwear and ties and shirts. He is barely aware of what he is collecting; he simply wants to make a pile. He slips another suit jacket from a hanger, wraps the untidy bundle in the jacket, knots the bundle with the sleeves of the jacket, puts the bundle under his arm. He does not look again at the bed, or at the bedroom that he has shared with his wife for sixteen years. He opens the door, listens intently for sounds in the hallway. He passes the rooms where his children are sleeping, knows he cannot bear to look at Jack in his bed, instead opens the door to Hadley's room. He sees her head on her pillow, her brown hair spread out behind her. Her eyes are open – watchful brown eyes, so like his own.

'Where are you going?' she asks from the bed. He thinks he hears a tremor in her voice. He does not know what she has heard.

'I'm not going far,' he says.

He walks to the bed, sits at its edge. He smooths her hair with his hand.

'What's wrong, Daddy? You look so sad.'

She sleeps on a pillow with a white lace ruffle; she cradles in her arm a worn and threadbare pink giraffe, a relic of her childhood.

He cannot tell his daughter he is leaving her. His throat feels swollen, suffused with its ache.

'I'm not sad,' he tells his daughter. 'You'd better try and get some sleep. Morning will be here before you know it.'

Hadley dutifully closes her eyes. His daughter, unlike his wife, will not ask to hear what she knows she cannot yet absorb. His daughter will wish away the voices behind the closed door, may come to believe by morning that they were only voices in a bad dream.

He kisses his daughter at the side of her face.

Holding his bundle, he descends the stairs, walks through the silent house. He finds his overcoat on the clothes tree, his car keys on the counter. Through the door of the family room, he sees his wife – a small, huddled shape on a couch. She is looking at her palms, which are resting on her knees, as if she were trying to read there what has happened to her, what will happen to her.

He says, 'I'll be back before the kids are up.'

She does not acknowledge this promise. He opens the door, leaves his house and family behind him.

And what can you say about a soiled shirt, a shirt that does not belong to your husband, hiding in your drawer?

He held it in his hands like evidence.

I said, my voice no more than a whisper, that I had taken the shirt from my father's laundry basket the last time I was visiting, that I had planned to knit a sweater for him for Christmas.

Stephen might have said, The size is wrong.

And I'd have had to lie again.

But he didn't. What was the point?

I remember that he sat down at the place where he had been, at his place within the family, near the fire. His eyes were inward, closed to me. My hands shook. I couldn't stop them. I hadn't meant for this to happen. But if I hadn't meant for this to happen, why had I kept the shirt?

I remember, too, that I was afraid. It was a kind of fear I had never felt before: a sense that glass would shatter, cutting each of us.

I had to go upstairs to get the gift for Lily. Stephen had forgotten to bring it down.

Lily felt the tension in the air. Looked at me and then her father.

The relatives came for the meal. They seemed, with their broad smiles and appetites, bright cartoon figures entering suddenly a darkened film – characters misplaced or lost. Or was it we who were misplaced, had lost our place?

I served the food that I had made. I smiled, said pleasant things. I could do this, had to do this for Lily, had to serve as a foil for Stephen, who could barely eat. From time to time I looked at his face, and it was white, preternaturally colorless. I thought to myself: How can I have done this to any man? And then I thought: Why, in choosing you, did it have to be something I had done to Stephen? What was the contract that Stephen and I had made? Where did it begin or end?

After the meal, the children dispersed to reinspect their toys. We were invited to go to Stephen's brother's house for dessert, as was the custom. I said yes too quickly. I wanted to be out of my house, away from the fear. I had set something in motion, and I did not yet know how it would play out. I wanted, too, to be away from the phone hanging quietly upon the wall. I thought that you might call, was more afraid that I would.

I bundled Lily up in her coat. I put my scarf on, then my boots. I looked at Stephen, who was not dressed for the cold.

You go on with the rest, he said, not looking at me. I think I'm getting another migraine. I'll just lie down, come along in an hour or so.

I did not believe him about the migraine, but I understood that he needed to be alone. I thought briefly that he might go looking for other evidence, the letters and the package that he now must be wondering about. I thought that now I should stay – but there was Stephen's brother waiting for us by the door, waiting to take Lily and me to his house so that Stephen could follow in our car later.

I hesitated, put my hand on Stephen's sleeve. You rest, I said. Come if you can. When I get home, we'll talk.

He turned away, said nothing. I looked quickly at Stephen's brother, who had heard.

The phone rang. I was paralyzed. Stephen glanced at the phone, looked at me. I walked to the phone. When I picked it up, my hand shook so badly I was afraid I might drop the receiver. I said, tentatively, Hello, praying it wasn't you. It was my father, wishing us all a merry Christmas. My relief was sharp, and I began to cry. I turned my back to the kitchen so the others wouldn't see.

In Stephen's brother's house, I saw blurred shapes and scenes, rushes from a film that was playing on furniture and faces, strange distorted limbs, bodies wrapped around an armchair, moving soundlessly against the shiny metal of a toaster or a teapot.

I hoped that Stephen was sleeping, knew that he was not. I did not know if he was opening drawers in his office, or pacing in the bedroom.

An hour passed and then another. I went to the telephone, called my house. There was no answer. I sat back down at the table.

I knew then. It was a feeling that came on like a chill, first along the hairs of my arm, then along my spine, and settling finally at the back of my neck.

I stood up, reached for my coat.

Keep Lily here, I said to Stephen's brother.

HE SLOWS THE CADILLAC where the tarmac meets the wood, wary of ice that may have formed on the bridge during the earlier storm. The night is still and dark, the visibility poor, no moon yet to delineate the bridge's span above the water. Beside him on the seat is the bundle of clothes. He is now, in all senses of the word, homeless – an alien and yet oddly comforting sensation, a state of being that seemed heightened during his solitary drive down High Street, his the only vehicle on the road, the windows of the houses he passed shuttered and closed to him.

He knows exactly where she is right now, exactly what she must be doing: lying in a bed next to her husband, waiting for her daughter to wake up. He knows he tortures himself with images of Siân with her husband, like a masochist poking a sore tooth, but he hopes that somehow if he looks at the images enough, forces himself over and over to examine them, he might finally be able to absorb them, defuse their power. On his way to the bridge, he passed half a dozen phone booths he knows well, slowed the car at each, thinking momentarily that he might impulsively call her despite the idiocy of the hour, had to will himself not to stop the car. He wants, needs, to hear her voice – to make the connection of now-familiar sound waves across a wire. He wants to call her to tell her what he has done, to tell her simply that he is not sleeping in a bed with someone else, will never do so again.

He parks in the middle of the bridge, halfway along its length. He emerges from the car, walks to the railing. Underfoot he feels a splintered board, a sliver missing. In good weather, walking across the bridge, one can see through the slats the water below, the shallow green water where the bridge meets the beach, the deep navy of the channel. When he takes that walk, and even when he drives the bridge's span, he often thinks of the pilings beneath the bay, of the force of the tides against the thick round wooden columns. He wonders how the engineers who maintain the bridge know when the pilings need replacing, how it is that their concrete anchors never seem to shift in the sand, causing a sudden give in the planking.

He feels rather than sees the rough surface of the railing. He remembers the first day that he touched Siân, on the bench, bringing his lips to her nipple, not knowing as he did so what was happening, what he was making happen. He had wanted a return to innocence. He remembers, too, the last time he lay with Siân, the last time they made love, how they both fell into a deep, seamless sleep, even though it was morning, how when he awoke he still had his finger inside her, and how he realized that for that to have occurred, neither one of them must have stirred even a fraction while they slept. Was there, or could there ever be, he wondered then, and wonders now, a reconciliation between innocence and sexuality?

A breeze drifts along the length of the bridge; below him he can hear the slap of waves. He cannot see much: a hint of land where there are lights at the shoreline. He looks over toward the east, where the sun will rise soon, where the dunes and the spit meet the other end of the bridge. In Portugal it's already Christmas morning, has been for some time. He knows little about how the Portuguese celebrate this holiday, other than that they must. He doesn't know much about Portugal at all actually, except for its food, or at least those dishes that have made their way across the Atlantic. He wonders when exactly he will ever get to Portugal: He cannot imagine traveling there alone now.

He raises his collar, leans on his elbows. He bends his head, shuts his eyes. He knows he should ask for forgiveness, that what he has done to Harriet and his children is reprehensible, that his wife is still probably sitting on the couch trying to comprehend the scope of this betrayal.

He turns around, rests his back against the railing. His coat falls open; he lifts his head to the sky, searching for a star. He wants to reach across a lifetime, to reclaim what once was forfeited.

In the overcast sky, he cannot find a star. He pulls his coat to, knows he needs a room now, if only for a few hours. He tries to think where there might be a motel open this time of year, winces as he imagines the thoughts of the night manager booking in a man alone on Christmas.

He walks to the car. He hears the clock tower ring three bells.

He remembers when there were prayers for different dilemmas.

The light was blinding on the surface of the snow, a painful light you wanted to ward off with your hands. I turned too quickly into the drive, skidded on the ice. The car thudded softly into the snowbank that Stephen's brother had made when he'd plowed the drive before the meal was served. I left the car door open, ran up the stairs to the kitchen. I called his name – once, twice, three times – and heard no answer. I thought he might be in the barn, did not want to think of what I might find there. I turned then and saw through the window that the barn door was open.

I left the house and walked quickly to the barn. The building was old, with wide plank siding, and sometimes in the winter, if the air was dry, the boards contracted, pulled away from each other, leaving thin seams of air and light from without or within. I hesitated at the barn's entrance, looked through a crack in the wall. I saw the ocher flannel shirt, a dark red stain.

I ran to where Stephen was sitting on an old wooden chair he had thought years ago to refinish and had brought to the barn, where it had remained all that time. There was a shotgun at his feet. The wound was to his shoulder; he was holding his arm limply in his lap. One sleeve was soaked with blood – a drenching, rusty spill.

He was barely conscious. His hand was already gray

beneath a blotting of the rust.

I said, Stephen.

He looked at me, tilted his head. The pain was visible on his face.

I touched his hand.

I'm so sorry, I said to him.

I watched the paramedics wrap my husband in warm quilts, tie him to a stretcher, and carry him out into the overbright sunshine of the yard. Later, the surgeon who stitched him said that he would lose the use of his arm. I wondered how it had happened: Had his hand shaken so badly that he had missed?

I understood that this was not for the shirt, nor for the onion sets that had been washed away, but for a life, a way of life, that might have to go with the onion sets.

I understood that it was for having had the farm at all. To release him from the farm.

And I understood, too, that it was for the missed connection – for an emptiness I had failed to fill.

When the paramedics had gone and I had said that I would follow, I went back into the barn. I scrubbed the chair and the floorboards. I think it strange now that I did not cry. I washed the chair clean, but I could not remove the stain from the wooden floor, from the tiny cracks where the color had settled in.

HE HAS WAITED long enough. Yesterday, Christmas Day, with its excruciating pain and elaborate pretense, was, he thinks, the longest day of his life. After his drive to the beach, he found a motel room at the edge of town, slept until sunlight blurred the edges of the shades, then drove back to his house for the charade of Christmas morning. He found Harriet, ashen-faced, an automaton, a smile frozen on her lips, sitting in a straight-backed chair, as the children, having demolished their stockings, were opening their presents. Only Hadley of his three children, on the floor with an unopened present on her lap, seemed to sense catastrophe in the air. He took off his coat in the kitchen, sat on the couch, and was immediately inundated with the squeals and queries of Anna and Jack, who pushed presents onto his lap, demanding his attention and scrutiny and, more than once, his aid in assembling toys. Normally that was a task he accepted grudgingly as a necessary fact of fatherhood, but yesterday he welcomed the work: It provided a focus, a distraction from the frozen smile.

When the presents had been opened, assembled, and marginally played with, he went into the kitchen and made pancakes – a ritual of Christmas morning that felt hollow this time. At the dining table, Harriet sat unmoving, a fork stabbed into a pancake, as if she were unable to cut it for herself. Even Jack and Anna began to feel the calamity, turning their gaze from mother to father to mother, then over to Hadley, who seemed, as the eldest, the repository of secrets. Catching Harriet's eye, Charles thought to take the ball from her, ease her task, by beginning the talk himself. (How, he had no idea; he had not prepared for this, could not even imagine the vocabulary with which one told a child this terrible thing.) But Harriet, seeing his intent, shook her head quickly. He didn't know if her gesture meant not now, or not today, or not at all, but it wasn't his place to question her, not his decision.

Awkwardly, after the meal, Charles stood in the middle of the family room, dispossessed, unsure of whether or not he had the right even to go upstairs to the bathroom to fetch his toilet kit, which, in his haste the night before, he had left. He had tended the fire, cleaned up the wrappings from the presents, finished the breakfast dishes, and was now unemployed. Normally they'd have gone visiting – to his parents, to her parents, for more food, to see the trees. He supposed that Harriet still planned to make these trips, was unclear if he should accompany her. Ought they to make a clean sweep, telling first the children, then each family – in the way they had once announced the impending birth of Anna?

But Harriet made the decision for him. She said simply, at his side, 'Go now.'

He turned to her, thinking he would ask her if she didn't want him to stay, to help her tell the children, but her face was impenetrable. She answered for him the unspoken query.

'I'm going to tell them when you're gone,' she said.

He left then, said no goodbyes. The children occupied, he slipped out the kitchen door, feeling small and mean. It was the worst crime, he thought, stealing away from one's children.

He'd driven to the motel, locked himself in his room. He'd wanted desperately to call Siân, knew that he could not. They'd made an agreement: They wouldn't call each other on Christmas Day. But what agreements were binding now?

He'd tried to sleep, a futile and restless effort. He'd gotten up from the bed, driven to the Qwik Stop for a six-pack, gone back to the room, drunk the six beers, one after the other. Still he couldn't sleep. There was nowhere to go, no one to call. It was Christmas Day, the one day of the year when everyone was occupied, everyone nestled into a family. And whom would he call if he could? Was there anyone to whom he would tell this story, anyone who could understand what he had done? He did not feel sorry for himself, did not want the companionship or understanding of other men. He wanted only to talk to the one person, hear the one woman's voice. He thought that if he could talk to her, he would be able to sleep. Everything would be all right.

He'd driven to the beach then. Straight across the bridge to the dunes. He'd walked the spit in its entirety, the air clean and chill, the sea gradually becoming rougher than it had been during the hours before dawn. He liked the sun on his face, even though it gave off little warmth. On his way back along the beach, in his crumpled suit and overcoat and soiled shirt, he walked at the edge of the hard sand left by the tide and thought of Winston. And when he thought of Winston, he was immediately mired in the imponderables left in the wake of his pronouncement to his wife: Who would keep Winston now? Himself? His children? And with those questions, immediately there were others: Where would he live in the interim until Siân could get free? Would she want to get free? Where would his wife and children live when the house was foreclosed? How could he keep his business going if the business was located in a house he could no longer enter? Did he have a business left at all? And how was he going to pay for everything?

The questions made him dizzy. Or perhaps it was his hunger. He hadn't eaten anything since the eclectic dinner of Christmas Eve. (Was that really only the night before? he

wondered in amazement; it seemed as though days had intervened.) And like Harriet, he had not touched the pancakes at
breakfast. It was – he looked around him for the sun – what
time now? He minded that he hadn't thought to collect his
watch when he was in the house earlier. He thought it must
be midafternoon, three o'clock, perhaps later. He'd driven
then to a bar outside town where he knew he would not be
recognized, had a sandwich there and a couple of beers in the
company of the saddest men he thought he had ever seen, and
when he'd emerged it was dark. Dark enough so that he could
return to the motel and imagine that the day was over, dark
enough to wish the day behind him.

He'd slept briefly, woken with a start. He called the motel
owner to find out the time, was disheartened to learn that
it was only seven-thirty in the evening. He'd driven back
then to the Qwik Stop, bought another six-pack along with
a toothbrush and a razor and, for good measure, a package
of over-the-counter sleeping pills. If he didn't sleep tonight,
he thought, he would go mad.

He *had* slept, fitfully, twenty minutes at a time, once waking
up in the midst of a nightmare in which his house was floating
in the bay and he could see Winston in a lower window,
drowning. He'd had another dream, a sort of erotic nightmare,
in which he and Siân were making love in his marital bed when
Hadley entered the room. He'd woken from this dream with
his shirt soaked. He'd sat up quickly, stripped the shirt from
his skin, had a shower. In the shower, he determined that it
was perhaps better after all not to sleep, spent the rest of the
night until dawn sitting in the dark in the only chair in the
room, finishing the rest of the beers.

It is ten minutes to ten now; he knows from the clock in the
Cadillac, the clock still keeping accurate time after 140,000

miles. He is parked beside the best-situated phone booth in town, a booth at the back of a small fish market at the end of a pier in the harbor. It is a phone people seldom use, chiefly fishermen calling home to their wives. In the half-dozen times he has called her from here, the only sounds he has had to compete with are the slapping of the waves along the dock, the frenzied cries of gulls looking for chum.

His heart racing, his fingers shaking more from nerves than from lack of sleep, he punches in the digits of her phone number, then his credit card. The phone rings once, twice, three times. He prays fervently and rapidly that her husband is out of the house. He brushes the hair from his forehead, looks around him from habit. The dock is deserted, this day after Christmas.

She answers tentatively, as she almost always does.

'Siân,' he says with enormous relief. He is afraid for a moment that he might actually begin to weep with relief.

'Charles.'

'I thought I'd go out of my mind if you didn't answer,' he says in a rush.

'Oh . . .' Her voice sounds guarded, careful.

'What is it?' he asks. 'Is your husband there in the room?'

'No,' she says, in a voice she might use to give information to a woman friend, an acquaintance. 'My husband's brother is here with his family.' She pauses. 'Visiting . . .,' she says carefully.

'Siân, listen to me. You don't have to say anything. I'll do the talking. But there's something very important I have to tell you.'

'What?'

'I've told my wife.'

'What?'

'I've told my wife.'

There is a long pause at her end.

'I don't understand.'

'I've told my wife that I'm in love with you. That I'm leaving her.'

The pause this time is so long he thinks she may have hung up the phone. Finally he hears her say, quietly, under her breath, as if she had turned her head away from the people in the room, 'Oh, no.' She repeats this – two low, sonorous syllables. 'Oh, no.'

'It's done.'

'No,' she says, again quietly. 'No.'

'Siân, it's done. It's over.'

'What happened? Why?' she asks, her voice rising.

'It was awful. Just awful.'

'You can't . . .,' she says.

He waits. 'What?'

'Listen,' she says, her voice barely a whisper. 'You have to get it back. You have to talk to her, get her to take you back. You can't have done this. We can't have done this.'

'Siân, it's done. I couldn't live that way. I couldn't keep lying, whatever happened. I'm not telling you you have to leave your husband. I'm just telling you what I had to do.'

'I know. I know.'

'Well, then.'

'I can't talk now. Something's happened,' she whispers. She says, in a louder voice, 'So how was your Christmas?'

'When can I talk to you? When can I call?'

'You can't. Not today. I'll write.'

'Write! I'll go out of my mind waiting for a letter. Let me call you later.'

'No, you can't. You don't understand.' And again, in a louder voice, 'Lily is fine.'

'OK, OK. But promise me this. You'll write today.'

'Yes.'

'And send it Express. I'll get it tomorrow.'

'Yes.'

'And listen, take down this number. It's the motel where I'm staying. Just in case. Call me anytime you can. From a phone booth. Any hour.'

'OK.'

'Siân, I love you.'

'I know.'

'I don't want to hang up.'

'I know.'

'I don't want to let you go.'

He hangs up the phone, unable to say goodbye. He picks it up immediately, hears the buzz of the dial tone. He stands with the phone in his hand, unable to move, reluctant to replace the receiver.

He looks out toward the end of the dock, takes a great gulp of air. What could possibly have happened that she needs to tell him about?

He replaces the receiver, walks to his car. He hits the steering wheel with the heel of his hand. There is nothing he can do but wait, a task at which he is remarkably poor. He has all but promised her he will not call her again. He could hear the fear in her voice. Something is very wrong, and she can't tell him what it is.

He puts the car in gear, heads down High Street, thinks of driving west to Pennsylvania. Instead he passes the street on which he used to live, makes the turn. He sees his house; Harriet's station wagon is not there. He takes a chance, pulls the Cadillac into the driveway. He hears no sounds, sees no faces in the windows. When he opens the kitchen door, the silence is complete: Not even Winston is here, bounding out to greet him as he normally would. Charles looks at the disarray in the family room – children's toys strewn about, abandoned. On the counter in the kitchen is a note in Harriet's hand: 'We're at my sister's. I don't know when we'll be back.'

Charles picks up the note, walks to his study, at the front of the house. Of course he understands why she has left with the children: she cannot bear the house now, a house so full of memories, a house she cannot have. He wonders if he should call, decides he should not, not today anyway. He hasn't planned on coming here, hasn't planned on working, but as long as he is here, he wonders if he oughtn't to try to get something done – something to while away the hours until Harry Noonan opens the post office tomorrow. He could fill some cartons with his papers so that he could sort through them back at the motel. Or perhaps, with Harriet and the children gone, he could work here for a couple of hours, listen to his messages, return the most important calls, get out some mail.

He enters his study, sees immediately another note on his desk. In his coat, he sits in his office chair, picks it up. It is written in purple crayon, on the back of a piece of his business stationery. The handwriting is Jack's.

He crumples the note in his fist, looks out his study window to the yard, where he can see the long rope swing he threw over the walnut for Hadley and the others. In the silence of his study, he opens the note, reads again the childlike scrawl.

The note contains only one word, a question.

Why?

The house was full of people, Stephen's brother and his wife, their children. They were solicitous and guarded. They wanted to ask, but did not, what exactly it was that had caused Stephen to be in the barn with a gun on Christmas Day. Stephen, in the hospital, would not say. Lily was told only that there'd been an accident.

I wrote the letter to you, as you had asked, and put it in the mail. I knew when I wrote it that it was irrevocable, and, when I mailed it, that it was irretrievable. I knew, too, that if a heart can be said to be broken, this letter would break your heart, because it had broken mine. And yet love – the love that we shared so briefly – lodges not in the heart but in the brain, and with the brain there are always thoughts, always memories.

The afternoon I handed the Express Mail package to the woman behind the counter at the post office, it seemed to me that I was giving over to her a great secret, forfeiting a mystery.

The next morning, the house still full of people, I dressed my daughter and put her in the car. We needed milk, cereal, eggs, bread for toast, and coffee. I did not want to think about when your post office would open, about how you would find the red-white-and-blue package, about how you would rip it apart, take it to your car. I did not want to think about your face when you had read the letter.

The A & P was not crowded; some early morning shoppers like myself, looking for their breakfast or thinking to get this chore done early. I put Lily in the basket in the cart, started down the aisles. Overhead was the piped-in music, a lazy drone I barely heard. I put bananas and oranges into the cart, potatoes for dinner. In another aisle, the next, I found cereal and coffee, put them idly in. I opened Lily's coat, I remember, shook open my own. It was hot inside the store; we were overdressed.

In the third aisle, the refrigerator aisle, I saw at its end a worker, a tall boy with pimples, in a white coat, whose task it was that morning to put prices on the orange juice, restack the eggs. I headed down the aisle, picked up a hefty gallon of milk, some yogurt, a container of cottage cheese. I was thinking about whether it would be more economical in the long run, since there were so many people in the house, to purchase cans of frozen orange juice rather than the brand in the carton that I preferred, when I heard the song.

Perhaps a bar or two had passed before it registered, before it stopped me, there in the middle of the aisle. I listened to its melody, its words, a simple pop song of no consequence to anyone else in the store, yet to me, at that moment, it was a call across the years, a cry across three states.

I began soundlessly to mouth the words. Lily looked up at me and smiled, then stopped smiling when she saw that I was crying. I put sound to the words, a hesitant, cracked sound that was something like singing. The boy, the teenage boy with pimples at the end of the aisle, heard my unfelicitous voice, saw me standing paralyzed with my shopping cart in the aisle. Another woman, an older woman with tight gray curls and wearing what we used to call a loden coat, turned the corner into the aisle, looked first at the boy, then at me, to see what was the matter. My voice is terrible; I am not a singer. But I didn't care. What was there to be ashamed of, what was there to lose? I opened my mouth wider. I sang as if I were not normally chagrined by my voice, I sang as if I had wanted to belong to a band all my life, I sang as though the song were a prayer and I a priest, begging for its meaning.

The song – a simple song with enigmatic words and lovely flourishes – finished abruptly, leaving me stranded in the aisle to no applause.

I picked up Lily, abandoned the cart with all that I had put into it. I carried Lily to the front of the store, looked frantically for a phone booth. It was twenty past eight. I had to reach you before you went to the post office. I was crazed, intent. I was crying too – I didn't care. I yelled up to the manager, in his booth above the shoppers, to let me use the phone. He said there was a pay phone just outside the store, around the corner. I ran with Lily past the startled woman at the register, ran past the long line of carts, found the phone booth against the wall. I put Lily down, reached for quarters in the bottom of my pocketbook. Lily started to wander away; I put my leg around her, held her to me. I found the piece of paper in my wallet, punched in numbers, fed the box with quarters as if it were a child you wanted to keep quiet with cookies.

The phone rang. A man answered. I asked for you. He said that there were no phones in the rooms, but he would be glad to give you the message. I told him very carefully what the message was: Don't open the letter. Go directly to The Ridge. I would meet you there.

I made the motel manager repeat the message. I told him it was essential that he give it to you. Essential. He said that he would walk straight over to your room, give it to you now, and that if you weren't there, he would watch for you, give it to you himself, in person, when you returned.

I thanked him, hung up the phone. I put Lily in the car, drove back to the house.

They were all in the kitchen, waiting for their breakfast, astonished I had returned without the milk and coffee. I said Hello and then Excuse me, and I ran upstairs to the attic.

In the attic, in addition to the trunk that had traveled from Springfield to Dakar and back to the farm, there were cardboard cartons of belongings from my father's attic that he had given to me several years before. The cartons had been placed along a far wall, behind other trunks, other boxes, in a position that had all but guaranteed their never being opened again. But I was on a mission, determined. No trunk was too large, no object insurmountable. I shifted heavy boxes, wedged myself in. I thought for a moment I might not get out. I made my way to the far wall where the cartons were.

When I reached them, I tore open their tops, upended the boxes onto the attic floor. There were showers of school papers and mementos. In one carton, I heard a promising clink. At the carton's bottom was a box of childhood jewelry – ropes of beads, a pin from the National Honor Society, a handful of gaudy rings. And there, tangled with a necklace, green and sticky with a substance that might thirty years ago have been Kool-Aid, I found the bracelet.

I held it in my hand, as if it were an ancient amulet I had excavated, its worth beyond understanding.

I put it on my wrist.

I went quickly downstairs to where the others were gathered. I hugged Lily, told her to stay with Stephen's brother's family. I told Stephen's brother I might be gone most of the day; it was important. Before he could think to protest, I ran out the door to the car.

I drove seventy, eighty miles an hour, hoping you wouldn't get there before me.

The lawns around The Ridge that day were covered in snow, a pristine snow with a crust that had not yet been trampled upon. I was sure that you would come. I remember feeling exhilarated with the knowledge that you would come, that within an hour or two you would be there with me. I did not precisely know how it would work, but I felt somehow that it would. We would talk, we would hold each other, and we would invent a life.

I thought that I would go for a walk around the inn, perhaps down to the lake. Then I went inside, asked the man at the desk, who knew me, if there was still the badminton court I remembered from childhood. He looked surprised, said yes, the court was still there, though not set up now, of course. But I could walk there if I wanted to. I told him I would like that. He gave me directions. It was across the lawn, down to the left. Behind a hedge. A flat grassy field in the summer, with a bench. I'd know it by the stone bench with the carvings, he said.

I walked across the lawn, making virgin footprints in the snow.

I found the hedge, covered with a thick frosting. I found the bench by the field, brushed off the snow with my gloved hands. I sat on the bench.

I looked across the grassy court, now covered with snow. The sun made a billion briiliant specks on the crust.

I looked across the grassy court. It was summer, and we were children.

And it was then, finally, that I could see it all.

A GUST CATCHES the metal motel door, slams it hard on his fingers. Charles winces, retrieves the door, pushes it against the wind, closes it. His topcoat billows out behind him. He bends into the gale, walking quickly to his car. In the parking lot, bits of debris and dust swirl and eddy, sending grit into the air, into his eyes. The ferocity of the wind surprises him, considering the clarity of the day. Overhead, evergreens sway and bend. A freak storm – a blow without the clouds.

He shuts the door, feels the sanctuary of the car, the quiet as well as the calm. He looks at his fingers, the bruised knuckles, the middle finger swelling already. Checking in the rearview mirror, he sees that his hair is wild about his head. He tries to comb it with his fingers. He notices, too, that his eyes are bloodshot – from too much beer, no doubt, but also from an almost superhuman lack of sleep. He cannot remember the last time he slept a whole night through, cannot really remember the last time he slept more than two hours straight. His face feels grainy, stretched, even though he has just shaved.

He puts the car in gear, heads toward the post office. If he has any luck left at all, Noonan will be there already, and more important, the Express Mail letter will have come in. As has happened to him before, he both dreads and hungers for the letter – hunger winning out. The open line of communication between them seems so fragile, particularly now, when he cannot talk to her on the telephone, when she has been so guarded, that he is eager to restore it, no matter what the cost. If he can talk to her, if she can talk to him, if they can be in each other's physical presence, then he truly believes that they will be all right.

He drives through town, the odd storm creating havoc in the streets. Townspeople, bent double, seem blown from open door to open door. Hats, newspapers, paper bags, trash, and Christmas decorations skim along the streets and lodge momentarily in doorways. He comes to a stop at the traffic light, doesn't like the perilous way it is swinging in the stiff blow. Harborside, he can see the water hit the seawall like a firecracker, explode in a spray that drenches everything within twenty feet of the wall – parked cars, hapless pedestrians, phone lines, the backs of shops. The tide is up. Any higher and there'll be serious flooding in a couple of hours. He thinks of the houses smack up against the water along High Street; there'll be anxious home owners there. He wonders if the spit will breach.

Noonan's Trooper is at the post office. *Yes.* If only his luck will hold, Charles is thinking, the letter will be there.

He opens the door to the main office. Noonan says immediately, 'Got a package for you, Callahan. How was your Christmas?'

Charles signs for the letter.

'Fine,' he says, relieved that not everyone in town knows yet about the debacle that was his Christmas. 'And yours?'

'Oh, the usual,' says Noonan. 'Too much food, too many relatives.'

'Know what you mean,' says Charles, holding the Express Mail package against his chest.

A breastplate.

'Watch yourself out there,' Noonan calls to Charles's back. 'Got a weird storm working itself up the coast.'

Charles nods, hurries to his car, his temporary retreat. (He reflects that his car is one of the few havens he has left now, though GMAC in its wisdom will probably want to repossess it; he could total the car, he thinks idly, before they get their hands on it.) He tears open the packet, sees the thin blue envelope inside. More delicately, he opens the envelope, unfolds the letter. Just the sight of her handwriting is somehow deeply reassuring.

He reads the letter through.

He reads it again.

And again.

He holds the letter in his hand, opens his car door, stands up for air. He turns slowly around, lays his head on top of his car. He looks up, starts walking. He completes a large circle within the post office parking lot, still holding the letter in his hand. His stomach feels hollow, as if he had taken a fist. Above him, tree branches whip against a power line. A woman pulls into the parking lot, emerges from her car. Immediately the wind snatches an envelope from her hand. The envelope rises and falls, slides along the tarmac, lodges in a bush at the side. The woman runs in its wake, a comical and ungainly dash. The letter must be important, Charles thinks distractedly.

He walks back to his car, the door still open, a little bell inside dinging to signal that something is amiss. He looks at the letter in his hand, thinks to fold it up, stick it back inside the thin blue envelope. Instead he reaches up to the cloudless sky, lets the letter go. He watches it loop and fall like a kite, skitter along the side of the post office, then disappear behind the back of the building. He thinks for a minute that he ought to run to catch it, that it is, somehow, valuable, a tangible thread to a precious thing he once owned, then he remembers suddenly that he owns nothing now.

He re-enters the Cadillac, no longer a sanctuary. He starts the car, pulls out to an intersection. Behind him a driver leans on the horn. Startled, Charles makes a right turn in the intersection, heading south and west toward the motel.

She has written that it is over. Totally, completely, irrevocably over.

She has written that her husband shot himself and will lose the use of his arm.

She has written that she has loved him.

He proceeds down High Street, unaware that he is even behind the wheel. He has no destination, no urgency at all. He thinks, oddly, that he will never get to Portugal now. He knows this for a certainty, though he is not sure why. He sees her skating in her boots, cannot bear the image, makes it go away. What is he doing? He cannot go back to the motel. Jesus Christ, he thinks, that's the last place he wants to be. He brakes sharply and suddenly, makes a U-turn in the middle of High Street, causing a long squeal of tires as he does so. He drives, nearly blind, out toward the beach.

To his right, along High Street, he is aware of the hammering of the surf. High upon a hill, he sees Lidell's lost Tinkertoy, rusted beams dancing above the town. He sees houses now with their windows boarded up, sandbags along foundation lines. He hopes his children are inside a house somewhere, hopes Harriet has had the sense to pull them in. The biggest danger is from power lines. He himself has seen them snap and fall, crackling along the pavement.

He sees her on a bed, the lovely tilt of her nostrils. He can feel her hand on his skin.

He sees an image he has often in his dreams: the nipples of her breasts bursting through the white cloth of her blouse. He had it when he was a boy, and then later when he met her again, and he had not had it in all the years in between.

He wonders if the dream will go away now.

In Portugal they might one day have sat at a café in the sun, eating braised octopus and Portuguese sausage. He'd have read to her, or she to him. They'd have drunk red wine and gone swimming and then made love.

Simple pleasures.

He ought to have known it was not possible. He ought to have known she wouldn't leave. She had said it, and he had not paid attention. *Neither one of us can help the other, and that's the truth*.

He sees the bridge in the distance, the surf battering the pilings. No fishermen against the railing today. He wonders if the blow could actually knock a man down. He thinks maybe he'll take the Cadillac straight across the bridge, pile it into the dunes, walk back to town and call GMAC, tell them where they can pick up their car.

He hits the bridge too fast. The rattling boards seem to want to shake the Cadillac apart.

The spray is beautiful at the railings. Splendid and theatrical. The sky above the spray is the darkest blue he has ever seen.

He reaches down in front of the passenger seat, snaps a Bud from its plastic ring. He brings the beer between his legs, pops the top. Eight-twenty in the morning. Perhaps his soul is in jeopardy now.

Looking up from the beer, he sees the sheet of ice. A sheet of ice that must have formed in the night from the spray, a sheet of translucent ice across the bridge. He brakes a split second too late and knows it.

He feels the brakes lock, the car skid. The railing gives with ease, splintering into a thousand bits of wood. He sees Siân's face; he hears his daughter's voice. The Cadillac sails in a magnificent arc, a graceful arc, out toward Portugal.

Timing is everything, he thinks.

For the first time in her life, at breakfast, she had not known how to be. Cal had sat beside her, so near, and yet there was a gulf between them. They could not touch, could not even speak, and within hours, she knew, they would never see each other again. All night she had lain awake in her bed, reliving the moments on the forest floor, unsure of their reality. It wasn't possible such a thing had happened to her, and if it had, what did it mean?

She had worn the bracelet. It had risen and fallen on her thin wrist as she moved her hand, a tangible sign that they had been together. She sat beside him, in her shorts and sleeveless blouse, her stomach knotted with memories of the night before, with a kind of bottomless dread of knowing that she had to say goodbye. She knew that he would not kiss her again, would not be able to in the daylight, and she knew that he would not touch her, not as he had the night before. That was over, encapsulated, a memory now – and it would be many years before she would let a boy touch her in that way again.

She said the word 'badminton,' and she could see that he was grateful. She spoke to him in a low voice so the counselor would not hear, and when she dared to look at Cal, he was smiling.

She left the dining hall with the others, as if she would walk down the path to the outdoor chapel, as if she would attend this last mass with the group. She walked alone so as not to draw attention to herself, and quietly, when the others were engaged, she slipped to the side, walked along the grass to the field where the badminton court was. She expected someone to call out to her, hunched her back a bit in anticipation, but miraculously, no one seemed to notice she had gone. The morning was hot and damp and still, the sun already high in the cloudless sky. Within hours, when the parents had arrived, retrieved their children, and taken them to their separate homes, the day would be a scorcher.

She saw him sitting on the stone bench already, a bench that had earlier intrigued her. One support was a death's head, a ghoulish face with lolling tongue, a face forever frozen in a grimace; the other was a madonna-like figure, except that the young woman, whose breast was bared, carried a stone rose, not a child. The boys tittered at the figure when they came upon it, and she supposed the church that owned the camp might demolish the bench one day. She hoped they wouldn't, because she liked the odd pairing, wondered at the mind of the stone carver who had created it.

Cal had rackets with him, a pair of birdies. She knew he had to have flown to get the rackets and be at the court before her.

He stood awkwardly, handed her a racket. She thought he wanted to say something. He looked at her but did not speak. Instead he gestured with his racket to take the court, choose her side.

She walked to one half of the mown grassy rectangle. It was a lovely court, surrounded on all sides by shrubs and hedges, some raspberry bushes. She heard the drone of bees, the hot sound of an early summer morning.

He served; they batted the birdie back and forth for practice. He asked her if she wanted to begin, and she nodded her head.

Her arm was long, and she knew how to hustle. No shot was beyond her reach, and that was her most serious flaw, going for shots that were clearly out of bounds. He played a steady game, his eye better than hers, running less, letting the long shots go, but she saw that he was playing for real, that he knew almost immediately that she could play the game, that she might beat him.

She liked the airy thwack of the birdie against the taut strings of the racket. She liked to smash it at the net, sending it to the grass before he could react. She laughed when she herself missed a shot. Once she ran backward for a high loop, the birdie vanishing in the sun, then lost her balance, tripped, fell onto the grass. He came to the net, asked if she was all right. Her shorts had grass stains in the back. She wiped them off. I'm fine, she said, laughing again, then served a brilliant shot, one she knew he would let go, would think was going over the line, and when it landed perfectly in the corner, he whistled in appreciation.

The score was 16–14, or perhaps something else, but he was winning, just. He stood poised for his serve, and she waited. He was looking at her through the net, and she thought that he was thinking about where to place his shot. He had the sleeves of his white shirt rolled above the elbows. He wore black pants, white sneakers. He held the racket and the birdie out, at arms' reach. He didn't move. She was going to goad him, then sensed something, stopped herself. All around them, there was quiet, a deep summer hush. He raised the racket and the birdie, made his serve. It was a terrible shot, she could see that at once. The birdie veered off to the side, hit the pole, ricocheted to the ground. Embarrassed for him, she ran to the place where the birdie had fallen, bent over from the waist to retrieve it. He ran to get it too, possibly apologetic. When she bent, her hair parted at her neck, fell forward over her face.

She felt it, shivered slightly.

A kiss at the nape of the neck. A butterfly.

His lips – his dry, boyish lips – made the shape of a butterfly against the back of her neck. She felt the light touch against her skin, thought, Butterfly.

She stood up, looked at him. She wanted to reach out, touch him on the arm. She wanted to take one step forward, kiss him on the cheek. She wanted to say again that it was all right to have done what they had the night before, that it was not all right that she was leaving him. She wanted to tell him that she would never forget him, no matter what happened to her.

But she could not move that one step closer. And he could not touch her. He shifted a fraction to the side, as if he would return to his half of the court. She smoothed her hair back off her face.

He said, Siân.

She meant to speak, couldn't, hesitated a fraction too long.

They turned simultaneously, took up their positions. She had the birdie; she had lost track of the score now. She thought that possibly he ought still to have possession of the birdie, but that didn't seem to matter.

She raised her racket. She would sail him a long one. She smiled, and she saw, through the net, that he was smiling back at her, in anticipation.

She hit the shot. She watched it soar into the sun.

And it seemed to her that it was then that the birdie, high above them both, stopped at its apex, stopped in time.

APPENDIX

Where or When

WORDS BY LORENZ HART
MUSIC BY RICHARD RODGERS

When you're awake
The things you think come from the dreams you dream.
Thought has wings,
And lots of things are seldom what they seem.
Sometimes you think you've lived before
All that you live today.
Things you do come back to you,
As though they knew the way.
Oh, the tricks your mind can play!

It seems we stood and talked like this before.
We looked at each other in the same way then,
But I can't remember where or when.
The clothes you're wearing are the clothes you wore.
The smile you are smiling you were smiling then,
But I can't remember where or when.

Some things that happen for the first time,
Seem to be happening again.
And so it seems that we have met before,
and laughed before,
and loved before,
But who knows where or when!

The Tape that Charles sent Siân

A Teenager in Love
Dion

Angel Baby
Rosie & The Originals

That's My Desire
Dion & The Belmonts

Where or When
Dion & The Belmonts

Mr. Blue
The Fleetwoods

Come Softly to Me
The Fleetwoods

What's Your Name?
Don and Juan

In the Still of the Night
The Five Satins

To Know Him Is to Love Him
The Teddy Bears

Here Comes the Night
Them

Don't Look Back
Them

Will You Love Me Tomorrow
The Shirelles

Crying
Roy Orbison

Love Hurts
Roy Orbison

Donna
Ritchie Valens